Praise for Divinity

"A truly rich, complex, and immediat
—Andy Peloquin, author of *Darkbla*

"Teeming with elements of the science fiction and fantasy genres, *Divinity's Twilight: Rebirth* is reminiscent of the compelling tales told in the Star Wars Expanded Universe mixed with the gripping stories found in the Final Fantasy universe. Magic and technology are blended in a way that feels organic and believable, with genuine characters you can applaud, despise, and revere."
—Robert Zangari, co-author of *Tales of the Amulet*

"Russell's new high fantasy launch is well written with a definite steampunk vibe and a sword-and-sorcery appeal. Readers of alternate-world fantasy will find this a satisfying read and a good start for a new author who's soon to have a loyal following."
—Library Journal

"*Rebirth* is just truly epic, beautifully organized, and just so darn polished. It's a truly brilliant debut novel and Mr. Russell deserves all the accolades for it."
—Rachel Rener, author of *Inked* and *The Lightning Conjurer*

"*Divinity's Twilight* is a delightfully ambitious epic fantasy that sprints right out of the gate and maintains an unrelenting pace throughout. The reader will find themselves mindlessly flipping pages as the stakes grow ever steeper with each subsequent chapter."
—The Critiquing Chemist

"*Divinity's Twilight: Rebirth* by Christopher Russell is the first book in what promises to be a breathtaking epic fantasy series... Top tier world-building coupled with well-crafted history and lore made Rebirth an enthralling read, with events and characters clicking into place at a breakneck pace... Classic fantasy archetypes are thrown to the wind while tropes are shattered and fused anew to create characters that reek of familiarity but brim with mystery, intrigue, and uncertainty."
—Reader's Favorite

Books By
Christopher Russell

DIVINITY'S TWILIGHT

Rebirth (#1)
Remnant (#2)

CONSTELLA

Gravitas

DIVINITY'S TWILIGHT

DIVINITY'S TWILIGHT

REMNANT

CHRISTOPHER RUSSELL

ILLYRIUM
PUBLISHING

Divinity's Twilight
Remnant

© 2022 Christopher Russell

Published in Williamsburg, Virginia, by Illyrium Publishing. Illyrium is a trademark of Divinitys Twilight Fantasy Novels, LLC. www.christopherrussellauthor.com

Written permission of the publisher.
ISBN: 979-8-218-06759-5 (Paperback)
ISBN:979-8-218-06763-2 (Hardback)
First printing edition 2022
Cover Design by: Chris McGrath and Allegra Pescatore
Book Design by: Ailish Brundage
Interior Maps by: Keir Scott Cartography
Interior Illustrations by: Raphael Luccini

Cover text set in Bureno. Interior headers set in Amerika Pro.

Interior body set in Minion.
Illyrium Publishing
Printed in the United States of America

For Nellie Conroe, my Mammaw,
In a book about all kinds of love, it's only fitting
I remember the woman who sat me on her knee,
and taught me all that love could be.

Table of Contents

9

Back Matter

Illustrations

NOTE: Many illustrations, titles included, contain spoilers for material that comes before them in the book. Look ahead at your own risk.

AUTHOR NOTE

Welcome back to the world of Lozaria! It's been two years since many of you last adventured with Vallen, Sylette, Matteo, and the rest of their dysfunctional crew, so a refresher is probably in order.

A summary of "The Story Thus Far" can be found on page 751 and will give you a brief rundown of the events of book one, *Rebirth*. A list of important characters can also be found on page 746 in the "Dramatis Personae" section. *Divinity's Twilight* is an *EPIC* epic fantasy, with lots of unique places, people, magic, and items you may not remember. Please reference the glossary on page 728 whenever you need a brain boost for the best possible reading experience.

If there are any themes or topics you'd like to avoid, check the "Content Warning" on page 756. Be aware that these content tags *may* contain spoilers.

Lastly, "Acknowledgements" are on page 757. I have an airship full of people to thank for their contributions to *Remnant,* including you, my dear readers. Without you, I wouldn't have the coolest job in the world.

That's all! On with the adventure, on with *Remnant!*

May wisdom ever light your path,
Christopher Russell

Legend:
- Sarconian Fleet
- Rabbanite Flotilla
- Regiment or Battalion
- Supply Depot
- Entrenched Defense Works

Seems like an easy victory. What am I missing?

Northern Corridors unusually quiet this year...

Syvas Bay

Sarconian Empire

Never gamb. / Ritterm 6th Fleet Yo

Gulf of Sostra

Sarconia

Arhus

New barracks and supply depots

Aldona Fortress

Lake Lovar

3rd Fleet

Weisvale

Aldona Survivors?

o Twin Lighthouse

Sarconian Province

Kingdom of Darmatia

Why does that fool Stetson still have his head?

Lyndwur Forest

232nd Mechanized Battalion

o Beiras

7th Fleet

Encircle Voras ASAP

o Etrus

Will the Blauers get involved?

1st and 5th Fleets o Dusan

Avoid Voras

Etrus

Marmoth Exclusion Zone

Ascendancy

Canal

o Nemare

o Seyla

Blockade Southern Rabban?

Magerium

Badlands

16

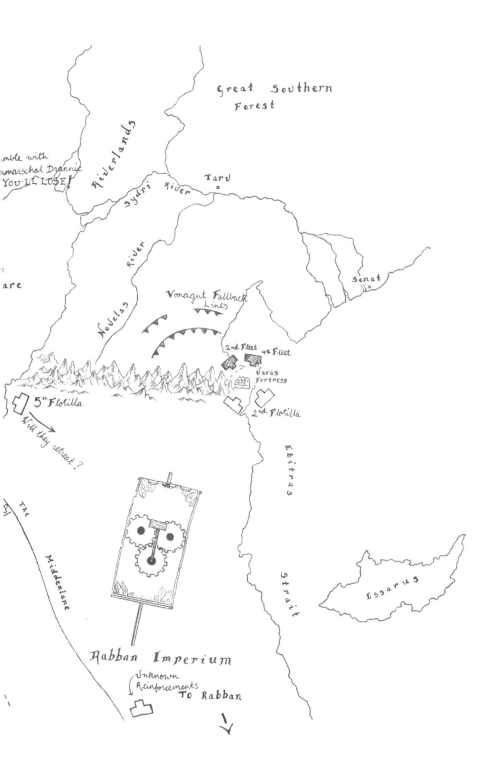

Great Southern Forest

Riverlands

...mble with ...marschal Drannic YOU'LL LOSE!

Sydri River

Taru

Senat

River

Novelas

Vonagut Fallback Lines

...are

2nd Fleet   4th Fleet

Varag Fortress

5th Flotilla

2nd Flotilla

Will they retreat?

Ebitras

Strait

Essarus

The

Middenlane

Rabban Imperium

Unknown Reinforcements To Rabban

Idyllic Days I

"**A**re you listening, Leon?"

"Hmm . . . what?"

Leonel Descar's eyes slowly fluttered open. Drowsiness clung to the lids like lead weights, and his thoughts were as murky as the wastewater left behind after cleaning the barracks latrines. Something slimy slithered along Leon's back, making him shiver. He felt cold. Wrong and out of place, even though he recognized the rust-colored stains on the darkened surface above him.

Vallen Metellus, his best friend, had put them there a year prior when he'd gotten fed up with cleaning and tried to stick his rag to the ceiling. Leon was *home*. Well, not his ancestral home—he didn't want to go anywhere near his father. This was his sanctuary. The place where he'd met Vallen, snorted menja juice when he cracked bad jokes, and finally felt like he *belonged*.

The carpet smelled of sweat-encrusted socks, the walls were painted a sickly shade of green, and the suite could barely fit their four-man squad, but Leon loved their dorm room at the Darmatian Military Academy.

"Yoohoo, Lozaria to Leon. Where are you at, buddy?"

A smug voice. Self-assured. And, beneath the surface bravado, trying just a bit too hard to maintain control. Leon sat up, swung his legs off their couch, and faced Vallen. "We'll need to get your eyes checked if you can't see me."

Vallen snorted. "My vision is perfect. I could fire a spark from my finger and hit a hovering rot-fly at fifty paces, first try." He raised his hand and mimed firing a gun, falling backward in his puke-colored chair as he did. "Besides, fixing your head should come first."

"Did I hit it?" Leon pawed at his messy hair. No swelling, no blood. Just . . .

He shivered again. Was he being watched? Leon scanned the shadows of the darkened room, but nothing seemed amiss. Four closed doors—one for each squad member—stood sentry in the corners. Two other chairs, their upholstery slashed and bleeding stuffing, sat on either side of Vallen. The sink in the washroom down the hall still leaked, drips echoing like gunshots.

Plip . . . Plip . . . Plip . . .

"No. Or at least, not yet," Vallen amended, oblivious to Leon's growing unease. "But you *did* fall asleep during our strategy meeting. As squad leader, I could give you demerits for that, you know?"

"You . . . you wouldn't give me demerits. Paperwork is the bane of your existence, and you'd have to fill out at least three forms to formally reprimand another cadet."

"Fair point," Vallen said. They both chuckled.

Something moved beneath the nearby table. On instinct, Leon's hand leapt for the rod he used to cast light magic. Only . . . it wasn't hooked on his belt. Where had it gone? He never let it out of his sight.

Vallen laughed again. "Jumpy much? It's just a scum-crawler— see?" He pointed as a thumb-sized, many-legged bug detached from the shadows and burrowed underneath the carpet. Neither of them made a move to stop it.

"Should we do something about it?" Leon asked. "Matteo told me that scum-crawlers like to lay eggs in moist environments, and you spilled your drink yesterday."

"And keep it from destroying the Academy, one floorboard at a time? More power to it, I say." Raising his fingers to his brow, Vallen mocked a salute.

His piss-poor attitude toward upkeep was understandable. The Academy's top brass—especially Commandant Hardwick Iolus—hated Vallen's guts. They scoffed at his abilities and the title of Triaron, which likely led to their current lackluster accommodations.

Leon could imagine how the dorm assignments had been decided: *That Sewertown trash is the spiritual successor to the Hero King Darmatus? Well, give him a room in the old wing. He's used to rooting around in the swill belowground, so it might even be a step up!*

Leon clenched his fists, his pulse quickening. There was little he desired more than to wrap his fingers around Hardwick's pudgy neck and *squeeze*.

Another shiver cascaded down Leon's spine, pimpling his flesh as it went. This time, it was accompanied by a prickling at the base of his skull. Like a prodding needle deciding where to stab. Leon was certain he'd forgotten something. Was it about Hardwick? The Academy?

"You mentioned a strategy meeting," Leon blurted. "With just the two of us? Where are the oth—"

A soft titter came from his left. "Right as always, Val," Velle'asa

Me'andara purred. "If he can't see me sitting here, he *does* need to be looked at."

She leaned across the gap between her chair and Vallen's, snagging his arm and snuggling in close. Once there, the Sylph pressed a crimson cheek to his shoulder and shook her head, tickling his neck with her long, lustrous black hair.

Leon blinked, another chill wind caressing the flesh between his shoulders. By all the Veneer, he could've *sworn* Velle hadn't been in the room a moment prior.

"Are you offering to heal him?" Vallen asked. "One glyph and he'd be cured."

"I-if I may, Velle's magic affects *cell division*, not—"

Storm clouds darkened Vallen's features. "Can it, Professor Night Light."

Glasses shaking atop his narrow nose, Matteo Alhan slumped in his seat. The wiry brown clump atop his head slumped as well, cowed like its master.

Under normal circumstances, Leon would have leapt to the awkward sensory mage's defense. But he couldn't focus right now. Not with the shiver racing through his body; the feeling of *wrongness* creeping across his flesh like spreading rot. Leon leapt to his feet, drawing the concerned stares of his friends.

"You weren't here!" he shouted.

"Who . . . who wasn't?" Matteo asked.

"*You* and *you*." Leon pointed to the . . . *things* on either side of Vallen. "Matteo and Velle. Vallen and I were alone, the doors were shut, and none of them opened. You couldn't possibly have gotten here without me knowing."

Velle released Vallen and calmly stretched her arm toward Leon, her beautiful scarlet eyes swelling with concern. "We were here the whole time, Leon. You're clearly under a lot of stress, so please, let me help. Let go and let me help you."

Soft fingers brushed against his. The touch was pleasantly warm. But before Velle could grab his hand, Leon jerked away. She *stank* of wrongness. The same scent that pervaded this room, that oozed from all of them.

"Tell me Vallen," he whispered, tone serious. "Tell me why we're in our room, with the curtains drawn and lights off, having a strategy meeting."

The room morphed. Ever so slightly, a ripple that coursed along the peeling walls like an ocean wave. When it passed, a dim illyrium lamp sat on the table between them, casting enough glow to drive away most of the darkness.

Yet a few stubborn shadows still clung to Vallen, hiding beneath his nose, tucked behind his uniform collar. "I pulled the curtains so nobody could eavesdrop. Since you seem to be forgetting everything else, I should probably remind you that it's Graduation Day. The day we take the exam that decides *everything* about our futures?" Vallen paused, waiting for Leon to respond, but he refused to speak. "Anyway," Vallen continued, "We have a match against Renar's team later, and I wouldn't put it past the dunce to spy on us to get an edge. Any of that make sense?"

"No . . . No, it doesn't." Ice formed in Leon's veins. The shiver now convulsed across his entire body. "Since when do *you* care about Renar? You've trounced him again, and again, *and again.* He disgusts you. You think he's lower than the chunky vomit sludge that seeps out of Sewertown pipes. And besides . . . "

Leon's mouth went dry. *And besides,* he thought. *Our exams are over.* Or, rather, they'd been interrupted. As if he was slowly tearing himself free from a swiftsand pit, Leon struggled to recall what *should* have happened. What *did* happen.

The Sarconian Empire invaded. We fought at Aldona Fortress. My father's prized airship, The King Darmatus, went down, and then . . .

Blinding light seared away Leon's memories, a blazing poker jammed *through* his skull that left him curled on the couch, gasping in pain. Vallen jumped to his aid, pressing his hand to his neck, shouting at the top of his lungs for help. Through the agony, Leon didn't feel gratitude toward his friend, only that clammy feeling of *wrongness.* Vallen would run for a medic. Who was this *fake?*

Soon, even those feelings of unease were burned away. Leon screamed, head swimming, vision going fuzzy. Indistinct shapes crowded above him, talking in hurried, anxious voices. Velle and Matteo, distorted and twisted, just like Vallen. But why were they even here? All of them should be on the Imperial landing ship preparing to escape the—

"*AAARRRGGGHHHH!*"

The blazing pain in his skull redoubled, casting Leon into the abyss.

"Let go," Vallen soothed as he faded away. "Let go and all will be well."

Part 1

Choices

Chapter 1

Kinloss

Hetrachia 12, 697 ABH
Somewhere Along the Phar Coast, Sarconian Province of Darmatia

Shaking and stench consumed Sylette Artorios' world, and there was nothing she could do about either.

The first she could forgive. Matteo's airship was a generation past its prime. Passing gusts whistled through tiny, impossible-to-locate holes in the fuselage. The engine on the deck below howled like a dying beast, all the while trying to rock the craft apart from the inside out. Every screw on her co-pilot's seat squeaked, the headrest was a swath of grimy bandages, and her seat cushion was missing, leaving her bottom resting on a plate of rusted metal.

Sylette gritted her teeth as each jolt of the craft was delivered *directly* to her already aching body. She was bruised, battered, and determined to hunt down and slaughter the mechanic who'd left the ship in this state. But the exiled Sarconian princess could deal with pain. Pain had been her constant companion for ten years, ever since her inexplicable banishment and her mother's execution.

Instead, what made the veins in Sylette's forehead twitch was dealing with that discomfort on top of the pungent odor of seven filthy cadets packed into a space little larger than a closet. She tried to focus on something—*anything*—else. Flocks of aether-swallows outside the viewport, sweeping by the vessel's port side. The vast tapestry of life hundreds of meters below, sea meeting land in the jumble of reefs and cliffs that lined Darmatia's Phar Coast. And ...

Sylette sighed, then nearly gagged as she sucked in a particularly potent whiff of the two men sharing the cockpit with her. Some combination of sweat, dried seawater, and a third element she had no desire to place.

I'm at my limit, Sylette thought, astral-summoning dust coalescing around her. *I can take the ship's shaking. None of us have bathed since we left Etrus yesterday. But I draw the voiding line at imbeciles bickering right next to me.*

"No, over there!" Renar yelled. Oblivious, he thrust his bare chest between the two pilot chairs—one armpit dangerously close to Sylette's face—and jabbed a finger out the viewport. "Take us closer to the cliffs."

Dear Veneer. Sylette spun away and held her breath. She barely heard Matteo Alhan's reply. "They're just rocks, Renar. Sharp limestone rocks, the kind we've been looking at since last night. Please, *please*, give me something more to work with."

If not for the unwashed brute hulking over her, Sylette would have complimented the Professor's display of nerve. Two weeks ago, the bespectacled Terran had been a sniveling coward, so unsure of himself that he'd allowed *Vallen* to lead him around like a pet crysahund. Now he might be useful to her, if only just.

Renar threw up his arms, releasing more of his musk to infect the air. "What part of the poem wasn't clear? It should be easy to find a *lighthouse*, Matteo." His hands traced an imaginary tower in the space above the dashboard. "And since it could be tucked under the cliffs, you're going to have to get closer."

"It isn't hidden under the cliffs."

"Why? People hide secret stuff underground all the time. Like buried treasure or evil relics."

But not lighthouses, you dolt, Sylette fumed, fingernails digging into her ragged armrests.

Born from her anger, clouds of silver slivers twisted around her head, clinking softly as they joined together. One dagger formed. Two. At the noise, Matteo glanced toward her. His cheeks blanched, and his grip on the airship's control stick tightened.

"You wouldn't fire those in a pressurized cabin, would you?"

No, but neither of them needed to know that. "Renar?" Sylette prompted.

Palms out, the burly Terran stepped back, allowing her a sweet breath of *slightly* cleaner air. "Yes?"

"If I'm not mistaken, Unter recorded an *exact* copy of Archelaus Heisden's poem. Why don't you go grab it from him and ask Lilith how his wounds look while you're at it, alright?"

The daggers twitched, honed edges glinting beneath the afternoon sunlight filtering through the transport's canopy.

"Oh, guess you're right. I'll . . . I'll go fetch it."

Turning sideways, Renar shuffled through the narrow cockpit door into the adjoining cargo hold. When he was gone, Sylette focused her gaze on Matteo, whose glasses did little to hide the thick bags forming under his eyes. Her brow furrowed.

"And you're not going to crash this time, right?" She let the blades spin about their cross-guards. "You're not going to fall asleep? You're feeling awake and full of energy?"

Matteo gulped and nodded.

"Good."

Satisfied, Sylette dispelled her summoned weapons and leaned back, eliciting a tortured squeal from her seat. It wasn't just Matteo—they were all tired and on edge, herself included. Lilith was dashing between the aft maintenance hatch, Unter, and Velle, stopping to check on their injuries whenever she wasn't fixing a broken steam pipe or sprung gasket. Reek aside, Renar was doing a decent job at navigating.

Which left Vallen Metellus, their eternal weakest link. He *did* save them in Etrus. Sylette would give the Triaron that much credit. Yet he'd done so by expending all his men'ar on a single spell, after which he'd limped along, sullen and brooding.

Thinking about him made Sylette's head throb. To have so much power yet be so useless! How was she going to turn Vallen into a valuable tool when he couldn't see anything but red mist?

The vibrations of the airship warred with the mallet beating against Sylette's skull. She started to let her eyes close, started to rest her head on the wad of bandages atop her seat. It certainly wasn't the worst pillow she'd used—a dirt-filled ditch had that honor. Sylette could . . . sleep for five minutes, and then . . .

She bolted awake, shaking violently to stave off exhaustion. Long silver hairs flapped back and forth, smacking Renar across the face when he ducked into the cramped cabin.

"Wha—*ptoo, ptoo!*" He spat several strands from his mouth, then glared at Sylette. "Watch where you're swinging that thing!"

Sylette snatched her hair back and held the loosely bound ponytail over her shoulder, inspecting a freshly soaked clump at its end. No . . . He'd sullied it; sullied the beautiful hair her mother had loved. For a second, Sylette considered slicing the clump off, then impaling Renar with the same dagger.

"That 'thing,' as you put it, is my hair. Hair which I would *kindly* ask you to not stick in unsavory places." Reaching beneath the dashboard, Sylette pulled out a wad of dirty cloth, which she used to wipe her locks dry. Then she tossed the rag at Renar's face—it *was* his shirt, after all.

His hand snapped up to catch it, a hand that clutched a wrinkled scrap of paper. Renar's eyes went wide. In that instant of indecision, he didn't drop the parchment. Nor did he block the flying garment. The sweat-stained, blood-crusted, drool-contaminated shirt struck him right on the nose and wrapped halfway about his head.

Sylette couldn't help but giggle. *Oh, how I needed that.*

"Yeah, yeah, laugh it up," Renar said, voice muffled beneath the fabric. "I'll get you back at some point. Just you wait."

Careful not to damage the paper, he unfurled the shirt and pulled it on over his tanned shoulders and chest. Sylette shuddered. That filth should be *burned*, not put back on without a second's hesitation.

"Anyway, this," Renar held up the scrap, "Is the entirety of the poem the Resistance broadcast. If we're going to find out where the meet-up point is, we have to figure out where Heisden wrote it."

The Resistance. Was it someone from the Darmatian army, trying desperately to assemble a rebellion against the Sarconian Empire's occupation? Or was it a cleverly laid trap, designed to lure in and eliminate surviving Kingdom stragglers like them? Sylette didn't know, but she'd always choose whichever option brought her a hairsbreadth closer to slaying the Emperor—the murderer she'd once called father.

Clamping down on her rage, Sylette nodded. "Read it."

"On distant shore, where mist a-abounds,
The god of wind and sea is found.
His jagged crest, worn and ... pocked,
Is lined in shadow where none may dock.
Beneath the yet eternal flame,
The wooden trappings of mortals came,
And only where his light did shine,
could they avoid the def's confine.
Stoic, stout, firm he stands,
Protecting all beneath his hands."

Renar read the first half of the poem aloud. He wasn't a court scop—one of those garishly dressed minstrels who'd frequented the palace halls, desperate for Emperor Sychon Artorios to grant them a recital. Sylette had summoned them on occasion, listening to their soothing songs while she ate fruit tarts in the gardens with her pet crysahund, Tyxt.

Even her limited experience was enough to expose the holes in his performance. The iambic was off, his pitch soared and dropped at random, and he was struggling with some of the words. But Sylette *could* see potential, not that his meaningless hobbies interested her.

"Wooden trappings are ships," she reasoned, "And the light—a lighthouse—protects them from reefs. What's next?"

Since there were only two seats in the small cockpit, Renar moved from the doorway and leaned against the instrument panel behind Matteo's chair. Even then, he was forced to hunch over, his shoulders and neck craned downwards to avoid smacking the low, curved ceiling. Squinting, he continued to read by the light of the blinking ceiling diodes.

"The serpents flee, their maws pull back,
The sea hems and . . . haws and must ret-retract.
Haze can but hide; the—there's a smudge here—*truth still remains,*
Both fear of man and—might be Unter's blood—*hope to claim.*
If one can but survive the perilo-lous quest,
In the—I can't read this wrinkle here—*they may find rest.*
The rest is a little blurry, but I think—"

Sylette cut him off with a wave of her hand. "That's enough. If I remember correctly, the rest is just some fanciful description and a little bit of the author's verbose flair. The only notable parts in there are about the tidal patterns and the mist common to the area."

Unable to see out the viewport, Renar squatted on his haunches and shoved his bulk into the gap between their seats. Too close! Sylette pushed against the opposite armrest, all but plastering herself to the shuddering bulkhead wall.

"So, we're looking for a lighthouse in a place with lots of mist and constantly changing tides," Renar said. "That should make things easier."

Do I have to do all the thinking around here? Sylette felt a sigh build in her lungs. It died on her lips. Exhaling led to inhaling, and she had no desire to take a hefty whiff of Renar's fermenting odor.

When Sylette spoke, it was to the bobbing needle of the altimeter on the panel in front of her—*away* from Renar. "What exactly do they teach you Darmatians in school? Tides are always coming in and out. That's kind of their thing. Besides, we'd have to sit and observe them in several locations to notice any difference or collect data from library repositories we can't access.

"Then there's the matter of fog. Tell me, Renar, what do you see outside?" Sylette pointed at the skyscape rushing past the airship.

"The sun, blue sky as far as you can see, the ocean and Phar coast, a paved highway a little farther inland, and some sandy bluffs spotted with small groups of trees. Why do you ask?"

Such a straightforward answer, and so *him*—quick, simple, direct. The coast he'd described was sheer limestone, fragmented in places where water rushed in to form tiny inlets and grottos. Their tops had been blasted by foam-laced wind, forming craggy dunes to which patches of shrubs and ivy—Renar's 'trees'—clung with rugged determination.

It wasn't until at least a league inland that green grass was even visible, and a league farther than that until the ground was level enough to site a road. And that road, the Pharus highway, was hardly a major thoroughfare. With Etrus at one end and remote Weisvale on the other, it saw scarce traffic, predominantly horses and wagons instead of magtech vehicles and airships.

But Renar could have stopped after describing the heavens, for that was all Sylette needed to make her point. "Yes. Clear sky, not a cloud in sight. In the month of Hetrachia, just before the start of winter, near both the sea and mountains of northern Darmatia. It's cold and there's no moisture in the air, Renar! There's no way mist is going to naturally appear at this time of year."

"Which means?"

Before Sylette could slug, stab, or otherwise assault the ignorant buffoon, Matteo came to her rescue. "She's saying all we have to guide our search is 'a lighthouse near Weisvale,' which we already knew."

The former princess closed her eyes and silently thanked whatever Veneer or deity was listening that there was someone else with common sense on the ship. "And," Sylette continued, "that's not much to go on. Renar, do you know anything about the poem's author or history or—"

"Actually," Matteo interjected. "We know more than you think."

It was the second time in a day that the timid sensory mage had cut her off or questioned her ideas and beliefs. The first time, just before the exile attempted to charge a compound filled with Sarconian soldiers, his suggestion had likely saved their lives. Even so, the fact that *anyone* would dispute her plans rankled Sylette like nothing else. Both then and now it raised her heart rate and made her blood boil—especially because of how inept the man-child was in every other situation.

But, Sylette let the irritation out through her nose. *But I'll restrain myself, simply because Matteo will probably say something useful.*

"Care to elaborate?" she asked.

"Well, combining what my father told me about the transport business, along with what we learned in our culture and society classes . . ." Matteo began in typical, roundabout Professor fashion. *Stay calm,* Sylette told herself. *Let him finish.*

" . . . After that, when the town of Weisvale was founded in the

30

third century to provide a settlement for those early logging pioneers, they needed to figure out a way to ship the rich lumber down south. Since there were no rivers, they had two choices—use roads or use the Phar sea. The first was impractical. The Pharus highway wasn't even built at that time. So, the frontiersmen decided to dump their logs into the sea and guide them down the coast to Etrus."

Sylette kicked the underside of the control panel, startling Matteo and cutting his *oppressive* dissertation short. So much for her staying calm.

"Are you *trying* to damage something important?" he squeaked.

"We'll pass the lighthouse before you're done. Just give us the lecture notes version."

Matteo looked crestfallen. "Those *were* my lecture notes. From Principles of Darmatian Industry? It was a required course our second year at the Academy." Neither Sylette nor Renar showed any signs of recognition. He might as well have been speaking Eliassi.

"You have your lecture notes *memorized*?" Renar snorted and shook his head.

"You ... don't?"

A snap of Sylette's fingers and an icy glare got Matteo back on topic. "Short explanation, got it. The Weisvale harbors were frozen most of the year—the town *does* sit up against the Great Divide mountains. This meant the settlers couldn't move their product by sea ... *unless* they constructed a road down the coast to a bay that didn't freeze. At that halfway point, ships from the south took charge of the timber and guided it the rest of the way to Etrus. And to keep those vessels from running aground on the cliffs or reefs, they would have built—"

"—a lighthouse," Sylette finished. "See? You can be brief if you try." Inside, she kept a firm damper on her hope. This might not be a fool's errand, but she wouldn't rejoice until they came face to face with the Resistance.

"You think Heisden's lighthouse and the one they built are the same?" Renar asked.

Matteo nodded. "I don't see why not. Heisden wrote that poem a century after it was constructed, so it was around at the time."

"And how long till we get there?" As he spoke, Renar stood and tried to stretch. His arms immediately smacked the bulkheads to either side. "Ow, ow, ow, that stings ..."

"It shouldn't be all that much ... wait, what's that down there?"

Easing off the throttle, Matteo slowed the airship and began an arcing descent toward the ground. The wispy cloud tendrils that had been whipping by slowed along with it, and the howl of the craft's tortured engine lessened to a wounded mewl. Sylette sighed as her seat—and the whole ship—stopped vibrating to pieces.

She leaned toward the viewport, and Matteo obliged her curiosity by pointing at the object that had grabbed his attention. "Start at the middle of the window," he suggested. "Then look down and left."

The scene below was a perfect match for Heisden's poem and the Professor's description. Ragged limestone cliffs topped by waving brown grasses wore their way to a broken black base that abutted the roaring sea. The lower levels were shorn bare of vegetation, gleaming dark teeth that cut the seething white waves crashing against them. However, Sylette's gaze was drawn to a solitary island that jutted out at least a hundred meters from the ridge itself.

It was no more than fifty meters in diameter, a circle rounded by the water lapping against its edges, with its upper reaches barely flat enough to support any manner of construct. Yet there stood a magnificent lighthouse, two rounded turrets clinging desperately to the side nearest the sea. The larger sported a burgundy cap half the size of the stone base beneath it. Within that glass chamber, currently dimmed, was mounted the largest illyrium crystal Sylette had ever seen.

Renar's eyes twinkled with the joy of a child unwrapping a Festivus gift. "I think we found what we're looking for," he breathed, moving next to her for a better view. Their shoulders brushed. Sylette bit her lip, counted to ten, and resisted the urge to shove him away. Loathe though she was to admit it, he had earned this moment.

"Maybe," she replied. "We'll have to get closer and look around. Matteo, can you set the ship down by that bridge?" The stone causeway extended from the open bluffs above the lighthouse down to the water's edge, then over to the structure itself. Made of a more grayish brick than the white marble of the towers themselves, it appeared to have been constructed at a later date, perhaps after the ravenous sea sliced the knob of land from its main body.

A drop of sweat trickled along Matteo's hairline. He licked his lips, and his fingers clenched and unclenched atop the airship's yoke. *Nerves*, Sylette reasoned. But of course he'd be nervous. His last flight had ended in a crash and a burning wreck—a wreck they'd been lucky to limp away from.

Yet the winds were light, the landing zone was flat, and there were no enemies to pressure him. If Matteo couldn't land now, he would *never* succeed as a pilot.

Reaching over, Sylette placed a hand on the control stick, preventing Matteo from pushing it forward. He glanced at her, eyes narrowed in confusion.

"You know," Sylette began, dredging up vestiges of compassion she'd long thought forgotten. "It's pretty tedious to call this flying wreck 'ship' or 'transport' or whatever every single time I talk about it."

"Flying . . . *w-wreck*?" Matteo stammered.

"It is. Don't interrupt." In the background, Renar snorted, but Sylette ignored him and pressed on. "She needs a name, Matteo. What is it?"

"My father called her—"

Sylette shook her head. "It's not his ship anymore. It's *yours*. What will you name her?"

Matteo gazed over his shoulder at the cargo bay door, through which could be heard the sounds of Lilith hammering a sheet of metal and Unter's deep, labored breathing. "We should decide it together. We are a team, after all."

Bile twisted in Sylette's stomach at the thought of being on a team with Vallen. This *wasn't* a team; it was a bunch of idiots and fools thrown together by happenstance. Their continued survival was a greater miracle than any the Veneer had ever performed.

"But *you're* the pilot. We don't get anywhere without you or"— Sylette waved her other hand at their surroundings, several tons of third-grade gestalt steel fixed in place by brittle bolts, bandages, and the collective prayers of its occupants—"Your ship. So, what's her name, Captain?"

"You called him *captain*." Renar started laughing again.

Daggers glared from her eyes, silencing him almost immediately. "Once. It won't happen a second time."

"*Him*," Matteo said. He was staring out the viewport, chest heaving, tears in his eyes. Trembling still shook the yoke they both held, but now from sadness, not fear. "Him," Matteo repeated. "Kinloss. I'll name the ship after Abbot Kinloss, the man who stayed behind— who gave everything so we could escape Etrus. He deserves that much, don't you think?"

"Yes," Sylette said.

No strong emotion compelled her agreement. Death stalked her. Her mother's, long past. Her father's, a promise to be fulfilled.

And, eventually, her own.

Suffice to say that Kinloss' sacrifice wasn't novel to her. Nor was Leon Descar's. She appreciated them, remembered them . . . and pressed forward. Looking back wouldn't bring her blade to the Emperor's throat.

Gently, slowly, so as not to alarm Matteo, she removed her hand from the control stick and allowed him to ease into their descent. The landing that followed was perfect, even though the pilot still had tears in his eyes.

Chapter 2
The Sea God's Crest

Vallen enjoyed watching others work.

Cupping his hands behind his head, he leaned against a smooth boulder, relishing the touch of cool stone on his back and the cushion of dried grass beneath his legs. The other cadets rushed around like Trillith, scouring the plateau and lighthouse below for clues to the Resistance's whereabouts. Sylette barked orders, her drones rushed to obey, and useless buzzes of information shot back and forth. If they all had chitin shells and mandibles, Vallen would be hard pressed to tell them apart from the insectoid species.

But that didn't bother him. They could waste their time if they wanted, so long as they didn't insist he participate. Vallen was a warrior. A fighter. The venerated Triaron, sung about in ballads, praised in myths. The long-awaited successor to the legendary King Darmatus' vast array of elemental magic. Rending the earth itself, he had annihilated a company of Sarconian soldiers and allowed them to escape Etrus. Vallen's comrades owed him their lives.

And therefore, the labor of turning over stones, searching cracks and crevices, and scrambling about a dank, dusty lighthouse was beneath him. Except ...

A crisp autumn breeze raced in from the sun-dappled sea, tousling Vallen's unkempt locks, making the nearby airship's landing struts groan as it continued its easterly journey. It carried with it some of the soot caught on his tunic, ash picked up when he'd fought bare-handed in the middle of a burning warehouse. He'd been out of men'ar then—unable to cast a single spell. Weak, gasping for breath, wild strikes fueled by adrenaline and rage.

The wind stilled, and with its passing, Vallen's facade of confidence shattered. Needles of pain lanced through his limbs, his head, his organs, a cacophony of agony that yearned to emerge as a tortured shriek. He bit his lip, drawing blood. His grasping nails tore fistfuls of grass and dirt from the ground. Cramps in his legs screamed for him to curl up, to lie in a sobbing heap until the suffering receded. But Vallen would *not* break. The world would break first.

Seconds ticked by, and the lingering effects of men'ar overuse— MIS—gradually faded. Vallen didn't move. Nearby, Lilith informed

Sylette they'd discovered nothing but cobwebs, dusty dishes, and crumbling furniture in the lighthouse. It was empty and hadn't been used for years. Neither glanced in his direction, but if they had, he'd appear to be lounging without a care. They wouldn't hear his groans. See the way his fingers shook or the dark caverns hanging beneath his eyes.

Since two nights prior, the last time he'd dreamed of Elaine, his mind had refused to let him sleep. *No, that's not quite right,* Vallen amended. *I've refused to sleep.* Some part of Vallen knew he was coming unhinged. The rest didn't care. It desired this self-destruction, this self-immolation in pursuit of vengeance for Leon. It wanted to blame something, anything, other than himself for the fates' of his friends. And it was this part that wouldn't let him rest, that wouldn't let him watch Elaine's death unfold in his visions, lest a worse cycle of self-loathing begin.

Burn the world rather than yourself, it cried.

"Nothing," Sylette grumbled after Lilith walked away. "There's *nothing* here." Her leg lashed out, kicking a pebble off the cliff. "Not a thing—no people, no supplies, no clues. Just a voided waste of time!"

Another pebble was condemned to the frothing waters, then a third. Though he'd never admit it aloud, Vallen could empathize with her frustration. Ravaged as his body was, he craved a fight. The frenzy of combat might bury his pain and self-loathing, if only briefly.

When Sylette ran out of stones, she stalked along the ridge, gaze sweeping the reefs below. What did she hope to find? The waves lashed the cliffs mercilessly, their roar thunderous at this distance. The princess would find no Resistance base or hidden airships, no matter how hard she looked.

Footfalls sounded to Vallen's left, boots striking on brick. Flipping over, he faced the pair of cadets at the top of the steps leading down to the lighthouse. Renar was fixated on the great illyrium crystal in its glass housing, his eyes narrowed and his lead-tipped scrivle scratching away at a palm-sized notebook held open in his left hand. Lilith approached him from behind with a curious grin on her lips.

"What's that you're doing?"

Vallen snorted as Renar jerked forward, bobbling his notebook. If not for the clips binding his page, he would have lost it over the edge. His scrivle was not so lucky. The writing utensil slipped through his thick fingers, bounced on the waist-high parapet lining the steps, and was caught by Lilith before it could plunge to its demise. She presented it with a flourish, prompting a sigh of relief from Renar.

"*Whew*. I only have two left. I can't thank you enough for saving that one."

"And . . . " Lilith prompted, staring at the notebook as Renar retrieved his scrivle.

"And?" Renar blinked, then tracked her gaze to the leather-bound booklet. "Oh, this. Promise not to laugh?"

I *might laugh,* Vallen thought. *No, I* definitely *will.*

"Why would I?" Lilith, as fast without her rapier as with it, dashed around to his back and bounded in the air to look over his shoulder. Even then, she barely cleared his back long enough to get a proper look. "Let me see, let me see!"

"Fine. Stop bouncing."

Renar tapped her head with the pad, then handed it to her with a nervous smile. She flipped through the pages, saying nothing for several moments. The longer the silence dragged on, the more agitated the muscular Terran became.

Vallen grinned. Lengthen his nose, give him some whiskers, and the fidgety brute would make a fine pipe-rat.

"Well?" Renar said.

Lilith beamed at him while pointing to an open page. "You're an *amazing* artist, Renar. You could even put these on display!"

"They're just scribblings, nothing that fancy."

"Is that the palace in Nemare? I've never seen it look so beautiful. Look here—this airship seems like it's *flying*! And I think . . . yes, that's a map of Etrus. When did you have time to make this? We came in at night and left in a hurry, and yet you still managed to record so much."

Vallen watched the exchange with one eyebrow cocked. Half of him wanted to gag. *This* bird sketching fop was his self-proclaimed rival? Every flag-brawl victory he had scored against Renar felt hollow now, like a poached egg absent its juicy yolk. It was little wonder the brute was a graceless warrior if he wasted his time this way.

The other half was amused. *A simple soul should have simple desires,* Vallen thought. Smirking, he pictured the horror that would twist Renar's face when he discovered his rival hadn't been sleeping. That he'd overheard every silly, childish word they'd spoken.

Renar blushed. "I-I may not be the smartest guy, but I like to think I'm good at drawing and figuring out things others might miss, like directional layouts or puzzles."

"Good doesn't begin to describe these!" Lilith gushed, eyes sparkling as she gaped at sketch after sketch. "Why become a soldier when people would pay good geldars for … Oh, that's right, you told us … "

Lilith's gaze fell along with her arms. Nodding an apology, she handed the journal back to Renar. Vallen couldn't quite make out what was on the open page, but it appeared to have two roughly shaded turrets in the foreground and choppy waves for a backdrop.

"Yeah, because of my dad," Renar said. "No need to get down about it, though. That's just the way he is. And I get where he's coming from. He wants me to follow in his footsteps. I just … " He paused, forearms trembling, focus fixed on the horizon where blue sea and sky met. "I just wish he'd let me enjoy the things I like along the way. That's not too much to ask for, right?"

A loud scoff escaped Vallen's lips, loud enough that Sylette stopped examining a cliff fissure and shot him an icy glare. Was Renar serious? Did he expect Lilith to say 'no?' For the first time, Vallen found himself agreeing with General Iolus—Renar's blowhard father. When the Void came knocking, no number of pretty pictures would save you.

"Of course not!" Lilith said, earning another snort from Vallen. Her short brown hair bounced as she darted forward, grabbed Renar's hand, and dragged him toward the lighthouse steps. "There's a whole bunch of crabs, urchins, and other sea critters gathered on the rocks around the towers. Maybe you can draw them for me?"

Renar's pale face brightened. In an instant, he was running alongside Lilith, two idiots dashing off without a care in the world. Vallen wasn't sure whether he envied or derided their ignorance. They were still innocent, unblemished by the taint of pain and suffering. Yet that meant the same trauma he'd endured awaited them when the lash of reality finally struck.

One person shared his sentiments. "Look at those happy-go-lucky fools," Sylette said. Her search abandoned, she mounted a nearby boulder and stared after the retreating cadets. "Off to draw crabs, rocks, and mud while we're not one step closer to finding the Darmatian holdouts."

Gusting winds whipped across the plateau, buffeting Sylette but failing to topple her from her perch. She leaned into the gale, braided ponytail floating behind her, the cinched-up ties of her bloodied blouse snapping against her chest. Vallen willed her to fall, or her silver hair to wrap firmly about her snow-white neck. But that was wishful thinking. Even in exile, a royal was still a royal, stubborn and prideful to the end.

"And you'd rather they kept flipping over stones with nothing but scum-crawlers beneath them?" Vallen asked, voice raspy. He hadn't spoken in nearly a day.

The smirk Sylette turned on him was wicked. "Ah! The useless lump we've been carrying since Etrus deigns to speak. How good of you to rejoin the land of the living *after* we've done all the searching."

"Injured reserve, remember?" Vallen waggled his fingers above his head. Dark splotches of flaky skin coated them, yet another aftereffect of MIS. "You woke me up, I shattered the square, and the Sarc panzcraft went flying like toys?"

"I remember. You mentioned it one or twenty times."

Curling his fingers, Vallen made a shooing gesture. "Then it seems I'm the only one pulling my weight around here. Come get me when you find the Resistance or have some Sarcs to kill." He rolled onto his side, facing away from the scowling princess and feigning sleep. In truth, he just didn't want her to look closer and see the blood on his lip or the sunken pits ringing his eyes.

Sylette inhaled sharply. It was likely she was debating whether or not to use Vallen's back as a target for her daggers. After a few tense seconds, the princess huffed and stalked past him toward the airship, her every step an anger-fueled stamp.

"Matteo!" She called. "How is the airship doing on fuel and supplies?"

The bespectacled youth was seated halfway down the transport's rear ramp, Velle—less haggard than she'd been yesterday—huddled close to him. A threadbare blanket, scavenged from one of the few cargo containers left on board, hung about their shoulders. Like the old hand-me-downs Matteo's family had given them to wear, the blanket would do little to repel the seaborne chill.

At Sylette's shout, Matteo jerked in surprise. His flailing arms caught the hem of the cover as he tried to stand, upsetting his balance and toppling him off the metal gantry. Velle wasn't fast enough to grab the blanket. It slid from her shoulders and fell atop Matteo, resulting in a vaguely Terran-shaped hump of groaning fabric. Stifling a laugh, the Sylph girl crawled over, reached down, and offered a shaky hand to help him up.

Jealous rage sputtered and died in Vallen's breast. Velle—Velle'assa Me'andara—had never truly been his. One of his lovers, perhaps, but nothing more than that. And he'd made his choice in Etrus, rejecting her when she'd extended a similar hand to him. The purpling welt on her cheek, only half hidden by her curling black bangs, was evidence of that. He'd broken their bond along with her beautiful crimson flesh.

There was no going back to the way things were before.

"At least you can land an airship better than your own two feet," Sylette said, stooping to grasp Matteo's other arm. Grunting, she heaved him upright. "Given your reaction, I take it we're low on everything?"

Matteo straightened his glasses, then shook his head. "It's not good," he admitted. "We barely have enough illyrium crystals to go twenty leagues in any direction, the extra synth-oil overheated and went bad because of its proximity to the engine—which is running *way* too hot, by the way—and there's no food on board. We're out of Sarc protein pouches, stale cracker packages, and I couldn't even scrounge up enough crumbs to feed the pipe-rats below deck."

Matteo's stomach loosed a supportive rumble that echoed off the surrounding cliffs. Matteo went red—only a shade lighter than Velle—as everyone stared at his midriff. Ten seconds passed. The echo faded. Then, unable to hold it in any longer, Velle burst out laughing.

"Oh, thank you, Matteo," she gasped, wiping tears from her eyes. "My gut hurts, but it's a good hurt. I didn't know just how much I needed that laugh."

Vallen tried to laugh along with her. A cough emerged instead. Hearing a growl or belch like that at the Academy mess hall would've left him doubled over, cackling at the top of his lungs. How much of him had died with Leon . . . and how much had been dead all this time, rot hidden beneath a mask of contentment?

Surprisingly, Sylette allowed them a moment of merriment, folding her arms and studying the curve of the airship's crescent moon frame. When the laughter stopped, she favored them with a frown that was only cold, not frigid.

"So, this was a waste of time *and* our supply situation is somehow worse than before. Fan-voiding-tastic." Sylette craned her neck upward, peering at the sky as if searching for celestial guidance. "We'll grab Renar and Lilith, then leave as soon as you've got the ship prepped." She turned toward Velle. "How's Unter? Did you take a look at him yet?"

Velle's smile disappeared. Brow knitted, she peered over her shoulder at the darkened opening of the cargo bay. "It's been pretty touch and go with him. The Moravi poison in his leg was allowed to spread freely, on top of which he took a bullet to the chest that was . . . only a finger-width from cutting a major artery. If I . . . If I'd been able to start working on him sooner, then he wouldn't be in such a . . . "

Tears welled in Velle's scarlet eyes and sobs choked her voice. Before she could curl up into a sniveling ball, Matteo climbed up the side of the ramp, knelt beside her, and passed her the blanket. "Here."

"Thank . . . you," she managed between sniffles. Matteo, face still flushed, nodded without looking at her.

Vallen wanted to chastise them for their weakness, but . . .

A spasm of pain shot through his right leg, knotting his muscles, arching his back as he gritted his teeth. Slowly, like a receding tide, the agony passed. Yes, in the state Vallen was in, he had no right to condemn *anyone.*

"Will Unter live?" Sylette asked.

The Sylph stopped dabbing her eyes. Blinking her dark lashes, she cleared her throat and continued as best she could. "I think so, but—"

"I can't plan based on a hunch."

"Yes," Velle insisted, tone hardening. "Yes, he will. I don't know a lot about Hue physiology, but Unter's strong and resilient. His body held the poison at bay until I could use magic to hasten his cell division and drive it out. But that took most of what little men'ar I'd recovered, and I need proper surgical tools to get the bullet out. *Unless . . .*"

She brightened, and her ears—longer and more curved than a Terran's—twitched where they poked through her raven locks. "Unless Lilith lets me borrow her saber and I can find a spoon in one of the crew's meal tins. We'll disinfect both with her flames and—"

"Excellent," Sylette said, "but we'll have to postpone the operation until we find someplace to lay low from the Empire." She gazed at the sky. Towering clouds, dark and ominous, dotted the horizon. A storm was coming.

Reaching up, Sylette knocked on the airship's side, a ruddy surface Vallen thought was more rust than paint. She ignored the scraps of corroded metal that dislodged at her touch. "Can the *Kinloss* get us to Weisvale, Matteo? The Empire shouldn't have a presence there yet."

Kinloss? Wasn't that the name of the frumpy monk who'd stuck his too-long nose into the middle of their—*his*—fight?

"Sariel's arse," Vallen muttered, covering his face with his hands. "*Please* tell me she didn't let the Professor name the ship after *another* whimpering coward. Leon would've . . . been . . ."

His voice trailed off. No, Leon wouldn't have been a better name. Vallen didn't need any more reminders of his failures. They could call it the *Randy Rittermarschal* or *Skipping Sarcon* for all he cared.

When Vallen looked up again, Matteo was drawing calculations in the air. *Bravo!* Vallen thought. *The Terran abacus is good for something!*

Circling his invisible answer, the Professor turned to Sylette.

"We could make it there, but just to the outskirts. We'd have to walk a league or more to the town itself. However …" He paused and gave his glasses a shaky shunt up his nose. "We'd be trapped against the Great Divide and Empire if we go that way. Won't they track us down and trap us?"

"Undoubtedly," Sylette replied. "Even so, we should have enough time to get back on our feet. Who knows?" She shrugged, a motion that pulled her blouse tight against the brown belt around her waist. "Maybe we can slip back past Etrus and into the Ascendancy. Or get to the Imperium by flying south of Nemare and through the Badlands."

"The Ascendancy *doesn't* like outsiders." Velle shivered as she spoke. Vallen hadn't seen any heated exchanges between her and Unter, but their people weren't on the best of terms.

"And *the Badlands?*" Matteo blurted, his eyes wide and mouth agape. "One, the *Kinloss* can't carry enough fuel to make that journey." He began counting on his fingers. "Two, if we *could* store enough fuel, we wouldn't have room for food or water. Things we kind of need to live. Three, if we have to land to get water—which is almost impossible to find in that desert, to begin with—the nasty beasties that live there will eat us and use our bones for toothpicks. I *don't* want to be a toothpick."

The complaints rolled off Vallen as his pulse quickened. His fatigued, tormented flesh needed a foe—needed to slash, rend, and kill. *Enough of this talking,* his soul raged. *Decide on a plan!* Either it would work out and he'd go on killing Sarconians, or it wouldn't. He'd follow a madman into the Void if there was blood waiting for him there.

No one heard Sylette's reply. The gusts lashing the plateau redoubled, interrupting their conversation. Silver and black hair whipping wildly, Sylette and Velle leaned into the wind, straining to hold their ground. Matteo shielded the Sylph with his body. Grasses danced around them—a freshly uprooted maelstrom of loam-scented green and brown mixed with the tang of salt. As Vallen rose to his knees and scurried behind a boulder, a high-pitched squeal reached his ears.

Their airship—the *Kinloss*, or whatever they bloody well wanted to call it—was teetering on its very old, very rusted struts.

"Where did this come from?" Matteo shouted to be heard above the howling gale. "That storm was at least an hour off! We should've had time to leave!"

A sheet of dark seawater crashed nearby. The tide was coming in, bringing with it a sea that was bucking and snarling like a chained-up dragwyrm. Waves half the size of the cliffs broke against the lighthouse, showering the bridge and steps with torrents of foaming water.

Vallen gaped at the pitch-black heavens, a darkness so complete it could blot out a moonless night. Was this a nightmare? Had he fallen asleep? Shadow shrouded everything, and the temperature plummeted, frosting his hurried breaths.

Then the fog rolled in.

Grayish-white tendrils spawned from the depths, coiling from the bay up about the reefs and crags. First, the lighthouse was consumed by the haze, followed by the bridge, and lastly everything beyond the plateau on which they stood. Visibility was terrible; Vallen couldn't see more than ten meters in any direction. Thankfully, the illyrium crystal atop the taller tower activated in response to the soupy mist, dispelling the suffocating veil as its beams started to rotate.

"Get on the shi—"

"AAAAUUUUGGGGHHHHH!"

Sylette's order was interrupted by two shrieks echoing up from below the ledge. *At last*, Vallen thought. Those cries could only belong to Renar and Lilith, and if they were in trouble, he would finally have the action he craved.

Grinning, Vallen stood and unhooked a gleaming cylinder from his belt. Formed from an alloy of unusual metals, it looked bronze, weighed as much as a dagger, and seemed no more useful than the average watchman's baton. *Seemed*. In the Triaron's hands, the rod could be—and do—almost anything.

Willing men'ar into his palm, he shoved it across the boundary between flesh and weapon, urging the rod to take on new life. Cool metal dissolved in his grasp, coursing around his fingers, flowing, extending, and at last reforming into the image pictured in his mind. Where once was a simple rod, Vallen now held a long, curved blade—a perfect imitation of a Vladisvar krenesh.

Good, he thought, flexing his fingers on the grip. *No needles lancing through my arm. I can fight.*

Not saying a word, Sylette took up a position near him, stance shallow and hands raised. The air about her head shimmered as she summoned four daggers into existence.

"Matteo and Velle?" Vallen prompted. He didn't want the blunderer shooting him in the back again.

"Prepping the ship to leave."

"How long will that take?"

The exile snorted. "Too long."

Adrenaline surged through Vallen, banishing the cobwebs of pain, invigorating his muscles and giving him sweet clarity. Part of him hoped the junker *never* started.

The smog ahead of them parted, revealing a pair of breathless cadets climbing the last steps to the plateau. Soaked down to their skivvies by sweat and surf, terror imprinted on ashen faces, they reached softer soil and churned their legs as fast as they were able. Renar took the transition poorly. He went down with a cry of pain, clutching his ankle, forcing Lilith to turn back to help him.

Not five meters from them, a massive spade-tipped tentacle rose past the steps and grasped the boulder Vallen had been laying against. Suckers the size of his head clasped on and the limb—itself the size of an ancient Weisse Elegoras trunk from the Lyndwur Forest—strained to haul the . . . *thing* it was attached to over the precipice.

The rock tilted, then ripped free from the ground entirely, leaving behind a deep rut that could double as a small canal. Though Vallen couldn't see it through the fog, a tremendous splash accompanied the impact.

Can we fight this monster? the logical part of Vallen's brain asked. It tried to make his heart waver and knees shake, but he shoved his doubts aside. The coming battle—its fury and carnage—was all that mattered.

Arm hooked across Lilith's shoulders, Renar was back on his feet. Together they staggered toward the airship, the burly Terran favoring his right leg the whole way. Lilith's fear-filled eyes kept darting back to the ledge. It wasn't hard to guess her thoughts: *How long do we have before the beast chasing us gets serious?*

Spitting and coughing, the *Kinloss* roared to life, its gravpads producing a downdraft that buffeted Vallen from behind. He cursed under his breath. *No!* he raved at Sylette as she shouted encouragement to the fleeing cadets. *No!* he fumed at Matteo as the transport's belly lights flashed the craft's readiness.

No! I NEED this fight!

When Renar and Lilith were halfway across the plateau, eight coiling tentacles—each a deep foam green more resplendent than any emerald—replaced the first. They shot over the bluffs and crashed around the pair, showering them with an eruption of soil and clay. In an instant, the plateau was bare—shorn to the skull-white limestone by the force of the blow. Greedy pink suckers latched onto the solid ground, suckling it like a babe at the teat.

Strong muscles rippled along the length of the tentacles, pulling at whatever titanic mass still hunkered in the waters below. A dark shape shot into the air. Vallen's eyes traced it through the sky. Up and up, then down, a hulking shadow that grew by the second. It could have squashed them all; crumpled the airship like a can beneath a Vladisvar's steel-shod foot.

Instead, it struck the center of the plateau. The shockwave from its landing hit like a cannon blast. Vallen nearly fell as the ground quaked, only managing to steady himself by digging his blade into the earth. Renar and Lilith tumbled head over heels, winding up in a pile of limbs at Sylette's feet.

A shrill cry came from the airship. Vallen glanced over his shoulder, where Velle clung to a mass of mesh cargo netting hanging from the left side of the vessel's cargo bay—a side that had become a ceiling when the craft collapsed onto its flank.

Two of the landing struts had snapped, the *Kinloss* was stuck, and there would be no escape.

Chapter 3

The Eastern Front

Hetrachia 12, 697 ABH
Outskirts of Beiras, Rabban Imperium Industrial Megacity

Patience did not come easily to Rittermarschal Ober Valescar, especially with the wounds he suffered at Aldona Fortress gnawing at his flesh.

The aging commander now wore two suits of armor. The first was the full plate of his station, a burnished silver breastplate, taloned greaves, and heavy steel boots that always heralded his arrival with staccato claps. Mail and gambeson padding formed the next layer down, and a simple, sweat-stained tunic clung to his skin.

Skin that had itself become armor. Valescar shifted in the command chair of the *Judicator*, trying in vain to quell the itch spreading across his ravaged left side. Healing magic and the soothing waters of a Sarconian medical bed could only do so much. The burns—and the stench of his own cooked flesh—would never truly leave him.

Flaking scar tissue covered his body from scalp to toes, a sore reminder of the exploding airship he'd narrowly escaped. The plate he'd worn that day was *seared* into him, bits of charred alloy welded to his shoulder, chest, and flank. Molten drips from the patch covering his missing left eye dotted his cheek, leaving ragged gaps in the dignified gray beard he'd once cultivated. They looked a bit like tears, but not a single soldier dared to say so in his presence.

When Valescar had laid on the butcher's table, staring up at the blinding light the surgeons held over him, a mousy doctor with a hooked nose had informed him they *could* remove the fragments. Pockmarks—quite deep in some places—would be left behind, but their magtech researchers were making great strides in the synthesis of alchemical flesh. It would only cost Valescar a few unavoidable nerves and the men'ar vessels underneath.

He'd crushed the light with a single magnetism-infused clench of his fist, brushed the doctor aside, and stormed from the facility. He was Rittermarschal Ober Valescar, commander of the Seventh Sarconian Airfleet, "Wall of the Empire," and staunch servant of His Majesty, Emperor Sychon Artorios. Death would claim him before he risked the power that protected the Imperial throne.

No metallic poison nor sliver of shrapnel would reach his heart—not with his magic keeping them at bay.

Which wasn't to say the wounds didn't irritate him. Valescar shifted again, his teeth set in a snarl, his eye narrowed in displeasure. Phantom flames licked at his left side, an agony made all the more aggravating by the simpering face of Lt. Colonel Stetson floating above the LDCT—Long Distance Communication Transceiver—projector in front of him.

"An' exactly what d'ya want me ta do 'bout it, Stetson?" Valescar growled, shaking his mailed fist. "This is yer mistake through and through."

The officer's cadaverous features tightened further, and his gaunt fingers twisted against each other as he spoke. "B-but sir, it was *you* who insisted I wait a week to pursue the girl despite the ironclad testimony I procured from the lizards. We knew where she was staying, but—"

"Need I remind ya who saved yer scrawny neck after the attempt on His Majesty's life?" Valescar half regretted that decision. One tug on Stetson's slicked-back mane would expose his weaselly throat for the executioner's axe, and his regret would be washed away. "An' even though I gave ya ample time ta cast a net ta catch 'er, ya still bungled the final stages. On top o' which, ya lost a warehouse full o' supplies, a platoon o' soldiers, *three* panzcraft, and damaged two o' yer warships in the most inane manner possible."

"But, Rittermarschal—"

Valescar slammed the armrest of his chair, warping the thin metal. "I ain't finished, Stetson! Then—after wastin' all them resources—ya had the gall ta fire on a civilian settlement. An' at their *church* of all places." Valescar shook his head in disbelief. "As if the Darmatians needed any more reason ta hate us. Do ya know how hard it'll be ta protect ya from His Majesty's wrath after this debacle?"

"Please, Valescar. You have to—"

"Don't screw up again." Valescar cut Stetson off before the man resorted to unsightly begging. "My patience will only last so long. End transmission."

Valescar made a dismissive gesture at his communications officer, Annell, who flipped a switch at her station. The image of Stetson disintegrated into millions of tiny yellow globules, which floated back down into the rounded basin of the projector from which they'd come. Ripples danced across the pool, then stilled, waiting for another image to display.

If only the real Stetson could be so easily eliminated. Pinching the puckered skin of his nose, Valescar once again questioned why he suffered the former captain of the imperial guard to live. The axe that claimed poor Lanara's life—an axe he'd wielded himself—should have meted out justice to Stetson on its second swing.

Valescar had . . . come to terms with the fate of Sylette's mother. But he'd spared Stetson for a reason. The man owed him *everything*, and therefore couldn't refuse a single bizarre request—like waiting an extra week to pursue a certain exiled princess.

A warm grin split his deformed lips. *Ah, lass. If only I could'a seen Stetson's face when ya gave him the slip. Ya outwitted me, ya foxed the bony weasel, an' all the Empire ain't gotta clue where've ya gone. Right proud, it makes me. How much like yer mother ye've—*

No, that wasn't a sentiment the Rittermarschal could indulge right now. Not while on campaign. Not while on the bridge of the *Judicator*, the flagship of his seventh fleet, minutes before she entered battle.

"Gadler!" Valescar called, rising to his feet without a groan. His body ached, but the men and women under his command wouldn't see his weakness. "What's the status o' our panickin' foe? Bring 'er up on the projector."

Captain Burntis Gadler, a lean man of middling years sporting a well-maintained chevron-shaped mustache, marched up the metal gantry from the bridge's lower deck and reactivated the projector. In place of Stetson's haggard form, a detailed three-dimensional portrayal of the landscape far below the *Judicator* sprang into existence.

Beiras' lofty skyscrapers dominated the far side of the image. In their shadow lay the hastily constructed Rabban Imperium defense works, the lower lip of Lake Lovare, and Valescar's own armada advancing across the Lozarian central plains.

Gadler drew a lacquered wooden baton from the belt binding his pristine uniform coat and used it to tap the far side of the yellow-tinted holograph. Valescar suppressed a chuckle. The baton was a relic, one belonging to the former war room era of muddy fields, staked-down tents, and static maps littered with carved tokens denoting friend and foe.

Now the *Judicator's* contingent of sensory mages fed that data directly into the illyrium crystal lattice that formed the projector's core. Maps, tokens, and yes, even Gadler's prized baton, had been rendered obsolete by the march of magtech. A part of Valescar wondered when *he* would become a fossil of war himself.

"Imperium reinforcements are still a day or two out at best,"

Gadler said, circling the edge of the projection with his baton. His tone was as clipped and refined as his mustache. "Our sweep through Darmatia, coordinated with a renewed offensive against Varas Fortress, has caught Rabban completely by surprise. If we engage now, all we'll have to deal with is their local forces."

"Which are?" Valescar focused his attention on the beads of ooze coalescing into hovering warships above the fake Beiras.

"A mere dozen airships—one dreadnaught, four heavy cruisers, and a smattering of smaller frigates. We can smash right through them."

Valescar nodded. With forty warships in his fleet and two army groups containing three panzcraft divisions, five infantry divisions, four mage battalions, and numerous support units on the ground, there could be no doubt of the outcome of today's battle. There would be no siege, only a slaughter.

He pitied his opposite, the Rabbanite commander who'd been ordered to stand and die for Beiras. They'd been fools to leave their Darmatian border undefended. Fools to think the Kingdom's neutral buffer could protect their soft heartlands. They would pay the price for their naiveté.

"No need fer tricks. That's precisely what we'll do," Valescar said. "Comm, signal all ahead one third ta the fleet an' let's see what their response is. Also, tell General Schutte on the ground ta hold till we've mopped up those airships."

Heels clicked together. Gadler saluted, then marched back to his post beside the ship's wheel on the level below—the second of the bridge's three tiers. Rorck, the flint-faced, burly helmsman, offered the captain control of the ship, but Gadler waved him off and began issuing orders to a group of deck officers at the stations around him.

"Ahead one-third!" Rorck shouted. One of his bulging arms, barely hidden beneath his sweat-soaked sleeve, pressed forward on the waist-high lever beside the wheel.

"Ahead one-third!" Annell echoed, directing her cheery voice into a series of bronze voicepipes surrounding her desk. At the same time, her deft hands tapped out a series of coded clicks on a brass knocker—a short-range communication to the rest of the fleet to adjust speed.

A sharp whistle came from the ceiling. Illyrium had been fed into *Judicator's* engines, and she was ready to accelerate. Seconds later, a deep rumble vibrated through the dreadnaught. It quickly subsided into a quiet purr as the ship reached a third of its maximum velocity but would return if they changed course or increased speed again.

An' now comes the fun part, Valescar thought. *Judicator*—her crew, not the ship—could all but operate without him. Technicians and engimages hastened hither and yon with resolute purpose. Hushed murmurs and energetic clacking came from the comm station. Bright lights flashed in the crew pits to either side of the bridge's central stairway as deck officers and mages pored over the data displayed on their instruments and crystals. The grating of boots on the metal gantries hung just below all the other sounds.

Each whisper, clatter, and hiss of steam added to the *Judicator's* symphony—the music of competence Valescar had cultivated over decades of military service. Gadler, Annell, Rorck, Hurgan, Ketric, Elias, Irine, and so many others he knew by name. He had followed their careers, plucked them from their units, and assembled them into the best crew the Empire over. They may not be his family, but their bonds were thicker than blood.

Valescar strode toward the front of the bridge, the crimson cloak of his rank trailing behind him. On his way, he complimented Ensign Annell on how swiftly she'd relayed his orders to the fleet. A clap on Helmsman Rorck's rock-firm shoulder brought a fierce grin to the man's scar-slashed lips. Lieutenant-Commander Hurgan, straight-laced as ever, jumped to attention as Valescar passed the fire-control pit. While he returned the salute, two pages of atmospheric data readings materialized in his other hand, key points highlighted with red ink. Sensor Ketric was a silent ghost, but there was no one the Rittermarschal trusted more when his ship found herself in the middle of a storm.

Ensigns Elias and Irine, twin spotters, glanced up from their bronze spyglasses at Valescar's approach. Both women clutched their fists to their chests and inclined their heads. From their tied back blonde hair, to their freckled cheeks, to the aqua crescent-moon catalysts that dangled from their left ears, they were always in sync. Valescar tapped his own breastplate, then waved them from their post.

"But sir," Elias protested. "We've only just begun our shift." Irine nodded in agreement.

"We're aboot ta enter combat," he replied. "The front's no place for a couple of unarmored lasses"—he clicked his gauntlet against his cuirass again for emphasis—"so why don't ya head topside an' join Lieutenant Yarric in the observation blister?" Valescar let a little iron creep into his tone, just enough to let Elias know his suggestion was an order.

"Yes, sir!" they said, snapping their heels together, then departing for the sliding doors at the bridge's rear.

Truth be told, it wasn't a matter of lass or lad, noble or commoner with Valescar. In his mind, ability was the great equalizer. No, he simply hated seeing his subordinates die, and being near the bridge's massive glass viewport when shells started flying was a quick way to go.

He shaded his eye against the glare streaming through the steel-reinforced canopy. The morning sun was catching up to them from the west, its rays setting the hulls of his 7th fleet ablaze. Intermingled with the dawn were the bright flares cast by the Sarconian host. Orange and red blossoms sprouted from their engines. Protruding illyrium power cores radiated bright yellow light. Lume barriers of all sizes shone with dazzling rainbow hues as they shimmered to life in preparation for battle.

Forty warships, roughly a seventh of the Empire's martial might. All about the *Judicator* they flocked, not unlike birds of prey on hunt. Though Valescar had seen this display on countless occasions, he couldn't help marveling at the grace and precision with which they soared.

Harrier skimmers and lancerjets screened for the larger vessels, flying above, before, and between them. Light cruisers paraded behind them, their sleek forms ready to plug gaps in the formation as needed. On either side of Valescar's flagship was the main line. Stalwart, with thick armor and innumerable guns, these heavy cruisers would bear the brunt of the battle. Still farther back were the reserves, freighters, and carriers. While the flattops were responsible for hauling and supplying their fighter-class craft, the lumbering transports kept the fleet afloat. Without their supplies, the illyrium and synth-oil that fed them, the warships would be nothing more than grounded hulks with guns.

Valescar's forces were reinforced today by one extra dreadnaught, the *Vindicator*. She was the sister ship of the *Judicator*—both were of the same design and were launched from drydock together—and was commanded by Vice Admiral Renfrow. Normally attached to the 1st fleet, the vessel had been released into his charge by Emperor Artorios for the campaign to subjugate the western reaches of the Imperium. Delighted at the reunion, *Vindicator* hung close to her sister's flank.

There ain't no way Beiras can resist all o' this, Valescar thought, shifting his gaze down. The Middenlane—the great highway that stretched from one end of the continent to the other—was a thin white line at this height. North of it was the great blue-green expanse of Lake Lovare, which bordered the Empire on its far banks, and to its south were the tiny bumps and stick-thin trees that dotted the expansive Lozarian central plains.

The view would have been beautiful—if not for the blackened craters, smoking ruins, and churned-up fields lining the approach to Beiras. Valescar's flesh itched anew, and a growl built in his throat. Scorched earth tactics. A smart move, from a military perspective. Absolutely disastrous for the ordinary people who called this land home.

Piles of charred white brick sat beside rain-filled shell holes up and down the highway. Little villages and hamlets, their tallest buildings two or three stories high, had been leveled, and what few thatch huts remained were being devoured by flames that cast inky smog up to greet Valescar's fleet. Trees had been reduced to stumps. No grasses swayed atop the plains; only mud and clay remained. Even without looking, the Rittermarschal knew that their precious fields had been salted. No crops would grow here for decades, maybe longer.

This was the cost of war. Beiras' wall of glimmering towers, resplendent in the morning sunlight, hid a darkness in their shadow, one that hugged its drab, factory-choked outskirts and pressed on toward the far horizon. *Dust,* Valescar realized. *They're kicking up plumes o' dust as they evacuate the city.*

And what then? After they made refugees of the whole population, did they plan to *destroy* the settlement? Set it back centuries just to deny resources to the enemy? Valescar's wounded side burned alongside the fire seething in his chest. He spun toward the helm.

"All ahead flank speed! We're endin' this *now.*"

Captain Gadler didn't balk at the change in plans. Reaching up, he pulled on a hanging rope, setting off piercing claxons throughout the *Judicator.* Every one of the vessel's thousands of crew members knew that sound: code red, all hands to battle stations.

The clamor of the bridge immediately rose from a murmur to a roar. Hurgan shouted orders at the grim-faced men manning the terminals around him, who in turn relayed orders to gun emplacements throughout the dreadnaught. Snaps and clicks echoed like pistol retorts, the sound of men and women racing to strap themselves into combat crash harnesses. There was no worse way to go than getting sucked out a shell hole at twenty-five hundred meters.

Judicator leapt forward, her engines straining for all they were worth. Grunts and groans rose from the crew as they were pressed into their seats, but Valescar leaned into the pressure, magnetizing his boots and armor to hold himself in place. Nausea that churned his insides was *nothing* compared to his disgust at the Imperium commanders.

Clouds of yellow illyrium dust burst around the 7th fleet, their exhaust magnified by the surge to maximum speed. The world around Valescar shook and shuddered, but he held firm, his eye trained on Beiras. The lofty, twisting spires of the city grew to dominate the viewport, and the stream of refugees became distinct enough for him to pick out humongous chained dragwyrms hauling artillery pieces and cargo bins. In the foreground, the blocky images he'd viewed on the projector resolved into trench lines, bunkers, and the Rabbanite airships protecting them from above.

"All ships reduce ta half ahead," Valescar called. He spread his legs to shoulder width and clasped his forearms behind his back. "Feed energy ta gun batteries, target enemy fleet."

"Half ahead!" Rorck repeated, slowing the ship.

Annell glanced up from her spread of comcrystals and code-knockers. "All vessels report one-hundred percent combat readiness."

The fleet drew together in a line, bands of light rippling across their almost overlapping lumes, an angry red glare pulsing from their thousands of weapon emplacements. Hurgan ordered one final adjustment, and the great turrets forward of the bridge swung left and leveled their cannons at the dreadnaught holding the enemy's center.

"Ready, my Lord," he announced.

Valescar held up a gauntlet, palm out. "Hold fire. The codes o' war insist that we give our foe the opportunity ta surrender. Annell, open a comm channel ta that dreadnau—"

Gouts of flame from the dozen enemy vessels—and from concealed bunkers on the ground—interrupted him. It took a moment for his brain to process what was happening, as often occurred when battle erupted. Vibrant explosions dimpled *Judicator's* lume, obscuring their vision. The sounds struck next. First, the roar of shells detonating on their shield, then—bizarrely—the blast of the Rabbanite guns firing.

Cause and effect went out the porthole the instant battle began.

"No damage to superstructure!" Ketrik cried, one hand on his ear, the other on a glowing illyrium crystal fused to the bulkhead. "Lume is operating at seventy-eight percent efficiency."

"Scum-sucking voidspawn!" Valescar cursed, watching one of his light cruisers, the *Threntas*, spiral out of control with a smoking wound in her side. Links of chainmail snapped as he clenched his fist hard enough to warp his gauntlet. "Fire at will! Blow them from the skies!"

Sarconian lumes lowered, and a weighty salvo flew back at the Imperium fleet. *Judicator* rumbled as her own cannons discharged, engines and gravpads firing in reverse to hold her steady in the sky. Bulkhead bolts rattled, the bridge trembled, and Lt. Commander Hurgan ordered their gunners to reload.

Caught by the gusting winds, the black smoke pouring from their cannons quickly dissipated. Valescar frowned. Their marksmen were good, but the opposing commander was canny. In between fusillades, he'd drawn his smaller wedge-shaped cruisers and snub-nosed frigates about his massive dreadnaught, forming a cluster of supporting lumes that allowed them to weather the Sarconian storm.

Dropping their shields, the Rabbanites fired again. At the same time, the enemy dreadnaught's engines engaged, and the entire Imperium fleet began accelerating toward them.

The *Judicator* quivered under the assault, and Captain Gadler swore as he stumbled into one of the four pillars supporting the bridge's roof. The *Cannavor* didn't take the exchange nearly as well. Her lume gave, and her front-mounted bridge was showered with shrapnel, ripping away the canopy and slicing a nasty gash down her side. She remained aloft but began listing heavily and drifting toward the rear.

Another update came from the sensor division. "Lume at fifty-four percent!"

"Alternate volleys!" Valescar's blood was boiling—half with fury at losing good men and ships, half with joy at facing someone *competent*. Loathe though he was to suffer casualties, he *loved* the thrill of the fight. "Battle groups one through five will fire in ten seconds. Groups six through ten in twenty seconds. We an' Renfrow's *Vindicator* will open up with the hammerers at twenty-five."

The 'hammerers' were the twin, side-mounted cannons the sister dreadnaughts had been built around. Running the length of each ship—a distance of several city blocks—they delivered a payload the size of panzcraft at mountain-shattering speed. One shot from the *Judicator* had once annihilated a Lusserian invasion from the north, collapsing a winter's worth of snow on them as they attempted to forge a narrow pass.

"Orders delivered!" Annell yelled.

Valescar took a deep breath and willed his plan to work. Still closing, the enemy fleet loosed another barrage. One of his light cruisers blipped out of existence, its magazine detonating in a blast that left behind nothing but ragged, earth-bound debris. To *Judicator*'s port, the *Vindicator* moved up and took half of the rounds meant for them on her lume. *Vice Admiral Renfrow's provin' ta be a capable ally*, Valescar thought.

Five seconds elapsed. The opposing warships continued to close with one another, their segmented decks, gun barbettes, and the colorful flags flapping proudly from their halyards resolving into view. Garish hull paints—greens, blues, even purples—clung desperately to rusted steel that had seen better days. Valescar had always *hated* the Rabbanite tradition of making sure their ships couldn't be hidden.

Ten seconds.

Reloading finished, the Rabbanite's lowered their lumes. Valescar smiled—a grin so wide it tugged at his scarred flesh and set his cheek to burning. *I have ya now!*

Half the Sarconian host blossomed with lances of flame and smoke. Their shields down and cannons loaded, the effect on the Imperium fleet was *devastating*. Cruisers split in two or three places, secondary blasts from their own munitions setting them ablaze as they tumbled from the sky. A carrier hanging to the enemy dreadnaught's rear took two rounds to the engine, sending its prow—and all the fighter craft lining its top deck—plummeting toward the plains below. In the back of his mind, Valescar could almost hear the pilots' screams.

When the smoke cleared, only five Rabbanite airships remained, and even they trailed fires that leaked from flickering lumes. The dreadnaught still hunkered at their center, engines still blazing, still rushing forward.

On closer inspection, it looked as though it had just been launched from drydock. Its swept wings were full of gaps—dark holes where weapons or lume projectors should be mounted but weren't due to lack of time. Several of her many decks were open to the rushing winds, the gestalt steel ribs connected to her arching spine laid bare for all to see. Of the engines Valescar could see, only two—one on each side—were operational. The rest leaked spouts of ebony synth-oil and wisps of unused illyrium discharge.

His left foot began to tap, his charred toes shrieking at the motion. *Why?* Valescar thought. *Why throw 'er inta battle instead of pullin' her ta the rear?*

The Rabbanites unleashed a futile, impotent salvo, then hunkered behind their faltering shields. At twenty seconds, the other half of the 7th fleet released *their* storm of fire and lead. Two more cruisers careened off course to explode in greasy fireballs among the trenches below, where Imperium ground forces continued to uselessly launch artillery rounds skyward. They would never reach, but perhaps doing something—*anything*—made their impending doom more bearable.

Three wounded warships rushed onward. Their commander, thinking the worst was past, that *all* the Sarconian vessels had fired, dropped their lumes to retaliate.

Valescar slashed his right arm across the viewport. "Fire the hammerers!"

"Fire!" Gadler and Hurgen echoed.

The deck beneath their feet *leapt*. Anyone not sitting was tossed to the metal gantry, and Valescar's teeth chattered as his brain tried to shake itself free of his skull and his eyeballs flattened into their sockets. The *boom* that followed would've shattered the canopy glass—and his eardrums—if not for the shock dampening techniques Sarconian engimages had used to forge the bridge.

The two remaining cruisers disappeared. Evaporated, disintegrated, the definition mattered little. The four hammerer rounds continued through their wreckage to strike the dreadnaught. It visibly jolted under the blows, seeming to halt in midair despite the immense power of its thrusters. Half a wing tore free and flipped end over end in its wake. One of the faulty engines became a shrapnel bomb that tore a quarter of the decks apart.

For a second, Valescar thought it would fall. Drop from the air to leave a crater the size of Sarconia on the fractured earth beneath them. Yet, with a gasp of black smog, fire, and yellow-red illyrium dust, it found some hidden reserve of strength and kept hurtling toward them like a vengeful missile.

Valescar's eye went wide. For a single second of chilling clarity, all the phantom embers scorching his left side froze in place.

Missile.

Toward us.

Toward . . . me . . .

A gasp came from the comm station. Valescar whirled toward Annell, who gaped at a sparking, staticky comcrystal on her desk. "They . . . they hacked us, sir."

"Who did?"

By way of answer, she pointed a trembling, white-gloved hand out the viewport.

A loud pop came from the crystal, followed by a garbled voice—a

Rabbanite voice. "... *sscrrkk* ... You think you've won, invaders ... *sscrrkk* ... Today? Yes, that is true ... *sscrrkk* .... Tomorrow? That is not a fate we need concern ourselves with, for ... *sscrrkk* ... neither of us will be ... *sscrrkk* ... around to see it! ... *sscrrkk* ... Come, my brothers! WE BECOME THE WIND!"

"Fire! Fire! Fire!" Valescar roared, spittle catching on the deadened half of his mouth. It dribbled down his chin and onto the clasp of his crimson cloak. "Don't stop firin' until that fool's ship is a pile o' slag on that piss-trough o' a trench they've dug."

Gadler shoved Rorck away from the helm while shouting into the voicepipe to the engine room. "Full speed astern! Give me all you've got!"

The old officers exchanged a look. A hint of fear lay in both their eyes, but not for themselves. It was already too late. They would die, and the crew they valued above all else would die with them.

Valescar turned back to the viewport. The enemy dreadnaught was a funeral pyre. His fleet had begun to encircle it from the sides, and fire poured into it from three directions. Its spine snapped. The other wing—and one of its two working engines—broke away in a spray of sun-touched sparks and silver.

Thrust unbalanced, the warship began to spin. Yet its forward trajectory retained a weighty inevitability. The *Judicator's* reverse thrusters engaged, tossing the bridge crew forward, but their sudden course change wasn't enough. They would soon be engulfed by the same inferno licking at the dreadnaught's hooked beak.

Raising his hands, Valescar prepared to push back with every drop of men'ar coursing through his veins. He'd never tried to move something the size of an airship before, but he would try. *By all the forgotten Veneer,* he thought through gritted teeth, *For my crew, let it be enough.*

As the *Judicator* rumbled backward, a familiar fuselage bearing a gold and crimson "1" on its flank cruised past in the opposite direction. Its three top deck turrets—one aft, two forward—were a match for the *Judicator's,* as was its command tower rising to a peaked bridge amidships. The only difference was the silver-haired man standing behind its viewport, fist across his chest in salute.

Valescar's jaw went slack. *Vice Admiral Renfrow? The Vindicator? What are they—*

A new sound burst from the comcrystal, this time a much-beloved sailor's shanty. Renfrow's gravelly, horribly off-key voice was the loudest, but thousands of different voices chipped into the tune along with his.

"Yo-ho-ho, Yo-ho-ho,
Yo-ho-ho, Yo-ho-ho,
Once upon a clear blue day, up I looked an' sighed,
The breeze was brisk, the sun was warm, what a day to die!
Yo-ho-ho, Yo-ho-ho,
Yo-ho-ho, Yo-ho-ho,
'Draw in the sails,' the captain said, 'Reef an' stow the lines,
A storm's a comin' with our foe, what a day to die!'
Yo-ho-ho, Yo-ho-ho,
Yo-ho-ho, Yo-ho-ho,
The cannons roared, the mast did snap, ol' Betsy screamed an' wept,
Our blood ran cross the tilting deck, what a day to die!
Yo-ho-ho, Yo-ho-ho,
Yo-ho-ho, Yo-ho-ho,
Crimson is the sea now stained, the fishies gnaw our bones,
Yet the breeze was brisk, the sun was warm, what a day to—"

By the time the shanty abruptly ended, Valescar and his entire bridge crew were on their feet, saluting *Vindicator's* bravery and singing along with them. The collision was brilliant. Hooked beak met pointed prow. Both were staved in, and as their guts intermingled, a detonation triggered deep within. Regardless of which vessel the explosion began on, an inferno swept outwards from the middle, casting fragments of their tortured bulkheads in all directions.

Valescar chanted a single word. "For'emag'wa."

The steel rain descending toward the *Judicator* halted, then reversed course. An entire dreadnaught was too much for the vaunted "Wall of the Empire" to stop. But the shredded remnants of one? Even two? Valescar could manage that just fine.

Yet the price in steel, illyrium, and cannons was one he'd willingly pay. The other . . .

Meaty thuds sounded against the viewport, the bridge tower, and the *Judicator's* top deck. Valescar held his revulsion in check. The stench of his own burnt flesh, real or imagined, filled his nostrils day after day. Seeing its like again wouldn't break his spirits.

The same could not be said of Annell, or Ketrik, or even the redoubtable Rorck. They fell to the deck, vomiting. Valescar couldn't blame them. No one should have to look upon the charred remnants of their fellow soldiers.

The rain—both kinds—slackened, then disappeared entirely as

Judicator continued her retreat. Valescar let his arms fall at his side. Then he fell to his knees, staring out the viewport at the smoking corpses of the Rabbanite fleet and the glimmering city they'd zealously defended to the last.

Beiras was all but won, and it had only cost him two light cruisers, the *Vindicator,* and Vice Admiral Renfrow and her loyal crew.

"A cost too voiding high," Valescar whispered. "A cost too voiding high . . . "

Chapter 4
Primal

Time slowed.

Or, at the very least, Vallen's perception of it did. The *Kinloss* had capsized. With a shrill whistle of protest, the engine screeched its disapproval at its treatment and went silent. Sylette kept screaming for Renar and Lilith to get up, crawl, or drag themselves to the ship. Her words were garbled, distant, like she was shouting from beneath the ebony waves that crashed all about them.

Vallen blinked, pulled his sword from the muck, and stared at the impossibility before them.

Gray smoke churned atop a white field—not made of snow or ash, but solid limestone. Cracks radiated along the sides of this pearlescent crater, and the rounded basin below was filled with fragments of splintered stone jutting at random angles.

And at its center was the *thing* from the deep.

As Vallen's gaze rose, the world began to tremble. No. Not the world. *Him.* From his knees, to his eyes, to the krenesh blade held at his side, every part of him was shaking.

Two pillar-sized legs tipped with serrated claws bit into the rock upon which the creature stood. Above them was a tan chest coated in glimmering scales—some small like coins, others large as suits of armor. They overlapped each other like chainmail and looked just as sturdy. It had no arms. Instead, four tentacles sprouted from each side of its long torso, their tips gliding through the air in mesmerizing patterns. Vallen had no doubt a blow from one would cleave his body in two.

At its peak was a visage he'd only seen in picture books, one he'd once mocked Elaine for believing in. Two ruby eyes blazed with power. A dark maw as large as Unter opened, exposing three rows of jagged fangs. Black mist poured from its throat and cavernous nostrils.

It was the face of a dragon, a mythical creature no one had seen in centuries.

"Elaine was right," Vallen muttered. "Dragons are real."

"That's not a dragon, you fool," Sylette shouted as she tugged Renar toward the landing ramp. She held one of his muddy arms, while Lilith clutched the other. "Look at the tentacles. It's a Draken, a Primal." Her voice dropped to a shaky whisper. "Still thought they were myths, though..."

Seeming to sense their awe and terror, the Draken shook its winding body, raising dozens of sharp spines along its back. Renar jabbed an excited finger at it as he slid through the muck. "HA! I told you the mist was an important clue. And see? There it is, the 'Sea God's Crest,' right on its back. I was *right.*"

Tentacles unfurled as Renar babbled, slicing through the air in lazy sweeps. Aiming at *him.* Vallen jumped back from the first, stepped aside as another struck the ground several meters to his left. Wind and stone chips struck his side, but the impact wasn't enough to knock him off his feet or send him flying.

Such slow movements, each blow telegraphed and weak. Its crimson gaze was locked on Vallen, attacking with two tentacles while another pair curled around him toward the ship. Was the Draken going *easy* on them? Herding them together, strike by strike, until it could finish them all off at once?

With a grunt, Lilith heaved Renar onto the grated metal of the *Kinloss'* ramp. "Never doubted you were right. Now, don't lose this again." She tossed him his grit-coated notebook, then raced into the ship, filthy trousers dripping slime with every step.

Sylette's retort was less kind. "Who bloody cares who's right? This thing is about to kill us!"

"I do!" Renar announced, taking a scrivle in his grimy fingers and stooping over a page that was only half smeared with clay. "If I die, I can take that knowledge—and this sketch!—with me to the Afterplane. Besides, Heisden wrote about this chap and it didn't kill *him.*"

The princess clenched her fists, and the daggers hovering near her twitched erratically. "It's the title of a *voided poem*! He could've made it up, he . . . *aaarrrgghhh!* Why in oblivion am I even arguing about this?"

The Draken clicked its teeth together in what might have been a laugh as Vallen continued to evade. Its four unused tentacles swayed back and forth without intent, even though they could have swatted them like rot-flies as they struggled—and failed—to flee.

There could be no doubt. The beast was holding back, toying with its food, and that *infuriated* Vallen. He clenched his jaw, banishing the tremble infecting his limbs.

Charge, the rage in his mind insisted as he dodged another overhead smash.

Crush it, his blood begged as his pulse quickened with every step, every meter he retreated. Vallen glanced over his shoulder at his

comrades, so close he could see their trembling eyes, their twitching fingers. Their sweat-soaked collars and heaving throats.

Soon they'd be out of room to move, and then . . .

Matteo's high-pitched whine came from inside the craft. "Lilith, help me get Velle down from the wall." A moment passed, accompanied by the scuffle of boots against the cargo bay's metal bulkheads. Then the Professor's mop of sandy-brown hair jutted out the hatch behind Renar.

"I can't get us airborne with the *Kinloss* on his side . . . " Matteo's voice faltered. "A *D-Draken*? What did y-you guys do? How could you bring an an-angry Draken down on our heads in the short t-time I was doing pre-flight checks?" Faced with a legendary monster, the Professor's jittery stammer was back at full force.

An unsteady Velle staggered into Matteo's back. "It's probably the illyrium on board," Velle explained. "Draconic species—including Primals—feed off spiritual energy. Illyrium is like a battery full of the stuff, so they tend to hoard it."

Enough with the talking, Vallen thought, walls of convulsing flesh closing about him. In a few seconds, the prison the Draken had constructed for them would be complete. Step, dodge, duck. Stumble back and back and then back some more. He could only evade for so long.

They needed to *fight*.

Fight!

"But it came after us by the lighthouse first." Lilith reemerged with her stolen Sarc saber gripped in white-knuckled fingers. "Why?"

"To protect the crystal in the tower!" Velle clapped her hands together. "That explains why the lighthouse is deserted. This is the Draken's home, and that's its favorite meal."

Renar waved his scrivle, flicking a clump of reddish mud onto his cheek. It joined the rest of the ooze dribbling around his stubble. "But this guy's been here *centuries*. Remember, it's the 'Sea God' Heisden wrote about in his poem."

"Just shut up, Renar!" Sylette shouted. "How does that useless tidbit help us in this situation? Does anyone have an *actual* strategy for defeating a Primal?"

No, Vallen thought. *But let's try anyway.* Krenesh held out and to the side, he stopped dodging, planted his right foot, and charged.

Moving with surprising swiftness, the Draken adjusted its stance to face the onrushing Terr, bleating out what sounded like a coarse mimicry of laughter. The piercing warble grated against Vallen's eardrums, threatening to drive him to the ground without a single blow. Vision swimming, he stumbled and raised his blade as if he could somehow drive off the sonic attack.

That saved his life. A tentacle soared in from his right, slamming into his weapon arm and the half-transformed shield morphing to cover it. Bronze alloy splattered around the strike, forming a liquid spray that absorbed most of the force.

Most. Vallen sailed across the plateau, fluid metal trailing him like a cape. One bounce. Two. He slid to a stop a meter from the cliff's edge, nothing broken but thoroughly shaken.

Metal pooled against his right side like blood, hastening to recombine with the rod's core clutched in his hand. Coughing, Vallen willed it to become a staff and used it to lever himself up on one knee. He was completely outclassed—even more so than when he'd faced Valescar, that blasted Sarc Rittermarschal who never stopped talking. How was he going to win?

Vallen staggered upright. Dirt, clumps of grass, and drops of blood fell from his torn garments. His ears rang like his brain was still jostling inside his skull. Whether due to the fog in his head or the fog on the plateau, his vision was hazy. He could see the dark outlines of his comrades, yelling and waving their arms at him, but had lost track of the Draken in the swirling mists.

"Void and Oblivion ... " he muttered.

Men'ar exploded from Vallen's body in all directions, transforming into a thin veil of lightning that clung near to his skin like a cloak. *Zzzt! Zzzt!* The crackling barrier didn't *halt* the tentacles trying to impale him. It *did* divert them, just enough to avoid a fatal wound.

One spade cut a deep furrow in Vallen's cheek as it passed. The other slashed the coarse weave of his tunic and glanced off his ribs. Blood seeped from the wounds, helped along by a slimy substance that burned his flesh and filled his nostrils with an acrid stench.

Grimacing, Vallen fell into a combat stance and summoned his krenesh blade again. The tentacles were like blades—hard as bone, quick as a rapier, and coated in a film of anti-coagulating acid. If he was cut, the bleeding wouldn't stop until he was drained.

The Draken reemerged from the smog with an enraged screech. Two of its tentacles were scorched, their tips covered in steaming, pock-shaped burns. Several of its other limbs crowded near their injured brethren, salving them with a bluish ooze that dripped from their suckers. Its head remained locked on Vallen, crimson eyes glaring with pure hatred.

Guess we're both hurt now, buddy, he thought with a sneer.

" . . . You imbecile!" The ringing in Vallen's ears faded, replaced by Sylette's nagging cries. "You can't beat it like that!" If he had a geldar for every time she said that he'd be a *very* rich man.

Ignoring the princess, Vallen sprinted straight at the Draken. He'd underestimated it, believing its gargantuan mass would make it slow and awkward. Now the Triaron had its measure.

He ducked the first tentacle swipe by bending to the left. Its close passage whipped droplets of blood and sweat from his face. The second was a slam, intended to crush him to a bloody pulp. Vallen let his duck become a fall, kicked off with his feet, and flipped out of its way, blade held to the side to avoid disemboweling himself.

Two tentacles were injured. Four were ministering to them, and two were retracting for their next attack. Vallen grinned. He had the smallest window of opportunity, and he would not waste it.

Flames burst from his krenesh, a tapestry of red, orange, and yellow born from his invested men'ar. Their blaze banished the mist around him, and the injured Draken reeled back, frightened by its heat and fury. A single needle of pain twisted in Vallen's skull as his spiritual energy drained, but he squashed it with an upward swing of his blade.

Fight! the voice in his head exulted, growing stronger the more magic Vallen used. *Burn! Destroy!*

One radiant stream of fire leapt from his sword, greedily lapping up what parched vegetation still huddled atop the plateau. He swung once more, then a third time, adding two more trails that couldn't possibly miss the immobile Draken.

Except they did. The first missed left, leaving behind a wall of flames two meters high. The second veered right, scorching the ground between the creature and the *Kinloss*. Only the last remained on target.

With an earsplitting roar, the Draken lurched forward and crushed the fire spell beneath its wicked talons, smothering it before it could grow in ferocity like the others. Tiny tendrils of smoke wafted between its claws as the beast leered at Vallen.

"Aqua Primals are strong against fire!" Sylette fumed. "It lives in the water. It came out of the water. I know it's empty, but you could at least *try* using your head for once."

I am! Vallen retorted silently.

His fire was *far* from ordinary. Fueled by latent men'ar and eager to consume the magic particles in the aether, the flames continued to expand, stretching their grasping fingers toward the heavens and bloating about their waistline like a Darmatian noble on Sariel's feast-day. Triumph evaporated from the Draken's features, replaced by fear as its snout and tentacles darted from one side to the other. It shuffled backward toward the cliff's edge to escape the blaze, thunderous footfalls reverberating through the earth.

Contrary to Sylette's deluded claims, Vallen *was* learning. He'd lost to her—something he was now willing to admit. He'd also been *thrashed* by Valescar. And the failures that haunted him, the deaths that mocked him whenever he closed his eyes, were strict tutors as well.

And *why* had Vallen suffered those defeats? Because he couldn't hit his opponents. They'd led him on a merry chase while evading every one of his flashy moves.

Yet this foe could not run. Vallen planted his feet in a wide stance, leaned over his krenesh, and urged it to change. Both ends expanded, the hilt morphing into a spiked pommel, the other blooming into a glistening head that was half jagged spear-tip, half curving axe.

A halberd, perfect for collecting and redirecting energy.

Vallen's face split into a gleeful smile. *Flames, off the cliff, or this,* he thought. *It matters not which you choose.* His left hand hovered over the spear-tip and began channeling men'ar into it. Electricity coursed through him, into his arms, then through the shaft to the crackling ball of blue-white lightning collecting at its end. More power, larger, stronger. Vallen fed all that he had into it, every last drop of men'ar in his blood's reservoir.

His migraine blossomed anew, hammering at his eyes, breaking against his temple. Needles stabbed at his stomach, urging him to vomit. But Vallen held on. Controlled the agony, directed it into the dense, sparking orb that could incinerate him if his focus slipped.

And then it was done. Soaked in sweat and covered in blood, Vallen admired his handiwork. Beautiful and wonderfully destructive, the bright sphere was so pure and white that he had to avert his gaze. He grasped the halberd in both hands and aimed it at the Draken. Reduced to its primal instincts, the poor creature was still floundering amid the flames, searching for a way out.

Vallen almost pitied it.

"Die!" he roared, thrusting the weapon forward.

Released from its constraints, the spell rocketed toward the Draken, unleashing bolts of wayward lightning that blackened the earth and vaporized the mist. Before Vallen could blink, the orb struck the beast square in its chest.

67

Power and light exploded, forcing everyone watching to avert their gaze. Vallen refused to look away from his moment of triumph. He leaned forward as buffets of heat and wind struck him, tearing at his clothes, wringing tears from his eyes. A tremor raced through the plateau; not enough to shatter it further, but the *Kinloss* gave a tortured squeal as another of its struts collapsed.

When the wind and quake had passed, all was silent.

Grinning from ear to ear, Vallen raised his halberd and staggered two steps toward his stunned companions. "How . . . was *that*?" he gasped.

They were speechless. Even Sylette—eternally cynical Sylette, who held *no* regard for his skills—could offer no words. Her jaw was in danger of dropping to the mud.

Vallen took another shambling step, chuckling at her surprise. *Dragon? Draken? Primal?* he thought smugly. *Whatever that thing was, I'm adding Wyrmslayer to my list of titles.*

His laughter caught in his throat, blocked by . . . Vallen tried to gag. Nothing emerged. He dropped his halberd—which reverted to its inert rod form—and pushed at his throat with both hands, trying to dislodge whatever was trapped there. The lump didn't move, and as he started to gasp for breath, he fell to his knees.

Was it the air? Vallen touched his tongue to it and nearly retched. The taste was like rotten fruit, fetid meat, and Sewertown sludge combined into one. He could smell the noxious combination; feel it crawling along his skin.

Panicked, his watery eyes darted around. The gray mist had darkened to black, becoming so dense he could no longer see the Draken, nor the far side of the *Kinloss*. Only his squadmates' shapes were visible. His squadmates! Shaking fingers stretched toward the glint of Sylette's silver hair. Vallen would swallow his pride and . . .

They were likewise collapsed, fingers scratching at their throats, legs kicking wildly. Sylette was still conscious, refusing to drop farther than her knees. Renar's notebook slipped from his grasp as he convulsed atop the ramp. Lilith, Matteo, and Velle were draped atop the benches in the cargo bay, illuminated by the eerie red flickering of the ship's emergency lights.

What . . . —his mind screamed— *. . . is going on?*

Before he could pass out, rain fell from the heavens—a few drops at first, then a downpour. The pressure instantly disappeared, and Vallen could breathe again. Thank the Veneer! Panting, he tilted his head back and gulped down a mouthful of air and water.

It was like drinking blood, slimy and full of iron. Revolted, Vallen spat it back up, then glanced at his sleeve. The tortured fabric—seam torn, white faded to a ruddy brown—was splotched with black goop. He pinched a bit and found it slimy and sticky, like ink. The smell was pungent, like seawater left to fester beneath the sun for days on end.

I...I shouldn't stay out in this stuff, Vallen decided. He crawled for the ramp, where a recovered Velle, supported by Matteo, had erected a glyph barrier above their heads. Every side of the runic circle dripped viscous grime, but those underneath were safe—for now.

Vallen stared at the crater as he crawled, searching for the body of the Draken. Was this deluge what was left of it after the explosion? The thought delighted and sickened him in equal measure.

The last of his flames were withering beneath the 'rain.' Past their fading wisps, past a screen of shifting black mist, something moved—a monstrous shadow swaying behind a thinning veil.

Thunder roared, and a gust of wind swept the mist aside for the briefest of instants. "I-impossible ... " Vallen stammered. "T-that's impossible ... "

At the center of the crater was the Draken. It had not moved a centimeter from where it had been when Vallen's blast struck it. Nor was it covered in gore, scorched, scarred, or injured in any way.

Through the fog, its two red irises glared at Vallen, mocking his pathetic attempts to slay a myth. Trembling consumed him. He was out of men'ar. His body was bruised, beaten, and battered. There was nothing he could do.

With a growl, a second set of red eyes, just a little farther back on the Draken's head than the first, opened wide. The ink droplets halted in midair. Intricate blue glyphs, each bearing sigils and signs Vallen had never seen, blinked into existence in front of the monster's tentacles. The first spell launched without warning, hammering Vallen's stomach with a stream of pure white water.

He went flying again, skipping across the mud and stones, crying out with every brutal impact. The blast didn't stop after he struck the ground. It kept driving Vallen toward the ledge, tearing his tunic from his back and flaying the skin beneath it red and raw.

Another sound pierced his screams—Sylette and the others screeching battle cries as they engaged the monster. Distracted by their pitiful resistance, the torrent buffeting his limp form ceased. Vallen spared not a thought for their safety. Mewling and whimpering, he curled about his bruise-blackened gut, desperate to forget the torment afflicting every fiber of his being.

"Velle, barrier to the front! Lilith, barrage it from above! Matteo, draw some fire, try to turn it! I'll take out its eyes once it's distracted!"

For some reason, Sylette hadn't given up. Explosions cascaded at his back, followed by a primal roar and the slicing *zing* of high-pressured water. Didn't she see they couldn't win? Unter was still comatose. Velle was casting on the dregs of her men'ar. Matteo was useless.

And I, Vallen sobbed. *The* legendary *Triaron of Darmatia, am lying face down in the mud of a nameless cliff.*

Pathetic, a small voice whispered from the depths of his mind. *Didn't you want people to shout your name? Hail you as a hero? Remember you for centuries to come?* The voice grew in strength as it spoke, silky tones echoing about Vallen's head. Were these his thoughts, or a delusion of his exhausted mind? *Where is your rage? Your desire to avenge your dead? There is no vengeance without power. Strength without the will to grasp it. Hatred without the passion to pursue it.*

Get up! it snapped. *Get up and go out in a blaze of glory!*

Vallen hurt. The weight of his past and the terror of the present stabbed through him as cleanly as any spear. But there was still breath in his lungs, fire in his heart. Payment for the dead was owed, and he would *not* relinquish his soul until his debt was cleared.

One shredded palm pressed against the rain-slick stones, then the other, which clutched his metal rod. Vallen loosed a growl and heaved himself up. At first, he staggered—forward, backward, and forward again. His vision swam, multiplying everything he saw. Vallen shook his body to clear his head, releasing clumps of grime from his hair and behind his ears.

He had no men'ar, was barely standing, and felt as if his pain-wracked limbs might crumble to dust at any moment. But . . . he was ready.

Blinking silt from his eyes, Vallen watched his comrades battle the Draken. Velle was backed into the airship's cargo bay, her last glyph blocking the hatch to protect those still inside. Matteo pushed against her shoulders as though he could prop up the Sylph—and by extension, her shield—with nothing but strength of arm.

Lilith strafed to the Draken's left side, shooting explosive flare after flare from her saber. The beast blocked every one of them using a rippling barrier crafted from the still suspended ink. On the opposite side from where Vallen stood, Sylette was harassing the creature with daggers fired from multiple angles.

Yet the Draken was capable of more than just defense. Two tentacles pursued Sylette, one snaring her blades in bubbles of ink, the other launching blasts of water to take her down. Silver hair flashed back and forth as the princess narrowly dodged each attack and retaliated with several more of her own. Another two limbs cast furious spouts against Velle's cracking barrier, while three more chased the greatest remaining threat—Lilith and her explosion magic.

Only one tentacle hovered above the skirmish, wary of the unexpected. *Like me,* Vallen thought, frowning. He hated to admit it, but this was probably part of Sylette's plan. She and the others would distract the Draken, and he—the foe it believed defeated—would swoop in and save the day.

No, Vallen thought with a laugh that made his jaw ache. *The ice princess would* never *design a strategy with me as the crucial piece.*

The dance of vibrant orange flares, whistling daggers, and blasting water continued for several more moments. Then Lilith stumbled. Sensing an opportunity, the Draken brought the last tentacle slashing in for the kill. Lilith parried the blow with her blade but was too small to resist the force behind it. She crumpled to the ground, saber bent, surrounding limbs moving in to finish her.

Vallen charged, rod morphing to a short-hafted spear in his hand. A slashing weapon would glance off the Draken's hard scales, but a piercing weapon—just like the spear's tip—might break through to its soft insides. He'd still need to strike a weak spot: an arm joint, its groin, or its eyes and head.

To strike the latter will require . . . Vallen clicked his tongue, the term as distasteful in his mind as it would be in his mouth. *To get its head I'll need the others to . . . cooperate.* He waved his spear at Velle as he ran, drawing her attention. "If you've got enough men'ar left," he shouted. *"Take me up!"*

It was the same tactic they'd used in their flag-brawl matches, a link to a past they'd once shared. Velle nodded her agreement and swung one of her hands toward him. Vallen couldn't help smiling as a pathway of glowing glyphs materialized between him and the Draken's head.

The Draken didn't notice Vallen until he was halfway to his face. A human opponent might have panicked; the Primal simply shifted all of its attention to the new threat. Spells cast at the others ceased, and the tentacles stabbing at the frantically rolling Lilith veered onto a collision course with the Triaron. He dodged left, right, then down, narrowly avoiding each slash as he made use of the limited space atop Velle's constructs. Small cuts opened all across his body from the near misses, but their stinging was nothing compared to the alternative.

Four tentacles penned him in, their surfaces sparkling with the glare of charged magic. As torrents rushed from them, Vallen jumped straight up, clearing their deadly wakes for the briefest of instants. He clenched his jaw and fell . . . onto a new platform Velle had summoned *above* the sloshing eddies.

"Yes!" Vallen cheered, springing to his feet and racing toward the goal.

The eyes of the Draken were now mere meters away, slotted pupils blinking furiously at the impossibility of his presence. He could smell the rancid odor of rot pouring from its half-open mouth. See the ranks of razor-sharp fangs as tall as his head and hear the hissing of air passing through the gill slits on its cheeks.

Atop its head was a crown Vallen hadn't noticed from the ground, one made of prongs of hardened cartilage that fanned out like the spikes of the late Queen Ephalia's diadem. The message it conveyed was clear: *I am king here.*

And I'm the kingslayer, Vallen thought.

Flourishing the spear, he pointed it at the monstrous crimson eyeball on the right. Vallen mustered men'ar beyond the dregs in his stomach, burned his lifeforce itself for one instant of power surpassing his limits, and propelled himself forward with an explosion of flame from his feet.

"AAAAAAHHHHHHHH!"

The Draken unhinged its jaw, revealing a runic circle that spanned the width of its gaping maw.

Void it all! Vallen cursed as the waterspout struck him. It blasted him *through* Velle's glyph—which shattered into thousands of shining particles—and straight down to the ground between its talons.

His body gave; the limestone did not. Vallen shrieked as his ribs cracked and his right arm snapped. Tendons tore with sickening pops, wrenching his previously injured shoulder out of place. Warmth sprouted beneath him, blood that was on the wrong side of his flesh. Pain became his world.

Through darkening eyes, Vallen tried to find his companions. Velle stared at him with horror marring her face—a face he still found so, so beautiful. One of her hands stifled a scream, while Matteo tugged at the other, desperate to get her even a single step farther from the Draken. Cowardly, but the right call.

Lilith and Sylette were on their last legs. Their spells were weak and infrequent, their evasions only by the narrowest of margins. The Draken would soon eliminate them and turn its attention to those hiding on the *Kinloss*.

This was the end.

"Spell 16, Glacial Prison!"

Everything went white—the air, the sky, the ground, even Vallen's breath. Freezing where they hung, the ink particles remained suspended for a surreal instant before gravity brought them clattering down. A shimmering layer of frost coated the dirt, the *Kinloss*, and his shrieking flesh. No more warmth gushed from his side; the leaking blood had stilled mid-flow.

Through his pain, Vallen felt a new sensation. Cold. He was colder than he'd ever been in his entire life. Frigidly, deathly cold, so much so that he began to shake uncontrollably despite the agony moving caused him. Was this real? Or had he fallen into a blood-loss-induced delirium?

Blinking frost from his eyelids, Vallen stared up at his puffs of rime-coated breath and the colossal statue above them. The Draken—a Primal-class beast of legend that had been on the verge of wiping their merry band of miscreants off the face of Lozaria—was frozen. Not just still. Encased in a solid block of ice.

Light refracted through the different planes of the block, showing distorted angles of the creature held inside. Even so, it was clearly the same monster that had nearly killed Vallen mere moments prior. Its tentacles were splayed like the frosted limbs of a great tree, its jaws open in shock, its claws even more firmly rooted to the ground.

Vallen's teeth chattered as he gaped. How in the Creator's accursed name had this *giant* been sealed away in an instant?

Cr-unch. Cr-unch.

At first, Vallen thought he was hearing things. He *was* on the verge of death, and the frozen Draken could very well be a feverish hallucination dredged up to comfort him as he drifted toward the Afterplane.

Crunch! Crunch!

The crunching of snow and ice became more distinct, the footfalls more pronounced and apparent. A blurry shape marched across his quivering vision, right up to the trapped Draken, and tapped on the glassy surface.

Matteo's flabbergasted cries tore through the wintry stillness. "B-but how? N-no, why, where, w-why are you, what a-are you—"

"I would advise that you ask a single question at a time, Senior Cadet Alhan. You're more likely to get a proper answer that way."

It was a woman's voice. Aloof, somewhat cocky, with a superior tone that seemed comfortable giving orders—or perhaps instructing others. It was familiar. All *too* familiar to Vallen.

No, he thought with a groan. *It can't be.*

He strained his eyes and the tall, imposing body and short black hair of Major Jis Reev resolved into view. Her 'catch' secure, the Darmatian Military Academy instructor spun to face them. As always, her keen emerald eyes were filled with scorn—their depths coolly judging each of them. She placed her hands on her fatigue-covered hips, the olive color of her gloves matching the greens of her combat garb.

"Cadet Alhan's incomprehensible queries aside, I'm not sure whether to be pleased or shocked at your arrival here. Of all the people I thought might hear my message, you fools are the last ones I expected to show up."

Major Reev shook her head, a display of resignation Vallen had often elicited from her when he slept through class. Then she waved them toward the lighthouse steps. "At any rate, come with me. We'll get you sorted down below."

"You mean this is the Resistance base?" Sylette appeared to be on the verge of tears, something Vallen never thought he'd see. "We made it?"

Major Reev's reply was short, sarcastic, and as cold and pitiless as the ice magic she wielded. "Yes, this is it, congratulations. You found the army." She turned to leave but paused to add one final thing. Even though her face was hidden, Vallen could hear the smirk on her lips.

"Well, what's left of it, anyway."

Chapter 5
What Remains

Twisting and turning, down and down, the narrow tunnel led ever deeper into the hidden expanse beneath the twin-turret lighthouse. Bathed in the dim light from strands of hanging illyrium crystals, Matteo stumbled along the slope, one hand on the smooth white limestone wall, the other dangling behind him in Velle's tight grasp.

Which doesn't mean anything! he quickly reminded himself, his cheeks red and chest tight. The battle against the Draken had sapped what little strength she'd recovered, and the close press of her body was *only* so he could help her reach the Resistance base.

His racing heart and clammy palms didn't get that memo. Velle sniggered at his discomfort, edging even closer as they rounded a steep bend. With their skin touching, everything Matteo thought or felt—or at the very least, a vague impression of it—was being directly transmitted to the Sylph empath. She'd made it clear the ability wasn't intentional or malicious, but knowing the girl he was . . . *fond* of knew that he knew that . . .

A weak giggle slipped from Velle's lips, echoing up and down the silent corridor. At the front of the column, Major Reev halted and turned, her footsteps clicking on the worn stone steps. "Is something funny, Cadet Me'andara?"

Cadet. The word sounded foreign in Matteo's ear. It had been a lifetime since they'd been called cadets. An eternity since those simple days at the Academy, when all he'd wanted was to curl up with a book in a forgotten corner of the campus library. 'Cadet' hardly defined who they were now—who *he* was now.

"Major . . . " Matteo began, rushing to Velle's defense before he realized his mouth was open. Cold emerald eyes—the harsh gaze of the Ice Queen of Darmatia, a living legend—shifted onto him.

His voice caught in his throat. At the same time, his wall-hugging hand slipped on something slimy. "*Gah!*" Matteo recoiled from the ooze. Not only did it stink like rotting fish, but it had scalded the skin of his fingers, leaving them red and raw.

Shaking his wrist, he came to an abrupt stop—one that lasted a fraction of a second. Velle ran into him, Sylette bumped into her, and

Vallen hobbled into Sylette. If Unter wasn't too large to fit through the passageway, he and his team would've been part of the pile-up as well. Instead, the Major had summoned a medical squad to bring him—and the *Kinloss*—in through a concealed hangar entrance, and the others had gone along to help move him.

The four cadets pitched onto the floor in front of Major Reev, Vallen screaming bloody murder about his injured ribs, and Sylette shrieking for the 'imbecile' to get off her. The Major's eyes narrowed to slits. Her lower lip twitched in disgust. "I saved you for *this*?"

An image of her kneeling over a badly wounded Vallen, one frost-coated hand hovering over his bleeding gut, the other tapping her chin, flashed through Matteo's mind. She'd obviously considered letting the Triaron perish then and there.

Pushing that thought aside, Matteo extricated himself from the others, adjusted his glasses, and assisted Velle to her feet. *Distraction*, he thought, watching Vallen winge and moan. *I need to get her thinking about something else.*

Matteo waved his injured fingers. Small white blisters dotted the most damaged, the flesh around them a stinging scarlet. "T-this isn't seawater, Major," he managed. "And these tunnels aren't natural. The sediment on the Phar Coast is composed of calcite and aragonite, which *can* form caves after millions of years, but not under these tidal conditions, and certainly not this far from the breakwater."

"You're . . . right." Major Reev blinked. Was she surprised to hear him say so much at once? "It's a type of acidic mucus young Draken secrete while tunneling for illyrium dust in the bedrock. They can't control its potency, unlike the adults. I suggest not touching or drinking it. Except for you, Cadet Metellus." Folding her arms, she leered at Vallen. "I won't stop you if you want to try it."

"I'll . . . pass," he grumbled, staggering to his feet while clutching his bloodstained side. A sling of dirty bandages secured his broken right arm to his stomach. If not for Major Reev flash-freezing his flank and Velle expending the last of her men'ar on him, Matteo wagered the Triaron wouldn't be moving.

A drop of slime fell from above, forcing Matteo to dodge. His gaze—only partially obscured by fog-rimmed spectacles—darted around the tunnel. Was the stuff all over the place? Fortunately, his search revealed that most of the dampness in the shadowy tunnel came from trickles of brackish water, not Draken gunk.

"Wait, you mentioned 'children.'" His arms began to tremble.

"The Primal *reproduced*? There are *more* of those things?"

"I bet they're . . . easier to beat," Vallen wheezed.

Sylette smacked him on the back of his head. "Don't even try, you imbecile."

Chuckling, Major Reev began walking again. Their team followed—*limped*—after her as best they could. "Nehalena," she said after a moment of silence.

"What?" Velle asked.

"Not *what*," the Ice Queen corrected, shaking her head. "*Who*. Nehalena is the name of the Primal you fought, and the one whose offspring formed this network of tunnels we're borrowing. I bet she's going to be furious when she thaws out."

Velle's cold hand—once more entwined with Matteo's—tightened. "Wait. All the stories say the Primals were created by a mad sorcerer who wanted the power to challenge the Veneer."

"I heard it was Sarcon," Sylette interjected.

"That's one theory," Velle agreed. "Either way, they were chimeras made from other creatures. Dragons, drakes, winged beasts, sea monsters, whatever the sorcerer could get their hands on. And the fusion . . . sort of broke them. Their minds, and their bodies. The legends say they couldn't have children."

The shadowy outline of Major Reev shrugged. "Myths are made to be rewritten. Nehalena has kids—the chubby slugs are pretty cute, too, in a weird sort of way." Matteo nearly stumbled into a gleaming patch of Draken mucus. The *Ice Queen* thought something was *cute*? This day was filled with more surprises than his sleep-deprived brain could handle.

"I'm more worried about her thawing out," Sylette said. "Won't she come after our—or the Resistance's—illyrium again? And how would she get free? That was a *Long Chant* you cast on her."

The exile's tone was awed, and Matteo understood her reverence. He'd seen two of the top-tier spells in his short life, and both had saved him: Leon's from a Sarconian prison cell, the Major's from a short trip into an acid-filled stomach. Few people knew the words to *any* of the numbered spells, and fewer still possessed the men'ar count, magic potency, and skill to use a Long Chant in battle.

Major Reev snorted. "I'll dispel my ice, of course. That's what a friend would do."

"*F-friend?*" Matteo sputtered. Velle staggered in shock, and Matteo slowed down so she could lean against his back instead of careening into the tunnel wall. "Thanks," she mumbled, her close breath sending shivers across his neck and ear.

"Yes, friend," Major Reev repeated. "Though I use the term loosely. In exchange for regular deliveries of pure illyrium crystals, Nehalena guards the surface of our base, which is an unused section of her nest. It's a deal the Darmatian army has maintained for generations."

Sylette's soft footfalls ceased. Concerned, Matteo and Velle turned toward her. Vallen *almost* plowed into her a second time.

"Don't just stop in . . . the middle of—"

A dagger materialized beside her head, its tip aimed at Vallen. A different instructor would've brought her up on charges for threatening a squadmate. Major Reev smiled and said nothing.

"And now *we've* jeopardized that arrangement." Sylette sighed. Then, almost as an afterthought, she flicked a finger to dismiss her floating blade. "Our—*his*—", she spat the word in Vallen's direction, "Reckless actions endangered the whole Resistance."

The little bands of illyrium bulbs lining the tunnel ceiling provided just enough light for Matteo to make out the faintest of smiles tugging at Major Reev's lips. It made her emerald eyes sparkle and dimpled the beauty mark on her left cheek.

"You *were* the best tactician in the bunch," she said. "Yes, I had to weigh the value of your lives versus the value Nehalena brings to the Resistance. It's why it took me so long to intervene . . . among other things," the Ice Queen added, smirking at bruised, battered, and filthy Vallen. She did *not* hide her loathing for the Triaron.

"Thank you for . . . choosing *us*?" Velle's nails dug into Matteo's palm. *Don't take it personally,* he tried to send through their connection. The pressure lessened, and she rubbed her cheek on his back.

"You're quite welcome," Major Reev replied as she waved them down a split in the path. Though *path* was a bit generous. What Matteo could see was little more than thin ledges sliced into the inside edge of a looping spiral. Breathtaking striations of glittering tan stone lined the curve's sides, but Matteo found himself too worried about clinging to the wall to truly appreciate the view.

A clatter accompanied Major Reev's jump to the floor below. She'd launched herself from a height of three meters without a second thought and was casually continuing on her way. They worked together to get Vallen down, then hurried after her.

"Though I would've expected someone to have the common sense to stop that overconfident buffoon," the Ice Queen called over her shoulder, voice booming in the narrow confines. "Not Cadet Iolus, his grades were only a fraction better than those of Cadet Metellus, but Velle, or Sylette, or . . . somebody."

"What do you . . . mean, Ms. Jis?" Vallen protested. "Her silver-haired Highness here . . . is responsible for most of—*Aaargghhh!*" His sudden cry was accompanied by the *clink* of metal striking stone and a swift rustle of fabric. A second *oof* came from the darkness, and Matteo peered back to see a lithe shadow pressing a taller one against the rocks.

"Shut up!" Sylette growled, just loud enough for Matteo to hear. "How many times did we have to save you when you got in over your head? Don't lie and try to pin any of this on me! And don't," her voice dropped to a deadly whisper, "Use *that* title around others."

"Give it a rest, you two!" Major Reev yelled. "I wouldn't want you to get blood on the welcome mat."

Welcome mat? Matteo mused. Realization brightened his eyes. "We're here?" He and Velle rushed ahead, trailed by Sylette and a very sullen Vallen who was massaging a red spot on his throat with his left hand.

Solid stone, smooth as the tunnel walls, blocked the way forward. Matteo didn't despair—not this time. The glittering grain flowing from left to right was a little *too* orderly and matched the dappled patterns on the passage's ceiling and sides with uncanny precision. Like the lighthouse above, the way forward was secreted behind an illusion spell.

Major Reev breathed in, then blew on the projection. Frost formed in the air, sparkles that caught and interfered with the rays forming the illusion. It shimmered, warped, and finally disappeared, revealing a metal hatch that matched the one beneath the lighthouse's muck-coated basement floor.

"Care to do the honors, Cadet Alhan?" The Major stepped aside and gestured at the gestalt steel plate. Thumb-sized rivets lined the door. The smallest of scum-crawlers couldn't wriggle through the gaps around its edges. It seemed impervious to anything but artillery fire, and worse still, there wasn't a handle in sight.

Matteo nodded. Letting go of Velle's hand, he approached the door and spoke the names he'd committed to memory. "Darmatus, Azarias, Vanineri."

"These words are accepted," a tinny voice from within the door announced.

With a ponderous grating, it retracted into the ceiling. Matteo felt a rush of joy. The password was the names of three of Darmatia's greatest rulers: Darmatus the Hero, Azarias the Architect, and Vanineri the Water-Blessed. He knew their exploits from stories he'd read until their pages were torn and smeared with ink—the tales that had convinced him to become a soldier.

And now, despite all the hardship and danger, Matteo was on an adventure just like theirs.

The smell hit him like a mallet. Sweat, blood, oils, rot, refuse, feces, urine, sewage, and a dozen other scents he couldn't place. His eyes watered, his hand leapt to his nose, and he nearly doubled over to unleash the vomit climbing up his throat.

Major Reev patted his back as she passed. "Yeah, the stench will do that to you." She walked to the lip of the wooden platform onto which they'd emerged and raised her arms to encompass the massive cavern unfolding before them.

"Welcome to the remnants of the Darmatian army, a ragtag band of idiots and fools that don't know when to give up!"

Coughing, Matteo pushed his glasses up the bridge of his nose, stumbled to grab the rickety railing behind the Major, and blinked up at the host of illyrium lamp panels affixed to the chamber's roof. Their almost blinding light drove away the underground gloom like a much too close sun.

His gaze followed the thick wires snaking from the panels down the cavern's sides. It was a massive dome, nearly the size of the flag-brawl stadium their graduation exam had been held in. Matteo's brain calculated a rough estimate in seconds: five hundred meters across, five hundred meters wide. Rocky outcroppings jutted from the walls and floor, forming dips and rills at random. Jagged stalagmites thrust from the ground, straining to meet their relatives from above. In one corner was a calm, quiet lake, its placid waters turning to rapids where they raced into the darkness of a rough-hewn tunnel.

But, Matteo thought, still fighting the odors making his head swim, *it's still too small. Smaller than the Academy, smaller than the Feywind, smaller than that nowhere base at the Rabban border checkpoint. You could only fit about—*

"How many soldiers do you have here, Major Reev?" Sylette's hushed tone reflected the knot of unease growing in Matteo's stomach.

"About a thousand."

One of the Ice Queen's gloves pointed at a tent city to their left. The ramshackle structures were constructed of dirty brown cloth and rope and supported by all manner of boards, pipes, and rocks. Some of them were long, full of patches and holes. It was evident they'd been stitched together from whatever material was on hand in a crude facsimile of a barracks hall. Near the wall, farther from the damp stone beside the pond's banks, the living situation was marginally better, with shacks made of plywood abutting the rising boulders in some rough semblance of permanent dwellings.

Before anyone could respond, the Major's arm shifted in the direction of the largest shelter—a giant square tent four times as big as one of the long barracks, backed up against the far side of the room. A flimsy fence surrounded it on three sides, creating space between it and everything else. The only people going in and out wore white robes and face masks.

"However," Major Reev continued, "of that thousand, a third is injured, and we're not sure how many will be able to return to active duty."

Secluded. People in white robes. Masks and robes with red splotches on them. *It's a field hospital,* Matteo realized. The suffocating miasma in the air took on new meaning as he imagined the horrors inside that tent. He dry heaved once, twice, then regained control of his breathing.

His next epiphany was more sobering than the last. *One in every three Darmatians here is a casualty. And what about the rest of the nation?* Matteo's heart hammered in his chest. More ragged breaths jetted from his lungs, one after another.

What about my parents? They'd left his parents behind in Etrus, left them to confront the Imperials so they could flee. *What if they were taken in for questioning? What if the Empire found evidence that we stayed with them? What if they're being tortured? What if they're already …*

Velle laid her soothing palm against his blazing cheek. The calm she sent him helped, if just a bit. Matteo gave a weak grin, took a deep breath, and vomited onto the stalagmites below the platform.

"What about the other cadets?" Sylette asked, ignoring Matteo's plight. "What about our fellow students?"

Major Reev spared a glance for Matteo. Did she pity him? "There are a few, but not many. Most of them were aboard the *King Darmatus* or stationed behind Aldona's walls. Those were supposed to be the safest points in our defenses, but . . . "

She paused, the slightest hint of moisture gathering beneath her emerald eyes. A shake of the head reset her steely countenance. "I'm sorry if your friends were among them."

"I didn't . . . know any of them," Vallen said.

He turned and started down the creaking steps, his teeth clenching with each impact. Sadly, Matteo hadn't known anyone outside their team either. Few cadets had greeted him in passing, and he'd replied with a curt nod and an anxious scamper to escape their notice.

Now, like Leon, they were gone—the opportunity to know them forever past.

Major Reev indicated they should follow Vallen in the direction of the tent city. Sylette, absently chewing at one of her nails, trailed after her. Matteo wiped his mouth on his sleeve—just one more stain at this point—and descended the steps along with Velle.

The clamor of barracks life drifted to them as they neared the dilapidated tents. Swearing, boasting, the clatter of cookware, and even the occasional grim laugh. Whatever they were cooking smelled heavily of wild onions and grease, the kind they used to over-flavor Darmatian army rations. Matteo immediately knew where their latrine trench was—the ditch off to their left *reeked* of fermenting urine and dung.

"Well, you've seen the overview," Major Reev said, guiding them toward the cramped avenue extending from one side of the makeshift camp to the other. "I'll take you through once and then assign you a berth."

Clang! Clatter-clatter-clat—

A rusty tin can with the faded image of a green ferras bean on it flew past Matteo to bounce end over end down the dusty stone 'street.' He spun toward its source: Sylette. Leg half extended, shoulders heaving, she stood in the middle of the path *glaring* at Major Reev.

"What about the ships?" Sylette shouted. "What about your equipment? This *can't* be everything. This can't be what I was holding out for."

Major Reev didn't reciprocate her rage. "There are a few craft in a hangar farther in, and a couple dozen vehicles and artillery we managed to salvage, but—"

"How could you not prepare for this? How could you not have a backup plan for losing Aldona?"

Matteo nervously glanced around as tent flaps opened and dirty, tired faces poked out. Other soldiers stood up from their campfires, their uniforms, fatigues, or simple undergarments torn and frayed. Dark stubble lined the men's faces, while deep bags—deeper than most trenches—hung under the glassy eyes of all present. The dented bowls and pots simmering atop tiny piles of coals spat drops of stew too clear to have any real taste.

Drawn by the commotion, they wandered over in groups of two and three until a ring of filthy bodies penned in Major Reev and the cadets. Vallen tried to push through, but a bare-chested Hue—older and more scarred than Unter, with a different beast tattooed on each of his four hulking arms—refused to budge.

Step by step, Matteo edged around the circle of onlookers until he could whisper in the fuming princess' ear. "Uhhh, Sylette? Look around. We're attracting a *lot* of attention."

Velle tried to grab Sylette's shoulder, but the girl shrugged free of her grasp. "Come on, Sylette. This isn't the right place. When we get to the tent, you can shout at Vallen all you want."

"No," Major Reev said, tone icy. "Let her say her piece."

Sylette stalked forward, arms waving wildly. "*My* piece? Everyone here is thinking the same thing I am. How could Steward Metellus botch things this badly? Why didn't your government see this coming? Why did the fleet waltz into what was obviously a Sarconian trap?" She stopped in front of Major Reev, her last question all but screamed into the stoic woman's face.

"Are you finished?" the Ice Queen asked.

A cruel sneer twisted Sylette's lips. "Yes."

Smack!

The slap hit before Sylette could react. She stumbled to the side, eyes wide with shock, fingers leaping to the stinging welt on her cheek. No tears tumbled to the ground—Matteo could tell she was too furious for that. Gaze filled with loathing, Sylette straightened up and thrust out her chin as if daring Major Reev to strike her again.

Would the Ice Queen take out her frustrations on *all* of them? Perhaps set them to hauling crates of munitions or cleaning the putrid latrines? *Anything but that,* Matteo prayed. *Please, dear Veneer, anything but that.*

"Did that wake you up?" Major Reev asked.

Sylette didn't respond.

Major Reev nodded, apparently satisfied by her student's

cold—but silent—defiance. "You think you're the only one who's suffered because of the Empire? Where in the seven hells do you get off acting like a teat-sucking lordling? You've got two arms, two legs, working eyes and ears, and"—she jabbed a finger at Sylette's twitching scowl—"a perfectly functional mouth, as you've just demonstrated."

"I—" The princess' protest died, slain by a single glare. Shimmers of frost glimmered in the Major's raven hair, beneath her eyes, and around her head. The temperature in the already damp cave fell further, and Matteo rubbed his hands together as his breath crystallized in the air. Interrupting the Ice Queen was *not* a good idea.

"But what of the people here?" Major Reev continued, raising one arm toward the noiseless spectators, the other toward the medical tent at the path's far end. "Look at the rot and decay. Look at the meager rations the men are eating, the pitiful conditions they sleep in, the wounded and diseased who have to be separated so their infections don't spread."

She turned to a group of soldiers on the left. Blood seeped from a poorly bandaged slash that had taken one man's ear. The Sylph woman next to him was missing half her uniform coat, the space beneath a mass of burns that had turned her red skin black from shoulder to waist. Grimy wraps covered her chest, and moldering leaves—the best poultice she could likely find—tried to stem the tide of pus oozing from the festering scabs. Others leaned on crutches, were missing fingers and toes, or were just so haggard they couldn't have had a proper sleep or meal since Aldona.

Matteo nearly retched a second time.

"Have you heard your comrades' screams?" Major Reev asked the soldiers.

A mumble. "Yes."

She spun to the other side. "What about the amputations? The bloody surgeries? Have you seen them?"

"We've been on the butcher's table ourselves!" A one-armed Terran shouted while his comrades grumbled their support.

Major Reev saluted the man, a gesture he shakily returned with the hand still attached. "Magic isn't a cure-all," she said, directing her words at Velle. "Unter, your friend, nearly died when your healing couldn't keep up. People in that tent *did* die. Spitting blood, leaking guts, going cold as our few salvators have to decide who will live . . . and who won't.

"And those are the ones who made it this far. What of the dead? The splintered families and orphaned children? The nation is in crisis, yet *you*"—The floating ice shards grew as the Major spat the word at Sylette—"dare to think *you're* special? You are a victim—that much is true—but no more or less than anyone else here."

Murmurs of agreement rose around Matteo. Heads bobbed in assent. Beneath the dirt, sunken gazes, and sallow skin, there was still fire, still passion. Legs twitched. Fists pumped. They might be beaten, but they weren't defeated. Not yet, at any rate.

The Major took a step toward Sylette. To her credit, the princess didn't flinch even though she was within striking range. "So, Cadet Farkos, do you still think you're special?"

"No," Sylette whispered.

"Will you follow orders?"

"Yes . . . " Sylette paused. The tension left her stance, and she sighed. "Yes, ma'am."

"Good to hear." As her hanging frost disappeared, Major Reev extended a hand to Sylette, which the princess reluctantly accepted. "Then you shall have your victory." She raised her voice. "*All* of you shall have your victory!"

Cheers erupted from the crowd, and the camp filled with the sounds of stamping feet, banging pots, and the upbeat strumming of one soldier's long, four-stringed instrument. Matteo couldn't help tapping along to the tune: *When Jelfo Went to Sea*, a favorite among the sailors in his hometown.

A fiendish grin spread across Major Reev's face. Instead of releasing Sylette from her grip, she pulled her closer. "As punishment for your tantrum, you'll be scrubbing dishes in the mess and washing clothes in the lake for a week. And just because I feel like it, the Triaron will be helping you."

Can the base survive them being together for more than five minutes? Matteo thought.

Silver hair flipping from side to side, Sylette tried to pull away. "What? Working with *him* is worse than latrine duty."

"Oh!" Major Reev brightened. "Thanks for the reminder. You'll both be scrubbing the privy trenches as well."

Vallen stumped forward, indignant. "Why should I have to help her? I did nothing wrong!"

"Didn't you?" Major Reev released Sylette, who staggered back three steps into the waiting arms of two soldiers. "Well, just think of it as payback for all the pain you've caused me the past four years."

Sylette immediately squirmed out of the soldiers' grasp, ducking beneath their arms and popping up a few paces away. They stumbled into each other but didn't curse or shout. Their stares—filled with an awe bordering on reverence—were fixed on Vallen.

The older one, his gray beard knotted with engine bolts that rattled against his oil-stained coveralls, found his voice first. "Did you say . . . the *Triaron*."

"I did," Major Reev said with a smile.

"*The* Triaron?" his companion breathed. He wore a similarly greasy outfit—the uniform of an airship engimage. "The one from the Academy?"

A freckled woman with red sergeant stripes on her sleeves shouldered her way alongside them. "Yeah, that's him! I saw a few of his flag-brawl matches on the telescriber at my old post."

Matteo lost track of the exclamations after that. He ducked the press of bodies as it closed around them, wanting nothing more than to be as far away as possible. An elbow grazed his ribs. He nearly tripped three times. But, with a gasp, he emerged on the other side.

"Telescriber?" Someone laughed. "I *went* to a couple of his matches. The kid's amazing."

"Amazin' don't cut it. He can use *any* kind o' elemental magic. I bet even high rankin' Imperial mages wud have trouble wit' him."

"Then . . . do we have a chance?"

"The Ice Queen is here. We *always* had a chance!"

"But now we have the *Triaron*—the only guy in the world with Darmatus' powers. That's some kind of sign, right?"

"It could be. Hey, tell Lesh to gather the rest of the lads. They have to see this."

"Sure thing. The whole camp'll know before the stew's done cookin'"

Most of that is drivel, Matteo thought, recalling all the foolish things he'd watched Vallen do. The gossip continued to spiral out of control, becoming more farfetched with every tongue it touched. Yet he couldn't deny the sudden surge of energy. This army had been one firm prod from collapsing ten minutes ago. Now they looked like they would charge Rittermarschal Valescar with nothing but pluck and a rusty shovel.

Matteo glanced over the jostling heads at Major Reev, who caught his eye and grinned. He shivered. Not at the underground chill, nor the effects of her ice magic.

She'd played them. Sylette, Vallen, him, the entire crew. The Major hadn't saved them out of any sense of altruism. No, she needed a symbol, something that would rally the Resistance back from the brink of despair.

The Ice Queen needed Vallen. The Triaron, spiritual successor of Hero King Darmatus, master of elemental magic.

Hope in the flesh.

Chapter 6
Affairs of State

Hetrachia 12, 697 ABH
Nemare, Capital of the Sarconian Province of Darmatia

A light rap at the chamber's double door wove its way through the canopy of gauze curtains, mounds of satin pillows, and beneath the silk sheets to brush against the ears of the bed's occupants.

Emperor Sychon Artorios wanted to ignore it. Gaze hungry, he stared up at the full lips, alabaster skin, and draping crimson curls dangling above him. Rose-tinted eyes that reflected his own passion narrowed, then blinked with resignation. A heavy sigh followed—one almost as heavy as their recent gasps of pleasure.

The rap came again, louder and more insistent. "We have to answer them, you know?" Rittermarschal Auvrea Titania purred. She leaned forward, her bare chest brushing against his as she traced Sychon's ear with her teeth. Lightning radiated from her touch, tingles of desire that made his fingers tighten atop her thighs and left him craving another minute, another second with her.

"You have an empire to run, my Lord," Auvrea whispered.

Sychon slid his hands up to grasp her slender waist. "Void my empire."

Another knock sounded, accompanied by two more that were practically *bangs*, the door's opulent elegoras wood shuddering under the impact. A growl formed in Sychon's throat, but Auvrea held a soft finger to his lips, one he *barely* resisted the temptation to bite.

"Look out the window. What do you see?"

Reluctantly, he tore his eyes away from her and peered between the canopy's folds. Light streamed through the balcony window, dappling the white and black marble floor with shimmering streaks. It was dawn. No, *past* dawn, perhaps late as eight or nine. Where had the night gone? Sychon could have sworn the hour of the Void had scarcely passed.

Chest still heaving, Auvrea rolled off him, gently sliding out of his grip and sighing as his hands caressed her retreating legs. She stood, wrapped herself in a scarlet cloak emblazoned with the seal of the Ritter

Order, and turned to Sychon, slowly, mesmerizingly tying the front clasp to afford him one final view.

Not final, the Emperor thought, rewarding her with a wicked grin. *This wasn't our first indiscretion, and it certainly won't be our last.*

Auvrea spun in place, cloak ever so briefly billowing up to reveal *everything,* then strode to the door with purposeful steps. The scent of lavender lingered in her wake—the aroma of oils that glistened on her skin, the bed, and now on Sychon's flesh. He breathed deeply of it while savoring the sway of her curves beneath the thin fabric.

Delicate fingers found the ivory handle of the door, then turned strong as they whipped it open in a spray of embers. Sychon wasn't sure which he found more alluring: Auvrea the sensual lover, or Auvrea the ruthless commander. Leaning back against his pillow, he settled in to watch the coming blaze.

The square-jawed, balding officer on the other side stopped mid-knock, his balled fist level with Auvrea's face. Shock twisted his features, followed by confusion and shame as his gaze fell on her hastily hidden cleavage. He glanced away—*not* a wise move.

Fire flared at the tips of Auvrea's curls. "I presume you have a good reason for bothering His Majesty in his private chambers, *Colonel* Eurik?" She ground his rank between her teeth, suggesting he might not hold it for much longer.

"I-I ... " Eurik stammered.

A mail-coated gauntlet shoved the remaining door open, revealing a sentinel armored from foot to helm in gleaming silver plate. Red and gold whorls danced along the cuirass, pauldrons, and tasses of the suit, while draconian talons curled from the vambraces to rest atop weighty gauntlets. The maw of a dragwyrm, fangs bared in a snarl, formed the visor and helm at the ensemble's peak.

"Grand Marschal," Auvrea said, bowing and placing her fist atop her breast.

The helm's black slit swung toward Sychon, who waved dramatically. "Come in, Zaratus. Have some wine, and maybe some grapes and cheese while you're at it."

He gestured at a sitting area near the door, where two chairs and a low table sat in front of a charcoal filled-hearth. On the table were an untouched pitcher of red Ithran wine and a plate of abandoned refreshments over which a trio of flies cheerfully buzzed. Placed by the servants the night prior, they had been ignored in the occupants' haste to reach the bed.

"The morning is already ruined," Sychon continued, "so you might as well invite the rest of my staff to join us. Perhaps we can have tea on the veranda and discuss possible festival themes that will appease the conquered Darmatians."

The towering Grand Marschal—first among Sychon's servants—ducked into the room. The longsword belted at his side clanked as he maneuvered it around the doorframe. "You jest, Your Majesty."

"Of course!" Sychon thumped the pillows at his side. "I gave explicit orders that I was *not* to be disturbed unless the Void itself started swallowing the city, yet all I see outside my window are sunshine and songbirds."

Zaratus turned to Auvrea, his red cloak rustling atop the marble in his wake. If the Grand Marschal was dismayed that his subordinate would use the mark of their station to hide her nakedness, he didn't show it. Nor did he show any emotion whatsoever. The dragwyrm hiding his face was for more than just intimidation, and only Sychon knew what lay beneath the mask—a fact that made him a pawn more loyal than any other.

One of the gauntlet's claws flicked at the still quivering Colonel Eurik. "Show her the report," Zaratus growled.

Eyes squeezed shut, Eurik hobbled closer until Auvrea huffed and snatched the wrinkled paper he'd pulled from his uniform's breast pocket. From where he lounged, Sychon could see scarlet drops bleeding through the parchment along with the ink.

"Are you *really* a Colonel? *Heh,*" she scoffed as she scanned the document. "You clearly aren't one of mine. No one in the Fifth Fleet would reach that rank acting like a beaten—"

Her voice trailed off and her luscious lips pursed in anger. Seconds later, the parchment burst into flame around her fingers, smoke rising as the ashes fell to the pristine floor. Sychon made a mental note to have one of the imprisoned Darmatian dignitaries—maybe old Steward Metellus himself—clean the tiles later.

"What did it say?" Sychon asked. "What happened?"

"It wasn't the Void swallowing my city," Auvrea fumed. "It was the blasted Creator."

Casually calling Nemare *her* city would've landed any other officer in boiling synth-oil. But Sychon had made her governor of the former Kingdom's capital. He would allow the claim to stand, provided she continued to . . . *convince* him of her capabilities at night.

"You don't believe in the Creator," Sychon noted.

"And I didn't believe in Sarcon's legend either. Yet the insufferable warlock's traipsing through the palace halls in the body of some blond dandy." She shook her head. "Not the *literal* Creator, my Lord. It's those foolish priests and Darmatians who still worship him and Sariel. They're calling it the 'Night of Sariel's Blades.' Hundreds of our men were murdered under the cover of darkness, slain while off-duty or during their patrols. Most knifed in alleyways, some strung up on lampposts, and even a few drowned in the city canals. All done by madmen dressed in white sheets who suffered a *fraction* of our casualties."

"A complete disaster," Zaratus interjected. "A colossal embarrassment."

Auvrea's eyes flashed. Cinders sparked across her hair. "I'm well aware of that. I . . . After the destruction of Sariel's Cathedral, I should have seen this coming. But . . . "—she brought a crimson nail to her mouth and nibbled softly—" . . . everything was so peaceful. They made no moves for almost a week, and . . . "

She stopped chewing and jabbed her finger at Zaratus. "Why didn't *you* stop them? Why wait until now to inform the Emperor and myself?"

The helm glared at her impassively. "I have been outside the walls constructing new airfields for the First and Fifth Airfleets. Airfields necessary to resupply our invasion of the Imperium." Zaratus leaned in, looming over his junior by two head spans. "And while I was handling the military affairs *I* was charged with, the *governor* of *this* city allowed a massacre to go unpunished. Is that not true, Your Majesty?"

Sychon blanched. He had no desire to reprimand Auvrea—not when the fault was half his to bear. Stalling, he rang the servants' bell on his gold and silver trimmed nightstand. Not three seconds later, one of two opposite doors flanking the balcony slid open and two young attendants in crisp black suit-robes hastened to attend him.

"Dress me," Sychon ordered as he stood and spread his arms. His toes sank into the lavish rug beneath his feet, its fibers ethereal as a cloud. *Another note,* he thought, undergarments rising about his legs. *Have the original rug-weaver make a replacement—exactly the same, but red and gold instead of Darmatian blue and silver. This is* my *palace now, not theirs.*

Trillith woven silk britches followed, and a gold tunic trimmed with silver complemented their untainted white. Ruffles were out of fashion this season. Instead, the servants fluffed a mauve cravat

91

about his neck, affixing it firmly—but not *too* firmly—with a precious illyrium gemstone the size of an egg. Once everything else was in place, Sychon bent slightly and allowed them to drape a regal crimson robe about his shoulders.

A flick of his wrist sent the youths scurrying for the balcony, and he stooped to retrieve his crown from the bedside. Pure silver, simple and elegant. Strong too. Like him, his magic, and his continent-spanning empire. Smiling, Sychon placed it atop his head and turned to his high commanders.

Auvrea and Zaratus bowed deeply. Eurik all but plastered himself to the floor. "Your Majesty," they chorused.

"I have reached a decision," Sychon announced. "Rittermarschal Titania"—he addressed Auvrea by her proper title—"who was in command of the city garrison last night?"

"Colonel Eurik," she replied with a grin.

The last brown wisps clinging to the officer's scalp seemed to wither along with his sagging chin. "If it p-pleases Your Grace, I do-don't have the authority to deploy the whole garrison without—"

Auvrea winked at Sychon as she rose from her bow, entrancing cleavage still very much on display. She stamped her bare foot in Eurik's face. Sparks burst around it, and the colonel scrambled on all fours toward the door. "Then you should have sought me out. It *was* an emergency, was it not?"

"Y-yes, I mean no . . . Yes? B-but, His Majesty issued orders h-he was not . . . not to be d-disturbed, and you were . . . with h-him . . . "

Her lips curled in a savage—and *beautiful*—snarl. "What are you suggesting, Eurik? Are you accusing *His Majesty* of impropriety? On top of your sordid failure to contain a growing rebellion in the Empire's newest capital?"

"N-never!" Eurik babbled, tears filling his eyes as he frantically glanced from Auvrea, to Zaratus, to the Emperor. "I . . . I wouldn't. No, please no. Forgive me. Not for my s-sake . . . for my family. J-just . . . Anything b-but that . . . "

Sychon relished the moment the light fled his gaze; the instant he realized his fate. The Sarconian Empire might have rittermarschals who wielded the power of judges and a Senate filled to bursting with conniving, capricious nobles, but *he* was its emperor.

And his word was law.

"You are stripped of your post as Nemare garrison commander," Auvrea declared. "You are demoted one grade. As soon as you leave this room, you will be immediately reassigned to the 14th Infantry Division besieging Varas Fortress. There you will take charge of a forlorn hope battalion scheduled to assault the outer wall. If you are successful in your new position," she bared her teeth in a crooked smile, "*Then* you might earn my forgiveness."

Life fled Lt. Colonel Eurik. He slumped to the ground, sobbing as though Auvrea had pronounced his date at the executioner's block. Which she had. Forlorn hope battalions were the place the Empire sent criminals, dissidents, and failures to die.

At a bark from Zaratus, two guards wielding ceremonial pikes clomped down the hall, hauled Eurik to his knees, and drug the blubbering husk of a man from Sychon's sight. It felt oh-so-good watching the condemned man crumble.

Almost as good, Sychon thought, exchanging a sultry glance with Auvrea. *As plotting Lozaria's conquest while wrapped tightly in your embrace.*

Chapter 7
Could Be Worse

Hetrachia 12, 697 ABH
Resistance Base, Sarconian Province of Darmatia

*B*ear it, Sylette thought. *Endure the pain and shame.*
The throbbing of her swollen cheek—so much like a little heartbeat—stoked the flames burning within her chest. It pulsed against the damp rag she held, along her fingers, and throughout her aching body. But like every obstacle she'd ever faced, it didn't stop her.

Silent and reflective, Sylette stalked after Major Reev, Vallen, and the other cadets. Step by step, gaze downcast, ignoring the crowds of soldiers packing in on either side of the wretched shantytown street. She had been chastised. Beaten, upbraided, and humiliated. And now, having seen the errors of her ways, the arrogant cadet was set on the path to reformation.

Or so Major Reev believed.

If Sylette had been alone, she'd have burst out laughing. Was Matteo so naive to think *she* couldn't control her emotions? She watched him walking side by side with Velle, both of them oblivious to the games going on around them. Major Reev had rescued them to use Vallen's name—the legacy of the Triaron the imbecile was wholly unworthy of.

And I . . . A ghost of a grin formed beneath the compress Sylette held, all but hidden from the world. *I plan on using the Ice Queen herself.*

Her tantrum had been calculated—a ploy to make Major Reev underestimate her. Sylette's grin became a grimace, and she lifted the rag so she could spit out a gob of scarlet mucus. Her lip was split near its corner, her flushed skin already purpling beneath the angry welt. The coppery taste of blood filled her mouth. Major Reev wasn't pulling any punches, and when the time came, neither would she.

Then there was the issue of Vallen's loose tongue. Sylette glared daggers at the fool's scar-mangled back as he hobbled along, wishing she could slice off the offensive organ and shove it down his throat. *Highness?* How could he screw up and call her *that* of all things? His mistake was half the reason she'd had to put on that ridiculous act. If the Darmatians discovered her true identity—that she wasn't Sylette

94

Farkos, but Sylette *Artorios*—they'd shove her in a cramped cell until they could barter her away to her father.

Or just put a bullet in her skull.

"Renar, Lilith!" Major Reev raised her arm to be seen above the throng. The two cadets, approaching from the direction of the hospital tent, hurried over. "Did you get Unter to the salvators?"

Renar's gaze fell. "He's looking pretty pale—for a guy who's already blue, I mean. Can they—"

"They're the best healers we have," she assured him. "And if they can't remove the poison, one of the nuns surely can. We had several members of the Way of the Will join us during our retreat."

Lilith gripped Renar's arm, and he smiled down at her. "A little bullet and some nasty goop aren't going to kill the big fella," she said, freckled face beaming. "He'll be fine."

"You-you're right."

With a satisfied nod, Major Reev strode past them and grabbed the flap of a particularly frail-looking tent. Its sides sagged like the chest of some malnourished steed, more ratty patches than cloth formed its surface, and the poles supporting it were not army-issue steel, but gnarled pieces of driftwood. And the fabric itself? Sylette had seen ancient texts that were less yellowed.

The Major's hand yanked the awning back. "Welcome to your new home. It's not an Academy dorm room, but it's probably better than whatever Sewertown hole Cadet Metellus crawled from."

"Hey!" Vallen cried. His origins were no secret among the army brass—he *was* the Steward's adopted son. Yet it seemed to Sylette that many, Major Reev among them, didn't look favorably on the rapid elevation of someone Nemare surface dwellers would sooner dump slop on than look at.

Renar shouldered past Vallen and disappeared into the shadowy gap. The other five cadets, Sylette included, followed him in, and Major Reev brought up the rear.

"*Oof!*"

"S-sorry!"

Sylette bumped into Matteo's back, prompting a stammered apology from him as he tucked in his shoulders and tried to scoot closer to Velle, who was herself wedged between Lilith and one of the tent's four supporting poles. The reek of sweat, clay, rotting wood, damp cloth, and body odor assaulted Sylette from all sides.

Cramped. The tent was impossibly cramped, with two listing

sets of hammocks made from sun-bleached netting and sail canvas dominating each side and leaving only a narrow, plank-covered walkway down the middle. Briny standing water pooled beneath their feet, the creaking pieces of moldy flooring barely keeping their ankles dry. A single trunk with a rusted lock sat at the tent's rear atop a foldable cot with one leg replaced by the sweeping end of a broken broom.

Six hammocks, three to a side. One collapsible cot—which might collapse permanently if Unter were to use it. This was their home now.

Velle's expression was horrified, her eyes darting from the floor, to the hammocks, to the host of dust motes swirling around five holes in the ceiling. Did she expect scum-crawlers or night-sliders to swarm her from under the boards? Matteo fumbled his glasses as he tried to clean the fog from them, gaze fixed on the alarming curve of the hammock supports. He probably hadn't spent a night out of a bed since the Academy's boot camp.

"I call a top bunk!" Renar shouted like an excited child.

He climbed the rickety ladder alongside the left-side hammocks, then launched himself onto the nearby sheet of sail canvas. Taut ropes bounced, the flimsy structure swayed, and the entire tent pulled in on itself for one tense moment before *barely* resisting his weight. If he'd brought the whole thing down on them, Sylette's boot would've had a pointed discussion with his chin.

Lilith wandered toward the trunk with careful, precise steps, avoiding the gaps in the haphazard flooring. With a mighty groan, Vallen lugged himself to one of the hammocks below Renar and flopped onto it. A curse burst from his lips. The blessed fool had somehow gotten his broken arm caught in the netting, flailing about until he freed the injured limb.

Hold your laughter, Sylette cautioned herself. It chafed her to let Vallen's misery go unappreciated, but her 'game' with Major Reev was more important.

Contempt oozed from the Ice Queen. "Yes, go ahead. Ignore protocol and make yourselves comfortable without being dismissed." One hand still on the flap, she parted it and stooped to leave. "Since you're settling in *nicely*, I'll take my leave and—"

"A moment, ma'am."

Major Reev paused and turned to Sylette. "Yes, Cadet Farkos?" Her attention wandered to the scrunched-up rag clutched in the exile's hand.

"This isn't about our earlier discussion, is it? Or your punishment?"

Controlling her fingers—willing them not to squeeze even tighter—took all of Sylette's focus. "Of course not, ma'am. I understand my place here."

"Good."

"But …" Sylette paused, chewing at her lower lip and refusing to meet the Major's stern gaze. Meek and timid, that's who *this* version of her needed to be. "Your strength!" she suddenly blurted. "The way you dominated that Draken, your magic, your … I'm babbling, aren't I?"

The Ice Queen let the flap fall. Whether it was up or down, the din of a camp preparing to eat came through clearly. "A bit, yes. Is there a point to this, Farkos? I have more duties than serving as nanny to the Triaron and friends."

Do not associate me with that imbecile, Sylette groused inwardly. "Do you think *we* could be that strong?" she asked. "No … what I mean to say is … could you train us to be that strong?"

The trap was baited and set. Major Reev needed powerful mages for her fight, the Triaron foremost among them. She wouldn't be able to resist the chance to mold them for the battle ahead, and while she was teaching them, Sylette would be whispering in her ear, planting suggestions, maneuvering her like a chess piece to the position where she would—

"I refuse."

"… C-come again?" Sylette spluttered.

"I—re—fuse," Major Reev repeated, punctuating each syllable with a harsh staccato. She stepped away from the entrance, a movement that nearly brought her to the small tent's center. "Why should I have to shoulder such an annoying burden? You had classes with me for the past four years and *now* you want to get serious? This must be a joke."

She thrust her arm at Vallen, lounging on his hammock with his back to them. "Besides, that one wouldn't even try to learn."

"And why should I if you're my teacher?" he retorted.

Major Reev ignored him. "Renar *can't* learn."

"Wh-what's that supposed to mean?" For some reason, Renar sounded more shocked than upset.

"Matteo would struggle with the application of anything I taught him."

A rather nice way of saying he's a coward, Sylette reasoned. Matteo started to protest, but clamped his mouth shut as the post beside him gave a disturbing creak.

"Lilith and Unter don't need more instruction, which leaves Velle, who would try her best, and . . . "

A creaking board was her only warning. Major Reev launched herself off the balls of her feet, head low, fist aimed at Sylette's chest. She dropped into a stance, swinging her right arm to deflect the blow, left arm pulled back to counter.

The attack never struck. Blinking, Sylette glanced down, then winced as the Ice Queen rapped a knuckle against her sternum. Her outer forearm block had been perfect! How had the Major evaded her guard?

" . . . *you*"—Major Reev tapped again—"who aren't the least bit interested in getting better. You never have been. So, I won't be participating in whatever little game you're playing."

Chilling emerald spears met fierce platinum daggers, their gazes each trying to peel back the other's mask and see what lay beneath. *We're cut from the same cloth*, Sylette realized as the silence dragged on. *We both dread losing control.*

"Major, if I may . . . " Velle began, shakily rising from the hammock Matteo had lowered her onto. She planned to insert herself between them, acting the kindhearted diplomat like she always did even though her legs trembled and she could barely keep her eyes open.

Sylette gave up. Holding her palms out, she dropped her guard and lowered her chin. There would surely be another opportunity to sway the Major. "It's fine, Velle." She glared at Matteo until he got the hint and eased the Sylph girl back onto her hammock. "I was being sincere, ma'am, but we can revisit the topic later."

"Don't bother." Major Reev straightened the ruffled hem of her uniform coat, restoring it to an immaculate state. Not a speck of dirt could be seen anywhere on her. What dark sorcery kept the Ice Queen so pristine in the middle of this *squalor*? "Even *if* I wanted to train you, I'm too busy keeping the Resistance running to focus on anything else right now. Most of the higher-ups are dead or captured, leaving me with far more responsibility than I care to have."

"My . . . my father." A reedy voice came from the top of the tent, where Renar's bushy eyebrows and mop of dark hair peeked over the lip of the tattered sailcloth on which he lay. "Is my father—is General Iolus, I mean—still alive?"

Major Reev sighed. "That's—"

The splish-splashing of boots on puddle-covered stone came from the street outside. Seconds later, a bob of neatly pinned blonde hair burst through the flap, followed by a sprinting soldier. Sylette sidestepped the woman's charge, who lurched to a stop centimeters from Major Reev. Flushed cheeks, tanned to a deep olive by the sun of southeastern Darmatia, brightened to a smile as her hand leapt to her high forehead in a stiff salute.

"Corporal Sayles." Major Reev took a step away from the huffing woman. "I may have made you a message runner, but that doesn't mean you have to *run* every message to me."

The woman—more a girl, as she seemed around Sylette's age—stayed stock still, her salute and grin unflagging. Major Reev cracked first, extending her arm for the letter. "Never mind. Just give it to me."

A yellowed piece of paper changed hands, and the Ice Queen glanced over it by the light streaming through the rips in the tent's ceiling. In the meantime, Sylette studied the corporal. Sayles remained at attention, uniform free of wrinkles despite a ragged, bloody tear on the left sleeve and several missing brass buttons. Energy radiated from her, an exuberance at odds with the low morale and poor discipline of the rest of the camp.

Is she loyal to the army, Sylette wondered, gaze following Sayles' eyes back to Major Reev. *Or to the Major specifically?* And more importantly, was there something about the corporal she could exploit?

"Ha, this is perfect timing." Snorting, Major Reev balled up the parchment and hurled it at Renar. He jerked in surprise, failed to block it, and almost fell from his perch when it struck his nose.

"What was that for?"

"Good news, Cadet Iolus," the Major continued. Her cheerful smile made Sylette shiver. It was quickly becoming apparent that the Ice Queen's pleasure meant misery for someone else. "Daddy dearest wants a word with you. You're to report to the brigade commander, General Iolus, immediately. Corporal Sayles will show you the way."

"Why is *that* blowhard in command?" Vallen groaned. "Getting eaten by the Draken would've been better than whatever he's going to put me through."

His hammock and the beams it was tied to swayed as he tucked himself tighter into its folds. Sylette wished the whole thing would come crashing down on his carefree skull.

Up above, Renar's shock twisted to dread. He appeared ready to resist the order until Major Reev barked a single ice-encrusted word.

"*Now.*"

With the speed of mud running down a dry riverbed, Renar heaved his bulk onto the ladder and dribbled to the floor. Much to Sylette's delight, his motion caused the lower hammocks to buck and shake, disturbing Vallen and coming *oh-so-close* to tossing him into the muck below.

When he reached the bottom, Renar turned to Major Reev, one hand raised in protest. "Major, I think visiting the General should wait until tomorrow. It's past dinner, he probably has a hundred things to do, and I need to go check on Unter up at—"

Major Reev flicked her sharp chin at him. "Corporal Sayles?"

A blonde blur lunged forward, caught Renar about the wrist, and began dragging him from the tent. Tears sprang to his eyes as his hand bent the wrong way beneath her skilled fingers. "Alright, alright! I'm coming."

The girl smiled, and the pressure lessened. As the tarp closed behind them, Sylette saw the breath drain from Renar's lungs. Deflated and defeated, he looked like he was walking the steps to the executioner's block—*not* going to see his father. She could empathize. Evidently, neither of them had drawn a winning card from the father deck.

Yet his loss was her gain. While Major Reev was proving far from pliable, General Hardwick Iolus was another story. Past his prime but still chasing glory, the former Academy commandant had proven ever so easy to manipulate. Sylette had once promised him victory, that she would take his brutish, dimwitted son and give him victory over the Triaron in the graduation matches.

She had held up her end of the bargain, even if the Empire had intervened. The General knew her capabilities. *And,* Sylette thought, turning away to hide her grin, *The bloated fool owes me a favor.*

The flap parted again, Major Reev stooping half-in, half-out of the entryway as she departed. "I'll leave the rest of you to settle in. Official orders will be along shortly, though we'll probably keep your unit intact to avoid sticking . . . *volatile* elements into other groups."

Chuckling at her own veiled insult, she started to let the tarp fall, then stopped abruptly. "Oh, two more things. When he's healed, Unter will be berthing with you. I leave figuring out the details of that to you." Major Reev waved grandly at the dismal, coffin-cramped quarters they'd been assigned.

"Second, there will be a memorial service for the fallen tomorrow. I *suggest* you attend, but if you so much as speak rudely to one of the attendees—I'm talking to *you,* Cadet Metellus—there won't be a frozen corpse left for them to identify you by."

Frigid threat lingering in her wake, the Ice Queen left, sharp boot clicks slowly fading into the general tumult of the camp. In unison,

Vallen and Matteo breathed a sigh of relief, then glared at each other for a tense moment.

"Not worth the effort," Vallen announced, turning to the dirty brown awning wall. Without replying, Matteo started sorting through the rubbish—old lumber, fragments of plywood, frayed rope, bent poles, and other odds and ends—around the tent and grabbing pieces that *might* help shore up the dilapidated structure.

The rest stewed in their thoughts, Sylette included. Getting slapped and denied by Major Reev—both within the space of an hour—didn't rankle her as much as what the woman had said.

"You aren't the least bit interested in getting better."

Irritated, Sylette tossed the crumpled rag she still held at the tent's rear canvas, which billowed at the impact. Lilith, sitting on a three-legged stool near the trunk, didn't even glance up.

What had the Ice Queen meant by that? What did *she* know that Sylette didn't? White hot fury bubbled in her veins, rage directed as much at herself as at anyone else. *I* am *trying to improve! I brought this 'team' together—kept them alive when they were voidbent on getting themselves killed. She should be* thanking *me for delivering her the Triaron on an illyriite platter.*

And what did her motives matter, if Major Reev had been keen enough to discern Sylette's true ambitions? Sarcon's sweaty sack! Didn't the Ice Queen want to defeat the Empire just the same as she did?

Lilith stood and started pacing, staring first at the sagging, hole-pocked roof, then at the haphazard, waterlogged planks that formed the floor. On one side of the central, muddy gap, Vallen lay in the bottommost hammock, while Velle occupied the one opposite him.

A little gasp burst from Lilith's mouth. Had she seen a night-slider? "What is it, Lilith?" Sylette asked. "Something wrong with our new home other than, well, *everything*?"

The freckled brunette walked from one end of the tent to the other, a journey of eight paces with her shallow stride. Her raised finger traced an imaginary line in the air along the way. "Not that I care, and it seems the Major doesn't either, but we're supposed to live here together, right?"

Sylette rolled her eyes. Why did she waste the slightest bit of concern on these fools? "Yes, obviously."

"Well, we have four boys and three girls. I just found it odd they didn't include a partition down the middle, but I guess we can't afford to be prudish in wartime. No big deal."

Oh, Sylette realized. *OH!*

She'd never once thought about mixing genders. When she was young, she'd possessed a *suite* of palace rooms many, many times this size. While running for her life, she'd slept wherever she could—even if that meant having to knife too-grabby hands. And at the Academy, their rooms had been split by sex though the teams were mixed.

This… Sylette glanced at Vallen and tasted bile. She could stomach living with him, just barely. Her hatred for her father and brother was a blazing sun beside the bonfire of disgust she felt for the Triaron.

"I-it's an easy fix," Velle soothed. "We could put up a barrier. Maybe an extra tarp or sheet of wood."

Matteo had turned a shade of red almost as deep as the Sylph's skin. "Er, I wouldn't—no, I mean *none* of the guys would look. And, you know, yeah . . . we could wait outside while you change, and you could do the same for us. We'll work it out."

"I make no such promises," Vallen said flippantly, his back still facing them.

The taste of bile intensified, its imagined reek spreading to her nostrils. Blood boiling, snarl on her lips, Sylette stalked toward Vallen. Whether she smacked him on the head or shot him full of daggers, she didn't want the senseless buffoon waking up anytime soon.

"He's joking," Matteo insisted.

Vallen sniggered. "You wish."

Velle staggered to her feet, trying to block Sylette's path with her arms. "What if we set a changing schedule? Won't that solve the problem?"

No, Sylette thought. *He* is *the problem.*

Something clicked in the rear corner of the tent. Lilith's elated voice followed. "Look! They included a few sets of clothes in the trunk. *Finally,* I can get out of this grimy outfit."

Sylette and Velle exchanged a glance, coming to an immediate, wordless accord. The Sylph grabbed Matteo and thrust his head beneath her hammock, then threw up a solid white glyph across the walkway. Unable to maintain his balance, Matteo screamed as he fell face first in a pool of cave sludge, his glasses clattering to a stop a few paces away.

Reacting to the shouts, Vallen rolled toward the noise. Two daggers materialized in the air in front of him.

"No!" he cried.

Yes, Sylette thought, firing them at the lines holding his hammock aloft.

The already strained ropes snapped instantly, dumping him,

shrieking, onto the next sling of netting down. Vallen could have still tumbled free, but he started flailing, becoming more and more entangled by the second. The remnants of his original hammock drifted down atop him, further muffling his pained, outraged yelps.

"What the void was that for?"

Sylette ignored him, her eyes wide at Lilith's brazenness. She was *undressing*—right in front of them, without bothering to kick the guys out first. Sylette had never known a Darmatian woman as carefree as she was.

Thankfully, Lilith was soon finished. She slipped a pair of drab fatigues over her snow-pale legs and tugged a white tank-top over her small breasts. A flick of her head shook out her short brown hair, which had been tousled by the shirt. With a swift kick, she sent her discarded garments flying against the rear of the tent, where they dropped behind the open trunk.

"I made a dirty clothes pile," she said proudly, stretching her arms in the air. "Blessed peaks, this feels *amazing*. You guys should clean up too!"

Sylette sighed. The bubbly girl was completely unaware of the crisis she'd caused. On the ground, Matteo cradled his glasses, wiping flecks of mud from the lenses while checking for new scratches. Vallen continued to moan, trapped like a fish in the pile of netting.

Her revenge had been postponed—perhaps derailed entirely. The list of headaches she had to endure continued to pile into a mountain.

And this, Sylette lamented, *this is my life now.*

Chapter 8

Deep Roots

Hetrachia 12, 697 ABH
Sarconian Occupied Beiras

Heavy mist filled the streets of Beiras, a choking pall mixed from furnace fumes, ash, and swirling gunpowder smoke. It reeked of iron and charcoal, and burned the eyes and throats of those it touched.

The first was normal. Beiras' countless factories, the lifeblood of their war effort, poured black smog into the sky day after day, rendering the city's lower levels a shadowy abyss that required masks and illyrium lanterns to traverse safely.

The second was not. Hundreds of smokestacks lay still, not so much as an ember leaving their mouths. Yet the smoke continued to thicken, fed by hungry fires that raced uncontrolled through the city and left charred ruins in their wake.

Beiras was burning, and it was *not* Rittermarschal Valescar's fault.

"That's an artillery factory," he yelled, pointing with his gauntlet. "Get the water truck over 'ere so we can save it!"

"Right away!" Irine glanced up and pressed a hand to her ear, relaying the order to her twin, Elias. Valescar had split the sensors up to help his teams communicate in the middle of this chaos.

Armor clanking, he strode toward the blaze, two great metal propellers—ripped from a crashed Rabbanite airship—whirling fast enough to blur in front of him. They drove back the flames and mist, allowing the soldiers with him to approach the factory's brick front. Fire jetted from the doorway and broken windows, obscuring whatever lay inside.

Wheels screeched on the pavement behind him. One of his firefighting teams had arrived. Hoses in hand, two lines of men came alongside Valescar, aimed their nozzles upward, and loosed torrents of water at the inferno.

Valescar moved on, directing the propellers ahead of him with both arms. He didn't have time to think; time to stop. A wooden tenement, four flimsy floors of apartments haphazardly shoved in an alley between two ball-bearing workshops, collapsed in a roar of sparks and cinders on his left.

Had there still been people inside? Workers that hadn't managed to pack their things and evacuate in time? Valescar waved at another building, one with a red engine engraved on its crumbling wall, and Irine called for more support. Two steps behind him, Captain Gadler and his aides hunched over a char-blackened map of the lower city, desperately trying to locate resources they should save before all was lost.

How could they do this? Valescar wondered. *How could those slimy slechers erase centuries o' progress ta make things a wee bit 'arder on us?*

More buildings were marked. Sarconian soldiers swooped in, doused them with water, and pulled out what they could. A dozen half-melted lathes for boring rifles. Four crates of ration packs meant for Rabbanites at the front.

Articles with no merit went back into the flames from whence they came. An oil canvas, sunset colors running like blood. A child's patchwork doll, black hair made from iron shavings, her clogs from whittled out bottle corks. Evidence of people's lives that Valescar had no reason to preserve, even though something twisted inside his mangled flesh as he watched them vanish.

An explosion erupted two streets over, making everyone flinch and glance around nervously. It could be stored munitions cooking off . . . or insurgents attacking another platoon.

"Get air cover there, stat," Valescar ordered. While Gadler relayed the command, he reached out with his magnetism magic, searching for moving metal in their vicinity—a sure sign that enemy gunmen were approaching their position.

Gadler stumped up beside him. Gray ash coated the man's mustache, making the *Judicator's* captain look older than he actually was. His once immaculate uniform was soaked with sweat, stained with soot, and singed along the legs and sleeves.

"Ya aren't supposed ta rush in with the troops, Gadler," Valescar admonished wryly.

The man snorted. "I could say the same about you, sir. Let me state once again that I disapprove of the theater commander leading a ground opera—"

"Noted. Fer the fourth time."

Shaking his head, Gadler glanced at Valescar's armor. He still wore the full plate, mail, and crimson cloak associated with his rank, along with two rapiers buckled to his back. "Aren't you hot?" The captain asked, pulling at his sweat-darkened collar.

Valescar was *always* burning, but his pain was more imagined than real these days. "I ain't felt hot since Aldona. Flyin' through a crashin' airship'll do that ta—"

He clamped his mouth shut. Something made of metal—or someone *with* it—was closing rapidly from their right. Valescar spun in that direction, metal blades prepared to repel bullets, the spools of wire on his hips loosening to retaliate.

No attack came. A flight of Sarconian lancerjets soared over the smoky rooftops, angling toward the source of the earlier detonation. Valescar relaxed, then winced as Irine's high-pitched shout assaulted his ears.

"I'm sorry, sir! Our comms are a mess with the battle still going on. I wasn't sure when support would arrive."

He waved her concerns away, gaze tracing the graceful arc of the lancerjets. The snub-nosed fighter craft did one loop before waggling their wings and departing. No enemy, all clear. They didn't have any forces in the area, and the blast could be ruled an accident.

More thunder roared in the distance. Beiras proper was his, but General Schutte was still clearing the Rabbanite trenches and nipping at the retreating enemy's rear guard. Fighting would continue through the evening and into the night, which would make the smog-obstructed visibility even worse.

The gunfire struck while Valescar was distracted.

Two of his men went down, one clutching his bleeding calf, the other plugged clean through an eye. Irine reacted quickly, grabbing the first under his armpits and hauling him toward the nearest cover—the chassis of their water truck.

Most of the Sarconians weren't armed, their guns stored on the truck's bed while they lugged log-thick hoses around. Another went down in a spray of blood as he ran to arm himself. Other stray shells pinged off the truck hood, the pavement, and the neighboring buildings.

Valescar raised his propellers in the air and spun them in a wide circle, hoping to catch as many rounds as he could. Bullets clanged against the blades like hundreds of weighty raindrops falling atop a metal sheet. He was catching most of them, but a few were still getting through—one into the truck's front right tire, which deflated with a furious hiss, and another across Gadler's shoulder. It sliced a golden epaulet off, leaving him stunned but uninjured.

Four, nay, five men, Valescar reasoned, listening to the clatter of striking rounds, feeling them whizz through the mist. *Semi-automatic rifles, five shots ta a clip, with a sixth reloadin' an' passin' them new guns.* Damage inflicted aside, they *weren't* trying to kill him. The fire was too sporadic, too unfocused for that. They were trying to suppress his unit.

But to what end?

Another group of Sarconians came rushing down the street, blazing green flares marking them as friendlies through the smog. With them was a huddled, frightened family. At the front limped a mother, ratty shawl wrapped around her wiry hair, infant clutched tight in her scraggly, burn-pocked arms. Next to her, a gangly youth of fourteen or fifteen too big for the tattered rags he wore ran with an even younger boy and girl on his left and right, their hands locked in his.

Refugees who didn't make it out of the city? Defectors? Spies who worked for Sarconian intelligence?

Valescar's thoughts ground to a halt. The hail of lead directed at his unit swung toward the unprotected squad. A lieutenant in a chainmail cuirass caught one in the chest and crumpled, nearly dragging the mother down with her. Only a desperate shove from another soldier pushed her free, and the man himself was hit in the ribs. He fell, clutching his scarlet side.

"Up there!" Valescar cried. He pointed with one of the unsheathed rapiers from his back, his propellers and wires already shifting to protect the approaching squad. "In the curved buildin' at the end o' the street, second floor balcony. Six men. Fire at will!"

All metal was his to know, to sense, to command. Every shell that struck his makeshift shields and cut through the smoke had brought Valescar closer to locating their foes. Now he knew exactly where the Rabbanites were, and they would pay for spilling his men's blood.

The enemy's diverted attention allowed Gadler, Irine, and the rest of his team to grab their rifles. Magazines clicked, bolts snapped, and cracks roared around him. The rounded building—once a tavern, if the blackened ale mug hanging out front was any clue—exploded in a deluge of flying brick splinters and wood fragments. One scream echoed from inside, followed by another. The rain of fire from the insurgent's nest halted immediately.

Nay, lads, Valescar thought, disfigured lips bared in a snarl. *Ya aren't escapin'. Not today, not ever.* He closed his eyes. He didn't need sight to see the metal canteens strapped to their belts, the ammo casings in their chest bandoliers. Their coat buttons betrayed them, as did the piercing in one's ear, the wrist bands three of them wore, and the cheap tooth filling on the fifth.

They were within Valescar's hundred-meter range, and he would have his vengeance.

"Ret'mag'wa," he chanted.

One hand kept the propellers suspended, spinning between the scorched tavern and street. The other *yanked*. Hard.

Surprised cries preceded the bodies by an instant. Arms flailing, curses on their lips, they came tumbling out the windows, banged against the balcony's heat-warped railing, and kept hurtling toward Valescar's outstretched gauntlet.

The first three never saw their fate. They struck the whirling blades—sharp, curved, meter-long hunks of metal meant to tug airships through the sky—and dissipated into a cloud of red mist that only added to Beiras' pervasive smog.

Seeing their comrades' demise, the last two insurgents dropped their rifles and unlimbered their belts, reducing Valescar's hold on them enough to reach out and grasp the railing. Their bloody fingers hung on for dear life.

Chuckling at their foolishness, Valescar adjusted his focus and wrenched loose the very rails they clung to.

"Aaaaaaaaaaaaaaa—"

Two shrieks rang out, then were abruptly silenced.

"Bit messy, don't you think?" Gadler asked, lowering his rifle and inspecting his clothes for crimson splatters.

"That," Valescar flicked a mailed claw at the two dead soldiers near their water truck, men that should not have had to die, "was messy. What I did ta those slechers was clean-up. The city's fallen. Don't they know when ta quit?"

"Apparently not." Gadler raised his voice and waved at the approaching soldiers. "Who's in charge? And who are these civvies?"

A woman with blood crusting her short black hair glanced over her shoulder at the dead lieutenant sprawled face-up on the street. "Lieutenant Snyder was in command, but she got slotted, so . . . " The three other soldiers around the Rabbanite family looked at her expectantly. "Well, I guess I'm in charge now, sir."

"And these?" Gadler gestured at the mother and her children. They closed about their parent protectively, the eldest son holding his arm out to shield her, and the little ones hiding behind her torn dress folds.

"Pulled them from a burning building. I know it wasn't our mission," she trembled a bit while staring at Valescar, "but we couldn't just leave them to die."

Gadler raised an eyebrow. "Were they in a factory you were searching? Did they give you any intel? Do they know where the fleeing Imperium forces are headed? Is it Varas Fortress, or Rabban, or—"

"Enough, Gadler," Valescar growled. "There'll be time fer all o' that later. Fer now, they've suffered plenty without us addin' ta it."

No father. The mother was sickly, her eyes dark, skin sallow, and chest sagging. She probably couldn't properly breastfeed the infant, and it would die in a few days. Her eldest son was the breadwinner, Valescar reasoned, given the lad was healthy enough to glare hatred at him and muscular enough to follow through on that hate if someone put a blade in his hand. If not for his work in one of these factories, the lot of them would have starved by now.

They could do better for these people. *The Empire* could do better for these people.

"Irine, I think there's a package o' ration bars in the truck cab. Can ya bring it here?"

"Yessir!"

The cheerful sensory mage made it two steps before an illyrium grenade flew into their midst. Valescar's eyes went wide. It was a crude device: a men'ar infused crystal attached to a smoking gunpowder satchel, long wick all but burnt through. No metal on it whatsoever.

"Glory to the Imperium!" the sixth insurgent screamed from the tavern steps. "Death to—"

Gadler shot him through the forehead.

Yet the charge he'd thrown would still detonate; still kill them all. The mother looked to Valescar, gaze pleading. She was right.

He *was* the only one who could save them.

Snaps echoed in the air like gunshots. Valescar used his magic to split his armor along the seams, then sent the fragments soaring toward the bomb along with his wires, rapiers, and the blood-dripping propellers. They wrapped around the charge in an instant, forming a steel cocoon like the one he'd used to survive Aldona.

One second passed.

Poompf!

The mass of metal expanded outward, weaker sections spiking like little mountains. For a tense moment, the peaks continued to multiply, and the whole orb shuddered and bucked as if it would split into a thousand pieces of searing shrapnel.

Yet it didn't. Valescar pressed his hands in from the sides, molding the air before him with the same magnetic forces being applied to the grenade. Sweat dribbled down his brow, across his scars, and into his ragged beard. Yet exhausted as he was, he held firm until, with a *pop*, the immense pressure pushing back against his magic disappeared entirely.

Valescar let the distorted sphere fall. It clattered across the pavement, and as it rolled, he breathed a sigh of relief. "I'm two fer two on survivin' explosions, Gadler!"

Something metallic struck his side. The approach, and the strike itself, had been perfectly concealed by his focus on the illyrium grenade and all the other clangs, clicks, and clacks around him.

Protruding from his side was a combat knife—the kind issued to Imperium special forces. Valescar glanced down at the red spreading from the gap in his gambeson, a tear under his armpit and directly in line with his heart. Attached to the blade was a shaking hand, which led to a quivering arm and a misery-hardened face of no more than fourteen or fifteen years.

The boy. The woman's son had stabbed him.

The brat's lips moved, his eyes twitched, but no words came out. With a startled gasp, as though not quite comprehending what he'd done, his fingers jerked from the knife and he stumbled backwards.

"Th-they told me . . . told me this w-was the . . . "

One step.

"The o-only way to k-kill . . . "

Two steps.

"You."

Three steps.

"Fire!" Gadler yelled.

"No!" Valescar screamed.

Like before, he caught some of the bullets in an invisible grip. But not all. Shells struck the lad's shoulders, chest, ribs, and hips, spinning him one way, then the other in puffs of red mist. He was dead by the time he struck the ground, by the time Gadler raised a fist to halt the gunfire and the boy's shrieking mother reached his side.

Eyes glazed over, bloody mouth agape, limbs sprawled at sickening angles, he was completely and unequivocally dead—unlike Valescar, whose shrapnel-littered left side had saved his life. The knife had hit metal and glanced away from his heart, rending flesh but leaving his heart unscathed.

Irine rushed toward him, calling for a medical team. Yet Valescar didn't feel the pain in his side, or the blazing needles prickling his tortured skin. Panting, blood-racing, he could only stare at the slain youth—too young to be drafted into any army—and his family crowded atop his broken corpse.

The little girl wept. Her brother clutched her hand while poking his eldest sibling, asking him why he didn't wake up. And the mother . . . A chill swept through Valescar. Her tear-stained eyes weren't glued to her son. No, they stared utter loathing *through* him, as if her despondent soul could tear into his and rip his heart out.

Deep ran the hatred of this war. Valescar's men had died, he'd killed the men who slew them, and then a child had attempted to end him and been butchered in turn. Now his mother would surely walk the same path.

What are we doin'? a tiny voice in the corner of his mind whispered.

Ignoring the woman, the voice, and the pain, Valescar picked up his fallen cloak, wrapped it around his neck, and *fled* in the direction of his ship.

Chapter 9

What's Best

"Whoa there!"

With a screech of iron on cobbles, the carriage lurched forward, then settled to a stop in front of the broad steps of the Heronah mansion. Renar Iolus hurriedly hid his silver pocket knife inside the sleeve of his fine coat. He'd altered the hem just enough to conceal it against his forearm, though the resultant wad of scratchy fabric chafed *miserably* against his skin.

He shifted to the left on the velvet padded seat, leaning against the window and feigning that he'd been staring at the passing city sights during the ride. When the cab door opened, he favored Ral the coachman with an innocent smile.

"Here already?"

The dusky-toned, bare-scalped courtier bowed at the waist, his twinkling black eyes a match for his impeccable servant's garb. "Yes, Young Master. Didn't you see us pass the estate gates?"

Renar scampered down the hanging carriage steps. At the bottom, he strained skyward, standing on his tiptoes to reach the second gold button above Ral's waistband. *Ha!* he thought. *I'll be taller than him in no time!*

"Obviously, Ral," Renar replied, waving the arm that *didn't* hide the knife. "The jalliper berry bushes lining the drive are in full bloom, their mauve buds contrasting beautifully with the thin sheathes of ice encasing their branches."

Ral's dark gaze flashed concern. He ducked into the carriage, and when he reemerged a moment later, he held a lace embroidered pillow. The same pillow Renar had used to cover up the carving he'd been etching into the interior paneling of the carriage.

"What is this?" Ral asked, tone accusing.

"A pillow?"

"Indeed. A pillow which you used to cover up vandalism of the Colonel's prized carriage."

Renar bristled. "Vandalism? My *art* is an *improvement* on the drab ornamentation my father thinks passes for culture in military circles." He jerked his arm toward the coursing waterfall scene he'd etched into the wood.

The *wrong* arm—a horrible mistake. Before he could snatch back the limb, Ral grabbed his elbow, pinched it hard enough to make Renar's eyes water, and rolled up the sleeve to expose the outline of his knife. Two tugs at the hidden pouch sent the blade tumbling toward the ground. Graceful as a sweeping brush stroke, Ral caught it between two fingers, raising it above his head which Renar couldn't reach even if he jumped.

"Colonel Iolus gave this to you as a gift." Disappointment etched Ral's hard features, but Renar heard something odd in his voice: an almost wistful sadness.

"Am I not free to do with father's gifts as I please?"

Ral inhaled sharply. " . . . No. This is a combat knife." He traced the tapered blade and tapped the channel meant to drain blood away from the cutting edge. Revulsion twisted Renar's stomach. Fighting disgusted him to the point of sickness. "You should not be using it to draw—"

"*Carve*," Renar insisted.

"—on the Colonel's carriage. You know how he views your . . . hobbies." Ral chose his final word carefully, kindly. Far kindlier than Renar's father, Colonel Hardwick Iolus, would have.

The boy's throat constricted, going dry as the desert wastes beyond Nemare's walls. "Will you tell him?" he whispered. Somehow, speaking the words aloud made Renar believe they'd come true.

"No."

Flicking his wrist, Ral tossed the knife into the air, catching it by the blade in his other hand on the way down. He passed it back to Renar—hilt first—but the wide-eyed lad was lost in thoughts of how to sketch the skilled attendant.

Charcoal for the skin, rubbing it in after application for a smooth finish. Long lines for the blade toss. Have to give the impression of motion, as Gabonni's Ten Techniques suggests. Highlight the gleam in his gaze by making the area around the eyes darker, and . . .

Renar blinked. The mansion's thick double doors were open before him, letting blocky shadows and the early spring chill into the grand, marble-floored foyer. Ral was at his side, and two similar servants flanked the opulent elegoras-crafted doors.

The courtier chuckled. "The Veneer took your senses again, Young Master."

There was no reason to argue. Whenever the compulsion to draw,

113

carve, paint—any type of creation—hit him, Renar lost all awareness of where and what he was doing. This time he'd merely pocketed his knife and climbed the estate steps in a daze, but at other times he'd disappeared from the Iolus estate or fallen down the manor stairs.

Unfortunately, his clumsiness was the *least* of his father's reasons for despising the pursuits that brought him joy.

"What was it?" Renar asked. Their host, the daughter of the Heronah family, had yet to appear. "I'm curious what gave me away. Father took my last sketchbook, and you had no reason to suspect I had anything else to work with."

Ral chuckled. "Your description of the julliper berries. Spring comes early in Nemare. There's no ice left on the bushes."

The colorful curse building in Renar's throat was stilled by the sunflower bouncing down the steps. Dainty slippers on pale legs carried a beaming girl in a yellow smock down the sweeping staircase before them. Golden light, slanting from the stained glass window on the landing behind her, bathed her in a radiant glow that perfectly complemented her bouncing flaxen curls and choice of dress. Renar had scarcely a second to appreciate her radiance before she hurled herself into his arms.

"Rennie!" she cooed. "I'm so glad you could come. I have so, so much to tell you. More than is written in a library worth of books ... probably."

"You're choking me, Angelie," he managed through her tight embrace. Angelie, a name derived from the angelic Veneer themselves. Like the lilac scent of her hair, it suited her well.

"Oh! We wouldn't want that." She danced back with agile steps, then clutched Renar's hands and began dragging him from the room. "Come, come! There's something in the ballroom for you, but you *must* promise not to peek. Oh!" She exclaimed again, pointing a finger at Ral. "You can stay here, Ral. I know he doesn't like to fight, so *I'll* protect Renar if any bad guys attack. Have scones with Maja, or something."

"I can't refuse a command from my future mistress," Ral soothed with an exaggerated bow.

"Good. We'll call for you when we're done."

"Open your eyes."

Light from the tall windows on the ballroom's left side made the majestic chamber sparkle like a pure shard of illyrium. Crystal chandeliers spread the midday sun to all corners, and the silver wall panels and diamond-infused floor tiles gleefully reflected the glow from ground to ceiling.

Renar felt like he was floating through the heavenly constellations, each pinprick of illumination a star. Only the hand-carved, stain-finished furniture—a massive table that could seat dozens, gold trimmed chairs along the walls, and a grand piano near the entrance—convinced him otherwise.

"Look *down*, Rennie," Angelie insisted. "Not at our stuff. You've seen it a hundred times."

A bit of an exaggeration. He'd been to visit Angelie Heronah, his fiancé, eleven times. Which also happened to coincide with their age. They wouldn't marry until they turned seventeen, but his father had arranged the engagement a year prior. Lord Heronah sat on the Darmatian Council of Overseers, a post which Colonel Iolus had designs on himself.

A pout formed on her pert pink lips. "*Down!*"

Before Angelie could grab his ears and tug on his head—which she *had* done before—Renar turned his attention to the leather-bound rectangle she'd placed in his hands.

A sketchbook.

He almost started weeping. "It's . . . it's *beautiful*, Angelie," he breathed. "Softened ek-leather, cepyrus pages, and . . ." A tear dripped onto the front cover, and he quickly wiped it away. " . . . my name engraved in gold. I'll treasure it always."

"You better. And don't let that nasty papa of yours get his grubby hands on it." Angelie stuck out her tongue for emphasis.

"He's not nasty. He just . . . wants what's best for me. Like your father." Renar's fingers twitched. He wanted to open the notebook and start sketching, but he didn't have a scrivle. His father had discovered every one he'd hidden, including those in the seams of his clothes.

A snow-white finger tapped the binding. Renar's eyes brightened, and he nearly leaned forward to kiss Angelie on the cheek. Getting infected with whatever girlish diseases she had was *almost* of equal value to the sleek metal scrivle snuggled into the gap in the binding.

"*My* father supports my dream." Spinning, Angelie flounced away, arms and legs tracing the movements to an elegant kata. No, not a kata—not a training form. She was *dancing*.

One hand up, one down, she went up on the point of her left

foot, the other hooked behind her knee. "I'm going to be the star of the Yoleshai Troupe—the greatest performers to grace the stage of Nemare's Moonlight Theatre. I'll dance and sing, the audience will cry and cheer, and I'll be showered with flowers night after night."

Renar cracked the fancy sketchbook and, with quick glances to track Angelie's flowing steps, began to draw. "You will," he said, not a shred of doubt in his mind.

"And you'll paint my debut. Both of us will be famous, and crowds will come from the ends of the continent to see us."

"Naturally."

Renar lost himself to the dance—*their* dance. Angelie leapt and twirled, his scrivle swept and darted. Faster, quicker, cleaner he drew, keeping up with her movements, leaving the details to be filled in later. Capturing her essence was the key. If he could grab hold of Angelie's life—her heartbeat, her soul—the rest would fall into place like pieces of a puzzle.

The world faded. They became breath and motion, the line between self and art blurring, then ceasing to exist entirely. Hours could have passed. Days. Renar didn't care. He and the page had become one with Angelie and her dance.

When Renar awoke from the trance, the jostling carriage materialized around him. Four walls, two windows, drawn curtains, Ral on the coachman's seat up front, and a too-plush bench beneath his rear end. In his lap lay the notebook Angelie had gifted him, open to the pages he'd been working on.

He nearly cried and ruined the drawing with his tears. It was the best piece he'd ever created—expression made manifest. And, staring at it, Renar knew with divine certainty what his life's calling was, his father be voided.

Kusselaf 19, 686 ABH
Nemare, Royal Capital of the Kingdom of Darmatia

Renar's father . . . no, *the Colonel*, as he insisted his son refer to him . . . didn't allow him to return to the Heronah estate for two months after his transcendent visit. He bided the intervening time patiently, obedient to the Colonel's whims and careful not to upset him by sketching in his presence.

Only at night, shrouded beneath his blanket in his darkened room, did Renar dare remove Angelie's special notebook from its hiding place behind the *Battle of Har'muth* painting hung above his bed. If a piece of art didn't depict war or violence, the Colonel thought it a waste.

Wilting vegetation lined the mansion's drive. The gorgeous julliper bushes had shriveled, their leaves falling to join the stinking bed of moss and fungus beneath them. Green grass was now faded to brown. Had the groundskeeper not watered since they were last here?

Not waiting for Ral to open his door, Renar leapt from the carriage and sprinted up the unswept, dirt-crusted steps. The great elegoras doors didn't part for him, no matter how he pounded and shouted for Maja to open them.

Boots clicked behind him. Expression grim, Ral turned the handle and let Renar into the foyer.

The room was dark. None of the illyrium lamps lining the walls glowed, and the stained glass window was covered by a paint-flecked sheet. Two workmen—one with a crowbar, the other with a clipboard—stood in front of it.

"Where's Angelie!" Renar shouted.

They spared him a brief glance, then turned back to their work. *Smack!* The crowbar bit deep into the window frame, and the laborer wiggled it back and forth until the first pane of glass came free.

Renar's fury grew. "What are you doing? Lord Heronah of the *Council* lives here, and—"

"It's fine," a small voice said. "They have permission to be here."

He spun in the direction of the ballroom, an exuberant greeting bubbling in his chest. The sight of Angelie stilled his lips.

Her dress was plain, an ash-stained, unornamented white that seemed to drain the color from her. Instead of gold, her hair was a dingy yellow. Gone were her dancing slippers, her feet bare and covered in dust.

Even Angelie's smile had faded, like she was forcing it out just for him. Hollow eyes, untouched by her grin, confirmed Renar's fears.

He ran to Angelie and wrapped her in his arms. Slowly, her hands crossed at his back, as though she was afraid he'd shatter if she squeezed too hard. Behind her, through the ballroom's open door, he could see another team of coverall garbed workmen unhooking the chandeliers, packing up the table, and wheeling out the grand piano.

"What happened?" he whispered.

Her false joy began to crack, her face quivering, her body shaking.

"I . . . my father, h-he . . . "

"YOU!"

The venom-coated shout echoed about the foyer, assaulting Renar and Angelie from all directions. As Renar spun toward the speaker, his fiancé pushed away from him, her fists clenched and gaze downcast.

"You . . . you did thiiiiiissss."

Lord Heronah slurred his words as he slid along the banister from the second floor. His eyes were hard, but the rest of him was soft. Shirt untucked, suitcoat ripped and soiled with red spots, he was a far cry from the dignified man Renar had met at the marriage meeting. Firm cheeks had gone flabby and were now covered in days-old stubble. His jiggling belly poked through where his belt had gone missing. While the Lord's right hand thrust a condemning finger at Renar, his left clutched a nearly drained bottle of translucent brown liquid.

The smell of unwashed flesh and intoxication hit Renar before Lord Heronah reached the bottom of the steps, making him gag and rush to cover his nose.

"Lord Heronah," Renar began, choosing his words cautiously. "I apologize if I have caused offense, but—"

"Yooouuu"—the finger whipped at him again—"convinced heeeerrrr"—it shifted toward Angelie—"to daaaaannceee while you dreeeeew. The Colonel didn't like that, noooooo siiiiiirrr, he didn't. Baaaaaaad influence, he called it."

The drunk stumbled forward, angling to put himself between Renar and his daughter. Stance tense, Ral moved closer to Renar, one arm held out protectively.

"I can fix this," Renar insisted. "Let me talk to the Colonel. I'm sure he'd be elated to help the family of my future wife."

Lord Heronah's filmy eyes narrowed. Lashing out, he smashed the liquor bottle against a nearby pillar, showering the floor with shards of glass. Renar stared at Angelie in horror. She was barefoot. If she took a step, she'd cut herself for sure.

The girl huddled down where she stood, trembling arms raised. This clearly wasn't the first time her father had exploded like this. "OUT!" he roared.

"But sir . . . " Renar tried.

Jagged glass jabbed at his chest. "I saaaaaid, OOOOOOUT!"

Renar turned to Ral. The former special forces operative could easily disarm Lord Heronah, then save Angelie. They would get her to safety, he would talk to the Colonel, and this whole mess would be resolved. If Renar had to sacrifice something to appease the man, he would give up the location of his sketchbook. Preserving his dreams wasn't worth putting Angelie through this trauma.

Firm hands gripped Renar about his waist. An instant later, he was on Ral's shoulder, and they were racing out the mansion door toward their parked carriage. Lord Haronah chased them with his broken bottle, but there was no catching Ral. No matter how loudly he or Renar screamed, the loyal courtier stayed true to his primary mission: keeping the Young Master safe.

If only Ral could have kept him safe from the one threat he could do nothing about.

Venare 8, 686 ABH
Nemare, Royal Capital of the Kingdom of Darmatia

The tight uniform chafed at his thighs, hips, and chest, but Renar refused to budge. He stayed at attention, eyes forward, arms firmly planted at his sides. To move was to incur the Colonel's—no, the *General's*—wrath.

General Iolus had been promoted and was now Commandant of the Darmatian Military Academy. A celebration was in order, one which Renar would have to plan. But nothing too fancy, and not with the help of Ral, his former attendant. Ral had been fired for disloyalty, for failing to report critical information about his charge to the General.

At first, Renar hadn't understood why the man had to leave, but he'd soon learned the price of disobeying orders.

The fire in the darkened study's hearth crackled merrily as it consumed the fresh fuel pinned to its logs by a long iron poker. Back turned to Renar, the General basked in its warmth. Shadows played across his half-hidden face, making his eyes sink, his nose elongate, and . . .

No, Renar chastised himself. *I mustn't think like that anymore. My art got Angelie into trouble, so I can't risk it.*

At length, the General spoke, voice calm and soothing. "I'm sorry, son. Angelie and her family have gone missing, so I have no choice but to cancel your marriage."

"I . . . understand, sir."

The General nodded. "Good. I'm proud that you've been able to adapt to recent changes so quickly. It means I can accelerate your training, get you bulked up before you enter the Academy. We only have seven years to get you ready, and given our . . . *predicament*, you'll need to be stronger than anyone else in your class to be of service to me when you graduate."

"Predicament?" Renar asked. "You mean that our family can't use magic?"

A brutish hand ripped the iron poker from the fire and slashed it in his direction. Stray embers caught in Renar's hair, but he didn't dare shake them loose. He was a statue. He was obedient.

"*Never* say that again," the General growled. "You *can* use magic—enhancement magic. When you're older, you'll use it to swing giant weapons no ordinary soldier can wield. Trust me. I know what's best for you."

"Yes, sir."

Thankfully, the General didn't press the issue further, and silence descended again. Renar kept staring at the fire, and at the gold etched name—*his* name—slowly being devoured by the greedy flames. The sketchbook pages beneath it were already ash and smoke, just like his dreams, Angelie's dreams, and the boy he'd once been.

Chapter 10

Unchanging

Hetrachia 12, 697 ABH
Resistance Base, Sarconian Province of Darmatia

Cold unease tightened Renar's stomach, its twisting claws a stark counterpoint to the cheerfulness of Corporal Sayles.

"Here we are, sir. General Iolus is expecting you, so go in when you're ready."

"I'm a cadet," he replied. His voice felt hollow, even to his own ears. "You don't have to call me 'sir.'"

"Of course, *sir.*"

She smiled, saluted, and strode away, leaving him alone in front of the large pavilion. *Leaving me to face my execution*, Renar thought, dread mounting.

The artist in him contemplated how he'd paint the scene. Vibrant, heroic reds and yellows for himself, marching resolutely up the rocky path from the tent city below, prepared to meet his doom. Ominous and foreboding, the pavilion would be smeared in shades of gray. Slate for the sides, like a tombstone. Ebony for the parted flaps, shadow curling from within hinting at the darkness he was to face.

An abyss that drained all life from the world.

In reality, a bright light shone through the gaps in the thick canvas—the fierce glow of several illyrium lamps. The only darkness here was that which Renar brought with him, darkness implanted in him by the man on the flap's other side.

He shook his head. Sweat trickled down his brow and moistened his underarms. No, this wasn't right. He wasn't ready to meet the General. Frantic, Renar began patting down the wrinkles of his filthy tunic. He tied the neck clasp to hide his bare chest, tucked the ragged hem into his equally tattered trousers, and knocked off what mud he could from his boots on a nearby boulder. Wetting his hand in a puddle, Renar smoothed his close-cropped black hair until not a strand jutted up.

The General expected perfection, and the price for failing to meet that standard was steep indeed.

A minute later, Renar was the stiff, dour, obedient soldier the General desired. He forgot the nonsense with Heisden's poem, the sketchbook tucked in his pocket, and the laughs he'd had after leaving the Academy. That short time, like the youth he'd once buried, was but misty dreams breaking beneath the sun's harsh gaze.

Yet no matter how hard his exterior, Renar could not wholly quash the terror needling him from the inside out. The General would *know*. Somehow, some way, he would find Renar's latest drawings. He'd see the weakness in his eyes. Divine his failures from the way he stood, the twitch of his hands, the haste of his breath.

Renar yanked the flap aside and strode into the pavilion before the last threads of his nerves could snap entirely. Taking two steps, he planted his legs at shoulder width, crossed his arms behind his back, and stood at attention with his chest and jaw out. He did not speak. The General would acknowledge Renar's presence at *his* convenience.

Scritch, scritch, scritch.

The sound of a quill darting across paper filled the tent along with the soothing smells of mahogany, burning incense, and aromatic oils. Signs of comfortable living—even opulence—were everywhere. Trillith woven carpets, adorned with intricate mandalas, covered a meticulously laid wooden floor that let not a drop of the cavern's moisture through. Ornate wardrobes bearing complex Sylph runes and bookshelves straining under the weight of expensive tomes lined the canvas walls.

Renar counted six brass illyrium lamps scattered around the room, while four crates of candles sat near a canopy bed in the corner—a contingency in case the crystals and electricity somehow ran out, of course. The bed itself was dressed in gleaming white sheets bearing a blue and silver floral pattern.

Subservience warred with disgust in Renar's gut. It was as though the flap at his back was the dividing line between a realm of plenty and one of poverty. Death, disease, and rot festered outside, but none of it could touch the General in his sweet-smelling tower.

He was, as ever, unchanging. Not even Darmatia's defeat at Aldona and the fall of the country could make the man prioritize anything other than himself.

Click, click.

With reluctance, Renar finally turned his gaze toward the General. He sat hunched behind a heavy elegoras wood desk, stacks of papers surrounding him like mountains, a half-filled inkwell almost glued to his right elbow. Beady eyes beneath thick black brows darted left and right, but never up, their world constrained by the margins of the parchment.

The General grunted, setting his flabby chin wobbling. *Scritch, scritch, scritch.* As his meaty fist scrawled across the page, the graying hair atop his scalp shifted, revealing the bald spot he normally tried to hide. *Shuup, shuup.* The signed paper shifted right, only to be replaced by another.

This was not a being Renar should fear, but it took all his resolve to stay still and *not* bolt like prey before a hawk.

BANG!

Renar nearly collapsed in shock at the sudden crack of the General's fist thudding atop his desk. Papers scattered at the impact, spilling onto the floor. Black ooze bubbled from the overturned inkwell, staining countless documents and rendering them illegible.

"How many times do I have to tell that Creator-poxed Tabitha we can't send her more anesthetic?" The General picked up a wad of dripping papers, ripped them in fourths, and flung the pieces in the air. "She and her nuns are nothing but a drain on my supplies. And then Major Reev has the gall to ask if I've petitioned the Hues or Sylph for aid? What business is that of hers, the blighted whor—"

In the middle of shredding another batch of forms, the General's red-rimmed eyes locked on Renar's. *Here it comes,* Renar thought, digging his fingernails into the palms of his clenched fists. *Three, two, one ...*

"How long have you been standing there?" the General demanded. He balled up the papers he held and threw them through the open grate of a wood fire stove behind him. "You should have said something when you arrived."

"My apologies, sir," Renar said softly.

"Don't mumble. You know how much I despise mumbling."

Renar raised his voice. "Of course."

"Good."

Mollified, the General rose and crossed to a washbasin on a tri-legged nightstand beside his bed, where he rinsed the ink smudges from his fingers. Renar overlaid a recent memory atop the scene. Tears streaming down her cheeks, Matteo's mother leapt from the porch of her house to wrap her son in a tight embrace. All was right with her world once she knew her son was alive.

The man before Renar betrayed not the slightest hint of relief at his return, of empathy of any kind. The General's cheeks were creased, but from irritation, not tears. *His* son was an inconvenience, one that upset his world instead of righting it.

Drying his hands on a pristine towel, he turned back to Renar, the rows of medals on his gallant blue uniform clinking with the motion. "Are you sick?" he asked.

The question took Renar by surprise. "Sir?"

"Your eyes." The General pointed at his face. "They're watering, and I know no son of mine would cry in front of another soldier."

Renar blinked, then sniffled. Huh. His eyes were moist, but he didn't raise a hand to wipe them. It had been a mistake to think about Matteo's family—to ever expect a fraction of their compassion from the General.

"Something in my eyes," he lied. "From when we fought the Draken."

"Voided abomination," the General swore. "If I'd had the firepower, we'd have blasted the beast on the way in." After a few slightly incoherent grumbles, the General waved at the pavilion wall in the general direction of the hospital tent. "When we're done here, go see Mother Tabitha and her . . . proselytizers to get some medicine. At least then they'd be doing something useful for me."

"You asked to see me, sir?" Renar prompted. He wanted nothing more than to be done with this conversation and escape the reek of indulgence assaulting him from every side.

"Yes, yes I did." The General did not immediately elaborate. Plodding around the table, he bent over his paunch and examined a latticework wine rack full of lavender vintages.

One of those bottles could ease the suffering of a half dozen dying men, Renar thought.

The General selected a bottle, uncorked it, and sniffed the contents. A rare smile tugged at his lips. "Care for a taste?" he asked, retrieving a long-stemmed glass from another shelf.

"No, sir."

Accepting was a trap. Soldiers—at least, any who weren't the General—were not allowed to drink while on duty. Renar felt a twinge of pain. His body remembered the bruises from the time he'd failed this test.

Scarlet liquid sloshed into the glass. The General took one delicate sip, hummed in satisfaction, and returned to his desk, the bottle still in his opposite hand. The clattering of glass as he sat down suggested this was *not* his first drink today. "Very well, down to business it is. First, did any of your companions discover our secret?"

Secret. It was a funny way of referring to their hidden shame. Their men'ar was inert; they could not use magic. Not with the most expensive of catalysts to aid them, nor enhancive drugs and tinctures, nor blood transfusions from powerful sorcerers. The General's legion of doctors had tried everything to fix them, but to no avail. His seed—the Iolus bloodline—was cursed, for Renar's mother was not similarly afflicted.

They were fle'bilis, in the old Eliassi tongue. The weak, infirm, and feeble.

Renar could almost laugh at the irony. Though he grasped at everything, the General had been denied magic.

"No," he answered. The lie might be the General's, but Renar had no desire to see the look of betrayal in his friends' eyes when they learned the truth. "I used the modified greatsword you gave me until I had to abandon it during the fighting, after which I used a rifle. None of them suspect a thing."

The General nodded and took another sip, setting the half-empty bottle amid his ruined papers. "I hope for their sake that's true. That Sylette Farkos is craftier than she looks."

A shiver raced down Renar's back. If they found out, he'd make them disappear—just like he did Angelie and her family all those years ago.

And what of Sylette's secret? The General was not a humble man. Had the name *Artorios* reached his ears, she'd already be clapped in irons, a bargaining chip for his next ploy at advancement.

He didn't know! Most of Renar was relieved, but a slithering, slimy thought bubbled up from the depths of his mind. *Tell him,* the Soldier said. The Soldier the General had molded into a mirror of himself. *Tell him and he'll praise us. You want his praise, don't you? Isn't that what you crave more than anything else?*

Renar bit his lip. Tightened his shoulders and pinched his eyes shut. *No!* he roared at the soldier. *He'd trade Sylette to her father. I can't condemn her to a fate like mine.*

"Spit it out," the General ordered. Renar's eyes popped open to find his superior leaning on his desk, teeth bared in a snarl. "You look guilty. Did they find out? What do they know? Tell me!"

"Why did you transfer Sylette to my team right before the exam?" Like sand cast to the wind, the words slipped from Renar's mouth, unable to be reclaimed. He tried to snatch them back anyway. "No, sir, that's not what I meant. I—"

One arm threw wine glass across the tent, where it shattered in a crimson spray against the taut canvas. The other *shoved* the desk aside with strength the bloated officer shouldn't possess. Three steps, a few heartbeats, and the General was in Renar's face. Veins bulged from his forehead as he rammed a finger into his son's sternum.

Spittle hit Renar before the roar. "How *dare* you question me, boy! You leave the nest for a week or two and think you don't need me anymore? That you can say and do whatever you want? I made you, you insignificant pissant, and I can unmake you too! You are nothing—*nothing!*—without me."

Renar tried to escape the tirade. Not with his legs, which were rooted to the floor, but by withdrawing into himself. He went back to that moment with Angelie, his fingers darting across his sketchbook, tracing the flow of her mesmerizing dance.

Back to when his life was bright and safe.

"Why are you clenching your fists?" the General screamed. "You want to hit me? Then *hit me*, boy! Or are you afraid? Terrified of fighting just like you've always been? *HIT ME!*"

His ears still heard the cries. Foul, spirit-laced breath still lashed his nose, and spit dribbled from his cheeks and chin. Renar's chest ached under the General's relentless prodding.

Taking a step back, the General threw up his arms, setting the baubles and frilly tassels on his uniform to shaking. "*Coward.* That's what you are. Raised a bloody coward . . . " He shook his head in dejection.

Renar didn't relax. The General's seething calm was a facade. If anything, what came next was always worse.

"So, you want to know why I put that uppity wench on your team?" The General peered intently at Renar, as if searching for a glimmer of intelligence in his son's dead gaze. Finding none, he laughed, a cruel cackle that echoed around the pavilion.

"That's exactly why!" he exclaimed with a snort. "She asked, and I had no reason to refuse. You're a failure. An abysmal cock-up who can't fight, can't pass your tests, and can't even follow my orders when I. Say. Them. Like. This." The general slowed his speech, enunciating each word with an exaggeration that twisted his face into a hideous mask of contempt.

"Her only condition was that I place you against that fool, Vallen," the General continued. "A match-up she promised me was a sure thing. And even though Vallen refused to throw the match, the clever little hussy pulled it off! If not for the interruption, it was the perfect plan. You would've passed. Vallen was humiliated. Well?" A manic gleam in his eyes, the General staggered toward Renar. "I did it for *you*, son.

Aren't you grateful?"

Revulsion, not gratitude, filled Renar's mouth. He wanted to vomit. To ram his skull into the cavern wall until whatever in him was broken oozed out along with his blood.

He couldn't draw. His father hated that useless passion, to the point of beating the desire out of him. He couldn't fight. He was too weak, too dim, and devoid of magic. Lacking a shred of faith in him, the General had cheated to ensure his son's victory not just once, but *twice*.

Tears welled behind his placid, emotionless features. *There's no place for you,* the Soldier crooned mercilessly. *Give in, give up, and find purpose in being daddy's unthinking little tool.*

You'll paint my debut, Angelie whispered.

The tears stopped. Behind Renar's eyes, the abyssal darkness brightened by the barest of margins.

Do you like poetry? Velle asked, voice full of compassion. *If you hadn't recognized that poem, we'd be sitting here none the wiser.*

Cracks appeared in the gloom. One shard slipped loose and shattered on the ground, exposing a blinding ray of light. The Soldier hissed and dodged away as the beam struck him.

A bouncing, freckled face smiled up at Renar. *You're an amazing artist, Renar,* Lilith said.

The wall crumbled entirely, flooding his mind with light. Shrieking, the Soldier disappeared in a puff of gray smoke. Both he and the wall would return—of that Renar had no doubt. They were constructs, his *artist's* brain manifesting the General's hold on him in tangible form.

Renar grinned, and the tension slowly drained from his body. He would not give up Sylette or any of his friends, even Vallen, so easily.

The General misinterpreted Renar's smile as acceptance. "Good, good!" His flushed face showed none of his earlier vitriol as he clapped his hands atop Renar's broad shoulders. "I'm glad you understand I was trying to help. I only want what's best for you."

"And mother?" Renar asked. He saw no signs that Leliet Iolus—a woman he hardly knew—was staying with her husband.

A shadow dimpled the General's lips and flashed across his eyes. "Visiting relatives in the country, far away from the capital and all this unpleasantness. She should be safe."

Renar nodded. Pressing the issue would only induce another outburst, and surely the General had taken steps to ensure the

Sarconians couldn't capture and use her against him.

"Yet you're here with me, which should work well." The General patted Renar's shoulders again, then gripped his right arm to guide him toward the pavilion entrance. "For now, keep your nose down. Don't get yourself killed, don't let Major Reev talk you into anything crazy. Manage that, obey my orders, and everything will turn out for the better."

"Sir?"

A distant gleam flickered in the General's gaze as if he was reliving a pleasant memory or imagining a triumphant future. Without warning, he turned and did something he'd never done before:

Hugged his son.

Alcohol came off his breath in waves. The sharp prick of medals and badges pressed into Renar's skin through his tunic. The grip was awkward and hard, and yet . . . it was an embrace nonetheless. One Renar had no idea how to respond to.

"Yes," the General whispered, almost directly into his ear. "You need only do as I say, just like you always have and just as you always will. If you do, things will always—*always*—work out for our family."

Chapter 11

Drop Off

Hetrachia 12, 697 ABH
Aboard the Judicator, Sarconian Occupied Beiras

Valescar dreamed.

He knew it was a dream because of the phantoms before him. The Sylette who sat at the other end of the chess board from him was a child, propped up on satin pillows and wearing a silver trimmed dress that complimented her hair and eyes. Delight brightened her features as she moved a bishop to capture one of his knights.

The real Sylette was over a decade older, hardened by rage and cruelty. And she would *never* look at him fondly ever again.

Instead of a headless, bleeding corpse, her mother, Lanara, stood beside Sylette's chair as she had in life. She brushed a gem-studded comb through her daughter's lustrous locks, glancing at Valescar every so often with a wink and a smile.

They'd both failed Sylette, and he'd failed *her* in turn.

Time ta wake up, Valescar decided. The joyous scene tore gaping wounds in him that burned fiercer than any of the fires that had lashed his flesh.

Before he could turn away, a familiar voice roared from the endless white sky above. "Fire!"

No, Gadler, this ain't—

Rifles cracked. Valescar reached for the shells with magic that wouldn't manifest, but couldn't find them. Where were the shooters?

Across the table, Sylette gasped. Pushing out of her chair, she stared at him in shock and confusion, spurted blood, and collapsed in a twisted heap. Crimson stained her pale chin and, like springs of water, sprouted in ringlets up and down her gown. The bullets had pierced her from the inside out.

Lanara tossed herself atop the girl with a strangled, heart-wrenching cry. No! This wasn't how this happened. Their roles should be reversed. It should be Lanara's glazed eyes accusing him from the bottom of a rancid, blood-crusted wicker basket, not Sylette's.

The mother's venomous glare turned on him, darker than the blackest pit in the deepest ocean. He saw two pairs of eyes then, overlaid

129

atop each other, their colors blending. As one, the women shouted.

"You let my daughter die!"

"You let my son die!"

Valescar awoke with a scream, tossing aside the sweat-stained sheets of his bed and jumping to the floor. Cold metal clanged beneath his bare feet. The walls of his stateroom echoed his bellow back at him until, like the racing of his heart and the heaving of his chest, they gradually subsided.

Just a dream, Valescar cautioned himself. A dull throb settled into his left side, along with a burning sensation that wasn't truly present. Both were good signs. Signs that he had, for now, escaped the ghosts of his mind.

He crossed the chamber to his wardrobe and began to dress. Orange light filtered through the porthole to his right. Outside the *Judicator,* evening was falling. He'd been asleep for several hours, but the occasional distant flash of light and retort of gunfire suggested the fighting still continued. It was time to put an end to this mess.

Once his gambeson and trousers were on, Valescar stretched his arms to the sides and summoned the rest of his ensemble. Clattering and clanking, they detached from a nearby mannequin and flew toward him, wrapping him from head to toe. In seconds, gorget, breastplate, tasset, cuisse, greaves, and gauntlets were all affixed in their proper places.

His crimson Ritter cloak, emblazoned with a pair of crossed white sabers, fluttered into place last, guided by metal clasps that cinched about his neck. A small smile graced Valescar's lips. Imagining the countless hours his fellow rittermarschals spent getting dressed and undressed was quite amusing.

He turned to the door, and his good humor faded. At the bottom of the wardrobe, almost tucked out of sight beneath a pile of tunics and jerkins, was a trunk wrapped in ivory chains. Despite the powerful scents of treated leather, rubbing oil, and sweat permeating the room, Valescar could immediately smell its contents: strong spirits, and lots of them.

Where a simple wooden block had served as Lanara's execution ground, they were his. He'd drowned himself in the bottle after her death and Sylette's banishment. Erasing all conscious thought and muddling through a swirling fog of endless carousing, crying, and feverish sleep had seemed better than bearing the pain of their loss.

Exactly how he'd recovered, Valescar couldn't say. But as soon as he reclaimed his senses, he'd ordered expensive polycarbonate chains—ones made *without* metal—for his liquor stores. He kept this trunk at his side as a warning, a reminder of what could happen if he ever slipped so far again.

Valescar shook himself free of the memory and waved his chamber door open. He had failed Lanara and Sylette. Had failed that Rabbanite boy and his mother. But by the Void, he was going to save what was left of Beiras.

Depending on the actions of Valescar's esteemed guests, what was to come would either be a polite discussion or grisly execution.

Two sets of double doors parted before his impetuous stride. At the third—half again as wide as those preceding it—stood a squad of heavily armed Ritter troops, rifles on their shoulders, twin short swords on their belts. Every entrance to the *Judicator's* hangar was similarly guarded. No one would enter or exit without his orders.

The thump of the guards' fists striking their chests was silenced by the thick portal shutting behind him. Yet a new sound immediately assaulted Valescar from the front: heated bickering.

Shouts rose to the hanging girders far above, intermingling with the racks of hawkish lancerjets and snub-nosed transports secured to them by thick cables. They bounced off the polished floor—so pristine Valescar could see his burned scalp reflected on its surface—and raced the length of the chamber to the rows of deadly panzcraft arranged against the far wall. To his left, where rushing wind would normally rip the words right from a speaker's throat, a segmented gestalt steel bulkhead blocked the hangar's wide mouth.

Valescar made straight for the source of the shouting. In the center of the cavernous room were two groups of Rabbanites surrounded by a loose ring of Sarconian soldiers. The first was somber, their backs slumped as they slouched or sat without speaking. Most wore factory clothes—grungy coveralls, patched coats, or thick, ragged trousers. They were not so much covered in dust and ash as caked in it. Few glanced up at his approach, but the eyes of those who did were sunken, defeated.

The second group kept their distance from the first, seeming to prefer the company of the Sarconian guards to their own people. A gap of several meters yawned between them—a chasm that spoke volumes. Noticing Valescar's approach, their internal squabble ceased.

131

As one they stood, straightened their colorful silk robes, and presented a unified front. One that was scornful, defiant, and unbroken.

"You command here, yes?" A lean man in a black robe tied with a white sash stepped forward from their ranks. Wrinkles carved his face like lines on a statue, but his hair, pulled from his high forehead and tied in a warrior's topknot, was only just beginning to gray.

Valescar came to a stop beside one of his guards. He jerked his head to the side, indicating the man should leave his post, which he did. Planting his legs at shoulder width, Valescar replied, "I do."

The Rabbanite spokesman nodded, then raised a thinning arm to his left—a gesture that seemed to encompass only his gaudily dressed countrymen, not their shabby counterparts. "At last!" he proclaimed. A murmur of relief spread among the men and women behind him. "If you release us now, we will ask the Ventrates to be lenient in your eternal damnation."

"Ventrates?" Valescar blinked, taken aback by the man's haughty tone *and* the unfamiliar term. Didn't he understand the situation they were in?

"Your people ignorantly refer to them as 'the Veneer,' a misguided label that reflects only a portion of their divinity. We, the Enlightened, know better." Bowing his head, the spokesman pressed his palms together in front of his chest, a motion mimicked by his brethren.

A few shards short o' a full crystal, this one, Valescar thought, trying *not* to roll his eyes. "Unless these Ventrates o' yers decide ta come aboard ma ship an' bargain fer yer release themselves, ye ain't goin' nowhere."

Beneath wispy, too-long brows, the Rabbanite's slanted eyes narrowed further. "For what other purpose would you summon us if not to grant our rightful freedom? We have given you of the . . . *Empire*"—he spat the word as if rancid sewage coated it—"no cause for grievance, even though the savages you lead have done nothing but heap injustice upon us."

Was he void-touched? His mind shattered until it saw a twisted version of reality none but the mad could fathom? Valescar resisted the urge to throttle the infuriating little man . . . or load him into one of *Judicator's* cannons and fire him at his own forces. Counting to three, he turned to one of the guards, a man bearing two red stripes on his cuirass.

"Unteroffizier, where did'ya find these fine gents and lasses?"

The low-ranking soldier saluted swiftly. "At the Sakuron building

132

in the city center, sir. They were burning files and destroying magtech experiments when our patrols stopped them."

"Lies!" a woman in the middle of the group yelled. Her robes, decorated with a repeating yellow solar pattern, were buttoned along the side in a way that accentuated her curves. Two jade pins were thrust through the bun atop her head. "We would never destroy the sacred blueprints gifted to us from above."

"We're at war, lady," Valescar said, shaking his head. Why did Titania get Darmatia while he was stuck dealing with these techno-zealots? "If I was in yer very fine slippers"—he glanced at her feet—"destroyin' info useful ta the enemy afore they nabbed it is *precisely* what I'd do."

"War?" The first man snorted, incredulous. "*We* are not at war with you. That is beneath us, a distraction from the march of progress the Enlightened have been tasked with. The *Guardians* are at war with you. As are . . . *those*, the charges of the Architects." He flicked a finger at the other, dirtier group of Rabbanites, then quickly drew it back as if afraid a speck of mud would fly across the gap to land on him.

Enlightened, Guardians, Architects. The strange titles bounced around in Valescar's head. It had been decades since the Empire had *any* contact without the Rabban Imperium except on the field of battle, where the primary objective was to stop the other guy from breathing before they could do the same to you. He knew next to nothing about how Rabbanite society functioned.

"So, yer sayin' ye"—Valescar held up one hand toward the speaker and the other toward the laborers—"are not related ta them. An' not only that, but none o' ya have fired a shot at ma men or in any way conspired ta bring harm against them or ma nation."

The spokesman clapped his hands. "Yes! At last, we seem to be speaking the same language. Though your accent and vocabulary could use some tweaking. More enunciation, less crassness."

"An' who led the voided fleet that rushed me like a rabid boar?"

"Deputy Shogun Obifuna Shai, a *Guardian*," the Rabbanite emphasized. "I am Jinsang Kazu, an *Enlightened*. Our roles couldn't be more different than . . . well, my intellect and yours, pardon the offense."

Valescar held up the palm of his right gauntlet. "It's no problem at all, Kazu." He smiled when the smaller man bristled. Rabbanite first names were given *after* their clan name. Even an uncultured, brutish heathen like Valescar knew that much.

He addressed the same unteroffizier as before. "Order Captain

Gadler ta launch the *Judicator*. We'll loop around the city and drop Kazu and his mates off at the Sakuron building." The man trotted across the hangar to a bank of several dozen bronze pipes that wended their way up into the ceiling and throughout the ship. Within moments of speaking into one, the floor lurched beneath their feet and the steady hum of the engines rose from the next deck down. *Judicator* was on her way.

"In the meantime, can ya clear somethin' up fer me, Kazu?" Valescar stepped closer to the fussy academic. His tone suggested they were old friends, not enemies. Kazu wrinkled his nose at some stench Valescar couldn't smell but held his ground.

"I exist to enlighten others."

"Swell."

Valescar's armor clanked as he gestured at the second group of Rabbanites. Most of them were men, but a few women in equally squalid dresses filled out their number, including a mother with a haggard infant held to her breast. Valescar pointedly looked away, focusing on a graybeard with a bulbous red nose and a puckered scar on his grimy neck.

"Whaddya call 'em?" he asked.

Kazu frowned and covered his mouth with the sleeve of his robe. "Nothing, if we can help it. If we must interact with them, we call them Casteless—hangers-on that cannot trace their lineage back to Rabban's chosen elite. In exchange for labor and military service, we are gracious enough to feed, shelter, and provide them what divine guidance their feeble minds can handle."

"'ow many o' 'em are still fightin'?"

"With Shai's death, I imagine most of the resistance you still face is from Casteless forces." The gleam in Kazu's eyes suggested he almost *relished* the thought of Sarconian troops wiping them out.

Valescar suddenly crossed the gap between groups, marching straight up to the squatting graybeard he'd been studying. "An' 'ow do ya think the fightin's goin'?" The metal the Casteless sat on seemed livelier than he did, with his slack jaw and thousand-league stare. Valescar kicked his foot until he got the man's attention. "I said, 'ow do ya think the fightin's goin?'"

His bulbous nose glanced past Valescar toward Kazu, and his open mouth clamped shut. Sighing, Valescar jerked a thumb over his shoulder. "Frumpy mc-dreary face back there *might* kill ya later if ya talk ta me, but I *will* kill ya now if'n ya don't."

The flush drained from the man's weathered face. "We're losin'. Don't take an Enlightened ta tell ya that."

"Would ya stop if ya could?"

"Sariel's blighted arse, o' course we would! We're gettin' butchered."

Valescar nodded, then casually sauntered back to Kazu. He gripped the Enlightened by his shoulder—lightly, like a war buddy he'd run into at the mess hall—and steered him toward the towering hangar doors.

"They don't seem too keen on fightin', Kazu," he said conversationally.

The man's hand leapt to his sash but recoiled upon finding nothing there. "If I still had my Ventrate given blade, I'd have cut that cur down where he sits. Death is the only recourse for a fool blind to his circumstances."

"Very wise," Valescar replied. He was no longer smiling.

Raising his arms, he clenched his fingers and *heaved* on the massive gestalt steel panels. A hangar tech could operate the doors from the glass-encased room on the floor above, but given Valescar's powers, this was faster and more satisfying.

Wheels screeched in their housings. Gaining momentum, the first panel retracted into the second, which rammed into the third. All three slid into a gap in the near wall.

Powerful winds immediately struck them, tearing at Kazu's robes and Valescar's cloak. He magnetized his boots and grasped the Rabbanite's shoulder more tightly to hold him in place.

"Is that the Sakuron building?" he roared, struggling to be heard over the whipping gale. Every gust was laced with smoke and ash. In seconds, the hangar reeked like a crematorium.

The skyscraper rose through the dark fog clogging the city streets and the encircling factory district. Made of silvery steel and thousands of opalescent glass panes, it looked a world apart from the fiery cesspit Valescar had fought through mere hours prior. The day's fading light glimmered off its sloping sides, making it sparkle like the rubies on the Sarconian royal scepter.

"It is," Kazu shouted back at him. Then he paused, squinting. "We're too high up. You'll have to bring your ship closer to drop us off."

"No, I won't."

A slight shove—not at all magic enhanced—sent Kazu over the edge. He dropped rapidly toward the roof below, his screams ripped from his throat by the twisting winds. Valescar's aim was true. The

Enlightened splattered on the pinnacle of the Sakuron building. He had been returned, as promised.

The rest of the Enlightened recovered from their horror quickly. They surged against the cordon of guards, but swinging rifle butts and slashing short swords forced them back. By the time the Ritter squads poured in from the three hangar entrances, a wash of blood was trickling across the glossy floor.

"Herd 'em!" Valescar shouted. He stepped away from the precipice and watched with grim satisfaction as the Enlightened were driven like cattle to slaughter. Some fought back, but their bare-handed strikes and kicks went only so far against professionals with bayonets and blades. More bodies in shredded scarlet robes struck the hangar floor, but more still found themselves trapped at the vessel's brink.

A group of five screeched prayers and jumped, hand in hand. Did they think they'd be welcomed to the Afterplane given what they'd done to the Casteless? Valescar couldn't imagine a just deity would so easily expunge their sins. Others were pushed, tripped, or went over with steel buried in their guts. In the end, not a single Enlightened remained aboard the *Judicator*, and not an echo of their final, pitiful cries could still be heard.

Valescar clapped his gauntlets together and made straight for the Casteless. They rose at his approach, clutching each other in fear but too tired—too beaten—to struggle or flee. The resignation in their gazes and posture spoke of a people prepared to die at any moment.

Grinning, Valescar addressed the red-nosed graybeard, though his words were for all of them. "Tell this ta every Casteless ya meet: throw down yer arms, give me yer masters, an' I'll give ya back yer lives."

Chapter 12

As the Water Lord Decrees

Jenuvant 26, 688 ABH,
Sewertown, Beneath the Royal Capital of Nemare

"As the Water Lord Decrees, so it shall be."
Whether it was said with admiration, loathing, or grudging respect, every scum-crawler in Sewertown lived by this singular commandment. You did not disobey any of the three Water Lords who ruled over the subterranean cesspit. To do so—whether through outright rebellion or just pissing off the wrong person—was a ticket to a slow, agonizing death.

Vallen licked his lips. They were dry and parched, just like his throat. Not a drop of water had entered his mouth in over twelve hours. At his side, Pockey groaned. He was whiter than a nobleman's bed sheets, all color having drained from his face. They needed to finish this job, and fast.

Pulling his tattered waterskin from his equally tattered belt, Pockey uncorked it and tilted it above his gaping mouth. Nothing emerged—just like the last three times he'd done the same thing.

"I could've sworn Bohomaz refilled my skin, Kit," the wiry pickpocket complained. His eyes bulged out of his small head, and his oversized shirt sagged down his shoulders, exposing a gaunt collarbone. Put whiskers on his acorn nose, and the urchin could pass for a pipe-rat.

Vallen shook his head as Pockey's gaze darted to his own empty skin. "You're hallucinating. Bohomaz won't give us our allotment until we retrieve the whisperwind amulet. He owes Vagley, and we owe him."

"But Kiiiiiiiit—"

"Vallen," he corrected for the hundredth time. "It's Vallen now, Pockey."

The youth shrugged, then started gnawing on the flaky leather hide of his waterskin. Most of the other kids at the *Safe Haven*—the thieving den Bohomaz operated out of the back of a Moravi pawn shop—had accepted his new name. The name Elaine had given him for his valiant . . . *almost* rescue. Even Bohomaz, who'd named him Kit, had simply boomed out a laugh and told him, "It fits!"

Ah, Elaine. Vallen could still picture everything about their first meeting. Her curious sapphire eyes, her lustrous brown hair bouncing around her ears, and the touch of her smooth hand in his radiating a warmth he thought he'd never know. Flowery scents had filled the room. They'd dressed him in clean clothes, not a stain, flea, or tear on them. Vallen closed his eyes, imagining—

No. He pressed his fist against the sand-coarse roof tiles beneath him, relishing the clarity pain brought him. Water Lord Balvin Vagley was not a patient man, and they would die if they couldn't deliver his requested item to Bohomaz. There was no time for insane dreams of another world.

Vallen stole a glance through the skylight into the murky, smoke-clogged building below. No movement. After hours of drunken carousing, the members of the Gutterpike gang had finally collapsed. Most lay unconscious at four long tables. A few were draped on the stairs to the second level or curled up in corners with half-naked women. Their boss, Scab Gutterpike, reclined atop a mauve sofa on a dais at the rear of the room, one heavily tattooed arm dangling to the floor.

In his massive hand, curled once about the stub of his missing little finger, was a silver chained necklace set with a bright green stone. Vallen smiled. It matched the description of the whisperwind amulet he'd been given.

"It's here, Pockey!" he whispered at a safe distance from the opening. The skylight wasn't covered with glass, just a thin tarp Vallen had briefly pulled aside. No one but a Water Lord could afford such a luxury down here.

The boy's munching paused. "What is? Water?"

"The amulet," Vallen hissed.

"You can't drink an *amulet*, Kit," Pockey said with a huff. "You can be pretty daft sometimes."

"Vagley hired Bohomaz to retrieve the amulet he accidentally gave to Scab in exchange for a . . . " Vallen trailed off. Whispering scratched at his already raspy throat, and the explanation wasn't getting through to Pockey anyway. He jabbed a finger at the tarp. "We go down. Get amulet. Give to Bohomaz. He gets Favorre medal. We get water. Make sense?"

Pockey dropped the waterskin, and Vallen lunged forward to grab it before it could hit the roof. The pickpocket's big eyes bulged further. "A *Favorre* medal? You can ask for *anything* if you have one of those."

Vallen secured the skin in one of his vest's pockets, which were filled with thieving tools: lock picks, fine twine, a mirror fragment, a torque wrench, a knife, and a pair of rusty pliers. Changing his name hadn't changed his role on the crew.

"That's right," Vallen soothed. "Now let's go earn it for him." Rising to his feet, he began edging along the roof toward the far end. A firm *'come here'* gesture convinced Pockey to follow him. Vallen had half a mind to leave his delirious friend behind, but he needed him for the next step.

Where one roof terminated, its neighbor began. Almost every meter of the sewer system was packed with haphazard construction, rotting boards and beams flung together with thrice-used nails, spit, and two curses for every prayer.

Vallen squeezed into the dark gap between tenements and lowered himself one story by pressing his feet to one wall and his back to the other. Grunting, Pockey came after him. Upon reaching Vallen, he set one foot on a jutting iron pipe—which blessedly held his weight—and the other on his partner's shoulder.

"Aarrghh," Vallen gasped, pinching his lips to stifle his shout. "Hurry it up!"

Above and to his right—even with Pockey—was a door. Yes, a door, and a locked one to boot. Rather than design an elaborate second entrance to their hideout like a tunnel, roof ladder, or sewer exit, the Gutterpikes had just shoved a door halfway up their rear wall. It was beyond idiotic since only one person could enter or exit at a time, but Vallen wasn't going to complain too much.

The thieves' lunacy was their way inside.

"Tools," Pockey requested.

Straining, Vallen used one arm to pass him the torque wrench and a lock pick. Within seconds, the sound of metal scraping against metal echoed down the narrow alley. Vallen's heart began to throb like the muscles in his legs and back. Would the Gutterpikes hear? Would Pockey break the pick or drop the wrench in his addled state?

Click!

"I've got it!" Pockey exclaimed a bit too loudly. "Now to . . ."

Something hard bounced off Vallen's forehead. He swore, resisted the urge to touch the swelling bruise, and twisted his neck to the side to avoid any more falling debris. Like the wrench, which would hurt a *lot* worse.

A muted splash came from below. As the noise faded, Pockey spoke a familiar Sewertown prayer. "It belongs to the sewers now."

"*You* don't get to say that," Vallen rasped. "That's the fourth pick you've lost or broken this month."

"Bohomaz doesn't seem to—"

"*Just get off me!*"

A minute later, Vallen was crouched inside the room, giving his eyes time to adjust to the musty gloom. While it was night on the surface, the giant illyrium crystal at the peak of Sewertown's dome never went dark. The oh-so-kind engimages who operated the shard did dim it while they slept, but their false sun was ever-present.

Vallen trusted Pockey to meet him at their rendezvous point. Well, he didn't entirely, but that wasn't something he could worry about at the moment. Footsteps muffled by felt pads, Vallen crept to the inner door, eased it open, and peered inside.

The cloying aroma of incense struck him like a physical blow. Vallen shut the door, coughed into the flap of his vest, and wiped his watering eyes with his sleeve. They were smoking hashim! Not much had entered his system, yet even that little bit had him seeing rainbow orbs that drifted from one end of the room to the other.

There's no doubt about it, Vallen thought, taking a thick rag and securing it over his nose and mouth with his twine. *They won't be waking up any time soon.*

Even so, he proceeded with caution. Out into the smog he skulked, one hand on the wall, the other probing through the mist in front of him. Two snoring brutes—their bald heads bearing a striking resemblance to a couple of boulders—slumped at the top of the stairs. Vallen tiptoed between their tree-trunk legs and onto the steps.

The first board creaked, its cry like an old woman's scratchy laugh. Every muscle in Vallen's body tensed. He was ready to bolt at the first shout, to sprint across the common room and out onto the street.

One of the men behind him snorted in his sleep. He scratched at his hairy armpit, inhaled sharply, then flopped onto his side and kept snoring. Breathing a sigh of relief, Vallen used the thief's sonorous log-sawing to cover the rest of his descent to the floor.

It was simple to chart a course from there. Most of the Gutterpikes were clustered on and around the tables and benches, so Vallen kept to the outside edge of the square chamber. He passed overturned tankards of mead, their sticky contents oozing through the floorboards to join the slime below. Articles of clothing, stolen trinkets, and discarded weapons were everywhere. There was even a huge wooden circle hung in one corner, throwing axes embedded in several of its concentric rings.

The pile of dull, low denomination geldars on a nearby stool suggested it was a gambling game, and part of Vallen wondered how it was played.

He reached the dais. In one corner was the hashim brazier—a wrought-iron cage with dried hashim leaves on the sides and a pile of smoldering coals at the center. Only thin tendrils of smoke still curled from it, a sign that the smog would soon begin to lift.

At the other end was Scab Gutterpike.

Scab was a nickname, but it fit the hulking Terran well. Like many of his men, he was completely bald. Unlike them, his condition wasn't voluntary. A swathe of crusty black scabs coated what was left of his scalp. Frantic gashes that seeped yellow pus cut through them at random, the result of one of Scab's tantrums. Rumor was he'd had a habit of tugging at his greasy hair before the Trenchdrakes burned down his old hideout with him still inside. Now, half-mad from his wounds, his outbursts were far worse—both for himself and those nearby.

Tattoo sleeves covered the lesser burns along his bare arms and chest. Vallen saw a dragon belching flame, a Sylph girl in an ... *indecent* position, and a six-spurred sewer junction, the symbol of Vagley's consortium of gangs.

Scab was fast asleep, one hand in his mead-soiled britches, the other loosely clutching the whisperwind amulet. The ovular green stone at its center was supposed to be able to read the flow of ambient men'ar, turning blood-red whenever someone lied in its presence. Vallen couldn't fathom why Vagley would give something so valuable to a deranged thief like Scab.

He wouldn't, Vallen reminded himself, stooping low to the floor as he approached. *Not permanently, which is why we're here to steal it back.*

Vallen circled the couch once, prodding at gaps in the rent upholstery to check for hidden weapons. A pair of throwing daggers rested hilt out in the pillow beneath Scab's scabrous head, and the sheath of a curved broadsword was hung around one of the sofa's posts.

No pikes. In fact, Vallen hadn't seen a single pike since he'd arrived. Plenty of knives, swords, crude crossbows, and whips—a veritable arsenal—yet not a single voided pike. Vallen considered shaking Scab awake to explain how names worked, but thought better of it when he realized the Trenchdrakes probably didn't have an elemental drake chained up in their cellar.

Two crouching steps brought Vallen within a handspan of Scab's ugly face. His breathing was slow and shallow. Even with the empty wine bottles stuffed beneath his legs and the hashim in his lungs, Scab appeared to be a light sleeper. Paranoia would do that to a man.

Glancing back and forth between Scab and the amulet, Vallen slipped a trio of tin geldars from another vest pocket. Each had a hole the size of a river-reed drilled in them near the edge. Soundlessly, he set two on the floor. The third stayed in his left hand as his right gently scooped up the amulet without tugging on its chain, which was still wrapped around what was left of Scab's pinky.

Too light, Vallen decided, comparing their heft.

He picked up a second coin and reassessed the weights. After a second's hesitation, he gave a satisfied nod. The difference was negligible. Returning the amulet to the floor, Vallen threaded the geldars together with the last of his twine. It wasn't cool to the touch like links of a chain, but it would have to do.

The moment of truth. Vallen licked his cracked lips beneath the mask, closed his eyes, and counted backward from ten. The ritual calmed his nerves and slowed his heartbeat. One wrong move and Scab would bolt awake, his daggers and Vallen's neck within easy reach. He had to be focused. Perfect.

Just like he always was.

His eyes sprang open. In seconds, the twine hoop was nestled beside the chain on Scab's hand, ready to slide into place when the amulet was removed. Now came the hard part. Placing one finger against either side of the chain, Vallen pushed out and up, lifting it from its resting place without scraping it along the scarred remains of Scab's pinky. And with one final tug, it was—

Scab's fingers began to close. If Vallen didn't get the chain out *now*, the brute's pipe-thick fingers would catch it in a vise grip. He did the only thing he could do: fall backward. The drop was quick and he barely felt the impact, but it produced a soft '*oomph*' that sounded in his ears like a crate shattering on cobblestones.

Vallen prayed to one of the Veneer Elaine had forced him to memorize. *By Sariel's sweaty arse, please don't let them hear.* That counted as a prayer, right?

Scab grunted and flopped onto his side, bottles beneath him clinking as they shifted. At the nearest table, a Moravi hissed and ruffled its head and neck spines. Nobody moved. Nobody shouted an alarm or tried to skewer Vallen where he lay.

Exhaling into his mask, Vallen cautiously rose to his feet and snuck back the way he'd come. The main door was to his left, but a guard hunched in the recessed hall, bulk draped across a rust-smeared bronze tank he was using as a makeshift pillow.

Vallen's mouth tasted like someone had poured sand down his throat. He'd do anything for a single sip of water, and it would be *so* easy to fill up his waterskin from the dripping nozzle taunting him from the base of the tank. He took a step toward it.

Crash!

The sound of glass shattering erupted behind him. *Void and Oblivion,* Vallen swore under his breath. He spun, knowing what he'd see. Shards of broken wine bottles glittered in the dim light coming through the countless cracks in the crudely built ceiling. Scab's restless sleeping had finally knocked them off the couch, and their remnants covered the ground around him.

Two huge, bloodshot eyes glared first at the smashed bottles, then the groggy shapes of the waking thieves, and lastly fell on the frozen form of Vallen. "Wha'dya think yer doin', boy?" Scab growled, his voice like thick sludge oozing from a pipe.

Vallen flashed a sheepish grin. "Would you believe I'm looking for the latrine? Blasted thing is hidden better than a priest's virtue in all this smoke."

A groggy Moravi lazily tasted the air with his forked tongue, blinked, and pointed a hooked claw down a hall beneath the steps to the second level landing—the opposite direction from where Vallen was going. The lizard's sickly green and yellow scales rustled as he tried to shake off a mead and hashim-induced stupor.

"Ze piss pot iz zat vey, hatchling," he said.

Scab jumped to his feet, glass crunching under his massive boots. "He ain't lookin' fer the pisser, ya dolt," he yelled at the Moravi. His shaking fists jangled the geldars on the hoop of twine wrapped around his fingers. Surprised by the sound, Scab raised the fake amulet in front of his burn-scarred face.

"*This. Ain't. My. Amulet!*" Scab roared. Spittle flew from his slashed lips, and veins bulged on his ravaged forehead. Vallen dodged as Scab threw the geldars at him, and heard the coins strike the dent-coated wall at his back.

"C'mon, Scab"—Vallen held up his palms, the real whisperwind amulet dangling from his right hand—"those are *tin* geldars. Go get yourself a shiny new necklace and buy something nice with whatever's left over."

They weren't worth as much as the spoiled mead spilling through the floorboards, and Scab knew it. With another cry, he grabbed his sword, violently drew it from its sheath, and buried it halfway in the couch in a fit of rage. Gray feathers burst from the wound to join the drifting smog.

Tattooed muscles bulging, Scab drove his blade the rest of the way *through* the sofa, dropping its halves to the floor. He jabbed its gleaming tip at Vallen and screeched, "Get 'im!"

By this point, most of the thieves were standing on wobbly legs. Some wore baggy shirts and pants stained by dirt and spirits. Others were bare-chested, or in nothing but their skivvies after a romp with one of a quartet of whores swiftly snatching their clothes and running for the back room. All of them brandished a deadly array of weapons as they laughed and jeered at Vallen.

"Not a single pike," Vallen lamented, shaking his head. "You guys need to think of a new name for your boy's club."

They charged him. Two slipped on a puddle of mead, taking down the four behind them in a mess of tangled limbs and grunted curses, but the rest leapt the tables or came at Vallen from the common room's side.

He didn't stand his ground. Scrambling toward the water tank, Vallen slipped the amulet into one vest pocket as he drew his knife from another. The blade's edge was dull, but he wasn't planning to kill anyone. That was one line he never intended to cross, no matter how desperate he became.

A wild cudgel swing came from the front, attached to a barrel-chested man with a beard like a tangled briar patch—the same Terran who'd been slumped atop the water barrel. Vallen ducked, charged under the thief's outstretched arm, and took aim at the nozzle near the tank's base. Its brass gleam had faded to the corroded blue of extreme rust, and white flecks coated the ground below it.

Small and wiry though Vallen was, he only needed a single swing to slice through the weakened pipe. Water jetted out as he passed, precious liquid sloshing uselessly onto the floorboards and dribbling to join the sewer sludge beneath the building. Vallen hated to watch so much go to waste, especially when he was parched as a Badlands riverbed.

Most of the thieves immediately dropped to the floor, casting aside their swords and daggers. They tried to cup the water in their palms, gulping down tiny handfuls so they wouldn't go to waste. The brightest among them ran straight to the tank. Hands clamped over the gushing pipe but only succeeded in making water squirt everywhere.

Their crestfallen faces spoke to the severity of the situation. A small fortune was slipping through their fingers. Reaching the entrance, Vallen threw open the door, then turned and mocked one final bow before disappearing into the fake Sewertown crystal-light.

"The Trenchdrakes send their regards, slime-swill!"

Chapter 13

Rising Flames, Departing Souls

Hetrachia 13, 697 ABH
Resistance Base, Sarconian Province of Darmatia

If not for Major Reev's barely veiled threat to turn him into an ice sculpture, Vallen would still be laying on his piss-poor excuse for a hammock in their ratty tent that was *just* one step up from some of the garbage-strewn Sewertown alleys he'd slept in as a child. Instead, he was wrapped snugly in three blankets—two of which he'd stolen—and huddling by a fire pit while waiting for a pointless memorial service to begin.

His ribs ached. A yellowed strip of cloth strained under the limp weight of his right shoulder and arm. Every muscle in his body felt like it'd been dragged back and forth through the cylinders of an airship engine more times than Vallen could count.

Not to mention he'd fallen asleep. For a minute, an hour, it mattered not. The second Vallen's eyes had closed, dreams of his past—of everything leading up to Elaine's end—had found him. *That* pain was worse than a hundred physical wounds, and he would *not* let his bloodshot eyes close again.

Summon your men'ar, a silky whisper soothed inside his head. *Banish the pain with your power.*

Oh, and his mind was playing tricks on him. Vallen ignored the voice, as he'd ignored every suggestion and order it had given him since their fight against the Draken. Whatever strength he'd summoned to launch his final attack on the beast, it had been his own, and no disembodied cajoling could convince him otherwise.

Though it was growing harder to deny that *something* was wrong with him—something tied to his overuse of men'ar. No matter how much of a fool Sylette took him for, Vallen could see a pattern. The first time he triggered MIS, the dreams of Elaine had returned. With the second had come the voice. Vallen had no intention of letting there be a third.

146

"Thank you for joining me on this most solemn of occasions ..."

Vallen's head snapped up as General Hardwick Iolus began his speech to the hundreds of disheveled soldiers gathered on the shore of the cavern's lake. The braggart possessed an impressive set of lungs, his words echoing among the glistening stalactites above and even reaching Vallen where he sat on a bench at the edge of camp.

"You have sacrificed much to be here, and those that aren't present have made the ultimate sacrifice for their country ..."

Chuckling, Vallen tugged his blankets tighter about his shoulders. Did the narcissist think he was winning any hearts and minds?

It was impossible to mistake the General. A wooden stage raised him above the unwashed masses, and as he strutted from one end to the other, the light of the stadium lamps turned the medals on his breast into a constellation of stars. His clean-shaven face, unwrinkled uniform, and puffed-out chest were completely at odds with the crowd before him.

Some wore Kingdom uniforms stained by grease, ash, or blood. Most simply wore whatever they could to stave off the subterranean chill. Dirty sweaters, torn jackets, bedsheets, even strips of canvas or repurposed camouflage netting. The least fortunate shivered around paltry fire drums clothed in nothing but thin tunics and summer-issue khaki leggings.

This was an army on its last legs, and Vallen didn't want to be nearby when it finally collapsed.

The service dragged on. Many soldiers cried. Their neighbors comforted them. Major Reev stood behind General Iolus on stage, unreadable face no more grim or serious than it ever was. A group of nuns dressed in white habits stood off to the side behind tables laden with what appeared to be grade school crafting materials. The whole charade was insipid, boring, and a total waste of time.

Leon needs to be avenged, *not mourned,* Vallen raged internally, gaze falling on Sylette's unmistakable silver hair. The others were nearby, Matteo weeping into Velle's shoulder, Renar sniffling while staring away from his father. *This distraction accomplishes nothing.*

" ... and the brave souls of the 292nd, who gave their lives to break the Sarconian encirclement above Aldona. None of them will be forgotten."

General Hardwick Iolus droned on. *Hardwick*, Vallen mused, picturing the letters in his mind. Who in oblivion would curse their kid with a name like *Hardwick*? With everything else going on, at least he could take solace in *not* eliciting a snigger every time someone spoke to him.

Vallen laughed at the thought of all the suffering little Hardwick must have gone through. A group of soldiers on their way to the memorial glared at him as they passed. The last of them paused, sized Vallen up from head to blanket-wrapped toes, and spat at his feet before moving on. Only the man's missing left leg and awkward, crutch-assisted hobble kept Vallen from chasing after him.

Injured or not, the phlegm-hocker *should* have recognized the Triaron. Major Reev had all but broadcast his name through camp, and the crowd of gawkers pretending to lounge around outside their tent had doubled in size since the previous night. She was using Vallen to boost morale. It didn't take a genius to figure *that* out. But he didn't care as long as they respected him, stayed out of his way, and he got another crack at the Sarcs.

The voice stirred again. *A demonstration of your power would surely earn their respect. And . . . their fear.* Not an entirely unappealing offer. Even so, Vallen ignored the hallucination.

"Good evenin', ma child."

Vallen spun, dropping his blankets and raising his arms to defend himself. He immediately regretted the decision. Only one of his limbs responded, and pain spiked from the gash in his side Velle had used the last of her men'ar to seal. Wincing, Vallen slumped back onto the bench in front of his assailant:

An old woman.

If she bore a weapon, it was concealed inside her baggy white robes. Ebony skin, gnarled by weather and weight of years, poked through where the vestments ended, and a mass of colored beads braided into her raven hair clinked melodically as she stifled a giggle.

She would have been beautiful—in a matronly way—if not for the burn marks. Where the left side of her face was carved with flowing wrinkles, the right was cratered by pink scar tissue, her dark flesh warped and pitted from her temple down to the edge of her withered gums. Vallen recoiled, half in embarrassment that she'd snuck up on him, half in disbelief that anyone could survive such a grievous wound.

"You don't look so good, ma child," the crone continued. "Why don't you lie down an' sleep?"

"I'm not your child," Vallen groused.

Another giggle slipped from her lips. "At *ma* age, ev'ryone is ma child. It is not about blood or relations. Time makes parents o' us all, often in ways we don't expect."

How in Sariel's accursed name do I keep attracting all these weirdos? Vallen thought. He was becoming a magnet for them.

Vallen shook his head. "I'm an orphan, lady. I didn't even know my parents. I can assure you I'm *no one's* child."

The fire beside them sparked, casting glowing embers into the cold cavern air. The nun's burns flashed beneath the glare, as did her deep blue eyes. They were radiant and fierce. Predatory, even, despite her years.

"Young boy, we are *all* someone's child. Big or small, Terran or Sylph, orphan or heir, we all came from da same place. We are all brothers an' sisters under da watchful eye o' our true parent, da Creator."

Walls slammed shut in Vallen's mind, and he narrowed his eyes. He wasn't wary because the old bag was a threat. No, it was because he'd heard the same sickening, worshipful drivel before. First from a girl that had meant more to him than his own breath, and again from a priest whose concern for others had gotten a church dropped on top of him. Their faith had been rewarded with death.

"Spare me the sermon," Vallen snapped. "Been there, tried that, didn't work. Still, be sure to tell Sariel 'hi' for me the next time you see him." He paused, tapping his chin as though an idea had just occurred to him. "Oh! Wait! That's right . . . he doesn't *exist*! So why don't you go find someone who will buy into your steaming pile of ek dung instead of bothering me?"

Leave! Vallen pled inwardly, turning away and pulling his blankets up around his ears. He couldn't leave the ceremony early and didn't want to abandon *his* fire, so he had to hope she'd get fed up and leave him alone.

A single gust of flame would—

The tempting whisper started to offer an *alternative* method to remove the hag, but Vallen silenced it. *He* was in control.

Jingling beads accompanied the woman's heavy sigh. "I would like nothin' more than ta find a more agreeable person ta talk to. Yet

I have come ta speak with da *Triaron,* with Vallen Metellus. Imagine ma surprise when such a bless'd man turned out ta be rotten as an overwatered dune-bloom."

"Give it a … "

The retort died in Vallen's throat. She knew him. Not just his title—*everyone* knew who the Triaron was—but his name. Smiling at his stunned reaction, the crone shuffled to the other end of the bench, brushed dust from the warped plank, and sat down beside him. The stones stacked at either end groaned in protest but held their weight.

"Ya have da look of revelation about ya, Triaron," she said, nodding at Vallen's face.

He gulped. "You're Sayri."

Like a rush of men'ar, recognition flooded through him and dragged his mind into the past. Reesa, Elaine's maidservant, had also been Sayri. She'd possessed the same warm umber skin, singsong voice, and ritually braided hair, each bead—each knot—a part of her story and her desert tribe's history. Her singing had once brought him no end of delight.

Now, the memory of her melodies haunted him.

"An' you are a rotten dune-bloom," the hag replied without missing a beat. "Too much water in da head softens da shell, ruins da crop, starves da village. Good food goes ta waste, jus' like with you."

"They're called *desarituses,*" Vallen corrected smugly.

She clapped her hands, firelight sparkling against her eyes. "Gud, gud! You *do* know something about our people, few though we are in yer lands."

Curiosity got the better of Vallen. "And why did you leave the Badlands? I've only seen one other Sayri in Darmatia."

"Hmmm, why indeed?" The old hag leaned forward, hands splayed toward the flames. How strange it was for a burned woman to not fear fire. "Yet I did not come here ta talk about me. I came to talk about you, Vallen Metellus."

"Who are you? Why do you care?"

"Who do you think I am, child?" Her eyes glinted mischievously.

Vallen matched her sarcasm. "An old crone playing dress-up?"

The elderly woman burst out laughing, a full-throated, hearty chuckle that Vallen worried could be heard from the lakeshore. Fortunately, none of the mourners turned around, and Major Reev's icy gaze remained fixed on General Iolus as he pumped a fist in the air

151

to emphasize some important point.

When her mirth subsided, a wizened finger reached up and wiped tears from her cheeks. "Hohoho, that's a good one. An' sometimes I feel that's da truth, feeble as I have become. It is hard ta keep things together when some days I even struggle ta walk. But enough beatin' around da bloom. I am Mother Superior Tabitha, da leader o' Da Way of Da Will."

The lyrical dialect took Vallen a moment to process, but the phrases, "Mother Superior," and "The Way of the Will," were unmistakable. A tingle cascaded along his arms and neck. This doddering, decrepit Sayri woman was *Mother Superior* Tabitha. Steward Metellus' religious equal. The leader of the Darmatian Church of Light. And without exaggeration, one of the most powerful people in the country—if not the *world*.

Vallen snorted to hide his shock. "Excuse my skepticism, but why would the grand proselytizer of the Church be slumming it in the mud with soldiers? Especially *this* lot." He jerked his usable thumb at the hunched backs of the crowd. The smell of char and ash *barely* hid the cocktail of sweat, rot, and urine pouring off them. "Getting involved with them is a death sentence."

"An' where else would I be?" Tabitha's reply was deadpan, her gaze firm.

"A villa, a cathedral, a royal palace," Vallen said, counting the possibilities on his fingers. "Negotiating with the Sarcs. You know . . . *anywhere* but here."

"But this is where da Creator's work is ta be done." The nun raised her arms, voluminous sleeves dangling beneath bone-thin limbs whose gesture took in the whole cavern. "Care for da injured. Visit da infirm. Comfort da sorrowful. Give peace ta those passed on. These are but four of da Seven Holy Tenets, but all o' them are personified in this camp. I can think o' no other place that needs ma efforts more than here."

From the depths of the past came Elaine's voice: *"Kindness. It's the act of doing something for another, for their own good, without desiring anything in return."* Vallen shook his head, eyes heavy, temple beginning to throb. Why were these whispers tormenting him? She and Leon were dead because of their vain attempt at saving others, and *still* they sided with this crazy zealot?

I am the only guide you need, Triaron, the whisper soothed. *Let me banish the rest.*

"This is work for professionals," Vallen insisted, massaging the bridge of his nose. "Let the doctors, salvators, and medics handle it."

"Do you think there are enough o' them?" Tabitha tilted her chin toward the field hospital, its canvas walls sagging like lungs straining to draw breath. "No more are comin'. Some perished at Aldona, but most are frightened. Scared ta do da right thing because o' what da Empire would do ta them in turn. But we can't judge them for it. Most have families ta protect, people that would suffer for their actions. So why shouldn't I—who have da capability and da will—serve da Creator's people where others cannot?"

So self-righteous, Vallen thought, rolling his eyes. "This isn't your job," he pressed. "You're *Mother Superior* Tabitha. You should be out"— he waved at the distant cave ceiling—"*there* convincing others to help. Or preaching about the Empire's tyranny, telling others that the Church has some grand plan to win Darmatia's freedom, or ... or ... something."

Tabitha steepled her wrinkled fingers and rested her chin atop them. Above the makeshift structure, her twinkling blue eyes shone with knowing amusement. "Strange that da child who doesn't care for da faith is now tellin' me how ta save Sariel's children. Let me answer yer question with a question: Do ya know da man who spat at you?"

"Of course not," Vallen fumed. Why would she bring *that* up? 'Crutchy' was in the wrong, no matter what she said.

"His name is Vert Cerna, brother o' Rasor Cerna. They served aboard da *Ananorae*, a Darmatian heavy cruiser that sank in da battle at Aldona Fortress. Before it went down, a launch managed ta get away an' dock with one o' da ships that escaped ta this base. Vert was on that transport. His brother was not."

"And why should I care about either of them?"

Tabitha clicked her tongue. "What manner o' fool wants ta know da endin' ta a story when it's hardly begun? By da time I'm done, you'll know why they should matter ta you—o' that I can assure you."

Vallen's head throbbed in tune with his aching side and battered arm. The smoke from the fire bent into unnatural shapes—airships, dragons, and the like—as his eyelids sagged and his attention waned. At best his conversation with Tabitha was a sparring match; at worst, it was a lecture. Did he have to sit here and listen to her blathering?

Down the hill, General Iolus' audience was getting restless, their melancholy giving way to impatience and boredom. Some at the fringes began to drift away in groups of two and three. Major Reev watched

153

them go, frown deepening, foot tapping as she stared holes in the back of the General's head. He didn't notice, instead beating his chest and shouting about, "Bravery and commitment!"

The Major was distracted. This was Vallen's chance to escape! He rose slowly, careful not to catch his foot on the hem of his blankets. One step brought him to the edge of the bench. A second saw him to the narrow gap between two listing tents. Once Vallen made it to the other side, he'd be free!

Frigid air rushed across his neck, its touch almost cold enough to burn and blister. He gasped, slapped a hand to the spot, and spun toward the Ice Queen. As expected, her piercing emerald eyes were locked on him from over a hundred paces away. Vallen didn't question how she'd spotted his flight. Mouthing a curse, he shuffled to the bench and plopped back down in his seat.

We can make her pay, the whisper declared. Vallen snorted at its absurdity.

"Back so soon?" Tabitha grinned, exposing lavender gums and sallow teeth.

"Let's get this story over with."

She nodded. "What do you suppose happened ta da second brother? Surely there was enough space on da ship for one more?"

"He died, obviously," Vallen huffed.

"Ah, but what *kind* o' death did he die?"

"Does it matter?" The frustration in his voice surprised him. "When you're dead, you're dead. The end."

Let your rage become action, the whisper encouraged. *Etch your point into her brittle bones.*

Mother Tabitha jabbed a finger at him. In the firelight, Vallen thought he saw a thick wooden ring—its surface coated in charred symbols—pressed against her knuckle. "Not so!" she said. "All beings are created equal, but it is not so with their deaths! Tome o' Testament, chapter seven, verse twenty-three: 'There is no greater love than ta give up yer life for another.'"

Quoting scripture now, was she? Vallen found it ironic that faith-addled zealots always tried to use their own holy books to back up their arguments. It was the same thing as screaming, *I'm right because I'm right!*

He humored her. "So, Ras—well, whatever he's called—sacrificed himself for his brother?"

Click-clack, click-clack . . .

Another nod set Tabitha's beads clattering. For the briefest of instants, Vallen thought he heard a melody in their random, disjointed impacts. "Jus' so. When da *Ananorae* was goin' down, a sudden explosion left Vert trapped beneath a pile o' fallin' debris. However, Rasor refused ta leave him and worked ta get him loose even if it meant dyin' himself. After several minutes o' shiftin' da wreckage about, Vert's leg, crushed under a pipe, came free.

"But then disaster struck!" Tabitha spread her hands. Before them, the fire seemed to crackle and flare to match her movements. "Movin' da rubble caused what was left o' da ceilin' ta come crashin' down, right on top o' da savior Rasor. Vert tried ta rescue him in turn, but there was little he could do. His leg was broken; he could nay put any weight on it. And unlike wit Vert, Rasor had been speared by metal beams. He would shortly bleed out."

The fire dimmed. The nun's voice grew soft and wistful. "So did da last group off da cruisa find Vert, unable ta walk, his body draped over da corpse o' his brother. Even though Rasor was gone, Vert fought them all da way ta da launch. They ultimately had ta knock him out ta get him ta safety."

"Got it." Vallen shook his head, feigning understanding to shut her up. "That explains why Vert was a *wee bit* peeved earlier, so I'll be careful next time I—"

"That is *not* da end o' da story, Vallen Metellus. I will tell you when I'm done, since you seem incapable o' figurin' that out for yerself. An' if you interrupt again, perhaps I shud tell Major Reev o' yer impudence?"

Vallen followed Tabitha's gaze, down the hill, over the heads of the soldiers, and onto the podium. He found Major Reev still scowling at them, and an involuntary shiver convulsed through him. Beneath the facade of the kindly nun was a cunning leader, the kind that dealt with not only the sick and infirm but with kings and emperors as well. It was little wonder Tabitha knew which of his buttons to push.

A moment of silence passed between them. Then, satisfied that Vallen would hold his tongue, the wrinkled old bag continued. "Vert's leg looked fine on da outside, but infection had seeped beneath da surface. Yet upon da lad's arrival here, he was triaged as healthy. Fit ta return ta duty after some bed rest. If he had followed da orders o' those docters you put so much faith in, he'd be dead—his brother's efforts but a temporary reprieve.

"Yet one o' ma nuns, searchin' da camp for any injured that did

155

not come forward, found him on his cot, sweat drenchin' his sheets and unable ta move, so bad was da fever. In da end, we had ta take his leg, but we saved his life. Da life his brutha had giv'n him. Da life he must now live for *both* their sakes.

"That is da end o' this story," Tabitha said, withdrawing her hands and crossing them in her lap. Her gaze remained fixed on Vallen, searching for some glimmer of understanding.

"Can I speak now?" he asked.

"Yes."

Smirking, Vallen shrugged. "I have no idea what you expected me to learn from that."

Tabitha skipped the disapproving glare this time. With startling swiftness, she drew a knobby walking stick from inside her robes, whipped it around, and smacked Vallen upside the head. The shock did more damage than the blow. He staggered, caught his foot on his bunched-up blankets, and nearly fell off the bench.

"What was that for?" Vallen yelled. When he regained his balance, he reached up to massage a swelling lump above his left ear.

The cane—a twisted length of lacquered oak with a fist-sized knot at the end—wagged at him in response. Vallen abandoned the bench entirely, rising and scooting out of the nun's range.

"Are you *blind* child?" Tabitha asked. "Or do you simply choose not ta see? How caught up in yerself must you be ta not recognize da truth starin' you in da face?"

Surging heat from the fire at Vallen's back coincided with the rising flame of anger in his breast and the pounding in his temple. Sweat dribbled down his chin as his throat went dry. "Lady, I'm not a mind reader. Just tell me your point already!"

"*You* are Vert Cerna, Vallen Metellus!" Mother Tabitha exclaimed with a jab of the stick. Its point, polished and sealed with a cherry stain, halted just below Vallen's chin, a hairsbreadth from his neck. "*You* lost your best friend at Aldona! *You* had ta run away an' leave him behind! An' now *you* find' yerself lost an' confused, unable ta come ta grips with his passin' an' blamin' anyone an' everything for it but da true culprit."

Her accusation hit Vallen far harder than her cane had. For an instant, he was reeling, drowning in his own guilt because some part of him knew *she was right.* His mind gasped for breath, struggling beneath the waves of despair torn from wounds he'd thought sealed.

The voice railed against his weakness, tone harsh like thunder.

It matters not if you're at fault. You've chosen your atonement. All this will end once the gravestones of your dead are festooned with the skulls of your foes.

Vallen smiled at the gruesome image. Knocking the rod aside, he stepped toward his assailant. "You don't know anything about me," he growled. "So don't preach like you can solve my problems, let alone anyone else's!"

Before he could take a second step, the staff snapped back up. "I *do* know you. Do you think I'd come here without knowin' yer past, hearin' yer story? Do you think I've never seen a child tormented by da same demons you carry with you?"

"And? What does it matter to you? Why do you care what I do, how I feel?" Snarling, Vallen batted the stick aside. It swung wide, scrapping across the cavern floor and nearly tearing free from Tabitha's shaky grip.

Yet the nun held firm. Like a vengeful goddess, she hauled the tip around until it once again pointed squarely at Vallen's neck. "You asked me why I'm here, *Triaron*," Tabitha spat the title, contempt oozing from her every pore. "I believe da Creator sent me here ta set you straight. Ta halt yer trajectory o' self-destruction an' help you become da instrument you were intended ta be."

Time for that stick to go, Vallen decided.

Cruel delight radiated from the whisper as Vallen launched forward, dumping his blankets as he charged. He snatched the club, ripped it from Tabitha's clutches, and proceeded to smash it over and over into the sparking charcoal of the fire pit.

"I. Don't. Need. Your. *HELP!*"

Each word was punctuated by a stab into the cinders, sending embers and ash dancing through the air along with the smoke. His eyes teared up, soot clogged his mouth, and his injured side and back ached horribly. But Vallen no longer cared. He cackled loudly, reveling in each splinter and shard ripped from the staff.

When he stood over the charred remnants of the cane, chest heaving, left hand dripping blood, Tabitha spoke in a voice that was little more than a breath. "If that is yer response, Vallen Metellus, it is evident that you very much do."

She . . . wasn't going to give up? Even after all that? The fight went out of Vallen.

No! Don't yield to this withered husk. Do to her what you did to her can—

Vallen silenced the voice with a thought. Shoulders slumped, he faced Tabitha, his movements slow as a glacial shift. "Fine. You win. Why do you want to help me?"

"I'd like ta say it is for yer own good, but if I did so, I'd be a liar." The blue pools of her eyes once again twinkled with amusement. Tabitha patted the bench beside her, beckoning Vallen over. "Come. Sit. Watch."

Sighing, Vallen sat. This was just one more defeat to add to the *great Triaron's* list of failures. "What am I supposed to see?"

"I cannot do all da work for you. What do yer eyes show you?"

Why couldn't the irritating crone just give him the answer she wanted? "The blowhard finally finished his speech, and the soldiers are shambling toward the tables your nuns set up. They're giving them paper and sticks to make"—Vallen squinted, then snorted—"*boats?* Is this really a funeral?"

"Not boats," Tabitha corrected. "Lanterns. Look closely."

The crowd was a haphazard thing. Scowling and cursing soldiers bumped into each other as Major Reev and several lower-ranking officers tried to form lines in front of nuns wearing strange pointy hats. General Iolus was nowhere to be seen.

Once the soldiers reached the rickety tables, the nuns passed them strips of leaf-thin parchment, a handful of driftwood fragments, and a small candle. Vallen watched a bizarre trio—a blond Terran man, burly female Sylph, and tall Hue that was a fair bit slimmer than Unter—carry their supplies to the shore. Finding a vacant spot, they sat on boulders and began weaving the sticks through the parchment.

"Why do they need more light?" Vallen asked, glancing up.

Though the tripod lamps scattered around the camp were dark, their generators still and quiet, the ceiling panels were beaming like the evening sun. He wagered it was bright enough for Matteo to sleep without a night light.

Tabitha waved at the crystal-clear waters of the lake. "They are not for seein'. They are for floatin' an' . . . rememberin'. Tell me, child, have ya ever been ta a Darmatian funeral?"

A soft titter and a flash of sky blue eyes twirled through Vallen's thoughts. Elaine, life personified. Elaine, casket draped in black, surrounded by white lilies on a funeral bier. The lid was locked tight, its contents too disturbing to be shown.

It had been a grand memorial. Hundreds had attended, the wealth and fame of her father clearly on display. Yet he . . . Vallen blinked, battling against the surging guilt. He had watched the service from a distant temple steeple, unable to bring himself to come a step closer. After what he'd done, he had no right to.

And it was worse with Leon. Not a shred of his body remained to mourn.

The nun didn't press the question. "Normally we cremate da bodies so da spirit might be freed from its prison o' rottin' flesh. Da ashes are then split. Most are offered ta Sariel ta keep from da Void until da time o' judgment. Yet some—a very tiny bit—are held back ta be mixed with a special paste, which is then eaten by friends an' family. Ta outsiders, da practice might seem barbaric. But I think it's essential. It helps us carry on, knowin' those we love are still with us, watchin' an' strengthenin' us from within. An' even shud da ashes giv'n ta Sariel somehow be lost, da part o' them inside us will be passed down, generation ta generation, never ta be destroyed."

"Meaningless." Vallen's despair bubbled over in a dark chuckle. "By that logic, the lanterns are useless. And what of those left at Aldona? Their bloated corpses litter the rubble—'un-freed,' to use your words."

"An' what would you do instead?"

"I . . . " The words froze in Vallen's throat. He *couldn't* do anything, not without leaving carnage and death in his wake.

"We make these tiny offerings because we must do *somethin'*," Tabitha asserted, weathered fingers clenching in her lap. "We cannot allow our loved ones ta wallow in death, trapped by da chains o' this world. Especially these brave souls, who gave their lives for a cause greater than themselves. An' so we launch these fragile flames into da shadows, prayin' that they will catch their forlorn spirits, gatherin' them up an' bringin' them to Sariel across time an' space."

On the shore, a man slipped, his lantern clattering across the stones along with his crutches. Wailing, he dived for the crude mess of sticks, twine, and paper, catching it before it could fall into the lake upside down. He paid no heed to the slimy ooze staining his uniform jacket, or the frigid water lapping at the bandage-wrapped stub of his left leg.

No, Vert Cerna's tear-choked gaze was fixed on the lantern he'd made for his brother.

You're nobody, Vallen thought as Vert's friends rushed to help him to his feet. *Your story, your brother, your life—they mean nothing to me. And yet . . . why are you so happy with that shoddy lantern? It can't bring your brother back, so . . . why?*

"Why?" Vallen's voice cracked. "Why do you want me to see all this?"

"So you can begin ta heal."

The illyrium panels cut off, dropping the cave into a deep darkness broken only by a smattering of scattered fires. Vallen expected the cavern to shake, rocks to fall, bullets to fly, and people to scream.

But it wasn't a Sarconian attack. As he lurched to his feet, Mother Tabitha grabbed him by the belt and yanked him back down. "Calm yerself. Wait an' look."

A small pocket of dancing light surrounded them, the dying fire pit casting long shadows that bobbed against the nearby tents. Vallen couldn't see anything. Not the lake, nor the masses congregated around it.

"Spi'ferat."

"Spi'ferat!"

"Spi'ferat ... "

Dozens of voices chanted spells, and with them came shooting arcs of flame that sliced through the gloom. Instead of dissipating as the magic expired, the radiance grew with each invocation, expanding until an orb of sunlight gleamed at the water's edge.

Not sunlight, Vallen realized. Like little heartbeats, hundreds of candles flickered inside the lanterns of the soldiers holding them. Mages had lit the first wicks, then each person had touched their flame to those beside them, passing the blaze on until not a single one remained unlit. Alone, they were insignificant. But together, they were bright enough to illuminate the whole cavern.

Major Reev stepped forward and knelt beside the lake, her lantern—and those around her—making the water and stalactites sparkle like gemstones. Pressing her palms together, she whispered something and sent her glowing raft floating across the pool. Others followed her example, first in ones and twos, then in a wave that clogged the whole shoreline.

With no winds or currents to propel them, the rafts drifted lazily, bumping into each other, running into rocks, or getting stuck farther down the beach. Their glow exposed a ponytail of silver hair alongside one of a handful of red-skinned Sylph. Sylette and Velle, and with them were Matteo, Renar, and Lilith. Velle and Matteo wept as their lanterns departed, and Renar and Lilith crouched to embrace them. Even Sylette stooped to place her hands on their shoulders.

Regret twisted in Vallen's chest. *He* was the odd man out. And while they launched offerings for *his* best friend, he sat back doing nothing.

Mother Tabitha read his mind. "Would you like ta offer a lantern for yer friend?" Vallen couldn't hear the kindness in her words, only the accusation.

"O-of course not. Besides, I'm the one who . . . who . . . "

Vallen pulled away from her, eyes darting, looking for a way out. The bench became the *Feywind's* hangar floor, cold, hard, and unforgiving. He'd lain there, defeated, as Leon had fought to save his life. Now, the lanternlight before him glared like the explosion that had claimed Leon's radiance.

The Empire wasn't to blame. Nor was the world, Sariel, or any other non-existent force of fate. There was only one place Vallen should aim his loathing over Elaine and Leon's deaths: *directly at himself.*

A sand-weathered, wrinkled hand reached into the darkness and grasped his thigh, dragging Vallen back to reality. "Earlier I said that you refuse ta recognize da cause o' yer friend's death. Do you know who I meant by that?"

"Me," Vallen said instantly. "*I* caused it. *I* got him killed."

"Perhaps," Tabitha replied, tilting her head. Black braids and beads slipped from her gaunt shoulders. "Perhaps not. But that is not da story *I* heard. Nor da story *they'll* remember."

"What do you mean?"

She gestured at the soldiers. "Until yer arrival, they were a shamblin' corpse, goin' through da motions without any belief that their actions would matter. An' who could blame them? Da Empire had smashed us beyond any chance o' recovery. Most didn't even have da strength ta grieve, for soon enough they'd be dead or captured too.

"But look at them now!" Tabitha exclaimed, arms spread wide. "You would think they could move mountains!"

Vallen looked, and listened, and heard . . . laughter? Music?

Another table had been erected on the shoreline, this one laden with dented supply tins, cases of grimy bottles, and a huge, steaming vat of what looked like stew. Men and women gathered around it, some still crying in each other's arms, but most eating, dancing, and singing at the top of their lungs. A quartet dressed in torn dress blues sat on a group of boulders playing a variety of stringed instruments. Major Reev stood nearby, not participating but tapping her foot to the up-tempo beat of their tune.

They were . . . happy? In spite of all the death and grief they'd just marched through?

Tabitha grinned at the disbelief on Vallen's face. "This came from a single spark: a legendary title, an announcement by Major Reev, and da story o' you an' yer companions, told once by her an' passed 'round da camp until throats were hoarse from repeatin' it. This scene was created by you cadets—those here now . . . an' those in Sariel's care."

"How can you say that?" Vallen shook his head, denying her with every fiber of his being. That story was a lie. His gifts had fallen into his lap. He had done *nothing* to deserve them. "I'm not like Darmatus. I'm not a worthy Triaron. How can I bring them hope when all I do is *take* and *kill*?"

Her shrug blunted his rage. "Who am I ta question why da Creator gave you da abilities he did? An' yet here we are"—Tabitha patted his leg and gave him a wink—"both o' us bearin' titles far more impressive than anyone deserves in spite o' all da mistakes we've made.

"But da funny thing about titles," her voice dropped to a whisper as she leaned toward Vallen, "is they have power in them, regardless o' whether they're deserved or not."

Her? Undeserving? A flashback of the knobby end of her cane whirling toward him popped into Vallen's head. Maybe Tabitha's violent behavior extended to people aside from a very stubborn, very rude Triaron.

Yet it was true Vallen did not deserve *his* title, at least. He was a symbol—to Major Reev, the General, and everyone else. And what lay beneath the symbol was foul and rotten. "Even if I accept what they think of me, I can't possibly live up to their expectations. I let Leon die. That's not something that can just be washed away."

"Nor should it," Tabitha retorted, blunting his argument again. "There is a second tale da men speak o'. One o' a young mage travelin' with da Triaron who went blow for blow with Rittermarschal Valescar— da 'Wall o' da Empire' himself!—an' survived long enough ta let his comrades escape."

Vallen's spirits sank as Tabitha's voice soared with passion and zeal. She didn't know where he'd been during Leon's last stand. Didn't know that he'd been carried from the ship like a sack in the arms of squadmates possessing far more sense than he. Everything Vallen knew about his best friend's fall was second-hand, and even then his companions had tried to hide the truth from him, knowing he was too weak to take it.

The second Triaron—prodigal mage, flamboyant womanizer, and rising star of the Darmatian army—was nothing but a scum-crawler who had *twice* thrown away those he cherished.

Lowering his head into his hands, Vallen prayed for the light to fade, darkness to fall, and for Mother Tabitha to leave him to fester in his misery. "Do you think I don't know how he died? Leon made that choice for *me*! If I hadn't charged in, if I'd worked with the others, if I'd—"

"So you *do* understand, at least in part."

"Come again?" The last thing Vallen had expected was for Tabitha to agree with him.

"You jus' acknowledged that yer friend made a choice. A choice ta save you. A choice that you"—Tabitha jabbed him in the arm—"Want ta deny him."

Her eyes, the same rich blue color as so many of her dangling beads, stared through him. It was clear the Sayri woman thought she knew him. Believed she could save Vallen from himself.

But she hadn't been there; hadn't made the choices that brought him to this moment or lived his countless failures.

"No!" Vallen roared into his palms. His voice emerged as a muffled plea. "No matter what he decided, Leon did it to save me. I'm guilty. There's no changing that fact."

Why am I telling her all this? part of Vallen wondered. He'd never been this open with anyone, including his own conscience. Normally he'd keep everything bottled up—shipped away to some distant corner of his thoughts never to be touched again. Life had always been easier that way, never worrying about others, never reflecting on the past, and never taking responsibility for his actions.

And yet something deep inside Vallen, buried layers beneath the rage-filled whisper in some forgotten crevice of his mind, was desperately shouting for someone to help him.

Leathery skin brushed the stubble of his chin. Bony fingers gripped his cheeks and yanked his face upward until his nose was almost touching Tabitha's. Her breath smelled of oranges, while the light scent of lavender wafted from her hair.

"How naive are you?" she asked, giving him a little shake. "By that logic, you might as well blame him for bein' born. Better blame yer companions, too. Did he not also save their lives? An' who's ta say ya would've done more on yer feet? It was seven against one an' it still took yer friend's life—all his energy an' men'ar—ta *halt* Valescar."

With a shove, Tabitha released him. "Don't you think it's selfish ta take responsibility for a decision *he* made? How is that not more o' da same?" She thumped her fist against her chest. "'I'm da Triaron, an' therefore everyone's lives are *mine* ta protect.

163

"How foolish! Don't take his free will from him. He made a choice, on his own, without you havin' any say in da matter. Yer friend *chose* ta sacrifice himself so that you an' da other cadets might live."

Tabitha paused, then leapt to her feet, robes swirling, braids swaying, beads clattering and clanging. She spun on Vallen with the force of a spring storm, and her voice boomed like she was speaking before a full congregation of worshippers.

"But he did not do so because he valued his life so little. *No!* He did so because he saw what you do not—your own potential! Now ask yerself this, Vallen Metellus: what will *you* sacrifice ta honor his memory an' ensure that final act was not in vain?

"These people, this world, desperately needs a hero, a second comin' o' Darmatus da Triaron. An' because you bear his magic, you are already seen as one. Will you be da light dey cannot find? Will you give them hope when all they see is darkness? Seize da gifts giv'n ta you an' become da symbol they need! Become da dawn that drives away da long night! Become da hero that everyone but you sees! *That* is yer atonement, da price o' da life Leon gave you."

Tabitha's knees buckled. Without thinking, Vallen jumped forward, catching her with his good arm. The pain was excruciating— like a hot poker had stabbed into his side and rooted around until *all* the muscles Velle had healed were torn again. Biting his lip, Vallen heaved them back onto the bench where they lay in a gasping pile of robes, blankets, and just a bit of blood.

"Why?" he panted, trying to roll off his screaming ribs.

"To . . . " Tabitha coughed. "Make you see sense."

"Killing yourself is a *brilliant* way to do that."

Two minutes of agonizing repositioning saw Vallen sitting on the bench with the nun braced against his chest, her head lightly resting on his dislocated shoulder. He bore the needles riddling his arm. She was far worse off.

Was Tabitha ninety? A hundred, perhaps? She appeared so much older now, her vitality drained and breath coming in ragged wheezes. Her skin should be darker but had lightened as it thinned with age. Sluggish black veins crisscrossed her arms. The burn on her face glared like an angry eye, and he could now see that it looped around the right side of her neck and beneath her collar. That cane hadn't been for show—it was a necessity.

"We need to get you to the salvators," Vallen blurted. He started to shout, but a trembling hand reached up to cup his cheek.

"Not yet."

"But—"

The revelry by the lake abruptly halted, shrouding the cavern in an unnatural stillness. Vallen could hear Tabitha's heartbeat. Water dripped from far above, striking the nearby stone like cannon fire.

"It's time," Tabitha croaked.

"Time for . . . ?"

Her finger tapped his lip, then hovered toward the lake. On the shore, the soldiers had fallen silent, their heads bowed and eyes fixed on the distant cavern wall. The lanterns had not drifted aimlessly. Guided by an unseen current, they'd floated across the breadth of the underground pool, gathering around an opening that had hitherto been invisible. Mist churned about the black maw, and the water turned white at its edge. A waterfall!

"The Rite o' Release," she answered at length.

A roar came from the crowd, the cacophony of boots striking on stone. Soldiers moved to either side, parting like reeds before a beautiful blonde maiden dressed in a shift of purest white silk. She strode through their midst like a goddess—steps sure, head high, garment whispering where it touched the ground. Snow lilies laced her hair, clung to her robe, and scattered in her wake.

Upon reaching the lake, the girl removed her sandals and continued into the frigid waters. Vallen gasped, but Mother Tabitha hissed at him. Not until the maiden was up to her waist in the pool, the distant lanterns wreathing her in a halo of light, did she stop.

Tabitha craned her neck to whisper in Vallen's ear. "A Darmatian memorial always ends with da Rite o' Release. One o' da Creator's chosen, a priestess, blesses da bodies o' da fallen before their final journey. This purifies their vessels so that nothin' can shackle them ta this mortal realm. In other words, ta release their souls."

Raising her arms above her head, the maiden began to sing. Rich in timbre, filled at once with passion, joy, and sorrow, her voice echoed off the cave walls until it filled every corner of the base. Vallen was stunned by how moving it was. Even though it was impossible, he could almost imagine Sariel descending from on high to claim the departed.

"Restless souls, now ascending,
go to be with those who went before.
Rise above, this mortal coil,
and at last, find your peace."

It was a short hymn, haunting yet hopeful. But Vallen couldn't help wondering if, beneath all the elegance and splendor, it was enough. "Does this truly give solace to the dead?" he asked softly.

A phantom smile formed on Tabitha's pale lips. "Magic—which you do put faith in—is very much like a song or prayer. It is a plea ta da forces o' da universe ta come ta yer aid and grant yer desires." The stanza repeated, louder, more fervent than before. Vallen pressed his ear closer to Tabitha. "Is there any purer medium for that wish than this? That yer loved ones may be joyous and blessed for all eternity?"

The whole crowd took up the hymn, adding their voices—their prayers—to the heavenly plea. It swelled, growing in strength, rising up to pierce the limestone and escape the pit the Resistance found itself in. Anything was possible, even the salvation of their fallen.

"Restless souls, now ascending,
go to be with those who went before.
Rise above, this mortal coil,
and at last, find your peace."

Just as Vallen began to lose himself in the melody, the floating lanterns reached the waterfall and disappeared from view. Not all at once, and certainly not every one, since some had become trapped on unseen islands or caught in still waters. Yet enough vanished to drop the cavern into darkness, reducing the maiden and soldiers to shadowy silhouettes.

The memorial was over. Whether or not the Rite had any power, the souls of the fallen had been released to begin their next journey. Who knew? Perhaps Leon was with them. Given that he was a master of light magic, he was sure to make the perfect guide.

As Vallen cradled Tabitha, the verse was sung one final time, carrying in it all the yearning, love, and hope the survivors could muster. Even he tried to sing, tone deaf though he was.

With his own voice grating in his ears, it wasn't nearly as pleasant as before . . . but Vallen found himself weeping just the same.

167

"Restless souls, now ascending,
go to be with those who went before.
Rise above, this mortal coil,
and at last, find your peace."

That night, after everyone had gone to bed, the lights still off and the fires but ash and smoke, a solitary lantern labeled '*Leon*' in crudely drawn charcoal lettering reached the far end of the lake and started its travels to wherever it might go.

Find your peace, Leon. Find your peace.

Idyllic Days II

With weighty finality, the large double doors of the Descar mansion closed behind Leon. They may as well have been slabs of stone rolling into place atop a crypt. Everything within these halls was dead and soulless—not just the magchines that thrummed and pulsed along the walls and ceiling, but the people too. Servants, staff, even Leon and his brothers. They were all tools for the master puppeteer: his father, Dr. Archimas Redora Descar.

Leon fidgeted in his fine suit-robe, tugging at the coarse hempen cotton covering his arms. His toes revolted at the cramped leather prison wedging them together. Why had he dressed up today? He *hated* wearing frilly vestments—at least those preferred by Nemare aristocracy. And yet Leon had done so anyway. What was wrong with him?

A sudden urge to flee crept across his neck like a chill wind. The door was still unbolted. No one had appeared atop the grand staircase or emerged from one of the gloom-filled passages leading farther into the estate. Leon could cross the immaculately manicured lawn, vault the boxwood hedge, and disappear into the encroaching twilight before anyone noticed.

Yes, that's exactly what he'd do. His hands twitched inside his finger-length sleeves. One foot slid backward on the dull, flint-gray tiles, squeaking ever-so-softly as he moved.

Clap! Clap!

All the magchines shut off at once, their gears and pistons grinding to an immediate halt. In the sudden silence, the squeak of Leon's shoes echoed off the bare walls and unadorned marble columns.

"Leaving so soon, brother?"

"You'll miss the festivities if you do. Like always."

Too late, Leon thought, standing up straight and trying to muster a smile for the two men striding down the staircase. He failed.

"Ernst, Julian," Leon said, greeting them each in turn.

Ernst, his eldest sibling, clapped his hands together again, restarting the magchines. As they whirred to life, the illyrium lights in the chandelier above them brightened, revealing a hawkish man with slicked back brown hair and calculating green eyes. His suit-robe, its color a match for his hair, was of a tight-fitting trim favored by young nobles.

Leon wanted to gag at Ernst's pristine getup. Where was the style in uniformity? Some part of the outfit should *scream*—should declare who its wearer was and why they were different from everyone else. It was why he'd worn gaudy cloaks to flag-brawl matches instead of armor and played the goompa horn when his classmates chose stringed instruments.

Their middle brother, Julian, was only slightly better. Layered sashes and silks cascaded from his shoulders, forming a robe of many parts that shimmered and flowed about him as he reached the floor. Leon gave him points for presentation but knew there was no soul in his wardrobe. Julian wore what he did out of a sense of vanity—to hide the slight gut he had no reason to be ashamed of.

Let's get this over with, Leon decided. He raised a hand to forestall whatever jibes or insults they were surely concocting behind their greasy grins. "Why did father send for me? I have my graduation exam tomorrow, and I can think of twenty better ways to get ready for it than wasting time here."

His words emerged through gritted teeth. The heady aroma of synth-oil hanging in the air, the too-dazzling glint of the chandelier crystals, and even the sound of his brothers' voices was too much for him. Each triggered memories in the recesses of his mind, phantoms Leon preferred stayed buried.

A hard bed, a plain sink, a locked door that only opened from the outside. Tasteless meals served on hard trays. Dark whelps on his skin from a rod he could *still* feel smashing against his legs and back.

They flooded in from all sides, threatening to drown Leon where he stood. *He* was responsible for his mother's death. *He* had to carry on her legacy. *He* had to become an engimage who could take her place at his father's side. If he didn't, he was more useless than the magchines that had failed to save her life.

The shivering rescued Leon. He jerked at the spectral touch of something slimy on his neck, half-spinning to look behind him as his father's whispers faded. Where had he felt that before?

"Brother?"

Leon faced Ernst, prepared for an outburst of mockery. It wasn't just father who blamed him for his mother's passing. The elder boys, who'd been four and six when he was born, had never forgiven Leon for taking away their sun.

"Are you alright, brother?" Ernst reached toward him, but Leon flinched away. His concern was a lie. A trick to get him to drop his guard, like it always was.

He stumbled into Julian's grasp. *Void!* Leon cursed inwardly. They'd take him out back, tie him to a tree, and—

"It's probably nerves," Julian suggested. Patting Leon's shoulder, he gave a little shove toward the hall in front of him. "Don't worry about who's watching the flag-brawl matches, Leon. Just fight hard and use that keen mind of yours to outwit your opponents. Like that light snare you set for Braena's Battlers last week. Brilliant!"

Julian chuckled and mimed a person caught in a net by clamping one fist overtop of the other. "You . . . you went to one of my matches?" Leon struggled to force the words out.

Ernst frowned. "We've been to *all* your matches. And your music recitals, tactics lectures, and every other event we could sneak away from the lab to see." His expression grew thoughtful, and he tapped a finger to his chin. "I've never heard of anxiety inducing memory loss, but perhaps some tests could—"

"No tests!" Leon insisted, waving his arms. *That* was more like the Ernst he remembered—ready to poke, prod, or dissect a 'problem' to discover its cause. In that regard, he was eerily similar to their father.

Julian's eyes lit up. "Hunger, then." Not waiting for a response, he strode down the brightly lit passageway, silks billowing around him like festival streamers. "In my experience, there is little a good meal can't fix, and we've prepared a grand one. Come along, come along!"

"Dinner?" Leon glanced at Ernst. "Father *never* hosts dinners. What's the occasion?"

A knowing smirk alighted on his eldest sibling's lips. "An early celebration, of sorts."

"For what?"

"Your graduation from the Academy! What? Did you think we wouldn't honor the occasion?"

Yes, Leon thought, a dumbfounded look on his face as he let Ernst guide him toward the dining hall. *That is* precisely *what I expected you to do.*

"And if . . . a drop of sakura jam . . . on a fresh menja slice doesn't ease your nerves . . . you can picture all the visiting dignitaries in their undergarments. Might make you . . . chuckle a bit to imagine old Metellus and Contus in their skivvies . . . but at least you won't be nervous anymore!"

Meat juices dribbled down Julian's chin as he alternated between giving Leon advice and tearing gobs from the moist chicken leg in his right hand. The way his middle brother attacked his meal was normal; his determination to ensure Leon was ready for his upcoming exam was not.

Wielding a fork and knife, Leon carved a much smaller slice from his own lemon-seasoned chicken, dabbed it in a crescent of mushroom gravy spread across the top of his plate, and brought it to his mouth. He chewed slowly. Every moment he was eating was a moment he didn't have to speak to these bizarre versions of his family members.

But are *they bizarre?* a part of him asked.

Julian and Ernst continued the conversation without him, predicting the nobles who'd attend the exam, which teams would win, and whether or not *this* would be the year Commandant Hardwick Iolus finally burst a blood vessel while screeching his speech and toppled from the stands. It sounded like the kind of nonsense banter a normal family would engage in. Had Leon simply imagined his father's scorn, his brothers' disgust, and the pain he'd suffered in this house?

The more he accepted the scene before him, the more the shivering along his neck and back receded. Only a small cold patch remained, pimpling the flesh beneath it.

Wood clattered on the tiled floor. Tapping his wine glass for silence, the man at the head of the long table pushed out of his chair and cleared his throat.

Leon didn't hear his opening lines. The mauve tunic, frilled neckpiece, and gold-laced suit coat the man wore belonged to his father. As did the thin pair of silver glasses perched atop his angular nose. There could be no mistaking his well-combed hair and beard—both silver like his spectacles and the delicate chains that dangled from them into one of his inner pockets.

This was his father, Dr. Archimas Redora Descar. But the beaming smile on his lips and the warmth he radiated toward Leon were completely foreign to him. The kind words he spoke, the joy in his tone . . . they *had* to belong to some other man. A stand-in, an imposter.

And if they didn't . . .

"I think I've named everyone present," Archimas said to the gathered ladies and gentlemen farther down the table. "But do speak up if I've missed anyone."

"When I polish off your delicious feast, you can mark me down as two!" shouted a stocky nobleman at the far end. He patted his belly for emphasis. "And you can count the wheelbarrow to cart me out as my third!"

Polite laughter filled the chamber. After a few seconds, Archimas held up a hand. "As much as Lord Khamerl enjoys the labors of my kitchen staff, this feast is not the real reason we are gathered this evening."

Archimas raised his wine glass, tilting it in Leon's direction. Red fluid sloshed around inside, its churning a mirror of his swirling, disoriented thoughts. "A man gets many opportunities to reinvent himself. For some, they discover themselves in their labors. For others, they find meaning in family, religion, or politics. I . . . "

His father paused, glancing toward the ceiling. Were those *tears* Leon saw welling behind his glasses? "I . . . nearly lost myself once. Anjalise, my darling wife, passed away twenty-one years ago. I was devastated. She was my core, my compass north, the first law in every theory I had ever conceived. I wanted to drown myself in my research, to shut everything else out until the pain . . . No, the pain could never disappear. Yet my work *could* have dulled it, if only just."

You made that choice! a distant part of Leon's mind cried. His eyes and ears told a different story. Archimas was not faking his grief. The clench of his jaw and the shaking of his shoulders spoke of a man barely restraining his sobs.

"Anjalise didn't depart this world in vain," Archimas continued, lowering his sparkling eyes. Fixing them on Leon. "She gave me the most precious gift an inventor can—a new creation, a new life. And once again, in the midst of my sorrow, I reinvented myself. I became a *true* father to my children, one of whom now has the chance to choose their future: Leonel Descar."

Leon froze. He'd never heard his father utter his name without scorn, derision, or at best, indifference. His heart began to race, and flecks of water dotted his vision. Snatching the carefully folded napkin from the table in front of him, Leon dabbed at his cheeks. *Sweat*, he told himself. *It's only sweat.*

Archimas smiled at him. "My youngest son will graduate from the Darmatian Military Academy tomorrow. From there, he will go on to serve our kingdom, defending its borders and keeping our people safe. Between his leadership and our airships, Darmatia will continue to be the crown jewel of Lozaria. A kingdom of reinvention. A kingdom of compassion. May wisdom ever light our way!"

"May wisdom ever light our way!" The party guests echoed. Glasses clinked, and wine flowed freely.

Leon didn't hear the following speeches, many of which were given in his honor. He didn't empty his glass, or the multitude of replacements servants continued to place before him. *My father . . . loves me?*

Slippery and difficult to grasp, the concept spun about Leon's head. A piece of him had always wanted his father's approval. Had craved it like a drunkard craves his next drink. And now that he had it, the memories—no, the *illusions*—of a darker past began to crumble to ash.

His dark bedroom cell disappeared.

The daily tests placed on his desk burned.

Bruises faded, turning from purple, to red, then blending into his flesh entirely.

A firm hand reached for him. Leon blinked, casting off the threads of his reverie. The toasts were over, and the guests were clustered in small groups as servants wheeled overflowing dessert carts throughout the room. Standing beside him was Archimas, his hand extended, bearded cheeks drawn back in a bright grin.

"Congratulations, Leon. I'm so, so very proud of you."

Tears streaming from his eyes, Leon stood, clenched his fist, and swung with all his might. The blow connected with his father's jaw, knocking him off his feet and onto the table. Plates shattered, half-filled dishes overturned, and wine and gravy mixed into a thick slurry that clung to Archimas' robes like blood.

When Archimas regained his senses, he propped himself up on an elbow and stared at Leon like he'd lost his mind. No, he'd *found* it. He didn't need that slimy feeling of wrongness to tell him this *thing* was not his father.

"Leon, what in oblivion are you—"

"You aren't my father." Leon gestured at Archimas, then at his brothers and the stunned nobility. "They aren't my brothers, and these aren't guests here to wish me well on the eve of my graduation. I am a tool to you. Nothing less, nothing more. And last time I checked, nobody celebrates when a wrench finishes tightening a batch of bolts."

The gasp on Archimas' lips died, morphing into a vile smirk. Shadows emerged beneath his eyes, under the chains of his glasses, and swelled in the creases of his robes. The silver of his hair darkened until it was but a shade lighter than pitch.

"I'll remember that," he sneered.

In an instant, Leon was writhing on the floor, his head an inferno of torment. It was as if a thousand fires had sprung up inside his skull, and he had no way to quench them. Distantly, the shadows above him receded, revealing a ceiling mural he could barely see through his tears.

It depicted black skies, a fractured crater, and three figures facing off in the middle of a circle of ebony pillars. One held a gleaming lance. Another, a crossbow. And on the horizon, almost directly behind the third, was a scar—a rip in the painting that seemed to suck in all the light around it.

The pain intensified. A pain that was somehow familiar, like it had been *branded* into Leon's flesh over months and years instead of mere seconds. Screams roared in the distance: his false brothers calling for a doctor. None would come. Though Leon didn't know how, that was a fact he knew with absolute certainty.

A blurry shape huddled over him, shrouding Leon in darkness. "Let go," Archimas cajoled. "Let go and enjoy the dream."

Leon's senses flickered, then failed entirely, hurling him back into the abyss of nothingness.

Part 2
What Lies Beneath

Chapter 14
A Thorny Subject

Hetrachia 13, 697 ABH
Nemare, Capital of the Sarconian Province of Darmatia

Emperor Sychon Artorios had to admit that Darmatians were the superior horticulturists. Pinching his fingers, he tore a lavender rose from its stem and brought it to his nose. Its fragrance was sweet yet strong, a honeyed scent bred into the buds over decades of magical engineering. If they'd put half as much effort into their military, it might be Steward Metellus strolling through the Nemare palace grounds this morning instead of him.

"For you, my rose," Sychon said, presenting the bud to Rittermarschal Auvrea Titania. She gingerly took the rose with her gauntlet and affixed it to her hair above her left ear. The flush of the petals paled in comparison to her dazzling curls, but it complemented her beauty nonetheless.

Auvrea's luscious lips curled into a slight frown. "An eglantine, my lord?"

"Is there a problem with it?"

"No, but . . . " She paused, eyebrows furrowed. "They were *her* favorite. The Third Consort's."

Sychon's heart clenched. He could almost *feel* the dagger entering his chest, tearing through muscle, and missing his core by a hair-thin margin. Despite the desert heat, he was suddenly cold. Cold as the clutch of death he'd nearly succumbed to that day.

And worst of all, he still didn't know why the blasted whore had done it.

"*Were*," Sychon growled. "There *is* no Third Consort, and there never was."

He lashed out, grabbed a cluster of eglantine stems, and ripped them from the bush. Shredded petals floated to the limestone walkway, followed shortly by their thorn-encrusted stalks and scarlet drops of blood.

"Besides," Sychon continued, tugging a handkerchief from the pocket of his red and gold tunic and wrapping it around his bleeding

179

hand. "They suit you far better."

Smiling, Titania gave a short bow, crimson cape fluttering behind her.

They walked in silence for a time, meandering up and down the garden rows without any clear destination in mind. Sychon admired the groundskeeper's penchant for order. Flowering shrubberies closed about them on the paths, often forming tight canopies to blot out the sun and creating sheltered grottos of greenery. Where the paths merged, the foliage gave way to meticulously pruned beds of roses, with bell-shaped neverfades and saffron bloodlilies hiding their roots like a dress hides a woman's legs.

The man's eye for topiary was also exquisite. Four of the Veneer surrounded a nearby fountain, their raised arms and halo-ringed heads facing toward it. Sychon couldn't tell how he'd made the shrubs so lifelike. Wires? A hidden talisman that altered the bushes' weight? Darmatian or not, the groundskeeper would be returning with him to Sarconia.

Boots clicked on the stone behind him—two clops as the man halted, and a third, sharper click as his heels rammed together. "Major Baumler, reporting with yesterday's casualty numbers as requested, Your Excellency."

"Read it," Auvrea ordered.

Sychon sighed. Duty, like defecation, could only be delayed for so long before things got messy.

He turned and sat on the broad, curved lip of the bubbling fountain. Auvrea was governor of Darmatia. She would command, he would listen, and if the Emperor's will was needed, he would interject.

Baumler coughed into his gloved hand, adjusted his square spectacles, and pulled a wad of papers from a briefcase tucked under his left arm. His voice was as thin and reedy as his frame. "The cultists inflicted another sixty-seven casualties last night, sixty-three of which were fatal. One group of four guardsmen was able to escape with minor stab wounds and lacerations. Our dead include fifty-two enlisted and eleven officers, all of captain rank or lower."

"And their losses?" Auvrea's tone was cold.

"Unconfirmed. We haven't recovered any corpses in two days, not since one insurgent was found crushed beneath Gefreiter Tremon . . ."—Baumler squinted at his notes—" . . . No family name on file."

"What excuse does General Novarre have for me today?"

180

Papers rustled as Baumler flipped through the stack. "He requests, and I quote, *'Take my voided kiddy gloves off and let me burn them from their holes.'* I've taken the liberty of translating on page six. Essentially, they know the terrain better, locals are giving them refuge, and temples are currently off limits to our forces.

"Plus"—Baumler wrinkled his mousy little nose—"tunnels through a place called 'Sewertown' are allowing them to evade our patrols at will."

The acrid tang of char filled the air. With a puff of smoke, the rosebud slipped from Auvrea's hair to burst into hundreds of bright embers. An instant later, the Veneer sculpture to her left likewise caught fire, shrub-carved robes, wings, and crown melting beneath the intense flames. Artyr the Sagacious, Veneer of the Sylph, collapsed in a rush of sparks and ash.

Scarlet curls flaring, Auvrea laughed. "He wants to be unchained, does he? Very well." Her cloak billowed as she turned to Sychon. Infernal eyes, red like blood, bored into his own without a shred of fear or indecision.

His hunger for her surged like magma through his veins. Alight with fire and dressed in gleaming silver armor, or naked on his bed, Auvrea was perfection. Beauty, power, and passion personified. Sychon cupped his chin in his hand and favored her with a wicked grin.

"What do you desire, Rittermarschal?"

"The Imperial Accords on Mysticism. Extend their effect to Darmatia immediately."

A wise request, Sychon thought, smiling. The Accords were one of the few laws enacted by his grandfather, Synard, that he agreed with. Under threat of death, they outlawed all forms of Creator worship, spirituality, or religion within the Empire's borders. Their citizens needed no master—no god—but him.

And now that Darmatia was an Imperial province . . .

"Granted."

Sychon unbuttoned the top clasp of his tunic, reached inside, and pulled out a tightly strung velvet bag that hung about his neck. It contained neither diamonds, nor rubies, nor highly concentrated illyrium. Rather, what he dumped onto his palm was a simple signet ring—one bearing more power than any mage in existence.

With a flick of his wrist, Sychon tossed it to Auvrea. "Draft the documents and affix my seal upon them. If closing their temples isn't enough, feel free to institute martial law. Imprison those who resist.

Establish a registrar of mages, confiscate their firearms and swords, and collect all the illyrium not being used to power Nemare. We will root out this rot infesting my city by driving the rebels into the open and crushing them once and for all."

Auvrea's grin widened as he loosened her restraints with every additional edict. The claws of her gauntlets twitched in anticipation, and sparks danced before her eyes. "Your will be done, my liege."

Bowing, she motioned for Baumler to follow her, then stopped at the archway leading from the secluded fountain patio. "I have one final request."

Sychon leaned back, draping one of his hands in the rippling water. This was such a refreshing place. So different from the firestorm Auvrea would soon release outside the palace walls.

"Anything," Sychon pledged.

"Let me unleash my Ritter troops on the city."

Warm rays of yellow sunlight bathed Sychon as he lay on a bed of satin cushions beside the gurgling fountain. His servants had brought them outside, arranged them in the shade of a broad-leafed spear-palm, and left him to his afternoon's repose. He couldn't recall the last time he'd rested as well in his Sarconia estate.

Consorts, ministers, children—someone always needed something there. Sign this, fetch that expensive portrait, come to my violin recital. The daily grind was never-ending. But here, with Auvrea and Zaratus to handle day-to-day military affairs, Sychon could finally take a moment to *enjoy* being emperor.

Yawning, he rolled over and sank deeper into the cushions while drinking in the wafting aromas of the garden. Honey, mint, chamomile, and the faintest whiff of . . . rot? Sychon blinked, bleary eyes unfocused. The sun was directly overhead, smirking down at him. But how could it? The dangling spear-palm fronds should completely shade him from the afternoon heat.

"Pleasant dreams?" the sun asked.

Sychon bolted awake, scrambling backward against the prickly trunk of the spear-palm. Pillows scattered haphazardly in his haste. *"You!"* he spat the word like a curse, heart thudding in his chest like the pistons of an airship engine.

"Me?" the youth said, his reply a mocking question. He straightened up, flicked his sandy-blond hair from his eyes, and cocked his head to the side. "If I'm not me, can I be you? Or perhaps neither of us are ourselves, in which case," he strode to the nearby sculpture of Sariel the Forthright and tapped its leaf-covered chest, "should we be them instead?"

The riddling, singsong words did not match the face that spoke them. Blue eyes, princely fair features, and the close-cut tunic and shoulder sash of a young Darmatian noble adorned the outside—the vessel. Inside the flask, beneath the mask, lay something altogether more sinister.

"Sarcon." Sychon growled the name, trying to hide the trembling of his fingers and legs. "What business do you have with me?" Wincing at the jab of the spear-palm's bark, he grabbed the trunk and rose to his feet. Dirt stains smeared the rear of his britches, evidence of his terrified retreat.

Sarcon ignored him, scrutinizing Sariel's chiseled jaw, majestic wings, and the long wooden lance gripped in his gnarled hands. "I have it on good authority that their thrones are empty. We could traipse over to their heavenly halls, choose the best seats, and do the work they were too afraid to complete. What do you say?"

How dare *he ignore me,* Sychon fumed. *Me! The most powerful man on the continent.* He glanced around the patio. Two guards stood by the fountain, another two by the entrance path. Their gauntlets clanged to their cuirasses in salute, but their eyes drifted elsewhere, avoiding his gaze. They had let Sarcon through unopposed.

Which meant they feared the resurrected founder of Sarconia more than him. Sychon's scowl deepened. He closed the gap with Sarcon, waving off the salute of a horrifically scarred officer who stood nearby. Harn, Hert, Hale. The name of Sarcon's insignificant lackey didn't matter to him.

At least Sychon still towered over the Descar boy, Archimas' son and Sarcon's current host. Amused blue eyes twinkled up at him, everything they saw just another game to the centuries-old immortal.

"I can send you back to your prison, warlock. It would be simple now that I own Darmatia."

"And who gave you that victory?"

Sychon saw the scene clearly. An ebony serpent, black and white in equal measures, lashed out across the battlefield, slicing through Darmatian warships and swatting them from the sky like insects. Lost Magic, a taboo spell banned by all the nations. The power Sarcon had displayed shocked Sychon to his core. He'd written it off as a necessary evil at the time, but now …

"You promised me Elysium when we conquered the Kingdom," he countered, pointing at the fountain's peak. A marble obelisk rested there, the arms and weapons of three Veneer—the fourth reduced to charcoal—reaching toward it. The shard, dark as a moonless night, was an artist's replica of the legendary wish-granting stone.

A stone that wasn't supposed to exist. "Where is it?"

"Precisely where I told you: Har'muth." Sarcon shook his head. "Really, Sychon, it's poor form to forget the things people tell you."

The veins in Sychon's forehead began to throb. He'd almost forgotten how pleasant the sorcerer's absence over the past few days had been. "And have you made any progress *retrieving* it? Our deal was—"

"Yes, yes. One shard for one body. My flesh is firmly trapped within the Elysium, so I am every bit as invested in its retrieval as you are."

"Then *show it.*"

Sychon immediately regretted his words.

The light in the garden *died*, shades of pitch creeping from the flowerbeds, dribbling, dripping down the shrubs and trees. Frost dappled the fountain, Sychon's breath misting as the desert heat fled like a whipped hound. His legs quivered, and he staggered backward, one palm raised to protect himself.

It would do him no good. Not against the *monster* glaring into his soul.

Ooze bubbled within the boy's eyes, corrupting blue into purple, then into void-touched black. Shadows slid from beneath the hem of his collar and twisted beneath his nose, ears, and chin. The putrid taint of decay grew overpowering, slithering down Sychon's throat and nostrils despite his best efforts to hold his breath.

"I," the corpse-man said, "am doing my best, given that I have a partner who wishes to handicap me at every turn. I have been denied the vapid Darmatian masses from which I would draw energy. I have been denied access to the files that would aid my research. I am beginning to think—Sychon Artorios, emperor of *mortal* men—that I made an agreement with the wrong man. A weak ruler no more willing to make difficult decisions than my misguided brothers were."

Sarcon raised a hand all but consumed by shadow. "Was I wrong?"

Enough! Sychon raged inwardly. *I will* not *be intimidated!*

Snarling, Sychon thrust his hand forward and clasped Sarcon's.

As soon as he did, the darkness evaporated, disappearing like morning mist beneath the sun's strong rays. Only the lopsided grin of the Descar boy stared back at him. "Good," Sarcon said. "Now, look at that letter in your hands."

When his arm withdrew, Sychon was surprised to find a folded piece of cepyrus paper in his palm. The grain was thick, of far higher quality than what a typical printer produced. He unfolded it, glancing first at the gold seven-pointed star painted on the back, then reading the neatly scribed note on the front. If not for the dried blood staining a third of the document, Sychon would've thought it an ordinary letter.

We, the Sect of Sariel, find the invasion of Darmatia by the Sarconian Empire to be in violation of the accord between the sentient races of Lozaria and the Creator. With their senseless destruction of fellow mortals, they spit in the face of the peace sought by the Veneer. With their desecration of Sariel's holy temple, they blaspheme against the very hands that wrought them. But no more! Though we break our sacred vows, we will become the blades of Sariel and do what he and the justice-loving Veneer cannot. As his divinely golden hair turned black to erase the sins of Terrans, so shall we tear down this vile empire and—

"I think I've read enough," Sychon announced. He began to crumple the paper up, then thought better of it and gestured for one of the guards to take it. "How did you get this?" he asked. "This should have gone to Major Baumler's office."

Sarcon chuckled. "Don't be such a wrench in the oil, or whatever it is you say these days. Enjoy the irony. How often do faith-blind zealots turn their backs on their most sacred teachings? Show me a man who won't debase himself for his ideals, and I'll show you a hypocrite."

"And your point?"

The sorcerer spun in a circle, sash twirling, arms raised to the blue sky above. The view was clear except for one heavy cruiser, the *Remelus*, circling the slums beyond the market quarter. "They've betrayed your trust. You extended the hand of benevolent rule, and instead of taking it, they cut off a finger. So, give them to me." A hint of the abyss returned to Sarcon's eyes. "Let me use them in my blood ritual."

"The cultists? That can be arranged, but—"

"*All* of them," Sarcon interrupted, tone hungry. "As I've said before, I cannot breach the Eliade defenses at Har'muth without an *army's* worth of men'ar. It is a spiritual void, dead in every sense of the word. The only magic we can use is what we bring with us."

Sychon cared little for the lives of Darmatians—or the lives of his *own* citizens, nobles, and soldiers beyond their usefulness toward his vision of Lozarian peace. But an empire without subjects was absurd. Power, without someone to exercise it on, was as valuable as ash.

"And as *I've* said before," Sychon turned, striding toward the Elysium-topped fountain, "you'll have to find another way. You may have the cultists and any other dissidents or rebels we capture. But the city will be preserved."

Sarcon's eyes narrowed. He began to pace, stopping briefly in front of each of the Veneer before circling back to Sariel. After running a hand along the length of the god's lance, he gazed at the distant palace dome—its bronze plates glimmering in the late-afternoon sun—and sighed.

"There is another way."

Finally! Sychon thought. "Go on."

"Weather patterns," Sarcon said, waving at a cluster of wisp-thin desert clouds passing over the city. "If we time our attack with the seasonal Kheofri storms gusting down from the Great Divide, we might be able to harness enough of their violent energy to keep your airships aloft within Har'muth. My former Eliade jailers will be no match for a modern aerial bombardment."

"But . . . ?" Sychon prompted.

He was rewarded with a mocking bow, one of Sarcon's hands plastered to his undead heart, the other swept off to the side. "The student learns, and the master applauds."

How Sychon wished he could snap the warlock's neck and be done with him. Clenching his fists to contain his rage, he replied, "*Your* master wants to know what catch lies behind your scheme."

Sarcon rose from his bow. "I require an esoteric text by Scharb Cimbri, the renowned astrologist who was executed by your ancestors for telling them the world was round. Good on them, by the way. Can't have peasants thinking they won't fall into the Void if they go too far past your borders."

Off to the side, Sarcon's scarred attendant twitched as if stung. Was he reacting to some lie, some deceit of his master's? Or was it merely a jab from one of the striped hornstings floating about the garden?

No matter.

"Is it in the Darmatian archives?" Sychon prepared to summon a guard to guide the sorcerer on his way. This tedious discussion was *finally* at an end.

"Of course not," Sarcon replied, picking up a gold embroidered pillow with silk tassels hanging from each corner. "He wrote it by hand in the 2nd century, and only one copy exists in the Sarconia National Archives. Since shipping it here would surely destroy the priceless tome . . . "

Up launched the pillow. Stunned, Sychon followed its trajectory through the air. It arced above the tall hedges, spun end over end as it fell, and—

Stopped, suspended by an invisible force. Sarcon grinned and made a slashing gesture. Unseen blades tore through the cushion, rending it from all sides. Feathers, strips of purple fabric, and strands of silk flew in all directions.

" . . . I'll need to travel to your capital to transcribe the information directly."

As the fragments slowed and drifted toward the ground, Sarcon remained fixated on their paths, watching little gusts change their course with childlike wonder. Sychon didn't understand the man. Couldn't *begin* to understand the man.

But he didn't need to know his heart to use his mind.

"I need you here. Instead," Sychon glanced at the 2nd lieutenant with the x-shaped scar disfiguring his face, "we'll send your aide."

That scar was a hideous deformity. Beginning above his eyebrows, the old wound crossed atop his badly smashed nose and ended near the corners of his lips. Sychon had known soldiers who'd died from lesser injuries.

Unexpectedly, Sarcon smiled. "Very well. But I imagine a junior officer will have trouble navigating the bureaucracy you've established. Why not promote him, say . . . two grades? And send him with your seal to smooth his way?"

There it was again. That twinkle in the mage's eye, that smirk that knew your thoughts before they were even the untapped seed of an idea. Sychon always found himself wondering who was manipulating whom.

"Agreed. Hart—"

"*Hans* Ulrich."

"Hans Ulrich is henceforth a captain in the Sarconian army, with all the privileges that rank affords. His first assignment is to collect your research materials from the capital while under supervision by an escort of my choosing. Is that satisfactory?"

Sarcon nodded. Captain Hans Ulrich's jaw dropped, and he fell to one knee on the hard limestone path, right arm glued to his chest in salute. And Sychon . . . he smiled.

He was still emperor, with all the power that entailed, including the power to give men the world—for a price. Sarcon himself may be unassailable, but his weakness was plain to see:

Young, naive Hans Ulrich. The man who would be his spy.

Chapter 15

A Higher Power

Jenuvant 26, 688 ABH,
Sewertown, Beneath the Royal Capital of Nemare

"Run!" Vallen screamed as he sprinted down the uneven Sewertown street. He skipped from one pile of shattered slate to another, narrowly avoiding tripping on jutting debris with every step he took.

Pockey slowly rose from an overturned crate on the next corner—little more than a crumbling storefront where someone had nailed up a mocking street sign in faded red lettering. It read "*Bleeding Void, This Way,*" "*Bugger All, That Way.*" The words didn't surprise Vallen, just that someone knew how to read and write down here. *He* had only recently learned, and only because Elaine had insisted on teaching him.

Haggard face twisted in confusion, Pockey held up a mud-smeared finger. Vallen didn't let him speak. Explaining the situation to the delirium-addled pickpocket would take more time than they had right now. He grabbed Pockey's wrist and pulled until the boy broke into an awkward, shambling run behind him.

"What's happening, Kit?" Pockey gasped as they turned onto the neighboring street. "Did you get the earrings?"

"Vallen . . . Amulet," Vallen corrected, boots pounding in sync with the thundering of his heart. Blood roared in his ears as he tugged in breath after breath of foul, refuse-tainted air. "Yes . . . Almost caught . . . No-pikes in pursuit."

"The *Gutter*pikes?"

"*No*-pikes," Vallen insisted with a wheeze.

As if to emphasize his point, a crossbow bolt whistled past and buried itself in the exposed axle of a derelict cart abandoned on the roadside. Two more followed, one glancing off a worm-eaten barrel of . . . mush, and the other plunging into a mound of rotting offal with a sickening *plop*. Angry rot-flies scattered in all directions.

Pockey glanced over his shoulder. "They're after us, Kit!"

Thanks for stating the obvious, Vallen thought. He looked back for a split second, gauging the distance between them and their pursuers.

There were four of them: three slate-faced Terrans and a green-scaled Moravi. Or was it mold? The lizard people tended to have difficulty keeping their scales clean in the oppressive humidity of the sewers.

Twang! Vallen discarded his musings when a third crudely fletched bolt launched from the handheld crossbow in the Moravi's left claw and missed Pockey's ribs by less than a handspan.

"Turn right!" he shouted, pointing at an alley. They skidded onto the shaded path, bouncing off a stack of slimy scrap metal to maintain their momentum. Vallen didn't want to consider *how* it had gotten coated in ooze, but a thin yellow stain traveled up the wall to a second-story window.

Slashed open cans, broken glass, and all manner of decaying food and excrement squished beneath their flying feet. If he wasn't used to the putrid stench, it would have made him gag. Two skeletal urchins, their skin tight across hollow cheeks, clutched dripping clumps of brown to their mouths and skittered beneath a lean-to formed from tattered blankets. They bared their teeth at Vallen and Pockey as they passed.

Vallen knew that look, the look of someone so hungry they'd chance disease for a morsel of food, even if it was rotten or maggot ridden. Sometimes the maggots were a hidden blessing—an extra bite in a scrap of bread.

If I don't get this amulet to Bohomaz, Vallen thought, feeling the trinket bouncing inside his vest pocket, *it won't be long before I'm in the same boat.*

A terrified scream echoed down the alley after them. "Out'ta da way, brats! We ain't got time ta deal with scum-crawlers right now." Iron clanged on the stones, and the first scream stilled, replaced by a second, far more plaintive wail. "I told'ya ta *move!* Kick the body aside and keep after 'em, Faerk."

Pockey's eyes went wide. He tried to turn around, but Vallen kept tugging him toward the bright slit of the street in front of them. "It's too late," he said, trying to convince himself as much as Pockey. "We have to keep going or we'll join them."

A line of fire raked along Vallen's left calf, making him gasp. He'd been nicked by a bolt, but not badly enough to down him. Wincing with every step, Vallen emerged on the next street.

He waved for Pockey to go on. "I'm limping. Get across the river . . . and have Singe cover my crossing."

"That spark-nut doesn't care a lick about you," Pockey said, casting concerned glances at the trickle of blood dribbling down Vallen's boot and onto the ground. "He'll just leave you to—"

Vallen interrupted him. "He will. I . . . have insurance." He patted the round bulge of the whisperwind amulet poking through his vest. Its dull green glow pulsed beneath the thin fabric.

A push sent Pockey into a stumbling run, and Vallen raced after him with a pained grimace, crimson droplets staining his wake. The stone street expired in the near distance, falling away into a long, dark pit that stretched in either direction between untidy rows of buildings. It wasn't a chasm leading to the Afterplane, nor was it a river any surfacer would recognize. And the bridge fording it was little more than a slapdash construction of old boards and prayers.

On the other side, a teenager slouched against a listing tenement painted in washed-out and peeling red paint. His close-cropped black hair clung to his scalp like bristles on a fancy surfacer brush, and his sloped shoulders and broad chest bulged against the buttons of his tan tunic. A clumsily stitched blue patch on his breast identified him as one of the lieutenants in Bohomaz's crew.

Vallen didn't like Singe, and Singe sure as oblivion didn't like him. They butted heads over everything, from heist plans to favorite foods, to abstract things like philosophy. Singe was always fight first, ask questions later. Vallen preferred to carefully sound out an enemy and avoid combat at all costs. But right now, he was glad to see the fire mage, explosive temper and all.

Twenty paces ahead of him, Pockey reached the rickety 'bridge' and began creeping across at a crouch. The wood shuddered beneath him but held firm. Singe uncrossed his legs and left the building's shadow, a wicked smile spreading across his face. Flickering balls of flame gushed from his raised palms.

The sadist is rearing to go, Vallen thought, pushing on through his spiking pain. He chanced another glance back. The No-pikes barreled from the alley, their gazes furious as they cast about to find the young thieves. One saw the trail of blood, then caught sight of Vallen at its end. A wild crossbow shot immediately flew at him as they charged down the street.

Ten paces to the bridge; twenty between him and a rusty blade. At the bridge's far end, Pockey gathered himself and leapt the final couple meters to sprawl at Singe's feet. Behind him, the beams bucked wildly but held firm.

Five paces. A nasty gleam popped into Singe's eyes, and he knelt beside the planks with a fire-shrouded hand outstretched.

"Don't!" Vallen and Pockey screamed as one.

A bolt fletched with spotted sea-pigeon feathers ripped at Vallen's hair and collar as it missed his neck and plunged into the sewer channel. Singe stared at where the arrow was still sinking into the thick brown sludge, then at Vallen.

"Sorry to do it, Kit, but I gotta keep them from getting the amulet back. Boss' orders."

One pace. Vallen could hear hard leather boots striking the stones behind him. Could hear the gruff panting of brigands with swords drawn back, ready to cleave him in two.

"*I* have the amulet," Vallen roared.

Singe's hand jerked to a stop a finger's length from setting the bridge ablaze. As relief blossomed in Vallen's chest, he sprinted onto the wobbling boards. There was no time to think; no time to plan out his steps. His left calf screamed as it nearly buckled under him. Not looking at the slowly drifting mire below, Vallen sprang onto his other leg and kept going.

To fall in the middle was death. The stagnant, pestilent filth was like a desert swiftsand pool. It would drag him under, flood his nostrils and mouth, and suffocate the breath from his lungs. And if Vallen somehow escaped its embrace, the slightest taste would leave him dead from disease in days.

The boards shook violently, upsetting Vallen's balance and leaving him flailing his arms. "I've got ya, ya bloody slecher!" came a hoarse shout at his back.

One of the No-pikes was on the bridge with him. Vallen threw caution to the stench-ridden wind, bent as far as his injured calf would allow, and launched himself for the far ledge with extended arms.

The breath rushed from his lungs when he struck the moldering channel wall. Fragments of stone tumbled into the sewage, and Vallen started to slip. The fingers of his right hand caught on the lip, but his left missed, leaving his body dangling. His toes went cold and damp, followed by his feet as strength fled his straining digits. Vallen was going to die in a Sewertown drain, just like he'd always known he would.

"We've got you!" Pockey yelled.

Two hands—one rough and uncaring, the other small and determined—gripped his shoulders and heaved him onto the hard stones of the opposite bank. "You better not have screwed this up," Singe growled. "If they kill us, I'll cook you alive."

A fit of coughing kept Vallen from pointing out the obvious: *If they kill us, you won't be alive to kill us again, you dolt.* His ribs were bruised, but he still propped himself on one elbow to watch Singe work.

Two No-pike brigands were on the bridge now, one at the middle, the other just beginning to test his footing. Singe called out to the nearest. "How fast do you think you are?"

The man's mask of fury briefly slipped, his bushy eyebrows rising in confusion. "Whad'dya mean, *fast*?"

Singe smiled as the flames in his palms burst back into existence. Not waiting for a response, he knelt, brought his fires together, and thrust the roiling blaze against the flimsy boards. Coated in greasy juices and globs of sewer slime, they burned like paper in a furnace, greedy flames flashing from one end to the other in seconds.

The brigands tried to flee. The farthest made it, tumbling across the cobbles with embers smoking on his leather jerkin. His friend was not so lucky.

Flames caught him before he could fully process what was happening, clawing up his pants, scratching at the long sleeves of his shirt. Screaming, he dropped his sword, then followed after it an instant later as his frenzied spasms pitched him head-first off the bridge. The grime swiftly swallowed his shrieks.

"Who's next?" Singe asked, sneering at the surviving Terrans and Moravi on the 'river's' opposite side.

The Moravi bared his fangs. Up came his crossbow, a bolt nocked and ready on its drawstring. His curved claw depressed the modified trigger and sent the jagged dart spiraling at Singe's head.

Singe raised a hand and shouted, "Spi'ferat!" Fire lanced from his fingers and incinerated the bolt, leaving only char behind. The Moravi reloaded but didn't bother firing again. His slotted eyes and flicking tongue remained focused on Singe.

"Zu vin zis one, fleshling." The lizard turned and waggled its spine-ridged tail at them—their race's equivalent of the Terran middle finger. "Enjoy itz vhile zu can. Ve'll be backz zu get vat's ourz zery zoon."

For once, Singe didn't rise to the taunt. Still smirking, he waved at the scorched corpse and broken planks disappearing into the rotten muck.

Vallen didn't resist as Pockey knelt and draped an arm over his shoulder. "You gonna be alright, buddy?" the pickpocket asked.

"Doesn't matter," Singe answered for Vallen. He cast a wave of crackling flame across the gap, which sent the No-pikes scurrying away while screaming curses. "We've got the amulet, *I* trounced the Gutterpikes, and Vagley isn't going to stick our heads on the pier beside the Grand Runoff. I'd say some dead weight taking a hit for the team is a mighty fair trade."

"Now ... " Singe stooped and made a 'give me' gesture in front of Vallen's face with his fingers. "The amulet. It's safer with me, so *I'll* give it to Bohomaz."

The iron edge to his voice left no doubt what the alternative was. Pockey started to protest, but Vallen squeezed his arm to keep him quiet. Singe was Sewertown in Terran skin. If they didn't do as he said, he'd torch their bodies, take the amulet, and dump what was left alongside the sinking brigand.

Swallowing his rage, Vallen undid his vest, reached into an inside pocket, and withdrew the amulet. Singe snatched it from his grip as soon as he held it out. "Pleasure doing business with you, Kit." Humming a raunchy tune, Singe sauntered away while spinning the amulet by its chain.

"And after all we went through to get it ... " Pockey moaned.

"Bohomaz will know the truth," Vallen assured him. "And Singe will get what's coming to him."

Even if I have to do it myself, he finished silently.

Two diversionary cutbacks, a trip through the neighboring slum, and an hour later, the exhausted boys pushed open the door to the *Safe Haven* pawnshop. The warped wood swung inward with a rusty squeak and jangled a tiny brass bell above to announce their arrival.

Its obnoxious ringing not only notified Jomori—the Moravi proprietor—of arriving customers, but also warned crewmates in the back rooms of potential intruders. A length of string ran from the bell along the shop wall and through a hole in the boards at the back where it connected to a second bell.

Jomori didn't glance up at their entrance. The aged Moravi was staring at the inner door leading to their hideout, his silver back spines quivering where they poked through his specially tailored doublet. Instead of organizing his wares, he stood on two legs behind the low counter, absently gouging furrows in its surface with a claw.

"Uncle Jomori?" Vallen said softly.

The lizard's head twitched, ear holes swinging toward Vallen and Pockey. One whitening eye-slit fell on them, then the other. His claw scraping halted, and the sweeping noise coming from behind the counter—his nervous tail swiping against the rows of shelves at his back—stilled.

"Zu are homez late, zung Zallen," Jomori wheezed, husky voice like the hiss of a nest of snakes. He brought a claw up to stroke his rubbery chin spikes, which everyone assumed was a beard. "Zinge returned halfz a clock-turnz ago. Vere haz zu been?"

Vallen shot Pockey a sideways glare, but the scrawny boy just shrugged in reply. If their gatekeeper could remember his new name after hearing it *once*, his best friend had no excuse to keep forgetting it.

"We were following *protocol*," Vallen emphasized. Not only was Singe an arse, he was also a bloody idiot who didn't obey the rules that kept their hideout hidden. Heading straight for the *Safe Haven* after a job was taboo.

Nodding sagely, Jomori picked up a draconic statue from a counter display and began cleaning it with an oily rag. His attention was elsewhere.

"What's got you shaking in your scales?" Pockey asked.

Asking a Moravi such a question was a tad insensitive, but Jomori didn't take offense. He blinked twice and jerked a claw at the ceiling. "A *zurfacer* guest." His scales bristled as he breathed the term. "An not juz dat, zung Zallen. Zey zeem zu be lookingz fer *zu*."

Vallen kept his surprise from his face. Someone from Nemare was here? And they came to see *him* of all people? He racked his brain, trying to figure out which bishop, bureaucrat, or noble he'd ticked off enough to track him into this subterranean cesspit. Surfacers, even the poorest among them, avoided Sewertown like the plague—which it kind of was.

Who in oblivion would be mad enough to follow me here? Vallen wondered.

He pulled a tin geldar from a pocket and slid it across the counter to Jomori, who took it while bowing his spiky head. Unless you intended to betray someone, Sewertown denizens always paid their debts, even ones as simple as the warning he'd been given.

"Thanks for the heads up, Uncle."

With Pockey in tow, Vallen undid the hideout's latch, opened it just wide enough for them to slip by, and closed and locked the bolt behind them. He turned toward Bohomaz's 'audience chamber'—a slightly raised platform centered around a wooden throne large enough to hold the Vladisvar's bulk. Excitement and dread filled Vallen in equal measures at the prospect of meeting his mystery guest.

He didn't make it far.

"Big bro Kit's back!"

"He goes by Vallen now, sludge for brains."

"Don't call him that. It's mean!"

The 'chore crew' swamped them. A dozen tiny hands from an equal number of small, grimy bodies grasped at Vallen and Pockey, childish exuberance radiating from their squealing voices and squirming fingers. One boy of no more than four tried to climb up Vallen's legs and onto his shoulders. Another two grabbed Pockey's arms and began trying to pull him down to their level.

All three had to be gently shaken off, but not without a sharp twinge of pain from Vallen's wounded calf. He'd need to treat it soon or risk infection.

Vallen waded through the children, returning their made-up handshakes, patting shoulders and heads. These were those too small to steal, pickpocket, or scout out marks to earn their keep. Six namedays or younger, they were treated as an investment by the crafty Bohomaz. In exchange for food and water, they scrubbed the floors, carried wooden utensils at mealtimes, and the oldest helped with laundry or dishes. Hence their collective nickname, the 'chore crew.'

Vallen thought it was a good deal for kids who would otherwise starve in a nameless gutter. Bohomaz might not be a saint, but he was a far better taskmaster than the other sleazy voidspawn who could have gobbled them up. Some called him a pervert for taking in so many children, but Bohomaz would simply smile at their shortsightedness. No one noticed children, making them the perfect thieves.

"Was the mission a success?" a girl wearing a baggy burlap smock asked.

"Of course the mission was a success!" Vallen answered with a grin, gathering a dark-skinned Terran toddler and pinkish Sylph girl in his arms. They adored and admired the older kids. He wouldn't take out his frustrations on them, no matter how horribly the end of their mission had gone.

Someone started tugging at the back of his vest. Without turning, Vallen grabbed the miniature offender who was starting to scale his rear and hauled him around to the front. "Where do you think you're going, Jaston?"

Having been denied its climbing handhold, one of the tyke's fingers found solace in his dripping nostril. "Up," Jaston said as if that explained everything.

197

"Up where?"

The finger withdrew and jabbed a gooey booger at Vallen. "Up Mt. Vallen."

Vallen held Jaston at arm's length to keep the slime from hitting *his* nose. "And where did this newfound fascination with climbing come from?" The booger jerked to the right, in the direction of Bohomaz's dais. Meal tables were pushed to the sides of the broad chamber so the floor could be cleaned, leaving a straight shot between Vallen and the diminutive figure standing near the throne.

He caught sight of glistening brown hair, sky blue eyes, and a bright yellow sundress at the same time the answer tumbled from Jaston's lips. "Her. Big sis Elaine. She's been telling us stories about places she's been on the surface."

Jaston dropped from Vallen's slack grip and scampered away with his goo-tipped finger safely tucked inside his mouth. He should've known. Only Elaine was naïve enough to risk coming to Sewertown, foolish enough to dress like a noble, and somehow still clever or lucky enough to reach the *Safe Haven.*

Questions and accusations formed in Vallen's thoughts, but not a single one could force its way from his throat. *Why are you here? Why did you come alone? Where's Reesa? How in the Void did you find me?*

A booming cackle came from the hulking Vladisvar reclining on the throne behind Elaine. "Hohoho! Felinx got your tongue, Vallen? You don't know how long I've waited to see that flabbergasted look on your stoic face. Certainly makes letting the little one in worth it."

Bohomaz's laugh matched his frame. Built of fading muscles, leathery gray skin, and crowned with two jagged horns, the Vladisvar nearly touched the ceiling and dwarfed the chair that barely constrained his bulk. Runes and sigils were tattooed across almost every open space on his body, which was bare except for a kilt the size of a bedsheet and steel plates grafted directly onto the flesh of his shoulders, back, and chest. Those symbols, along with the host of scars marring him from head to toe, told his story—a history of long-ago triumphs from when the crime lord was a proud, noble warrior.

And the weapon that forged Bohomaz's legacy? Vallen's gaze shifted from Elaine to the vicious, four-clawed gauntlet welded to the stump of the Vladisvar's left arm. Calm as the giant was these days, Vallen didn't want the girl who held his heart *anywhere* near an instrument of brutal murder. Or Sewertown in general.

"Who's she?" Pockey asked, children still hanging from his arms and legs.

Vallen didn't answer. Elaine was all he could see. Leaving the forest of kids, he walked toward the platform in a daze. "Elaine," he said, trying to find the right words. "Why are you here?"

She'd been smiling since Vallen saw her, but her lips bent into a frown when he spoke. "Why am *I* here?" Elaine held a pale hand to her breast. "I'm here to find *you*! You're four hours late to the reading lesson we had scheduled today."

Lesson? It took Vallen a moment to process what she meant. *Oh,* he realized, sweat beading on his forehead. *That lesson.* They'd made a deal, one which he'd forgotten during the pressure of the Vagley mission. Vallen would visit Elaine on the surface every week, and she would teach him how to read and write.

He'd been more than happy to accept the arrangement. Something about Elaine breathed life into him. Her cheerfulness, energy, and innocence were such a massive departure from all that Vallen had known. And unlike every surfacer he had known, she seemed to *care* about him. That she had given him a *real* name proved that to him.

We only agreed to expand our skillset, a tiny, cynical part of his mind insisted. *So we can understand the ledgers and notes of the surfacers we rob. It wasn't for her.*

Elaine started tapping her foot, gleaming black shoes starkly contrasting with the faded, splintered boards of the platform she stood on. Immaculate white socks stretched over her knees, ending beneath the hem of her dress, and a necklace bearing the sigil of the seven-pointed star hung around her neck. She was like a gem-studded ring some surfacer lost down a water drain only for it to turn up in the muck of a Sewertown channel—completely out of place.

"I'm sorry, Elaine," Vallen said. He felt warm and dizzy, but it was probably just nerves. "A job came up at the last minute and . . . I"—he gulped—"sort of . . . forgot about our lesson."

"What kind of job?" Elaine asked, crossing her arms.

Vallen looked to Bohomaz for support, some form of believable lie about what they'd been doing, but the Vladisvar's crimson eyes just twinkled amusement at him. The crime lord was having *way* too much fun with this.

"The, uh, normal kind?" Vallen hedged. Elaine's brow furrowed, and the tapping sped up. "Where we go and pick up . . . things . . . at one location and transport them t-to . . . another . . . " His voice trailed off under the aristo girl's wilting glare, and his arms slumped to his sides in dejection.

"Fine, we stole something. Happy?"

Elaine's features softened. "See? Doesn't it feel good to be honest?" She let the question hang in the air just long enough for Vallen to think he'd gotten off the hook before hitting him with the follow-through. "But what did I tell you about stealing? It hurts others, which breeds resentment and fuels the cycle of hatred. You need to give it up and focus your efforts in a positive direction, like your studies."

A gravelly bellow made her spin around. "Vallen can't," Bohomaz said. "He owes me his life until I choose to relinquish it. I have given him Lysham, which he must balance out with Rashakh."

Please don't retaliate, Vallen pleaded inwardly. Gulping, he clenched his clammy fists and prayed Elaine would stay silent.

She didn't. Imposing size, muscled knots of leathery sinew, and a titanic claw almost as big as Elaine did nothing to blunt her righteous fury. "You make *children* steal for you? What about child labor laws? Are you feeding them properly? Educating them? Vallen didn't know his basic letters, which means these younger kids"—she waved at the 'chore crew,' who were still bouncing around the common room—"are going to end up the same way. Are you alright with that?"

"I am." Bohomaz straightened to his full height and loomed over Elaine. Even with one horn sheared through at its middle, the elderly Vladisvar looked like a voidspawn—a demon. "The universe would snuff out their insignificant flames without my intervention. Should I do more? And without asking anything of them in return? I see no equity in that, youngling."

"Besides"—Bohomaz bared his fangs—"your surfacer logic means *nothing* here. On your journey to our lovely home, did you see any public bread stations, baths, or schools? None of your 'common' conveniences exist below ground, and none of your leaders care to visit to construct them. We are beneath their notice, Miss Elaine."

For the first time since Vallen had met her, Elaine took a step back, head bowed in shame. She bit her lip, then glanced at him. Why . . . were there two of her? "That's—"

Her blue eyes went wide as she pointed at the ground beneath him. "You're bleeding, Vallen!"

What? Vallen's gaze dropped to his blood-soaked pant leg. *Oh, that's why I'm dizzy*, his mind sluggishly processed. Rivulets of red

201

dripped from the hem of his britches, ran along his boot, and pooled on the floorboards. He'd lost at least . . . The math proved impossible, his sight blurry and filled with pulsing spots.

Elaine lurched across Vallen's twisting vision. Leaping from the stage, she gestured for the kids to move aside, clearing a circle around him. Only Pockey remained, catching Vallen by his shoulder before he could collapse.

"I know you," Pockey suddenly blurted at Elaine. "You're the girl from the Festival of Sariel, at the temple in the Upper West End. The one we tried to steal from!"

"*Elaine*," she said, tone hard. "And I don't care right now. Just get me some water to clean his wound."

Pockey went deathly still, acting as if she'd suggested they take a swim in the Darmatian royal treasury. Which she effectively had. Water was worth as much as gold to them.

"*Water*," Elaine hissed. "*Now*." Without waiting for Pockey's response, she knelt beside Vallen, gripped his ghostly pale hand, and lowered him to the ground.

Bohomaz sighed and nodded at Pockey, who sprinted into the neighboring kitchen. One of their four water tanks—the only one accessible by crew members aside from their leader—squatted in its corner, along with a stack of much-dented pails. Unfolding his massive hand, Bohomaz dangled the whisperwind amulet, its emerald gemstone smaller than one of the Vladisvar's obsidian fingernails.

His message to Vallen was clear: *Consider this water your payment for the amulet.*

If he recovered, that was fine by him. Sweat beaded along his arms, his teeth chattered, and he was so, so cold. As Elaine ripped open Vallen's pant leg and raised his foot to rest on her knee, his nausea swelled and frigid darkness took him.

Chapter 16

Burns

Hetrachia 14, 697 ABH
Resistance Base, Sarconian Province of Darmatia

Quiet.

Sweet, blissful quiet.

Major Jis Reev craved the stillness of early mornings. They were full of potential that had yet to be realized, opportunities that had yet to be capitalized on. Every distant clatter held meaning. The cook, rising to grease his pots. Water droplets plopping on the floor, heralding the incoming tide outside the hidden cavern. Whispers, the guards changing shifts, some headed to well-deserved rest, others rising to begin their duties.

And her, flowing through the moves of a training kata. Jis punched, air rushing around the blow. Planting her foot produced a precise *tap,* and she pivoted into a reverse side kick that snapped the hem of her sweaty leggings tight.

Every sound and movement energized her further, and the racing of her heart added another beat to the symphony of silence.

Bad-ump, whoosh, tap, whoosh, Bad-ump, snap-snap!

The tempo changed. Falling back, Jis blocked high, grabbed an imaginary attacker's wrist, and pulled them down onto her driving knee. *Smack!* Her hands mimed the blow by clapping her thigh, and Jis stepped into a lethal elbow aimed at their throat. Guts pulverized, windpipe crushed, her foe fell to the floor. *Stamp!* A stomp of her heel finished them.

Panting, drenched, but grinning ear to ear, Jis brought her bare feet together and bowed to the empty lakeshore.

A new sound, applause, shattered Jis' peace. "Perfect as always, ma child."

"My hook-round-kick combo was a half-second slow," she replied. "If my opponent evaded the first, they could have lunged in and grappled me to the ground." Stooping, Jis picked up a towel, wiped her face, and turned to Mother Tabitha.

"It was perfect ta *me,*" the nun countered, tapping her walking stick for emphasis. "Allow an old woman a moment ta enjoy 'er little Jisarivel's accomplishments."

Jis' emerald eyes went wide. She glanced from side to side, scanning for other early risers on the chilly beach. Fortunately, they were alone.

She closed the gap between them and gripped Tabitha by the shoulders. "If you let anyone—*anyone*—hear that name, I won't give you the supplies you asked for."

"Bot it's a pretty name," Tabitha lamented, shaking her head. The beads threaded into her braids clinked together, another melody joining the day's sounds. "All da other girls at da Hermitage House wished I had given them such lovely, wonderful names."

With a sigh, Jis dropped her arms. She couldn't stay mad at Tabitha. Not at the woman who had raised a stubborn orphan girl to become the Ice Queen of Darmatia.

"Just . . . don't say it too often, Mother."

"Of course, *Major Reev*."

On the ground nearby stood a single stool piled with Jis' belongings: her boots, calf-length socks, and uniform jacket. As she cleared it to make room for Tabitha to sit, the nun *tut-tutted* under her breath. "Put some clothes on, child. You want ta freeze ta death?"

Jis glanced down at the thin gray camisole she wore. Soaked with sweat, it clung to her pale chest. Her muscular arms and neck were similarly slick with perspiration. Yet she didn't feel a thing. Cold, sleet, and rain meant *nothing* to the Ice Queen. Her men'ar just . . . worked differently than other elemental mages.

"That joke is getting stale."

Tabitha harrumphed. "Then wear a coat for propriety's sake. Every man in this camp can see down yer shirt."

"They wouldn't *dare* look," Jis scoffed. "They know what would happen if they do."

Swinging her arm, she sent a wave of frost across the cave floor. It turned white in an instant, sparkling like a field of crystals, and the lake began to freeze where it touched the shore.

The nun slowly lowered herself onto the stool, glaring at Jis over the knob of her cane as she did. "*This* is why ya can't find a husband."

"You can't find what you aren't searching for."

"Perhaps you are lookin' for da wrong future, then."

Why did they keep coming back to this? Yes, Jis was still young and attractive. Her figure was slim, she wasn't too tall, and there was just enough curve in the right places to attract the male gaze. And while her black hair was kept short, it was quite striking when combined with her shining emerald eyes.

But none of that was important. Her body was just another weapon, and Jis had no desire for a suitor—not with the wound from . . . *that man's* betrayal still festering in her heart.

She doubted it would ever truly heal.

"I'm a *soldier*, Mother," Jis said, adopting the resigned tone of someone who'd spoken the same lines again and again. "My duty is to my nation. I have no desire for a life beyond the one I have."

"And if you *weren't* a soldier?" Tabitha asked, her blue eyes twinkling.

Jis recognized the question for the trap it was but bit down on the bait anyway. "Come again?"

"I'm not jokin', Jisarivel." Tabitha's voice hardened, adopting the same sternness she'd used to chastise the orphanage children when they'd misbehaved. "Yer parents were soldiers, an' they died for their ideals. Yer comrades perished by da droves at Aldona an' you were helpless ta save them. Why must *you* fight? *You* specifically? What can *you* do except die along with them?"

"You'd bring my *parents* into this?" Jis growled through gritted teeth. "You hid the truth about them from me for years. And the only reason I found out was because you thought their story might somehow dissuade me from enlisting. *You. Were. Wrong.*"

The scene appeared before Jis like a ghost. The long table at the Hermitage House stretched out before her, a simple white bed sheet hiding its numerous dings and dents, grubby-faced children of all ages lining the sides with joy in their eyes. They sang to her, wished her a happy nameday, and cheered as Jis blew out the sixteen candles jammed into her apfel-sized cake.

Afterward, she'd told Mother Tabitha of her intent to join the Darmatian army. There were so many injustices in the Kingdom: Sewertown, the market slums, and even their underfunded orphanage. But merit was everything in the army, and with her magic she swore she'd rise to the top and change things from within.

Tabitha had tried all she could to stop her. And when that had failed, she'd shown her the mud-stained linen basket and an ink-smeared note left on the House's doorstep sixteen years prior. Jis' parents hadn't died—not immediately, at any rate. They'd left her behind, sacrificing their lives with her to fight against the Empire in the Rabbanite foreign legion. All for the sake of creating a better world for their daughter to grow up in.

And then Tabitha had passed her a crinkled newspaper clipping with two names circled in red. Her parents were two among thousands, their deaths a footnote in a larger article debating the merits of Rabban's latest attempt to take Varas Fortress.

Jis sneered at the memory. Both then and now, Tabitha had expected her to give up. She'd rather drown in a Sewertown sludge pit. "After hearing what happened to my parents, my resolve to enlist only grew stronger. They did fail. But . . . they weren't wrong for trying. *No great thing can be accomplished without ignoring the risks involved.* That," Jis chuckled wryly, "I learned from *you.*"

"And did I also not teach you that violence begets violence?" Tabitha jabbed her cane at the cavern ceiling far above. With the illyrium panels dimmed and the tripod lamps turned off, the darkness seemed to extend on and on forever. "Look at where this war has brought you. I exist ta serve da downtrodden, da injured, an' da weak, but what chance do you have o' winnin'? This is *suicide,* child."

"Should I tell them that?" Major Reev pointed at the ramshackle camp and the hospital tent beyond. "Should I tell them that all their suffering was for nothing? That their comrades died for a lost cause? And what about the families who will have to smile and wave at the Sarcs who killed their loved ones, hiding their grief because it's *inconvenient*? Do *they* get a say?"

Tabitha held up a pacifying hand. "I was not tryin' ta insinuate that—"

"And that's assuming they *let* us surrender," Jis continued. Her eyes saw a placid sapphire lake, but her mind saw exploding airships, toppling towers, and screaming soldiers. The only record of their passing was the lanterns they'd launched from this shoreline—their number a fraction of the Darmatian dead.

Why had they ever brought the cadets along? *Her* cadets. Jis shuddered, and her voice dropped to a whisper. "You weren't at Aldona, Mother. You didn't see the ships that ran up the white flag and were blasted anyway. You didn't see them use Great Magic to obliterate half our fleet and the fortress itself. Maybe they'll let civilians like you live in their new regime, but for us, for the Darmatian army, this is a war of survival."

Jis stared at the distant shadows across the lake. They twisted and morphed, forming into the shades of faces she would never see again. Students she'd scolded, their tests marked with red ink. Grinning officers she'd studied alongside at the Academy.

You're too stiff, they teased her. *Lighten up, Reev.*

We'll let you practice your incantations, but you better join us for a drink next time, another said.

There would be no more drinks for them. No more 'next times.'

Trembling hands, feeble and spindly, grasped Jis about her waist. She stiffened, preparing to execute a Vladisvar arm break, but relaxed when she smelt the familiar fragrance of oranges and lavender. No matter how skilled she became, Tabitha always managed to sneak up on her.

Coarse braids brushed Jis' neck as the nun nestled her head against her daughter's back. "You know," Tabitha said after a few moments. "I call everyone ma child, even that rotten dune bloom Triaron you asked me ta visit."

Jis snorted. The insult fit Vallen perfectly. Sayri would use every part of the spiny-shelled plants they grew, but water them just a bit too much—like with Vallen's ego—and they collapsed into a mush of rotten paste that was no use to anyone.

"But you"—the grip on Jis' stomach tightened—"you *are* ma child. More so than any o' Sariel's children. An' so I don't want *yer* body ta be mangled, ta see *yer* face beneath a white shift on a salvator's table."

Though the sweat on her back had begun to dry, Jis felt a damp warmth spreading through the fabric. "That ... " Tabitha croaked. " ... is why I want *you* ta stop fightin'."

The Ice Queen's frigid resolve nearly shattered. Her heart thumped, her lip trembled, and she had to choke back tears. Carefully, Jis reached up and cupped her mother's hand in hers. It was so small and shriveled, fragile and delicate.

She held it for a while, enjoying the sensation. Then, one by one, she pried Tabitha's fingers free and stepped away. Jis did not—*could not*—meet her gaze, for more reasons than one.

"I can't stop," she said. Her muscles tightened, and she pinched her eyes shut, bracing for the outburst she knew was coming.

It never arrived. "I understand," Tabitha replied, sniffling slightly. "I don't agree, but there is no one on Lozaria I trust more than you."

Disobeying her own rule, Jis spun around. Words of reassurance tumbled from her mouth. "It's not like we don't have a chance, Mother. I've reached out to the Hues and Sylph through some of my old Academy contacts. And if one of our messengers gets through the lines to the

Imperium, we can coordinate our efforts. Hit the Sarcs in Darmatia from both sides. And . . . . and . . . ”

What she was about to say tasted like some revolting mixture of bile and sewage, but Jis spat it out anyway. “And we have the . . . Triaron. He may be a fool, an imbecile, and a total twit, but his powers are real.”

“Providence is at work in that one.” Tabitha chuckled while glancing at her staff. It looked different than the one Jis had gifted her. The grain was rougher, had an oak finish instead of cherry, and the brass inscription beneath the handle was missing entirely.

“*He didn't*,” Jis breathed.

“He *did*,” the Sayri nun confirmed, laugh deepening. “Just like another frosty hothead I know.”

No one treated her mother like that. Fatigue banished, Jis took a step toward the camp. She would do to Vallen what he had done to Tabitha's cane.

The replacement stick swung up to block her path. “Calm down. It was not wholly 'is fault. Da boy doesn't understand why he has 'is powers, what they are, or how ta use them properly. He needs a teacher.”

A prod came at Jis' chest, behind which Tabitha's gaze was set like flint. Orphans had always called her “Lady Dragon” when she was out of earshot, and that was *before* she suffered the vicious burns that scarred her face, neck, and shoulder.

Burns that . . .

Jis took a step back. She couldn't get upset—not now, not near Tabitha. “You can't be suggesting *I* take that role? Being his instructor was the worst four years of my life. It was like training a foglip to dance. A foglip! Those things don't even have legs and I'd probably have more success with them.”

Tabitha followed her, cane tapping on the stone floor, and Jis continued to retreat. Her hands came up in a warding gesture. *Please,* she begged inwardly. *Don't ask that of me. And don't come any closer!*

“Who else is there?” Tabitha asked.

Jis grabbed the first excuse she could think of and flung it out like a shield. “This army has a dozen elemental mages. Renerv, Peloqun, Hazal, Pesca, Kohanek . . . ”—She listed possible candidates on her fingers—“And all the elements are represented between them, so if they took turns training him, then—”

Tabitha's breath crystallized in front of her face. “But they don't do *this*,” she said softly, swiping her staff through the hanging shards of ice between them. It was too late. Glittering frost dappled the already cool air of the cavern, every molecule for ten meters around Jis frozen into twinkling pinpricks of ice. Blue-white cracks spread from her feet in every direction.

As a child, she'd marveled at how her emotions manifested in gorgeous displays of magic. In an instant, she could turn her closet bedroom into an icy castle, or a simple tree into a wintry delight that coruscated with refracted light.

Then Jis realized that she didn't feel cold . . . but everyone else did.

Enraged that an older orphan had stolen her straw-stuffed doll, young Jis had collapsed in a bawling heap. Tabitha had made it for her, even using one of her braids for the doll's hair. It had seemed like the end of the world to her.

Minutes passed. Or perhaps hours. When Jis came to, she was wrapped tight in Tabitha's embrace. But her clasp wasn't warm. The quivering nun was barely breathing, just rocking back and forth while muttering, "*I-I've . . . got y-you . . . I've g-got . . . you . . . ,*" through blue lips.

The angry pink scars were the mark of Tabitha's kindness. Her beautiful ebony skin—now hard, black, and dead—had to be chipped away, and still she had barely survived.

Even now, Jis hadn't perfected her control. She glanced at the shivering nun, swore, then pictured her men'ar as a cloud being sucked back into her chest. The splinters of ice clattered to the ground, and the temperature around them returned to normal.

"Stay away," Jis warned, stumbling farther down the beach. "You shouldn't get close to me, Mother. Not after what happened before."

Tabitha sighed and shuffled after her. "Not you too. Like I told that fool Triaron, people get ta make choices, an' savin' you from yerself was mine. This"—she dragged a finger down her scar—"is a badge o' honor. It's how I knew my little Jisarivel was special."

Jis' right foot struck water—and beneath it, an unexpected spur of rock. Flustered and distracted, she slipped and lost her balance, arms flailing as she fell. Something wooden rattled across the limestone. Two gnarled hands snagged her left wrist and hauled her back upright.

"Why do *I* have ta do all da savin' around here?" Tabitha asked when they were a few paces away from the lake.

A laugh tore itself from Jis' throat. "Because it's what the Creator called you to do?"

"Clearly," Tabitha said, bending to retrieve her discarded cane. She leaned heavily on it when she rose. "But since I'm not gettin' any younger, *you* need ta take up sum o' my slack."

"Mother—"

"No buts! You are a prodigy, Jisarivel, gifted with powers so strong they manifest subconsciously. Even so, you trained tirelessly ta control yer gift. Da Triaron did not. Yet da world needs him, an' we are out o' time for him ta figure things out on 'is own. Give him da push that I gave you. Help him ta save us all."

Jis stared at Tabitha as the seconds stretched into moments, then minutes. To say she loathed Vallen was like saying a dragon was dangerous: an understatement of epic proportions. But he *was* her student. All the cadets were.

For the sake of those who would never return, her life debt to Mother Tabitha, and the whole Kingdom of Darmatia, Major Jis Reev the Ice Queen would swallow her stupid pride and train the Triaron.

I am so *going to regret this later,* Jis thought, plastering her palms to her face. She inhaled slowly, then released a monumental sigh. "Fine. *If* he listens to me, I will train him. The whole lot of them, in fact. Doesn't make sense to do things halfway."

Mother Tabitha started laughing, setting her beads to clanking in that disjointed yet melodic way Jis loved. Her morning quiet was shattered, but the culprit was her precious mother—not her birth parent, but the only one who mattered.

"However," Jis held up a warning finger. "I do have a stipulation."

"What might that be?"

Jis grinned. "This time, I get to teach them *my way.*"

Chapter 17

Every Man Has His Price

Hetrachia 14, 697 ABH
Nemare, Capital of the Sarconian Province of Darmatia

The twin gold bars and single diamond-shaped pip of the new captain's epaulets felt like lead weights on Hans Ulrich's shoulders as he stood at attention in the Emperor's study. He didn't deserve the promotion, nor did he deserve the crisp hepam-cotton dress uniform he now wore or the expensive P-22 Lerchis pistol attached to his black leather belt. Like most things in his life, he'd lucked into them.

Or been cursed *with them,* Hans considered. He didn't need a degree from the Royal Academy of Sciences to realize he was a pawn in a game—a crude, cracked stone piece being whipped around a board by gem-studded fingers.

Though Hans' salute was stiff, inside he was a nervous wreck. His pulse quickened with every passing second, and the dampness beneath his armpits threatened to become a swamp to rival those of the Moravi Atoll. He could almost hear the buzz of rot-flies scouting out a potential home.

Why had Emperor Artorios summoned him? *Just* him? Lord Sarcon was noticeably absent, and the only other being in the study besides His Majesty was the looming armored form of Grand Marschal Konig Zaratus, which made Hans *more* anxious, not less. He prayed to their ancestors—Sarcon included—that he hadn't caused the most powerful man in Lozaria some unknown offense.

"At ease, Captain Ulrich." The Emperor made a pacifying gesture as he lowered himself into a high-backed chair behind his large elegoras wood desk. "I asked you here to talk, not bark orders at you."

Hans said nothing. One didn't start blabbing to monarchs and potentates unless *they* specifically gave you permission to. He lowered his right arm, crossing it behind his back with his left and assuming a parade rest position. The stiffness in his legs softened from the immovability of steel girders to the firmness of mere concrete.

After a moment of silence, the Emperor coughed and waved at the room around them. "What do you think of my new office? It's a fraction the size of the reception hall at the Imperial Palace, but I think I've

211

managed to spruce it up since the departure of its previous occupant."

'Departure' was a kind word for 'imprisoned.' After signing the Kingdom's surrender, Steward Rowan Metellus had been relegated to a prison cell beneath the building—a precipitous plummet in status.

The Steward's chambers had suffered a similar fate. Blue and silver wallpaper, artwork, and furniture had been removed in favor of the reds and golds of the Empire. Two banners bearing the Imperial crest—an avenging angel holding aloft a scepter of Illyriite amid a tangle of burning thorns—hung on either side of a broad window overlooking the vacant city square. Sitting areas flanked the room on either side, plush satin couches, likewise upholstered in shades of crimson, arrayed around low tea tables.

Floor-to-ceiling bookshelves covered the walls. But instead of tomes, maps, or scrolls, martial artifacts littered their shelves. Helmets, sabers, pistols, and bayonet-tipped rifles were the most common, but a full suit of golden armor hung on a mannequin inside a glass case. On the far side of the chamber, rack after rack of glittering illyrium crystals shone beneath the focused lighting of a twin display. The smallest of those shards, the size of Hans' fist, was likely worth enough for his family to live comfortably for the rest of their lives.

It was an intimidating display of wealth and power, one matched by the imposing stature of the Emperor himself. Hans' roving gaze fell on his master. Broad shoulders filled out an immaculately tailored military uniform that accentuated His Majesty's muscular build. His jaw was strong, face unblemished, and his flinty silver eyes complemented the imperial circlet resting atop his head. While streaks of gray dotted his pitch-black hair, they only enhanced his regal bearing.

Hans was suddenly very conscious of the ragged scars deforming his nose and cheeks. He didn't belong here, for more reasons than one.

"It-It's quite impressive, Your Majesty," Hans managed.

His lack of elaboration made the Emperor's brow furrow. Did he expect a man who'd been a lowly second lieutenant a day prior to begin spouting a treatise on the ratio of window drapes to pillows in a room? Hans had been a machinist in a ball-bearing factory before enlisting. He didn't know the first thing about style.

A gruff, metallic voice came from the Emperor's right. "Congratulations on your promotion, Captain Ulrich," the Grand Marschal said. "We expect great things from you." His molded dragwyrm helm inclined ever so slightly, and Hans all but threw himself into a low bow in response.

"I'm honored by your trust," Hans said, words gushing from his mouth onto the Trillith-silk rug below. "I will strive daily to be worthy of my new duties, and to serve His Majesty and the Empire with all that I am, from this breath to my last."

"For the Empire, from this breath to the last," the Grand Marschal echoed.

As Hans rose, the Emperor *smiled* at him. "As I accepted your oath at your commissioning, so do I accept these words of fealty, Captain Ulrich."

That day in Sarconia's capital square, Hans had been one insignificant man among hundreds staring up at the stone dais extending from the acropolis—the bluff upon which the palace and Senate dome sat. His sensory and healing magic was the only noteworthy thing about him, and it was because of it the recruiters had made him an officer instead of cannon fodder.

Now the same Emperor who'd seemed an eternity away on that balcony sat before him. Spoke not to a crowd, but to him alone. Hans had never been a zealous patriot, but he couldn't stop the chills racing through him. The adrenaline thundering through his veins.

The Grand Marschal shattered his euphoria. "Unfortunately, we have pressing need of your loyalty."

Hans blinked in confusion. "I thought I was to return to Sarconia on your orders, sir?"

"And so you shall," Emperor Artorios said. Still speaking, he opened the top drawer of his desk and removed four items: a cepyrus letter, a cork-sealed inkwell, a clinking velvet bag, and a wooden plaque the size of a book engraved with gilt lettering. "What we ask of you today is a minor *addition* to your current mission. It won't require you to do anything different than what Sarcon has already instructed you to."

"What *has* Lord Sarcon instructed you to do?" the Grand Marschal asked suddenly. "Did he mention any documents or resources he wanted aside from Scharb Cimbri's weather charts?"

A pawn in a game, indeed. Trying his best to *not* appear stressed, Hans took a steadying breath, set his jaw, and told the truth. "I haven't spoken to my liege—my *superior*," he corrected hastily, noting the Emperor's narrowed eyes, "—since yesterday. As far as I'm aware, organizing a team of scholars to transcribe the Cimbri texts is my only objective."

"You now have another." The Emperor leaned forward, his

gaze hot enough to sear flesh. "I fear that our dear founder might be becoming . . . *unstable.* I worry the strain of swapping bodies has addled his mind, and he may no longer have the best interests of the Empire at heart. Which is where you come in, Captain Ulrich."

Hans' didn't need a mirror to know he was white as a sheet. *Me?* he thought, holding in a laugh. *You want* me *to do something about an immortal wizard who can swat ships from the sky like flit-gnats?* Never mind that Sarcon had saved his life and was oath-bound to carry out his former squad leader's—Vahn's—final wish. Would his conscience allow him to betray them both?

"Wha-what would you have me do, Your Majesty?" he stammered.

"For now, nothing," the Grand Marschal said. Before relief could wash over Hans, the armored sentinel pushed the inkwell across the desk toward him. Clear fluid sloshed around inside the flask even after it came to a rest.

"The first of our gifts: invisible ink. During your trip to the capital and after you return, you are to begin exchanging letters with one of your old Academy drill instructors, Major Trenno Sart. The front will be innocuous trivialities. The back"—the Grand Marschal tapped a steel claw to the flask—"will be messages written with invisible ink, informing us of everything Sarcon does, who he meets, and what he tells you. Not a single detail of his activities is inconsequential."

It was clear that Major Sart would never receive Hans' letters. He would address them, drop them with an imperial postmaster, and somewhere along the line they would disappear into the clutches of the Ritter Order, the Emperor's personal agents.

For an instant, Hans' conscience bypassed his brain, and he blurted, "Isn't Sarcon on our side?"

He cursed his foolishness, fully expecting to be accused of treason and sentenced to execution. *You can't speak your mind,* Hans chastised himself. *Not when Elycia needs a husband, and Meira and Sirus need their father.*

Surprisingly, the Emperor nodded and favored him with a weak, warm smile. "That is our hope as well. To have our great founder at our side gives legitimacy to the Pax Sarconi—the great Lozarian peace—we desire. But a wise ruler," he reached up, removed his crown, and stared at it with tired eyes, "must prepare for any eventuality. Even frightening ones."

"You want me to spy on him?" Hans asked, digging his grave ever deeper and praying the dirt wouldn't be tossed in behind him. "The greatest mage to ever walk the continent?"

The Emperor bristled, grip tightening on his circlet, but the Grand Marschal raised a gauntlet to forestall an outburst. "A crude word, yet not an entirely inaccurate one. Let us present our other gifts, after which you can decide for yourself whether or not to aid us."

They were . . . giving him a *choice*? Hans held his tongue as Emperor Artorios gestured him forward. He strode to the edge of the desk, where a late afternoon sunbeam turned the golden trim, buttons, and medals on his uniform into tiny stars.

The biggest medal on his chest—the Imperial Obelisk, a monochrome plinth attached to a white ribbon—had been awarded to him for bringing Sarcon home in the face of *'severe threat of personal harm.'* It marked him as a national hero, yet another accolade Hans didn't deserve.

After replacing his crown, the Emperor passed Hans the next item in line: an official-looking document filled with flowing script, signed with his name, and bearing a crimson seal. The dried wax bore the letters 'S.A.' beneath the combined shield and sword of the Artorios household.

"My seal, as promised," Emperor Artorios said. "This should open any door in Sarconia you need access to."

With shaking fingers, Hans took the parchment, folded it reverentially, and slid it into his jacket's breast pocket. It added another weight to his load that didn't belong—this time the crushing weight of an entire empire.

Hans recognized the thick, lacquered wooden plaque that the Emperor picked up and started reading from. A housing pass, effectively a property deed in a place like the former Kingdom where the state didn't own everything. Though he'd never seen one this fancy. In addition to the oil-rubbed surface, the edges were smoothed and rounded, and the words *'Upper Ring'* were emblazoned at the top in gilt letters.

" . . . is presented to the undersigned, Captain Hans Ulrich, this fourteenth day of the month of Hetrachia on the Imperial calendar," the Emperor read. "Rights to this domicile extend to his wife, Elycia Ulrich, and their children, Meira and Sirus Ulrich. They may use the property within the bounds of Sarconian residential regulations until such time as they return this pass or the Housing Bureau requests its return."

"Excuse me, Your Majesty," Hans said, certain he'd misheard. "Is this pass addressed to *me*? A pass for a house in the *Upper Ring*?"

"Of course."

If his jaw hit the plush carpet or his eyes tumbled from his head, Hans didn't feel it happen. He'd lived in Sarconia's lower ring since birth, staring past the filthy storefronts and countless smokestacks at the gleaming inner wall and the orderly towers and mansions that peaked above its battlements. Every soldier, factory worker, and peasant in the outer district dreamed of life in the Upper Ring. They traded stories about what it must be like and made plans for lives there that would never come to pass.

Hans had gawked at the broad boulevards, marble fountains, and tree-lined sidewalks as guards rushed him and Sarcon through the district to the palace months earlier. Now he and his family would *live* there. No more worrying about schools, his kids' safety, or—

The Grand Marschal spoke as if he knew Hans' thoughts. "You are a staff officer now, Captain Ulrich. We can't have someone of your station living in the lower ring, especially in the unruly Trevellian quadrant. Why, within a league of your current tenement—3429 Central Gate Square, if I'm not mistaken—there has recently been a rash of drunken assaults, home invasions, and worse. Most of those affected were defenseless families whose husbands were deployed, so the faster we move your wife and children, the better."

With every raspy statement that emerged from the Grand Marschal's elegant helm, Hans' spirits sank lower and lower. The housing pass listed the names of his wife and children. They knew where he lived, and what commonplace crimes they could blame an unfortunate 'accident' on.

Of course they do! Hans' guts twisted as he tried to keep his fists from clenching. He wanted to kick himself for being so blind. The Emperor and his Grand Marschal *were* the state. He wasn't bargaining with a superior officer—he was staring into the sneering face of Sarconia itself.

From the very beginning, he'd never had a choice.

"And the sack?" Hans asked. His voice sounded foreign in ears, as though reaching him from far, far away.

A tug of the Emperor's ring bedecked fingers undid the silk drawstring, revealing a small fortune in glittering *gold* geldars. Hans could draw a captain's salary for a decade and not see half that amount.

"New homes require new furnishings," Emperor Artorios said as if it was the most obvious thing in the world. "Now, if you're quite finished dawdling, *Captain* Ulrich, I would appreciate it if you'd pick up your ink and get on with your mission."

Hans hadn't lied to his Emperor.

Technically.

He hadn't *spoken* to Sarcon since they'd parted ways in the palace gardens the day prior, and he truly didn't know what the inscrutable immortal was planning. Which wasn't to say the crafty mage didn't have other ways of contacting him.

You're getting better at this, Sarcon's voice, soft like falling snow, whispered directly into his mind. *Sychon and his pet never suspected I was present even as they schemed against me.*

Probably because I didn't know you were listening, Hans thought as he descended the spiral staircase to the building's lower level. Streaks of sunlight from slotted windows dappled the marble steps at even intervals. It had taken a while, but he was finally getting used to the sun's daily presence. In Sarconia, whole weeks could pass without a single ray breaking the clouds, with lazy, ash-choked rain being the only thing to fall from the heavens.

A pang of homesickness struck Hans. When had he last embraced Elycia? Last gazed on Meira's latest charcoal drawing, or clutched Sirus' too small hand? Why was he half a continent away fighting in a war he didn't care about when his family needed him?

You'll see them soon, Sarcon soothed, interrupting Hans' thoughts.

No, interrupting was the wrong word. Rather, his ancient ancestor was *in* his thoughts, beaming his consciousness into his head from wherever his host body was. The first time Sarcon had contacted Hans in this manner, he'd gone milk white and leapt halfway to the ceiling before collapsing against a suit of antique mail. Two nearby guards had rushed to support him, Sarcon's mad cackle rattling around his skull as he regained his feet.

When Hans had asked Sarcon why he hadn't used telepathy before, he'd merely replied that the men'ar capacity of the Descar boy was larger than Vahn's, allowing him to access more of his abilities. Just how many types of magic could the sorcerer wield? Most mages could only use spells from one or two of the ten schools, yet Sarcon

217

had already shown proficiency for four: degenerative, light, dark, and blood.

Reaching the bottom of the staircase, Hans marched along a breezeway that skirted the inner courtyard. The gurgle of one of the city's innumerable fountains floated through the open archways of the wall on his right. Water cascaded down the fountain's tiers and into a series of four channels that flowed throughout the surrounding greenery, creating isolated islands accessible by small footbridges.

Nothing like this exists in Sarconia, Hans thought. *I wish Elycia and my kids could see it.*

Sarcon hummed his agreement. *Your Empire has forgotten the natural order of things. Blood and spirit will always prevail over smoke and metal.*

Blood. The word left a sour taste in Hans' mouth, like the orage plums his wife loved but he couldn't stand. A scowl must've crept onto his face, for the gefreiter stationed at the next intersection went stiller than a statue as he stuck out his chin, straightened his back, and smashed his fist against his cuirass in salute.

Hans halfheartedly returned the gesture and walked on. The kid was only six or seven years younger than him. Without the horrid scars, captain insignias, and the phantom weight of the men he'd seen killed, they weren't all that different.

You still intend to go ahead with the blood ritual, Hans thought. *To turn the people of Nemare into living energy for your spell.* It was a statement, not a question. After several months at Sarcon's side, he was beginning to understand him—insomuch as one could understand a seven-century-old immortal who'd lived alongside legends and fought in battles that were now more myth than history.

Yes, Sarcon admitted. A smile accompanied his mental projection, the kind a teacher would turn on a student who'd, at last, solved a simple math problem. He wondered how he could see Sarcon's knowing grin in his mind when all he heard were words.

The Emperor won't allow it.

Another smile. *Not now. But if desperation can make murderers of honest men, what do you suppose it will do to those already rotting from the inside out?*

Hans shivered despite the desert heat. It was cool beneath the palace eaves, but the hepam cotton of his uniform—designed for more temperate Sarconia—made Nemare feel like a sauna.

We needn't revisit that subject now, Sarcon continued. *You are not wrong to cherish life, Hans, but be careful not to mistake chaff for wheat when the harvest comes.*

A left at the end of the hall brought Hans to a carpeted corridor lit by hanging braziers chained to the high ceiling. His room was the third door on the left; Sarcon's, the one before it. Once he packed his trunk, the ink and coins in his side satchel the last items to stow away, he'd be ready to depart for the capital—to return to his wife and children.

So why send me to Sarconia at all? Hans asked suddenly, curiosity getting the better of him. *Are the Cimbri texts just a ruse to distract the Emperor from your true intentions?*

Laughter echoed in Hans' mind as his hand grasped the latch to his chamber. It grated on his senses, making it hard to turn the knob or concentrate on anything but Sarcon's voice. *A ruse indeed. You're quite clever, one of the shrewdest mortals I've ever had the pleasure to meet.*

And you're absolutely right. As Sarcon spoke, the flames above Hans' head shrank and the metal beneath his fingers turned cold as a frost elemental's heart. He jerked away, massaging warmth into his frigid digits while glancing with trembling eyes at the encroaching shadows.

You aren't going to recover a musty old tome, Sarcon said, obsidian gaze boring through Hans' skull, his mind, his *soul. You're going to break into the Emperor's vault and unravel the secrets of Darmatus' supposedly lost lineage—secrets that will at long last give me back my flesh and blood.*

Chapter 18

Chance to Change

Jenuvant 26, 688 ABH,
Sewertown, Beneath the Royal Capital of Nemare

The ceiling of the *Safe Haven* was much the same as always. Holes—ranging in size from the tip of a finger to the girth of the juicy flarkis melons preferred by Moravi—dotted its surface, and stains from thrown food, splashed liquor, and at least three different kinds of fungus made it a patchwork of dark brown hues. The sight made Vallen want to vomit: partially because the barnacle mushrooms in the crack directly overhead looked like a man's guts turned out the wrong way, but mostly because he was still nauseous from blood loss.

"Drink this," a soft voice beside him said.

Vallen opened his chapped lips and let them tip the contents of a dented tin cup down his throat. He should have been wary. *Everything* in Sewertown came at a price. Yet right now, he was too thirsty to care.

Lukewarm water splashed over his arid tongue. For a moment, he couldn't taste the tang of iron, or the bitter bite it gained from sitting in the tank too long. To Vallen, it was the nectar of the gods—the best thing he'd ever drunk.

"Another," he croaked.

When the refilled cup hovered in front of his mouth, he snatched it and downed its contents in one go. Vallen was nowhere close to satisfied, but it was a start.

"Whew. I thought Kit was a goner."

Blinking, Vallen raised his head from the lump pillowed beneath his head, and his surroundings resolved into focus. Pockey, standing over him with a relieved smile on his mousy face. Elaine, kneeling at his side, tears welling in her beautiful sky blue eyes. A crowd of grubby faces and greasy hair formed a ring around them, and across the room Bohomaz sat like a terrifying temple statue, ready to spring to life and gobble up non-believers.

"Vallen," he corrected Pockey for the third time that day. "What happened? How long was I out?"

"A couple hours," Elaine answered. She somehow managed to

sound upset, worried, and gladdened all at once. "Pockey brought water, I cleaned and bandaged your wound, and these little ones"—she smiled as she gestured at Jaston and the other young orphans—"prayed you back to health."

Jaston stuck three fingers in his mouth and gave an extremely self-satisfied nod. "Sar'el keep ya from harm, an' may the voo-man never bite your leg."

Laughing, Elaine ruffled the tyke's curly blonde hair. "And may the Void never blight your path. We'll work on that second part some more." Her eyes twinkled, but tears still clung to their corners like a beggar to his last coins. Vallen reached out to brush them away, then winced as he shifted his left leg.

"Ouch . . ."

"*You*"—Elaine's gaze hardened—"need to stay put. Hit him with another pillow, Pockey."

"Literally?" the pickpocket asked. Pockey grabbed a cord of straw that had been tied at both ends and made ready to bash it into his friend's head. Hopefully, he was just suffering the lingering effects of dehydration.

"If he tries to move again, yes. For now, slide it behind his back."

The boy complied, and Vallen held still while the scratchy cushion was shoved between the pillar he was leaning against and his bare back. *Bare?*

Vallen realized he was naked from the waist up. A patchwork blanket slid down his chest as he leaned forward, and a variety of pillows—made mostly of straw, but with a few fancier ones they'd stolen mixed in—tucked around him. His injured leg was propped up on a particularly fine sample. Yellow filigree traced whorls around the edges of a rising sun sewn from satin, and silky gold tassels draped from the corners.

The pillow would've been worth upward of twenty *silver* geldars, if not for the crimson droplets spread all over the sun and the sky around it. Vallen ripped the blanket away and made to stand.

"Why'd you let her use *that* pillow?" He glared at Pockey accusingly. The pickpocket should have known better. None of them were worth sullying a valuable score.

"I—"

Vallen cut off his excuse. He'd noticed something even worse. Overturned and empty at Elaine's side was a water bucket—one large enough to quench the thirst of *five of them* for a day. "*All* that water was used on *me?*"

His mind raced, compiling just how far into the Vladisvar crime lord's debt he was now. Given the awful geldar to water exchange rate, the tiny sack of coins hidden beneath his bunk—a pouch intended to eventually *free* him from this fetid abyss—would barely cover a tenth of his dues.

"Why?" Vallen asked, staring first at Pockey, then Elaine. She looked hurt, confused. It wasn't her fault, but he couldn't stop the words tumbling from his mouth. "Why waste all of that on—"

"It wasn't a waste," Bohomaz rumbled, bass tone vibrating parts of the wall, floor, and ceiling that weren't properly nailed down. "Your leg is patched. You are alive."

"But the cost—" Vallen began.

The Vladisvar's faded gray hide quivered, old muscles straining as he leaned forward and pointed at Elaine with his clawed gauntlet. "She has paid in full. Balance has been maintained, and not even the Karakhtahm would rule otherwise." Vallen gulped. What could she have offered that the most important of Vladisvar courts would rule the exchange a fair trade?

Please, he begged to any deity that would listen. *Anything but her freedom. I can't see my sun chained down here with me.*

"What did she give you?" Vallen whispered.

Bohomaz shook his head. "I won't tell you, little graftless. Not until you recognize the price she has already paid."

The price she's already paid? The Vladisvar's words were cryptic and infuriating, as they so often were. Frustrated, Vallen glanced at his now exposed legs. Gauze wrapped his left calf, its bright yellow color at odds with his pasty skin. A furrow of red scored the muscle beneath it.

The crossbow bolt had taken a bite out of his leg, rending a nasty gash in his flesh as long and deep as the arrow itself. Vallen blinked. It was a miracle he'd made it across the sewage channel; a miracle he'd stayed upright long enough to make it back. The pile of blood-soaked poultices piled near Elaine spoke the same truth Vallen already knew: *I shouldn't be alive.*

"I'm sorry."

He turned at Elaine's apology. But his eyes didn't stay rooted on her face. They drifted down, and whatever unnecessary self-recrimination she was spouting swept away from his ears like smoke.

The girl was a mess. She curled on the floor atop bare legs, her shoes and stockings missing. Her pale thighs were exposed, the hem of the dress above ripped over and over again until it could barely be called an article of clothing—even in Sewertown. Streaks of blood coated the rest, running down her stomach, arms, and smearing her forehead where she'd likely wiped sweat from her brow as she cared for him.

Weeks earlier, Vallen might have blushed and turned away. Now he just chuckled lightly and asked, "Elaine, why is your hair soaked?"

She paused, then glanced up at the mop of brown strands clinging to her head and neck. "There isn't any soap here," she explained matter-of-factly. "Pockey didn't even know what soap was when I asked him for some."

"I knew!" he protested. "We just call it something else down here."

"Well," Elaine continued. "No 'mythical white squares' were available, so I got my hair wet and squeezed whatever leftover shampoo oils I could from it to clean your wound. The rest"— she waved at Bohomaz, who held up a flask of cinnamon-brown spirits—"of the sterilization was done somewhat . . . distastefully. Given the circumstances, I'll ignore that he drinks that swill around children."

"Mighty kind of you, Miss Elaine," Bohomaz said, taking a swig.

Elaine turned back to Vallen, who hadn't stopped staring at her. She began to redden, and for the first time seemed to realize her situation. "Stop staring, Vallen. It's—"

He tossed the blanket over her legs. Then, ignoring the pain spiking in his calf and the cynical voice in his head screaming for him to stop, Vallen wrapped Elaine in a tight embrace. Bohomaz laughed, Pockey gasped, and the 'chore crew' launched into a raunchy song about a sailor and his mistress they had *no* right to know, but he didn't care.

She was his everything, and nothing else mattered.

After stiffening, Elaine relaxed and hugged him back. "You need to be in bed, Mr. Patient."

"And you need to dress more warmly when you visit." Vallen opened his eyes and peered down Elaine's back at her feet. Surprisingly, a ruddy, segmented line circled the milky skin of her right ankle. A birthmark?

"Or better yet," he continued, ignoring it. "Just don't come down here at all. Sewertown is no place for a girl like you." Slowly, like a man climbing the steps to the gallows, Vallen loosened his grip and held Elaine by her shoulders. Those enthralling eyes and radiant smile of hers had now saved him twice. "I don't know what I'd do if I lost you."

A sly grin split her lips. "So come to the surface more often. Then I won't have to come down here to find you."

"That's . . . " Vallen turned to Bohomaz, expecting an immediate denial.

"Within the terms of our arrangement," the Vladisvar finished.

Vallen's arms slid down Elaine's before falling slack at his sides. "What?"

Once again laughing at his underling's shock, Bohomaz took a wax-caked candlestick from the small table beside his throne and held it to his chest. The flickering light revealed several carvings etched into his hide:

A dragwyrm mounted by a claw-wielding warrior, whose off-hand clutched the haft of a spear piercing the beast's massive eye. A horde of Moravi fleeing back aboard their ships, the receding tide taking the blood of their countless fallen with them. And in the space between them were two fresh letters, the lines still oozing red.

E.G. Elaine Gennesaret.

Vallen's heart sank. Whether Elaine realized it or not, she had entered into a jekhat with Bohomaz—a contract of flesh sacred to the tribal giants. The only ways out were to fulfill the jekhat or die, and that death would come at the hands of a special squad of mercenaries dispatched by their blessed shaman, the Rhashim.

"What have you done, Elaine?" Vallen sank down amid his pillows, barely feeling the hand the girl placed on his shoulder.

"*HA!*" Bohomaz bellowed his loudest laugh yet. "You may be noble, Vallen the Valiant, but by Sondek's matchless might are you daft." He set the candle on the table, then replaced it with a cloth-covered object that seemed like a toy in his monstrous grasp. "She has paid the debt outright. No one will come for her pretty hornless head."

It took Vallen a moment to process the crime lord's words. *Outright?* Had Elaine bought him? Was the wrapped item Bohomaz held worth as much as the ruined pillow, the water used to treat him, *and* the years of service he still owed?

More importantly, Vallen wondered, gazing into Elaine's gleaming eyes. *Am I her slave now?* He'd once accused her of saving him from the depths of a river only so she could sell or keep him as a slave. Now he was past believing she'd do so—not intentionally, not maliciously, at any rate. But to hold his debts . . . that was essentially the same thing.

And Vallen was done being the property of others, even if his owner was the girl he loved.

"I'll pay it back in full," he promised her. "But that means I can't go with you. Not now, at least. I can't keep being a slave." The weak smile he gave her was more for his benefit than hers. If he dropped the facade, he feared he'd break.

"Vallen," Pockey said quietly. "It's a book. Though it must be a pretty valuable book, seeing as it's worth as much as you and all."

The fact that the pickpocket had *finally* gotten his new name right didn't register in Vallen's mind. He stared at Bohomaz's face, where the giant's fangs were pulled back in the grin of a man who'd just beaten the house in a game of sleds. Then he looked at the now unwrapped book in his flesh-and-blood hand.

It *was* a fine book. The spine was bound in cherry-stained ek-leather, the title was rendered in gilt script, and the pages bore the creamy color of cepyrus paper. At auction, such a quaint little pocketbook would go for a handful of silver geldars.

But it was still just a book, and not of equal value to Vallen's debts.

"It's not a fair trade, Bohomaz," he said, shaking his head.

"Hey!" Elaine had her hands on her hips and a scowl on her face. "My father illustrated and signed that book. Plus it's full of wise sayings from Steward Metellus and other Darmatian scholars."

"Like this one." Bohomaz carefully flicked the book open with one of his gauntlet's claws, bending closer to read the cramped text. "*Do not let your eye for value supplant that of your neighbor. Just as your eye belongs in your head, so too does his eye belong in his. Were they to swap, neither eye would fit the others' skull, and both would be rendered furious and half-blind.*

"Or," he continued, turning the page, "*keep to yourself your judgments. For to one merchant, the pearl is most beautiful, while to another, the emerald is divine. No created thing has value until we assign it, and therefore everything is at once worthless and priceless.*"

Vallen held up his hands to forestall another insipid quote. If he ever met Steward Metellus, he'd tell the man exactly where he could shove his 'wisdom.' "Enough. I get it. You like the book."

"I do," Bohomaz replied. "But not enough to completely let you go. This is an investment. You will learn from Miss Elaine, and in turn teach the next generation."

He gestured at Pockey and the 'chore crew,' who were holding hands and giggling while dancing in a circle around them. "Miss Elaine has offered to help in that capacity. If she does, I recommend she dress the part of a tramp and you escort her to and from the surface. She can only thank the Equilibrates that flashing *silver* geldars while asking for directions didn't result in her untimely demise."

"What?" Elaine asked when Vallen shot her an incredulous glare. "How was I supposed to know that paying for directions wasn't a thing down here?"

Common sense? he thought, silently thanking Artyr, Sondek, Sariel, and the other four Veneer he couldn't remember for watching over her. If, of course, they existed.

"*That* will balance the scales, young Vallen," Bohomaz finished. "*That* will satisfy Rashakh and Lysham. *That* will earn your freedom."

Freedom. A word Vallen had never dared utter, lest it turn to rancid ash on his tongue. He had believed it impossible to achieve. Believed he would die down here as Kit, known only by his role in the crew, another nameless corpse drifting with the sewage down the Grand Runoff and out to Erimos Bay. It was both the first and final journey all sewer scum embarked on.

But now he was *Vallen*.

And soon he'd be *free*.

Taking Pockey's arm with one hand and Elaine's with the other, Vallen pulled them close. "Why wait?" he asked, grinning at Elaine. "Let's start that next lesson right now."

The smile she favored him with was electric. Euphoric. It made him feel like he could do *anything*. "Alright," Elaine said. "But first I'm going to need some chalk." She looked at both of them in turn. "You guys *do* know what chalk is, right?"

The dream ended, but Vallen didn't wake up.

He wondered whether or not that was progress. He also wondered why he understood the memory *was* a dream, or why he was now stuck in a pseudo-space between the bliss of his past and the bleakness of his present.

Elaine, Pockey, and the 'chore crew' were still present in this space, clustering about an injured Vallen—about him, ten years prior. He circled his naive self, taking note of the sparkle in his eyes, the smile on his lips. The cynic was dead, but it wouldn't be long until he rose again.

A small glowing circle wreathed their static images, beyond which everything vanished. Floorboards fell away into a dark, yawning abyss. The light streaked, then shook as if afraid, and at last disappeared entirely as the surrounding void devoured it. There was no Bohomaz. He and the rest of the room had already been consumed.

Only one other image lurked beyond the darkness: a shadow slouching in a nearby hall, a single flame bursting alive and snuffing out atop one of the shade's fingers. Vallen knew who it was, and what role they'd play before this was all over.

You lost her when you accepted her hand, the darkness said. Its sultry, silky voice didn't surprise Vallen. It was the same one that had spoken to him since he'd dipped too deep into his lifeforce in Etrus.

"Are you showing me these dreams?" he asked.

The darkness chuckled, a deep and sonorous sound, weighty enough to shake the entire space. *I deal in far greater aspects of reality than mere—*

"Get up!" a different voice shouted.

Around Vallen, the abyss began to warp and twist. Wood boards shot into the air, fluttering as though made of cloth. Black ooze gushed from the holes they left behind, rising about the legs of the images from his past, reaching for their waists. It seemed a thing alive, tendrils shooting up to grasp at arms and shoulders before swelling to consume them.

Vallen knew they were phantoms. Illusions of people long gone. Yet that couldn't stop the gaping wound in his heart from *wishing* they were real. From praying that *this* time, he could save them.

He leapt to Elaine's back and hooked his arms under hers. Had she always been this small? This vulnerable? Vallen tugged, pulled, and yanked, his full strength available in this alternate dimension where no injuries constrained him.

It wasn't enough. Sweat beaded his brow, his back began to ache, and still, she didn't budge. In seconds, the ooze would enter her mouth, nose, and ears. Elaine would suffocate and die . . . again.

Her head turned, and hope blossomed in Vallen's breast. Her sky blue eyes once more gazed into his.

"It's too late," she said, before promptly bursting into flames.

No acrid stench accompanied her passing. No cry or yell of excruciating pain. She just . . . evaporated in his arms. And somehow, that was worse.

Vallen screamed himself hoarse, raging against the darkness until it swallowed him as well.

Hetrachia 14, 697 ABH
Resistance Base, Sarconian Province of Darmatia

Vallen woke face down in a puddle of cold mud, his ribs and right arm ablaze with pain and a hard boot tip buried halfway into his gut. He spluttered, spitting gobs of cave goop from his aching mouth, blinking water from his burning eyes. He'd need to flip a coin to decide which was worse: the foul taste or the phantom needle-pricks jabbing *inside* his limbs.

The boot heaved upward, flipping Vallen onto his back. He coughed, blinked, and stared at the frost-ringed shape hovering between him and the top of the darkened tent.

"I won't say it again," Major Reev said, words pitiless as bullets. "Get up and get moving. Training begins in five minutes."

A chorus of groans rose from the rest of Vallen's squad. What did *they* have to complain about? At least they hadn't received Major Reev's royal treatment—one hammock-to-floor ejection and two boots to the ribs for the price of one.

As bodies heaved themselves to the floor and the sound of hurried dressing filled the tent, Sylette pointed out the obvious. "I thought you weren't going to train us. In fact, you gave us a laundry list of all the reasons we were the *last* people you wanted to have anything to do with."

"I changed my mind," Major Reev said without humor. "I've been known to do that on occasion." Bathed in the dim blue light of a wrist-mounted chronometer, Vallen saw the Ice Queen smirk. "Four minutes now, by the way. I'll be outside."

The temperature in the small space rose noticeably when the tent flap closed behind the Major. As soon as it did, Sylette growled and fired a dagger into the thick side of their heavy clothes' trunk. "That woman, she . . . Arrgghhh!"

Vallen could sympathize. Waving away Matteo's outstretched

hand, he grabbed hold of the nearest tent-pole with his left hand and dragged himself to his feet, teeth gritted the whole way. Ignoring his soaked tunic, grimy hair, and clammy skin, Vallen took one step toward the exit. Then another.

Some things were beginning to make sense. After the lantern vigil, he'd been unable to keep his eyelids from closing, and he'd fallen asleep the instant he flopped onto his hammock. When he did, the dreams of Elaine had returned, picking up *precisely* where they'd halted in Etrus. Vallen wasn't going mad. There *was* some logic behind the memories.

And it was likely caused by the whispering voice—the same darkness that skulked in that shadowy dimension between his dreams and the waking world. Vallen didn't know what it was, or how to stop it, but one thing was certain:

He needed to be stronger. For Tabitha, who had seen a glimmer of potential beneath the mire of his despair. For Leon, who had paid the ultimate price to save him. For Elaine, who had given him life and whom he'd failed in turn. And for himself, so he'd never need to light another lantern.

I'll swallow my pride, Vallen decided, picking up his pace. *Whether it be the Ice Queen or the Void, I'll gladly take all the power they'll give me and make it my own.*

He passed Renar, who was stumbling from his berth, half-dressed and half-asleep. Sylette hounded him, threatening harm if he wasn't ready in time. Still tugging on her second boot, Velle glanced up at Vallen, then glanced away just as quickly. He felt a pang of regret at the gulf between them, but that distance was his fault as well.

Lilith nodded to him as he neared the flap. Her saber rested in her lap, and she ran a whetstone along the blade with the gentle care of an attentive mother. She was always the most prepared among them.

"You look ready," Lilith said.

"I am," Vallen agreed. It was the most they'd ever spoken to each other, but he felt a bit better after the exchange.

He took one more step, raised the flap, and left the tent.

Shading his eyes against the glare of the illyrium lamps lining the cavern's ceiling, Vallen squared his shoulders and faced Major Reev. She let out a low whistle as her emerald eyes roved over his dirt-smeared features.

"I didn't expect you to be the first, Cadet Metellus. Though I *did* have a hunch you might look like a drowned rat when you did arrive."

Vallen's retort died on his lips, replaced by a grimace masquerading as a grin. "I'm always eager to learn."

That earned him a snort of disbelief. "Since when?"

"Since now."

The Major's lips parted in a frosty smile. After a few seconds of consideration, she nodded. "Alright. If that's how you want it, I'm more than happy to oblige. We'll see what you can do and maybe—just maybe—you won't be such an embarrassment when we're finished."

Chapter 19

Wise Fears

Hetrachia 16, 697 ABH
Aldona Fortress, Sarconian Province of Darmatia

Night had already fallen when the transport trawler *Hartvale* gave a momentous lurch and lumbered into the gray sky. Inky blackness clung to the mountains on either side of the Theradas Pass, but the landscape around Aldona Fortress was illuminated by countless construction spotlights, including the airpad where the *Hartvale* had refueled.

Well, what's left of Aldona, Hans supposed as he gazed out the circular porthole of his traveling quarters. The ruin of the once magnificent fortress was strewn across the narrow valley like the desiccated bones of a fallen Primal.

Its head lay cracked, the white tower that had formed its crown strewn across all three of the bastion's walls. The castle wings that extended to the mountain cliffs were snapped, a dozen or more breaches in the battlements gaping like bloodless wounds. Half of the dreadnaught *King Darmatus,* the blade that had slain Aldona, protruded from its corpse like a spear.

The rest was being picked clean by circling vultures. Three heavy cruisers hovered over the mass of shattered marble, crashed airships, and abandoned artillery pieces. Beneath the bright glare of their spotlights, crews of engimages scurried like Trillith, peeling salvageable steel panels from wrecks and harvesting glowing illyrium crystals from dead engines.

There were mounds of bodies too, whole heaps of twisted limbs wearing uniforms so dust-stained they were practically white. The putrid stench of rotting flesh popped into Hans' nostrils unbidden, and he nearly gagged. Get one whiff of weeks-old carcasses, and the smell would haunt you forever.

As the *Hartvale* banked south, preparing to circle the fortress before turning north toward Sarconia, another group of carrion appeared. They wore gasmasks, thick wool uniforms, and long black gloves that came up to their elbows. As one they chanted a spell and shoved their arms toward a mountain of bodies. Fire leapt from their fingertips, turning the corpses into one more blazing light in the darkness.

A mage battalion. Hans shivered—partially at the chill seeping through *Hartvale's* creaky bulkheads, but mostly at their brutality. Yes, the dead had to be cremated to prevent disease, but couldn't they give them a proper ceremony first? It's the least he'd expect when a Rabbanite bullet inevitably found his skull.

"Cold?" a voice asked.

Hans jumped to his feet, dumping the blanket and heavy officer's coat he wore over his uniform. His head banged on the low metal cargo rack above him, and his trembling fingers missed the grip of the Lerchis pistol on his hip. Head ringing, he slumped against the porthole, then collapsed back into his seat.

"If I was an enemy, you would be dead, Captain Ulrich. It is fortunate I am not."

Major—no, *Lt. Colonel* Baumler now—didn't laugh at or mock Hans as he soundlessly entered the chamber and shut the sliding door behind him. The lock *should* have clicked. But for some reason, it made no noise whatsoever.

This was not the first time Hans' traveling companion had surprised him. Nor would it likely be the last. Using one hand to massage the growing welt on his head, Hans glanced at the three gleaming diamond pips on Baumler's epaulets and started to stand and salute.

"Oh, none of that, my dear Captain." Baumler waved Hans down and took a seat on the plain wooden bench across from him. "We are companions on this journey, you and I. Were I to insist on following proper protocols, you and that juvenile lieutenant piloting this vessel would be popping to attention like the lizard-folk when a rot-fly buzzes past."

Hans ignored the veiled sleight against the Moravi and sat back, tugging his coat and blanket about his shoulders. "Yes, I'm cold," he said at last, unable to think of a better reply. "The *Hartvale's* walls are so thin I can almost feel the wind rushing past us."

Baumler opened his briefcase, took out a stack of papers, and adjusted his glasses before flipping through them. In the short three days they'd been together, Hans had never seen the cherry-leather, combination locked case leave the spindly man's presence. He ate with it, slept with it, and even took it to the washroom with him. Was Baumler just that fastidious, or did the case contain a secret he couldn't let out of his sight?

"The *Hartvale* wasn't designed for transporting people," Baumler said. "She was manufactured nine years ago with the designation of 'produce hauler,' and her bulkheads were sheared down to the minimum to assist with refrigeration at high altitudes. Your discomfort is perfectly understandable, Captain."

"Then why is she carrying us now?"

Baumler glanced at Hans over the rims of his spectacles. "Necessity. You try fighting a never-ending war without having to repurpose a piece of equipment or ten. It is a wonder our troops get fed at all anymore, given how many supply ships this or that admiral or general have commandeered for their 'crucial' operations." Baumler snorted. "They seem to forget their fleets would plummet from the skies without the synth-oil the quartermaster corps provide."

"Uh-huh," was all Hans could manage. Every conversation they'd had turned to topics of logistics, bureaucracy, and economics. It wasn't that he found those subjects boring, it was just . . .

No, that's exactly it, Hans decided. He went quiet, turning to stare out the porthole again, and Baumler quickly forgot there was a world outside of his papers. The joyous *scritch-scratch* of a scrivle echoed around the small compartment.

The *Hartvale* completed her ponderous circuit and charted a course north. Yet as they moved away from Aldona, the bright glow around them didn't diminish. Other airships of all classifications streamed along above the Middenlane highway, their lights—blinking red and blazing yellow—painting smears across the crystal-clear sky. One massive carrier passed so close to *Hartvale* that Hans couldn't tell whether he or the ship was shaking more.

Below, the broad road was clogged with traffic. Magtech trucks and carts hauled by scale-covered mounts jostled for space in a chaotic jumble that was one wrong move from a massive pile-up. Every few leagues or so, a mass of tents and rickety plank barracks appeared beside the road, and Hans could see numerous fires dancing among crowds of tightly packed soldiers.

"Where is all this coming from?" Hans whispered, words misting on the porthole glass.

Somehow, Baumler heard him. "The Ascendant Bank," he answered without looking up.

"The *what?*" Hans faced the other officer. "Aren't those divisions coming from the provinces north of the capital?"

"Oh. You meant literally. I sometimes forget that not everyone can see beneath the surface of things."

Hans was an expert at not taking offense. Even so, he bristled at the implied insult, intended or otherwise. "Could you explain your meaning, sir?"

A smile tugged at the corner of Baumler's razor-thin lips. "Nothing would delight me more," he said. A white-gloved hand reached into his briefcase and removed a single gold geldar. "Yes, the actual troops, ships, equipment, and supplies are filtering down from the Drahej and Yelnarm provinces. The Lusserian tribes have been quiet since the last culling, so our garrisons are wasted there."

"And the coin?" Hans could feel the weight of his own sack of golds, resting in his pocket like a mass of wriggling maggots. Would he really be forced to choose between the Emperor and Sarcon? And if he was, would his family survive his choice?

Baumler raised it in the air. "This, my dear Captain, is the true source of everything you see outside. The Emperor may order a fleet into battle, but this tiny coin buys the steel, builds the ships, feeds the crews, and pays for their spilled blood. Without this, that"—Baumler gestured at the line of men and vehicles approaching Aldona—"wouldn't be possible."

"Isn't that semantics? The Imperial Mint produces the coins, and the Emperor owns the mint."

"Do they?" Sly smile on his smarmy face, Baumler set the gold piece on his palm and held it out for Hans to inspect. "Whose name and crest are on the top?"

Hans played along. "Emperor Sychon Artorios, and the crest depicts the Imperial angel. Do I need to recite the oath as well?"

"*One state. One people. One mission*," Baumler read for the benefit of absolutely no one. Then he clapped his hands together. When they parted, the coin was in his opposite palm, reverse side up. Etched on this surface was the high dome and four minarets of the Senate chamber, with curling laurel leaves along the edges.

"There's nothing odd here, either."

"They wouldn't make it obvious." Baumler's free hand pulled a magnifying glass from his case and held it over the coin. As Hans leaned in to use it, he wondered if the man had something in his satchel for *any* problem or situation.

The Senate dome expanded in size, individual bronze panels and the sweeping buttresses along its flanks coming into view. Even the tiny windows atop the minarets could be seen, and a crowd of robed men congregated on the broad entrance steps.

"The attention to detail is extraordinary," Hans breathed.

Baumler nodded. "The die used to stamp them was made by a master, one with enough *arms* to engrave, hammer, and stamp coins at the same time."

"What do you mean?"

"Look just below the dome."

Hans squinted. As Baumler suggested, there was barely legible lettering inscribed into the border of a triangular slab set atop the entryway columns. Twisting his neck, Hans followed the words.

"Minted at . . . the Ascendant Bank . . . in Elonce." He paused, then blurted, "*Elonce?* As in, the capital of the Hue Ascendancy? *Their* bank?"

"The same," Baumler said, returning the coin to his briefcase. "We do not produce our own currency. Nor have we in almost seven centuries. Every coin in circulation—from lowly tin to glimmering gold—comes from the Blauers."

Ignoring the racial slur, Hans slumped back against the frigid bulkhead wall. If Sarconia didn't make its own money, why did the Imperial Mint exist? Was it just another lie perpetuated by the Artorios house and their cronies?

"Why tell me this?" Hans asked. "Isn't it better if people don't know?"

"Indubitably," Baumler replied, picking up his scrivle and resuming his note-taking. "But as a captain, you have level three clearance, and I do so dearly love explaining my work to people."

"*Your* work?"

A passionate gleam blazed behind Baumler's glasses. Between his angular jaw, black widow's peak, and vicious grin, the staff officer looked almost predatory. "Indeed. It is why I am on this journey with you, Captain. His Majesty has tasked me with solving the problem, and I do not intend to disappoint him."

Overzealous as he is, he's still more deserving of his promotion and post than I am, Hans decided. Competence—and a bit of arrogance—practically oozed from Baumler's pores.

A gust of wind shook the *Hartvale*, and Hans clutched his blanket close. The freighter that caused it steamed past, running lights pulsing green, Sarconian flag proudly rippling from her bridge-top halyard.

Distant honking rose from below. A tri-horned dragwyrm had become irritated at its handlers, muscling free of its restraints and curling up in the middle of the road. Trucks lined up on both sides, their drivers waving fists while soldiers armed with raw meat, shock batons, and more courage than sense approached the beast. None of them wanted the delay reported up the chain of command.

"Even if the Ascendancy minted our money, I don't understand why you'd say they own our armies," Hans said.

"How do you finance a war?"

Another question. Hans considered turning back to the porthole, but he had no desire to watch young, ignorant recruits get torn apart by their own beast.

"Taxes," he said simply, suppressing another shiver. Hans remembered what happened to lower ring workers who couldn't pay their quarterly tithes. Ritter squads hauled them screaming from their homes, and they were sent to the northern labor farms, western illyrium mines, or were pressed into forlorn hope battalions.

"That is one method," Baumler agreed. "But what if there's no wealth left to tax? We have been at war with Rabban for nearly seven centuries. I would not be surprised if a whole host of our border villages could not produce ten tin geldars between them."

A shiver of a different sort raced along Hans' arms. "Seven centuries . . . The same amount of time the Ascendant Bank has been supplying us with currency."

"You begin to see the problem, my dear Captain. The Blauers have been *bankrolling* our wars. Nine in ten rifles are paid for by their loans. Seven in ten uniforms, four in ten cruisers, five in ten panzcraft, and *every* dreadnaught launched from our shipyards."

"And not just us." Baumler chuckled, and Hans swore the temperature in the cramped cabin plummeted another ten Kels. "To match us, Rabban has borrowed just as much—perhaps more. We are both in debt to the tune of a *billion* gold geldars, Captain, a bottomless pit from which we cannot hope to escape."

Hans suddenly felt very small indeed, as did the purse of coins hidden inside his uniform jacket. The Emperor commanded fleets, Sarcon wielded arcane sorceries, but the Ascendant Bank—and therefore the Hue Ascendancy—*owned* Lozaria's two largest empires. The puppets might dance of their own accord for now, but the gossamer strings were still there, waiting to be tugged.

Baumler did not seem displeased by this revelation. He continued to scrawl figures on his papers, plotting some solution Hans couldn't fathom. The *Hartvale*, likewise, plowed onward through the night toward Sarconia. Neither could be deterred from their mission.

But Hans merely sat and shivered, uncertain about a great

many things. Who his true master was. Who owned him. And, more pressingly, how in oblivion he was going to break into the royal vault when he arrived in the capital.

Chapter 20

The Instructor and the Drunk

Hetrachia 17, 697 ABH
Resistance Base, Sarconian Province of Darmatia

*F*orty-seven ...
   With a soft *whump*, the top of Matteo's foot rammed into the hanging sack of grain. There was no power behind the round-kick. Not after three days of conditioning drills, sparring, and weight training. They'd run laps through the caverns, balanced atop rickety rafts set adrift on the frigid subterranean lake, and hauled back-breaking crates of supplies from one room to another only to be told to return them to where they'd started.

Forty ... eight ...
   It took all of Matteo's focus to maintain his balance. Up came his knee, thighs and hamstrings screaming bloody murder. Out lashed his foot, bare toes curled back, skin raw and bruised on top where it impacted the makeshift bag. He winced as it struck, cringed as he re-chambered and lowered it to the ground. The water-worn stones were ice cold, but the blistered soles of his feet had long since gone numb.

Forty . . . eight? No, Matteo realized, blinking away the sweat dripping from his sandy curls. *Already did forty-eight. Forty-nine.* He wouldn't lose his count, not now, not when he was so close to finishing. Breath ragged, fire scouring his lungs, and blood thumping in his ears, Matteo loosed a guttural growl and kicked as hard as he could.

FIFTY!
   The heavy bag—half as tall as him and almost as heavy—recoiled sharply from the blow. It swung right, straining against the rope binding it to the frame Major Reev had constructed for them, and tapped the next sack in line, which belonged to Renar.

   Months ago, the slope-shouldered youth would have come after him for, "Invading his space." Now he flashed Matteo a grin, planted his right foot on the ground, and drove his bag into the smooth cave wall so hard the entire apparatus shook on its four posts.

"*That's* a kick," Renar said, catching the sack as it returned.

Matteo clapped. It wasn't a competition. And if Renar could do to the Sarcs what he'd done to that bag, he was more than welcome to the small victory.

Leaning on his knees, Matteo turned and surveyed the rest of their practice chamber. Hundreds of these alcoves existed throughout the base, rounded caves ranging from the size of a closet to larger than a flag-brawl field. Like the long, twisting corridors connecting them, they'd been hollowed out by the Draken, Nehalena, or one of her brood. Major Reev insisted this had once been a play area for slug-like Draken pupas the size of Unter, but Matteo couldn't tell this space apart from any other he'd seen in the Resistance base.

The only novel thing about the room was what they were using it for. Beneath the dim glow of a single panel of illyrium lamps, the rest of Matteo's squad engaged in specialized training.

Lilith and Vallen sparred in a circle marked with small stones. He ducked a kick to the head, responding with a side kick of his own that missed wide as Lilith nimbly spun around it. Her follow-up chop would have knocked Vallen unconscious, but she slowed at the last second and tapped him on the neck. Raising his good arm—the other was still fastened to his chest by a sling—the Triaron yielded.

Matteo rubbed his eyes, certain exhaustion was making him see things. Sure, they'd been forbidden to use magic and Vallen was fighting a limb down, but had he just given up *gracefully*?

"Again," Vallen demanded, pushing his soaked hair back and settling into another stance. Lilith smiled, licked her lips, and rushed him.

Elsewhere, Sylette stood at the center of an array of circular targets. Some were fastened between gleaming stalactites, some hung at head height, and still others were propped up on the ground by piles of stones. Matteo counted twenty, all of which sported deep gouges—the result of countless dagger barrages.

His eyes fell on Velle last, and as they did, his heart skipped a beat. She was stunning. Crouched low to the ground, slender red arms outstretched, Velle directed two shimmering white glyphs up, down, and sideways to block every flight of glinting ice shards Major Reev threw her way.

The Sylph's fingers jerked, altering the barriers' size, shape, and angle like a conductor changing the tempo of a symphony. Her footsteps were precise, mimicking the Major's movements without wasting any extra energy. Keen crimson eyes tracked the frost materializing in the air, anticipating attacks *before* they were launched, glyphs arriving in place with plenty of time to spare.

As the combat continued, the space around Velle began to sparkle. Every impact shattered crystal barbs and sent splinters of astral dust flying from her shields. It was mesmerizing. *She* was mesmerizing. Her glistening black hair billowed as she twisted and turned. Her long ears twitched at each summoning, each strike, and each step of her opponent, sensing what would come next.

And Velle's *face*. Matteo knew she was beautiful, but there was something captivating about the grim set of her lips, the ferocity in her gaze. She had never craved battle like Vallen, yet now she clearly wanted to *win*.

Unfortunately, her practice partner was the Ice Queen of Darmatia. Matteo watched Major Reev nod, the curt bob of a master satisfied by their student's performance. A normal instructor would've ended the lesson there.

Major Reev was *not* a normal instructor.

The deluge of frozen spears intensified, forcing Velle to shift both her barriers to one side. As soon as she did, a half dozen more wickedly sharp blades crackled into existence at her back.

"Behind you!" Matteo yelled. He'd sensed the collection of men'ar at the spot a half second before Velle did, but his warning still came too late to make a difference.

A leathery, vein-covered wing sprouted from a gap in her shirt, and with it, a flickering glyph. The desperate shield caught two of the frigid needles. The rest bypassed it, aiming for Velle's spine and neck.

They halted a hairsbreadth from impaling the woman he cherished. "That's enough," Major Reev announced. "Good glyph strength and control, but that last assault would've killed you."

With a snap of her fingers, the shards turned to water, which splashed harmlessly around the trembling Sylph. She collapsed to her knees, as did Matteo. Until that moment, he hadn't realized he was leaning forward, one arm straining toward her. All his fatigue was gone, but somehow his heart was racing even faster than before.

"You."

Matteo glanced up, and his pulse quickened further, as though his heart wanted *out* of his chest. He didn't blame it. If his legs worked, he'd flee the storm bearing down on him too.

Major Reev stopped in front of Matteo, emerald eyes evaluating him with her usual frosty disdain. *She's going to punish me for helping Velle,* he decided. Would it be sprints? More kicks? Five minutes freezing his stones off in the lake?

"He was only trying to save me," Velle said, rising to her feet.

Renar stepped up beside Matteo. "That's right. He's a sensor, so he saw your attack before—"

"Precisely," Major Reev interjected, holding a hand to her head as she closed her eyes. "Cadet Alhan's a sensory mage, and a telepath on top of that. Which makes my mistake in wasting his time doing the same training as you even bloody worse."

She reached down, grabbed Matteo's wrist, and yanked him upright. "Enough punches and kicks. It's time you met the drunk."

Crisp autumn wind whistled through the forest glade, rustling piles of fiery-hued leaves from their stupor and making naked gray branches sway lethargically. The smell of salt hung heavy in the air along with the rhythmic crash of waves against the nearby cliffs. Birds squawked overhead, maintaining rigid formations as they flew south to the Etrus Peninsula or Moravi Atoll—away from Darmatia, away from the Empire's wars.

Like we should have, Matteo lamented, staring up at the flock through the thin canopy. But they were committed now. *He* was committed now, and regrets were meaningless.

Another icy gust pimpled the flesh of his neck, and Matteo hunkered into his thin coat like a goose-turtle into its shell, hoping the frayed wool would keep out the cold better than it would a blade. His breath misted in the air, fogging his glasses as he gazed with envy at Major Reev.

She stalked back and forth across the clearing in the same outfit she'd worn all morning: olive-green fatigues, a tight white tank top, and calf-length combat boots. Anyone else would be blue-lipped and shivering. Major Reev was just pale and irritated. Whoever they were waiting on was clearly late.

Against his better judgment, Matteo broke the awkward silence. "Why are we in the middle of the woods?" he asked. "I thought everyone was confined to the base to avoid Sarc patrols."

The glare she shot him seemed to say, '*Do I* look *like everyone?*' Matteo supposed since she made the rules, she was free to break them.

"We have aerial cover," Major Reev waved at the interwoven boughs above, "and it's unlikely that the Empire will commit ground troops to such a remote area when they need all the guns they have to pacify Nemare and win the war against Rabban."

"Makes sense," Matteo agreed, glancing away before his eyes could betray him. There was a certain silver-haired princess in their company who might warrant a significant diversion of Imperial resources this way.

The Major's attention shifted to a couple of small brown rodents scurrying amid the fallen leaves. "That's the other reason we're up here."

"Wood voles?" Matteo recognized their short ruddy fur and pink button snouts from a Darmatian nature guide he'd once read.

"*Life*," Major Reev corrected. "The kind that isn't Terran-sized."

"Which is important *because* . . . ?"

A scowl alighted on Major Reev's lips. Abandoning her irate circuit of the glade, she marched toward him like a charging boar. Matteo was about to dodge to the side when her hand snapped out and drew the combat knife on his hip from its sheath. She brandished it at him, tip glinting menacingly.

"A single soldier can kill with this," she said. *Except me,* thought Matteo. He only kept the blade for cutting vegetables for their evening stew and wouldn't know what to do with it in a real fight.

Before he could respond, finger-length shards of ice formed in the space around them. "A mage can down whole squads, platoons, or even companies with their magic," the Ice Queen continued. She fired the jagged splinters harmlessly into the ground, but Matteo couldn't help flinching as they struck the loam with meaty *thwacks*.

"But a sensor," she tapped the flat of the knife on his arm, "Can command a host of soldiers or mages, directing them against positions where the flow of men'ar is strong or weak. They can find enemy ambushes before they're sprung, detect advancing magtech vehicles, or"— Major Reev smiled, a wistful, somber smile—"they can try to save a fleet, only to be ignored."

Matteo sucked in a breath. "At Aldona? You mean they heard my warning?"

She disregarded his question, raising the blade to touch the top of his head. "And then there are *telepaths*, the rarest of the rare. A soldier is a weapon. A mage is an arsenal. A sensor is a commander. Yet you, Cadet Alhan, cannot only feel every breath, spell, and beating heart on a battlefield, but you can *direct* them as well. Speak into their minds and guide them to victory. You are a *general*—one worth more than a dozen Vallen's."

Me? Matteo thought, shock rippling through his veins like wildfire, electrifying every fiber of his being. *I'm worth . . . more than Vallen?* He'd held the Triaron on a pedestal for so long that the very idea threatened to topple him to the ground.

But at the same time, it was invigorating. Rapturous, even.

"No-no-no," Matteo stammered. "You must be mistaken. I can barely—"

Crack!

The sound of a branch snapping came from behind a clump of thick elderberry bushes. Major Reev immediately launched Matteo's knife at the noise. It flashed into the undergrowth, drew a string of vile curses from someone on the other side, and thudded into a tree trunk. Moments later, a man teetered through the bushes on unsteady feet, the dagger clutched in one hand, a mostly empty bottle in the other.

The drunk, Matteo surmised.

It was an apt description. While the Terran wore a blue and red Darmatian naval coat, its collar was half ripped off and dangling, four of the buttons were missing, and a variety of stains—green, yellow, and other colors Matteo didn't want to guess the origin of—streaked its tattered fabric. Smushed berry juices dribbled down the sleeves, and in place of an ammo bandolier, the man wore three glass flasks filled with various shades of brown liquor.

Matteo could almost smell his hair on sight. It was long, draping past his shoulders, and matted with either gobs of grease or synth-oil. The scruffy red patches on his cheeks and chin couldn't be called a beard, but it was clear he didn't own—or couldn't use—a razor. Sunken eyes, a bent nose, and a fresh red slash on his right ear completed the ensemble.

Oh, and he wasn't wearing pants, just a pair of holey briefs.

"Sondek's mangled manhood!" the man shouted, voice part growl, part slur. "Stop throwing bloody knives wherever you voiding please, Jis." He chucked the dagger at Major Reev with an underhand throw, which she caught using a block of summoned ice.

She appeared ready to sling it right back at him. "*Major Reev*," she said curtly. "We are still an army, not a tavern or a brothel."

"I've called you—*hic*—worse," he replied with a slimy leer. "And I can recall a few times you dropped *my* title, among other things." The drunk glanced down at his missing outerwear, and for the first time in his life, Matteo saw Major Reev's cheeks flush red.

"You lush," she spat.

He chuckled. "You vixen," he returned.

Taking one or four swigs from his bottle, the drunk stumbled forward with his arms raised as if to *hug* the Ice Queen. Then he saw Matteo, and his eyes went wide. "Who's this bloke?"

"Cadet Alhan," Major Reev answered with the strained patience of a tired parent.

"Why's he here?"

"To meet you, even though I knew it would go like this."

He stopped moving, and his arms fell. "You mean you didn't invite me out here away from the camp to, you know . . . "

The glare Major Reev gave him would freeze a fire elemental *and* the volcano that spawned it. "Never again, Holcomb. Not with this . . . *thing* you've become."

Whatever she meant, it gave the irrepressible sot pause. He walked to a nearby stump, brushed the moss from its surface, and sat down with a thoughtful look on his filthy face. Even as he struggled to uncork a new flash, he appeared to be wrestling with her words.

"So why should I give a void about Cadet Alabaster here?" he asked.

Matteo bristled at the blatant butchering of his name but stayed silent. No one he knew was as strong, noble, or courageous as Major Reev. If he couldn't trust a living legend, a national hero, who could he trust?

"He's a sensor," she said.

Another gulp of spirits washed down the drunk's throat, and a laugh bubbled back up. "Ha! You got half a dozen of those sorry scumsuckers left, even with the army's stones kicked halfway to its teeth."

"And a telepath," she added, tossing it out like bait on a fisher's line.

The drunk bit down. His eyes narrowed, and he sat just a touch straighter on his stump. If not for his missing pants, Matteo would have thought he looked like a proper officer. "Sariel's suckling sacks," he breathed, gazing at Matteo with a glob of drool slipping from his open mouth. "You mean it?"

"I do."

Pocketing his flask, the drunk hopped up, staggered two steps to his left after slipping on some leaves, then righted his course and made for Matteo, hand outstretched. "Pleasure to tickle your tendrils, young Alaric. I'm—"

Major Reev stepped forward, blocking his path. "Colonel Rodale Holcomb," she finished. "The best sensory mage we have left."

Scowling, Holcomb jerked his arm back as if the Ice Queen would freeze it off. Which she might very well do. "You could have stopped at 'have,'" he groused.

"Then I would've been lying," Major Reev said with a grin.

"Are you still sore about the Kharit Incident? They gave you a bloody medal for your theatrics. You should be *thanking* me for showing up late."

"*Theatrics?*" Major Reev roared. "*That's* what you call saving lives?"

Her face reddened again, and frost danced on the already chilly breeze. Matteo slid backward one step at a time, recalling the terror he'd felt at the sight of a mythical Draken encased in a solid spike of ice.

Holcomb noticed his retreat. Ignoring Major Reev, he pointed at Matteo. "You. Alembic. What can you see while Major-ly unstable here is preparing to freeze our bollocks off?"

"Major *what*?"

"See?" Matteo babbled as they argued. "Crystallizing shards, swirling rime, but I don't see how that matters right now."

"Not with your *eyes*," Holcomb said, sidestepping Major Reev and running his fingers through his grimy hair. "Your magic. Your mind."

Oh! Matteo realized. He often forgot he could use sensory magic, given he had to be stationary *and* calm to use it, both of which rarely occurred at the same time. Trying to tune out their bickering voices, he stilled his body, slowed his breathing, and closed his eyes. The world faded away as he fell into himself. He heard the whoosh of his lungs, the thump of his heart, even the rush of his blood.

That was what he was looking for. Like a wispy white thread, men'ar encircled his blood, forming a massive tapestry of twine spreading to every cell in his body. It was bright and warm, like a miniature sun.

Only sensors could see the true nature of magic. How it was intrinsically linked to life itself and flowed through every living thing. With the smallest of pushes, Matteo sent a handful of threads soaring from his body to touch the outside world. And as it did whenever he saw it, the explosion of colors nearly blinded him.

The forest was a quilt of fading greens, verdant near the ground and almost gray where their branches scraped the sky. Birds were sapphire blue, as were the wood voles, insects, and other skittering creatures that had escaped Matteo's normal sight. Drained of all but the last vestiges of life, the dried leaves, stones, and the stump where Holcomb had sat were black, representing the absence of men'ar.

An absence that sent a chill down Matteo's spine, like he was standing atop a gaping chasm as frigid gusts pushed him ever closer to the edge. Shaking his head, he turned his attention to his companions.

People, especially mages, were more vibrant than all the other threads combined. While Holcomb was a pulsing yellow beacon, Major Reev was a brilliant star. She radiated waves of men'ar, forming a constellation of twinkling orbs—small and large—that orbited her like celestial bodies around a planet. It was breathtaking, perhaps even more so than when Matteo looked upon Velle with the sight only he possessed. And as one orb flashed and disappeared, more threads of men'ar rushed from the Ice Queen's surroundings to keep her radiance from dimming.

"I see greens for the plants and forest," Matteo said aloud. "Blues for wildlife, yellows for sentient beings, and grays and blacks where men'ar doesn't touch."

Holcomb grunted, then hacked a ball of phlegm and spat. "Artyr's blistered buttocks," he swore quietly. "I knew it."

"Knew what?" Major Reev asked.

As their voices cut through Matteo's tranquility, his second sight vanished, replacing her incandescence with the much duller hues of reality. He briefly wondered if Holcomb had a derogatory curse for *every one* of the hallowed Veneer.

Blinking, Matteo shook off the fog of regret that always accompanied waking from the other world and tried to figure out why Holcomb was grinning from ear to ear.

"Us sensors only see in black and white, Jis," the drunk said. "White for men'ar, black for everything else. Your boy ain't a sensor. He's something else entirely."

Chapter 21

No Love Lost

Hetrachia 24, 697 ABH
Resistance Base, Sarconian Province of Darmatia

The smell of the soup was positively unfair. Renar took another whiff of the strong, gamey aroma wafting about their campsite, imagining he was about to eat a meal from a renowned Nemare bistro instead of thin broth seasoned with whatever non-poisonous herbs and fungi the scouting parties could find. In response, his stomach roared its frustration.

It was tired of wasting away on an herbivore's diet, losing belt size after belt size to Major Reev's nightmarish training. The pants Renar had worn upon arrival no longer fit, and though he was becoming faster and more agile, his muscles and feet were on the verge of open rebellion. His toe calluses had blisters, and those blisters had their own bloody pustules growing out of them.

Yet Renar would bear all those agonies and more with the stoicism of a Badlands hermit if he could just

eat

real

meat.

By some arcane miracle, the Ice Queen's frosty heart had melted just enough to give them a gift: two small squirrel-hares they'd trapped on the surface. And the occasion for this kindness? Unter's discharge from the hospital. Renar wondered if one of them would have to *die* for her to give them something larger, like a chicken or wild turkey.

He shuffled closer to the fire pit. "Are you sure I can't help with anything?" Renar asked again.

"Yes," Matteo and Unter grunted as one.

"Well, just let me know if you need another log or more pails of water." Chastised, Renar circled the two cooks and sat down between Lilith and Vallen.

The quiet brunette was cleaning her saber, which she'd used to defeat *two* Kingdom swordsmen while sparring earlier that day. Vallen was taking a knife to a length of gnarled driftwood, carving a grip at one end and a tapered point at the other. Little red gashes coated his

247

fingers, some wrapped in bandages, others freshly oozing. He clearly wasn't very good at it but kept whittling away, his lips pursed, his brow furrowed in concentration.

Clenching his fists, Renar resisted the urge to pull out his notebook to sketch the scene. He couldn't risk it. Not here, not in the General's camp.

His gaze roved to Unter's broad back. This gathering was a celebration of the Hue's recovery, but there he was, making dinner and taking care of them all once again. Renar had wanted to help, though *hinder* was a better definition of his contribution.

It hadn't occurred to him that the squirrel-hares needed to be gutted and butchered before going into the pot, nor did he realize cutting a potato involved more than a single slice down the middle. Matteo had quickly taken over his duties and ordered him to get firewood from the camp depot—which Renar had done four times, resulting in the stack beside their listing tent.

Why can't I do more? he pondered.

The sight of Unter standing brought a smile to his lips. Renar's Renegades was *finally* at full strength again! But the blue giant now walked with a terrible limp, the flesh of his left calf black like rot. Every second or third breath he took was a wheeze, the result of the bullet that had pierced his chest.

Velle and the nuns insisted Unter would fully recover with continued treatment and rehab, but Renar couldn't help thinking *he* was responsible. If he could use magic, or fight better, or had spent more time studying strategy and tactics, then maybe his best friend— his *only* friend—wouldn't have to suffer like this.

I'll ask the General, Renar decided, squashing the pangs of anxiety the thought stabbed through his heart. *He'll get better physicians to care for Unter. And since he's a Hue who can use magic, he'll be treated well. Not like Angelie. Not like my last friend.*

"Finished, dinner is!" Unter declared in a booming voice.

The sounds of the camp poured onto Renar like a waterfall. Clattering cookware. Cheerful shouts and soldiers laughing at an unheard joke or story. The all-pervasive buzz of the illyrium lamps scattered throughout the cavern. Renar shook his head. Whenever he thought about the General, the rest of the world faded to gray—quiet and washed out.

Vallen was the first to rush the pot, Sylette on his heels.

"The ones who trained the hardest should eat first," she yelled, trying to cut in front of him.

The Triaron waved his right arm, which was now in a composite brace instead of a sling. "I'm glad you feel that way, *Your Highness*, since it means I'm in the right spot. Plus, I'm injured. I need the protein more than anyone."

"If you're basing it on wounds, Unter should eat first," Velle said, emerging from the tent. Her eyes met Vallen's, then darted toward a group of Terrans singing sea shanties around a nearby fire barrel. *What's going on with the two of them?* Renar wondered.

Lilith stood and sheathed her sword. "Those who don't cook don't get to complain. They also have to do the dishes afterward." At her approach, Vallen grinned and raised his palms in a gesture of surrender.

"Fine, but only because you beat me once yesterday."

Raising a hand to her brow, Lilith pretended to swoon. "Who's replaced our dear Triaron with this chivalrous prince? My racing heart is sure to burst from my chest if I come but a step closer."

"For the record, it was more than once," Sylette said with a snigger. "Vallen's been on his rear more than he's been standing the past week."

"Talking less," Unter commanded, banging his ladle on the side of the pot to silence them. "Eating more. Can bicker when full bellies are."

A chorus of muted grumbles met his words, but no one disagreed, not even Vallen. Matteo handed each of them a crude wooden bowl and Unter used his lower arms to distribute soup. Within minutes, they were seated around the fire on an assortment of benches, boulders, one splintered trunk, and their solitary cot, which Renar had drug outside for the Hue to sit on. Everything else was too small for him.

They ate in silence for a while, flickering flames painting them in orange and shadow. Renar guzzled the soup, spooning pieces of stringy meat into his mouth along with piles of gooey mushrooms and potatoes. Juice gushed from each bite, delivering an earthy flavor accompanied by chunks of salt that grated against his teeth as he chewed. It was a far cry from the gourmet dishes served by the General's chefs.

But it was still the best thing he'd eaten in weeks.

When all the big bits were gone, he tipped his head back, brought the bowl to his lips, and downed the savory broth in one gulp. "Ahh ... " Warm and rejuvenated, Renar hopped to his feet and made for the still steaming pot. "I'm getting seconds if anyone wants me to—"

Something caught his eye. Something that didn't quite belong. Narrowing his eyes, Renar scanned the group. Vallen was jabbing his spoon in Sylette's face. Velle and Matteo sat on the same piece of driftwood, the Sylph laughing as the Professor blew on a bite of stew. Finished with her food, Lilith grabbed a pail of water and began rinsing her bowl in it, despite what she'd said to Vallen. Bowls of soup in two hands, spoons in the others, Unter wore a smile of contentment.

As did the man in the tattered naval coat sitting beside him. Though long, greasy hair hung over his bowl, Renar could hear the telltale slurp of someone enjoying the last dregs of their broth.

"Who are you?" he exclaimed.

"Me?" the man asked. He flipped back his hair, revealing a crooked nose and cheeks dotted with patchy red scruff.

Most of the group seemed surprised to see him. Matteo just glanced up and sighed. "At least you wore pants today, Colonel."

The Colonel gave an experimental waggle of his legs—which were covered in enough mud to count as soil—then resumed tucking into his soup. Renar couldn't blame him; it *was* good soup.

"Wait," Renar murmured. "Did you say *colonel?*" He focused on the man's ripped collar. The left half dangled down his back, but the right showed the unmistakable silver falcon pin of a Darmatian colonel set against a red lapel.

"Sir!" Renar shot to attention, fingers on his brow, back straight, stomach sucked in. If the General caught him disrespecting an officer, more than his spirit would be broken. The others also grudgingly rose and saluted, with the exception of Vallen and Matteo.

"He's not worth it," Matteo said.

The Colonel shrugged. "'Fraid the boy's right," he mumbled around a spoonful of soup—soup from a second bowl that had seemingly materialized from nowhere. "Don't want or deserve the title, so you're better off praying to Sariel's dangling duds than giving me a lick of respect."

Matteo sighed again. "That's a new one. Bravo."

"You know this fool?" Sylette asked. All pretense of decorum gone, she flopped back onto her bench.

"Unfortunately. He's Colonel Rodale Holcomb, my sensory magic instructor. Or to hear Major Reev tell it, '*The best sensory mage we have left.*'"

"Not exactly a vote of confidence," Lilith said, hiking up her sleeves to resume dishwashing. Unter leaned forward and passed her both his bowls without getting up.

"I don't care who he is," Vallen said. The same spoon he'd leveled at Sylette was now aimed at their guest. "At that rank, you're only a stone's throw from running this army. Why are you eating our food instead of dining with the big gut himself?" Renar didn't know whether to laugh or take offense at the Triaron's reference to the General, so he stayed silent instead.

Velle did her best to *not* scrunch up her nose or turn downwind of the Colonel. The smile she beamed at him was as compassionate as a Veneer's. "It's just a couple bowls of soup. We can spare that much, especially given how little there is to go around."

Not just two bowls, Renar saw. A third bowl was clutched in Colonel Holcomb's grimy fingers, the others upturned on the ground beside him. "Mighty kind of you, miss ... "

"Velle," the Sylph supplied.

The Colonel glanced up at her, gaze lingering longer than was polite on her breasts. None of the girls' shirts fit her well, and the tight tank top she wore now was no exception. "Pleased to meet you, Miss Velle," he said with a nod. "And I came prepared to pay for my dinner."

Unhooking a clasp on the leather bandolier across his chest, Colonel Holcomb removed a flask of almost see-through yellow liquor and set it by the fire. "Badlands whiskey. The good stuff, the kind ol' Hardwick never lets the troops get their hands on."

"He's good in my book," Vallen announced, grabbing the bottle and taking a swig. He started coughing an instant later, giving Lilith a chance to dart over and swipe it. Winking at him, she tipped it back, licked her lips, and smiled.

"Where do you get all this booze?" Matteo asked. "You drain it while *I'm* training and then somehow have more the next day."

Sylette pinched her nose. "And how much of it ends up on his clothes? He *reeks.*"

"Colonel's secret on both counts," Colonel Holcomb said, winking at the silver-haired princess.

Lilith offered Unter the flask next, but he pointed to his blighted calf and shook his head. Setting aside his bowls and spoons, the Hue faced their guest, lower hands planted on his thick knees. "Spirits good are. But old Darmatian custom this is: at table recline, a story provide. Payment for meal, this be shall."

If at our table you freely repast, a story from your lips is the least we can ask, Renar corrected silently. Though Unter had simplified the saying considerably, it excited him that his friend was taking an interest in poetry.

251

The Colonel placed a hand over his heart. "With Vida's bountiful bosom as my witness, you will not find a finer storyteller in the whole of the Kingdom. It would be my honor to repay your kindness with a tale of depraved debauchery the likes of which will leave your tips tingling till Taensday."

"How about a heroic story instead?" Velle suggested.

"*Or* a tale of heroism, as the beautiful lady requests."

Light on his feet, Colonel Holcomb stepped to the center of their campfire circle. He made a shooing gesture at Lilith—who sat down beside Vallen, liquor in hand—and reached into the depths of his uniform pockets. Out came three small sacks tied with strings of different colors: green, blue, and red. Tucking them between the fingers of his right hand, Holcomb swept back the frayed train of his coat and bowed.

"This is a story of a greedy officer, a noblewoman, and a legend that persists to this day," he began. "Our stage is Darmatia. Our set the tiny fishing hamlet of Kharit on the shores of emerald lake Lovare. Love was lost that day, but life was gained and—"

Matteo tapped his chin with the butt of his spoon. "Kharit . . . " he murmured. Then his eyes went wide. "That's the place you mentioned to Major Reev! The Kharit Incident! This isn't a story, it's *true*."

The Colonel's sunken eyes glared at Matteo from beneath his scraggly bangs. "Plague and pox, boy. A true story is still a story. Don't get your knickers in a knot and go spoiling the surprise for everyone else."

"Major Reev. Love lost." Sylette put two and two together. "You and Major Reev *dated*?"

Vallen chuckled wickedly. "Oh, I am *never* going to let her hear the end of this."

Renar found the idea equally hard to stomach. Diligent, razor-focused Major Reev and this embodiment of sloth and indolence had been an item? His fingers itched again as his mind painted the contrasting image.

Bright whites and blues for the Ice Queen, a sweeping vortex of frost and light that surged from her half of the canvas. And at her side a pit—dark and dismal, like a putrid swamp. Bubbles floated to the surface, their languid pops the only sign of life. The two of them were as different as the Creator and the Void.

"Shut your gaping holes before I shove something in them," Colonel Holcomb demanded. His outrage quickly faded, replaced by a distant, forlorn stare. "I was a different person back then. Not . . .

this"—he traced a line from head to toe with his left hand—"as she so eloquently puts it. Now, can I tell my story? Or should I take my hooch and leave?"

Lilith clutched the bottle protectively, and Unter made a chopping gesture to silence the others. "His tale. Not ours. Let tell, talk then."

"Much obliged," the Colonel said, stalking around the fire until it was between them and him. The metal grate and the stew pot that had sat upon it had been shifted to the side, allowing the flame some space to breathe. Its tallest tendrils danced just above his knees.

"You're right. This *is* real. And that's why you should pay close attention to the lessons of our past."

Colonel Holcomb cast the red-stringed sack into the fire. It burst open, scattering a cloud of powder, and the flames grew in response, surging out from the stone pit in a ring. Renar threw up his hands instinctively, shielding his face. Yet no wave of searing heat washed over him. The air around him was as cold as ever.

Curious, he opened his eyes and watched the fire come *alive*. Shapes of red, orange, and yellow moved within it. People. Animals. Airships. They were small and indistinct, with clothes and features that fluttered like the living embers they were.

How was Colonel Holcomb doing this?

"A talisman," Sylette said, mouth agape. "Why are you wasting priceless magic-infused illyrium dust to tell a *bloody story*?"

The Colonel shrugged. "Because I can." Before she could protest further, he spread his fingers like a conductor and urged his fire puppets into motion. Two dominated the flames: one balding, with medals making a pincushion of his chest, the other with a full head of long, silky hair and a new uniform coat.

"As I said before, this is the tale of a greedy officer. He already had a good life. He'd graduated from the Academy near the top of his class, was in love with the brightest mage of his generation, and was considered the leading candidate to one day run the very school that had blessed him with all that fortune.

"But something changed." The balding man raised his arm, pointing to something in the sky above the fire. "The officer's superior came to him with grave news. The Ruling Council was considering someone else for the position the officer wanted. He sympathized with the officer. He wanted him to succeed. So, he offered the officer a deal he couldn't refuse."

The balding man's hand stretched out to shake the officer's hand,

and Renar's breath caught as he recognized General Iolus, fire sprite though he was.

"At first he asked the officer to look the other way." The miniature officer covered his eyes. "Then he asked the officer to collect payments for him from his 'friends.'" A bag of gleaming yellow coins appeared in the officer's arms, only to be passed to the balding man. "The requests grew more and more outrageous. Bribe a Councilman. Change the company assigned to an airship contract. Divert guards from a supply cache on a specific night.

"In time, the officer began to question the deal. But it was too late. He was in too deep and, somewhere along the way, he'd gotten a taste for the 'goods' they were exchanging." Another ember-clad sack changed hands. Only this time, the officer poked a hole in the bottom, grabbing the sparks that slipped out and pocketing them. The thin line that was his lips grew, and grew, and grew until it was a dark red sneer spreading from ear to ear.

Though the tale made Renar's skin crawl and his veins flood with ice, the artistry of it spoke to his soul. He tracked every move Colonel Holcomb made in the shadows, and grinned as he drew the green-stringed pouch back and tossed it into the mix. Emerald dust swirled around the cackling red figures, drew away from them as if disgusted, then pranced to the edge of the flames where it formed into a poised woman with short black hair and striking eyes.

"Enter our heroine," the Colonel declared. "She saw her love. Saw him advance in rank and prestige, even as she—who was his better in every matter of heart, mind, and skill—lagged behind. Yet she assumed he deserved his success and loved him all the more for it."

The woman skipped over to the officer, planted a green flower pin on his uniform collar, and moved to the periphery once more. Hungry red flames instantly devoured the flower.

"Seems like she was an idiot," Vallen said. Two elbows caught him in the ribs at the same time—one from Lilith, one from Sylette. He collapsed to the ground, hacking and clutching his right side, and Unter gazed around the circle, daring anyone else to interrupt.

There were no takers.

"*She* was not the idiot," Colonel Holcomb said wistfully. "She was ready to give anything for their love, a love she thought might change the nation when they were the ones leading it. The officer took advantage of that love."

Glittering coins dripping from his sleeves, the officer stalked through the fire to tap the woman on the shoulder. She turned, smiled up at him, and nodded at the crackling words oozing off his fiery tongue.

"It was *his* turn to ask *her* to look the other way. The balding man had friends at a large shipping firm that didn't want to abide by military transport code. 'There haven't been any storms on Lake Lovare in a week!' they argued. Yes, its tempests could rage for ten days a month, but nary a cloud could be seen from shore to shore. Why should their ships sit at airdock when they could be making money?"

The Colonel's voice fell. "She had the final say, and he convinced her to let them go. The blame for all that followed lies squarely on his shoulders."

With a lazy flick, he dropped the blue-stringed bag onto the coals. Dark storm clouds rose alongside the flames. Obsidian waves crashed back and forth, buffeting tiny red airships that should have been beyond their reach, snatching them from the sky like a child's toys. Renar swore he could hear the fierce winds howling, even though the sizzle of embers was all that reached his ears.

"The storms hit on the ninth day of Lovare's cycle, fifty leagues from shore. They should have perished. Every single ship should have gone down with all hands. But her lover's command hadn't sat well with the woman, and she was the void-forsaken Ice Queen of Darmatia."

White swept through the flames, freezing them in the middle of their violent spasms. All was still. The waves, the airships, even Renar's eyes and mouth. Neither he nor his companions dared to speak or breathe. To make the slightest noise would ruin the moment.

Down the chasm created by the ice flows strode the emerald woman. Determined, confident, and very much in control of everything, including the forces of nature. She touched the red airships buried within the glaciers, freeing them and turning them green. Within seconds, hundreds of little green figures spilled from inside them to gather, cheering, at her feet.

"She . . . " Colonel Holcomb's voice cracked, and he brought a stained sleeve up to wipe his face. "She didn't save them all. But she *did* save most of them. And for that, the balding man gave her a medal, a fraction of the glory that was to be the officer's, and petitioned the Council she be bestowed with the title others had once mocked her with: The Ice Queen of Darmatia."

The balding figure ascended through the flames, taking a seat at the top of a tower with the Academy's flag dangling down its side. On a lower level stood the emerald woman, a sparkling medal on her chest, but a haunted look in her eyes. And at the tower's bottom slunk the officer, his red glow fading to gray, his hair matting and knotting, and his fine coat ripping with every step he took.

"This is the story of Major Jis Reev's heroism, and of the greedy officer who justly took the blame for his mistakes, disappeared from her side, and all but abandoned his career as penance for his sins."

Chapter 22

Kindling

Hetrachia 25, 697 ABH
Nemare, Capital of the Sarconian Province of Darmatia

Broken bodies lay strewn up and down the winding Nemare boulevard. Most wore white stained with crimson, sightless eyes hidden behind matching hoods, and lifeless hands clutching short daggers with curved blades. A few wore Sarconian red and gold, their chainmail rent by knife thrusts or crossbow bolts. Over all hung the faint shadow of night, darkness held at bay by the lights of a city whose peace had once again been shattered.

Ritterbruder 2nd Class Mikus Garax heard the twang of bowstrings an instant before he felt them strike the bale of hay behind which he crouched. He winced. If not for the overturned wagon and its cargo of ek-feed, those bolts would be sprouting from his back.

His sergeant, Dar, grinned at Mikus as his railing-thick fingers drummed against his Rekhert rifle stock. The soldier's bushy beard and dark eyes made him look like a voidspawn in the dim light. "Up?" he asked, one finger caressing the trigger with a bit *too* much fondness.

"Up," Mikus agreed.

As one, he, Dar, and their two squadmates sprang up, leveled their firearms, and loosed lead at the Sariel cultists defending the next intersection. Two went down in sprays of blood, their robes turning scarlet, but most ducked into doorways or behind the bullet-shredded remains of a passenger rickshaw. The whir of crossbow windlasses winding came from behind it.

"Go," Mikus said to Dar, nodding at the low-hanging roof beside them. Another grin and the big man was off, tossing his rifle up and following it with dexterity belying his muscle-bound frame. They'd fought together long enough to understand what the other was thinking.

A cultist emerged from a half-collapsed archway, sighting down their raised crossbow. Mikus twisted his Lerchis pistol left and plugged the insurgent between his eyes—or at least between the slits they'd cut in their mask. These cultists were fools. What was the point of hiding your identity when you couldn't see to shoot straight?

"Aaarrrghhhh!"

Across the cobblestone street, a Sarconian infantryman caught a bolt in his shoulder that whipped him around like a child's top. His captain barked an order to retreat, and three of his men grabbed the fallen soldier, hauling him down a flight of nearby cellar steps. One took a shaft to the bum for his trouble but still made it to safety.

Not complete fools, Mikus lamented, waving his men back behind the hay and wagon before they could be targeted. He tossed his empty clip aside, then slotted a fresh one from his belt into the butt of his pistol.

This dance was getting old. They'd been hunting the cultists for almost two weeks and had nothing to show for it. A troop of guards would get ambushed making their rounds, Ritter squads responded, and Darmatian blood flowed like a river. For every Sarconian slain, five cultist bodies were burned in a mass grave.

But it didn't end. Instead, there seemed to be more of the sheet-clad lunatics every day, and Mikus sorely regretted deciding to serve another tour of duty last year. The extra retirement pay wasn't worth the cultist dagger he could almost *feel* coming for his insides.

Screams erupted amid the rebel lines. Mikus smiled at the familiar wails and leaned around the wagon's tin-shod wheel. Sure enough, an armor-clad bear was dropping on the cultists from above. One already lay on the ground, a smoking hole in their chest, while those nearby hauled their crossbows around to face the new threat.

Silver flashed as Dar's bayonet-tipped rifle went to work, each thrust and stab accompanied by a gruff insult or laugh. They might call Mikus the 'Hound of the Ritter,' but Dar was its jester, a former criminal who enjoyed his work far more than the company doc said was healthy.

"Hold," Mikus whispered to his squad. Gesturing with his pistol, Mikus caught the attention of the 'boot grinders'—Sarconian army regulars—in the cellar stairwell. "We've got them flanked. Get after them! Go, go!"

A few of them surged upright, only to be met with a hail of bolts. Not *all* of the cultists were focused on Dar. The overeager regulars toppled back, some dead, some dying.

One of their comrades—little more than a boy—gazed at their bodies in horror, his freckled cheeks quivering and mouth agape. A feather-fletched bolt was lodged in the throat of the man convulsing beside him, and try as he might, his flailing hands couldn't tug it free. Blood spurted everywhere, soaking his tabard, splashing on his neighbors, coating the ground. Eyes wide, the boy's hand shot to his own throat.

Then he emptied his guts at his feet.

Mikus ignored the glare the army captain shot him. His responsibility was to *his* men, and his men alone. Roaring, he rose and led his squad down the street at their reloading foes.

It was quick work. Dar had dispatched half the cultists himself, and the first volley fired by the charging Ritter broke the rest. They fled perhaps a dozen paces before Mikus' squad pounced on them with vengeful zeal. Bayonets and short swords swung with brutal efficiency, severing limbs, splitting stomachs, and silencing the zealots' final prayers to their gods.

By the end, Mikus stood amid a charnel house. Twenty or more cultists lay on the cobbles, their blood dribbling down adobe housefronts and painting the sandy stones red. The only sounds were the dripping of blood, the creak of the wagon's lazily spinning wheel, and the sobs of the boy shattered by his first taste of combat. If any civilians were still in the neighborhood, they'd been wise enough to lock their doors and stay quiet.

"What have we got?" Mikus asked Dar.

The hulking man ripped his bayonet free from a cultist's gut and wiped the blade on a still white patch of their robes. Ironic. Dar himself was soaked in blood, his brown beard and hair oozing scarlet, his cuirass smeared with red, purple, and even green streaks.

"Just a bunch of slechin' sheeters," he cursed, using the . . . *affectionate* nickname he'd coined for the insurgents. "Got most of them, but a few"— Dar jabbed his rifle at a dark, refuse choked alley— "beat tail when they saw me. Might find the balls they left behind if they haven't fallen down a gutter drain."

The other Ritter chuckled at Dar's dark humor, and Mikus allowed himself a wry grin. "Search them," he ordered, kicking over the nearest cultist and ripping off his hood.

It was a middle-aged Terran man with calloused hands, thinning black hair, and sightless blue eyes. There was no symbol on the front of his robes. No seven-pointed star to mark him as a Bishop, one of the Sect of Sariel's leaders. Mikus moved on without closing the corpse's eyes or whispering the Oath of Repose. The Void was welcome to every sheeter soul they sent it.

Unteroffizier Jotun found a silver star necklace and prayer beads in a Sylph's pockets, which he slid into his own before flipping the next carcass in line. Gefreiter Hursch, their youngest squad member, plucked an ivory tooth filling from the mouth of a Terran who wore a velvet doublet beneath his sheets. He started to cut the fine fabric free, but Mikus touched Hursch's shoulder and shook his head.

Unlike other stiff-necked officers, he had no problem with looting—even did it himself from time to time. But take something too big, and the brass would notice and drop a mountain of regulation violations on him. Mikus had no desire to fill out more paperwork than he already had to.

They didn't find any Bishops among the dead. There were a few oddities, including a couple Sylph drenched in an extra layer of red and a lone Moravi with a tail hole cut in his robe, but not a single cult leader with a golden star on their chest. Mikus was beginning to think their intel was bad.

"We need to take one alive next time," he said, shooting Dar a pointed glare.

The sergeant shrugged, then spat the black wad of chewing shag he'd been working on since before the fight. His teeth pulled back in a grin, exposing purpled gums. "But they're so eager to die. They practically throw themselves on my darling Lida, and she doesn't appreciate their sloppy advances."

Mikus rolled his eyes as Dar stroked the barrel of his rifle. Did he *have* to name it? "Hit them with *that* end"—he pointed at . . . *Lida's* wooden butt—"instead of the pointy one. Simple, yes?"

Turning the rifle around, Dar hefted the stock, a thoughtful look on his face. Then he slammed it down on the scaly head of the slain Moravi. Tough as the lizard's skull was, it shattered in a spray of green goop and sharp bone.

"Still broke," Dar said.

Enough, Mikus decided, pinching the bridge of his nose. He started to summon the regulars—why should *they* have to burn the bodies?—when something caught his eye: a strange splotch on the wall of the alley Dar had indicated earlier. Praying it wasn't just peasant piss or spilled liquor, Mikus wandered over and activated his enhancive magic.

"Auger Noc'tanu."

The colors of the world shifted around him as men'ar modified his sight. Yellow light from the lamppost on his left faded. Shadows whitened like snow, and reds and blues bloomed like spring flowers. Everything in the alley was instantly visible, a world of perfect clarity accessible only to him.

The Hound of the Ritter wasn't just a mocking title, though Mikus *had* broken the nose of the first of his Imperial Academy classmates to call him that. He was the best tracker the Empire had, with the eyes of a hawk, the nose of a hound, and the ears of a bat. Sensory mages could follow the flow of magic, but Mikus could follow anything—or *anyone*—else.

More bright splotches littered the alley. He ignored the sludge seeping from an overturned waste can, sidestepped piles of broken glass that shone like constellations, and stooped near a wad of shabby blankets that appeared to have once been someone's home. This wasn't the fancy part of Nemare.

One blanket bore a stain in the shape of a massive palm print, its center an angry red, the edges violet or purple. "What has the Hound found?" Dar rhymed in a sing-song voice as he approached.

"Were any of the sheeters big?" Mikus asked, ignoring the jibe. "*Blauer* big?"

"One might've been, but I was a little too busy to watch what I was stabbing."

"Just be sure not to hit *us* when you're in the zone," Jotun said, stalking down the corridor without disturbing any glass. The wiry soldier could move like a ghost when he chose to.

"Stay out of Lida's way and I won't."

Mikus' eyes tracked the purplish blood down the alley. Violet fingerprints, twice as big as his, painted the adobe wall to their right. Thick droplets congealed among the broken bottles. The streaks on the cobbles meant the Blauer was limping, his boots and robes slick with blood loss he couldn't staunch. He'd taken a blanket, hastily bandaged the wound, then gone in search of aid.

Aid no Sarconian-controlled hospital would give him.

Aid only the Blauer's comrades would provide.

"We've got a live one!" Mikus said, jumping up and motioning his men to follow him. "He's leaking a bit and moving slowly, but hopefully he'll lead us to his friends before the rest drains out."

At some point, the blue giant stopped leaving a trail of blood behind—even a body that big had a finite amount of the stuff. But that didn't stop Mikus.

He switched spells, activating Auger Olv'era and letting the scents of Nemare wash over him. Sand, spices, perfumes, and the ever-pervasive aroma of fresh water. One sniff of the Blauer's blood was enough. The stench was overpowering, like vinegar left to sour beneath a hot sun.

Mikus tracked it deeper and deeper into the slums until they found the Blauer. He'd made it a fair way on the last dregs of his life, but his luck had run out. A dilapidated shrine beside an algae-coated canal was now his tomb.

"Take his pulse." Mikus snapped his fingers at one of the surviving regulars. He was fairly certain the sheeter was dead, but it didn't hurt to check.

The sandy-haired gefreiter hesitated, glancing at his captain. "It could be a trap," the captain pleaded on his subordinate's behalf. "The body could be rigged with explosives."

Mikus surveyed the shrine. The water nymphs carved into the flanking columns had faded or been chiseled away and pawned by locals who preferred bread to art. The triangular slab they supported listed left, and a jagged crack ran across it, shredding the mosaic of a bubbling urn at its center. Worse still, ages of black gunk clung to every moist surface like rotting flesh.

The whole thing could collapse at any minute.

Which wasn't Mikus' problem. "It *could* be," he agreed, nodding at the doorway and the Blauer a few meters inside. "Now, take his pulse."

With a sigh, the unfortunate regular handed his rifle to the dazed lad who'd emptied his innards at the earlier skirmish. He took one timid step into the shrine, then another.

"*BOOM!*" Dar shouted.

The regular screeched and scrambled backward, arms raised to ward off falling debris. His terror was completely unbecoming . . . as was Dar's trick. Mikus elbowed him in the side.

"The body, gefreiter," he ordered when the boot grinder regained his senses. Was that water on the infantryman's britches, or had he soiled himself? Either way, the regular hurried to the Blauer's side, knelt, and placed two fingers on the beast's cannon-sized neck.

"Dead," he squeaked a moment later.

Dar practically beamed with pride. "Ha! Knew I put a slug or two into something big. That arm he's missin' was Lida's work, too."

"We wanted him *alive*," Mikus reminded him. "Anything else?" he asked the gefreiter.

Standing, the regular peered into the gloom, his head angled down. "The floor drops away past here. Looks like . . . steps, and I can't see the bottom. I don't think this is a shrine, sir."

"Does it matter what it is?" Hursch asked. The kid had his short sword out and was using it to scrape the black ooze from a pair of nymphs in a compromising position.

"Yes," Mikus said, suddenly excited. A long passage leading underground? This had to be an entrance to the cultist base, just as he'd hoped. Mikus would report this directly to Rittermarschal Titania, then shove her glowing praise right in his infuriating commander's face. She would *finally* have to recognize his value.

And when she does, Mikus thought, sneering. *I'll see if I can't tear her down a peg or two.*

Ready to explore the tunnel, he chanted, "Auger Olv'era."

The reek hit Mikus harder than a royal prizefighter, knocking the air from his lungs and making him see double. Take week-old carcasses bloating in the sun, combine them with the musk of a hundred unwashed slaves milling in a dark pit, and sprinkle in rot-fly-infested feces, and the stench would *start* to approach what he smelled now. Mikus immediately released his spell and fought down the urge to cry, retch, and run all at once.

"That bad, huh?" Dar slapped his back until he began to cough. When he finished, Mikus sucked down a breath of sweet slum air, then gagged as the memory of the foul smell burned inside his nostrils.

"What *is* that?" he gasped.

Jotun emerged from the shrine like a revenant from a grave, wiping long, pale fingers on his tabard. He'd likely gone in to find something to steal, and if he did, none of them would ever know.

"I have a theory," Jotun said, voice raspy. The regular he'd passed jumped as he spoke. Like the rest of them, the gefreiter hadn't noticed him enter or leave. "Your average Darmatian won't speak a lick on the subject, but the less reputable clientele at the taverns say Nemare has a shadow beneath it. A sister city covered in warts, ugly as sin, and all but forgotten by the people up here. I think this leads there."

The regular captain scoffed. "You're saying people live down *there*?" He pointed through the murky archway.

"Would explain why the cultists disappear like smoke and we can't find their leaders," Mikus said, straightening and pushing the rancid odor as far from his thoughts as he could. "How deep does it go?"

Jotun chuckled. "I came back after the fourth landing, and all I could hear was dripping water."

"We'll report it."

Mikus started to walk away, but the captain called him back. "Shouldn't we post guards? What if they come back before we do?"

A foolish idea. It might be night, but the slums of Nemare never truly slept. The Sarconians were already drawing a crowd, a few scraggly boys armed with sticks and some rough Terran men with more dangerous weapons on their belts. None wore sheets, but they didn't exactly appear pleased to see their occupiers outside their homes.

"They'll just get killed." Mikus stared pointedly at vomit-lad and sandy-hair.

Dar grinned. "Five bronze geldars say they don't last thirty minutes."

"Raise to ten," Hursch said, looking up from the erotic mural he'd exposed. "Five for the time, five that it's street rats with shivs—not sheeters—that do them in."

The captain bristled at their insults, and Mikus could almost see steam leaking from his collar into the cool desert air. There was no love lost between the Ritter Order and the regular army. One had the Emperor's ear, commanded the seven fleets, and received the dragon's share of equipment and funding. The other was just expected to fight and die when told.

But at the end of the day, they were all Sarconians. "We'll blow it and leave," Mikus said, holding up a gauntlet to forestall further argument. "There's only seven of us left and they"—he gestured at the slowly growing mob, peasants drifting into the square in twos and threes—"don't seem to want us here."

Dar beamed like a new recruit after his first spin at Sarconia's most infamous brothel, *The Florid Flower.* "Now we're talkin'!"

Out of the pouch at the small of his back came an illyrium grenade. He licked his fingers, teased the fuse from its shell, and began entwining it with a long strand of detonation cord hanging around his waist. Dar was *always* prepared to make things go boom.

"Will that keep the cultists contained below ground?" the captain asked, fidgeting with his sidearm while glancing at the listing tenements and boarded-up shops around them.

"Doubt it," Mikus said. "Those insects probably have a few dozen holes to crawl from."

"Then why—"

"Better to report we did something than go back to the Rittermarschal empty-handed. Unless *you'd* like to tell her we found their nest and did nothing."

The captain gulped and shut his mouth.

A throng encircled them as Dar worked, stretching from the channel bank on their left, in front of a row of two-story houses covered in the same rotting gunk as the 'shrine,' and blocking off the street on their right. Women and children joined their men, haggard mothers clutching thin boys and girls to their sides, aged elders holding kitchen supplies like swords. Those in front whetted their lips and shook an array of cudgels, knives, and fist-sized stones.

They had the numbers and were a hairsbreadth from choosing fight over flight.

Mikus flicked out two fingers from his left gauntlet, the signal for 'standby, weapons ready.' Jotun and Hursch casually pulled their bayonets from their belts and slotted them around their rifle muzzles. They made no sudden movements, nor did they roar battle cries to startle their foes. The kindling of a riot was primed, but Mikus had no desire to see it lit.

"Go back to the West End!" a hunched geezer shouted, waving a cane. The left half of his face was a rash of pockmarks and diseased flesh. "The Kingdom didn't bother us, so why should you?"

A boy whose ratty tunic was sliding off his frail frame threw a rock that skipped past them into the canal. "Get out!" he cried. Others quickly took up his chant.

"Get out! Get out! Get out!"

"How's that charge coming?" Mikus called over his shoulder while popping open his holster. He *would* shoot his way out if he had to, he just hoped it wouldn't come to that.

"Got it set," came Dar's reply. "Right under the Blauer's crotch, which is ironic because I'm going to blow the stones he doesn't have into—"

"Lay out the wire as we move. Forward!"

The time for subtlety was over. Mikus whipped out his Lerchis and waved it at the crowd, who parted before its glaring barrel like sheep before a wyvern. *Good,* he thought, marching toward the street they had entered from. *They still fear guns, at least.* Hursch and Jotun menaced the peasants on the flanks with their bayonets, while the captain and his surviving troopers formed a timid rearguard. Dar walked in the center, playing out loops of acrid-smelling detonator cord, smile never leaving his face.

They were about ten paces from the street when Dar came to a stop. "What is it?" Mikus hissed, unwilling to look at his sergeant and give the peasants an opening to throw something at him.

"Out of line," the big man huffed.

It was just about the worst thing that could happen. On the side street—more an alley, really—no more than three of these scumsuckers could attack them at once. But if they lit it here, the Darmatians might realize they had a bomb and rush them from all sides. Someone would die. *I could die,* Mikus thought, which definitely wasn't an acceptable outcome.

He hesitated for only a moment. "Light it!"

Steel struck flint. Sparks flew, illuminating the twisted grin of a man who craved his next violent thrill, his next explosive rush. The thread burned, hungrily consuming the oil-soaked line, racing toward the shrine where its feast awaited. Wide-eyed peasants dodged out of its blazing path. A few, recognizing what it was, stamped at the line to snuff it out. They were too late.

KABOOM!

The ground shook with the force of a crashing airship. Children wailed, men collapsed, and the stars above seemed ready to shake themselves from the sky. A gout of flame erupted from the shrine, consuming the wharf and anyone in its path. Then the pillars collapsed, the walls blew out, and with a mighty wheeze the stairwell to the lower city tumbled in on itself.

Mikus didn't look to see how many bodies had been shredded by splinters of stone sent flying by the blast. He didn't turn toward the shouts for help or deny the roars of outrage. Cocking the slide of his pistol, he calmly pushed through the dust cloud, shooting each and every Darmatian that came between him and his way out.

At his side, Dar lowered his shoulder and shunted a charging knife-wielder back into the smog. Hursch spitted the pockmarked elder on his bayonet. Two retorts rang from the right, and Jotun stepped over a pair of sightless corpses as he slotted a new cartridge into his rifle.

Did Mikus want this? No, not really. But kindling, once ablaze, was almost impossible to extinguish.

"We lost Drannic!" the captain called above the chaos.

Mikus shot another outline in the mist, which twitched and fell to the ground. One of them had died, just as he'd predicted. But it wasn't him, and he wasn't going back for the lad. He was the Hound of the Ritter, and his responsibility was to himself, his men, and no one else.

Chapter 23

Where I'm Needed

Hetrachia 26, 697 ABH
Resistance Base, Sarconian Province of Darmatia

It was a rare day that Jis forwent her usual morning training session. She did so now because a piece of her heart, Mother Tabitha, had decided it was time for her and her Way of the Will sisters to move on.

Jis stood at a distance as they completed their preparations, tying what little they possessed onto the backs of mules with patchy hides and gaunt frames. The white-robed sisters had come here with healthy animals and crates full of medical supplies—bandages, salves, and ointments that had saved many of her soldiers. Now they left with barely enough to see them to the nearest town, let alone the Kingdom's capital.

This is wrong, Jis thought, seething inside. Ice crystallized around her as she surveyed the underground hangar bay, searching for the culprit.

Dock workers called out instructions to engimages on the scaffolding around two light cruisers undergoing repairs. A maintenance tech directed soldiers with trolleys bearing engine parts to piles of equipment staged around the long chamber, making marks on her clipboard as they came and went. Sparks flew from welding tools, metal clanged on metal, and laborers cursed, grumbled, and laughed as they began another day.

But of course, the man in charge was nowhere to be seen. Jis figured General Iolus was tucked snugly beneath his silk sheets, sleeping off whatever rare wine vintage he'd gotten plastered on last night. And did he care that Tabitha had preserved his army? Salved their scars and put them back on their feet? No. The ungrateful toad had denied every single supply request Jis had sent on the sisters' behalf.

Why? Why was she shackled with nothing but incompetents, ingrates, and drunks?

Unbidden, an image of a younger—*cleaner*—Rodale Holcomb surfaced from the depths of her mind, and her chest ached like it was being crushed. The unseen wound hadn't hurt like this in years, not since she'd frozen her naive love beneath the ice that was the wretch he'd become. Drink, sex, and more drink were all Rodale cared about now, and given that all three were in short supply here, Jis couldn't fathom why he'd responded to her coded summons—why he tormented her with his presence.

"Even Vallen is better than that lush …" she mumbled.

"Glad to see I'm winning you over."

Jis spun toward the voice, arms raised in a staggered Viette defense, but relaxed when she saw who it was. "I'm surprised to see you up this early, *Triaron*," she said, tone mocking. Had thoughts of Rodale truly distracted her to the point *Vallen* could sneak up on her?

"I *did* make your morning lectures at the Academy."

"Less than a third of them," she corrected. "And if you were there, you slept through them."

"Ah, but showing up is half the battle. I'm sure the Professor would agree that a half beats a third."

Flashing a roguish grin, the bane of Jis' existence walked over and stood beside her. He was looking better than he had in weeks, color returning to his tan cheeks, a mischievous twinkle back in his brown eyes. The long-sleeved tunic he wore hugged muscles undiminished by the time he'd spent recovering. Rodale had been just as handsome when she met him, with a square jaw, lengthening chestnut hair, and—

Jis squashed the memory. The two of them were disgustingly similar. End of subject, no more comparison required.

"You don't look like you slept," she said, pointing at the dark bags under Vallen's eyes. "I could park an airship on those things."

"I …" His grin faltered. Whatever quip he'd prepared died on his tongue, and the twinkle fled his gaze, replaced by a distant hardness. "Sleep has been a … *grim* place for me lately."

She fought the urge to laugh—to tell Vallen it served him right for all the misery he'd caused her. "Nightmares? Is it because of Cadet Descar?"

"That's part of it."

Vallen fidgeted, adjusting the straps on his sling even though it was already cinched as tight as it would go. For all his ego and bluster, something had shaken him and he did *not* want to discuss it.

Just as well, Jis decided. She loathed giving sappy encouragement. People either had the strength inside them to conquer their problems, or their problems would conquer them. A few smile-coated lies wouldn't matter one way or the other.

So, she told a half-truth instead. "You're getting better. Lilith's still putting you on your rear, but it takes her at least thirty seconds now."

"You forbade using magic," Vallen groused. "And I'm fighting with an arm tied behind my back." He waved his right shoulder back and forth.

"Tied to your front, technically."

He opened his mouth, then clamped it shut again. That was the second retort he'd swallowed. What was wrong with him?

"Are these it?" Vallen asked a moment later, nodding at the spear-shaped hulls of the light cruisers. "Everything the Resistance has left?"

A strange question. He'd never once shown an interest in military tactics, strategy, or logistics. Jis would know; she'd graded his tests.

She looked up, tearing her eyes from the nuns' preparations and raising them to the cavern's high ceiling. Steel girders ran the length of the chamber, dangling thick cables that held the two cruisers suspended in mid-air. Other craft—small fighter-class airships and blocky transports—hung on the room's flanks, but the cruisers dominated the space.

Neither looked like much. The closest was missing one of her four aft engines, and in its place was a gaping tear that stretched halfway to her pointed nose. Scorch marks blackened the warped panels around the wound. Wires, pipes, and other important components spilled out like guts from a disemboweled man.

Her identical sister was in better shape, with an upper gun turret melted into sludge and only a couple truck-sized breaches in the outer hull. But both had a long way to go until Jis would be comfortable seeing them in the air again. She prayed that the engimages clambering over them like insects could fix them—and that General Iolus wouldn't reassign them to some imbecilic fancy of his before they did.

"*Conviction*," Jis said, pointing at the more damaged vessel, "and *Dharmasya*. I was aboard the latter at Aldona, and thankfully she was on the right flank opposite that Sarc death beam. After the fortress fell, we stuck to *Conviction's* side, knocked out an enemy heavy cruiser, and fled with all the transports and fighters you see here."

Vallen chuckled. "That's a lot of words to say 'yes.' Do you think they're enough?"

"To win?" Jis paused, then sighed. "No. Not even with Sariel at the helm and the rest of the Veneer manning the guns."

"Then—"

Jangling beads and the rhythmic tapping of a cane on stone interrupted whatever Vallen had been about to say. "What little trust you place in our deities, Major Reev," Mother Tabitha said as she hobbled toward them. Jis whispered a silent word of thanks the nun

269

hadn't called her Jisarivel in front of her worst student. "If yer faith were but da size o' a tiny ferras grain, perhaps da Empire would already be vanquished."

"And if we're the instruments of the Creator's will, praying will accomplish nothing unless we act," Jis countered with a slight smile.

Vallen started chuckling, prompting her to raise an eyebrow. "Is something funny, Cadet Metellus?"

"You're better off not arguing with her, Major," he said, wiping his eyes with his free hand. "She'll win every time. Even"—he turned to Tabitha with a grin that was out of place on his normally smug face— "when she's trying to lose."

Tabitha came to a stop and raised her walking stick, tapping its tip against Vallen's chest. "I can see a flower startin' ta blossom on ya, ma once rotten dune bloom."

"And you look spry enough to survive the week, old crone." He lightly batted the cane away, and they both snickered at some shared joke.

"Didn't he destroy your last cane?" Jis asked.

Vallen glanced away. Was that *shame* in his eyes? "Yes . . . but I *did* replace it. How's it feel?"

A soft smack caught him on the forehead before he could dodge. "Weight's off," Tabitha replied, continuing to swing the walking stick around. "But da reach is fine. I can still whack unruly scamps until they're not so insufferable."

Jis stepped forward to intervene, but Vallen simply rubbed the spot and continued trading barbs with Tabitha. Retaliating didn't seem to have crossed his mind. *What's happening?* Jis thought, blinking to make sure it wasn't a mirage. Had her mother somehow done the impossible: tamed the Triaron who refused to listen to *anyone* but himself?

Seeing her expression, Tabitha winked. "Please excuse me, Triaron. I need ta speak ta yer lovely instructor fer a moment."

"Lovely?" Vallen scoffed. "She's anything but—"

Beads clattering, Tabitha grabbed his sleeve and leaned in until their noses almost touched. "Ye are destined for greatness, Triaron. Yet do not forget this: ye are *one* man. No matter how ya shout, da waves crashin' against da shore won't move. Alone, they'll swallow ya whole. But," she smiled around bright pink gums, "if ya add a thousand, a million whispers ta yers, da tide *will* turn. It will break, an' bend, an' twist however ya will it. An' that, my dear Triaron, is how ye will win."

Vallen sniffled, nodded, and grasped her frail arm in his. "No promises, old crone."

"Seven Blessings guide yer path, dune bloom."

Left hand in his pants pocket, Vallen shuffled toward the tunnel on the rear wall that led back to the base's main room. He did not raise his head. Nor did he look back. If he did, someone other than Jis might see the tears welling in his eyes.

By the Veneer, he'd come to *say goodbye* to Tabitha.

Jis turned to her. "What did you do?"

"Showed him kindness. Met him in his pain. It's not a difficult concept, Jisarivel."

"Uhuh."

They stood in silence for a few minutes, watching the sisters tighten the saddles atop their mules, listening to the sawing, hammering, and clanging of the repair efforts. Jis had no idea when she'd see her mother again. *If* she'd see her mother again. One well-aimed Sarconian bullet was all it would take to separate them forever.

She glanced down at Tabitha. Strength radiated from the nun despite her hunched back, wrinkled skin, and the dreadful burns marring the right side of her face and neck. Jis winced, but she was done fleeing from them.

Appearances be voided! Jis stooped and wrapped her mother in a tight embrace, not caring who could see them. She couldn't feel the warmth of their closeness, even as Tabitha hugged her back, but in her heart she knew how it felt: *right.*

"You don't have to leave, Mother," Jis whispered. "We still have injured. The army needs you and your sisters."

A leathery palm cupped her pale cheek. "Ya mean *ye* need me, daughter. An' yer wrong about that as well. That boy still needs ta find da voices that will join with his. But ye?"

Tabitha pushed on Jis' face, guiding her gaze across a cavern filled with life. The nuns chatted excitedly in spite of their meager supplies. Her engimages kicked off a bawdry hauling ditty as they winched a fresh plate of steel up *Dharmasya's* side to plug her wounds. A man in greasy coveralls noticed her, called to his buddies, and the whole group paused and saluted.

"Ye've already found yer place, much as I disagree with it. An' I know yer voices will sing a song this land desperately needs ta hear."

Jis couldn't stop the tears. They flowed freely, and she buried her face in Tabitha's braids. Smooth beads rubbed against her skin, while the twin scents of her childhood—lavender and oranges—filled her nostrils.

"Where will you go?"

She could hear the smile in her mother's voice without seeing it. "Where I'm needed."

When they parted, Tabitha reached up and unhooked a chain of six painted beads from her hair. Jis recognized five of them: Sayri shapes and runes that, when combined, were said to give certain protections to their wearer. The sixth—flat like a coin—was unfamiliar.

"But even though others need me now, my heart is always with ye, my first an' greatest child. Feed men'ar inta this"—Tabitha tapped the sixth bead—"an' ya will be able ta find me, no matter da leagues that separate us." She placed the trinket in Jis' hand, curled her fingers over it, and kissed her daughter on the cheek.

Then Tabitha returned to her sisters. They helped her into the saddle of a white mule, mounted their own beasts, and began leading them toward the far wall—a sheer limestone curtain that ran from floor to ceiling.

Burying her emotions, Jis barked an order to the hangar operator stationed on a raised platform nearby. "Open the doors!"

With a squeal, the massive doors shielding the hangar from prying eyes slid apart, revealing the wall for the cliff-face facade it was. Light streamed in, along with the squawking of gulls and a crisp salt-laced breeze. Waves lapped against the reef-lined path just beyond the hidden cavern.

Tabitha and her sisters rode into the light—so bright Jis had to shield her eyes to watch—and disappeared from sight. *Farewell, Mother,* she thought, remembering something the nun had once told her. *But not goodbye. Never goodbye.*

Chapter 24

Desperate Measures

Hetrachia 27, 697 ABH
Sarconia, Imperial Seat of the Sarconian Empire

NEWLY ADMITTED PROVINCE OF DARMATIA
RALLIES BEHIND BENEFICIAL IMPERIAL REFORMS
IN WAKE OF COWARDLY TERRORIST ATTACKS

With a world-weary sigh, Hans Ulrich folded the zeitpapier in two and placed it on the empty tram bench beside him. It started shaking as soon as he set it down, as did his legs, back, teeth, and everything else. The outer wall rail line was many things, but smooth was not one of them. Closing his eyes, Hans grabbed a nearby railing and waited for the turbulence to cease.

Propaganda. The capital zeitpapiers—from the upper crust *Sentinel's Bugler* to the often crass *Factory Factoids*—had ceased to report the news. Or perhaps they never had, and Hans was only now beginning to notice. Wig-bedecked court ladies buried in powder were more genuine than what he'd just read.

Were they *really* calling what had happened a terrorist attack? According to Sarcon, the Emperor himself had ordered the strike on Nemare's cathedral. And now the lady governor's Ritter squads were roaming the streets, slaughtering half as many ordinary citizens as they did Sariel cultists. It was madness to believe the Darmatians possessed anything but *hatred* for their conquerors.

Hans stifled a grim chuckle, then glanced at the tram's other tired occupants to make sure they hadn't heard him. A mother hushed her jabbering child. Across the narrow aisle, a wrinkled man who looked like an extension of his weathered seat yawned as he rolled with every buck and bump of the railcar.

Hans relaxed—as much as the hard bench and constant jostling allowed him to, at least. Outside the dust-caked windows opposite him, Sarconia bathed in the orange evening rays of a rare clear day. The inner Balastine wall, pure and white, shone like glittering stars. Long crimson and gold banners hung from its battlements, above which the twisting towers of the palace and the senate dome could barely be seen.

The sight always took Hans' breath away, just as the squalor it overlooked always made his chest feel tight. Thousands of ashen chimneys spat smog into the air, creating a dark pall the sun struggled to pierce. The lower ring's factories never closed. Their furnaces never cooled, and one exhausted shift was merely replaced by the next in a never-ending cycle.

Once, Hans had been among their number. Punching his timecard, tuning out the foreman's ceaseless roars, pulling the heavy lever of his magchine press until his arms mimicked the motion in his sleep. The old and slow disappeared, their names scoured from their rusty lockers and never spoken again. The young and fast survived, but only until their money ran out, their luck dried up, and they became old and slow themselves.

Yet by some miracle, Hans had escaped. *And I'm not going back,* Hans swore to himself. *No matter what I have to do, I'm not going back to that living void.*

Darkness fell as the tram shot through one of the numerous keeps built into the outer Humbrad wall. Without looking, Hans reached up and yanked the yellow cord dangling above him. Years might have passed, but he still knew that Trevellian station—his destination—was the first stop after passing through the line's fifth tunnel.

"Now stopping at Trevellian station," a tinny voice announced from a box on the car's ceiling. "Please exit at the rear door and follow the arrow marked signs to reach ground level. Again, the tram is now stopping … "

When the railcar coasted to a halt, Hans rose and did as the voice instructed. The old man glared at him suspiciously as he walked past. The mother clutched her child close, covering his eyes with her hands.

I understand, Hans thought, stepping off the rear platform onto the stone surface of the Humbrad wall. *It's not a pretty scar.*

The ruddy-cheeked soldier guarding the station entrance shooed him by without a second glance. "Get a move on, razor-face. We've got a load of vittles bound for the Ritter barracks comin' through, an' you're blockin' the way!"

Hans turned around at the top of the steps. He saw no sacks or crates of food being winched up to the wall-top station from the ground far below. The loading zone for military deliveries, adjacent to the illyrium-powered elevator, was also sectioned off from the civilian side by a series of yellow railings. Hans couldn't 'block the way' if he was a fully-grown swift-lizard hooked up to its cart.

A protest died on his lips. Dressed in brown britches, wool tunic, and a plain duster jacket, Hans looked the same as any other disgruntled outer-ringer. Without his uniform and military ID, he had no more power than the poor sods milling about the market square in the wall's shadow.

The guard cleared his throat, then noticed Hans as he turned to spit over the parapet—directly onto the crowd beneath him. "Didn't I tell you to leave? Looks like that slash cut a bit deeper than yer face. Nothin' for it, then. I'll speak slowly so ye can understand. *Bugger off before I get angry.*" His questing hand bypassed the hilt of his sword and rested on the handle of a metal-studded cudgel clipped to his belt.

Hans wondered if the brat had ever seen combat. Unlikely, given his loose grip on the weapon. But he couldn't start a fight. Not now. The entire reason he was here—out of uniform and with no identification but the Emperor's seal—was to commit treason, and attacking a guard was a good way to get caught before he even started.

Thoughts of what he had to do weighed on Hans as he followed the winding, back and forth trail of the downward steps. He had spent the past week searching for a way to enter the Royal Archives. Flashing the Emperor's seal had earned him admittance to the palace grounds, but the Royal Guard kept him from entering His Majesty's personal suites. The restricted wing of the Compendus Archives had also been a bust, containing nothing but accounts that spoke the same history Hans already knew:

"*The line of Darmatus is dead, ended with the assassination of Queen Ephalia during the Theradas Dispute of 603 ABH.*"

As far as the world was concerned, not a drop of the blood needed to lift Sarcon's seal remained.

Would the immortal accept that explanation? No, and he'd probably disintegrate Hans on the spot for his failure. So it was time for desperate measures. While a team of scholars transcribed the useless Cimbri texts that were his cover story, he would call upon the shadow of Sarconia's sordid history: the Orabairos.

If they exist, Hans thought with a snort.

The sounds and smells of the Trevellian quarter hit Hans before he touched its streets. Shopkeepers desperately hawking their wares. A pot-bellied sergeant extolling the virtues of volunteering for the army *before* the draft could find you. Greasy aromas from a dozen bubbling cauldrons mixed with the acrid stench of burning coal and timber that permeated the cloud Hans was descending into. Few factories could afford illyrium power, and the fuel they could buy didn't burn as cleanly as the crystals.

A beggar wearing a lopsided tricorn accosted Hans the second he reached the ash-caked cobbles. "Spare a tin for a veteran?"

His clothes were ragged, a patchwork mismatch of spirit-soaked uniform pants, a blanket with armholes sliced in it, and more scarves than Hans had seen on a nobleman's coatrack. Rot-flies buzzed around his hairy ears, and his gap-toothed smile was bordered by gums stained black by chewing shag. A simple tin wouldn't fix his problems, even if he spent it properly.

Hans flipped him a bronze. "No tins on me, friend. Take that and stay somewhere warm tonight."

The man's eyes went wide. He nodded his thanks—so furiously Hans thought he might lose his hat—before hobbling toward the enticing fragrance of the nearest stew vendor. Hans' satisfied grin faded as he realized what he'd thought was a limp was actually a missing leg. The beggar's pant leg clung so tightly to the crude prosthetic replacement it looked like skeletal remains.

Not a bad comparison, Hans decided as he started weaving through the market throng. *He's a skeleton from the last war, or the war before that. A remnant the inners are perfectly happy to let disappear in the smoky mists outside their wall.*

Something thudded into Hans from the front: a child, eleven or twelve namedays old. "Sorry, sir," he muttered, pulling a dirty gray cap down over his eyes before disappearing into the forest of legs.

Hans smiled, knowing he'd been robbed. But he'd once been a Trevellian stray himself. His right hand was firmly wrapped around his silver-laden coin purse. What the lad had taken was a backup, one filled with no more than two or three tin pieces. The pickpocket would eat tonight, and Hans was no worse off for it.

"Two squirrel-hares for six tins!" a haggard woman in a dirty apron called from her booth made of rotting boards, rusty nails, and spit.

"Rip-off!" someone replied. "I've eaten more in the past week than those scrawny rodents have."

"Exotic spices!" yelled an olive-skinned man wearing a clean robe and a yellow turban. "Add some zest to your ordinary meals!"

"Crap covered in gold still tastes like crap," a passerby mocked, prompting loud guffaws from those around them.

The sergeant held up an official-looking document with a long line and a red 'X' at the bottom. " . . . and if you sign up today, I can guarantee you a posting in sunny Darmatia. No suffering through the whipping winter winds outside Varas Fortress, icicles growing from the tip of your nose, toes turning black with frostbite. Yessirree! Sign here, sign now, and travel to where the days are hot, the food is plentiful, and the women wear almost nothing at all!"

Young men, most dressed in little more than rags, rushed the recruiter's stage, pushing and shoving to be the first to sign. The first contract was ripped to shreds as they clawed at it, but the guards behind the sergeant brought forward stacks of papers that they casually tossed into the crowd.

Hans knew it was a lie but couldn't speak against them. Few could read, and those that could wouldn't find the hidden clause in the enlistment agreement. By sunrise, all of them would be bound for where the Empire needed bodies: the Eastern front and Varas Fortress.

Skirting the soon-to-be corpses, Hans walked up the steps to the only stone building on the square. He didn't make for the open door—from which wafted the sounds of clinking glasses, squealing girls, and venom-coated curses—but for the long bulletin board beside it.

Layers upon layers of cheap paper covered it. Most were torn or ripped in some way; *all* were coated in ash, soaked by rain, or some combination of the two. In the space between the board's two splintering posts, Hans saw wanted posters, bounties, recruitment propaganda, hiring flyers, and every kind of advertisement in between.

Taverns seeking busty serving wenches. Factories searching for strapping men. A hand-drawn sketch asking if anyone had seen Mrs. Garretil's lost porcupine-cat. Hans had no idea why anyone would keep an animal that spiky as a pet, but he dearly hoped the woman found it.

By far the strangest posting was an ad touting the 'stirring' effects of Tarric's Terrific Trigger Tonic, the use of which he didn't wish to speculate on. Shaking his head, Hans removed two items from inside his jacket: a sharp dagger and a gold geldar worth a hundred times what he'd given the beggar.

The Artorios House had tried to outlaw stories about the Orabairos, but the rumors swirling around the lower ring couldn't be silenced. Every time a noble perished under suspicious circumstances, or a general went missing on his way back from his mistress' apartment, they spoke of the assassins' guild in hushed tones. In those stories, *anyone* could die—not just the outers. And that gave them hope.

Hans had heard many accounts about the Orabairos in his youth, all of which had three things in common. They were founded in the

277

early years of the Empire. They would assassinate anyone, anywhere, provided the coin was right and the target deserved it. Lastly, their services could only be requested in a very specific way.

He took a deep breath. Then a second. Hans tried to steady his nerves, but his heart kept racing like an out-of-control tram. His fingers trembled, as did his legs. *We have no choice!* he shouted at his traitorous hands. *We either commit treason, or we—and our family—will die. It's that simple.*

Before he could run away, Hans raised the gold coin, pressed it to the center of the board, and rammed the knife through it. The steel sliced cleanly through the soft metal, pinning a small fortune before the eyes of the entire marketplace.

Hans turned to the crowd and roared, "This gold I raise for all to see! A sign of treason, my sincerity! Come Orabairos and grant my plea!"

The mob went silent, staring at him with rapt attention. One of the squirrel-hares slipped from the shopkeeper's grasp to strike the street with a sickening crunch. Enlistment papers rustled as a light breeze swept them across the square. Hans swore he could hear the sergeant's plump jaw drop and his teeth clatter together as he snapped it shut and yelled:

"Arrest that man!"

"Gold!" a hundred voices screamed.

As one, the guards, beggars, pickpockets, shopkeeps, factory workers, and what seemed like the whole of the Trevellian district charged at Hans.

Chapter 25
Sensor's Labyrinth

Hetrachia 27, 697 ABH
Forest near Resistance Base, Sarconian Province of Darmatia

"Ellara's teats, boy!" Colonel Holcomb cursed, blaspheming against the matriarch of the Veneer: the resplendent Eliade, Ellara. "Use your magic, not your eyes."

"I'm try—"

Matteo ran into a wall. Again. Since it *was* almost invisible, he could forgive the mistake. His shoulder, however, screeched in pain, informing him of yet another bruise he'd be massaging the next morning. Thick as his jacket was, it wasn't thick enough to fully mitigate the blow.

Velle's concerned voice was his only solace in this misery. "Sorry, Matteo! I'll try to make my barriers easier to see!"

"No you don't, missy," Holcomb countered from his tree-top perch. "Make 'em even clearer. And toss more in his path. Doesn't help either of you if you don't take this seriously."

Matteo glared up at his perpetually tipsy trainer, who waggled fingers wrapped around his latest flask of brown liquor and flicked his chin to the right as if to say, "*The exit is that way*." Ha! As if he'd fall for the same trick a second time.

Kicking aside a pile of rotting leaves, Matteo went left. He hopped over a moss-covered trunk, wove through a thicket of large ferns with spear-shaped fronds, and caught sight of the clearing where Velle stood.

The goal! he thought, running toward her. Velle's mouth opened, her men'ar bright hands started waving at him, and Matteo slammed into yet another of her glyphs with a splash of white light and an explosion of pain.

"Sorry!" she yelped for the . . . Well, it was happening a *lot*.

Matteo slid down the barrier to the ground, the cool loam welcoming him into its embrace like a doting mother. He felt a sharp pang of unease at the comparison—one that had nothing to do with his accumulated aches.

Logically, Matteo hadn't expected to receive any communication from his parents. Just asking after him, a wanted fugitive, could bring down the Empire's wrath. But to not know whether they were alive or dead, free or imprisoned, was a burden that weighed on him daily. A burden that sat in his stomach like a steel plate, pinning him to the ground, tempting him to never rise again.

"Told you which way to go," Holcomb mocked.

Hooking his legs around the thick branch, the Colonel rolled to the side—out over a four-meter drop. Velle gasped and threw out an arm, spawning a platform beneath him. But Holcomb was fine, dangling upside down with his loose hair and tattered robes spilling toward the forest floor like vines.

"Oh," Holcomb said, squinting. "This is what things look like when you're constantly on your backside, right boy? Guess I should have taken that into account."

Matteo gritted his teeth, thoughts of his parents banished. No one—with the possible exception of Vallen—could infuriate him like this drunkard could. Brushing off his pants, he stood, grabbed a handful of leaves and dirt, and cast them in Velle's direction.

Little ripples of light spread outward where they impacted her glyphs. And where they didn't . . . Matteo threw a second clump of debris. This time, a clod of soil bounced between two clouds of ripples. An opening! His scowl turned into a smile.

"Oh, well done." Applause came from the treetops. "As if *no one* ever thought to escape a Sensor's Labyrinth *that* way. Switch the barriers around, Velle dearie. And randomly alternate their height. Then add some motion into the mix."

"That's more than I've—"

Holcomb's tone softened. "If you can block all of the Ice Queen's attacks, you can do this easily."

Velle nodded, closing her eyes and extending her palms. Wide-eyed, Matteo watched her work, even though it meant more hardship for him. Sweat beaded on her brow, where only a single, curling raven lock draped across her crimson skin. Her lips pursed with concentration, and the wisps of energy around her hands began coalescing into solid shapes.

Into *runes*, Matteo realized. He saw the vague lines and arrowheads for *up, down, forward*, and *back*. Across her knuckles glowed the empty circle representing *clear*, and at the center of each palm was the filled block meaning *solid*. They were rudimentary, hazy and faint, but they told Matteo something incredible: Velle was making the *air* into a catalyst for her magic, and her spells would only get stronger.

Holcomb whistled. "The girl's got it. What about you, boy?"

Shaking fingers found his glasses as Matteo slowly spun in a circle.

The trees quivered, invisible glyphs bouncing into them and hurtling away again. Dead branches showered around him. Though winter's chill had begun to still the forest, Velle had brought it back to life with dozens of flying shields no one could see.

Terrible as Matteo's vision was, it was what he'd always relied on. To read about his storybook heroes. To write essays and scrawl formulas. To aim his rifle. And, of course, to run away.

But he was done running.

Matteo pulled the glasses from his face, closed their wire frames with a soft *click*, and slid them into his jacket's inner pocket. When he looked up, the world was grainy, unfocused. Was that a smile on Velle's blurry face? He couldn't tell, but he grinned at her red-black blob. In a way, this was a showdown between the two of them.

"Close your eyes," Holcomb said. Matteo did, slowing his breathing, tuning out the noise from Velle's soaring glyphs.

"Touch the world."

He sent his threads spilling into the forest, connecting him to all that was. The ground turned green, the squirrel-hares hiding in a snarl of roots beamed sapphire-blue, and the sky became a misty gray, all but lifeless.

One brilliant yellow glyph—square and thick as a balled fist—zoomed past at chest height. Another rose and fell between two nearby tree trunks, acting like a makeshift gate. Matteo stepped toward it. Instantly, the colors faded, the drab hues of the real world blending with them until he couldn't be sure what was where. New age art that was nothing but random paint streaks splashed on a canvas made more sense than what Matteo was seeing.

A barrier clipped his arm, sending him whirling. "You've got this, Matteo!" Velle called, voice strained. He planted his legs and tried to make the colors *sit still*.

"Why are you struggling?" Holcomb asked from far away as Matteo's ears tolled like the bells of Etrus' destroyed chapel.

The flashes of green, blue, and yellow began to settle, calming as Matteo stopped moving. "I can't move and maintain my sensory magic—or whatever it is," he amended, "at the same time." As if to prove his point, a yellow glyph swung toward his midriff, and the colors exploded again as he rolled over it.

"Reshal's six scalded scrotums," Holcomb swore. Matteo heard liquid sloshing around, followed by a hearty belch. "Alright, boy. Let's look at things this way: are magic and science the same thing?"

"What?" Matteo screeched, barely dodging another glyph—only to slam into a tree trunk. "If you want to talk nonsense, stop the exercise first!"

"Don't you dare lower your arms, missy! I'll ask again: are magic and science the same thing?"

Matteo hugged the tree, bending left and right to avoid glyphs. The trunk shook as some rammed the far side. "Of course not, you drunk!"

"Reeeeaaally?" Holcomb said, drawing out the word long enough for Matteo's thundering heart to tap out at least five beats. Was this how he died? If so, he wouldn't blame Velle. It was all Holcomb's fault.

"Both have rules," the Colonel continued. "Both have a cost. And above all else, both are balanced. Burn something, and you get carbon dioxide, heat energy, and some sort of char. Pour men'ar into a fire spell, and it's consumed to produce flame, which in turn gives off the same elements. Mighty similar, I'd say."

"That's—"

Matteo swallowed his retort: half because he would've bitten his tongue as he ducked beneath the next rampaging glyph, half because the drunk wasn't entirely wrong. Magtech functioned on the principle that spiritual energy was just another form of energy, one born of men'ar and capable of being converted into electrical or heat energy, among others.

But knowing that was of absolutely no help in his current situation. As it was, Matteo was balanced on a razor's edge. The next glyph could . . .

Balanced! he realized. Holcomb had used the same word to describe magic. Was it a coincidence? One of the drunk's random fancies? Matteo turned and started climbing the tree, hoping to get above most of Velle's barriers.

Assuming his magic was balanced while he was standing still, why did it become unbalanced when he started moving? Nothing was wrong with his process. He sent the threads of his consciousness out in all directions, mapped the men'ar in a circle around him, and then focused it on the path he wanted to take. It was—

"Focus isn't balance!" Matteo shouted. "I'm trying to pack all the sensory information around me into one direction, and it's getting overloaded!"

He craned his neck to glance at Holcomb, a blue blob sitting on a brownish line with a glinting bauble pressed to its lips. Void, his eyesight was *terrible*. "How should I know?" The blue blob shrugged.

"Sure, sounds right, give it a shot. Can't turn out any worse than yours truly. Unless, of course, you die."

What a resounding vote of confidence, Matteo thought. As a shimmering glyph passed beneath him, he let go of the tree, bounced on the platform with an "*Oomph!*" and landed awkwardly in the clearing below.

Time to test his theory. Matteo flung the strands of his magic wide, dappling the forest in the bright colors of his sensory vision. Then he tugged them all back in with the exception of two: one to the front, and one to his back. The one pointing forward brushed the closest emerald tree before weaving through a copse of shoulder-height bushes. The one behind centered on Velle, who was a yellow star exuding bursts of golden light.

Two threads.

Forward and back, equal and opposite.

Total balance.

Matteo took one step. No explosion of colors. No jerking, bouncing, or intermingling of his two sights. He'd done it! For the first time in his life, he'd been able to move without his magic going haywire.

Two more experimental steps brought him between a pair of barren tree trunks, and still his vision remained unclouded. Movement, and the colors of his secret world, were finally under his control.

"I've got it, Velle!" Matteo said. "I've—"

A rock-hard glyph clubbed him on the back of his head, and accompanied by Velle's cries and Holcomb's laughter, Matteo toppled into darkness.

Chapter 26
Balance the Scales

Hetrachia 27, 697 ABH
Sarconia, Imperial Seat of the Sarconian Empire

The market square in front of Hans had become a battlefield. A guard leapt from the recruiter's platform, expecting the crowd to part for him. He got an elbow to the teeth, a punch to the kidneys, and a shove from the shopkeep who'd been hawking the scrawny squirrel-hares. His helmet went flying, and he toppled to the cobbles as a trio of youths—two redheads and a blond who'd been signing away their lives seconds before—grabbed his rifle, short sword, and cudgel.

The rest of the soldiers were hesitant to follow his example, but that didn't stop the mob. Filthy beggars swarmed the steps to Hans' right. Four or five broad-shouldered, heavily tattooed factory workers in rubber coveralls sauntered up the center, knocking smaller rivals aside. Greedy shouts came from the tavern door, and Hans glanced over to see a gaggle of sallow-skinned whores beckoning from the shadows like wraiths come to collect his soul.

Hans gulped. He'd known nailing a gold geldar to the board was foolish, but he'd done it anyway. So much for the Orabairos legends.

He left the knife buried in the wood and spun to his left, searching for an exit. The pitiless gaze of a Rekhert rifle brought him up short. Another guard stood at the mouth of the adjoining street, gun aimed at Hans, no peasants blocking his line of fire.

"Stay right where you are, traitorous scu—"

The guard jerked in surprise. His rifle tumbled from shaking fingers, and his hands went to his throat. Though Hans couldn't see a wound, the soldier began foaming at the mouth and collapsed against the garbage-stained wall of the tavern.

What in oblivion is going on? he thought. Shaking his head, Hans started to run toward the downed man. He'd slip out of the square, down a side alley, and board a tram at a different station to get home.

Someone grabbed his arm. "Are you daft? That way's no good—guard station a block up the road."

Hans recognized the stench of urine and old alcohol. As he

turned, the sight of a red tricorn, blanket shirt, and half-dozen scarves confirmed his suspicions.

The peg-legged veteran he'd tossed a bronze coin was on the steps with him, holding his wrist like a vice. Hans didn't think. He swung his trapped arm like a windmill, intending to free himself.

It didn't work. Peg-leg pulled back, robbing Hans' swing of momentum. The scowl he wore was irritated and impatient—*not* the expression Hans expected to see on a coinless vagrant.

"Stop resisting," the veteran growled.

Hans peered at his face. The hovering rot-flies, the shag blackened gums . . . they looked so real. Wasn't this man a beggar? "Who are you?"

"Ask me later."

A bald-headed factory worker with a mallet in his hands rose from the crowd like a surfacing sea monster. "Get gold," he ordered a companion whose head was the size of his bare biceps. "I take void-touched inner who thought flashing money here was good idea."

He marched toward Hans, who balled his opposite fist and brought it down on Peg-leg's grasping arm. "Let me go!"

Peg-leg obliged. As Hans flailed backward, the veteran lashed out at the approaching brute, slamming his heel into the man's gut. Only . . . it was the heel of his missing left leg. The factory worker doubled over in surprise, spittle launching from his lips. Peg-leg left no opening for retaliation. He brought his other knee up under the thug's chin, laying him out cold.

That gave the crowd pause—a long enough pause for one of the recruiter's men to level his rifle at Hans. Light glinted off something silver, something Peg-leg pulled from the folds of his blanket and threw without hesitation. Just like the last guard, this one clutched his throat, dropped his weapon, and stumbled off the wooden platform.

"Who are you?" Hans asked again.

The veteran flicked his tricorn into the face of another grungy laborer, throwing him off balance, then gestured for Hans to follow him down the narrow street opposite the one Hans had chosen for an escape route. "Ask me later," Peg-Leg repeated, breaking into a sprint.

Hans spared one look for the encroaching throng, then took his advice, all the while wondering how a beggar who smelled of piss and didn't have a leg up on anyone could run so fast.

"It's . . . later," Hans wheezed, planting his back against a brown brick wall that *might* have been red before the tenants on the floor above started tossing their waste into the alley.

He was tired. Too tired to care he was resting on crap, and far more tired than any soldier his age should be. Months of desk life and stress were catching up to him.

Across the dung-clogged lane, Peg-leg stood with his head cocked, listening to something beyond the ever-present dripping pipes, rattling magchines, and mumbled curses of the Trevellian district. He wasn't breathing hard. In fact, he didn't seem to be breathing at all. The mysteries surrounding him continued to multiply.

Until Hans' exhausted mind stumbled onto the only logical conclusion. "You're Orabairos," he said.

Peg-leg gave a curt nod. "Not here."

"Not *here*?" Hans laughed. "We've circled the district three times, incapacitated another five guards—"

"That was me, not you."

"*You* incapacitated another five guards," Hans corrected. Had he struck a nerve? Did this killer even *have* nerves? "And now we're so deep in the Pits that even *I* don't know where we are, and I grew up here."

"Good," Peg-leg said. He started walking deeper into the alley, toward a wall made of moldy boards, rusted wire fencing, and piles of rot that almost smelled as bad as the trenches outside Varas Fortress. Hans gagged, and for an instant, he was back in that nightmare. Shells exploding overhead, men wetting themselves in the muck, corpses caught in—

He shook his head. "It's a dead end."

"Looks that way."

Peg-leg disappeared. Earlier that day, Hans' jaw would've dislocated from shock. Now he just sighed, pushed off the bricks, and approached the back of the alley. It was a clever illusion, two different walls—one slightly in front of the other—arranged to look like a solid surface. Hans turned sideways and shimmied through the gap.

"Not completely daft," Peg-leg said when he reached the other side. In his hand was the open lid to a trapdoor disguised as a section of dirty cobblestones, beneath which was a shaft leading into darkness. "Get in," he added as if his intent wasn't obvious.

"The sewers?" Hans pinched his eyes closed and sucked in breath—which he immediately regretted because it tasted like a rotting rat. "Is that necessary? I'm sure no one will find us . . . wherever *here* is."

"It's necessary," Peg-leg replied. "Remember, you summoned *me*. In the hole or I leave."

With a final glance at the soot-choked sky, Hans lowered himself into the shaft and began working his way down the slimy metal rungs embedded in its side. The climb felt like it took half an hour, but that was just his aching legs talking. Hans' feet found solid stone in a matter of minutes, and he stepped out of the access-way onto a long platform paralleling a murky river of sludge. A lit torch was propped in a nearby bracket, evidence that someone—or some*thing*—had known they were coming.

"Wonder which is worse?" Hans mused aloud. "Down here, or up there?"

"Up there," Peg-leg answered, stepping to the sewer's edge. "It stinks just as bad, and the rats down here don't bark orders like the ones up there."

Bizarrely wise, *and* the most words the secretive man had said to him. "Can we talk here?" Hans asked, tone mocking.

Another nod. "Here. Now."

"Are you Orabairos?" Hans asked. He needed to confirm what he already suspected.

"Yes."

Hans could almost cry. Though that was probably due to the noxious sewage fumes, *not* relief. When would he learn not to doubt legends? Sarcon was real. Elysium was real. Now he had met an Orabairos assassin. Watched him dispatch half a platoon of soldiers and rescue him from a greed-crazed mob. If a pure-bred dragon stalked around the next corner right now, breathing fire and casting spells, Hans probably wouldn't bat an eye.

The Orabairos agent blinked. "Is that all you wanted? To verify our existence?"

"Void and Oblivion, of course not!" Hans snapped. "But before that, why were you even there? Why are you dressed like . . . ?" He waved at the assassin's outfit, which dripped grime the same color as the walls around them.

A faint grin split the man's rotting lips. "Fooled you, didn't I? People don't notice what they expect to see, and the Empire has put beggars aplenty on these streets. As to my presence, you're not the first dolt to make our pledge in broad smokelight. Most get killed." His smile widened, exposing jagged yellow teeth.

I could have done it at night? Hans fumed inwardly. He wanted to kick himself for relying on tavern gossip and children's stories to plan his moves. "Why save me?" he asked.

As if from thin air, a bronze geldar materialized between two of the Orabairos agent's fingers. "You took pity on me, which is more than I can say for most of our prospective clients. We care more about ethics than it would appear."

The guards you slaughtered might disagree on that score, Hans thought. "And your leg?" It still looked like a mud-caked, torn pant leg plastered to a spindly wood stump, but the assassin had been running on it faster than the Academy's best athletes.

"I can't say."

Hans recalled the coin he'd stabbed into the bulletin board. "Aren't you worried about the military using your calling card against you? They could have someone pose as a client, leave troops in wait, and—"

"They tried. They died. They don't try anymore. I can't say more than that."

"And how did you take out those soldiers? What did you throw at them?"

"I can't say."

Hans wanted to scream, but the sound would echo endlessly through the old sewer system, and some said there were worse things than thieves and patrols down here. "What *can* you say?"

"I have permission to accept or deny your request," the assassin said, taking a step back toward the entry shaft. Shadows cast by the torch twisted around him, blurring his already faint outline. "I suggest you make it before I grow weary of idle chatter."

Idle chatter? They'd barely exchanged a hundred words between them. Hans ran a hand through his rumpled hair, slicking away sweat and sewer ooze. "Your name," he said. "At least tell me your name."

"Vier," the shadows answered without hesitation.

"The number 'four?' Really?"

"It suffices. Your request?"

Hans took a breath. It was a crazy mission, treasonous and suicidal, but if the Orabairos refused to aid him, he was finished—both as Sarcon's second and the Emperor's spy. Pleasing the latter was dependent on surviving the former.

"I need you to break into the Royal Vault, find the Emperor's private archives, and return to me with any documents pertaining to the lineage of Darmatus Aurelian." Hans emptied his lungs in one continuous stream, then clenched his eyes and fists, waiting for the inevitable rejection.

"Will this act save more lives than it will cost?" Vier whispered.

Hans' eyes burst open. "Come again?"

"Will this act save more lives than it will cost?"

The hushed question echoed along the curved sewer walls, growing in strength, battering at Hans' ears. He heard it inside his head. Felt it within his heart. It was the same impossible question Sarcon had asked him in Nemare, and even in his nightmares, Hans still hadn't found an answer.

Vahn and his men had died to free Sarcon, though they hadn't known it at the time. Thousands of Darmatians had perished at Aldona, and more would fall—be *sacrificed*—if Sarcon had his way. What was the cost of peace? Was it a price worth paying?

And when that peace came, what would it look like for Sarconia's wretches, the men and women who trudged about with bent backs right above them? The poor were the first to suffer from war, but what benefit would peace bring them?

Three searing lights tore through the chains of indecision: Elycia, proud and radiant, her arms wrapped around the small shoulders of their children, Meira and Sirus. They were the only lives that mattered.

"It will," Hans said.

Vier nodded, holding out a hand. "Then shake on it."

"No cutting of palms?" Hans scoffed. "No blood-signed contract or exchange of ceremonial coins?" Now that he'd made his choice, it was as if an anvil had been removed from his chest. He felt liberated.

As he took Vier's hand, the assassin leaned in close, murmuring in his ear. "Nothing so pointless. But know this, Captain Hans Ulrich." A chill stabbed through Hans' chest at the mention of his name. "If we do this for you, and the scales are *not* balanced in favor of life, as you say they will be, then no power on this continent will keep you safe from our retribution."

Hans stumbled away. Though Vier's diseased gums were pursed in a grim line, he swore he could hear the assassin's cackling bouncing around his skull. How? How in Oblivion's seventh damned name did he keep making deal after deal with void-touched immortals and hired killers?

Vier's hand pursued him. "Payment. And the seal."

A dozen questions died on Hans' tongue. It didn't matter how the Orabairos knew his name, or how they'd discovered he possessed the Emperor's seal. The sack of silver clinked merrily as he passed it over, and Vier pocketed the wax-stamped letter without checking its authenticity.

"Expect the documents before you return to Nemare," Vier said.

The shadows swallowed him whole, leaving Hans alone with sloshing sewage, scurrying rats, and a host of new fears and worries.

Two small bodies barreled into Hans the second he opened the door to his townhouse.

"Papa, see shuup!" little Sirus jabbered, peeling away from his father's leg and holding up a toy airship. The craftsmanship wasn't great, just a carving with little pieces of metal tacked on for cannons, but the three-year-old was wholly enamored with it.

"I do!" Hans replied. He knelt and flicked the ship's miniature steering wheel, making it spin. "Where did you get it?"

"*I* found it at the market," his daughter Meira announced, hand to her chest. "I told the shopkeep that my papa was flying south on one with the Emperor, and he was so impressed he gave momma a discount."

Or afraid, Hans thought, darkness creeping back into his mind. No. He wouldn't think about those things. Not here, not around his family. Smiling, Hans ruffled Meira's scarlet hair. "You did very well. Remind me to bring you along next time I visit the grocer so you can talk *them* down a few geldars."

The girl beamed at him, dimples rosy, sea-foam eyes twinkling. She was more her mother's child than his, and for that, Hans was grateful.

A tiny finger poked at the scar tissue on his nose. "Papa get hurt?" Sirus asked. His precious ship hung at his side, and he was staring intently at his father's disfigured face.

Oh. Right. Hans hadn't spent more than a couple days at home in . . . ancestors knew how long. Last time, Sirus could barely speak, and now . . .

Tears sprang to Hans' eyes. This war had taken so much of his children's lives from him, and it threatened to take ever more. *Worse still,* a dark voice whispered. *It could take* you *from them entirely.*

Meira must have seen him weeping, for she grabbed Sirus and started pulling him away. "It's an old scratch," she told him. "Nothing to worry about. Don't ask Papa about it again."

Wiping his cheeks with one hand, Hans reached out and pulled them close with the other. "Ask as much as you want, Sirus. Anything, anytime. Just . . . not today," he added, his tears threatening to overflow again. "Papa needs to rest."

They nodded as one, then wandered down the hall into their small common room, Meira asking Sirus about airships the whole way. She was an amazing daughter, so mature for her short five winters. Hans didn't deserve her.

He hung his jacket on the coatrack beside his dress uniform and trudged to his bedroom door. The wallpaper was peeling off the wall on his right. Above, the illyrium lights flickered, their circuits not properly welded to the central crystal. More things he'd failed to do. More things the war had left him without *time* to do.

Humming and the sounds of splashing water came from beyond the kitchen door. Hans paused, debating whether he should sneak up on Elycia while she was washing dishes or just throw himself into bed.

He chose the latter. Not bothering to remove his boots or foul-smelling clothes, Hans flopped onto the creaking mattress and buried his face in his sweat-stained pillow.

Minutes passed. Or perhaps hours. The next thing Hans knew, a slender form was snuggled alongside him, one arm draped protectively over him, the other stroking his hair. In the darkness, it was impossible to miss Elycia's sea-green eyes, and Hans stared into them with the desperation of a drowning man.

"Elycia, I—"

She pressed a finger to his lips, then went back to stroking his hair. "It's alright. Whatever happened, whatever you did, it's alright."

The tears overwhelmed Hans, and he curled his chin to Elycia's chest, thanking whoever would listen for a love that needed no words.

Chapter 27

Respite

Hetrachia 27, 697 ABH
Forest near Resistance Base, Sarconian Province of Darmatia

Fluffy clouds cradled Matteo's head as he dreamed, and the evening sun—warm and red—hovered over him, stroking his hair with its beams. Wind caressed his cheeks, carrying with it the fragrance of the white jasmine flowers his mother loved, and liquid dribbled down his forehead and neck, cooling him as it went.

"The Afterplane isn't so bad," he murmured. "Seems I got to skip all the awful stuff in Kinloss' sermons."

Raising a long sunbeam to its mouth, the sun laughed. "You aren't dead, silly. I wouldn't let that happen on my watch."

"Then why am I laying on a cloud?"

"You mean my lap?" The sun chuckled again, a familiar, pleasant sound. "Let's get these glasses back on you before you start asking Sariel to help you cross over."

Rough metal scraped against his skin as two glass orbs settled over Matteo's eyes. He blinked—once, twice—then felt his flesh flush hotter than the wet rag on his forehead could hope to cool. Velle's head and shoulders hung above him, less than an arm's length from his face. And if her belly was beside his head, then her legs were beneath his ...

Matteo started to rise, but Velle prodded him in the forehead with a black-nailed finger and forced him back down. "No. You're resting. That was a nasty blow my glyph gave you, and I'm not letting you go until my treatment is finished. But when it is"—she glared into the darkening forest, its shadows multiplying as the sun started to set—"Holcomb is going to get a lump to match yours."

He gave up struggling. Her finger was remarkably strong, and the situation wasn't wholly uncomfortable—not after their combined trek through the Etrusian sewers. Add to that all the time they'd spent together these past few weeks, and Matteo was getting used to being near Velle.

Even if he was going to be nearly as red as she was throughout the entire experience.

"Holcomb's only trying to help," he said. "And since I figured out how to walk and use my magic at the same time, I'd say he succeeded."

"Funny. His 'help' looks like everyone else's definition of 'harm.'"

Matteo sniggered, and Velle's gaze softened as she turned her mesmerizing ruby eyes on him. One glance was enough to make his heart pound like it had when he was dodging her glyphs.

She moved a hand over his chest and released a burst of men'ar. Within seconds, his pulse slowed, and his nerves were only slightly—instead of completely—frayed by the touch of her thighs on his neck.

"You're still like an open book, Matteo," she said. "You don't have to be anxious around me."

"That's . . . difficult."

"Because of what your mother said? About finding a wife?"

Matteo's cheeks flushed as his emotions spiraled out of control. Surprise, embarrassment, concern, and countless others. Velle must have felt them all through her empathic abilities, for her own lips and eyes twisted along with his.

"How did you find out about that?" Matteo asked.

She stared at the sky, nibbling at her lower lip like she did whenever she made a mistake. He was beginning to understand Velle's quirks the same way she could feel his. "You may have noticed Lilith is, shall we say . . . light on her feet. She overheard your conversation with your mother—among other things she probably shouldn't have—and told me because she thought, you know . . . "

"I know," Matteo interjected before she could say those three damning words aloud: *I love her.*

Silence fell, lengthening along with the shadows of trees and ferns. Somewhere, a nochlow hooted, and the pounding of the surf below the cliffs seemed to grow as daylight ebbed. Despite his wool-lined coat, Matteo shivered, and Velle once again placed a hand on his breast. This time, warmth flowed into him along with her blood magic, the same Sylph spell she used to keep her bare arms from freezing. How strange that something that could stop a heart could heat it in equal measure.

Her other hand slid along his scalp and began absently stroking his hair. "Could you . . . " Matteo gulped, considering. "Could you block out the pain with your magic?"

"Physical pain?" Velle's electrifying touch traced to the spot on his neck where he'd been struck by her glyph. The skin was smooth, no bump, no bruising. "I've healed all the injuries I could see. Do you want me to take a look at the bruises on your chest?"

"No-no-no." He waved her off, afraid she would start removing his coat. "I was referring to . . . *unseen* aches. Like"—a pang of regret swept through him—"Like leaving my parents behind."

"Oh, Matteo." Velle gazed at him, eyes dangerously entrancing, and he had to look away. "I can treat the symptoms. Make you calm, drive away the depression, give you the feeling that everything is bright as crystal. But it'll be a lie, and the pain will always return. No cure will be enough until you come to terms with the past.

"But they're still alive," she insisted, her fingers running through his curls, making Matteo's tension bleed away with every second, every breath. "I know they are. Anathea has your determination, and Martan has your strength. They'll survive until the Resistance gains the numbers to challenge the Empire, and then you'll be reunited."

He nodded. There wasn't much else he *could* do. Velle was right, and his worrying wasn't accomplishing anything except upsetting them both. Forcing a smile, he changed the subject. "What about your parents, Velle? What are they like?"

Nails dug into his scalp. Not hard enough to draw blood, but enough to make him squirm. A second later, Velle gasped and the pressure disappeared. "I'm so sorry, Matteo. I got . . . distracted."

He didn't press, and the head-scratching resumed as she stared into the forest. Wherever Velle was, she wasn't with him anymore. The chittering of nocturnal insects filled the glade, yet another sign they should head back to base, but Matteo let her have the time she needed.

"You don't want to meet my parents," Velle said. "My mother would treat you like a chair. Something that exists, but that she couldn't care less about until she needs one. My father would despise you. It's not a pleasant situation, especially with my younger sister in the mix."

Mother, father, sister. It occurred to Matteo that he knew nothing about Velle's past—or that of any of the other cadets. Vallen was from Sewertown. Renar was the Commandant's son, and Sylette had . . . *issues* of a different magnitude.

But what of Lilith, Unter, or Velle? Did her family live in Nemare, like many other Sylph in exile? He'd heard the Magerium cut ties with any citizens who left their borders without an official assignment, and living apart from one's people must be difficult—as difficult as it was for him to be separated from his parents.

Matteo reached up and clasped Velle's wrist above the silver circlet she wore. The crescent moon charm attached to it brushed against his skin, cold as the coming night. "I'd still love to meet them," Matteo said, seeking her crimson eyes amid the ruddy twilight. "Once this is all over, once Nemare is liberated, we can get all our families together and—"

Velle took his hand in hers, leaned down, and kissed him. It was abrupt. Shocking. But Matteo could feel *everything* in that instant. Raven curls tickling his cheeks and neck. The touch of soft fingers intertwined with his. Velle's lips tasted sweeter than the most succulent jam, and her sensual scent—like fresh jasmine—flooded his nostrils.

The kiss was everything he'd wanted. Everything he'd imagined in his wildest fantasies.

But it still felt *wrong*.

Velle pulled away before he could object. The separation felt like a yawning chasm, one deep enough for Matteo to fall into and never climb out of. He nearly chased her, craving another second of her lips on his.

Instead, he asked, "What was that, Velle?"

She bit her lower lip, and Matteo could swear she was a couple shades redder than she normally was. "I . . . that was . . . "

Thump!

Matteo's head hit grass as Velle shoved him off her lap and jumped to her feet. "*Ack!*" His cry halted her sudden flight. Velle turned around, one trembling arm stretched toward him.

Her movement brought her into a sliver of light filtering through the branches—the day's last gasp. Matteo's eyes went wide. Velle's reaction mirrored his own, and her hand snapped back, covering her right cheek. Hiding the three-pronged black star and crescent moon sigil tattooed on skin that had always been smooth and unblemished.

"You saw *nothing*," Velle hissed, then vanished into the forest.

Chapter 28
Two of a Kind

Hetrachia 28, 697 ABH
Resistance Base, Sarconian Province of Darmatia

"V-void," Sylette mumbled through pale, frost-dappled lips. "Voiding void. Void-v-void-void. Voidity void. *Void! VOID!*"

Step by step, she limped across the ice-slick stones of the training room. Out of the sparring circle, past Renar's pitying gaze, and over to the wall beside the hanging practice dummies. They didn't have true faces, but Sylette could almost *feel* the knots on their wooden "heads" condemning her.

Weak, they whispered. *Slow. Foolish.*

They chastised her with the haughty voice of the Emperor and teased her with Vasuron's sweet, honeyed words. *Inept. Talentless. Failure.*

But what was she supposed to do against *that*? Sylette glared over her shoulder at her opponent, raven hair tucked behind her ears, emerald eyes still boring through the princess' skull. Major Reev bore not a scratch—not a scuff, cut, or scrape to indicate Sylette had so much as *touched* her.

"Voiding monster," she muttered.

Sylette collapsed atop a pile of sacks filled with sand, her whole body shivering, her legs trembling and convulsing. Every hair on her arms and legs stood on end. Not a drop of sweat beaded on her skin, even though she'd just finished fighting.

No, Sylette's whole world was ice and frost. Shards clung to the frazzled ends of her silver hair, twisting it, knotting it in snarls and curls. Patches of gleaming frost painted her leather chest guard in blue-white and crusted her loose trousers and blouse, making them crack and crinkle with every move she made.

Rubbing her hands together barely helped, as did curling her legs to her chest and wrapping them in her quivering arms. Void it all. Void her misting breath. Void her chattering teeth.

But most of all, Sylette thought, plucking slivers of ice from her clothes with aching fingers, *void that sneering, emerald-eyed witch who didn't move a single voiding step no matter how many blades I tossed at her.*

296

"Next," Major Reev called, gesturing for Velle to step into the ring. The Sylph girl shot Sylette a glance. Winked and gave her a weak smile.

Did Velle feel *sorry* for her? Well, void that too. So what if Sylette's daggers weren't as effective shields as the Sylph's glyphs? So what if the Ice Queen had overwhelmed her, had all but *frozen* her to the cave floor?

Sylette had other talents—her mind, tactics, and foresight. If they were to fight for real, things would go differently. She'd choose an environment that favored her: hot and steamy, a place where Major Reev couldn't use her magic. Smoke canisters would render her eyes useless. Clanging daggers would mislead the Ice Queen's ears, isolating her. Then Sylette would stalk her from the shadows, summoning daggers one by one, encircling her foe with a net of steel from which she couldn't—

Sighing, Sylette shook her head. Her pride was a distraction. Like her temper, it only ever served to get in the way of her revenge. She needed to internalize Major Reev's lessons. Take them and use them against her *true* enemies.

Sylette chipped away at the ice on her leathers as she surveyed the room. Velle was *advancing* on the Major, pushing forward with one brilliant white glyph while three more circled her blind spots, catching any frozen spears fired at her from behind. She wasn't going to win— *that* wasn't in doubt. But she *was* improving.

Which was more than Sylette could say for Renar. His form was fine, barrages of heavy punches and kicks which left cracks on the wooden mannequins and spilled sand from the hanging bags. Yet he didn't seem any stronger than the martial artists who'd trained her as a child, who'd taught her the basics of stances, forms, and strikes before her men'ar ever manifested.

Was there some reason Renar was holding back?

Not her problem. Sylette kicked her boots against the ground, shattering the ice clinging to their soles. Grunting, she heaved herself to her feet. *Void.* It hurt to walk, to breathe—even *shivering* made her muscles twinge.

Not even Sylette's pride could keep her training, not after that thrashing. Placing one hand on the wall, she shuffled toward the cavern entrance, desiring nothing more than to curl up in her hammock with her ragged blanket.

"Void." Step.

"Bloody void." Step.

"Void." Step. "My." Step. "Life." Step.

Sylette paused by the last of the training dummies, leaning against it for support. Ahead of her, Vallen and Lilith circled each other in a sparring ring drawn from white chalk. Could she get past without them seeing her?

Vallen sprang forward, whipping his front foot in a head-high roundhouse kick. Ducking low, Lilith moved inward, angling toward Vallen's brace-wrapped arm.

Taking advantage of his injury, Sylette thought, smiling. *Very smart.*

Arresting his momentum, Vallen dropped his outstretched leg down in a vicious axe kick. Lilith deflected the blow off her arm, rolled with the impact, and scythed out with a sweep kick of her own.

The Triaron didn't stand a chance. His pivot foot flew out from under him, knocking him to the stones in a heap of sweat-soaked fabric and grimy bandages.

"Enough of this," Vallen snarled.

Reaching up, he grabbed his brace and sodden tunic and *ripped* them free. He tossed them away, flexed his right arm until it popped, then settled into a defensive stance. "Again," Vallen said.

Void, Sylette thought, eyes wide.

He *was* a muscle. Corded sinew covered Vallen's body from head to foot, bulging at his shoulders, taut and lean around his chest and abs. He was like one of her blades, razor-sharp, gleaming as sweat dribbled down his cheek and trickled along his stomach, tracing every unyielding curve. Down toward his baggy, rope-tied trousers which hung just a bit too low. Down toward ...

A flush crept down Sylette's neck, banishing the cold, quickening her pulse. Why was she ... ? What was she ... ?

NO.

She tore her gaze from him. No, she was *not* going to deal with those kinds of urges, *especially* involving this voiding imbecile.

Across from Vallen, Lilith slowly settled into her own stance. Her grin was wicked, her eyes roving over him bit by bit. "Are you trying to distract me?" she asked.

Vallen blinked. "Huh?"

Lilith charged him, grabbing him by the wrist, trapping his newly freed arm in a brutal hold. He tried to pull away, to flee. Too late. Lilith slid her leg behind his and slammed him to the ground so hard *Sylette* groaned. Laughing, Lilith sat on top of Vallen and bent his elbow until he gasped: "I give! I give!"

Sylette turned away, hand raised to hide her giggling. After that 'manly' display, it was fitting Vallen end up with his face kissing the cave floor.

What's that?

The gold-tipped corner of a leather notebook glinted at her from among a stack of sparring staves they'd been using earlier. It lay face-down, pages spread wide, tattered binding jutting out. Gritting her teeth against the pain, Sylette stooped and picked it up.

A quick brush of her fingers cleaned the dust off, revealing ...

Sylette nearly tore the ink-and-charcoal sketch from the book. Valescar stared up at her from the open page, face shrouded in shadows, solitary eye glowing like an ember. His wires snaked up and out of view as he hurtled from the notebook, his teeth bared in a savage growl. Sylette could almost hear the excuses he'd spat that day as the *Feywind* burned, begging her to return to the Emperor's side.

At least then he'd dropped the mentor's mask.

Lied to her face instead of in her ear.

"Void," Sylette said again.

It was quickly becoming her favorite word, despite her mother's insistence that she speak like a noble lady. Decorum hadn't saved her from Valescar's axe. So, void him, void Major Reev, and void maidenly language, too.

Tucking the notebook under her arm, Sylette limped from the cavern. She knew who it belonged to, knew what they'd give to have it back. Now she simply needed to wait for them to notice it was missing.

The yellowed, hole-ridden ceiling of their tent was as ugly as ever.

Sylette stared up at it out of the corner of her eye, half her attention on the sketchbook she was lazily flipping through. Wrapped in two blankets, a sailcloth, and wearing *three* extra shirts she'd ... *borrowed* from Velle's stash, the chill was finally draining from her bones.

Her teeth ceased chattering, color returned to her fingers, and her heavy eyelids were ... starting to ...

Someone threw open the tent flap, shaking the flimsy poles holding it up, threatening to bring the whole thing down. Sylette tugged the notebook beneath her blankets and pulled the sailcloth over her head, hiding her from sight. The hammock continued to bounce as the intruder cast around the room, knocking aside stack of pots and dishes, pulling up the muddy floorboards with a wet squelch.

"Where is it?" they grumbled. A man's voice, gruff, uncertain.

Renar, just who Sylette was waiting for.

She let him stew awhile longer. Listened as he overturned Unter's cot, combed every hammock on the 'boy's' side of the tent, then started rummaging through the one dilapidated trunk their squad owned. Clothes soared across the room, landing in puddles of murky water. Coins—what little remained of the funds they'd received from the Alhans—clinked on the stones as Renar tossed them aside.

"It has to be here," he breathed, voice ragged. "If it's not here, then ... Then the General already has ... "

Renar spun round, heading for the 'girl's' hammocks—for Sylette. She sighed. Best to stop him before he stooped to rifling through their unmentionables.

Throwing back her blankets, Sylette leaned forward and held up the notebook, its pages open to a frothing sea, high cliffs, and a lonely lighthouse clinging to the reefs beneath them. "Is this what you're looking for?"

The boy froze, face red, arms just a few hand spans from her face. A criminal caught in the act, a deer staring down the arrow aimed at its head. "This isn't what it looks like," Renar babbled.

"Then what is it?" Sylette waved a hand at the destruction he'd wrought. "Why are those pants—*my* pants, I might add—soaking in our cave's finest vat of muddy water?"

Renar licked his lips. Glanced down at the wads of filthy clothing, the scattered dishes and chipped or bent utensils. He started to speak, then threw up his arms and collapsed onto his backside.

Right into yet another puddle.

"What do you want?" Renar asked.

"Excuse me?"

"I'll do anything, just ... " He ran a grimy hand through his sweat-mussed black hair. "Just don't give my sketchbook to the General."

Sylette bristled, fingers tightening on the sketchbook. "You're smearing the ink!" Renar shouted, crawling forward as she raised it even higher.

"Why do you assume I want something?" she asked.

Renar clenched his teeth, saying nothing.

"Well?"

Glancing toward the tent roof—perhaps toward the heavens beyond this wretched pit—Renar let out a long breath. "You *always* want something, Sylette."

"That's not—"

"It *is* true," Renar insisted. "For us to follow your orders, find the Resistance, fight the Empire, on and on and on. It's kind of who you are—the girl with an angle."

Did Renar understand the situation he was in? That *she* held his sketchbook? That *she* had the power to shred it with daggers, toss it in the lake, burn it in a campfire, or—as Renar seemed to dread—simply hand it to his father?

And yet he threw caution to the wind, crawling through the mud while trying to snatch the sketchbook from her, insulting her all the while. Sure, maybe Sylette never did anything without purpose. Maybe they did see her as a heartless voidspawn.

But Sylette certainly didn't need to hear the truth from this incompetent mound of muscle.

Waving an arm, she summoned a platform of daggers beneath her hammock—a step to help her descend to the ground. Sylette swung her legs over the side. Dropped onto her blades, then to the rotting planks beside the still kneeling Renar, sketchbook clutched in her right hand.

What favor will General Iolus trade me for bringing him this? Sylette wondered as she hobbled toward the tent flap.

Then she stopped. The boy behind her wasn't rising, wasn't moving to stop her. Renar was an enhancive mage, wasn't he? Why didn't he try to overpower her?

Sylette turned to glare at him. Tears were building in his eyes, slipping down his cheeks. His throat and chest heaved despite his best efforts to hold in his sobs.

"Why aren't you trying to take back your sketchbook? Isn't it important to you?"

Renar nodded. "It . . . it is. But I couldn't win, and if we fought, the General would find out anyway."

"The *General*?" Sylette scoffed. "Why not call him father, dad, or any of those other sickening nicknames children use?"

"He insists I call him by his rank."

Sylette's grip on the sketchbook loosened, her sneer softening. The *General*. The *Emperor*. Seems they both had lousy, arrogant dungheads for fathers.

She took a slow step toward him, careful to keep the prize he sought just out of reach. "What will happen if I give the General your sketchbook?"

"He'll destroy it," came the instant reply. "Then punish me for daring to defy his orders."

A pang of white-hot guilt pierced Sylette's gut, digging through her insides. It was only for an instant. The briefest flicker of nausea and pain.

Of shared understanding.

I will not become You, Sylette vowed, picturing those whose throats she would slit: the crown, the false uncle, the traitorous brother.

Turning the sketchbook spine-down, Sylette rapped it against Renar's bowed head.

"Ow," he yelped.

"It hurts? Good." Sylette struck him again, lighter this time, then pressed the leather-bound pages into his trembling fingers. "Remember that pain whenever you're about to do something bloody foolish like losing your beautiful art."

Renar glanced back and forth between Sylette and his sketchbook, mouth agape, looking more confused than a lesser drake who'd finally caught up with a dreadnaught. "Why?" he asked.

Sylette tossed her hair over her shoulder as she turned to leave the tent. "*You* found the Resistance camp. I always pay my debts, so consider us even."

"Thank you."

"Don't."

A pause. Suddenly, Renar leapt to his feet, boots clomping on the floor planks as he raced after her.

Dear ancestors, what now?

"Just now, you called my sketches 'beautiful,'" Renar said, stopping Sylette beside the tent flap, pointing at a drawing of the *Kinloss* with all of them gathered in front of it. That scene had never happened, but . . . it wasn't an *awful* likeness. "You did, didn't you?"

Sylette chuckled. "I said no such thing."

Chapter 29
The Traitor

Hetrachia 28, 697 ABH
Nemare, Capital of the Sarconian Province of Darmatia

W henever Sychon left the palace, a flock of crows went with him.

He was fine with the soldiers. They didn't speak and kept to the fringes of the mob, their bayonet-tipped rifles facing out toward the still buildings and silent streets lining the broad thoroughfare leading to the Imperial Airfield. The others were hangers-on. Sycophants that wanted a minute of his time to endorse a piece of legislation, approve a construction plan, or sign off on a new provincial anthem dedicated in his honor. And like crows, they cawed incessantly.

"Will it rid me of these confounded cultists?" Sychon asked the anthem's composer, cutting the bard off before she could thrust her sheet music at him.

The feathers on her lopsided maroon beret seemed to wilt along with her smile. "No, but—"

Sychon snapped his fingers and two of his royal guard—dressed in puffy silk uniforms and armed with useless halberds—pushed the bard back into the surrounding mass of petitioners. They were clothed much as she was, medals and baubles pinned to their chests, gaudy capes draped from their shoulders. The city's director of public affairs had a ruff sprouting from his neck like an overgrown rose petal, and the minister of social wellbeing could hardly be seen behind her spiky collar.

Even the military officers looked ridiculous, festooned with enough gold braid to rig a sailing ship. Had any of them seen combat? Or was Sychon forced to keep them around because of pledges to noble houses whose levies he needed to win the war?

He ignored the call of a mustachioed general—whose name he couldn't be bothered to remember—and scooted closer to Auvrea and Zaratus. Their twin armored bulks discouraged the man, who began jabbering angrily at his unfortunate aide.

"You look dashing in white, my lord," Auvrea said, crimson eyes roving over him.

Sychon snorted. "I look like a target." He tugged at a gold-wrought starburst pinned to his breast as they walked. "See? A marker for my heart."

"It's a solast, Your Majesty." Zaratus' voice boomed inside the dragwyrm helm he never seemed to remove. "Each gold needle represents one of your royal ancestors, while the central star—"

"Represents the Empire they served," Sychon finished. "I know *what* I'm wearing, I just don't understand why we're celebrating Ancestors' Day with no audience."

He waved at the dead government offices around them. Their white marble facades and proud columns were quiet and cold, no sounds of labor issuing from within. Festive red and gold banners fluttered from their eaves, but no crowd cheered the passing procession or threw traditional reed-woven wreaths at their feet.

In their place, riflemen patrolled the rooftops, scanning for potential threats. Two hulking panzcraft chugged along on their flanks, belching steam into the air as their treads tore up the sidewalks. Even the gray skies were covered. A heavy cruiser bearing the name *Fidelity* hovered overhead, belly cannons tracking the Emperor's retinue.

Zaratus' helm swung to follow Sychon's gaze. "A necessary precaution. After the destruction of the cathedral, we can't be certain when or where the insurgents will strike."

Sychon glared at his Grand Marschal. Who was he putting on an act for? No one except the two of them—not even Auvrea—knew the truth of the holy landmark's destruction.

"I agree," he said.

As they approached the mound of jagged rubble, shattered statues, and countless shards of stained glass that had once been the Cathedral of Sariel, Sychon ordered his court to halt. He stooped over an effigy of Sariel—his handsome face cracked in twain, both wings and one leg missing—and picked up what had once been the Veneer's eye.

Raising the fragment, he turned to his subjects. "The cultists will be brought to justice," he shouted. "Not one more stone of Nemare will be destroyed. Its citizens—*our* citizens—shall soon know lasting peace. With our ancestors as witnesses, I swear this to you. Glory to those who came before us!"

"Glory to the ancestors!" the crowd shouted.

Applause erupted among the gathered dignitaries, and out of their ranks rushed a man in dark suit-robes. Glancing around, he found a rubble-free space, ordered a pair of servants to erect a tripod, then set a sapphire recorb atop it. Sychon smiled just before the device flashed white, documenting his sweet lies for posterity.

He dropped the eye back onto the pile, shielding the motion with his cloak. The cathedral would soon be gone, replaced by a new Ritter Order chapter house. Sychon had no need for such a senseless memento.

"And where is the *first* among our ancestors," Auvrea asked when he rejoined them. "I don't see our dear Lord Sarcon anywhere."

"Otherwise occupied, thankfully," Sychon said. "He's found something below the palace that intrigues him and hasn't bothered me in a week."

"Ah, the unopened door," crooned a voice from Sychon's side. "A mystery, to be sure. One even *I* haven't been able to solve."

Zaratus moved to block the new arrival, but the Emperor gestured for him to stand down. "Dr. Archimas! So good of you to join us before your departure."

With the grace of a dancer, Doctor Archimas Redora Descar placed one gloved hand to his breast and executed a deep bow. The train of his snow-white suit-robes flapped as he tucked one leg behind the other, and the silver chain of his spectacles jangled against the matching buttons on his coat. Like always, he wore a rough gray beard—the kind that suggested he'd been so caught up in his research he'd forgotten to shave.

"Your Majesty," Archimas said. "Lovely Lady Titania," he continued, kissing the gauntlet she proffered. "And well met, Grand Marschal." Zaratus jerked his helm in a terse nod.

"Unopened door?" Sychon prompted. He started walking again, and Archimas fell in between him and Auvrea.

"A solid stone wall deep beneath the palace covered with ancient Eliassi runes and old murals," the engimage explained. "What we've deciphered suggests that Darmatian royal blood should open the path, but we don't exactly have any of that lying around these days, now do we?"

"Did you try blasting your way in?" Auvrea asked. Sparks flared among her crimson curls as if she were imagining attacking the problem herself.

Archimas smiled. "Of course, my dear. Brought down the floor above and killed half a dozen workers in the process. And what do you suppose we found when we finally dug the door out again?"

"No damage," Zaratus grunted. "Old magic—*blood* magic—is not to be trifled with."

He would know, Sychon thought. *His people practically invented the School of Oaths and Pacts.*

"Just so," Archimas agreed. "We started experimenting with the populace's blood after that, drawing it under the guise of a men'ar census. Yet no matter how we combined it, no matter how much we used, none of it satisfied the door. Eventually, I had to give up, as much as that rankles me."

No matter how much we used, echoed in Sychon's mind. Here was another sociopath, so much like Sarcon. Both were quick to spend lives with no tangible benefit—when there was only an astronomically small chance of their wild schemes succeeding. Sychon shivered, and Auvrea blew a gust of warm wind at him. What a perfect woman.

"Can he get in?" he asked Archimas. The last thing Sychon needed was Sarcon obtaining another advantage, especially when their partnership was growing frayed.

"Not without Aurelian blood." Archimas bent forward, clasped his hands behind his back, and stared at Sychon over his lowered spectacles. "You wouldn't happen to know where Sarcon could obtain some, do you?"

His tomb was the obvious answer. Sarcon was Darmatus' brother, and since they shared a bloodline, what flowed through his veins should work on the door. Rabban had died with no heirs. Which left . . .

Sychon shook his head. Yes, Hans' first coded message mentioned Sarcon had an unhealthy fascination with the Royal Archives. But even the Imperial seal wouldn't enable the inept captain to enter his vaults, and what was stored there was hardly conclusive evidence of anything.

Still . . . it wouldn't hurt to send a message to the Ritter in Sarconia.

"Do you have any progress for me?" Sychon asked, changing the subject. "I'd hate to think that you accomplished nothing in the weeks leading up to your promotion. My chief researchers may find it difficult to accept a superior with fewer contributions than they have."

"Then I simply need deliver." Reaching into his robes, Archimas produced a blueprint covered in sketches, formulas, and cramped annotations. He handed it to Sychon with a flourish. "Behold, the future!"

It didn't *look* like the future. The device seemed to be nothing more than a slender tower, one surrounded by concentric rings and topped by a giant orb. He started reading the engimage's notes. *Brass tubing . . . store energy in central housing . . . produce waves . . . equal and opposite forces . . .*

Nonsense, nothing but scientific nonsense and gibberish. At least until Sychon reached the bottom of the page. His grip on the paper tightened, and he nearly ripped the page as he scanned the final line over, and over, and over again.

"Where did you build this?" he breathed.

Archimas grinned, clearly pleased at the Emperor's reaction. "Etrus. We believed it would be an effective deterrent to the Ascendancy or Magerium if either decided to test the border."

Void him, Sychon thought, chills pimpling the flesh of his neck and arms despite Auvrea's magic. *The arrogant blowhard is right. This is the future.*

"Can it be moved?" he asked.

"Not yet. The prototype is too heavy to lift without heavy cruiser class propulsion, and we'd need to build a special storage container to keep it from—"

Bells rang out across the government district, startling Sychon from his scheming. Noon already? He glanced up and was surprised to see the broad steps of the Imperial Airfield in front of them. At their crest was a tall archway flanked by Sarconian banners and topped by a newly erected effigy of their guardian angel—the mistress of war wielding her Illyriite scepter. As Sychon watched, a sleek silver transport alighted on one of the smaller landing pads beyond the arch and deployed its ramp.

"Ah, my ride has arrived," Archimas said. A figure with slick brown hair appeared at the top of the ramp and waved at them. "My eldest son," he explained. Facing Sychon, he sketched another bow, this one somehow deeper than the last. "Please excuse me, Your Majesty. I go to create even greater wonders than the one you now possess."

Sychon patted the blueprint. "I look forward to it. Go with my blessing."

Minutes later, the arrow-shaped airship launched into the sky and sped away at impressive speed, wisps of yellow illyrium dust drifting in its wake. Sychon marveled at how quiet its engines were. The bubbling waterfalls in the palace gardens made more noise than Archimas' personal vessel.

"He's dangerous," Zaratus said as the procession turned toward the palace. Marching the length of the district and back was symbolic of carrying their ancestors' will with them in all that they did. "Are you certain we can trust him?"

"Once a traitor, always a traitor," Auvrea mocked playfully.

Rolling up the plans, Sychon handed them to Zaratus. "For all his brilliance, Archimas is easy to understand. He wants to play god, and as long as we give him the resources to do so, he'll never consider betraying us."

Auvrea lifted a gauntlet to her lips and laughed into it, muffling the sound so she wouldn't disturb the crows still flocking around them. "Perhaps you should rename the holiday to *Traitors' Day*, my lord." The Rittermarschal pulled a scroll from a pouch on her belt which hung beside the ceremonial sword she never used.

Grinning wickedly, she passed the letter to Sychon. It bore the official Darmatian seal: the silver chalice of wisdom and lance of Sariel imprinted onto ocean-blue wax. "Two traitors in one day," she said. "The first promised you the future. *Mine* promises to deliver you the rebellion."

Chapter 30
Breaking Curfew

Adamantele 1, 697 ABH
Resistance Base, Sarconian Province of Darmatia

Hard, calloused fingers closed across Vallen's lips, tearing him from the suffocating embrace of dreams better left unseen. His whole body tensed, blood thumping, heart pounding as he lashed out and clenched his assailant about their wrist. It was small, delicate. No matter. Size meant little when it came to killing.

Vallen jerked the attacker forward, pulling them toward his shaking hammock. A headbutt would disorient them, and then—

A palm struck Vallen's nose—not hard enough to break it, but enough to make him hiss. "Quiet!" his opponent whispered, close enough for their breath to tickle his neck. "Do you want to wake the whole tent up?"

Vallen recognized the voice. He should after all the times he'd heard it snickering down at him as he lay on his back. "*Lilith?*"

"Who else would it be? You think an *assassin* could make it this far into the base unnoticed?"

A fair question, one to which Vallen had no good answer. "Your hand is on my mouth."

"To keep you from making a fuss." Lilith flicked his upper lip. "Which went *brilliantly*, by the way."

Her hair caressed his cheek as she whispered into his right ear, breath smelling of citrine spirits, skin dappled with freckles that shone in the pale light filtering through their threadbare tent. The camp outside never truly slept—distant patrols exchanging reports, soldiers cursing as they stumbled to the latrine, the illyrium lamps bolted to the ceiling casting their false evening glow long after the Void's hour.

"What do you want?" Vallen asked, breath quickening as he glanced lower.

Her loose blouse billowed beneath her neck, dangling against his bare chest. Each time Lilith shifted, the brush of the coarse fabric—the sight of the sweat-slick mounds beneath her shirt—sent shivers arcing across his arms.

Hazelnut eyes met his. Smiling, Lilith followed Vallen's gaze down to her unkempt clothes, his own half-naked body. "To watch you sleep without a shirt on? I *envy* that you boys can get away with that."

"Why not try it?" Vallen whispered, grinning. "I'm an advocate for complete equality in all—"

Lilith traced a fingernail along his lip, his cheek, his skin sparking—burning—at her touch. Then, she flicked his nose.

"You wish," Lilith said, rising and tossing a grimy tunic at Vallen's face. "Now get dressed. I need a drinking buddy."

"How far are we going to walk?"

Lilith spun around, one eye flashing. The rest of her all but blended with the shadows of the tunnel they were following. Illyrium bulbs hung from the stone ceiling at regular intervals, but their misty glow was a poor substitute for a proper lamp.

"For a legendary warrior, you sure complain a lot."

"For a girl who never said one word to me at the Academy, you sure talk a lot," Vallen replied, reaching down to massage his calves.

After weeks of grueling training, traipsing through the endless passages of the base on aching, blistered feet wasn't quite how he'd imagined this trip. Was Lilith toying with him? Or was he so . . . *pent-up* he was imagining the furtive glances she'd been casting his way?

"You seemed like a shallow philanderer back then," Lilith said, stretching her arms above her head as she started moving again. Vallen swallowed as the motion tugged her shirt tight across her breasts.

Stay calm, stay focused, he thought, trailing after her. "And what about now?"

"A shallow philanderer *and* a hopeless fighter."

Vallen's retort died in darkness along with his pride. He could make a thousand excuses for his losses: Major Reev's magic handicap, his healing arm, the lack of weapons. But the fact remained that this slip of a girl who only came up to his shoulders kept knocking him on his backside no matter *what* he did.

She was a blade. A fighter who thrived in combat, relishing its thrills, drunk on the challenge of every second in the ring.

Just. Like. *Him.*

Up ahead, light carved an orange silhouette on the tunnel wall. Lilith stole up to the opposite opening on whisper-soft feet, making not a sound to betray her presence. Clangs and clunks came from the chamber beyond, along with the shrill hiss of jetting steam. Vallen counted at least a dozen rusted pipes coating the ceilings, the walls, clattering and clanking as they wove their way toward the base they'd left behind.

"Why would Holcomb keep his booze here?" Vallen asked, hugging the wall beside Lilith.

"Because no one wants to deal with—"

BOOM!

The whole tunnel shook, limestone dust falling from the ceiling, pipes banging against one another. Vallen grabbed Lilith, wrapping her in his arms and forcing her to the ground. Pinching his eyes shut, gritting his teeth, he waited for the rain of rubble to strike his back.

None came. The trembling subsided, replaced by a cloud of inky smoke wafting from the nearby cave. "Blast it all!" someone inside shouted. They coughed a few times, then started whacking something with a metal rod. "Bloody kerium won't take. Keeps—*cough*—blowing open the first piston. Need to—*cough*—reinforce it some more."

"You can get off me now," Lilith said, quiet enough the whacky explosion guy couldn't hear her.

Vallen looked down. Saw that his body was pressed atop hers, their noses barely a hand span apart. One second passed, two, her eyes twinkling, grin growing with his every racing breath. Sweat trickled down his neck, dripped onto her shirt. She was so close, so warm. Like a fire blazing against his chest, his stomach, his—

"Well?" Lilith asked.

Slowly, Vallen pulled away. He shivered at the sudden absence—the chasm yawning between them. Should he have tried something? Leaned in instead of retreating?

Still smiling, Lilith reached up and brushed a hand through Vallen's hair, knocking off the chalky dust. "My hero," she teased, fluttering her eyelashes.

"You could have told me," Vallen said, rising and then hauling Lilith to her feet.

"About explosion-boy?" She glanced over her shoulder as the clanging, cursing, and mumbling intensified. "That's why no one comes down here. They're afraid to get caught in"—she waved her hand at the thick smog clogging the hall—"whatever it is he's doing."

"I don't blame them."

"Which is why," Lilith said, taking Vallen's hand. "We have nothing to worry about. No one will see us breaking curfew."

Laughing, she tugged him through the smoke and down the hall.

311

Vallen didn't protest. Each moment he spent with Lilith was a little brighter than the last. The darkness of his past receded, the agony of his dreams faded, and he started to see the *present.* Her next kick or punch. The tightening of her jaw as she struck, the fire in her gaze as they exchanged blows.

The way I lose myself as she drags me along, Vallen thought.

'Lose' being the key word.

"We're lost," Vallen said, blinking at the solid stone wall in front of them.

Lilith winked at him. "Do you trust me?"

"Have you thrown me on the ground in the past five minutes? Sat on my chest while breaking my newly healed arm?"

She tightened her grip on his hand, drawing a gasp from his lips as her nails dug in. "Is that a request? I'd be happy to oblige."

Vallen tapped the wall. "I give, I trust you."

"Good."

Lilith stepped forward, jabbing her hand into a narrow crack running from the tunnel floor to its ceiling. Limestone shattered, splitting apart, folding onto itself as she shoved it aside. Vallen gaped. What strength, what ...

"Oh," he said. "It's a painted curtain."

"It's a curtain." Giggling, Lilith flipped it back and forth a few times. "What? You aren't going to gasp anymore? That little '*huh*' you made ... those wide eyes ... They were *so* cute."

Eyes narrowed, Vallen pushed past her into the room. Unlike the hall, there were no wires draped with illyrium bulbs or crystals. The chamber was shrouded in total darkness.

"Flar'a," he murmured, holding out his hand.

A soft, flickering flame appeared in his palm. It was the first spell Vallen had learned from Metellus—simple, but enough to light the space around him.

No, something whispered deep inside him. *That* wasn't *your first spell. Try to deny it, try to forget. Nothing will change the fact that—*

Vallen squashed the voice. Buried it under his yearning, his desire. "I need a drink," he snarled, more forcefully than he intended.

Wielding a flar'a spell of her own at the end of a short dagger, Lilith stepped up beside him. "Shouldn't be a problem. Take your pick."

The cave was about the same size as the common room in his Academy dorm, ten paces deep and about half as wide. *All* of it was filled with liquor. Wooden racks bearing lavender wines, tall barrels of ale stacked in the corner, crates stuffed with bottles of whiskey, flasks of gin, and vials of almost translucent liquid even Vallen had never tasted before. Several of the barrels lay on their sides, lazily closed taps dripping brown fluid onto a growing puddle on the floor.

"Where does Holcomb get it all?" Vallen breathed, spinning around like a child at his first grand Festivus. Whole bandoliers—complete with three or four silver flasks each—hung beside the entrance, ready for the Colonel to take with him when he left.

Lilith strode to the wine racks, bending over to examine the labels. "Ithran, Jinale, Truvant . . . " She kept listing names. "These are all top-shelf—the kind you serve to fancy nobles in fancy clothes at fancy parties where they serve even fancier cheese plates. Someone has to be helping him."

"General Iolus?"

She selected a bottle, uncorked it with her dagger, and took a long draught. "*Ahhhh* . . . I'd say he's about the only one with enough pull to do this. Care for some?"

The bottle was flying through the air before Vallen responded. Dousing his flar'a, he jumped forward, tucking the wine to his chest as he caught it.

"Careful!" he hissed.

Lilith picked up one of the clear vials, sniffing at its contents. "There's more where that came from."

"And what happens when they discover we were in here?"

"Relax. Holcomb told me I could visit."

Lilith took her own advice, plopping down on a pile of blankets at the center of the room. Sliding a grimy rag onto her flame-wreathed blade, she turned over her shoulder and rammed it hilt-first into a crevice in the wall a few hand spans from the nearest booze.

Picking up a square bottle of golden ferras-grain whiskey, Vallen joined her on the floor. "The liquor-fiend gave up his stash. I find that hard to believe."

"He might have been drunk at the time."

"*That* I believe."

"Anyway, stop worrying and pour," Lilith said, snatching two short glasses out of another crate and smacking them atop the central blanket. "It's cold, I'm thirsty, and we are *way* too sober right now."

Vallen popped open the whiskey, filled the glasses, then passed one to Lilith. "Too sober for . . . ?"

She knocked it back, auburn curls bouncing, pale, freckled neck stretched taut. "Another." She slammed the empty glass down, batting her eyes at Vallen until he complied. "Here's the game, Triaron. I ask a question. If you answer, I drink. If you don't, you drink. Then we switch. Easy?"

Vallen stared at her. At her shirt slipping off her shoulder, exposing skin that shimmered in the dancing light of her makeshift torch. At her deep hazel eyes, glowing cheeks, and the crescent-moon-thin smile that set his veins on fire.

"Sure." Vallen poured, slid the glass back to her, then picked up his own whiskey.

"Was Velle your first?"

The sip he'd just taken spluttered back out, spraying over the blankets, leaving him coughing and pounding his chest. "Drink goes down, air comes up," Lilith suggested, demonstrating with her own whiskey. "I don't recommend reversing the order."

Spitting, Vallen glared at her. "*That's* what you want to start with?"

"Fun, right?"

"No, she wasn't," Vallen spat. "Not by a long shot. Now drink."

A wink, a blown kiss, and Lilith drained the rest of her glass, bowing at her waist afterward. "And for my next trick, I'll—"

"My turn," Vallen interrupted.

Should he ask the same? Perhaps something raunchier? Lilith tucked her legs beneath her, laying on the piled blankets as she stretched like a cat. The gleam in her eye, the way she crossed her hips as her tongue traced her lips . . . that was clearly what she wanted.

"Where did you come from?" Vallen asked.

Lilith blinked. The question seemed to surprise her almost as much as it did him. He was defying the mood, her efforts, his desire for . . . what, exactly? Curiosity?

Rolling onto her back, Lilith stared at the ceiling. The shadows jerked and twisted, blending, parting, forever locked in a battle of pushes and pulls.

"I was a merchant," she said at last. "We weren't wealthy, but business was steady. Our caravan traveled up and down the Middenlane, trading with the Empire, the Imperium, and every kind of people in between.

"Eventually, my father . . . " Lilith paused, leaning over and taking a sip of whiskey. "My father saved enough geldars to send me to the Academy. He didn't think the nomadic life of a merchant was for me, so he decided I should try being an "*Educated, noble officer*," as he put it.

I think he was wrong."

Lilith laughed, a harsh snort absent her usual cheer. "I *know* he was wrong. Just look at us now." She thrust her glass at the damp, moisture-slick walls around them. Even here, the smell of salt and sea and earth overwhelmed everything else. "Trapped in a hole."

Did Lilith think her tale was *sad*? A caring father, a childhood exploring the world, enough coin to give her a promising future? *He'd* been stuck in a hole. *He'd* been trapped in a subterranean cesspit where children killed each other for half-rotten scraps and a mouthful of water.

Vallen emptied his glass, barely tasting the harsh fluid burning its way into his stomach. "And where did you learn to fight?"

"One drink, one question," Lilith replied, wagging a finger at him. "For my turn, hmmm … " Rising to her knees, she crawled toward him, shoulders and hips swaying. "Where are *you* from?"

Without answering, Vallen picked up the whiskey bottle and took a swig.

"No luck, huh?" Lilith reared up in front of him, her honeyed, spirit-laced breath blowing directly in his face. "Then I'll use the other question you asked: where did you learn to fight?"

Same answer, Vallen thought, suppressing another stab of pain. Another phantom knife in his gut, rooting through his insides, forcing bile up his throat. Though his head swam, he tried to drown it. Tried to drain the rest of the whiskey in a single gulp.

Vallen didn't want to feel. Didn't want to think.

Numbness was all he longed for.

Lilith snatched the bottle from his fingers, holding it beyond his reach as he swiped and grabbed at it. "That's a rules violation, Cadet Metellus."

"And what's the punishment?" Vallen growled. "Another drink? Maybe some more of your teasing?"

Setting the whiskey aside, Lilith cocked her head and smiled at him. "Your punishment is … another question: Do you—"

"Spare me," Vallen said, planting one boot on the blanket and starting to rise.

"—want to take a roll?"

He paused. "A … roll? Like sparring? *Here*?"

Lilith laughed, taking his hand, leading him back to the floor. "Where I come from, rolls normally involve hay. Or, in our case"—she glanced around as Vallen's heart started *pounding* on his ribs—"blankets."

315

"Oh," he said.

"'Oh,' indeed."

The makeshift torch burned low, casting them in threads of light and shadow, setting Lilith's eyes ablaze. She traced her mouth with her tongue, shifted so her blouse exposed more of her glistening neckline. One final invitation, a pause so short Vallen didn't breathe, so long his heart belted out a half dozen beats.

They leapt at each other, arms wrapping, bodies crashing together with the force of desperation. Lips met, their tongues clashing, seeking to go ever deeper as they sought warmth, heat, *life*.

Lilith tasted like fire—a medley of bitter spirits and passion that flooded Vallen's mouth. He drowned in her flames, the embers of her touch, the inferno blazing everywhere their skin met.

And then they parted, gasping, panting. Not from exertion, but from yearning for what came next. Vallen traced downward from her smoldering lips, kissing her cheeks, chin, neck as his hands roamed to her belly.

"Yes?" he asked, fingers trembling.

"*Yes*," Lilith begged, raising her arms.

Vallen slid stone-cold hands up her molten flesh, drawing a shiver from her body, a sigh from lips he swiftly silenced with his own. He wove circles with his fingers, teased her with little flicks and scratches just as she'd done to him with her words. Up and up and up until he reached her soft mounds, her small breasts that barely fit in his grasp.

He stopped. Pulled away from Lilith's mouth, halted his hand a hairsbreadth from giving her another surge of pleasure. He stared at her heaving chest, blouse pulled up to expose her sweat-slick abs, her toned stomach. His eyes worshiped her sun-touched hair and the freckles that painted her face like constellations of stars.

"Why stop?" Lilith breathed, pulling him toward her, taking his hand to guide it further in.

Vallen smiled. "To appreciate your beauty."

"Corny . . . but I'll allow it."

Their lips met again, biting, pulling, *hungry*. Placing one hand on Lilith's searing back, Vallen lowered her to the blankets as his other hand tugged off her blouse, then roamed down toward her trousers.

This was the natural end of their short rivalry—a craving that had begun as they circled each other on the sparring floor, now ended in a victory that satisfied them both.

And, for a night—if *only* for a night—the agony of Vallen's nightmares was far, far from his thoughts.

Chapter 31
Unbridled Curiosity

Adamantele 2, 697 ABH
Resistance Base, Sarconian Province of Darmatia

When Matteo was thirteen summers old, his mother had told him that the key to understanding women was to listen. "Words get in the way," Anathea had said. "What *you* want. What *you* expect. But still your lips, open your ears, and invite the girl to tell *her* story, and you will discover a bond between you like never before."

Only . . . Velle didn't seem interested in talking to Matteo. She shunned him at their campfire meals, putting Unter's bulk between them. She no longer woke him to take morning walks along the lake, traded duties with the other cadets to avoid working alongside him, and even hung a sheet in front of her hammock so no one would bother her. Though their daily lessons with Colonel Holcomb continued, Velle said nothing as her glyphs punished his every misstep, each blow seemingly harder than the last.

What was going on? Matteo had thought they were becoming closer—that there was a spark developing between them. And that kiss? A roaring inferno, a brush of divine nectar. He could feel the specter of Velle's touch, haunting his lips, gliding through his hair, warming the blood inside his veins.

That symbol had changed everything. A three-pronged star, perfectly symmetrical, with a crescent moon curling around it from top to bottom. Matteo had no idea what it meant. He'd never seen it in textbooks related to the Sylph Magerium, and not a single story about her people mentioned such a tattoo. Yes, they were reclusive—even xenophobic—but surely *someone* knew about the crescent-star sigil.

Like those records, the tattoo itself had vanished by the next time Matteo saw Velle. In its place was smooth red skin, unblemished as a placid sea. Her eyes had burned at his scrutiny. Blazed with a fury that had sent him scurrying from their tent. If not for Velle's unrelenting anger, Matteo might have thought he'd imagined the mark.

But it was real, and she was hiding something. From the group. From *him.*

His curiosity quickly got the better of him. Yes, Velle had warned him away. Made it clear that she would brook no snooping into her personal affairs. Yet if the Sylph already hated him for simply *seeing* the tattoo, how much more could she loathe him for finding out what it was?

A lot, Matteo's common sense told him. He ignored it.

Matteo's instincts—which had voted with his common sense before being swayed by his heart—took him straight to the people most likely to have an answer. There were three of them, two female Sylph and one male, gathered around a bubbling pot that smelled like they were cooking their boots. A fourth, a Terran man, sat on a flat boulder beside one of the women, arm draped across her bare shoulders.

They glanced up at his approach, and Matteo nearly ran. They looked like they belonged here, muscular frames chiseled from the stone, jackets and pants dirty as the cave floor. Scars and tattoos—more colorful, more extravagant than Velle's—coated the exposed flesh of their necks, shoulders, and arms.

"What do you want, kid?" the Terran asked in a gruff voice. Unlike the Sylph he held close, he was shirtless, a golden visage of Ellara the Eliade imprinted across his chest. Her flaxen locks and flowing robes were a match for his short beard.

The Sylph woman beside him chuckled, shaking the long braid of raven hair that sprouted from her otherwise shaved scalp. "Here to gawk, most likely. Darmatians don't see a lot of our kind in one place very often, and when they do, it's at a pleasure house. Keep moving, boy." She shooed him with fingers tattooed by blue shoots of ivy that twisted around her knuckles and up her arms. "We're soldiers, not whores."

"Is that so, Siena?" The Terran's fingers strayed lower, brushing the top of the Sylph's—Siena's—strapless garment.

"Not now, Herj," she chastised, smacking his wandering digits with a hand more pink than red. *A half-breed,* Matteo assessed. Her hoop-pierced ears were shorter and less pointed than Velle's, another sign of mixed heritage.

The other woman laid aside the rifle she'd been cleaning and looked Matteo over from head to toe. She was older, wine-toned skin just beginning to crease around her mouth and eyes, and her bob of midnight hair curled forward beneath ears sharp as blades. Matteo flushed at her gaze, and a smile twinkled in her crimson eyes.

"This one is but a sprig budding on the tree," she said. "Green. A cadet, and one of those traipsing around with the Triaron, if I'm not mistaken. Run back to Major Reev, little greenling."

That irked him. Matteo was trying desperately to tear free of Vallen's shadow, yet everyone in the camp seemed to define him by their association. He'd lost count of the number of soldiers who'd approached him about the Triaron, asking what he was like, if he was single, and so much other void-forsaken drivel.

Matteo straightened his back, stuck out his chin. "I'm here for answers."

"Temple tent is that way," Herj said, jerking his thumb over his shoulder at a small awning slightly less filthy than the rest of the camp. An iron-wrought seven-pointed star dangled above the entrance. "But given all the death and disease around here, I'd wager the Creator is out to lunch. Or maybe on vacation? Either way, he don't exactly seem the answerin' type these days."

Siena giggled. Matteo bristled. "I have a question about the Magerium—something I can only ask one of you."

"Can you pay?" the male Sylph asked.

He turned from the pot and fire, staring at Matteo with dark, disinterested eyes. His face was as smooth and sensuous as Siena's, fair as a marble statue. The cut of his loose tunic exposed the taut, sleek muscles of his back, a gap that would enable him to grow wings without ripping the fabric. If not for the slight bulge at his throat and flat chest, Matteo might have mistaken his gender.

"How much?"

Two slender fingers rose in the air. "Twin bronzes."

"That steep? You haven't heard the question yet!"

The older Sylph shrugged, her shoulder muscles rippling unnaturally with the motion. "Trees do not grow from nothing. Neither do answers. One bronze now, one bronze after."

That was almost all the money Matteo had on him, the money his parents had slipped him as the cadets fled out the back door of their home, abandoning them to their fate. Matteo gritted his teeth but tossed the woman a bronze geldar anyway. He had to know what was wrong with Velle.

Siena's lips turned up in a predatory grin as her squadmate caught the coin. "Why don't you come closer, greenling?" She patted the boulder beside her, opposite the Terran. "We don't bite."

"Much," Herj added.

"I'll stand," Matteo said, taking a step back for good measure. He now understood why the man tattooed with Ellara's likeness was half-naked despite the cavern's chill: Siena was feeding warmth into Herj's blood, and possibly a few other suggestions beside.

I trust Velle not to manipulate me, Matteo thought. *But these Sylph . . .* But these Sylph *what?* The hidden sigil, Velle's secrets, and her sudden frostiness were all signs he didn't know the girl as well as he'd believed. Could she have been tugging on his emotions, stoking his desires, bending him to her will?

Matteo shook his head. He wouldn't board that airship—not yet.

"Your question?" the older Sylph asked, steepling her glossy, black-nailed fingers.

He took a breath. Steadied himself for an answer, all the while wondering if he truly wanted one. "I need to know about a tattoo I think originated in your home country."

"*This* is our home now," the pretty male Sylph interrupted. "Darmatia is our only mother. We know no other, and it certainly knows not us."

The others nodded their agreement, and Matteo kicked himself for forgetting something so basic: every Sylph who left the Magerium without approval was dead to them. An exile, an outcast.

"The *Magerium*," Matteo corrected. "My mistake. This tattoo isn't normal." He gestured at Siena's ivy-inked arms and the silver-laced feathers he saw as the older Sylph shifted her back toward him. "Nothing like what you wear. It was on the face, right side, just below the eye"—Matteo tapped the spot on his cheek for emphasis—"and until the wearer lost their composure, I think it was hidden with magic."

Siena leaned forward. "Interesting. Describe it."

"A three-pronged star cradled by a crescent moon."

Frigid. That was the best way to describe the atmosphere around the campfire the instant Matteo spoke those words. The fire continued to crackle, the thin stew kept bubbling. But the three Sylph stared straight ahead, gazes blank, frozen like a bubble on the verge of popping.

What is going on? he thought.

Herj seemed as confused as Matteo. He chuckled at first. "Alright, good joke, mates. You got us." No one moved, and his laughter died. Turning to Siena, Herj took her by the shoulders and shook her. "Siena? Love? What's got hold of you? *Siena?*"

As if waking from a trance, she gasped and began to cough. "You need to leave," Siena growled once she could speak. "*Now.*"

"But I paid you," Matteo protested. "Just tell me—"

320

"*No*," the older Sylph said. The rifle was back in her hands, barrel pointed at his gut. "There are things about the Magerium you are better off not knowing. This is one of them, little greenling."

"But *why* is he asking?" The male stood and took a step toward Matteo. He had the look of a man frightened enough to do anything to save his skin. "He's seen it. And recently." He paused, then the light of realization brightened his dark eyes. "I was there when Major Reev brought them in. It's her! The Sylph girl in their group. She's one of *them*."

Venom—hatred, disgust, and revulsion all rolled into one—dripped from the word and ate away at Matteo's resolve. He regretted coming here. Regretted pursuing the tattoo's secrets in the first place, for now Velle might be in danger.

He didn't wait for the Sylph to lunge at him. Coward that he was, Matteo bolted, bouncing off soldiers who hurled curses in his wake, stumbling and slipping on the damp rocks. He didn't know where he was going. To hide in a corner? To warn Velle?

At the moment, none of that mattered, and Matteo simply ran because running was what he did best.

Matteo didn't know how long or how far he ran. All the tents looked the same—tired and listing—and the tunnels branching off of them weren't much better. White limestone, cold and wet, twisting and turning endlessly, ever deeper into the ground. He ran until his lungs gave out, and when they did, he collapsed.

He awoke to the sound of humming. If it was a tune, Matteo didn't know it. The notes seemed random. Discordant and jarring, like the singer was deliberately bouncing from low to high octaves without stopping anywhere in between and rhythm was a concept they'd never heard of.

"Make it stop," Matteo groaned. His blood thundered in his ears, and the spear wedged inside his skull blazed like the sun. Not since Aldona had he felt such agony.

The humming ceased, and for a second, Matteo's pain receded. Then the hammering began.

"No!" he yelled. "That's even worse. Stop making *any* noise. Stop *everything*!"

Once again, the noise obliged. Mumbling his thanks, Matteo shifted onto his side, snuggling deeper into whatever he was wrapped in. Blankets? Though they stank of synth-oil and grease, he wasn't particularly picky right now.

Something prodded him in the back. "Try some of this."

"Leave me alone . . . "

"It'll help." The prodding grew more insistent, more annoying. "Besides, I need someone else to try it."

Matteo flipped toward the voice, waves of pain crashing against his skull. "*Leave me—*"

A hot mug found his lips, parting them and forcing blistering liquid onto his tongue, down his throat. Matteo gagged and his eyes popped open. What a bitter brew! His mouth pulled in on itself, shriveling as the strong taste clung to his teeth and gums.

Then the drums belting in Matteo's brain grew softer. The pressure in his temples eased, and the ambient sounds around him—groaning pipes and hissing steam—hurt just a little bit less. He took another slurp of the drink before it was hauled away from him.

"Slow up, buddy. Caffe's too strong to guzzle all at once."

"Caffe?" Matteo blinked. The world beyond a few hand spans from his face was blurry, full of blobby shapes and diffused colors. One shape, tall and white, set something down with a *clink* and picked up an object that looked like two twigs glued to thin sheets of glass.

"You'll be wanting these."

The shape slid the twigs onto Matteo's face, and the world grew clear.

A man no more than a few years older than him stood at the edge of the cot on which he lay, blond stubble peppering his ruddy cheeks, a grin splitting his lips. Fiery hair curled from his head in all directions, some mushed, some matted, and some sticking skyward like a mast on a ship. He looked ridiculous, but not as ridiculous as the multicolored crystal lenses attached to a monocle overtop his right eye. Blue, red, green . . . Matteo had never seen its like.

Sensing the scrutiny, the man swept his white lab coat behind him and gave a deep bow that would put most noblemen to shame. "A thousand blessings upon your recovery, my dear friend. It's not every day I find some poor soul stranded outside my door, but when I do, it is my sworn duty as a doctor to mend what ails them."

"Doctor of medicine?" Matteo asked. It made sense that something as bitter as what he'd been fed was an herbal remedy of some sort.

The man shook his head, the hair upon which didn't flinch. It gleamed from too much grease. "Science! I am one 2nd Lieutenant

Jayden Darres of the Royal Engimage Corps, at your service . . . "

"Senior Cadet Matteo Alhan, sir!" Matteo saluted and made to stand, ashamed of his previous rudeness, but Jayden waved his arms until his guest flopped back onto the cot.

"None of that, none of that," he said, bringing two fingers up to massage his temples as if *he* were the one with a migraine. "Invention stands on no ceremony such as rank, age, or any other sort of stuffy categorization. Three geldarless brothers in their teens found a cure for Red Plague, while hundreds of rheumy-eyed graybeards had their noses jammed so far in books they could almost smell the forest they came from. We're all equal travelers on the paths of knowledge."

Matteo chuckled, the veins in his forehead throbbing less and less with each passing second. "You called it 'caffe?'" he said, pointing to the still steaming mug on a nearby stool. The fluid was brown and frothy, like mud after a caravan passed by on a stormy day.

"For the chemical in the beans I distilled." Jayden picked up the mug and—contrary to his own advice—drained it in one go. "Whew-wee! That's the stuff right there. Perks you up, sharpens the mind, and gets you ready for just about anything. Say . . . do you think I could convince Major Reev to test it on the troops? Let me collect some data on their reactions?"

It was easy to see how that conversation would play out. The Ice Queen would take one sip, blanch, and throw the blazing contents of the cup right in Jayden's face. "I don't think that's a good idea, Jayden," Matteo said.

"Jay," he corrected. "Never know when saying that extra syllable will cost someone an eye or finger during a dangerous experiment. Be bright, be brief, be gone is my motto. Except when explaining too little will have the same result."

Matteo studied Jay's face for a sign he was joking, but the man neither smiled nor blinked. "So, Jay," he said as the engimage started getting a distant look in his eyes. "Where are we?"

"My lab!" Jay boomed with an auctioneer's boundless enthusiasm. "Well, technically the power room for the whole base, but so long as I keep the lights on, the Major lets me use it for my projects." He stepped aside and raised his arms, granting Matteo a view of the whole space.

Pipes, wires, and cables spread through the rounded cave like spiderwebs, clinging to the limestone walls, hanging from stalactites, and winding around the floor in thick bunches tied together with lengths of sodden rope. Matteo instantly yanked his feet away from the floor, afraid a stray spark might hit a puddle and electrocute him.

In the far right corner was a great beast of an illyrium furnace, red-hot flames surging behind its slotted access hatch and jets of steam spewing from loose seams. Most of the pipes and wires jutted from the magchine's back before racing around the room, into the walls, or out the tunnel to the rest of the base. If not for this coughing, shuddering device, Matteo suspected the Resistance would already be voided.

The rest of the room was a direct glimpse into the mind of its occupant. Papers scrawled with tightly packed numbers, sketches, and formulae were tacked anywhere there was space. And where there wasn't, they were stacked in piles that, more often than not, had toppled and spilled across the floor. Half-eaten ration bars were everywhere, including—Matteo shifted slightly and felt a wax-paper wrapper brush his leg—in Jay's bedsheets.

His mess continued elsewhere. Overturned boxes of bolts, crates of pistons, sacks of gyros and screws. A workbench dominated the left side of the chamber, and projects in various stages of completion dominated it in turn. Hunks of metal with what looked like plungers jutting from holes drilled in their sides. Next to these was a solid approximation of a soothsayer's crystal ball, arcs of blue lightning coursing against its glass sides, and a metal rod as long as Matteo's leg surrounded by rings of bronze that became smaller closer to the solid orb at its peak.

I've seen something that looked like that, Matteo thought, eyes glued to the bronze tower. *But where was it?*

"I see you've discovered my latest creations," Jay announced. He stepped over to the workbench, carefully avoiding his scattered notes. "Care for a demonstration?"

Anything to take his mind off Velle. To distract from the mystery of her tattoo and her fellow Sylphs' violent response to it.

Matteo nodded. "Sure."

Jay tilted one of the blocky metal contraptions toward him. It seemed heavy—the kind of thing you didn't want to be wearing sandals around like the quirky engimage was. Tip it too far and *smash*. Squished toes.

"This is an airship engine," Jay said proudly. He gestured for Matteo to come closer, and he rose and picked his way across the room using the same meandering route the inventor had. "Look at it closely. What do you think is missing?"

Matteo leaned in, examining the device. Four holes the size of his fist had been drilled near the top, two to a side. Pistons had been inserted into them, and a thin metal spoke extended from them up to a single steel shaft that connected all four. It looked like nothing Matteo

324

had ever seen, even working with his father's shipping company.

"Where's the illyrium?" he asked. "Inside those holes?"

"Knew you were a clever one," Jay said, clapping Matteo on the back. The blow nearly sent him stumbling. "That's the secret." He moved closer and whispered, "There *is* no illyrium."

"What? That's impossible."

Jay clicked his tongue. "Not a word I like to use around here, my friend. As my former master used to say, '*Impossible is, by definition, just another kind of possibility. Simply keep working until the 'im' falls off.*'"

Huh. There *was* a kernel of wisdom in that saying. "Who was your master?"

"Archimas Redora Descar—a thief, a cheat, and a liar," Jay rattled off without a hint of remorse. "Stole a fair bit of my research while I was apprenticed to him and passed it off as his own. But enough about that," he pulled a wrench from one of his coat's many pockets and clanged it against the engine. "Demonstration time!"

Matteo's thoughts strayed to Leon as Jay ducked under the workbench and began rustling through his things. Did Dr. Descar know his son had perished at Aldona? The *Feywind* had exploded in a fireball on the Theradas plain. The rest of the fleet was ravaged, and the official reports likely listed them all as killed or missing. Matteo couldn't imagine any parent who wouldn't be grief-stricken on learning that.

"If you don't use illyrium, how do you power it?" he asked.

A red canister preceded Jay from beneath the table, fluid sloshing noisily inside. With a flourish, he unscrewed a cap on the back of the engine, inserted the nozzle extending from the canister inside, and began to pour. After precisely five seconds, he stopped and set the canister aside.

"Synth-oil," he said, raising a hand to forestall Matteo's coming protest. "But not synth-oil at the same time. We make the sticky, explody stuff by using men'ar to change the properties of shale we drill around Dusan. That whole procedure is a long story, so I won't bore you with the details.

"Anyway, since 'synth-oil type-two' is not a terribly fun name and 'Jayrium' is a tad self-serving, I ended up calling this"—Jay tapped the canister—"kerium. It's made using a different sequence of spells than the usual kind, and is a bit more, well …"

Jay pulled flint and a small dagger from his coat, held them over the dark gap exposed by a raised piston, and crashed them together. Sparks dropped into the hole. " … Volatile," he finished, racing for the far side of the room.

Matteo saw him go. It took him an instant to realize what was happening, but when he did, his eyes went wide and he dived behind the cot, flipping it over so it was between him and the engine.

BOOM!

The kerium ignited, filling the room with acrid smoke. Yet the wave of fire never came. No shrapnel tore across the room to shred the cot, blankets, and Matteo's quivering flesh. Hesitantly, he peeked over his flimsy barricade at the engine. It was thumping around atop the workbench, pistons pounding, the din *almost* as loud as the furnace in the corner.

"Dear Creator," Matteo breathed, crossing himself with the seven-pointed star.

Then a secondary explosion erupted deep in the device. One piston shot out like a bullet, burying itself in the ceiling. The fuel cap went flying in another direction followed by a gout of steaming black goop that melted a constellation of little holes right *through* the metal workbench.

Matteo gaped. "That could have killed us!"

"Ah, but it didn't," Jay said, emerging from behind the furnace. He grabbed a sheet from beside Matteo, dunked it in a bucket of standing water, and tossed it over the engine. A sizzle like meat on a frying pan drowned out every other sound in the room.

"Five seconds! A whole *five* seconds. That's more than twice as long as last week's test."

Crossing himself again—more protection from this lunatic couldn't hurt—Matteo rose and slunk toward the door. Two steps into his escape, he stepped on another void-forsaken ration bar. Its wax wrapping crinkled like a spring thunderstorm, snapping Jay's head in his direction.

"Are you a mage by any chance, my dear Matteo Alhan?"

With a sigh, Matteo turned around, a smile on his lips and a prayer in his heart. "I'm a sensor, but not a very good one."

"Excellent. Just the kind of mage I need." Jay waved him closer. Cringing at every *pop* and *crack* coming from beneath the steaming sheet, Matteo obliged.

Jay held up the crystal ball, which Matteo could now see was etched with hundreds of runes, white shapes and patterns that dimpled its otherwise transparent surface. "This is a menetric—a device that measures the men'ar count in crystals or people. The latter just needs to touch the surface, while the former gets placed on a bracket inside the sphere." A little yellow shard sat at the center of the orb, jagged streaks of blue light jetting from it toward the glyphs on the menetric's edge.

"And the color?" Matteo asked.

"White for high capacity, blue for moderate, and green for low. If a crystal is dun, or a person has no men'ar, the menetric won't react at all."

"If that thing can read the quality of something's magic, why do you need me?"

That earned another grin from Jay. "Stupendous. Another fine question, my fledgling engimage." Matteo swallowed a retort. If being an engimage meant being around explosive materials all day, he wanted none of it.

Jay walked along the workbench until he was standing beside the bronze tower. He placed one hand on a switch at its base. The other raised the sphere, holding it in front of his face.

"Use your magic to examine the menetric, if you would."

"Will it explode?"

"It's not *impossible,* because—"

"'Impossible is just another kind of possibility,'" Matteo groaned.

He closed his eyes. The pain in his head was now a gentle pulse, a slight tapping above his eyes he could barely feel. Jay had hauled him from the halls, let him sleep in his bed, and given him his special brand of medicine. Assisting in one last experiment was the least Matteo could do to repay him.

Colors blossomed, painting the world in shades of magic. Yellow was everywhere. Blazing from the furnace like a cluster of stars, oozing from the menetric and Jay, whispering through the pipes. The limestone walls were a faint green wherever tiny clusters of lichen hung, but the rest was black, including the engine. Magic may have been used to create kerium, but there was no men'ar left in it.

"Alright, I can see the men'ar in the sphere," Matteo said.

"And how about ... " Jay's golden outline—almost like a skeleton, painted in yellow along his veins—twitched ever so slightly. " ... Now?"

The world went black. Pitch-dark, not a pinprick of radiance in sight. Matteo screamed at the sudden loss of input. There was no men'ar, no light, no *life* any way he swung his head. And his magic? Matteo stared down, searching for the threads that should be there, connecting him to everything that was. Nothing stared back. Emptiness, a hollow at his center that went on and on and on forever.

He might have screamed for a moment. Or an hour. Suddenly, he was being shaken, and Jay's frantic voice battered at his ears. "Open your eyes, Matteo! You're not blind. It's the effects of my device, nothing more."

Slowly, Matteo did as he was bidden, cracking his eyes and gazing around the room. He was certain the world had vanished along with his magic, but that was not the case. Here it was—true and real and touchable. Matteo scraped a finger along the stone wall, then reached up and lazily flipped one of the lenses on Jay's monocle over the engimage's eye.

But like a hole gouged from his chest, he still couldn't feel his men'ar.

"I'm . . . alive."

"That you are, lad."

"But my magic . . . "

Jay shook his head, good cheer gone. "I hadn't foreseen this side-effect," he said, rising and marching straight to the bronze tower, which seemed to hum and shake as Matteo watched it. "I'll need to recalibrate and run more tests to avoid a repeat, but the theory is clearly sound. I only hope that foolish master of mine does similar tests before putting it in the field. If not . . . " Jay shuddered.

"What is that device?" Matteo asked. "What did it do to me?"

"It took your magic," Jay replied, flipping the switch back the other way. "Temporarily, of course. It stores up electrical energy in a power-cell here"—he pointed at the square base—"which keeps it running once the men'ar canceling waves begin to flow. It's difficult to find the right frequency, but . . . "

Matteo was barely listening. It was as if a breath of pure light had entered his body, rushing through his blood, making him whole again. The tear in his chest sealed shut as though it never was.

He closed his eyes, and . . . Yes. The colors—*his* colors—were back. Matteo breathed a sigh of relief.

" . . . this is the future," Jay said as Matteo's ears came unplugged. "A world where those with magic don't oppress those without"—he touched the bronze tower with one hand . . . "And a world where our devices aren't dependent on a crystal those same people guard like jealous lovers." . . . and the sheet-covered engine with the other.

A noble goal. One Matteo *would* have supported with all his heart mere minutes prior. But that hole in his chest? That ache, an irresistible craving for something he thought he'd never miss?

No. Matteo had no intention of being parted from his magic ever again.

Chapter 32
Absence

Adamantele 5, 697 ABH
Forest near Resistance Base, Sarconian Province of Darmatia

The Soldier was back, and with him came the veil of darkness that threatened to smother Renar's mind.

It had approached slowly, softly, creeping upon him with velvet-padded soles. Shadows sprouted in his vision when Major Reev complimented Velle on her improving glyph work. Pitch dripped in his thoughts when Vallen finally removed his brace, scored a blow on Lilith, and was given grudging permission to resume magic practice.

And now a swell of midnight loomed on the horizon, preparing to drown Renar as he watched Matteo run through his Sensor's Labyrinth. This wasn't the same boy he'd known before graduation. A man had taken his place, with determined eyes beneath his glasses, sweat-mussed hair, and a tightly belted tunic that could no longer hide the fruits of his training.

Matteo closed his eyes as the next set of glyphs raced toward him, converging through the trees from all directions. Velle wasn't pulling any punches with her attack. But just before they could strike him, Matteo started moving, sidestepping the first, ducking the second, and twisting so the rest passed him on either side. He was a leaf weaving through the trees, wind at his back, sun on his face. Inspiring. Breathtaking.

Revolting . . . the Soldier whispered.

Renar's fingers stopped twitching. The urge to draw Matteo's triumph died, the notebook hidden in his jacket suddenly a weight heavier than he could bear. What had he been doing these past weeks? He'd hauled stones larger than he was, kicked bags until they bled dirt, run for leagues through the corridors of the base. His feet were blistered. His knuckles were ripped and bruised.

And despite it all, if Renar took three steps forward—past the dirt line Colonel Holcomb had scrawled with a stick—he'd get clobbered by the first glyph to pass his way. General Iolus had lied about his son's abilities. Renar possessed no enhancive magic to resist the power of Velle's runes. Dodging like Matteo was out of the question, for he couldn't feel his men'ar, let alone that of others. Wielding destruction like Vallen? Renar snorted. The best he could do was destroy others' lives with his ignorance, as had happened to Angelie.

At that moment, Renar finally understood the General. Here was Matteo, the dunce of the Academy practicals, a mage who'd been his kin in failure. Neither could use magic. Both were hindrances to their teams instead of assets.

But when the crucible blazed, Matteo hadn't burned or shattered. He'd hardened into the sensor before them, swinging around trees, leaping invisible glyphs, and *smiling* with the rush of it all.

Renar was the General's son through and through. Talentless, weak, and full of envy for the absence that had dwelt inside him since birth.

"Five tins say he doesn't last another thirty seconds," Vallen said.

Lilith grinned. "I could use some spending money. You're on."

"If you have time to gamble, you have time to study their technique," Major Reev said, her arms crossed. "Figure out what you'd do if it was you in there instead of Matteo."

"Get above Velle," Sylette said. She was sitting away from the others, knees tucked to her chest, silver eyes not missing a single move the training duo made. "Use the branches to obscure her sight, fire daggers from multiple angles, and drop on her while she's distracted."

The Ice Queen nodded. "Excellent strategy."

"Do you have a plan to kill *all* of us?" Vallen taunted.

Sylette flashed him an icy smile. "For you, you mean? Not sure I'd need one."

The voices of Renar's comrades pulled him from his thoughts. Shaking his head, he straightened and peeled his fingers from the ashen trunk he'd been leaning on. Bark came away beneath his fingernails, and a few droplets of blood smeared the surface below. Had he been digging in that hard?

His confusion didn't go unnoticed. Unter stooped forward, ducking beneath a barren branch as he brought his lips near Renar's ear. "Amiss, something is?" He pulled a bandage from one of his oversized pockets—wraps he carried in case one of his wounds reopened—and offered it to Renar.

"No, just thinking about how I'd draw the scene," he said, which was only *half* a lie. *Lots of charcoal black and bog green,* the Soldier suggested. *The colors of sin and envy.*

Unter peered at the journal-shaped bulge on Renar's chest. "Think why? Could draw just. Once start, scene will come natural to you."

Let instinct take over. It was sage advice . . . *if* Renar could sketch right now. His well of creativity was dry, its desiccated bed cracking further with every dodge Matteo executed, with every day his fellow cadets continued to improve, leaving him behind. Rotten ooze bubbled through those cracks, refilling him with thoughts of a darker sort.

Matteo was breathing hard now, sweat plastering his tunic to his heaving chest. A close miss swept the curls from above his eyes. Another clipped his elbow, tearing a grunt from his lips. Renar hated that a part of him reveled in the inevitable conclusion.

It arrived all too soon. Matteo crouched to the loam-covered ground, discovering too late that Velle had secreted a second glyph in the shadow of the first. The invisible barrier caught him in the chest, drove the air from his lungs, and sent him careening through a stand of spear-fronds.

"Sondek's heartbroken hemorrhoids!" Colonel Holcomb spat, clambering down from the treetops. "Any man who's only concerned with slaking his own thirst is going to get walloped. Anticipate your partner, boy. Their steps. Their moves. It's a *dance*—one that needs to satisfy you both."

Major Reev scowled at the drunk. "You couldn't satisfy a clump of mud." She turned to Velle, who was clenching her fists and smiling. "Well done! Your control and precision continue to improve. Though"— she glanced at Matteo's limp form—"you could hold back a touch with your teammates."

Velle tilted her head. "Didn't you want us to train like it was actual combat?" One of Matteo's legs twitched, and he popped out of the ferns with a hundred tiny nicks on his cheeks, hands, and clothes. Renar found it strange that the Sylph wasn't rushing to his side, ready to heal his every ache and pain.

Yet another incredible ability he hadn't been blessed with.

"*I* think Velle has the right idea, for once." Sylette sprang to her feet, her braided silver ponytail bouncing against her back. "The Empire won't go easy, so neither should we."

Vallen glanced up from his quiet exchange with Lilith. Renar could see five tin geldars sparkle in her palm before they disappeared into a pouch beside her saber scabbard. It wasn't the first bet the Triaron had lost to the freckled girl, and it likely wouldn't be the last.

"We got away from Valescar, didn't we?" Vallen said. "The rest of his ilk can't be that bad."

No thanks to us, the Soldier jabbed, stalking around Renar in the gloom of his mind. *We could barely do more than stand and watch.*

Sylette laughed. "How many times do you have to be reminded that you spent most of that battle *on the voiding ground*?" She shook her head. "And you know *nothing* about the other Rittermarschals. There are at least three mages in the Empire stronger than him when he's going all out. And his fight with you?" Another harsh cackle burst from her throat. "He was playing with his food."

The forest glade seemed to still. Matteo stopped scrabbling around in the spear-fronds. Vallen's brows rose to his hairline, realization painted on his face. Velle's hand drifted to her mouth to stifle a gasp, lest the Major turn around and see her horrified expression. Only Holcomb continued to make noise, swearing as he stared into the dark mouth of his empty liquor flask.

"You speak like you know Valescar," Major Reev said. "Why is that?"

Her emerald gaze was cold, the air around her beginning to shimmer, the dead leaves under her boots crackling as they frosted. Renar knew—*all* of them knew—what was coming next.

Unter shifted, trying to block Sylette from the Ice Queen's view. "Gut instinct," he offered, holding up four index fingers. "When Hue warriors clash, get we sense for foe—their style, drive, strength. We in their head see, and they in ours. Surely warrior great as you experience this?"

"Perhaps. Though many things about your escape have never quite added up. Like how a ragtag band of some of my least favorite cadets weren't simply butchered by the man *you* claim is the fourth most powerful mage in the Empire. That's info army intelligence hasn't even managed to pull together."

Matteo staggered to his feet. "We got away because Leon—"

"I'm asking Cadet Farkos, not anyone else," Major Reev snapped.

She stalked toward Sylette, grass freezing with each step. Renar wanted to defend Sylette. To say something that would allay the Major's justified suspicion. And failing that, he wanted the power to protect a friend who'd already been through oblivion, both past and present. She may be an Imperial heiress, but she'd suffered under her father as much as he had.

But you can't, the Soldier mocked. *You aren't clever enough to find the right words. Aren't gifted enough to turn the Major aside. And—*the shadows enveloping him smiled, exposing too-sharp teeth—*you aren't brave enough to even try.*

"*I* told her those things," Vallen said.

Major Reev whirled toward him. "Stay out of this, Cadet Metellus."

"It was a one-on-one. I told Valescar I was the Triaron, and he was intrigued enough to grant me a duel."

"Metellus . . . " The shards manifesting around Major Reev changed direction, spinning toward Vallen as they grew in size.

"I got my stones rocked," Vallen laughed. "And when the voidspawn didn't put a bullet in the back of my head, I realized he was toying with us. Almost wish he did, with the way the blowhard yapped about how 'proper mages' fight and me 'wasting my gifts.'"

The temperature plummeted, dappling the forest in rime, misting the cadets' breath. Holcomb gave up on his bottle and turned to Major Reev, clutching his tattered uniform robes against the chill. "Hey Jis! Stop giving me blue balls for the thousandth—"

A jagged ice spear impaled the tree beside the Colonel's head, instantly silencing him. "I'm warning you, Metellus. Stay out of my way."

"But that got me thinking." Vallen unclipped the metal rod on his belt and twirled it between his fingers. "If I can go toe-to-toe with a Rittermarschal and live, I must have something going for me. And he told me he's number *four* in the biggest empire in the world. That means a lot of people are beneath him—beneath *us.*"

And Renar saw it. In Vallen's lopsided grin, his twinkling eyes, and his patented slouch. The lies he spewed without hesitation. He was doing what Renar *would* not. *Could* not.

And you hate him for it, the Soldier condemned.

"How about it, Jis?" Vallen raised his weapon, pointing it at Major Reev. "I've gotten better since then. *You've* made me better since then. So now I want to know: who's stronger . . . the Triaron, or the Ice Queen of Darmatia?"

Chapter 33

To Catch A Snow-Hare

Adamantele 5, 697 ABH
Nemare, Capital of the Sarconian Province of Darmatia

Ritterbruder 2nd Class Mikus Garax had been inside precisely two palaces during his years of military service. Which, of course, made him an expert on their design and what it said about the people who built them.

The palace in Sarconia was a subdued but stately affair. Red and gold carpets, banners draped from every column, dangling wrought-iron chandeliers casting out every shadow with a bright illyrium glow. The halls were all hard angles, with evenly spaced alcoves that could double as defensive positions during a siege. And the throne room conveyed not wealth, but strength. The whole of the triangular room rose toward the simple marble throne at a slant, forcing supplicants to gaze up at their ruler no matter where in the room they knelt.

Not so in Darmatia. Mikus found their palace garish, filled with useless tapestries, murals, and other explosions of color that made spots dance across his sensitive eyes. Their throne room was covered in dust, unused for the better part of a century, but the furniture left behind was worthy of condemnation.

Seats of darkwood inlaid with gold, silver, and ivory were arranged in rows before a throne whose opulence put all of them to shame. Recessed archways lined the walls, each depicting a glorified moment from Darmatian history. Gem-studded incense burners hung from the high ceiling on chains, and though they'd burned nothing in decades, Mikus nearly gagged on their phantom aromas.

He wanted out. Out of the throne room, out of the palace, out into the cool night breeze where he could be free of extravagance, duty, and his superiors' insipid bickering.

" . . . one fleet *must* remain behind," Grand Marschal Zaratus insisted, tapping the table-long map before him with one of his gauntlet's claws. "We can't risk the cultists becoming emboldened by an undermanned garrison and organizing a coordinated assault."

"And what if the rebellion escapes our net because we didn't commit enough troops?" Rittermarschal Titania countered. "Better to burn out one nest of adders than to kick both and purge neither."

The argument went back and forth, Mikus listening with only half an ear. He was in the second row of a gaggle of well-dressed officers, all with close-cropped hair, pressed uniforms, and gold lace in abundance. An itch started shrieking at him from his crotch, and Mikus had to pinch his eyes shut and count backwards from ten to resist the urge to attack it before the Emperor and his command staff.

Closing his eyes didn't make much of a difference. He couldn't see Emperor Artorios or the governor over the heads of his fellows, just a flash of vermillion against the drawn curtains whenever Titania became irritated. Zaratus was impossible to miss. The Grand Marschal stood a full head taller than everyone else in the chamber, his dragwyrm helm glowering as it stalked around the central display.

Mikus sighed as the itch bid him a pleasant farewell, and relief flooded his nethers. An elbow immediately rammed him in the gut.

"*Pay attention!*" hissed the bane of his existence as Mikus strained not to groan or double over. He gritted his teeth, nodded, and reminded himself that Terrans only needed one functioning kidney to live.

Rittermark Silesia Marta said nothing else. Smoothing the hem of her uniform jacket, she turned her hard azure gaze back to the meeting. Not a strand of chestnut brown hair escaped the black cap on her head. Her gold buttons glistened with fresh polish. Silesia Marta was the perfect Sarconian officer, and Mikus rued the day he'd been assigned to her brigade.

A portly vice-admiral in navy grays stepped out of line, raising a piece of parchment close to his beady eyes and bulbous nose. "The latest casualty reports, Your Majesty. I think they're pertinent to this discussion."

Titania huffed a cinder-laced sigh, but the Emperor waved for him to continue. Mikus saw his liege through a gap between two headquarters aides he didn't recognize. He did not sit on a throne or bed of cushions, as many rulers might, but leaned over the map table along with his commanders. Another sign of strength.

"Two-hundred twenty-seven dead in the previous fortnight," the vice-admiral read. "The 106th infantry was ambushed when they mobilized to put down the South End slum riot last week, losing a third of their complement to arrows and homemade liquor bombs. When they tried to retreat, the rioters collapsed the buildings around them and charged in with an assortment of daggers, knives, and crude spears.

The butcher's tally was high on both sides."

Mikus felt a pang of guilt—a spike of indigestion in his gut that was there and gone in seconds. He and his men had caused that riot, shooting their way out of a packed crowd of Darmatians to save their own skins.

Would I do it again? Mikus wondered, listening to the lengthening list of death and damage. *Of course I would.*

At his side, Silesia shifted uncomfortably, and Mikus gulped. He didn't fear the cultists or the censure of his peers, but he was *terrified* of what she'd do to him if she was in hot water due to his actions. Dung rolls downhill, and all that.

But what truly got him shivering was her magic. Her magic that . . .

Mikus blinked. What *did* her magic do again? He tried to focus on the question, but a dense fog flooded his mind, making coherent thought difficult. Pain pounded against his temples, a symphony worse than the most egregious of Dar's explosive masterpieces, and with it came the faint scent of cinnamon.

Cinnamon? Mikus glanced around. The vice-admiral was droning on, Zaratus was nodding his helm, and the Emperor was pushing a wood-carved dreadnaught across the map of Darmatia by its thin stand. No embers swirled in the air about Titania's ruby curls, and not one of the four braziers in the throne room's corners were lit.

So why did Mikus smell burning cinnamon sticks?

The aroma grew more powerful, swelling into a wind that gusted from the Hound of the Ritter's nose straight into his thoughts. It struck the fog. Shredded it to ribbons that slowly dissipated like mist before the rising sun.

And suddenly, Mikus understood. *Oh, that crafty little harlot,* he thought, glaring sidelong at Silesia. *She did it* again.

" . . . another riot occurred last Savonday, led by the canal workers' union. I fear this has—"

"Enough," Zaratus commanded, holding up his fist to silence the vice-admiral. With a bow, the man folded his parchment and returned to his space in the front row.

In a flurry of motion, Zaratus snatched a tiny wooden rifleman whose stand read, '*106th Infantry*,' and flung it against a statue of the betrayer, Darmatus Aurelian, resplendent in silver plate. The carving splintered into halves.

"We still have plenty," Titania replied, gesturing to the stack of

336

wooden airships, soldiers, mages, and panzcraft clustered atop a city on the map labeled, *'Nemare.'* "What's your point ... *my lord,"* she added, almost as an afterthought.

"In case you haven't noticed," the Grand Marschal growled, "our adoring new citizens outnumber us fifty to one. I'd rather not make that a hundred to one by sallying out on a fool's errand brought to us by a *traitor."*

Titania threw up her hands. "What more do you want? The intel is sound. The defector listed every vessel and unit that escaped us at Aldona by name, and our analysts have cross-referenced their info against official Darmatian records. It's a perfect match."

"Or a deception."

"Why do you think *they*"—Titania jabbed a finger at several white painted spikes jutting up throughout Nemare—"are challenging our rule? It's hope," she answered before Zaratus could respond. "Hope that someone is coming to save them. Hope that the old regime isn't dead. We should have nailed Metellus' head on a spike in front of the palace on day one, but now we can do the next best thing ... "

A red tongue traced red lips as the Rittermarschal smiled. " ... Toss the bloody bodies of their heroes at their feet."

"Who?" the Emperor asked, glancing up.

"The Ice Queen and Triaron."

Whispers raced through the room like the stench of rotting flesh on a humid day. Some were excited. Others, hesitant. All bore the sickly-sweet odor of self-interest Mikus had come to associate with the Sarconian military.

What can I get out of this?

How will this affect me?

Mikus understood them because he *was* them. He had no desire to go get his stones frozen off in the middle of winter by the Kingdom's legendary she-demon, nor a craving to meet the rumored spawn of Darmatus' long-shriveled loins.

Which was why Mikus cursed every god, ancestor, and poxed whore he could think of when Silesia started pushing her way to the front of the room, his sleeve clenched tightly in her gloved fist. She murmured as they walked, and instead of casting surprised glances, the officers in front of them parted with bowed heads.

Spicy and fragrant, the smell of cinnamon once again wafted through Mikus' nostrils.

"Pardon, Your Majesty, Your Eminences," Silesia said, saluting when they stood exposed in the gap between the officers and the map table. All eyes were on them. Displeasure furrowed the Emperor's brow. Zaratus' reaction was inscrutable, hidden behind the fangs of his menacing visor. While the commanders opposite them scoffed at the breach of protocol, sniggering behind gray beards and mustaches that were already wizened when Mikus was a boy, Titania maintained a coy smile. Silesia was one of the governor's favorites.

"Rittermark Silesia. I trust you have something important to share?"

The young woman inclined her head, clutching her hand to her breast. "I do, Rittermarschal. A two-stage strategy that will rid us of both our plagues at once."

More snorts erupted from the generals and admirals nearest the Emperor.

"A babe scarcely off the teat wants to lecture *us* on strategy?"

"Who *is* this upstart?"

"Your Majesty, you can't possibly be granting the floor to—"

"*Silence!*" Zaratus ordered, stomping his sabatons so fiercely Mikus thought he might punch through both carpet and wood to the floor below. The high commanders of the Empire fell quiet, but jealousy still simmered in their hateful eyes.

Sighing, the Emperor waved Silesia toward the map. "Continue." When she bowed lower and approached, Mikus stayed behind. He couldn't avoid being dragged into her crazy scheme, but he could avoid being caught in the initial explosion.

"Where are the rebels encamped?" Silesia asked.

The Emperor raised his palm, and four unused tokens—two airships, a rifleman, and a mage—slid unaided across the map to rest atop the northwestern coast of Darmatia. *Gravity magic,* Mikus assessed, holding in a gasp. The most powerful magic known to mortals, an ability that, more than the crown on his brow and the armies at his disposal, gave this man the right to rule.

Silesia nodded. "Close to the Great Divide. Home turf for a genius ice mage, especially at this time of year."

"Which is why we can't attack," Zaratus interjected. "You only prove my point."

"I said nothing about attacking, Grand Marschal." Silesia strode around the map of Darmatia, gloved fingers—milk-white like her skin—tracing the province's borders. "Have you ever hunted snow-hares?"

"I don't see how that's relevant."

"If you haven't, I don't recommend it," Silesia continued. "But for those of us from the northern provinces, up past the Velt River and Soder's Forest, we sometimes had to when our winter larders were nearly bare.

"Of course, a snow-hare is just a hare with pristinely white fur. They have no fangs, no claws, no means of defending themselves against predators. So how do they survive while foraging in the snow?"

When no one answered, Silesia stared straight at Mikus, an order writ large in her cold azure eyes: *speak*. "Camouflage," he said, trying to ignore the attention shifting onto him. "They look like snow and— once they've rolled around in the stuff—smell like snow, making it hard to find them. There could be a hundred in a field touched by maiden winter and you wouldn't be able to see them."

"I grow tired of this diversion," the Emperor said, tapping the table. "Skip to the end. How does one catch a snow-hare?"

"You don't."

An assortment of chuckles met Silesia's reply, but she wasn't listening. Her hand was drifting down the jagged reefs of the Phar coast south of the rebel camp, toward a small port city whose name Mikus couldn't make out at this angle.

"Not directly, anyway. You see, snow-hares are unique among their brethren in that they can feed on both plants and men'ar. Since the latter makes their coats glow, even after death, some couturiers will raise them in captivity and glut them on illyrium crystals before weaving garments from their lustrous fur.

"The stuff is like sel-spice to them—a drug. They can't get enough and will chase a hint of illyrium like a hound chases meat." Silesia glanced at Mikus, favoring *her* hound with a sly grin. "So, catching them is rather simple. Take a crystal, put it in the middle of a patch scraped down to dirt and mud, and wait for the snow-hare to take the bait. And when it does"—she mimed raising a rifle, sighting down its imaginary scope—"you plug it with lead, skin it, and throw it in a pot."

Silesia recoiled, her fake bullet fired directly at Mikus' forehead. He didn't move. Didn't laugh along with the other officers now warming to her ingenious ploy. Without Auger Olv'era and the scent of cinnamon he'd tied to it, he'd be nothing but this harlot's plaything— just like almost everyone else around her. And for that, he hated her even as he obeyed her.

"Where do we place our bait?" the Emperor asked, approaching the table beside Silesia. She stiffened for an instant. Her jaw clenched ever so slightly. Then she was all smiles, oozing confidence as she circled a spot on the map with her finger. "Right here, Your Majesty."

Her reaction had been a blip; a motion impossible to track for anyone without a hound's eyes. But Mikus had seen it, and he knew what it meant. He understood Silesia because, in that instant, she'd glared at the Emperor the same way he glared at her:

With utter loathing.

And once Mikus figured out the *why* behind that glare, he might finally be rid of Rittermark Silesia Marta for good.

Chapter 34

The Five Rules

Adamantele 5, 697 ABH
Forest near Resistance Base, Sarconian Province of Darmatia

Blazing emerald eyes bored through Vallen as the lips beneath them split into a fiendish smile.

"Oh, you foolish, foolish boy," Major Reev moaned, pent-up delight oozing from her words. She almost seemed to shiver with anticipation. "You don't know how long I've waited for this."

Her chains snapped.

Ice flared around the Major, stretching to the treetops, framing her like angelic wings. The other cadets dived for cover as she *exploded* across the clearing at Vallen, shards of blue-white crystal scattering in all directions. Her raven hair flapped wildly. Her olive fatigues clung to her body like a second skin, and her pale flesh became an extension of the frost swirling around her.

Vallen had time for one thought before they clashed:

How beautiful.

He struck out with fire, wrapping the krenesh blade he summoned in flame and whipping it toward his teacher's face. A sword of ice met it—a chilled sheathe that encased Major Reev's left arm to her elbow. They exchanged several fierce blows, embers dropping to the loam at their feet, frozen splinters filling the air.

The Major was the more experienced mage, but Vallen was the better swordsman. He pressed her back, using his weight and reach. Lunge, swing, parry, strike. Vallen fell into the familiar rhythm, a smile ghosting his lips as she retreated around a thick ash tree.

Rule two, he recalled from Major Reev's lessons—lessons she'd drilled into him through sweat, blood, and pain. *Use the terrain to your advantage.*

Urging more men'ar into his blade, Vallen sliced *through* the tree, cutting high to low so it would fall in her direction. Branches snapped in the canopy as the great ash dropped, and the Ice Queen was forced back toward him.

The boom was tremendous. Wind rushed around them, Vallen's teeth chattered, and Colonel Holcomb was knocked square on his backside.

"Void fondle my sister! I think the Sarcs felt that one in Nemare."

"We have scouts," Major Reev growled between strikes. "There's not a single Sarc patrol for leagues. No one will notice."

Rule four, Vallen thought. *There is more to your opponent than their attacks.* They had a mind. Thoughts, feelings, and emotions. All of which could be exploited.

While her attention was split, Vallen sidestepped her downward slash, then severed the tip of her blade with one of his own. A twist of the grip, and his krenesh was swinging to blood her chest and end the duel.

Shards of ice struck Vallen in the face. He gasped, shutting his eyes, staggering away through the waist-high ferns and waving his sword to keep her at bay. A kick made his ribs scream. He stabbed in that direction, only to howl as three sharp jabs raced up his opposite flank.

Major Reev was ignoring her own rules! *Rule one: Men'ar is finite. Guard it jealously, and only cast without an invocation in an emergency.*

"Rule one!" Vallen cried, words an accusation.

"Rule five," she countered. As she spoke, a blast of frigid snow lifted him off his feet and slammed him into the trunk of a tree. *"Your opponent always gets a say."*

Something cracked in his back. Warmth sprouted from his head, little rivulets of fire that coursed down Vallen's neck to soak the collar of his tunic. It was like fighting Valescar all over again. The Ice Queen was more experienced, more powerful, and loved by ambient men'ar. He couldn't best her in a straight-up fight.

"Flar'en," Vallen breathed. Heat surged in his chest and spread through his veins like molten ore. The frost on his face melted, and he blinked open his eyes just in time to roll away from an arm-length ice spear that would have pinned his shoulder to the trunk.

"Are you trying to take my arm off?"

Major Reev came sprinting after him, perverse pleasure in her manic grin. *"You* wanted the real thing, Triaron. Don't complain now."

Her arm swung forward, releasing a wall of ice that shot past Vallen to block his retreat. Each spike was taller than he was and thick as Unter's legs. With a sigh, he turned to face his teacher, brandishing a staff in place of his krenesh.

Rule three, he thought, whipping his men'ar into a storm, driving it into his weapon. *The cornered drake fights fiercest.*

"Zeph'for'sla," Vallen chanted.

Concentrated blades of wind—sharp as Sylette's daggers, strong as an airship engine—erupted from the staff's tip. They clawed great gouges in the forest floor as they passed. More slashed branches rained from above, their ends cleanly severed.

But Major Reev didn't turn aside. She whispered something, and two slanted ice shields appeared before her. The wind struck. Hunks of rime went soaring, and clouds of sparkling dust covered the glade, obscuring the duel. Vallen could hear the confused shouts of his companions, echoing from all around.

"Did that hit her?" Renar asked.

Sylette scoffed. "She blocked first."

Lilith hushed them both. "Quiet. I can hear someone moving in ther—"

"Spi'fros'at."

With a noise like a thousand wine glasses shattering, a shaft of gleaming ice shot from the cloud and pierced Vallen's side. He spluttered, glancing down to see crimson spreading around the wound. Ice immediately surged from the shaft, plugging the hole in his ribs, creeping up his body to snare his right arm.

"It's over," Major Reev said. The mist parted for her like a door and she marched toward Vallen, ivory fingers grasping the other end of the spear impaling him. Trembling consumed him as the frost spread. He was cold. So very cold, weak, and . . .

The Ice Queen halted a meter from him. "Do you yield?"

Blue lips parted in a smirk. "N-no."

. . . thrilled she'd let her guard down. The ice crawling across him like vines stopped. It was men'ar made manifest, a tangible product of spiritual energy given will by the mage who created it. It had no mind of its own, and any mage who gave it direction—should their men'ar align with its essence—would be obeyed.

And the Triaron was master of *all* the elements, even if he loathed using water.

Reverse, Vallen willed it, pouring almost all his men'ar into the ice to drive out the Major's.

Drunk on the Triaron's men'ar, the ice happily obliged. It retreated to the wound in haste, then shot back at the one who birthed it, snaring Major Reev's arms and legs in glittering binds. Vallen lunged forward. He had one shot at this. One chance to win before the Ice Queen figured out his trick.

She spat at him and yelled. "Gla'cena!"

A hundred tiny needles launched from the wad of frozen spit, lancing Vallen's limbs and chest, shattering the shackles that held Major Reev fast. He stumbled, muscles refusing to cooperate. His staff tumbled from his hardening fingers, reverting to an ordinary rod as it struck the churned-up muck at their feet.

Was it poison? Some sort of capsule she kept in her mouth as a last resort? He barely had time to think before the first punch landed on his cheek.

"You *are* the Triaron," Major Reev said, her assault continuing. Chest, side, gut, face. On and on. "I've never seen you use water, but I was wrong to think you wouldn't. Now *yield*."

He wouldn't. With a snarl, Vallen surged under the Major's arm, wrapped her up, and slammed her to the ground. This was no longer about protecting Sylette and returning the favor she had done him in Etrus when she'd snapped him free of his despair. This wasn't even about winning or humiliating Major Reev.

Vallen just didn't want to go down. Not again.

She punched at his nose. Vallen reared up and blocked with crossed arms, then snagged her arm and tugged her into a headbutt. Darkness swelled at the edges of his vision as they both fell away, groaning. Aches in his back, head, and arms shrieked at him, while the hole in his gut burned like a hot poker.

But Vallen wouldn't go down. His men'ar was thrumming with a need to be released, the voice in his head whispering so softly it could barely be heard above the pulsing of his blood. *Strike, strike, STRIKE!*

He did, a hook that hit Major Reev's shoulder as she rolled to block. Quick and strong, her legs snagged behind his waist and twisted to the side. In an instant, their positions were reversed, Vallen on the bottom, the Ice Queen on top, flinging punches like rain. Frost came with them, slicing his cheeks until warm blood threatened to blind him.

"*Yield!*"

"*No!*"

Give me control! the voice railed. *I can give you victory!*

Vallen ignored it and lashed out with an electric shock, stunning Major Reev long enough for him to throw her off. He wouldn't accept the help of whatever the voice was. He would win with his own power.

Rising to his knees, Vallen crawled toward Major Reev. The clearing was a mess of ravaged trees, flattened bushes, and slick mud. Scorch marks marred the thick ash trunks. Dripping icicles hung from what few branches remained above.

"Stop, Vallen!" someone yelled. It sounded like Velle, but he didn't care who it was.

He was going to *win*.

Men'ar raced to his hand, gathering dirt and silt, molding it into a gauntlet. Vallen raised it over his head, then swung it at the Major's slumped head.

The Ice Queen twisted. The gauntlet missed.

And with a grim smile on her bloody lips, Major Reev jammed a dagger of green ice into his exposed gut. "Sleep well, Triaron," she murmured as Vallen collapsed against her, sight failing, consciousness fading. "For once, you've earned it."

Jis let the dagger melt, leaving just enough ice to staunch the flow of blood from Vallen's wound. A night's rest, a healing session with Velle, and the imbecile would be back to ruining her life like normal.

Only ...

She glanced down at his scarlet-smeared face, hair slick with grime, his teeth clenched in pain felt even in his dreams. He'd fought with *fire* today, as well as cunning she hadn't thought him capable of. The lessons she'd taught him were etched in every move and decision he'd made.

Velle flung herself in the muck at Vallen's side, thrusting Jis aside. "What did you do? What did you stab him with?"

"Liquefied hazewort, martyr's bramble, and a touch of illyrium dust." Jis rattled off the compound's ingredients as she rose and looked herself over. Scratches and bruises coated her arms, and her fatigues were ruined. A small price to see the Triaron *finally* coming into his own.

"Knock-out venom." A soft sigh slipped from Velle's mouth. "Thank the Veneer that's all it was. Did you have to stab him, though?"

"Did he look like he was going to go down otherwise? It was that or freeze him solid."

Kindness and compassion. Velle was the rock of the team, their shield and guardian angel. If she fell, they all did, which was why Jis had been so hard on her when they sparred. Survive the Ice Queen's fury, and you could survive *anything*.

She turned to the rest of the cadets. Matteo was gaping at the destroyed clearing, which was now littered with gnarled branches and blackened by stray flames. The boy had probably thought he was gaining on Vallen in combat prowess. Jis shook her head. No, *his* gifts lay in a completely different direction.

"Unter. Renar."

The sentinel and his chain. They stepped closer, the latter's gaze glued to the mud. Jis knew what ailed him—had known for years, despite the deceit his father peddled among the other Academy instructors. She just hadn't the heart to shatter the illusion he so clearly clung to.

"Haul this fool to the medic station," she ordered. "Lilith?"

The girl hopped off the downed ash tree. "Yes, ma'am?"

This one was a firecracker, strong, fast, fierce. Jis was swiftly running out of techniques to teach her, though the grace with which she moved suggested this type of training wasn't new to her. She was their vanguard—the combat nut who'd blaze a trail through all their foes.

"Head to the quartermaster and ask him for a 'special' parcel," Jis said. "He'll know what I mean."

They deserved a reward tonight. A few slices of ek-meat and a couple pouches of cheap spice were the least Jis could do to honor how far they'd come and what they'd accomplished in the scant few weeks they'd been in her care.

Lilith raced off, dodging through the trees. Which left . . .

Sylette was gone, not a trace of her silver hair visible amid the gray trunks and oncoming autumn dusk. The little harpy who'd caused all this trouble had vanished the second Jis was no longer paying attention.

No matter. She watched Unter and Renar heft Vallen onto their shoulders, Velle trailing behind holding glowing hands to his stomach wound. This was *his* day, and Jis wouldn't concern herself with anything else. Raising two fingers to her brow, she sketched a mocking salute at Vallen's back.

Rodale came up beside her and held out a fresh bottle of piss-yellow booze he'd pulled from nowhere. Jis jerked away, pinching her eyes, scrunching up her nose against the scent of stale spirits and unwashed rags wafting off him.

"No thank you," she said, trying not to gag.

Rodale shrugged. "Suit yourself. More for me." He took a swig, then two more for good measure. When half the bottle was gone, he glanced at Jis, something approaching respect in his drink-addled gaze.

"You did well today, Jis."

She bit back her automatic retort: *You don't get to call me Jis anymore.* Instead, she asked, "What do you mean?"

"With the kids. I figured someone should tell you that, even if it's

347

just void-tickled ol' me. So, you did well, Jis." Rodale took another hit and belched. Some of the piss-colored liquor spilled from his mouth, dribbled into his scruffy almost-beard.

Jis nodded. Like with Sylette, she could ignore his slovenly appearance, stench, and their history for one evening. *Just* one evening.

After all, you were right, Tabitha, Jis thought, smiling as she stared at the emerging stars in the twilight sky, each a fledgling light slowly coming into its own. *That brat was worth teaching. They* all *were.*

Chapter 35
Illusions and Falsehoods

Adamantele 5, 697 ABH
Sarconia, Imperial Seat of the Sarconian Empire

Numbers were the soul of the Empire.

Its fleets were its arms and legs, its citizens its blood, and the Emperor its keen and discerning mind. But its soul—the essence that kept all the other organs working—was the numbers scrawled on the spreadsheets, ledgers, and maps tacked to every surface in Commissioner-General Gustav Rudolf's office.

He sat hunched over his desk, magnifying lens in one hand, a red-tipped quill in the other, tracking seven tin geldars missing from the 22nd Mechanized Company's coffers. Most would call Gustav a fool for fussing over such a trivial amount—barely enough to buy soup and bread at a capital tavern. What they didn't realize was that one error often hid another, which hid another, and so on.

Whether by mistake or malice, someone in the Twenty-Second's headquarters was misallocating funds. And not just any funds. *His Imperial Majesty's* funds.

Such a sin was too much for a patriot like Gustav to bear. It made him sick to the point he'd *almost* skipped his roast pheasant lunch, and had taken his second shot of schnapps to go so he could return to his labors a few minutes sooner. Yes, Gustav would hunt down the wayward tins, smear their trail with red ink, and jab his quill through the very heart of the bookkeeper who thought to sully the soul of the Empire.

Gustav flipped the page, smacking his lips as his pen traced cramped figures down a page of ammunition tallies. He could feel his mutton chops graying with the stress of his search, the tips of his waxed mustache wilting like the candle flickering on the corner of his desk. Beneath the polished darkwood surface, his stomach growled, complaining that if Gustav worked much longer, he'd miss his dinner reservation at his favorite winery, *Chateau de Chasseurs*.

Just a few more minutes, Gustav told himself, undoing a few of his uniform's buttons to give his belly room to breathe. *A few more minutes and I'll have this tin-thief by their troublesome tail.*

As he patted sweat from his cheeks with a gold-trimmed handkerchief, an errant record caught Gustav's eye, one two tins less than should have been issued for the company's payroll. His lips creased into a smile. His eyes twinkled like a schoolboy reciting the Imperial pledge for the first time. Here was the prey he'd been hunting! Now to drag it into the light.

The double doors of his office slammed open, sending loose papers whipping around the room, tearing a map of the Eastern Theater from Gustav's wall. There had been no preamble. No knock from his secretary, ring from the projectostand on his shelf, or notice from *any* of the dozen officers on his staff.

And as if to spite Gustav for his lethargy in finding the missing tins, the gust from the door blew the payroll ledger from beneath his fingers, over his shoulder, and out the second-story window behind him. It disappeared, swallowed by the darkness of a moonless night.

Gustav shot to his feet in a rage, medals on his chest bouncing wildly. "Who in the Emperor's blessed name *dares* interrupt my work without authorization?"

"I do."

A man wearing the same uniform—staff officer black trimmed with red and gold—marched across the long office, not bothering to avoid the stray documents scattered beneath his boots. Gustav's hands balled into fists. This *cretin* was stomping on the *soul* of the Empire—*His Majesty's* soul.

He glanced past the officer, a captain by the insignia on his shoulders, to scowl at Henriette, his secretary. She peered in from her desk outside his door, one hand playing with the hem of her skirt, the other tugging at her braided hair. Useless. Both her and the gaggle of staffers behind her, staring at the captain while whispering amongst themselves.

All of them would be fired come the morning.

And this rapscallion, Gustav thought, sizing up the captain, *will be on the first transport to the Varas Fortress trenches by then.*

He glared at the officer as he halted in front of Gustav and reached into the folds of his jacket. A weapon? Such a barbaric threat would be a perfect match for the ugly scars slashed deep into the captain's face.

"Ha! Do your worst, *gefreiter*," Gustav mocked. "Nothing you do will make me betray His Majesty, and by this time tomorrow I'll have you stripped to rags and on your way to the Eastern Front."

"Funny you should mention His Majesty, Commissioner-

General," the scarred man said. He drew a scroll from his coat and unfurled it, revealing an Imperial writ imprinted with a crimson seal.

The wax was dried and flaking, but the sword, shield, and angel of the Artorios household were impossible to mistake, as were the flowing initials: *S.A.* By some absurd twist of fate, this *brute* bore the personal seal of Emperor Sychon Artorios, First of His Name, Ruler of the Twin-Walled City and all its Lands. A seal that was only superseded by edicts straight from His Majesty's sovereign lips.

Numbers were the soul of the Empire . . . but the soul was ever slave to the mind.

Gustav bowed until the tassels and medals of his uniform touched his desk. Ground between his pride and his duty, his words emerged with a pained gasp. "How might I be of service, Captain . . . ?"

"Ulrich," the scarred man finished. "Two things, General, both very simple matters. First, I require you to file a form for an infantry squad to visit 3429 Central Gate Square tomorrow at dawn to move my furniture to my new Upper Ring lodgings."

"What? That's a gross misallocation of—"

Captain Ulrich shook his head, one finger tapping the seal he held. Gustav instantly swallowed his tongue. "I wasn't done speaking. But not to worry, the second task is easier than the first." The man held out his bare hand, fingers covered in calluses, weathered by hard labor and sun. "You need only shake my hand, General. After that I—and the Emperor's writ—will disappear from your life forever."

Cursing whatever whim had led His Majesty to entrust this ignorant knave with his mandate, Gustav grabbed Captain Ulrich's hand and squeezed as hard as he could.

Captain Hans Ulrich cinched his greatcoat to his neck and stepped off the stoop of the Ministry of Logistics onto Central Plaza, the beating heart of the Empire. Each of the six faces of the plaza, including the building he'd just exited, represented a pillar of Imperial might.

To his left was the Compendus Archives, a library with four wings containing all the knowledge Imperial scholars had collected over seven long centuries. Further in that direction was the headquarters of the Ritter Order, a stately building fronted by four massive columns, each carved from top to bottom with one of the organization's core values: *Strength, Obedience, Honor, Victory.*

Hans wasn't so sure they embodied honor anymore, but like a smart Sarconian, left the thought unsaid. Saluting a passing sergeant and the squad of clean-shaven recruits tromping behind him, he turned right and strode along the wide boulevard in front of Fleet Headquarters—the center of military operations. Its windows remained lit throughout the night, and many dedicated commanders simply slept in their offices rather than return home for a few brief hours.

Next was the Royal Airfield, with a steady stream of airships coming and going beneath its bright spotlights. The roar of cruiser engines was just one more sound in the cacophony of Central Plaza. Projectostands attached to illyrium streetlamps belted orders about curfew, carrying identification papers, and other important notices. The clomping of army-issue boots echoed off the pristine edifices and scrubbed cobblestones, while the titter of whispered conversations came from small gazebos and secluded benches scattered between buildings.

Directly across the square from Hans, past a three-tiered fountain topped by the gorgeous angel of Sarconia, was the plateau housing the Royal Palace and Senate dome. No matter how many times he saw it, the sight still made his skin tingle.

Wine-colored neverleave trees lined the edges of a massive elevator platform leading up to the top, where two panzcraft and an array of heavy guns guarded the entrance to the Emperor's private estate. Flying buttresses and high towers rose beyond the gate, vaulted halls and gabled roofs reaching for the pitch-black sky. Every archway cradled stained glass windows that glowed ruby, sapphire, and emerald when illuminated from inside. Hans couldn't see what they depicted from this distance, but he'd soon get a closer look.

For the Royal Palace—and the vault it hid—were his destination.

Hans turned down a side street, searching for a nook where he could change. Ritter agents were everywhere these days, and the last thing he needed was to bungle his mission by carelessly using his magic in public.

There. A small gap appeared in the bushes lining the lane, exposing a patio where officers could eat lunch, share a drink, or—more than likely—entertain their mistresses far from the prying eyes of their wives and families. Hans had collected enough blackmail on Sarconia's elite to know that their passions often exceeded their reason.

Wait. *Hans* had never blackmailed anyone in his life. He was only concerned with protecting his family, lovely Elicia and little Meira and Sirus. He was—

The flimsy, oft-patched wall in his mind cracked, the personalities on the other side crying, clamoring, screaming to be free. Not now, not here. Not while he was on a mission!

Hans stumbled, one hand on his face, the other gripping the back of a wrought-iron chair. It was patterned after twisting homle fronds, with jagged leaves and clusters of berries like she'd—like Elise—had once grown for her shop in the lower ring.

Why was she here? Elise glanced around at the unfamiliar surroundings, the bright lights, the airships rumbling overhead. This was the Upper Ring, about as far from her grandmother and their store as she could get.

Elise went to run a hand through her unruly curls, only to knock a black officer's cap from her head. The captain's pips attached to its front stared at her, accusing her of the truth she knew deep down. Elise staggered backward and fled into—

Barthol. He was a Royal Academy professor of mathematics, the very same man who'd cracked Khaleesa's Conundrum, once called the unsolvable algorithm. Calm, cool, and collected, he was precisely the person they needed to get through this confusion. Barthol adjusted his non-existent spectacles and raised his arms, staring at the gold cufflinks and silver buttons of a uniform he'd never worn.

It was simple, really. He was on a mission. He was *always* on a mission, like when Barthol had gotten them into that lecture on gravpad propulsion systems. Who had been their target then?

Elise shrugged, and Barthol scoffed. No matter. Now they just needed to switch into their latest persona, that insufferable General—

Kres popped out, gasping as he fell to his knees. Where was the blood? He'd been staunching it with both hands—both hands!—but there was too much, pouring and pouring and pouring. How much blood could Fritz's slashed neck possibly have in it?

Five liords, Barthol answered without missing a beat.

Elise rolled her eyes. *You aren't helping, Bart. He needs to get the blood back in Fritz, not know how much is supposed to be there.*

Yet Kres failed. He *always* failed. And then the stench came, foul, rancid. He fell on his backside and scrambled away from Fritz's cackling skull, what skin still clung to it bleached by the blazing sun. Flies buzzed around, procreating, laying eggs. Then came the maggots, squirming and feeding. Kres bore it all. Lay still as they crawled over him. Breathed

353

not a sigh as the bayonets fell around him, silencing those still screaming for their mothers. They wouldn't get him, they wouldn't get him, they—

You're going to faint, Kres, Elise warned.

Let me sing him a ditty, Clara, the Bard of the Riverlands, said as she strummed an invisible lute. *The king was a silly old fart, who placed all his wives in a cart. He pushed them to town, charged eight tins a round, and got rich off the fruits of their—*

"*ENOUGH!*" Vier yelled, staggering to his feet. "Enough, all of you, enough."

They mumbled apologies, sliding away to the corners of his mind, retreating until the next episode occurred. It was inevitable. Like Elise, one of them would see, hear, or smell something that reminded them of their true life—the one they'd lived before Vier copied them—and surface to live a long-lost lie.

But they weren't real. They were a part of Vier, manufactured by his magic.

His *curse.*

Only Hans remained. The flesh he currently wore, a persona not quite as realized as the rest. Not yet, at least.

Vier shook his head, clearing away the whispers of his other lives. He closed his eyes, took a deep breath, and visualized his men'ar congregating in his belly. A strand of black thread ran from his right palm down his arm, through his chest, and blended with the roiling ball of energy. Then it expanded outward, pushing against Vier's skin.

Oozing through his pores.

His stomach bulged. Silver-black hairs sprouted from his cheeks, forming into sweeping mutton chops and a well-pruned mustache. Blue eyes clouded to black, his nose flattened, and the calluses fell from his hands, replaced by smooth, ink-smeared flesh. Even Vier's uniform changed, sprouting medals and lace Hans had never received: the Imperial Star, the Herald's Bugle, the Lusserian Campaign Bronze Cross, and too many others to name.

And with this fresh illusion came its memories. Poring over accounting ledgers day in and day out. Sipping wine with other silver-haired officers in a smoky lounge, making wagers about which units would survive the next assault on Varas Fortress. Descending dark steps to a basement filled with rattling chains, private rooms decked out in red silk, and young girls—

Vier banished the swirling recollections. He was *Vier.* Not

Commissioner-General Gustav Rudolf, not Hans, not any of the faces he wore.

And this curse of his made him the best assassin the Orabairos could call upon.

Three times a day, Vier could cloak himself in another's veil. Three times a day, he could add to the maelstrom of voices chattering in his head. All it took was contact with a target's skin—a direct conduit to their men'ar, the signature of their existence.

In other words, a simple handshake.

I came up with the handshake play, Clara insisted.

Elise raised an eyebrow. *Did you now?*

Are any of the rest of you smooth enough to pull it off?

Vier ignored them. The bard was a genius, but prone to claiming credit for others' accomplishments. But whose accomplishments were they, really? Who *was* Vier? Just like he wasn't sure who the face beneath his mask belonged to, he wasn't sure which story matched the blank eyes of his reflection.

Was Vier—four, in the common tongue—the number of days he spent hiding beneath corpses as Lusserians pillaged his village? The hours he was beaten by the guardsmen for filching food? How many times he was cast out of the settlements he wandered into?

Or do all those stories belong to other people, too? a voice whispered from the deepest abyss of Vier's mind.

He set about checking his gear, ensuring that none of his weapons or tools could be seen beneath the men'ar illusion he wore. Vier's appearance hadn't changed at a molecular level. Rather, a layer of light had settled atop the black jumpsuit he wore, hugging him like a second skin. When he moved, it moved, down to shuffling his toes and blinking.

His bandolier of chemical-laced needles was tight against his chest, and the dagger strapped to the small of his back was covered by the very real greatcoat he wore. The last thing Vier needed was a grunt trying to earn a favor by fetching a cloak for a General wandering around in the cold without a jacket.

With a final count of the various powder bombs lining the coat's hem, Vier stalked out of the secluded patio and straight across Central Plaza. His steps were loud and purposeful. His expression grim. Soldiers took one look at him and jumped aside, smacking fists to their chests in salute.

And why shouldn't they be nervous? He was Commissioner-General Gustav Rudolf, the man who controlled every bullet, meal kit, and pair of combat boots in the Empire. The rittermarschals might execute the war, but it was he—the master of numbers, the Empire's soul—who gave them the tools to do so.

Passing the fountain, Vier nodded to a pair of aristocrats in crimson frock coats, lesser nobles of House Julian. They possessed mineral rights Gustav wanted, so a little politeness toward the family went a long way.

At the base of the palace plateau, he met Countess Baduaire and her escort. The youth was ten years her junior, muscles rippling beneath his satin robes, but the Countess was still his match. Gustav 'appraised' the ample 'assets' prominently displayed by her gown for a polite second before bowing to kiss her hand. She chuckled at his manners, insisted they meet for tea the following week, then continued dragging her paramour toward a waiting carriage.

It was all part of the illusion. All part of the act. As Vier approached the elevator, the lieutenant manning the first security post waved for his men to unlatch the gate and allow the Commissioner-General aboard. He looked like Gustav, acted like Gustav, and knew everyone entering and exiting the palace. The young man wasn't about to make the mistake of delaying him by checking his identity papers.

The lift rumbled to life and whisked Vier upward, gears clanking beneath the metal platform on which he stood, steam hissing from the valves along its sides.

A marvel, Barthol breathed, taking control and walking over to study one of the four great wheels ratcheting them toward the summit. It spun so fast the teeth lining its edge were practically a blur.

Kres pressed a hand to his mouth. *I don't like heights. I think I'm gonna hurl.*

Smell this, Elise said, holding up a clove of non-existent fenroot. *You'll feel better.*

Laughter bubbled from their throat. *This is a toy!* Shogun Rashige of the Rabban Imperium proclaimed. He was a rare guest, one who only emerged to insult the Sarconian magtech that had been his undoing. *These silly Sarcs waste illyrium on an impressive approach to the palace when they could put the entrance underground. One airship assault would smash this lift into a scrap heap.*

"There *is* a hidden lift inside the plateau," Vier said aloud, unsure why he bothered. "Only the royal family uses it. Everyone else has to ride or"—he pointed at a set of steep, switchback stairs carved into the sheer cliff face nearby—"climb up."

As the elevator ground to a stop, the voices fell silent. His madness—for what else *could* Vier call this?—hadn't yet completely taken hold, and the others knew not to jeopardize the missions that kept all of them alive.

For if they lost the patronage of the Orabairos, it was unlikely they'd find another home.

Vier approached the next checkpoint with Gustav's characteristic swagger: chest out, hands clasped behind his back, eyes dissecting the numbers behind everything around him. Each of the panzcraft flanking the steel gate was comprised of one hundred and seventy-eight individually machined parts, not counting screws and welds. Their main armament was a S/48 Farschel Cannon, for which they could store seventy-six rounds. It had a crew of four, cost seven silver geldars to operate a day, and—

"Commissioner-General? Is everything alright, sir?"

Blinking away the statistics swimming before his eyes, Vier scowled at the flint-faced colonel of the guard. He was a burly man with a close-cropped black beard, matching hair retreating from his stony gaze, and a nose that had been broken more times than Gustav had visited the warfront.

Which wasn't a lot, but it was still pretty crooked. "Colonel Malkep," Vier said. "Thank you as always for your diligent service as His Majesty's guard dog."

The officer bristled but didn't retort. These two had a history— one in which Gustav's rank gave him a slight edge.

"What brings you to the royal plateau at this late hour?" Malkep asked.

Vier sighed and rubbed his chin, playing up how irritated Gustav was to be here. "The war, Malkep. What else could it be? I had to cancel my reservation at *Chateau de Chasseurs* to look over some shipments Prime Minister Tallis *insists* have to arrive in Darmatia within the week."

"You mean you haven't heard?"

"Heard what?"

Malkep frowned. His aide, a captain with a scar across his chin, stiffened, and the soldiers inside the stone guard post looked up from their logbooks in surprise.

"Tallis had a resurgence of the white plague," Malkep answered. "He's quarantined in his quarters, unable to see anyone. You'll have to return another day, sir."

357

Inwardly, Vier cursed. How could Gustav know everything about every little crap-hole outpost in the Empire, but not know the most important minister in the land was on his deathbed for the third time? He glanced around, gauging the odds in case Malkep saw through his deception.

The soldiers manning the gate were wide awake, either standing at attention or glued to their gun emplacements. A pair of concrete bunkers sat behind their panzcraft, entryways piled with sandbags, slits lined with rifles. It would take a squad of mages or a heavily armed company to break through.

Which meant Vier and his needles, dagger, and bombs had no chance whatsoever.

He threw up his hands. "The old coot is *always* dying, Malkep. I don't keep track of when he's in bed and when he isn't, just like I don't always pay attention to which of your boys"—Vier stared pointedly at the scar-chin captain—"is keeping you company when you visit your family estate."

Malkep's eyes widened at the implication, but he was wise enough to avoid looking over his shoulder. If he had, rumor would have quickly turned to fact. "Void your underhanded accusations and threats, Rudolf. I don't know what you're up to, but you aren't getting in, general's sabers on your collar or not."

"I don't deal in threats"—Vier growled, reaching inside his greatcoat and yanking out the Emperor's writ—"I deal in absolutes. Like the seal on this writ, for example."

When Malkep didn't speak, Vier leaned closer, shoving the wax emblem right in the colonel's face. "It's real. Smell it, taste it, or even jam it up your bum if you don't believe me. Now, if you don't want to head south in disgrace like the last head of the Imperial Guard, I suggest you open the gate."

"Tell me the real reason you're here," Malkep said, standing his ground. "The Emperor isn't in residence, so are you here to meet his so—"

Vier waved the writ at the captain, who saluted and rushed into the guard post. A moment later, the massive steel gate cracked with a boom and opened wide enough for two men to walk through side by side.

"Write that I went to see Tallis' staff," Vier ordered as he walked away. "Or whatever you want. I don't care."

"His Majesty will hear of this!" Malkep called after him.

Vier stepped through the open portal, then took the path leading toward the central courtyard. He smiled. Malkep could report whatever he wanted, and all the flak would fall on a bewildered Gustav Rudolf—one who hadn't visited the royal palace and couldn't tell his interrogators what they wanted to know, regardless of what they did to him.

He skirted a patch of topiary shaped to look like angels playing musical instruments, passed under an ivy-covered archway, and took the next left. A broad chest thinly veiled by a gossamer robe sprang up in front of him. There was no time to dodge, no time to change course. Vier collided with the man, and both of them—as well as the serving girls clinging to his arms—collapsed in a pile of tangled limbs.

A curse died in Vier's throat as *all* the voices in his head recognized the man he'd struck.

The first prince! Elise gasped, blushing as she fussed with her dress.

Rashige started to draw his sword. *Vasuron Artorios! Now you pay for sinking my lord's fleet!*

Clara tried to burst into a song glorifying the crown prince. Kres shied away, hiding his face. Barthol sniffed. Why did the people love a man who cared nothing for the sciences?

And Vier, mind racing, numbly rose to his knees, held out his bare hand, and said:

"I humbly beg your forgiveness, Prince Artorios."

Chapter 36
Hidden, but Never Gone

Darkness stretched in every direction, on and on and on forever. There was no horizon. Nothing to delineate up from down, left from right. Just pitch black as far as Vallen could see.

He was back in the space between, that warped reality that lay at the intersection of his dreams and the waking world. But it was not so strange as it once was.

Vallen waved his hand and the glassy floor beneath him—like crystal or stilled water—began to glow. A handful of holes appeared in the surface, and from them emerged portals of light. They were mirror-shaped, but instead of reflecting his appearance, they showed moving images, blurry and indistinct. Sound echoed from their depths, a muffled laugh here, a muted cry there.

These were Vallen's memories of Elaine. Blurred by his attempts to forget. Muffled by time, liquor, and pleasure-seeking. Hidden, but never gone.

None of the portals showed scenes Vallen recognized—none but the one at the end. It was darker than the others, its edges charred to crumbling ash, its light obscured by clouds of smoke. Twisting tendrils of crimson, orange, and yellow swam among the shapes huddled at its center.

Vallen turned away. Whatever the darkness wanted, whatever it promised him, he was *not* going through that doorway.

Why? the voice asked. *I can help you conquer anything that lies within.*

The shadows around Vallen seemed to lengthen, stretching into yawning chasms and endless abysses. It was as if he were suddenly on Lozaria's tallest peak, and all around was an ocean of nothingness. Bleak, desolate, and empty.

He shut his eyes. Centered his mind and focused on not moving. Somehow, Vallen knew that if he fell into one of those pits, he'd end up as empty as it was.

"Nothing you say will make me relive that day, *voidspawn*," Vallen spat.

Voidspawn? The darkness seemed . . . offended. *You Lozarians have such a pitiful understanding of your own myths. But perhaps Elaine should be blamed for that. She was your teacher, after—*

"Shut up!"

Vallen's eyes snapped open. He flung his arms forward, unleashing a torrent of scorching flames into the gloom.

Nothing emerged from his palms. No embers, not even a wisp of smoke.

The darkness laughed. *What vitriol. Try that a few thousand more times, and you* might *be able to warm the place up a bit. Now, imagine for a second you had accepted my offer for aid against the Ice Queen. You could have* melted *that insignificant Vestige. Instead ...*

Plop. Plop.

Vallen glanced down, following the sound of dripping water. Only ... it wasn't water. The same black ooze that had once swallowed his phantom Elaine was gushing from a wound in his gut—the hole where Major Reev had stabbed him.

He tried to plug it with his hands, but the flood just pushed through his fingers, sticky and warm. With every passing second, Vallen grew weaker. His thoughts slowed. His legs grew unsteady, shaking as strands of ooze slipped down them.

He was going to fall. He was going to die. He was going to—

Shall I help you with that? the darkness asked.

"Void you."

Abandoning his efforts to staunch the flow, Vallen flipped the darkness a crude gesture, stumbled forward, and toppled into the nearest glowing portal.

Charkur 17, 688 ABH,
Nemare, Royal Capital of the Kingdom of Darmatia

Vallen adjusted his fine hepam-cotton britches for the eleventh time that hour, noting with displeasure that the chafing along his thighs did *not* disappear. Worse still, his arms—trapped in Darmatian-blue suit sleeves—could barely stretch past his knees, making the removal of the pebble in his stiff dress shoe as improbable as the existence of Elaine's beloved Veneer.

"*Save me,*" he begged the girl in question.

She looked down at him from the landing of her parents'

townhome, pity and amusement clashing on her fair features. "It's just a few more steps," Elaine encouraged. "You can make it!"

And make it Vallen did, but not without several mumbled curses and a threat to burn her brother's wardrobe to cinders. It was his cast-offs the Sewertown orphan was wearing, though the original owner was none the wiser. Elaine's maid, Reesa, snuck the lad's old outfits from his room, tailored them as best she could, then passed them to her young ward. Aside from buying Vallen clothes herself—an expenditure her parents would have to be *blind* not to notice—this was the only way to make him presentable for his surface study visits.

Though the subterfuge chafed at him for an entirely different reason. "Can you tell me why we have to deceive your parents again?" Vallen asked.

Elaine glanced away, fingers twisting the handle of the white parasol she carried over her shoulder. The useless sunshields were all the rage this season, or so Elaine had told him. "They might be pretty open-minded, Vallen, but they're still surfacers. Let's break them in slowly."

"*You're* a surfacer and still seem plenty fond of me."

The girl shifted the parasol to hide her blush. "True, but I'm me and they're them. I promise we'll tell them soon."

Clanking locks interrupted Vallen's retort. They turned just in time for Reesa to throw open the door and sweep them both into an embrace.

"If'n it isn't ma two favorite children!" the Sayri woman boomed, dark braids scratching against Vallen's cheek, the colorful beads woven among them clattering with a melody all their own.

"Hello, Reesa," Elaine said, dropping her parasol and returning the hug.

"Hello, bear-woman," Vallen gasped, struggling to wriggle free. No matter how hard he tried, he couldn't escape the grip *gluing* him to her apron. Only when she released him was Vallen able to stagger away and grab a much-needed breath.

"I cannae believe it's been two months since ya first visited, not-so-little Vallen," Reesa said, stepping back and evaluating him with hands on hips. "Ye've sprouted like a dune bloom. An' are those *whiskers* I see?" She rubbed an ebony-colored finger across Vallen's chin, making him snarl. "Ya gonna be a handsome one. I can already see it, yes I can."

Elaine pointedly looked past her, into the foyer beyond. She immediately fell into a curtsy, hands drawing up the hem of a blue dress that matched her eyes. "Greetings, father, mother."

"Let them by, Reesa," said a crisp male voice. "We mustn't keep Elaine and her guest waiting on the stoop."

"O' course, Mister Gennesaret."

The Sayri woman hustled them inside, where Vallen sunk into a well-practiced bow. His head might be bent, but his eyes roved about the room before settling on his hosts.

Mister and Missus Gennesaret were a match for their surroundings and each other. He wore a suit-robe of the same gray as the crystal chandelier and a blue waistcoat emblazoned with gilt initials: *H.G.* His silver-laced hair was slicked back with some sort of gel, and his close-cropped black beard was styled with curling edges—a little artistic flair to spice up an otherwise subdued appearance. He struck Vallen as aloof and reserved, like one of the twin moons.

But if he was a moon, Elaine's mother was the sun. She was positively *radiant,* wearing a shimmering dress that sparkled like the crystal glassware on the marble-topped bar to their right. Flaxen hair, so very different from Elaine's tawny locks, flowed down to the small of her back with little white flower buds laced in along the way. Deep brown eyes smiled at him from a face like the goddess Ellara's, unblemished but where joy-etched lines lightly touched her skin.

"Thank you for inviting me," Vallen said. "May Sariel bless this home, and you, its keepers."

The smile on Missus Gennesaret's lips widened. "So polite as always. The pleasure of your company is entirely ours, Vallen. May our hospitality be as warm as our faith."

"Though we would like to meet *your* parents soon," Mister. Gennesaret said, rubbing his beard as he stared at Vallen. "To think you've been escorting our daughter around town for the better part of two months and they haven't bothered to—"

"Harold!" Missus Gennesaret lightly touched his arm. "That's no way to treat someone with whom we've shared Sariel's blessing."

"Quite right. Please accept my apology, young Vallen."

Vallen straightened and made a pacifying gesture. "No need. *I'm* alarmed they've been gone so long. It seems the art exhibit they're displaying in Rabban is more engaging than their only child. Though"—he glanced at Elaine—"your daughter has ensured my studies haven't lapsed during their absence."

"Art, you say?" The tip of Mister Gennesaret's beard seemed to twitch with excitement. "Any pieces I might know? I have several friends from the Rabbanite Neoclassical school of design, so it's possible some of them are at the show. I could even have them pick up a new piece or five for our gallery."

Missus Gennesaret sighed. Slipping her slender arms through her husband's, she started pulling him toward a nearby door. "Enough, dear. Let them get on with their studies. Besides, you still have to finish the centerpiece for Steward Metellus' upcoming festival."

"Right you are," he grumbled. "Be diligent in your studies, children."

"Yes, father." Elaine curtsied again, then grabbed Vallen's wrist and drug him upstairs to her room. Reesa followed behind and took her place on a chair outside the door. The wink she gave him suggested the Sayri woman didn't understand or didn't care about the duty she'd been assigned.

Elaine rushed in and threw herself onto her bed, unleashing a muffled scream into one of her frilly, lace bedecked pillows. Vallen entered the room more slowly, checking that everything was still in the same place, evaluating potential escape routes.

It was much the same as he remembered from his past visits. A wide, tiled floor stretched across a space as large as the *Safe Haven* pawn shop, complete with a fluffy bed, mirror-topped set of darkwood drawers, and an adjoining bathroom that still smelled of flowers Vallen didn't recognize. The window near the bed overlooked a lush garden filled with vibrant colors, some he'd never seen in Sewertown: bright yellows, cheery pinks, and even royal purple.

"It's like a dream," Vallen whispered, walking over to the window.

Elaine rolled over and snorted. "My father's bad manners? More like a nightmare."

"I meant your garden. Nothing in Sewertown comes close to this." He paused, considering. "Except maybe Bohomaz's toe gunk. Vladisvar skin produces *all kinds* of weird fungeses."

"*Fungi*," Elaine corrected. "And ew. Should you be sharing that stuff with a girl?"

Vallen narrowed his eyes to slits, staring at her until her cheeks reddened again. "What?" she asked when he didn't say anything. "Something on my face?"

"You're a *girl*? I mean, the dresses and shoes *would* suggest that, but Pockey told me that—"

A pillow whacked him upside the head. Laughing, Vallen caught a tassel as it fell and heaved it over his shoulder, preparing to fling it back at its owner. Elaine squealed and held up a textbook—*On Darmatia's Founding, 5-88 ABH*—as a shield.

"You think I won't hurt a history book that dull?"

Elaine shook her head. "Study first, fun after."

"But . . ." The pillow slipped from Vallen's fingers. "*You* started it."

"I start many things, Sir Vallen, which means I also have the right to end them." She flipped open the book and pointed to a random scrawl of text that was gibberish at this distance. "Our ancestors say so right here."

Vallen mocked a bow, then flopped on the bed beside Elaine, sending the lighter girl tumbling into a pile of pillows. "Woe to him who defies Elaine, chosen of Darmatus, heir to his legacy and lord over all who want to enjoy life. Long may she reign."

"Long may I reign," she echoed, giggling amid silk sheets and soft velvet fabrics. They both grabbed books—hers four times as thick as his—and settled in to read.

Half an hour later, Vallen tossed his tome spine up on the bed and loudly announced, "Boring!"

Elaine grabbed a long, thin piece of sanded wood carved with swirling symbols and stuck it in her book to mark her place. Laying it aside, she picked up Vallen's, checked the page number, and quirked an eyebrow at him. "Really? You stopped after *three* pages?"

"I think those pages taught me everything I need to know about the rule of King Azarias Aurelian."

"Oh?"

"He was a great architect. Built most of Nemare's canals, her walls, even her peerless sewer system. But"—Vallen pointed to himself—"he did void all for the poor, who started living in those sewers to avoid his ridiculous taxes. I don't need to read more to know how that turned out."

Elaine placed her hand on Vallen's thigh—a little too close, but he didn't freeze or flush as he once had. "Vallen, I'm so sorry. I didn't mean to give you a lesson that—"

He patted her hand. "It's alright. Besides, with everything you're teaching me, I can probably write my own version. Now"—Vallen glanced around at the leather-bound books on the bed, then at her shelves which were filled end to end with neatly arranged volumes— "how about one with some battles?"

"Boys and their violence." Elaine brushed her hair back as she sighed. "You better not become a soldier when you're older, Vallen."

"Don't waste your worry. I doubt they'd let Sewertown slime enlist."

"Even so …" She paused, studying her shelves. Vallen wondered if she'd read all the books here. There were hundreds of them covering all manners of topics: history, science, rhetoric, religion, and even novels about outlandish quests and adventures. To finish them would take …

Vallen started counting on his fingers but gave up when he reached ten. Without paper and a scrivle, any math more complicated than that was still beyond him. *It would take a long time,* he concluded, which was as satisfying an answer as any.

"Aha!" Elaine bounded to her feet, raced to the shelf, and snatched a gold-trimmed volume from the third shelf. When she returned, she placed it between them and curled her bare legs beneath her. The scene was achingly similar—almost an exact replica of that first evening they'd spent together.

The night she'd saved him.

Tears started welling in Vallen's eyes, and he turned away so she wouldn't see. "Are you going to read to me again?" he mocked playfully.

"Might be the only way you'd finish a book," Elaine countered as he dabbed his eyes with his scratchy collar. Why did shirts *need* collars? They were almost as useless as Singe. "Not this time," she continued, tilting the cover so he could see it. "My father just finished the illustrations and gave me this special copy. No text yet, nothing but pictures.

"Perfect for you," she added, sticking out her tongue.

Vallen clacked his teeth together. "Don't make me bite that tongue."

"You *wouldn't.*"

He leaned in, seeing how far he could push things before they were *both* crimson as Sylph, but Elaine yanked the book up and thrust it so close to his face he could smell leather and paint. "Book. Look. *Now.*"

With a huff, Vallen obliged. The seven-pointed star stamped on its cover marked it as a religious text, the kind usually overflowing with platitudes about aiding your neighbor, tithing at temples, and abiding by a list of rules longer than the train of a noblewoman's gown. Ignoring Elaine's glare, he took the book and opened it so they both could see.

"Once upon a time, there was an expensive tome with no words," Vallen started, pretending to read. "People had no idea what to make of it, or why it was created, so they decided to use it as firewood to warm themselves on the darkest night of Jul, when the snow was deep, the winds frightfully cold, and needle-toothed monsters roamed the streets searching for little children to feast on."

Elaine flicked his ear. "Very creative, but no. These are a collection of paintings commissioned for the upcoming Feast of Sariel, hosted by the Steward. You *do* know about his feast day, right?"

Vallen shrugged. "Sariel loved vittles so much he declared a special day for nobles to loosen their belts, let their paunches free, and grow even larger than they already were?"

The irritated tapping of Elaine's fingernail on the first page drew Vallen's gaze down. It was a breathtaking piece, and like always, he found himself wondering how a pipe in the sludge like Mister Gennesaret could produce such magnificence.

Blackness swallowed the sky, a maw that flashed with lightning and churned with malicious intent. Two armies clashed below it, tiny iron-helmed splotches that thrust with spear and sword, crimson staining the jagged rocks at their feet. Mouths gaped in wordless screams. Tattered banners were frozen in the act of falling and twisting beasts of scale and claw were trapped forever in their dives.

Vallen's breath caught. He could hear the shouted orders, feel the fear gnawing at his flesh, taste the blood and ash. It was so vivid, so real—as if the artist had been present at this very moment.

"What is this?" Vallen asked, tracing the spines of a snarling drake.

Elaine waited for him to withdraw his hand, then flipped the page. "The Battle of Narempi Plains. It was here that Sariel ... "

" ... shattered the Grand Alliance, putting an end to their crusade to eradicate all Terrans," Vallen finished with a smile. "Your lessons are beginning to take root, Your Highness."

"I only pray the tree above them doesn't rot, my ungrateful subject."

A bright light strode through the carnage of the next painting, silver lance raised in one alabaster arm, the other bearing a shield of holy radiance centered on the sign of the seven. Gold hair tumbled across Sariel's shoulders, down his back, and swept the battlefield in his wake. Wherever it touched, the ground was purified. Blood disappeared. Blossoms of white, blue, and yellow sprouted from solid stone and the wounds of the dead. It was an impossible miracle, but beautiful nonetheless.

The page turned again, revealing a gap in the fighting, a ring formed by Terrans, Sylph, Hues—warriors of *all* races—as they drew back to give space to two mighty combatants. One was Sariel, resplendent in a breastplate as handsome as he was. The other was a fellow Veneer. Vallen struggled to remember his name until he noticed the familiar horns on his head, the shining tattoos engraved into his armor-hard chest.

"Sondek!" Vallen exclaimed.

"Very good," Elaine said. She reached over and grasped the corner of the page, but stopped mid-flip when she noticed Vallen's frown. "Is something wrong?"

"Why would the Veneer fight among themselves?" he asked, pointing at Sariel and Sondek.

It was Elaine's turn to frown, her brow creasing and lips pursing. Vallen found her frustration adorable. "Do we need to revisit Alsance?" She pointed at a nearby tome heavy enough to double as a weapon. "You can't have forgotten his . . . *detailed* summary of the battle already."

I wish I could, Vallen thought, shaking his head. "Nothing like that. It's just . . . " He chewed on his words, trying to choose them carefully to avoid upsetting Elaine. " . . . They're supposed to be the good guys, right? The heroes—the servants of the Creator, saviors of the world."

"Who *you* don't believe in," she jabbed with a smirk.

Vallen grinned. "As long as they keep you safe, I don't much care if I ever find out whether they're real or not." Elaine glanced down, blushing, and Vallen pressed on through her endearing silence. "So even if the Creator told the Veneer to support both sides in the war, even if he told them to make the conflict so bloody no single race would *ever* dream of trying to annihilate another again, why would *this* happen?"

He'd caught a glimpse of the next painting as Elaine began to turn to it. Now Vallen flung back the page, exposing the illustration in all its gruesome glory.

Sariel stood over Sondek, splattered in mud and streaks of purplish blood. His robes were rent, the gleam of his lance dulled by gore, and his golden mane plastered to his back by rain and sweat. In the darkness, the filth lacing his hair almost made it look black.

But it wasn't Sariel's appearance that gave Vallen pause. He was *smiling*. With Sondek gasping at his feet, gray flesh shredded by countless blows, he *smiled*, delighting in his triumph. That exultant mask, twisted with glee, was *not* the face of a god. Vallen had seen that same grin on murderers, thieves, and more nobles than he could count.

It was the face of someone reveling in the pain they'd caused. The face of a mortal sinner.

He flipped through the pages in a rush, each depicting another of Sariel's victories:

"The Veneer are supposed to be better than us Elaine."

Ripping Artyr's right wing from her back as she tried to flee.

"They're supposed to be noble and just."

Smashing three of Chi'Chotath's chitin legs and tearing free his mandibles.

"They aren't supposed to crave anything. Want anything. Gods should have *our* best interest at heart, otherwise they aren't worthy of the worship you give them."

With Sariel's Veneer brethren put to flight, the Grand Alliance crumbled, routing before the Terran host. They didn't give chase; they no longer possessed the numbers to do so. But alongside a blood-slick Sariel hoisting his lance in the air, they cheered the close of the darkest chapter in their history.

Elaine listened quietly to Vallen's accusations, statements that he knew flirted with the offense of blasphemy. She pulled her legs up and wrapped her arms around them. Wiggled her bare toes and drummed her fingers atop her porcelain shins. Her eyes betrayed not a hint of the thoughts swirling behind their mesmerizing panes.

Yet Vallen found his eyes wandering elsewhere as the seconds ticked away. Past Elaine's eyes, beneath her dress, lower and lower still.

"They're infallible, Vallen," she said at last. "Pieces of divinity are divine themselves, and everything in creation acts according to the will of the one who made it. Perhaps Sariel's rage was part of that plan—to show us how wretched and disgusting our hate really is. Yes, that must be—"

Vallen lunged forward and grabbed her right leg. Elaine yelped in surprise, but he slammed the girl back on the mattress, clamping a hand on her mouth lest she summon Reesa with her wails.

"Vallen," she gasped between his fingers. Her cheeks were scarlet, her breath coming in heaves. "I know we've gotten closer these past few months. And I like you, I do, but—"

Pulling his hand back, Vallen held a finger to his lips. "This isn't what you think it is," he whispered, then bent over her right ankle and the bruise-colored birthmark wrapped around it.

Only . . . it wasn't a birthmark.

"Void and Oblivion," Vallen cursed, running his palm over the brutalized flesh, marred by the weight of something too heavy for *any* person to bear.

Every time he'd seen it, his suspicion had grown. Piece by piece— like the links of the chain that had once been secured around Elaine's ankle. The wounds were old. Faded by time and coated in glossy scars.

Hidden, but never gone.

Vallen was a fool. He'd been so fixated on *his* freedom, *his* future, that he hadn't noticed the obvious truth in front of him.

Elaine knew what it meant to be a slave better than he ever could.

"This is a slave mark," Vallen said dumbly.

Tears coursing down her cheeks, Elaine nodded and threw herself into his arms.

Chapter 37

The Crimson Door

Adamantele 5, 697 ABH
Sarconia, Imperial Seat of the Sarconian Empire

The crown prince of the Sarconian Empire, first in line to the throne, gazed at Vier's outstretched arm as if it were a rotting corpse covered in dung, swarming with maggots, and gushing fire. He stared up at the heavens, closed his eyes, and, with an exasperated huff, grabbed the offered hand.

Vier tugged him to his feet, then fell to one knee. "Please accept my profuse apologies, my prince. I was distracted by the splendor of your gardens and didn't see you around the corner. What can I possibly do to make up for my carelessness?"

"Lick my shoes," Vasuron Artorios said.

Behind the eyes of Gustav, Vier watched for a flicker of amusement from the first prince. A twitch of the lips, a wink, some hint that he was joking. Yet Vasuron stood still as a statue, flowing black hair blending with the night behind him, muscular chest half-exposed to the winter chill as his white robe slipped from his left shoulder.

"My lord?"

Vasuron's dark eyes narrowed. "Did I stutter? Lick it." He slid one satin slipper forward, its sole scraping on the marble walkway.

Despicable, Rashige spat. *He dishonors my dead lord with his vulgar orders.*

Elise blinked. *H-he never acted this way during his speeches.*

Oh love, Clara laughed as she tightened the strings of her lute. *He's a prince. They never show you their darkness until you're trapped in the shadows with them.*

Vier tuned them out. They might have pride and morals, but he did not. He was a blank slate. Bowing his head, Vier reached for the slipper.

"A jest, General," Vasuron said, withdrawing his foot behind the folds of his robe. He held out his arms and the two serving girls, who had risen without assistance from either man, snuggled back against his sides.

One blonde-haired with pale skin, the other scarlet with dusk-toned flesh, they were much like the rings on the prince's fingers or the gold lace dappling his vestments: decorations. They didn't speak, their empty eyes gazed down at the saffron Bloodlilies wilting beside the path, and not a shiver shook their bodies though Vier could see their bosoms through the sheer nightgowns they wore.

When Vier stayed on his knees, Vasuron sighed and waved for him to rise. "Get up, get up. If you stay rooted to the ground for much longer, I'll have to plant you in the garden as a spirit ward. A very *ugly* spirit ward," the prince amended, cocking his head to the side as he studied Vier. "Also . . . who *are* you?"

"Commissioner-General Gustav Rudolf at your service, my prince."

Vier pressed his fist to his breast and bowed. It didn't surprise him that Vasuron didn't remember Gustav. For all the power the Orabairos claimed the crown prince possessed, he was rumored to be quite eccentric—even mad.

I heard he once filled a palace swimming pool with chocolat from the Moravi Atoll, Elise murmured.

That's trivial, Barthol scoffed. *He ordered the Royal Academy to turn over all our astronomy globes just so he could play a giant game of sphereball with his mage friends.*

Kres peered out from between his fingers, eyes quivering. *I saw. I saw s-something* far *worse. When he last returned from the Lusserian Wilds, he . . . he attached a hundred captives to the bottom of his flagship, the Hedon's Sacrifice. Told them he'd free them if they survived the voyage.*

How awful, Elise said, voice a whisper.

Right before the outer wall, Kres paused, whimpering. *He commanded the Sacrifice drop altitude so she would barely clear it. All of them smashed into the battlements, and the blood, the blood . . .*

"General Rudolf, then," Vasuron said, grinning as one of his fingers tugged at the top of the blonde's gown. "What brings you here so late?"

Vier gulped. If this ended the same way it had with Malkep, flashing the Emperor's seal wouldn't save him. "I was on my way to the—"

"Actually, I can't tell you how little I care what you were doing," Vasuron interrupted, not bothering to stifle a yawn. "I just got in from the front, that little brat Alain has been riding me like a warhorse, and I haven't had a proper dip in a bath in weeks." He glanced from one girl to the other. "Isn't that right, my flowers?"

"Of course, Your Highness," they replied as one.

Alain, Vier processed. *Rittermarschal Alain, commander of the Second Fleet.* If the crown prince and third most powerful mage in the Empire were back in Sarconia, the Orabairos needed to know about it.

He stepped aside, head still bent, and yielded the path to Vasuron. "Apologies for delaying you, my prince."

The crown prince nodded, then continued on his way. When he was even with Vier, he abruptly stopped and fixed his obsidian eyes on the Commissioner-General.

"By the way, Rudolf, you have the most even vibrations of anyone I've ever met, including my father and all the rittermarschals. They're smooth, calm, like the surface of a lake at dawn before even the water-skippers have begun to frolic. I've never met a man without ripples, so I'm not sure what to make of you."

"I'm nothing special, my prince," Vier said, feigning fluster. *Vibrations?* What was the prince talking about? He tugged at Gustav's collar and chuckled. "A measly man of figures who fights wars with ink and quill, unlike your courageous self."

A grin split Vasuron's soft lips. "And still the water's surface remains unbroken. You are so much more than you say, General. When we meet again"—the prince's dark gaze seemed to flood with pitch, growing into a chasm that swallowed Vier's lies whole—"I plan to discover exactly what you're hiding."

Vier was left breathless and sweating as Vasuron and his servants disappeared around the corner.

Him. Breathless.

Had the crown prince seen beneath his mask? Peeled back his skin and glimpsed the lifeless husk it hid? No, that was impossible. The crown prince was not a sensor. While the Orabairos didn't have much information on Vasuron, all data suggested his gifts lay in the same direction as his father—spatial manipulation.

Calming his heart, Vier straightened and waded into the bushes, pushing aside carved dragwyrms and half-naked nymphs in search of a secluded spot. The third of his three charges remained unused, and he had the perfect face to wear into the Royal Palace—a key with black eyes, black hair, and a black heart.

As Vier expected, the palace reacted to Vasuron's presence like a lock fitted with its one true match. *Whirs* and *clicks* trailed him through the halls, as if some mechanical traps or magical runes had begun to activate and, recognizing the flesh he wore, disengaged. Vier's confidence grew with each step, and he began to believe his encounter with the crown prince was actually a stroke of fortune. Between Vasuron's men'ar signature and the Orabairos map of the estate he'd committed to memory, he'd arrive at the vault well ahead of schedule.

A left past those portraits, Rashige suggested, fingers drumming against his sword hilt. *We can steal up on that cur Sychon. Slit his throat as he sleeps.*

Barthol pulled at his goatee. *Your blade is clearly sharper than your mind. The Emperor's not here.*

And a good thing, too, Clara added, casting around for something small and valuable to pocket. *Otherwise, this place would be swarming with guards. It's empty as a tomb and*—she tried to grab a silver candelabra off a marble-topped windowsill—*filled with just as many treasures, ripe for the taking.*

Vier snatched his hand back before he could touch the gem-studded piece. "We take *nothing,*" he whispered to the shadows. "Nothing except the documents we were hired to find. Who knows what traps and alarms are tied to the items in here."

The wispy, half-formed persona that was the crown prince sat quietly in Vier's mind, content to listen to the others bicker. He said nothing about their mission, even though he now had as much access to the assassin's thoughts as the rest of them. A smile curled his lips, and a mischievous twinkle glimmered in his dark eyes, as if he were enjoying a clever joke.

I've got a joke, Clara said. *What's the difference between a lord and a pig?*

Will you keep it to yourself if we don't say anything? Elise asked.

The pig's a bit choosier about the mud it ruts around in.

A few of the voices chuckled, but most groaned. It had been years since Clara joined the collection and her material was growing stale. If the real Clara had possessed cunning superior to her wits, Vier suspected the girl wouldn't have lost her hands.

The whispers continued to toss advice, complaints, and insults back and forth as he climbed the sweeping central staircase. Its rails were stained mahogany. The carpet cascading down its center was Trillith silk woven into patterns of red and gold. Wealth was everywhere in the dark palace, but no one was around to appreciate it.

Busts and portraits of past emperors stood in recessed alcoves on the next floor, their stern gazes preserved so they could still pass judgment on their progeny from beyond the grave. Vier bustled past them, ignoring Rashige's demands to smash them to pieces for their crimes against his people. Lonely furniture, little table settings and gloomy bookshelves, stood in between the old rulers. Vier could see his reflection in the curve of a teapot left on display, not a speck of dust left to mar the image.

The Emperor's chambers were close now. Vier turned right, passing the imposing doors of the guest study and the stained glass windows overlooking the central courtyard. Outside, the clouds had parted, and the light of the rising moons revealed a large garden. Vier saw spear-tall razor-fronds, purple-laced bellflowers large as his head, and a dozen other species of exotic flora lining the walls and walkways. The bright display of color was a stark counterpoint to the usual bleakness of Sarconian design.

Yet at the garden's center hunched a tired old oak tree, its branches bare, its limbs curled over a pond clogged with algae. In its shadow rested a bed of eglantine roses that had been left to die, brown-capped mushrooms sprouting unchecked among their rotting stems.

Why did the groundskeeper abandon those eglantines? Elise asked, reaching toward them even as Vier hastened onward. *The rest of the garden is immaculate, but ...*

"Hate takes many forms," Vier said grimly.

Bright red lips, long brown hair, and a voice like a song danced through his memories, impossible to forget. Hers had been one of the only contracts he'd ever refused, and a very small part of him—the sliver that still cared, that hadn't been slaughtered to forestall madness—regretted that terrible decision.

We're here, Barthol announced, bending to study the silver-trimmed murals painted on the massive doors of the Emperor's suite.

Vier didn't bother looking at them. He pushed through one set of doors, making straight for the next. Then the next, and the next after that. Dining room, reading room, parlor, bedroom, so many rooms, so many sets of doors. All were done up in the livery of the Empire, gleaming gold and red the color of their enemies' blood. By the time Vier reached Sychon's study, he was nauseated by the thought of seeing just one more sofa, curtain, or bedspread in those colors.

It's like someone bled out on a pile of coins, Rashige said in agreement.

Clara laughed. *You're not wrong. You can't see it, but everything here reeks of blood.*

One final door barred their way. It was notable in its simplicity, made of two flat darkwood panels that, while certainly expensive, bore none of the carvings of Sarconian greatness Vier had seen on his way in. No locks were embedded in its surface, just two simple bronze handles.

This is where our map ends, Barthol said, pulling up a floating blueprint of the palace for all of them to see. *A hole four floors deep—straight into the heart of the plateau. Redacted on each and every set of plans by order of the royal family.*

Clara flexed her fingers, eager to see what lay beyond. Elise slid behind Rashige, while Kres continued to babble nonsense in a corner he'd conjured for himself.

Only two minds reached for the handle: Vier and Vasuron.

Time froze when his fingers gripped the cold metal. No, it wasn't time that was frozen. Vier glanced at a chronometer in a glass tube on a nearby shelf. Its gears continued to whir, its arms continued to spin.

He was frozen. Trapped in place by some supernatural force, able to blink and breathe but nothing more. Before Vier could react, blue light shot out from an eye-shaped illyrium crystal bolted above the door. Beginning with his feet, it roved up his legs, chest, face, and vanished once it cleared the top of his head.

"Crown Prince Vasuron Artorios identified," a tinny voice from the ceiling announced. "Now deactivating vault security protocols."

With an audible *click*, the door popped open and swung inward under its own power. Gasping, Vier regained control of his muscles and slipped inside the dark gap, lest it close as quickly as it had opened.

Illyrium lamps blazed to life at his entrance, casting the chamber in an otherworldly glow and illuminating the treasures stacked around its edges. Suits of primitive iron plate flanked the entrance. An octagonal mosaic of the Sarconian crest covered the ground. A detailed map of Imperial expansion covered the entire right wall, and flags from every nation, noble line, and military order Vier knew of hung from the ceiling.

Barthol urged him toward the map, Rashige wanted to inspect a rack of ancient weapons stacked behind a crate of southern silks, and Clara was calculating how much the set of ruby-studded goblets on a nearby dresser carved from elegoras wood would fetch from an outer ring fence. Yet none of these exquisite artifacts were what Vier sought.

He hastened toward the room's far end. More. There had to be more to the Emperor's archives than this pitiful collection. Lamps continued to come to life at his approach, and those behind winked out as he moved on.

How are they doing that? Elise asked, eyes wide with wonder.

"Runes," Vier answered without pausing. "Magic formulas scrawled onto the crystals or their sconces and Imbued with men'ar. They allow for simple commands like 'on,' 'off,' or 'on when someone's close by.'"

That last one doesn't seem very simple.

Vier shrugged. "Add enough runes and you can order magtech to do just about anything you want."

Instead of a solid stone wall, Vier found a railing at the end of the chamber, beyond which was a precipitous drop into a black abyss. Rashige tried to shout a battle cry into the void, but Barthol clamped a hand over his mouth.

Let's not tempt fate, yes?

The Rabbanite warrior nodded, and Barthol released him.

Supported by a grinning Clara, Rashige wrenched control of their body from Vier and roared, "Shogun Ashikari Rashige has come for your heads, Sarconian snakes!"

Bright light flared within the chamber, banishing the dark, stretching down and down, deeper and deeper. Rashige's echo went with it, growing in strength as it bounced among the countless floors extending into the shaft before them.

Vier gripped the rail and stared at the true form of the Royal Archives. A square gap supported by four giant pillars had been bored straight through the palace. But it didn't stop at the first floor. No, it continued onward, burrowing into the plateau, hollowing it from the inside out.

Vier watched as illyrium braziers continued to activate in the distance, so far below ground he could barely see them. Their light revealed floors upon floors that expanded from the central chasm in every direction. He saw dust-covered glass cases filled with strange instruments on the next floor down. Bookshelves crumbling beneath the weight of knowledge on the floor below that, and a space cluttered with stacks of yellowed scrolls on the floor after that.

On and on and on for what seemed like forever.

At last, a gold flicker came from the bottom of the shaft, reflecting off whatever the final batch of lights had illuminated. Barthol immediately began calculating the size of the archives.

Given the height of the plateau, plus the four floors of the palace, I estimate that it's eighty-four floors deep and likely just as wide. Assuming a perfectly square space like this shaft, and allowing for even three-meter tall floors, I'd wager the Royal Archives are—

Gigantic, Clara finished, cutting off an indignant Barthol. *Keep your numbers in our head, old man. Unless*—she winked—*you want to calculate how much we'll make off the trinkets in here.*

Where do we even start? Elise whispered.

Kres let out a manic giggle. *Hehe ... We don't! We don't! If we were a hundred Kreses with a dozen lifetimes, we'd still not be able to search the whole thing.*

The unhinged lad clapped his hands as Vier's fingers tightened atop the railing. Kres was right. He didn't have time to search the whole of the archives. The eleventh bell of fading would soon arrive, and the palace would flood with day staff come the sixth of dawn. Vier hadn't the hours to scour a single floor, let alone this *labyrinth* that rivaled the Compendus Archives.

"An index ... " he mumbled. "This place must have an index."

Inside his mind, Vasuron rose from the throne of satin cushions he'd begun constructing. It alarmed Vier how swiftly the prince's persona was developing. Even Hans, who he'd copied days prior, hadn't materialized to the point the Captain's voice could be heard above the ever-present maelstrom of murmurs at the back of his skull.

There is no index, Vasuron said, tapping his head. *It's all in here, passed down from ruler to heir in each generation.*

Rashige growled. *I'd be delighted to dig it out for you.*

No need, no need. I want to see where this adventure leads as much as the rest of you. Vasuron pointed at a metal stairway that wrapped around one of the four pillars in a spiral. *The most valuable treasures are always buried deepest. To the bottom, Vier.*

Vier wanted to argue. To howl and rage about how he could never trust someone as twisted as the crown prince. But he was a blank slate, one who'd accept aid from Oblivion itself if it meant completing his mission. Vier started down the stairs without another word.

Time ceased to have meaning beyond the flickering crystals on the walls and the seemingly endless floors he passed. Clara tried to stop on the instrument floor, whining that she saw a bone-hewn half-harp begging for her touch. Barthol desired *'Just a peek'* at the cepyrus scrolls, some labeled with dates preceding the modern era, and Rashige spotted a blade in a black scabbard he insisted belonged to the first ruler of the Imperium.

Vier indulged none of them, pressing on regardless of what wonders he saw. Floors of torture implements crusted with blood. A magically chilled level stocked with wines produced by every vintner in Lozaria, from South's Last Gasp to Laslicht in the frigid north. Old firearms, stacks of framed portraits, and a floor filled with perplexing ash-filled glass bulbs went by with barely a glance.

And then came the books. Floor after floor of shelves packed end to end, top to bottom with every kind of written word imaginable. Tomes, ledgers, and diaries. Legislation, scripts, and novels. Vier saw a stone tablet propped upright in a display case, next to which was a pile of animal hides covered in what looked like blood-scrawled symbols. If something had been scribed, scribbled, or carved in some way, he suspected the Royal Archives possessed a copy of it.

Scratching started following Vier down the steps, the sound of something heavy being dragged across stone floors. He raised a mental eyebrow at Vasuron, who held his arms out as if to say, *Why look at me?*

The source of the noise soon became clear. Some levels had their shelves neatly arranged, sorted into straight rows that allowed Vier to see from the stairs to the plateau's distant edges. Others were haphazard. Shelves stood at perpendicular angles, rotated back in on themselves like whirlpools, or were purposely arranged into a maze to the frustration of anyone attempting to peruse them.

Vier stared in surprise as one such set of shelves rearranged before his eyes, sliding across scarred slabs to take up their new positions. More runes were at work here—a spell intended to confound and trap would-be thieves. Clara gulped, and a little of her earlier bravado bled away. There were worse things than guards down here.

As they neared the bottom, the clatter of the shelves was gradually swallowed by the sound of a thousand skittering insects. *We have to turn back,* Elise said, trying to spin them around. *I hate bugs.*

You grew plants for a living, Clara said, hands on her hips. *You should be used to them.*

My grandmother handled them for me. Whenever I'd see one, I'd yell for her, and—

"They're not bugs," Vier interrupted. He let go of the winding metal railing, stepped onto the cold stone floor, and began walking down an aisle between rows of wooden desks.

Hundreds of scrivening magchines were bolted to tables throughout the ground floor, each one chittering like Trillith engaged in a heated trade dispute. Their skeletal brass arms hovered above piles of papers, ink-dipped quills tracing the same pattern over and over again. Vier snatched one from the nearest magchine, which calmly turned, selected a new page from the stack at its base, and continued scrawling where it had left off.

More runic symbols, Barthol assessed. *The Emperor is crafting talisman spells by the thousands.*

To what end? Rashige grumbled.

"And where will he get the men'ar to Imbue them?" Vier added. He pocketed the half-completed talisman, yet another secret the Orabairos would want in their arsenal.

The aisle led straight to the far wall, no deviations leading to hidden artifacts, no shelves stuffed with esoteric texts to block his way. Vier made straight for the end—both the end of the walkway and the end of his search.

For what else could the blood-red door towering before him be?

Chapter 38

Trapped in a Hole

The crimson door was like nothing Vier had ever seen. Like nothing *any* of his lives had ever seen. Framed by the dark stone of the plateau, it stood twice as tall as a man and wide as four standing shoulder to shoulder. As with the study entrance above, Vier could see no keyholes, but this door was also absent any handles, knobs, hinges, or any means of opening it at all.

Only one thing told him it was a door: the razor-thin line separating its two halves from each other.

This was the Emperor's vault. Of that Vier had no doubt. He turned to Vasuron. "How do we get inside?"

The princeling toppled onto his mound of cushions, wispy, shadowy robes fluttering down around him. *I can't help you there.*

Rashige stalked over to Vasuron, grabbed him by his collar, and heaved him into the air. *You* will *answer us, scum.*

Or what? The crown prince started laughing. *I'm you. You're me. Are we going to start slugging ourselves, now?*

They were getting nowhere with this tactic. Waving Rashige aside, Vier turned and approached the crimson door. He held out his arms, hoping it would scan him like before. No crystal emerged from the smooth stone above the door, and the only light illuminating him was that of two glowing illyrium braziers, one on each side of the portal.

Vier tried pressing Vasuron's palms to the damp, smooth stone. No response. Leaning forward, he jammed his eye to the crack, wondering if some new age magtech would scan the prince's eye. Again, no response.

The next half hour saw Vier try another dozen ideas. He snapped the arm off a scrivening magchine and used it as a crowbar, which broke on the first attempt. Prying it open with his dagger didn't work, nor did melting it with a vial of acid from the bandolier beneath his second skin.

At last, he gave into the maddest of Rashige's suggestions:

Blow it up, ya?

Removing the illyrium crystals from four wall-mounted lamps, Vier bound them with wires from a scrivening magchine and stuffed one of his powder bombs in the center. He planted it right against the base of the crimson door, spread another bomb's worth of powder in a trail leading away from it, and took refuge behind a heap of overturned tables.

"Ready?" Vier asked, though no one else was truly listening.

Elise huddled beside him. *Do we have to—*

His flint and dagger crashed together, sparks flashing onto the powder. The flames caught quickly, racing around the corner, across the room, right up into the core of the makeshift illyrium grenade. One second passed. Two.

Then a massive gout of smoke and flame erupted from the crimson door. Dozens of tables and scrivening magchines blew past Vier, tumbling end over end. Sparks shot so high they reached the next floor, where they fell among stacks of crinkly, brittle parchment—pieces of history that could never be replaced. A fire started almost immediately.

But Vier couldn't care less about a few thousand moldy tomes. With Barthol screeching at him to smother the flames, he rushed into the smoke to find . . .

. . . the crimson door unscathed. Not a scratch on its surface to indicate he'd done a thing.

"Hands on your head," said a voice Vier didn't recognize. Not one of his, then. He couldn't forget the whispers in his head no matter how much he wanted to.

Raising his arms, Vier slowly spun around, the robes of his illusion gliding softly over the soot-blackened floor slabs. "Is that any way to speak to your crown prince?" he asked, drowning his words in contempt.

The soldier opposite him was dressed all in black: black mask covering his face, a black-stained cuirass belted to his chest, and a black jumpsuit underneath. Though the mask had slits for the man's eyes, it left his mouth exposed so he could breathe during combat.

A Ritter commando—the Emperor's special forces.

"If you're the crown prince," the agent said, aiming a Lerchis pistol at Vier's breast, "use your magic."

Vier's cover was blown. If they hadn't already encountered the prince up above, they would never have questioned his identity for fear of what horrors Vasuron would wreak on them for insubordination.

Did the first prince see through us? Barthol jabbered, hands raised to surrender.

It doesn't matter! Rashige bellowed. He drew his phantom sword and clutched it in both hands. *We fight!*

And fight Vier did.

Popping a needle from inside his sleeve, he caught and threw it at the commando even as he dodged to the side. The agent's shot pinged off the door behind him. Vier's needle found purchase in the man's armpit.

Such a blow should amount to little more than a bloodstinger bite. Yet the man started foaming at the mouth, dropped his pistol, and collapsed in a quivering lump that swayed back and forth like a discarded puppet. All of Vier's needles were coated with eshap extract—a delicacy to drakes, highly poisonous to Terrans.

I told you not to use my remedies to kill! Elise yelled. Her tiny fists beat against his skull, setting his temples ablaze.

Clara stepped in and bumped her aside. *Fighting time, love. We can hash this out later.*

Vier's gaze roved up, following the nigh invisible cord still holding the commando aloft. He'd rappelled down while they were trying to blast open the door. That explained why Vier, despite his too-sensitive ears, hadn't heard him coming.

Him, and the dozen other members of his kill-squad.

Muzzle flashes came from the next floor up, forcing Vier to take refuge behind his table barricade. He was already at a disadvantage, and if they flanked around to the sides, he'd be finished.

This is why you bring guns to a gunfight, Lt. Colonel Urdell mocked. She only appeared when she thought Vier was going to get killed, standing over him with hard eyes, gritted teeth, and the baton she'd used to whip her cadets.

He'd jammed half of that broken baton through her right ear to complete a contract.

Another commando landed in front of Vier, knees bending to absorb the impact, Lerchis rising to plug him full of holes. He dove at the man, drawing his dagger as they rolled. One jab to the kidneys, one to the neck, and blood was gushing onto the stones.

Vier twisted the still dangling body and crouched behind it. Bullets thudded into the other side, but not into him. Keeping a tight grip on the corpse's belt, Vier pushed it ahead of him until he reached the safety of a different table.

Blood! Kres shrieked, staring at his scarlet hands. *B-b-blood is here again! Pouring, spurting, f-flooding! Blood-blood-blo-blo—*

Two down, who-knew-how-many more to go. Vier popped the clip from the pistol he'd just acquired, counting the rounds in the magazine. Eight rounds, but small in caliber.

"Keep track of them for me," he ordered Barthol.

A shadow moved on the walkway above Vier, circling to his right. He let Arceas, the crack-shot of the 273rd Infantry, take the shot for him. Tossing aside his imaginary shag, Arceas stilled his breath, clutched the Lerchis in both hands, and dropped the commando through the railing.

Seven rounds! Barthol called.

Yes, Vier might be on the brink of madness. He might hear hundreds of whispers, recall thousands of memories he'd never lived, and couldn't remember who he was beneath it all. But until the darkness claimed him, he had the *experience* of hundreds of people as well.

Feet locked about his neck—a brute of a soldier dropping on him like a spider on its prey. Vier jammed a needle into his calf, then grabbed his knee and ankle and broke his leg with the Sva-Anat techniques of Master Jo-Rung-Ti. Blood jetted from the man's lips as he fell away, only to be replaced by another foe swinging a Sarconian army short sword.

Vier backed away, using Sva-Anat footwork to dodge each blow by the narrowest of margins while staying close enough to his enemy to discourage stray fire from above. His dagger lay abandoned in the neck of the agent he'd stabbed. There was no time to draw more needles or bring his pistol up to fire.

Fortunately, Vier knew where to find an extra arm. Skirting a table, he baited a gut stab that would have left him spitted and gasping for breath. But instead of piercing him, the blade sank through the edge of the Vasuron illusion, clipped his side, and snagged between the halves of a scrivening magchine's bony arm.

Cursing, the commando tried to jerk it free. A costly mistake. Vier brought the Lerchis up under his chin and pulled the trigger, blowing a hole in the man's skull and sending Kres into another bout of hysterics.

Oh, the b-blood of the saints, it purifies, it does. Swim in it, b-bathe in it ...

Six rounds!

Another corpse shield in hand, Vier marched straight toward the second-story shooters, emptying his clip at them when he got close enough. The first round clanged off the railing. Its partner lodged in the belly of a female commando, her gender betrayed by her dying scream. Vier applauded her mettle in persevering through the Ritter ranks, if not her decision to oppose him.

Five rounds! Four!

Running didn't save the next in line, though his cuirass ate a shot Vier was loath to waste.

Three! Two!

The last rounds were precise. Perfect headshots that shattered the commandos' masks before burying lead in their foreheads. Yet Vier didn't exult in the momentary reprieve. He cast away his empty pistol and glanced around, frantically searching for another dropped weapon.

"Enough," a gruff voice—presumably the squad leader—shouted from several levels up. "We burn him out."

"But what about the devices His Majesty has stored down—"

"We can beg his forgiveness when the spy is dead. Now *cast!*"

Hurried chanting echoed from above, and a roiling mass of flame began gathering in the shaft between Vier and the next floor. The chamber became a furnace. Sweat coursed down his back beneath the illusion. Acrid bubbles foamed inside the scrivening magchine inkwells, while their spindly brass limbs sparked and sagged in the shimmering haze.

Clara wiped a hand across her brow. *If we don't move now, we're toast. Literally.*

Jokes? Barthol clicked his tongue. *At a time like this?*

Vier slotted two discarded pistols into his hidden bandolier and dashed for the spiral staircase. His opponents were smart, staying well away from the railings as they directed streams of men'ar into the blazing cloud slowly drifting toward him. To kill them—to simply *survive*—he needed to escape this hole.

A fact the Ritter commandos were well aware of.

Light flared beyond the flames followed by the roar of an explosion. Vier skidded to a stop, then dove aside as the metal staircase blew free of its moorings and toppled across the room below. Its mangled remains crushed most of the remaining magchine stations, sending boiling ink spilling across the floor, casting countless sheets of expensive parchment into the air.

Why? Barthol cried as Vier staggered to his feet. *Don't these heathens have any respect for the knowledge they're destroying?*

Flight was no longer an option. Dexterous as he was, Vier couldn't climb the columns or walls while under assault from bullets and spells. Only a miracle would save him now.

Lashing out, Vier snatched a falling talisman—both sides coated in completed sigils—and thrust it at the orb of fire. The runes started to glow as he fed it men'ar. Gifted it all the energy remaining in his body. Ice sparkled in the air, and his breath misted as it left his lips.

Then Vier collapsed, curling into a ball, spitting blood. The Vasuron illusion enveloping him popped like a soap bubble, exposing the grimy, soot- and blood-stained shadow beneath. Vier's true self.

Thr-three charges, it was, it was, Kres babbled, rocking back and forth, legs tucked to his chest. *Hans, G-Gustav, Vasuron. Three masks, three s-skins, they were, they were. We broke the rule. We p-pay the pri-price!*

The blathering fool was right, though Vier hated to admit it. He'd tried to go past his men'ar limit—a wall all of them knew not to touch. And the result? Pain, like thousands of searing needles stabbing him from the inside out, frying his nerves, making it impossible to concentrate.

Vier tried to move anyway. Gasping with every twitch, every motion, he drew one of his pistols and aimed it at the maelstrom of orange and red.

Barthol didn't need to count. Vier fired every shot in rapid succession, praying to gods he knew were lies he would hear the telltale shriek of lead meeting flesh. The flames swallowed his rounds, but no scream came.

So that's it? Elise said softly.

Clara sighed. *I reckon so. Nothing left to do but sing the audience out of here.* She picked up her lute, tested the pitch, and began a somber dirge unlike anything she'd played before.

Darkness clouded the edges of Vier's vision as the smoking pistol tumbled from his fingers and his arm flopped to the floor beside him. The men'ar imbalance in his blood wouldn't kill him, but the fireball blistering his skin would. His throat went dry. If he had tears left, they turned to steam before they could fall. Everything was fever and choking and torment.

Don't wanna go, Kres sobbed. *Don't wanna go.*

There is not a thing that begins that does not end, Barthol mused while listening to Clara's singing. *And if one has lived—*truly *lived—there is no reason to fear that end's arrival.*

To life, Rashige toasted, raising a clay cup of sake to his lips.

Barthol joined him. *To life.*

Kneeling beside Vier, her form wispy and ethereal, Elise stroked hair whose color he had long forgotten. *Brown,* she whispered in his ear. *Brown like damp soil, fresh and pure. Brown like chestnuts, ready for harvest. And brown like your mother's face, beaming with joy as she named you ...*

The inferno never fell. Distantly, Vier heard a cacophony of snaps, cracks, and shrill screams. Was *he* screaming? Were those *his* bones snapping?

"Why would you—"

SNAP!

"But, my lord—"

SNAP!

A shiver convulsed through Vier's body—a chill that had nothing to do with the dwindling men'ar in his veins. He blinked, then blinked again to make sure he wasn't hallucinating.

The fireball was gone, only a few thin tendrils of reddish light left to suggest it had ever been at all. Shadows and quiet reigned. Most of the illyrium lamps had been upended or destroyed in the fighting, and the cracking and crying were eerily absent.

Vier took a deep breath of soot-laced air, then rolled onto his side and—bit by excruciating bit—levered himself into a sitting position. He didn't know how he was alive, but he was. Questions could wait. For now, he needed to—

Something thudded on the stones in front of him, followed by more blobby shapes that landed with sickening splatters. The first smashed into one of the few tables still standing. Another snagged on the rope tied about its middle, bounced once, then split into two halves before hitting the floor. Sticky warm fluid splashed across Vier's face and hands. The bitter tang of iron filled the room, along with the steady *plop-plop-plop* of water dripping from somewhere high above.

Only it wasn't water, and these shapes weren't artifacts dumped by the Ritter commandos.

They *were* the Ritter commandos.

The shape near Vier resolved into a decapitated head, its eyes and mouth frozen in a wordless scream. A dark cap pinned with a silver rittermark claw clung to his blood-matted scalp, the hair poking from beneath it black streaked with slivers of gray. This was their commander, but what had killed him?

Those wounds, Barthol suggested, peering intently at the man's severed neck. *The skin is twisted. Battered. Like something grabbed his head and twisted it off with brute force.*

I didn't need that image in my head, old man, Clara huffed.

In the background, Vasuron leaned forward on his throne and smiled. *This is about to get very, very interesting.*

Vier frowned. "What do you mean, you snake?"

"That's a rather rude way to refer to me," a voice boomed from the darkness.

The breath caught in Vier's throat. It was as if something were pressing down on it, forcing the air back into his lungs, holding his neck in a vice grip. He tried to grab the invisible weight with his hands, but they were held fast to his sides, rooted in place by the same unseen power.

"Better," the voice said as Vier's eyes flitted about the shaft, searching for its source. "Now, let's shed some light on things."

Clara snickered as every surviving lamp in the archives blazed to life at the same time. *Bad joke. Great execution.*

When Vier's eyes adjusted to the glare, they were immediately drawn to a shadowy figure *hovering* several meters off the floor. Yet the shadows didn't touch the man's body. They flowed around it like water in little streams and rivulets, separating and joining as they continued their never ending loops.

Not shadows, Rashige said, sniffing the air. *Blood.*

And suddenly the fluid slithering around the man took on a horrific connotation. Vier watched as globs of blood lifted off the floor to join the macabre dance, leaking from still open wounds, floating down from corpses draped on railings floors above them.

Cracking and snapping. Fluid manipulation. Squeezing Vier's throat and binding his limbs. He knew with startling clarity who the man cloaked in blood was, even before he dropped his gruesome shield to the floor with a nauseating splash.

Crown Prince Vasuron Artorios, first in line to the Sarconian throne, and heir to his father's gravitation powers.

A foe Vier could not fight.

Chapter 39

Thank You

Vallen woke with a strangled cry, fresh tears wetting his cheeks where Elaine's had once fallen. Ache and loss hollowed his chest. His mouth was as dry as it had been on that day when no comforting words would come, and her phantom touch still lingered as if it were etched into his flesh.

He half expected to hear the darkness whispering from the shadows, taunting him with the countdown to the final portal. There weren't many left, and each time he visited a memory, its glowing gateway disappeared for good. Soon Vallen would close his eyes and see nothing but that charred, flame-filled door.

Yet for now, he was back in the land of the living. The camp around him was silent. Dawn was still some way off, and the last of the cooks and mess crew had retired for the night, leaving only the occasional patrolling guard to break the army's peace.

Snores reigned within their tent: loud like loggers from Unter and Renar, soft whispers from the rest. Hushed breaths came from Vallen's right. Confused, he turned toward the noise, and realization sank in when he saw pale skin dappled with freckles and a tangle of sleep-mussed brown hair.

Lilith lay beside him in his hammock, discarded clothes bunched to her chest after the events of the previous night. Vallen vaguely recalled Velle mending the wounds in his shoulder and gut, then staggering back to their bunk like a drunkard. Lilith had met him on the other side of the awning.

Without a word, she'd leapt at him, burying his lips with hungry kisses, fumbling at his belt and britches. Vallen hadn't resisted, returning her aggression with a passion born of every frustration, failure, and setback he'd suffered since graduation. It came roaring out as he tossed her onto his hammock and roamed the curves of her body, worshiping her toned stomach and taut hips.

After their first time in Holcomb's hidden stash, it was only natural there'd be a second.

Vallen reached out to trace the beautiful constellations spotting Lilith's back, but drew his hand away at the last second. The pit that was Elaine yawned in his chest, reminding him of what happened when he cared, when he got too close to someone.

Flirting and fun were fine. They buried the pain for a bright, incendiary instant. Made Vallen recollect what life *could* be like if he hadn't become a thief in every sense of the word.

He shifted away from Lilith, from the girl who smelled of snow and seashores, winter and spring. An odd combination, one he'd have to ask her about one day.

Carefully, Vallen dropped to the floor, then steadied the hammock so it wouldn't sway. Lilith moaned, blinking a few times before falling back asleep. Donning his cast-off britches, Vallen mumbled, "Flar'en," to keep the cavern chill at bay and stalked from the tent.

He needed a walk to clear his head.

Leagues upon leagues of open water stretched out before Sylette, their dark depths a mirror reflecting the glory of their heavenly mistress above. The sky was gorgeous tonight, the million diamonds of her dress sparkling with nary a cloud to mar their brilliance, and her powdered cheeks—the moons, Esta and Exal—played a melody of light across the sea's surface.

The exile almost gagged at the thought. Were those *her* musings, so close to poetry like something Renar or a bard might sing of? Sylette was getting soft. This place was *making* her soft.

Major Reev spouted nonsense about training to fight the Empire, but what progress was the Resistance making? They drilled, the engimages repaired their cruisers, and General Iolus grew ever more bloated, drinking himself into an early grave with whatever vintages he'd spirited away before Nemare's capitulation.

There *was* no plan. And even if Sylette could now summon a few more daggers, even if she could control them better, it amounted to but a single drop of water cast at the blazing furnace of the Empire.

Snarling, she grabbed a stone from the pile on the pier beside her and cast it across the glass-still waters. They shattered as the pebble skipped—once, twice, thrice before sinking—and she smiled at the now ruined image. The reflection came apart, moons twisting, cliffs dancing, stars disappearing entirely. Sylette retained some power over her surroundings, though it was but the power of a child throwing a tantrum.

The reflection split again, this time farther from the pier connecting the twin-turret lighthouse to the mainland. A draconic head covered in gleaming scales burst from the sea, its nostrils blowing white foam into the air, dark torrents of water coursing around the spines on its back. Tentacles followed as the Primal heaved itself toward shore, its beady ruby eyes fixated on the illyrium crystal at the lighthouse's peak.

Sylette no longer feared the Draken—Nehalena, as Major Reev had called her. Provided they didn't interfere with her meals, the beast was content to ignore them. Seven cadets hadn't proven a match for her, so what could Sylette possibly do to Nehalena on her own?

More shapes, like oversized worms, followed in the Primal's wake. While she kept most of her bulk in the sea, the little blobs wriggled onto the rocky shore at the lighthouse's base. Tiny heads—like pointed guard helmets with eyes and needle-teeth—popped out from their segmented shells.

They immediately began crying. Sylette plastered her hands over her ears, but the deafening warble pierced through anyway. It struck at her core, making her teeth chatter and her insides shake. *Make it stop, make it stop, make it—*

Like a good mother, Nehalena slipped a tentacle through an opening in the lighthouse glass and removed the giant illyrium shard within. Sylette watched with pinched eyes as the Draken larva gathered below it, leaping like seals, flopping over each other to get at it first. Nehalena set it on the shore, and the crying ceased as they opened their mouths and streams of yellow energy raced from the crystal down their throats.

"To think a bunch of infants could down an heir to the Sarconian Empire," a voice said from behind her. "My, how the mighty have fallen."

Sylette recognized those words. They were her own, ones she'd once used to mock an arrogant fool as she stood over his limp form. She unplugged her ears, returned to a sitting position, and asked that same fool the first question that came to mind:

"Why aren't you wearing a shirt?"

Vallen took that as an invitation to approach. He walked down the pier, swung his legs over the side, and sat down a meter from her. Just looking at his bare chest made Sylette shiver, and she pulled her wool-lined jacket tighter while praying Vallen wouldn't notice.

He did. "I think better the fewer clothes I have on. Maybe you should try it."

"Is that what you and Lilith were doing earlier?" Sylette countered, breath misting in front of her. "*Thinking?*"

"So you heard."

"*Everyone* heard, imbecile. We don't exactly live in a giant palace, and there's nowhere else for us to sleep."

Instead of retorting, the Triaron leaned forward and sighed. "Sorry," he said, so soft Sylette thought it might be a trick of the wind or the waves lapping against the shore.

"Excuse me?"

"Sorry," Vallen said again, loud enough it was impossible to mistake. "If it happens again, we'll figure out some way not to bother the rest of you."

"That's . . . awfully responsible of you," Sylette choked out.

"And the shirt thing? It's a Flar'en spell. Heats my insides. Just one more perk of"—Vallen paused, then gave a mirthless laugh—"being *me,* I suppose."

Something was off about him. Sylette scooted closer, watching Vallen's chin drift to his chest and his shoulders slump like they might melt. Shadows ringed his eyes, dark caves that had nothing to do with a single sleepless night. His hair seemed brittle as tinder, and the scars on his chest, shoulders, and back looked ready to gush fresh blood. Some were old. Too old for Sylette to know what had caused them.

Vallen was a single push from toppling into despair. She could tell because she'd been there—because she *was* there, even now. Sylette wanted to jeer at him, spit in his face, and tell Vallen his pain served him right. If he wasn't such a void-touched arsehole, none of this misery would've befallen him.

Sylette did none of those things. Her father would have picked at Vallen's weaknesses. Torn him apart using his failures and insecurities until nothing but an obedient husk remained. It was what he'd tried to do to her, and she would *not* pass on that legacy. Her vengeance would come on her terms.

The astral dust coalescing around her dissipated, banished by a deep breath and a decision. Packing her rage into a tiny ball, she attached it to another stone and cast it past Nehalena and her feasting children.

She pointed at the Draken larva, their carapaces glowing yellow as they glutted themselves on illyrium. "How did you block out their crying?"

"Vor'spa," Vallen answered, glancing up. "It's a little disk of wind I can place anywhere. Put one by each ear, and any sound coming in will be forced in a different direction."

"Very clever," Sylette acknowledged. The admission was like a punch to the gut, but she bore it and kept going. "And the same could be said of your fight with the Major. You thought about your surroundings, using your strengths, the terrain, and even her own magic against her. That's a far cry from the imbecile I took down in our graduation match."

Vallen chuckled, a hollow noise that didn't reach his dark eyes. "*Down* being the key word, Your Highness. I fell both times." He stared straight down at the murky water, as if preparing to cast himself in. "*Every* time ..."

This wasn't working. Sylette switched tactics, hoping their usual banter might cheer him up. "I've never seen you use water magic before. Perhaps the great Triaron hasn't mastered *all* the elements?"

"Water's too valuable to waste," Vallen replied. "I grew up in a place where people would kill for half a glass of water, sometimes less. I'm also a terrible swimmer."

"Is that something you should be admitting right next to water filled with hungry Draken larva?"

"You might be doing me a favor if you push me in."

So, she did. Tired of Vallen's moping, Sylette threw off her coat, pressed her hands to his back, and shoved a very surprised Triaron over the edge. He screeched as he fell, a scream that sounded like the sweetest of symphonies to her ears. But he didn't have far to go.

Right before Vallen hit the water, a net of floating daggers caught him. He quickly scrambled upright, face flushed, hands sparking with embers as he glared pure hatred at Sylette.

"What was that for?" Vallen yelled.

"The bed of daggers?" Sylette tapped her chin thoughtfully. "You said your swimming's lousy, so I think summoning them was rather kind of me. I was even nice enough to face the flat sides up."

"No! You shoved me off the pier. When I get back up there, I'm going to—"

Sylette waved her hand, and several blades on the edges melted into dust, shrinking the hovering platform. Vallen nearly lost his balance as one beneath his left toes vanished, but he managed to yank his foot to safety just in time.

"Careful," Sylette warned. "I didn't *completely* dull the blades, and I would hate for you to lose any bits you might end up missing."

"Why did you push me?"

"You asked me to."

"I didn't mean it literally."

Sylette prodded her chest. "And *I* didn't ask you to defend me against Major Reev. *I* didn't want to incur another debt to you after the last time you bailed me out of trouble."

A few more daggers faded to ash, and Vallen retreated another step toward the platform's narrowing center. "What are you talking about? I owed *you* for Etrus, not the other way around."

"Your math is screwed up, as always," Sylette said, shaking her head. "Waking you up and wiping out a couple of Imperial platoons are *not* equal. And then you go and jump in the way of the Ice Queen's wrath? Are you insane? How do you expect me to pay that back?"

Vallen spared her a glance. "What are you trying to say, Your Highness?"

She took another three daggers for constantly using that title— one she'd *specifically* forbade him from speaking. They plopped into the water between Vallen's feet, leaving him straining to stay standing atop two floating islands.

"Can't you figure it out?" Sylette asked.

"I'm not a mind-reader. Go see Matteo if that's what you're looking for."

Sylette sighed. Then, twisting her head so her silver braid shielded her reddening face, she mumbled two words she'd never expected to utter to the ek-turd in front of her. "Thank you."

"I can't hear you," Vallen said, more focused on his trembling legs than her.

So she thrust her chest out, whipped back her hair, and roared like the proud banished princess she was. "*THANK YOU, VALLEN METELLUS!*"

Her cry echoed off the cliffs, around the bay, and out over the midnight sea. A few of the Draken larva perked up at the cry, tiny snouts swinging in her direction. Even Nehalena tilted her gigantic head in what might be the Primal equivalent of a raised eyebrow.

Vallen snorted, which became a chuckle, and finally devolved into a gut-clutching bout of laughter. Shadows still clung to his eyes, but at least a twinkle of light glowed in their depths.

The Triaron would not succumb to his darkness today.

"You said it," he gasped. "My name! You finally called me

something other than 'fool' or 'imbecile.' Guess you're warming up to me, eh, Your Highness?"

"Don't count on it, imbecile."

Sylette swung her arm like a sword. In an instant, the rest of the daggers reverted to astral dust, and Vallen Metellus, second Triaron and heir to Darmatus' legacy, plunged shrieking into the frigid waters of the Phar Sea.

Chapter 40

This Changes Everything

Adamantele 6, 697 ABH
Sarconia, Imperial Seat of the Sarconian Empire

Vier bit down on his false molar without hesitation. He'd been prepared to die minutes earlier, and he was prepared to die now. The arceni poison within would quickly spread to his heart, still its beating, and kill him in a matter of minutes. Yet his tongue would fail him far faster, and Vasuron would get no information about the Orabairos from his purpling lips.

Vier's teeth never connected, his mouth wedged open by the same force that bound his body. "Really?" Vasuron sighed, shaking his head. "That's your first reaction when someone tries to have a conversation with you? You must not be much fun at parties."

The prince landed on the floor, the blood parting before his feet like wheat before wind. His white robe was immaculate—not a speck of dirt, not a scarlet drip anywhere on it. No sweat beaded his brow, his gleaming raven hair was smooth against his back, and his chest rose and fell in an even rhythm. Slaughtering an entire squad of Ritter commandos hadn't troubled Vasuron in the slightest.

"I'll be taking that." The crown prince raised his left hand, and a spike of pain lanced through Vier's skull as his poison-filled tooth was yanked from his jaw. Vasuron cast it into the mound of crumpled desks and magchines.

"Now," Vasuron continued, "I shall ask you some questions, little spy. Answer well, and you shall live. Answer poorly, and . . . " Shadows clouded the prince's fair features as he grinned. " . . . well, the experience will be enjoyable for one of us."

Wait, Barthol said. *This madman set his men on us, then killed them. What game is he playing?*

Clara's eyes lit up. *He's right. He could have let those soldiers finish us off. He can slay us at will. Play our sleds right, and we might get through this.*

You just want to live, Elise pointed out.

And you don't?

"Nod for yes," Vasuron said, holding up a finger. "Shake your head for no. Are you ready?"

The weight disappeared from Vier's neck, and he sucked in a sweet, glorious breath. It tasted like death but meant he still lived.

Vier nodded.

Vasuron clapped his hands. "Splendid! First and most importantly, are you here on my father's orders?"

Vier shook his head.

"That makes sense. The Ritter are my father's loyal dogs, barking when he says, happily leaping off cliffs when he tells them to. If they attacked you, there must not be a connection."

Clasping his hands behind his back, Vasuron started pacing around Vier. Blood, ash, and bodies tumbled out of his way without him lifting a finger. It was possible his abilities exceeded the Emperor's— exceeded any mage Vier knew of. The shadows behind the Sarconian throne might be far more dangerous than what sat on it.

"And my father's ministers?" Vasuron asked. "Do you work for Prime Minister Tallis? The rittermarschals?"

Vier shook his head, not wincing, not trembling as the crown prince stooped low to study him.

"It seems you don't," Vasuron said, resuming his pacing. "Yet you came here in the guise of Commissioner-General Gustav, and these commandos"—he kicked the commander's head without touching it, sending it careening off the crimson door—"stopped still upon seeing a mirror image of me. So, you're a mimeo?"

Vier nodded.

Hiding his magic when the prince had seen through him served no purpose, nor did taking offense at the slur for users of morphic magic. Those who played with the truth of things had always been looked down on.

Vasuron halted directly in front of Vier, towering over him like a monster out of legend. At that moment, the black of his eyes seemed to grow, merging with the shadows around his nose, creeping toward his wicked mouth. Darkness wafted from his hair like smoke, clung to the hem of his robes like tendrils of ooze.

The crown prince was *this* creature's mask, just as Vier's illusions were his. This sadistic aberration, reveling in the blood of those he'd slain, carrying it around like a second skin, was his true form.

"Last question," Vasuron said. "Why are you here?" He raised a finger, and Vier's tongue could move again.

"To find the truth about the line of Darmatus," Vier answered instantly. "The truth"—he nodded at the crimson door—"behind that door."

"No vibrations." Vasuron's grin widened as he shook his head. "Not a single lie, not a single half-truth. How positively refreshing in this city that is nothing but masks, illusions, and lies."

The prince laughed, spun in place, then reached down and grabbed Vier's wrist. He expected pain. For his nerves to erupt in piercing agony at the sudden contact. Instead, a wave of cold washed through his veins, renewing his men'ar, revitalizing his muscles.

Bringing him back to life.

"How did you do that?" Vier asked dumbly after Vasuron heaved him to his feet. The words were his, though every voice inside his head was yelling the same thing, Barthol loudest of them all.

Impossible! he railed. *Given what we know of men'ar mechanics and physics, it's simply ...*

"Everything is made of vectors," Vasuron said, cutting into Vier's thoughts. "Blood, gravity, men'ar. I simply changed the direction it was flowing inside you—pushed out the old, brought in the new. And of course, the same is true of this door."

Vasuron approached the door, Vier trailing numbly at his heels. To think that the crown prince would not only slaughter his own men but *aid* the spy invading his home. What a bizarre turn of events, even for him.

What does he hope to gain? Clara asked. *That's what we need to be focusing on now.*

At a few meters distant, Vasuron halted, held up his palms, and began twisting them in opposite directions. A *boom* rumbled from within the red stone. Then, as Vasuron clenched his hands into fists, the door began to *move*.

Long slivers—wide as Vier's thumb and several times as long—split from the stone. There were layers upon layers of them, some hugging the original face of the door, others jutting out several hand spans. Before Vier could begin to marvel at how perfectly the hundreds of pieces had fit together, they started shifting.

Up and down, left and right, out and back. Like pieces of a children's block puzzle, only a thousand times more complex. The shapes at the center folded into the ones at the sides as Vasuron eased his arms in either direction, each movement precise, each part an exact match for those sliding in beside them.

In seconds, the door was gone. Vanished into hidden alcoves deep within the walls on either side. Vasuron gestured at the dark hole in the wall. "Go on. Find whatever it is you seek."

Vier obliged him, stepping into the gloom beyond. The air was stale. Dust coated the floor, a few cloth-covered paintings, and a single darkwood chest large enough to hold a child. No one had been in the vault in months.

Which makes sense, Barthol said, eyeing some of the exposed blocks in the doorframe behind them. *These are carved with runes I don't recognize, and the locking mechanism could only be triggered from* inside *the door. No one outside the Artorios bloodline can get in here.*

Except us, Clara corrected. *We got in.*

But Vier had no interest in the door. He marched straight to the chest and heaved it open. It had no lock, but given the security Vier had overcome to get here, he didn't think it needed one.

The chest was packed with files from end to end. Little tabs jutted up from each, cramped black script hinting at what secrets lay inside. Vier rifled through them like lightning, memorizing each title, searching for the one he needed.

- *Plans to repeal the Imperial Accords on Mysticism, 631 ABH.*
- *Letter to Marquis Steffenholt about his daughter's death in the Imperial Harem, 652 ABH.*
- *Plans to disrupt peace talks with Darmatia, 603 ABH.*
- *List of Attendees at Queen Ephalia of Darmatia's funeral, 603 ABH.*
- *Edict Granting Extra-Judicial Powers, Subject: Ritter Order, 692 ABH.*

It wasn't in the first batch. There were several documents related to Darmatia, but none were what Hans wanted. Vier picked up another pile and leaned against the wall. As he did, Vasuron entered the chamber and began sweeping the sheets off of paintings, filling the room with dust that the prince sent flying away from him.

- *Plans for Invasion of Darmatia, 697 ABH.*
- *Plans for Re-Conquest of Varas Fortress, 697 ABH.*
- *Operation Dragwyrm's Maw, 697 ABH.*

Strategies for the war, operations that were either already finished or currently underway. Vier made note of the names and military units involved. The Orabairos would appreciate the information.

- *Lineage of the Royal Consorts, 685 ABH.*
- *Petition from Third Consort Lanara to Send Aid to Drahejd Province in the Northern Reaches (Currently Under Lusserian Threat), 685 ABH.*
- *Blood Tests of Royal Offspring, 685 ABH.*

Yet another pattern, one that smacked of court intrigue. If Vier had more time, he would have gladly taken all these secrets back with him.

- *Lineage of the Artorios Bloodline, 12 ABH - 697 ABH.*
- *Lineage of King Darmatus, 105 EOM -* 603 ABH *685 ABH (corrected).*

That's it! Elise squealed, bouncing on her toes. *That's the one we want!*

Vier tugged the thick folder from the pile, careful to keep its tattered binding from crumbling. As he did, another, smaller folder fell out, scattering its papers when it struck the ground. Where the pages in the first were crinkled and yellowed with age, those in the second folder looked like they could have been drafted in the past few years.

He stooped to gather the papers, only to have them jerk away from him onto Vasuron's outstretched palm. After reading the first page, a wide, fiendish grin split his lips.

"You do not know how long I've waited for something like this," the prince breathed, face contorted with pleasure.

"Like what?" Vier asked. He was desperate to see the document for himself, but knew he couldn't snatch it from the crown prince's grasp.

"Something . . . far, far more interesting than I've experienced in a long time."

Vasuron passed the records to Vier, then tapped the aged file he still held in his hands. "Read this, then look at the tree and dates in there," the prince said. "I'm sure you'll find it enlightening."

If the kid grins any harder, his face is liable to split in half, Clara quipped before being hushed by her fellows. They packed together, reading the documents along with Vier.

He scanned the first page. The second. With each paragraph, his eyes got a little wider. His breath a little shorter. Vier reached the end of the new records and practically tore open the yellowed ledger, which revealed an artist's depiction of Darmatus' lineage, complete with lacy branches and gilt leaves.

Down, down, down he traced. Back to the legendary king himself. And when he arrived there, his finger quivering atop the faded golden script belonging to the first Triaron, Vier was forced to confront something inconceivable.

A truth that, like him, shouldn't be.

Couldn't be.

For it would shake the foundations of their society to their core.

This changes everything, whispered every voice inside Vier's head.

Idyllic Days III

"No . . . " Leon whispered, his staff clattering against his greaves as his arm swung limp at his side.

The fading light of his magical flare painted the flag-brawl stadium lume in rainbows of color, a vibrant background that highlighted the dark shape plummeting toward the arena's floor. Air tugged at its arms and legs as it spun end over end, dark hair fluttering wildly, streams of molten bronze chasing it down.

And down.

And down.

Leon wanted to scream, but that wouldn't help his friend. Willing strength into his numb legs, he broke into a half-stumble, half-run. He had to save him. He had to—

Vallen struck the street of the abandoned village zone. A plume of dust shot skyward, followed by a flash of red light that brought Leon to a breathless halt. The Triaron would live—the systems in his combat suit would see to that.

Yet this was the end for him. Vallen Metellus had been eliminated from their graduation match with Renar's Renegades, and their entire squad was doomed.

"Vallen is *DOWN!*" the silky voice of Tannen Holler boomed from projectostands around the stadium. "I cannot believe what we are witnessing, folks!"

Major Jis Reev, his co-caster, snorted. "Just payment for his arrogance. You can only use the same tactic so many times before someone comes up with a counter. It's a miracle it took this many matches to happen."

A hush descended over the crowd. They huddled at the edge of the field's high walls, pushing as close to the lume as they dared, straining for a better view. Colorful pennants hung limp in their hands. One little girl's "Vallen's Vanguard" sign slipped from her fingers and floated over the side. It struck the shimmering barrier below, sizzling and smoking until it was naught but ashes.

Gasps and cries of shock rippled through their ranks, growing louder, more frenzied by the second. They couldn't believe their eyes. Leon couldn't believe *his*.

"No …"

Hand pressed to his face, he staggered backward—a single, swaying step.

Two daggers shot past, silver blades glittering in the stadium's light. The first clipped a lock of blond hair from his fringe. The other glanced off his breastplate, tip burying itself in the grass nearby.

Leon's eyes went wide. Vallen might be out, but the match hadn't ended. What a fool he'd been to lose focus.

The fool you've always been, Leon's father whispered in his ear. *The fool you'll always be.* Chills swept down his neck, slithered down his spine despite the sweat plastering his undershirt to his chest.

Leon ignored the sensation, raising his staff above his head. The orb-shaped gemstone at its crown radiated golden light as he channeled men'ar through his arm and into its sturdy darkwood shaft. Muttering an incantation, Leon swung the staff in an arc, tracing a circle from which a screen of gold exploded. It wrapped around him like a sphere, an egg—a translucent barrier that protected him from every direction.

More daggers struck the shield, dimpling its surface, spreading ripples of brilliant white as they bounced off. Leon exhaled in relief, fingers tightening on his staff as men'ar bled from him. The shield wasn't a permanent solution. If he didn't find a way to escape or counterattack, it would drain him dry.

Leon cast around, trying to piece together what had happened. Behind him, in their home zone, Velle lay in a crumpled heap. Her armor glowed scarlet, a color eerily similar to her skin, and her daggers lay discarded within reach of her listless fingers.

The Sylph must have been the first to fall. As soon as her suit locked, any spells she'd cast would have disintegrated—*including* the aerial glyphs Vallen had been charging across.

Another prickle of unease snaked down Leon's back. *He* was Velle's defender. *He* was the last barrier between enemies and their home zone.

How had Renar's squad plunged through three zones—cruiser, village, and swamp—without him noticing? His breathing quickened and his pulse raced, thundering in his veins. Leon was *cold*, ice crackling in his ears, frost creeping across his chest, down his stomach, piercing his flesh like hundreds of needles.

What's going on?

Where's Renar's squad?

Why doesn't any of this make—

A storm of blades launched from the shadows of a gnarled swamp oak, all aimed at a fist-sized spot on Leon's shield directly in front of his head. He twitched his staff. Shifted men'ar from the other sides of his lume to reinforce that point.

The daggers struck, a hail of clattering and clanging and almost blinding ripples that seemed to last forever. Yet just when Leon thought the barrier would crack, the onslaught ended, replaced by loud, mocking applause.

"Looks like I focused on the wrong enemy."

Leon glanced up, a gasp slipping from his lips as he caught sight of a silver-haired girl descending on a platform of interlocked blades. At a snap from her fingers, the daggers spread to the sides, allowing her to drop the last meter into a nimble crouch. When she rose, both her steel knives and her platinum glare were fixed on him.

"Sylette Farkos," Leon blurted. Why did he say that? Why did he know her name?

Flicking her braided ponytail over her shoulder, the girl nodded. "I asked them *not* to announce it. How do you know my name?"

No, that was wrong. *Farkos.* It tasted bitter on Leon's tongue, like overripe plums or his father's lies. It stank of rot and filth, turning his stomach, urging him to retch.

Clutching his throat, Leon spat the first word that popped into his head. "Artorios . . ."

Streams of dust materialized around Sylette, jerking and spasming as they combined into jagged slivers of metal. There was no form to them, like with her daggers. They were vicious and ugly, just like the grimace twisting her face.

"Who," Sylette snarled, "told you that name?"

Leon blinked, breath misting in the cold inside his bubble. "I . . . I'm not sure."

"How? How do you know?" A shard shot forward like lead from a rifle, penetrating a finger-length into Leon's lume before rebounding. "I'm not associated with that man, with that *voidspawn*. Don't. *Call me. That! NAME!*"

Leon wanted to answer. Wanted to pick through the dark smears in his memory, the deep chasms he couldn't seem to plumb. But frigid gusts forced him back. Kept him rooted in the present, his attention on the danger before him. If he didn't feed more men'ar into his barrier,

Sylette's assault would carve him to ribbons.

"Calm down, Sylette!"

A large, gloved hand settled on her shoulder. The darkness vanished from Sylette's eyes, replaced by irritation. She shook out of the man's grip, brushing the spot afterward as if to clean away the residue of his touch.

"That's a good way to lose your fingers, Renar," Sylette said, continuing to pick at her combat suit. "And *don't* give me orders. My strategy, my command."

Renar raised one of his bushy eyebrows. "Yes, yes, princess."

That earned him another acid-coated glare, though Leon couldn't fathom why. "What took you so long?"

Unter—their squad's giant, four-armed Hue—marched up on Renar's right. "Triaron still move try. Out knock, pin with wreckage."

"He did *not* seem pleased with the outcome, so I drew a smile on his face." Lilith bounded along in their wake, her auburn curls bouncing, a saber clutched in her left hand.

"With scrivle?" Unter asked.

"Of course." Flourishing her sword, Lilith chuckled. "What? You think I'd use this?"

Renar turned to Leon, arms spread wide. He'd already resheathed his greatsword in the scabbard hung across his back. "Seems you're the only one left."

"There's still Matteo," Leon said, glancing over his shoulder at their flag tower. His heart sank into his stomach.

Their flag still flew, twin swords coated in fire and lightning— Vallen's design—flapping proudly atop a white backdrop. The same couldn't be said for Matteo. One limp arm hung over the tower's edge, a long-barreled rifle discarded beside it.

Leon was the last one left.

Tannen's commentary confirmed his fears. "Here comes the end. One versus four, nowhere to run, nowhere to hide. How long can Leon Descar hold out against these overwhelming odds?"

"Not long," Major Reev said, words lashing him like shards of ice. "A draw is his best bet, and there's still five minutes on the clock."

Leon looked up at the central match display, where four massive telescribers showed clips of the flag-brawl match transmitted to them by recorbs floating around the arena. Beneath each of the device's four faces was a timer counting down the minutes and seconds remaining in the game.

5:02, 5:01, 5:00, 4:59 ...

The seconds ticked off, one by one. If Leon could remain standing and protect their flag until it hit *0:00*, the officials would declare a draw, which would look far better on their exam report than a loss.

But what were the chances of that?

"Care to let me go?" Leon joked.

Shaking his head, Renar pointed at a white-robed official on the sidelines. "You don't have to take a beating for that idiot, Vallen. Just surrender."

A kind offer, far kinder than the Triaron would've ever offered Renar. Leon's hands started to rise. If he clasped them behind his head and knelt, the match would end.

You ran away from the future I gave you, his father sneered, glasses chain clinking as he stood over Leon. *Now you run away from this too? Typical.*

Leon froze.

If he gave in, Vallen would fail and have to repeat his final year at the Academy. Their squad would break up. And he . . . Leon cringed, shivering as visions of a windowless cell, a hard bed, and a metal table covered in endless formulas and equations swam before his eyes.

He would *not* go back.

He would *not* become his father's magchine, another tool for his ambitions.

For too long he'd dwelled in the shadows, supporting others, obeying their whims and commands. Even with Vallen—the one who'd torn him from the doctor's clutches—he'd always played moon to his radiant, blinding sun.

But no more, Leon decided, splitting his focus, channeling men'ar through his staff and into the center of his lume.

Today

The spot started to shake, to sparkle.

it's my turn

Sweat beaded on his brow, trickling down his nose and off his chin. The crystal orb on his staff glowed. Too bright to hide, too powerful not to notice. Sylette tensed, backing away. Unter swung his arms forward, four massive bucklers shielding him and the freckled girl in his shadow.

to stand

Only Renar stood firm. "Don't do it. You're just going to make this more painful for all of us."

in

the

LIGHT!

"Sorry," Leon said. "I have to try."

His barrier disintegrated, globules of floating light collecting in a cone before the rod's gemstone. Then they fired like a dreadnaught cannon.

Anyone who blinked missed what followed. Dense golden radiance struck Renar's chest plate, bowling him over and removing him from the competition. Unter was brushed aside, two of his shields half melted, his right arms scorched free of both suit and armor. Behind both, trees snapped and crashed as the beam plowed through the swamp zone.

"A four-on-one is *instantly* reduced to a three-on-one as Leon launches a blistering surprise attack," Tannen roared. "Convinced they were still negotiating, Renar stood there and took one to the chin. You won't find any honor on this battlefield, dear listeners!"

"Honor?" Major Reev laughed. "There's no *honor* in war. Leon made the right call, but eliminating one opponent doesn't increase his chances much."

Right and wrong didn't matter to Leon. He charged toward the blazing forest, smoke wafting from ferns and bushes set alight by the heat of his blast. Disappearing was his only chance at victory—the possibility of turning the fight into a series of chaotic, single bouts instead of a coordinated pincer.

"Stop him!" Sylette yelled as daggers swished through the smog.

Leon waved his staff. Felt more power drain from him, his skin pimpling as a chill settled in his veins. His lume popped back into existence in time to repel the daggers, but Leon winced even so. Why was Sylette aiming all her attacks at his *head*? Was she trying to kill him?

Probably.

Unter moved to block Leon's path, a great fortress of flesh, metal, and enhancive magic that he couldn't hope to beat head-on. The Hue thrust his shields forward, their faces glistening with the orange glow of a protective spell. Any blasts Leon threw at them would bounce right off.

Which meant it was time for some wonky, logic-be-voided creativity.

Smiling, Leon *fell* backward, dispelling the front of his light barrier as he did so. What remained was half a shimmering egg. Or, as he liked to think of it, an unbreakable sled.

An engimage needs creativity, Leon's father had told him time and again. *More than any other skill,* that *is what will let them craft the future.*

Well, his dear old dad had never thought of anything like *this.* Leon bounced once, the momentum of his sled disappearing as it carved a furrow through the grass. Unter loomed over him, swinging down with his bucklers to pummel Leon's suit until it locked.

"Licht'lashen," he mumbled, unable to activate two spells without an incantation.

Light sprang from Leon's staff like a whip, coiling first about Unter's bulging left calf, then his right. The giant glanced down, blinking confusion at the pulsing threads attached to his leg. They didn't burn or sting, so he clearly had no idea why Leon had cast them.

Tapping his staff with his forefinger pulled the chains of light *toward* him. Except . . . he'd wound them tightly around Unter's legs, and the hulking cadet weighed *far* more than Leon, his staff, and his shining sled.

"See ya!" Leon said.

His sled launched forward, racing beneath Unter's bucklers, hurtling below his crotch. As he passed his lasso points, Leon dissolved the chains, then cast them at the nearest tree. Another pull, and he was speeding along even faster than before.

Lilith cast fireballs from her saber as Leon disappeared into the smoke-wreathed bowels of the swamp. Each blast showered him with plumes of water and clumps of charred dirt, but none of them came close to striking him or his sled.

Soon, Leon was alone amid the burning trees, Sylette's angry shouts and Unter's thumping footfalls the only signs of pursuit. Should he push on and try to take their flag? No. If they suspected he'd run, they'd double back to grab his. Luring them into an ambush was his best chance.

Stretching out his staff, Leon sent long strands of light soaring across the forest. Binding trees together with shining nets. Laying tripwires between stumps, along the marsh paths. Dappling the smoke-filled canopy with enough crisscrossing lines to snare a flock of pigeons.

Leon was an Ilfaen frost-spider, and this was his nest—his hunting ground. While the smoke would impede the visibility of his foes, simply *touching* one of his threads would tell him where they were. All of the strands were connected, and all led back to the illyrium orb on the end of his staff.

The cord of light twitched. Unter—or perhaps one of the girls with him—was barreling through the threads behind Leon, snapping them as he came.

Time to disappear. Standing, Leon raised his staff, dragging the remnants of his lume along with it. He let it flow up his body and around his head, forming it into a sealed helmet that trapped enough clean air for him to breathe for the next few minutes. Then he launched one final chain into the forest canopy and dragged himself onto a sturdy branch.

To the south—toward Leon's flag—the forest burned, orange flames chewing through the underbrush and casting embers into the murky, ankle-deep waters of the swamp zone. Yet here, near the forest's center, the trees seeded by their proctors were still strong and hardy, their trunks heavy with the weight of years.

Matteo might have pondered how the Academy had transplanted them onto the field, but Leon couldn't care less. They were here now, and they would serve as the perfect trap.

Unter blundered into the clearing below, shields slashing apart light-threads like strands of yarn, trunk-thick legs splashing mud in all directions. The Hue didn't seem to fear Leon—not with a shell of orange magic clinging to his skin. If Leon attacked, he'd give away his position without inflicting much damage.

But, he smiled, men'ar rushing out from his body and across the forest, *I never planned on a direct assault.*

Leon pulled on his staff. Willing the men'ar back into it, back into himself. Drawing his web down atop his prey.

The trees shook, frail branches snapping, dry leaves tumbling from the smoke-shrouded canopy. Trunks began to groan, their bark shivering and cracking as golden strands pulled taut against them. Unter stopped. Glanced at the net of light closing about him. More threads, more chains than could be counted, so bright it was like staring at the sun.

Too late, the Hue turned to run.

Gnarled roots popped free of the earth as the great oaks toppled inward. Taking a wide stance, Unter raised his bucklers. One trunk struck. Two, three, four—a whole copse of ancient wood bearing down on the blue giant. His legs sank into the mossy muck. With a groan, Unter collapsed to one knee, his teeth gritted as purple blood oozed from beneath his shields.

"Fall," Leon muttered, pouring more men'ar into his threads. Strengthening them until they were hard as dragon scales.

Unter stayed standing.

"Fall."

Leon cast more golden coils over the pile. Another, *another,* and then more still. He tugged on them as chills seeped closer to his heart, as heat dribbled from his neck, arms, and legs. Perhaps only a quarter of his men'ar remained, each thread Leon cast bringing him closer to the darkness, to that edge no mage should cross.

Yet he was all but beyond caring.

He would win.

Today, *he* would stand in the light, consequences be voided.

"Fall!" Leon roared, dashing forward.

He jumped onto the center of the mound of light, wood, and straining muscle. Unter opened his mouth to speak, but Leon shoved his staff in the Hue's face, summoning a shimmering plate that pressed down on him. Forcing Unter's other knee to fall, plastering him into the swamp.

A few more seconds and his armor would lock. Just a few more—

"Fire!" Sylette roared from somewhere nearby.

Something glinted amid the cinder-laced trees. A dagger? A bullet? Leon ordered a light thread to yank him to his left, a short dodge that wouldn't ease his pressure on Unter.

Then a blast of hot air washed over Leon, scalding his fingers, ripping sweat from his scalp. Flames *split* the ground beneath him, a pillar of fire that wrapped both him and Unter in its embrace as it reached for the heavens. Leaves turned to ash. Branches withered, trunks burned to char.

And, for a brief instant, Leon blacked out.

No, a harsh whisper spat in his ear. *This is* not *how this story ends.*

Tannen's shouts brought Leon back from the shadows. " . . . Lilith hit *both* of them with an earth-shattering blast of explosive magic! Unter's suit locked up, knocking him out of the competition, but what about Leon?"

"He predicted she'd hit him when he went to finish off her squadmate," Major Reev replied.

I . . . I did? Leon thought, blinking. A soft barrier of light surrounded him, its surface faded, cracked, and flickering. Ash coated the clearing beyond the sphere, and flames licked the blackened trunks of several toppled oaks.

Unter lay beside him, warped armor pulsing with a weak crimson glow.

"A practical choice by Lilith," Major Reev continued as if discussing how she preferred her tea. "But an even better tactic from

411

Leon. Friendly fire was one of the few ways he was going to overcome his—"

Another glint drew Leon's attention, the same metallic flash that had preceded the last attack. In an instant, he was running through the forest, staff glowing as he fed men'ar into its crystal.

BOOM!

Heat seared Leon's neck *through* the failing lume, drawing a hiss from his lips. He heard more trees snapping, crumbling. Stumbled as a wave of smoking soil and clumps of dirt crashed over him, shattering his shield and nearly driving him to the ground.

How were they hitting him? Where were they? Leon glanced left and right, searching for answers in the chaotic, blazing forest. Acrid smog filled his lungs, ripped tears from his eyes. The heat haze hanging above the waters made it almost impossible to tell which way he was going.

Leon saw the glint again, this time for what it truly was: a hovering silver mirror with jagged edges, as if it had been formed by welding the flat edges of blades together. *Or* daggers, Leon realized. These were *Sylette's* doing.

Sylette can only make daggers, a distant sliver of his mind protested.

Huh? Why did Leon know that? *And why*—a shiver crawled across his scalp, pricking it with needles as it went—*is that the total opposite of what I'm seeing here?* The mirrors might be framed by daggers, but their faces were pristine glass.

None of this made sense.

He swung his staff forward, lashing a coil of light around a listing oak below the mirror and pulling himself in that direction. Leon's shoulder protested the movement. His fingers blistered and bled as he struggled to hold onto his rod.

But this time, Leon avoided the explosion entirely, and a plan was taking root in his mind.

He watched the mirror as he flew past, its glinting face tracking his motion as he reached the tree, unhooked his chain, and took off in another direction. Yet it didn't follow or float after him, staying rooted in the air.

Which meant there were *more* of them, a whole series of mirrors arranged by Sylette so Lilith could target him anywhere in the forest. Leon saw another in the crook of a drooping swamp willow. One hung over a pond beside the main path, while two more draped from the canopy like bulbs on a Festivus tree.

All of them turned to follow him, featureless faces painted with fiery brush strokes. Leon couldn't trace the reflections from one mirror to another. There was too much smoke in the air, and he was too disoriented from leaping over fallen logs, wading through waist-high ferns, and sprinting in random directions to avoid Lilith's blasts.

But Leon didn't need to. If Lilith could see him, that meant the mirrors traced a line back to wherever she was.

He would get one shot at this, one chance. Smoke seared Leon's nostrils and throat. He coughed into his free hand, tasted blood from some scrape or cut he hadn't noticed. Each breath hurt worse than the last. Each step was a little slower, his throbbing legs a little heavier with every passing second.

The chasm in Leon's chest yawned, tugging at his eyelids, frigid talons biting ever deeper into his flesh, his veins. His next spell would be his last. Any more would kill him, regardless of the prototype magtech armor he wore.

Light filtered between the trees ahead, a gap through which Leon could see the sandy clay hovels and straw-thatched roofs of the village zone. He cleared the final tangle of undergrowth. Charged onto the empty street, footfalls casting clouds of dirt in his wake, and stumbled against a broken fence post.

Leon looked exhausted.

As intended.

There were no structures he could easily snag with light-threads, no way to execute a miraculous dodge.

As intended.

Leon planted his back against the dilapidated, rotting fence, sliding to the ground while fixing his gaze on the forest he'd left. Only a single mirror hovered at its edge, its burnished surface glinting.

"Leon's had enough," Major Reev remarked. "He made it far, but there's only so much one man can do on his own."

"Is this the end of the road?" Tannen asked, riling up the fans. "The hero's last gasp? The fading of a flag-brawl miracle, the sun's final rays, the—"

"They get the point, Tannen."

The crowd hushed once more. Leon could hear banners snapping in the wind above the stadium, flames crackling as they devoured the forest, the gentle hum of the arena lume high above his head. Every noise was a thunderclap, each beat of his heart loud as a drum.

413

Tannen was right. One way or another, this *was* the end.

And

he

would

win.

Leon grinned as the ground beneath him quaked, surface cracking, tongues of fire licking at him through the gaps.

One second.

He raised his staff, expelling *all* the men'ar inside in a concentrated rush of golden radiance. The beam jetted across the clearing. Struck the mirror, then bounced away into its depths faster than his eyes could follow.

Two seconds.

The earth exploded, tossing Leon into the air. Gouts of flame and earth caressed him as he gave away what was left of him—as he fed every drop, every speck of men'ar left in his well into his staff.

Three seconds.

Blood dribbled from Leon's nose, his eyes. Chills swept across his face, stealing sight from his left eye, numbing his lips so he could no longer smile. Everything was cold. Everything was pain.

But . . . Leon only needed to stay conscious.

Four seconds.

He went soaring through the sky on a golden disk, borne aloft by light and flames and heat.

Five seconds.

His illyrium crystal shattered, fragments scything in every direction. One scored a deep gash across Leon's chin. Another struck his chest plate with such force he feared the suit would lock.

Six seconds.

The flames spent their wrath, fading to wisps of smoke through which Leon fell. End over end, blond hair fluttering wildly, shards of translucent gold chasing him down.

And down.

And down.

Leon struck near Vallen's limp body, the last of his lume splintering into a thousand pieces at the bone-jarring impact. Groaning, he rolled onto his side. Spat blood while staring at the two halves of his crystal-less staff.

The staff, the road, the swirling clouds of smoke and dust—they all swam back and forth, hazy and unfocused. Every sound was muffled, as if someone had stuffed wads of Trillith wax into Leon's ears.

"*Aamaaziing!*" Tannen belted from the next country over. "*Hee hiit heer. Hee reeaally diid. Boounceed aa beeam of liight off eeveery miiroor Syylette suumooned aand knoocked Liiliith off the Vaallen's Vaanguard flaag tooweer. Shee's doown. Fiiniished. Briiliant, siimply briiliant!*"

So, he'd done it. Leon smiled, though he wasn't sure if the smile reached his lips. Everything was cold and—

Someone yanked his collar, dragging him into a sitting position.

"Bravo, Leon."

He stared into Sylette's flinty eyes, at the dagger drawn back in her right hand, ready to strike. The world rushed into focus. The gleaming edge of her blade. The roar of the crowd, bellowing their approval, chanting *his* name.

"*LEON! LEON! LEON!*"

Sylette glanced up at the stands, obscured by the smoke from Lilith's final attack. The crowd couldn't see he was at the girl's mercy. They only knew what the telescribers above the field told them—that his armor was still active.

Leon gritted his teeth, rage bubbling up through the chills, the pain, and the nausea. He'd been so, *so* close to winning. To saving his team. To freeing himself from his father's clutches, claiming a life that was his and his alone.

And now . . .

"You know, I could *let* you win."

Slowly, Sylette lowered her blade. A snap of her fingers summoned a simple white pillow from the ether, which she placed behind Leon's back before pushing him onto it.

Leon wanted to resist, to lash out at Sylette with his splintered staff. But his body wouldn't respond. He could only glare at her. "Excuse me?"

"Oh, did I speak too quickly?" She sketched a mocking bow, then materialized an iron-wrought chair fashioned to look like a stand of falling ivy. Taking a seat, she steepled her fingers and leaned toward him. "I'll say it again:

I. Could. Let. You. Win. You caught it that time, right?"

Sylette can only summon daggers, Leon recalled once more. The thought was accompanied by a blistering stab of pain, like a hot poker rammed into his skull.

"*Arggh!*" he gasped.

Sylette nodded. "I bet that fall hurt a lot. So why don't we wrap this thing up? I yield, you win, and then some salvators come patch you up."

"Why would you do that?"

It made no sense. Leon was unable to fight, so . . .

" . . . a single stab to your breastplate would lock your armor and give me the win?" Sylette finished. "I bet you're thinking something along those lines. But I'm not interested in this match. It's a skirmish—a prelude to something much bigger. Instead of a hollow victory, I'd rather make an ally." She extended a hand, her fingers spread. "An ally like *you*."

"It wouldn't be a win," Leon growled. "It would be a farce, a lie."

Sylette grinned, a deep smile that seemed to stretch just a bit too far. "Does it matter?" She pointed up at the stands. "Listen to them cheer."

"LEON! LEON! LEON!"

The crowd was still shouting for him, drowning out Tannen Holler's attempts to speak, shaking the entire stadium as they stomped their feet. Goosebumps pimpled Leon's skin, accompanied by an electric rush, a *thrill* unlike any he'd experienced before. Was *this* the kind of worship Vallen received? Was this what it felt like to be him?

Sylette saw the wonder twinkling in his eyes. "It doesn't have to end, Leon. You gave them the story of a lifetime—an impossible victory they'll be retelling in the streets, singing about in taverns, recording in their histories. And in return, they'll shower you with their favor. Their adulation." Her voice dropped to a silken whisper. "Their *love*. You want that, don't you?"

Did he? Leon's father considered him a tool. His brothers, a nuisance. Leon owed *everything* to Vallen, cherished him as no one else did for giving him the only taste of freedom he'd ever known.

But was that love?

Was *this*—the roar of the crowd, the reverence of their cries—truly love?

Could he possibly understand that which he'd never received?

Yes, Leon decided, glancing down at the phantom chasm piercing his chest. *Better a beautiful falsehood than an ugly truth.*

Fingers twitching, Leon raised his right hand, extending it to meet Sylette's. He stopped a hairsbreadth from grasping her palm. "Why me? Why pick me?"

The shadows beneath Sylette's bangs, lips, and collar lengthened and twisted until they mimicked the smirk she wore. "To take down an Empire. *To save the world.*"

Like pieces from one of his father's puzzles, Leon's memories slotted into place, one by one.

Empire.

Sylette.

Artorios.

Leon remembered. Dear Veneer, he remembered *everything* they'd been through. The canceled match, the massacre at Aldona, the sacrifice he'd made for his friends.

The *love* he'd shown them.

And this—snarling, Leon smacked aside the hand before him—*is not Sylette.*

With that realization came a crashing wave of pain, pouring through his body, setting his blood aflame. Leon remembered this agony as well. A perfect torment that sought to unmake him, ripping him apart scrap by scrap like a pack of ravenous boerwolves until naught remained. His memories were its prey. The life he'd lived its sustenance.

And every time Leon remembered—every time he broke the glittering facade laid across his eyes—the pain returned to cast him back into the abyss. Flaying him open. Laying him bare for his new master, the one to whom the shadows bowed.

Through his tears, Leon saw it. The creature inside Sylette, the thing that had taken her form. Dark ooze dripped from its bottomless eyes, slipped from its too-wide smile. Glistening silver bled from its hair, plopping to the ground, exposing raven locks black as pitch and deep as the Void. Mist coiled from beneath its armor plates, hugging its rot-pocked flesh like a second skin.

Leon scrambled to escape, scratching at the dust with his fingernails. He would fail. He *always* failed.

Again.

And again.

And again.

"Another mistake," the creature said, voice vast as the oceans. "Each time I correct my errors, yet each time you still see through me. Do you know how many times you've repeated this day?"

"Not . . . enough, clearly," Leon spat through his suffering. "I'll never take your hand, and neither will they." He flicked his chin at Vallen's body, which was starting to fade away like the rest of the illusion.

"That couldn't be further from the truth, but I'll allow you your delusions. Soon, those will also be no more."

"Perhaps. But someday . . . they'll discover I'm alive. When they

417

do," Leon chuckled around a mouthful of blood. "I certainly wouldn't want to be you."

Not-Sylette shrugged, ebony daggers forming from the shadows around her. "I am you, and you remain a small part of me. What happens to one will also befall the other."

"I'm alright with that."

Not-Sylette swept her arm forward. A dozen obsidian daggers sped through the smoke-choked air and plunged into Leon's gut, slicing through his useless armor, mangling his insides. Blood spurted from his lips. He toppled onto his side, shivering uncontrollably, his vision fading.

Even this was a familiar end: laying in the dust as not-Sylette planted a boot atop his blade-riddled ribs and ground down *hard*. From the fringes of his consciousness came a new chant. *"SYLETTE! SYLETTE! SYLETTE!"*

"Fickle crowd," not-Sylette murmured, kneeling beside Leon as his life bled away. "Now, let go. Let go and the pain will finally cease."

Part 3
Thread of Hope

Chapter 41

Over the Abyss

Adamantele 7, 697 ABH
Lighthouse above Resistance Base, Sarconian Province of Darmatia

*W*hat does a man do when he's lost sight of his future? Renar pondered that question for the umpteenth time as he sat on the steps of the lighthouse guarding one of the entrances to the Resistance base. He held a scrivle in his right hand, a piece of charcoal in the other, and his notebook lay open across his knees.

Open to two blank pages.

The tools of Renar's trade trembled in his hands, itching to be used. No one was around. Not Vallen, Major Reev, the General, or anyone else who might scoff at his dreams. Who would tell him his passions were useless and inane.

Renar was alone with his creativity and the soft snow floating from the heavens. It gathered in the cracks and crevices of the cliffs, blanketed the gray slabs of the pier, and speckled the obsidian reefs around the lighthouse with patches of pristine white. The way it fell was mesmerizing. Entrancing. Renar's gaze was drawn upward, attracted to each unique flake drifting toward his eyes, latching onto his nose, lips, and wool coat. There they melted, their instant of life—of grace and beauty—ended all too soon.

Such a brilliant metaphor.

Such a perfect scene to capture on his page.

And yet Renar couldn't draw. For while no one was around to scoff at his dreams, *he* was more than capable of doing so himself.

The dimwit finally starts to understand, the Soldier whispered. *The General knew you'd arrive at this point. Knew you'd see he was right. Pity it took you till now to see it.*

Sighing, Renar laid his scrivle and charcoal on the step beside him and pulled on a pair of thin gloves. They were made of sail canvas stitched in the shape of gloves, too thin to truly keep out the cold, but the best the Resistance could make right now. He had no cap except his unruly black hair.

Unable to draw, but too stubborn to go inside. Renar was every bit the fool the General thought he was. Rubbing his palms for warmth every few seconds, he started flipping back through his past sketches. Back to a time when he was a little surer of himself.

This notebook wasn't an old one. The General had discovered and burned its predecessor a few weeks before graduation, so all the drawings in it were fairly recent. Renar saw thick brush strokes in the shape of Unter, hunched atop a bench minutes before a flag-brawl match. Lilith was on another page, slashing at a training dummy, and across from her an angry Sylette loomed over an Academy orderly who'd filed a book on small unit tactics in the wrong section of the library.

Then there were the pictures he'd sketched while on the run. They were hurried, a few quick lines used instead of hundreds, but they'd gradually gained something his art had been missing for years: emotion. Regardless of subject, the drawings *breathed*.

Grass and leaves crunched beneath Renar's feet as he stared at a picture of Lyndwur forest. He could hear the hiss of Grozza's tongue and click of his claws as Sylette negotiated with the Moravi. Taste Mrs. Alhan's splendid seafood cannelloni with just a glance at a bowl overflowing with pasta and sauce, immortalized forever by his hand.

Those were good memories. Times when Renar had felt like he belonged—like he *deserved* to be with the other cadets.

Ah, but there are bad memories in here as well. The Soldier reached out, turning the page with misty fingers.

Face twisted into a sneer, one eye blazing like an iron poker, Valescar dashed at him with metal cables frozen mid-flight.

You can't use magic, the Soldier mocked. *You're weak. Useless. Dead weight.*

The page turned again, half-melted snowflakes tumbling off between Renar's legs. He needed to put the notebook away before it got soaked.

No! You need to see this. See what everyone else sees. What the General sees.

An invisible hand grabbed Renar's head. Forced him to look at the page. But there was no hand, and there was no Soldier. This was all him—his guilt trying to make him recognize what he should have known from the beginning.

A shattered chapel gazed up at him. The holes in its roof were sightless eyes, the mangled gate and missing doors its screaming mouth. Fires blazed in its gardens, and the bloody hand of a monk was draped across a splintered altar.

"I didn't see Kinloss die," Renar mumbled.

The Soldier smirked. *And yet you added that detail anyway. You feel responsible: for his death, for Unter's injuries, for all of it. They think you have magic. They make plans assuming abilities you don't have. But instead of telling the truth, you keep letting them believe a lie.*

Mist poured in from the sides of the next sketch, obscuring the bulk of a vicious, crimson-eyed Primal. Its fangs dripped viscous ink. Its bladed tentacles shot through the dark, aiming for Renar's treacherous, deceit-filled heart.

Where were you while everyone else fought? The Soldier circled Renar, lashing out at him from the swirling snow. *You sprained your ankle running from it! From liar to useless to outright hindrance. They would be better off without you.*

Renar slammed the notebook shut, then stuffed it in his pocket. Tears welled in his eyes, mixing with the flakes of snow already clinging to his stubble-lined cheeks. The voice was right. The General was right. It was time for him to admit it, and for his dream of freedom—of choosing his own path—to come to an end.

Ducking into his coat, hiding from the world, Renar tucked his knees to his chin and started rocking back and forth.

"I know," he whispered in response. "I know they would be. I know, I know, I know ... "

"What know?" boomed a voice Renar would recognize anywhere.

Like a rocktoise emerging from its shell, he poked the top of his head out of his jacket. Unter was limping down the pier while favoring his left leg, the one that had been injected with Moravi venom. Every step imprinted a huge footprint in the snow, a trail that led from the plateau above.

"Nothing," Renar murmured.

Unter cupped one of his four hands to his ear. Another arm gestured at the winter storm around them. "Up speak! Can no hear in snow." His words echoed around the harbor, bouncing off the sheltering cliffs, burying themselves in the dark blue waters. *UP SPEAK, Up Speak, up speak ...*

Renar had no desire to discuss his shortcomings, even with his best friend. The blue giant was like the rest: a mage, chosen by men'ar. Unter wore the same patchwork tunic and multi-colored trousers the quartermaster had sewn for him when they'd arrived, thin garments that exposed his thick neck, bulging arms, and the rot-black wound on his left calf. A normal person would freeze if they dressed like that, but

423

not an enhancive mage. Not someone who could turn their skin into a barrier against the elements.

"Seat taken?" Unter asked. Renar shook his head, and the Hue climbed the stairs he sat on in two long strides. A brush from Unter's lower right arm sent snow flying as he cleared himself a seat.

"You're still recovering," Renar said once his squadmate was settled. "Why are you out here?"

"Medic say good for injury is fresh air."

Jet black eyes blinked twice in rapid succession. Was that the Hue equivalent of a smile? Or was it a sigh? Renar couldn't remember despite the body language chart he'd written to avoid offending the hulking transfer the General had put on his team.

After a few seconds, Unter's lips creased into a stiff grin. He pointed at it. "I joke. Air do little for injury. Medic don't give clearance, I just come up to visit way-any." Unter blinked slowly—one eye and then the other—before holding a finger to his lips. "It secret. Tell don't."

More secrets. *Exactly* what Renar needed when he couldn't handle his own.

"Sure," he said, glancing at the water lapping against the pier.

Unter reached down and picked something silver out of the snow between them: Renar's scrivle. It looked like an oversized needle in his pipe-thick fingers.

"Drawing done?"

A weight settled atop Renar's shoulders. "No."

"Then where notebook is?"

The weight pressed harder, bending his neck, hunching his back. "Away."

"But ... "

Unter bit his tongue, frustration evident from his hurried blinking. Renar could see he wanted to say something clever, something that would cheer him up or inspire him. Yet the words the Hue sought failed him in their foreign tongue.

"Snow," Unter said at last, waving around them. "Cliffs, water, lighthouse ... "

"It's picturesque?" Renar supplied. "Scenic? Beautiful?"

The Hue snapped his fingers as he snapped his eyes open and shut. "*Beautiful!* That is word. Why you no draw beautiful scene before forever gone?"

"I ... can't."

Renar's arms pressed into his knees, the weight on his back—and the notebook in his coat—growing heavier by the second. How easy would it be to fall forward? To let gravity take over, drag him down the steps, and roll him into the icy water?

In that moment of frigid, refreshing clarity, there would be no more lies. Renar wouldn't be beholden to the General anymore. He wouldn't have to worry about letting his squadmates down or fouling things up and getting people he cared about—people like Unter—hurt.

All it would take for Renar to be free was for him to stop hanging over the abyss and throw himself in instead.

A large blue arm caught him across the chest. "Where you go, friend?"

"I'm fine," Renar insisted. "Anyway, let's get in before the storm gets worse or a Sarc air patrol wanders by."

He tried to stand, but the pressure on his chest increased, pinning him where he was. "Not until something draw you," Unter said, deep obsidian eyes set like stone.

"What? I told you, I can't right now."

"*Won't,* can't not."

Renar sighed. "Those are pretty much the same—"

Holding Renar in place with one hand, Unter grabbed his collar with another and shoved a hand inside his coat with a third. He didn't realize what was happening until his dingy old notebook, bound in cracked leather with a faded spine and some damp pages, was dangling high above his head.

"Give it back!" Renar yelled instinctively.

In an instant, the years fell away, and Renar was back in the General's dark study, begging him not to toss his first sketchbook into his hearth. He'd failed. Failed again and again and again, until finally, the beatings that followed made him mute.

No blow came. Unter gripped the tired, worn journal in a hand as large as it was, but made no move to cast it into the harbor or rip it into pieces. Instead, he placed it on his knee, hefted the scrivle, and began scribbling on a blank page.

Renar leaned into Unter's arm, suddenly more curious than upset. "What are you—"

The Hue's free arm put a palm in his face. "Wait."

"It's *my* notebook."

"Wait."

After two tense minutes, Unter held his sketch up for Renar to see. He squinted, cocked his head, then snickered despite his best efforts to hold it in. "Is that . . . two blobs?"

"You and me, it is."

"And where are we?" Renar asked, still trying to stifle his giggles. "One of the moons? Those holes look like craters. Or maybe we're standing on some holey cheese. We should probably ask the next priest we see to bless it."

Unter didn't appear offended at the wild guesses. Calmly, he pointed at a little, lopsided tower in the background. At its peak was a very stiff flag.

Everything slotted into place for Renar. Unter had drawn a flag-brawl match—the *first* flag-brawl match they'd played together after the Hue entered the Academy. The holes in the ground were shell craters, mimicking an artillery-shelled battlefield. The blobs were the two of them, one surrounded by jagged lines, the other raising a stick-thin arm in the air.

Only . . . those jagged lines weren't accents Unter had added to improve his sketch. They were sparks coursing from his combat suit, one 'specially' modified for the first Hue to ever enroll at the school. Normal suits were designed to lock up when their wearer sustained too much damage. But Hues were stronger than Terrans or Sylph. Able to take more punishment. And a certain Commandant decided to see just how far he could push the magtech toys he'd been given.

"I'm so sorry, Unter," Renar babbled. "I didn't know he would—"

The Hue waved until he fell silent. "I see that look before," Unter said, pointing at Renar's crestfallen face. "Defeated look. 'I up give' look. I what it means know. You on edge are teetering, and you know don't if on cliff top you stay should."

There it was. Leave it to Unter to see right through him. And in that instant, Renar didn't care what secrets or lies he revealed. The dam burst, his tears fell, and he unleashed all the pent-up darkness he'd been collecting inside his soul.

"I'm useless, Unter. *Useless.*" Tears garbled his words. Renar sniffled, trying and failing to stop the warm snot dripping across his lips and chin. "T-the General thinks so, and so does Major Reev, Sylette, Vallen . . . the w-whole lot of them! And they're right. I'm a—"

Not that! the Soldier roared, grabbing Renar's lips, ripping the vile truth away with shadowy digits. *Never that. They'll never look at us the same if they discover we aren't mages—if they discover the General's deceit.*

" . . . I-I've been dragging the team down," Renar sobbed instead, pier swaying as he wept. "I couldn't do anything to h-help stop Valescar. At Etrus, I just swung my sword around and w-wildly fired a rifle. I . . . I don't know if I even hit anyone."

Wiping snot away with the back of his hand, Renar laughed, a harsh, mirthless cackle. "When the . . . the Draken attacked, I sat in the ship, injured and unable to do anything. A-and now I'm back under the General's thumb—a p-pawn in whatever schemes he's been crafting. Useless, useless, useless."

Renar buried his head in his gloves, relishing the cold tickle of snow on his scalp and neck. The abyss behind his eyes yawned, ready to swallow him whole. Release, escape, and freedom rolled into one gaping black pit. All he had to do was jump.

Booming laughter made Renar crack his fingers and glance up at his friend. "What's so funny?"

"You!" Unter shouted, his peals of mirth still echoing around the harbor. "You are blind man who searches for cane only to realize in hand whole time it was."

"So, a fool? That sounds about right."

Unter blinked more laughter as he spoke. "But best kind of fool. *You* convinced Matteo fly he could. When we what to do knew not, *you* the Major's message deciphered. *You* this base found. And way I hear it, if not for *your* warning, Draken would others unprepared have caught."

No. The Hue was wrong. None of those proved Renar was capable. They proved he'd manipulate others to survive, that he'd run away at the first sign of trouble leaving others to fight for him. He *was* the General's son, through and through.

Renar turned away, but Unter thrust the sketchbook in his face. "Then this there is."

"An amateur's first attempt at modern art?"

"First *great* attempt," Unter countered. "But no. You raise hand, throw match. Save the life of stranger you know for barely one day."

Renar saw past the crude blobs, the twisty towers, and the random black holes on the sketch. The other team had charged straight at Unter, flinging every spell they could, ignoring the rest of his squad. It was clear that something was wrong, and with one glance at General Iolus' smirking face up in the stadium's VIP box, Renar knew he'd bought their loyalty.

Sparks flew from Unter's suit, flames and astral energy bashing into him from all directions. But his armor didn't lock up. It continued to absorb damage, turning red-hot where the plates met on the Hue's chest. Whether the suit melted or exploded, it wasn't going to end well for the mage inside.

Ich'oth—the Moravi student Sylette had later replaced—hissed for Renar to rush their opponent's open flag. An easy win, one their fans in the stands were practically frothing at the mouth for. And what did he owe the Hue? No one in the Academy seemed too keen on getting chummy with him, and the Commandant had already made his distaste for the foreigner clear.

One second. That was all it had taken for Renar to thrust his hand in the air and shout, *"Renar's Renegades surrender! We give up!"* The ref had immediately called the match to a halt.

In the present, Unter mimicked the motion, raising the notebook high into the snow-filled sky. *"Up we give,* said you. But a different look on your face had you. Defeat not. Loss not. Yes, that is one." He jabbed a finger at Renar. "That is face. A smile. *Victory."*

For in losing that day, Renar had beaten the General. The crowd had booed him, but it didn't matter. He had saved a life. He had gained a friend.

Standing, Renar walked down the steps and leaned over the edge of the pier. The slate gray water was like a mirror, a solid sheet of crystal broken only by the ripples of tiny snowflakes. And in that mirror, he saw his reflection.

Tears stained his cheeks. His eyes were puffy, and his red nose was dripping an unseemly amount of snot. Yet Renar could see nothing but the smile on his lips. He *did* matter. He *could* make a difference, even if he wasn't a mage.

In his mind, Renar made a crude gesture to the Soldier, ignored the apparition's enraged reply, and took a single step back from the abyss. The darkness wasn't gone. It wouldn't disappear overnight, not with the General so near at hand. But Renar no longer desired escape so desperately that he'd take that route.

His reflection shattered. The water beside the pier danced with ripples, started to froth white, then erupted as something massive burst from the sea.

Renar barely had time to scream before the ensuing wave hit him.

Chapter 42

Bekshak

A white-crested wave of frigid water knocked Renar from his feet and stole the breath from his lungs. In an instant, he was sliding across the pier, washing toward the far side like a fish caught in a strong current. Renar scrambled for purchase, trying to catch a mooring ring, a loose block of stone, anything he could.

Chills carved through his flesh, nipping at his veins, purpling his lips. His clothes clung to his flesh like soggy chains. Vision clouding, Renar made a desperate attempt to grab a snow-slick bollard, only to cut his fingers bloody on its rusty surface and go sailing over the edge anyway. He could almost feel the icy embrace of the sea before it reached up to kiss him.

Two of Unter's arms snagged him by the armpits and heaved him back onto the dock. Renar hit hard, gasping in pain. Brackish water spurted from his lips as he tried to speak.

"Breath save," Unter cautioned, smacking his back to force the fluid free.

Renar coughed, trying to rise. He was so, so cold. His vision trembled as he shook. His teeth chattered and he couldn't feel his toes inside his waterlogged boots. Fire and hot soup were all Renar could think of, and if he couldn't have them, he just wanted to curl into a ball right here.

"To go, we need," Unter urged. "*Now.*" He sounded nervous. Worried.

"W-was it Nehalena?" Renar stammered through drawn lips. "Is s-she back to . . . to finish us off?"

His world was dark, blurry, and quivering like a first-time flag-brawl player. Renar thought he saw Unter shake his head and point a short distance past the lighthouse. There was something out there. Long, cylindrical, with a sheen to it like burnished silver. It floated atop the obsidian waters, bobbing back and forth without sinking.

"What i-is it?" Renar asked, craning his neck.

"Later ask."

"B-but—"

Unter placed a palm on his bare neck, chanting, "Num'fleis."

Warmth coursed through Renar's veins as his nerves were

429

numbed, restoring his clarity, taking away his aches and chills. It was an enhancive spell—one he knew well but couldn't cast on himself.

Across the bay, the metal cylinder resolved into a warship, one with a central tower, stubby wings halfway down its length, and a long-barreled cannon mounted on a forward platform. Blue-skinned men wearing sailor whites, black berets, and tall boots were swarming out of an open hatch at the tower's peak.

This was an attack. They were being invaded!

Renar stumbled to his feet, leaning on Unter for support. "We have to get back inside! Warn the others, get Major Reev to organize our defenses."

Unter nodded. Then a rapid *clicking* filled the air, and the Hue sighed. "Too late."

"Katcha, uns fa la niett!"

The strange shout startled Renar, but it was Unter's hand on his shoulder that stopped him mid-flight. He turned and found himself staring down the barrel of the shipboard cannon. One of the soldiers had the deck gun pointed in their direction and was jabbering at them in a language he didn't understand.

"Order us to surrender, he is," Unter said. His blinking was slow, dejected.

Renar glanced at him. "You know what he's saying?"

"Haead, speak they. Or Hue. Tongue of my own."

The soldier shouted again, and Renar stared at him while raising his arms above his head. The cannon he had trained on them was huge, yet he'd swung it around like a toy, two muscular arms on the aiming wheels, one adjusting its scope, the last on its trigger.

Four arms, blue skin, a foreign language. Renar felt like a fool for not realizing the truth sooner. "They're Hues," he whispered out the side of his mouth. No reason to yell and give the cannoneer cause to shoot. "Why in Sariel's name are they here?"

"Soon find out, will we."

Unter tilted his head at the tower. Now that the pier had been 'secured,' two more figures emerged from the hatch and began descending a web of netting to a small dingy crewed by two of the white-uniformed sailors. The boat rocked as they dropped to its deck, and when they straightened, Renar swore they stood a head above their comrades.

Of course, he could just be intimidated by their full plate armor and the heavy shields—each as tall as him—they carried.

430

"Their leaders?" Renar murmured.

Unter blinked twice in short succession: a no. "Ascendant Guard," he said. "Protectors of, say you would . . . *important people.*"

"Like whom?"

His answer came quickly. The next Hue out of the hatch wore a sleek, long-sleeved black uniform trimmed with gold lace. He was large, but not so large as Unter or the Ascendant Guardsmen, and had silver hair and a well-trimmed beard where all his soldiers were bare-scalped and clean-shaven. Control and dignity oozed from him as he gazed around the harbor like a conquering hero.

He immediately stooped, extended his arm back into the ship, and withdrew the slender, white-gloved arm of a beautiful Hue woman. She climbed onto the platform with grace, descended the netting with effortless ease, and alighted on the dingy without making a splash. Every soldier or sailor she passed dropped to one knee and didn't rise until the train of her long yellow gown had slithered by.

Where Unter was broad, she was toned and petite. Where Unter's arms were built like stone slabs, she was lithe and supple. Her chin was pointed, her cheekbones sharp as the reefs around her vessel, and gleaming black hair jetted from her scalp in a single braid that stretched halfway down her cerulean back.

Renar's fingers twitched. Though he had a gun aimed at him, though he was faced with several dozen hostile soldiers, he wanted nothing more than to sketch this woman. For an instant, the darkness was gone. Inspiration flooded his head, fire blazed in his veins, and Renar came *alive.*

Only . . . Unter had his notebook.

He turned to his friend, and his request died on his lips. The Hue was limping down the pier, heading for the narrow jetty that jutted toward the strange warship. He was moving faster than before, leaving long drag marks in the snow with his injured left leg, hastening toward some objective Renar could only guess at.

In the harbor, the dingy cast off, ferrying the Haead noblewoman toward that same jetty. If nothing were done, Unter would meet her the second she stepped on the dock. Was there history here? Some secret the blue giant had never confided to Renar?

"Ja ilga reht fa nu, Katcha!" the gunner roared, tracking Unter with the cannon.

Whatever he said, Unter didn't slow or turn from his course. If anything, he sped up, breaking into an awkward half-run, half-shamble.

431

Renar didn't hesitate. He rushed after his friend, waving his arms, screaming loud enough to wake a Draken. "Stop, Unter! He's going to shoot!"

"Las wargan, Katcha!"

Unter didn't respond to either of them. He bent his head and dashed around the bend, hopping the two small steps joining the pier to the jetty.

The force and sound of the shell firing struck Renar's chest before the round exploded against the limestone cliffs. Rock splinters flew in all directions. Whole chunks splashed into the churning waves. A gasp of flame shot skyward, and an extra layer of smoke settled over the bay.

Warning or simple miss, Renar wasn't keen for them to get another chance to shoot. And apparently, the Hues weren't either. The black-uniformed officer jumped from the tower, landed on the metal deck with a thump, and charged the cannoneer. Grabbing him by the collar, the officer threw him aside and started shouting at him while pointing at the noblewoman in the dingy.

His message was clear: *Don't voiding shoot anywhere near our mistress.*

The small launch cut its engines and coasted to a stop alongside the jetty. Two sailors hopped out—one fore, one aft—and began securing the ship with mooring ropes. A small entourage followed: the two Ascendant Guardsmen, a slim male with a bundled pennant in his arms, and a skeletal male hauling a length of rolled-up carpet almost as thick around as he was.

The guardsmen noticed Unter and Renar, but they only seemed concerned with him. One reached behind his massive shield and hefted a long rifle whose stock wrapped around his forearm like a gauntlet. Its barrel was pointed at Renar's chest in a matter of seconds.

"Halt!" he yelled in garbled Common.

Renar obliged, skidding to a stop. A thousand thoughts swirled through his mind. *What's Unter doing? Why aren't they stopping him? Is it just because he's a Hue, or were they expecting him?*

You don't trust your friend, the Soldier said, laughing. *You were right about Sylette, so go with your gut. Accept that he'll betray you too.*

The gaunt male, dressed only in a simple white shift that left his sides exposed, grunted as he heaved his carpet forward. It unfolded down the length of the jetty, continuing until Unter stopped it with a raised boot. Stepping over the mound of fabric, he kept walking toward his kin.

Don't go, Renar thought, heart beginning to crack.

The second guardsman produced a pole, and the pennant was tied to it and raised into the air. Snow-laced wind caught the fabric, unfurling it into a banner Renar didn't recognize: a balanced gold scale on a blue field, coins evenly stacked on both hanging plates.

Please come back.

Renar caught a glimpse of jet-black hair in the dingy. One guard shoved aside the skeletal male, while the other reached into the dingy and helped the noblewoman onto the jetty. As soon as both she and her dress were safely on land, all of the Hues once again dropped to their knees. Awe shone on their downturned faces. Awe, worship, and *fear*.

I need you. Please . . . please come back.

The thought faded as Renar narrowed his eyes, left his mouth hanging just a *bit* too open. One Hue wasn't kneeling. One Hue wasn't throwing himself at this woman's feet or losing himself to reverence.

Unter marched straight up to the Hue woman, who raised a dark eyebrow at his defiance. He smiled in reply.

"Hello, Taala, my dearest sister."

"Hello, Taala, my dearest sister."

Unter barely kept the tears inside, tears his brethren would only see as weakness. How he'd longed for this moment. To see Taala of clan Lyadrin fully grown, a beautiful, graceful woman bending her immense talents to the good of the Ascendancy.

She still had that same black mark above her lip he'd joked about when she was a child. The braids in her hair were their mother's style made over, and her ebony eyes—so full, so deep—had all the kindness of their father in them.

This was the Taala he'd dreamed of meeting, if only under different circumstances.

Realization flashed across her face like a storm, marring her beauty, twisting her lips into a snarl. Two hands leapt for the gilded sash at her waist, eager to draw the curved blades hanging there.

"*Bekshak!*" Taala cursed.

Then she spat in Unter's face.

433

He made no move to wipe it away, nor did he raise his arms to block or retaliate. To do so was instant death for a Bekshak, and he would more than likely meet his end anyway. Right now, protecting the Terran at his back—protecting his new clan—was all that mattered.

Shields slammed on stone as the Ascendant Guards rushed to flank their mistress. Two wicked scimitars appeared in the hands of one, while the other swung his rifle away from Renar and onto him. Good. That was one less gun aimed at his friend.

"Why here, Taala?" Unter asked. "What Ascendancy want?"

She hissed again, baring her sharp teeth. "Only Haead may use that name, Bekshak. You dishonor me with your presence, with that vile tongue you use. After what you did, it is only by the benevolence of the Prime Factor you still draw breath."

Taala spoke in Hesed. It sounded like a sweet lullaby to Unter's ears, melodic despite the rage in her tone. He wished he could join her, but they'd cut out his tongue for trying.

"Grace to Vida for that breath," he praised, pressing his palms together in prayer.

The Guardsmen growled. "Let us kill him, Adjudicator!" one said. "He slings filth on both your good name and that of our goddess."

One of Taala's arms rose in the air, and when it fell, Unter would die. They didn't need an excuse to execute a Bekshak—an exile, an outcast. His very existence was a sin.

"Or . . . " Taala's voice emerged as a raspy whisper. "We could shame you further."

Unter followed her eyes to her slave, the sheet-clothed male with sunken eyes and ribs that pressed against his skin like blades. If only his malnourishment and the purple bruises he wore like tattoos were the worst they had done to him.

Both his upper arms were gone, the flesh at the joints puckered and scarred by burns. He was crippled. The mark of his shame clear for all to see.

"I suffer not Castrati," Unter said. "Sooner die. Sooner off pier jump."

His sister nodded. Callous though Taala was, she would spare him that indignity. Perhaps, buried deep under her mask of contempt, she loved him still.

But not enough to defy their customs. Taala's arm started to fall, her men leaning forward, eager to cut him down.

"I Darmatia clan serve now!" Unter yelled.

Her arm jerked to a stop. "You dare flee your fate, Bekshak? You wish to heap the stigma of cowardice on top of the crimes you have already committed?"

The words stung. Unter was no Bekshak, and he was no coward. Any crimes he had committed were void before the gods, and he'd gladly indulge in them again. No just deity would ever declare the bond he'd shared with Jesrah a sin.

But to go silently to his end would endanger Renar, who even now huddled against one of the pier's support pillars, unwilling to abandon Unter though fear was writ large on his quiet features. Taala glanced at the Terran, a wicked sneer ruining her gorgeous face. Yes, she'd already bound their fates together. If he perished, so would Renar.

"I but of you think, of Ascendancy," Unter said, treading carefully. "Kingdom like us not. Laws have, but none so strict as Bekshak or Castrati. Me kill, Terran kill, red pall over negotiations cast. Plus, injured am I." He slowly shifted one of his lower arms, pointing at his blackened calf. "No honor in such kill."

"Bekshak have no honor, so honor need not be afforded to them."

Taala moved her arm. But instead of swinging it like a headsman's axe, she lowered it to her side. "I cannot let you roam free," she said, voice softening. "I am an Adjudicator now—an agent of the Prime Factor and her Assembly. And the law is clear: any Bekshak encountered outside our borders must die. As Vida cast them aside … "

"So shall she collect them back," her subordinates said as one. Unter knew the saying well. The scales of the Veneer Vida must be balanced, whether they be those of the Ascendant Bank or those of life and death.

Taking a deep breath, Unter pounded all four of his fists to his chest. "Then request I the Trial of Scales."

The scimitar-wielding guard stepped toward him, blades raised. "A clanless cur cannot demand the Trial. You do nothing but deepen your disgrace with every word you speak."

"Part of Darmatia clan am I. Them deny"—Unter blinked amusement—"is same as denying mission here."

Taala snorted, but her eyes blinked the same pattern he had. "Who says I'm here to parley with the Darmatian rebels?"

"Out here, who else there is?"

The echo of their voices bouncing off the cliffs answered them, as did the swirling snow, dark seas, and the biting chill his magic kept at bay. The lighthouse watched over them, silent as a sentinel, and not a single airship disturbed the skies above.

A small glint on the plateau caught Unter's eye, a flash of glass directed at his face. Something moved in front of the glare, clipping it into long and short bursts of light—a code he'd learned at the Academy.

Watcher gone to get aid. Will return ASAP. Hold out for help. Delay.

One of Major Reev's scouts was watching them, observing the situation while waiting on reinforcements. Well, Unter would do exactly as they asked:

Survive as long as he could.

"I cede the point, Bekshak," Taala said. Her blinking shifted, becoming slow, resigned. "You shall have your Trial, and I shall have my execution."

"Believe me . . . you do?" Unter said. He'd thought she'd declare him a liar, kill him, and then try to explain the mishap to Major Reev or General Iolus later.

Taala tapped her right eye, which changed colors in rapid succession. Red, blue, green, yellow, and finally back to black. "Bekshak lie as easily as they breathe. It is second nature. Yet my Alteration says you speak truly. For that, I will honor the honorless and grant your final request."

And she believes I have no honor, Unter lamented, staring at his sister's false eye as it flashed like a telescriber screen flicking on and off. Was the device reading his heat signature? Tracking the subtlest hint of motion, searching for a nervous tic?

It was a dark sign—a sign that the Alters were gaining power in the Haead capital. For a high-ranking Adjudicator to bear a magtech implant meant that the Haead definition of perfection had changed. That rather than attempting to better their surroundings with magtech, they had at last given in to the allure of desecrating the sacred bodies Vida had bestowed on them.

How long had he been gone?

And what else had Taala done to her precious flesh?

"Don't look so sad," Taala mocked, misinterpreting the sorrow in his gaze. "Death is a release for your kind. I shall be gracious and even let you choose the Guardsman who will deliver your soul to the Afterplane."

He jabbed a finger at the rifle-armed guard. Muscles bulged in the gaps between his armor plates, but his arms were short and the top of his helmet only reached Unter's nose. Grinning, the guard holstered his rifle and dropped his shield. It landed with a thud that cracked the end of the jetty, knocking fragments of stone into the harbor.

A thought occurred to Unter, one only an older brother would be concerned with. "Mated, are you? Maybe one of these?" He waved at the Guardsmen.

Taala chuckled and shook her head. "No. But like a Bekshak who tried to reach beyond their station, they wish they could be with me."

She went right for his oldest, deepest wound. Then, with a parting smirk, she turned and marched to the end of the pier, her servants and slaves trailing behind, careful to avoid the long train of her elegant gown.

Unter and his opponent were left glaring at each other.

"Bekshak, I formally challenge you to ritual combat," the guard growled, voice like a rockslide slathered in condescension.

Unter blinked acceptance. "Under Vida's solemn gaze, charges state."

"You are Bekshak," the guard spat, gauntlets clinking as his fingers clenched and unclenched. "You spurned our laws. You defiled our motherland. And then you ran, fleeing the justice you were due. What need have we of charges?"

Once, Unter would have agreed with him. Blindly, frothing at the mouth, and ready to dispense his mistress' judgment without any consideration of his own.

The old him had been a fool.

"Your witness?" Unter asked.

The guardsman raised his arms and a deafening roar erupted from the Haead warship. Several dozen sailors crowded the rounded deck, sitting on the gun platform, hanging from the netting. After weeks at sea, they were looking forward to a fight.

"Yours?"

Unter waved at Renar, who didn't seem to understand what was happening. "Terran friend watch for me."

"*Friend?*" Beneath his helm, the guardsman's lips twisted in a grimace. "To call an outsider friend . . . You have truly fallen far, Bekshak. Worse than a magic-drunk crimson witch, perhaps."

Ignoring the slight, Unter held up one of his fists. "With these, fight we. No weapons. No armor." The Trial of Scales granted the one challenged the right to select the method of combat, and he'd be at a disadvantage without a weapon. Fighting bare-handed was his best chance.

"Good. Wouldn't be much fun fighting a wounded dog otherwise." His foe pointed at Unter's venom-scoured calf, the skin splotched with dark, creeping sores.

The soldier set about discarding his armor, removing plates that thunked to the pier like cannon rounds. His ek-skin belt followed, along with a padded gambeson and a sweat-stained tunic. When he was down to his trousers, the guardsman grabbed four handfuls of snow, smashed them to his naked blue chest, then bellowed at his comrades on the ship. They cheered him, stamping their feet, baying for Unter's blood.

"Interfere not, Renar" he called over his shoulder. If the Terran moved—if he tried to help his friend in any way—Unter knew Taala would kill him.

"Ready to die, Bekshak?" the guardsman taunted, circling right, bouncing on the balls of his feet.

Unter mirrored him, maintaining his distance while studying his opponent. Scars covered his arms and torso. The worst was a jagged slash from his left shoulder to his opposite hip, a wound that could have been delivered by blade or beast. He held his arms up, palms out, and kept his right foot forward. His sneer was arrogant, but his stance was strong.

This was a veteran. A man who'd been killing when Unter was standing guard outside the Assembly hall, drinking with his friends, and chasing after the one who'd doomed him. Down a leg, he stood no chance unless his foe made a mistake.

"What name?" Unter asked suddenly.

The guardsman blinked confusion. His movements slowed, and he stopped bouncing. Combatants never spoke during the Trial of Scales, and no one would shame themselves by giving a Bekshak their name.

Unter used the opening to charge, a stumbling lunge off his good leg. His foe blocked high. Unter dove low and drove his shoulder into the guardsman's gut.

Breath whooshed from his lungs, and they went sliding backward toward Taala and her attendants. With his head under his foe's armpit, Unter could see her disdain writ in bared teeth and smoldering eyes.

"You cheating cur!" she snarled.

At her side, the other guard drew his rifle and aimed it not at Unter, but past him—at Renar. By law, they couldn't interfere with two Haead engaged in a Trial. Their fates would be decided by the gods.

A Terran hanger-on, however, was fair game.

Two fists pounded on Unter's back, attempting to dislodge him. He staggered under the blows, letting them drive him down. Then he let his left leg buckle entirely. The next strike glanced off his falling shoulder, and his opponent staggered left. Right into the line of fire.

The sharp staccato of a gunshot rang out across the harbor. Unter glanced back, watched Renar reel to the side. But he wasn't hit, just frightened. Small shards of stone tumbled from a bullet hole in the pillar beside him. At the last second, the guard had jerked his rifle to the side to avoid hitting his comrade.

"*Hide!*" Unter yelled. Nodding vigorously, Renar dived behind the pillar, shielding himself from Taala's sniper.

Light exploded across Unter's vision. He released the guardsman and lurched away, hands raised, head spinning. Another punch came in, but this time he managed to take it on the forearm instead of the ear.

"Forget about me, Bekshak?"

The guardsman kicked low, aiming at Unter's injured calf. He went to one knee. Took it on the thigh, then scrambled a few steps farther down the jetty. The area around his chest wound was starting to ache, each breath a little harder, a little fierier, than the last. Velle's magic had healed Unter's wounds as best it could, but the scars—both inside and out—remained.

Through his swimming vision, he watched Taala raise her arm again. In response, the deck gun on the ship cranked toward Renar. A stone pillar wouldn't stop an artillery round.

"If he touches those steps," she roared, pointing at the spot the two sections of the pier met, "blast his Terran pet to dust."

"What should we have expected?" the guardsman mocked, pursuing him. "He is Bekshak. Coward. To think he'd honor the Trial was foolish."

Three paces to the stairs.

Unter turned aside a strike at his face, retaliating with a high-low combination to the ribs and throat. Four arms made fist-fighting easy . . . except when your enemy could match you blow for blow.

The guardsman deflected both attacks, then launched another kick at the same spot. Unter screamed as it met his knee. Something popped, and he retreated again, barely able to stay upright. He held out his hands, trembling, begging.

"Please . . . " Unter gasped. "Me spare, please . . . "

One step to the stairs.

Laughing, the guardsman aimed a third kick at Unter's injury. It was fortunate he had a bit of a sadistic streak. Otherwise, Unter's plan wouldn't have worked.

As the leg swept in, Unter lunged forward to meet it, grimacing from the pain lancing through his calf. He caught it with two arms and locked it to his side. Strikes immediately rained on his bent head, shoulders, and back, but his foe was off-balance. Stumbling on his pivot leg, he couldn't put any real power into his punches.

"Let me go!" the guardsman shrieked.

Unter obliged. Surging upright, howling at the agony blazing through his body, Unter lashed out with his right side arms as the guardsman toppled like a dead tree. He didn't punch. He *pushed*. And that push was just enough to spin the screaming soldier over the edge of the pier.

Water splashed. The screams cut off, replaced by flailing arms and churning white bubbles. Unter looked to Taala, who crossed her arms while gazing at the spot where her champion was floundering in the frigid waters. He saw not a shred of pity in her eyes.

"Won have I, sister," Unter declared.

She gestured at a thrashing blue arm, desperately clawing at the frost-rimed side of the jetty. "The Trial hasn't ended. You both still live."

Unter blinked disbelief. "He soldier yours. You serve. Toss his life away, you would?"

"Our laws are absolute. He lost to a Bekshak. His life is already over."

Ignoring the jeers of the sailors, ignoring his pain and common sense, Unter dove flat on his belly and thrust an arm into the water. At first, he found nothing. The surface was stilling, the guardsman's struggles weakening.

Then strong fingertips burrowed into his forearm. Unter latched on to the soldier in the same manner and heaved with all the strength he had left. A gasping face cleared the surface, spraying water everywhere, while another arm reached for the pier's lip.

But even pulling together, it wasn't enough. The guardsman started to slip, his chin sinking, his eyes blinking panic. Where they gripped the stone slabs, Unter's other fingers began to ache and bleed. If he didn't let go, they were both going to the depths.

"Renar!" Unter yelled. "Me help! Now!"

Without a moment's hesitation, the Terran broke cover and sprinted toward them. There was fear in his gaze. In the haste of his breath, the twitch of his lips. Yet still, his best friend came. For *him*.

This is my clan now, Unter thought, grinning and grimacing in equal measure. *My* true *clan.*

"Shoot him!" Taala ordered.

440

The guardsman beside her raised his rifle, sighted on the running Terran, and . . .

"*STOP!*"

The booming voice of Major Reev echoed from the top of the plateau, but Unter couldn't turn to look. Out of the corner of his eye, he saw Taala frown. Then, with obvious reluctance, she placed a hand on her guardsman's weapon and pushed its barrel down.

Renar skidded to a stop, flopped to his knees, and hooked an arm under the drowning Haead's other shoulder. He gasped as his flesh touched the freezing water, a sign that Unter's spell had worn off, but kept tugging until they deposited a panting, shivering guardsman at the feet of his former mistress.

"A-Adjudicator . . . I'm sorry . . . I . . . " he mumbled, skin turning an unhealthy shade of blue as he crawled toward his discarded garments. Unter pitied him, for he knew what was coming. What he had condemned him to by saving a life claimed by the Trial.

Taala kicked him in the face with the jagged tip of her laced-up shoe, breaking his nose, spraying blood across an undisturbed patch of snow. "*You* are Bekshak now. You will leave my sight, and the next time I see you, you will die."

"Trouble with your men?"

Unter turned toward the Ice Queen but didn't rise or salute. He didn't have the energy, and hopefully the Ice Queen would understand.

Major Reev marched toward them along the pier, a contingent of armed Kingdom soldiers at her back. She wore her full naval dress uniform, medals pinned to her chest, a ceremonial saber clanking against her hip. Her dark hair spilled from beneath a red beret bearing her rank insignia.

Though the Major was dressed for a military ball, her pursed lips and flinty eyes suggested she'd much rather freeze everything for several leagues.

"A minor dispute," Taala said, smiling. Her Common was clipped and precise—not a stutter, no hint of an accent. "A matter pertaining to Ascendancy Law. Nothing you need concern yourself with, Major Jis Reev."

The Ice Queen raised an eyebrow. "It concerns me when two of my men"—she waved at Unter and Renar—"are assaulted by a foreign delegation. Since you know who I am and what I can do, give me one good reason I shouldn't seal your ship in a block of ice."

Taala's smile deepened. And though Major Reev wouldn't

understand, Unter saw his sister blinking amusement. In the Ascendancy, politics were a game, and she was enjoying herself.

The callous Adjudicator who had consumed his compassionate sister raised a gloved hand, palm open in offering. "I would suggest you didn't, Major. If you did, I wouldn't be able to cast your faltering rebellion a rope from the heavens."

"A rope?" Major Reev snorted.

"Indeed. For if you accept my terms, my country will do everything in its power to grant you victory against the Sarconian Empire."

Chapter 43
Hangman's Bargain

Silence reigned in General Hardwick Iolus' pavilion, a stillness broken only by the crackling of a small wood fire stove in the corner, the sloshing of liquor in the bottle Colonel Rodale Holcomb was sucking like a babe at the teat, and the fraying of Jis' patience. Each strand snapped with a twang that made her head throb, and it took every bit of self-control she had *not* to snatch the flask and throw it into the flames.

"Refreshments!" General Iolus said suddenly, clapping his hands. "How could I be so inconsiderate? We can't start our talks without a good drink."

Jis glared at Rodale, who was already partaking of the Void's nectar. Why was the lush even at this meeting? He'd worn a set of *slightly* less stained uniform-robes, complete with pants, but hadn't bothered to fix his matted curls or hide the rings around his eyes.

Bowing to their guest, General Iolus rose from the table at which they sat—stained darkwood inlaid with traces of sparkling Darmatian silver—and crossed to his fully stocked wine cabinet, one of many luxuries secreted away in his private quarters. His other excesses included a canopy bed and feather mattress, exotic carpets adorned with mandalas, and an unlit brazier surrounded by vials of aromatic oils.

Jis took a deep breath. Reminded herself it was natural to try to impress foreign dignitaries. If only the bloated fool, strutting around with more metal on his uniform than a rifle squad had bullets, cared half as much about his hungry soldiers.

"Is a 627 Seylan red to your liking, Adjudicator Lyadrin?" Iolus asked, stooping to reach the lower shelves. "Or perhaps a 614 Evenacht rose? It might be Imperial made, but I hear the eastern vineyards are second to none."

Adjudicator Taala Lyadrin waved dismissively. "I must decline. I never indulge during official Ascendancy business."

The Hue ambassador sat straight in her chair, four arms folded in her lap. General Iolus had been forced to cede his cushioned high-back seat—more a throne, really—to her since no other chair could contain her height. Even seated, the drooping tent ceiling was but a few hand spans short of her ring-bound ebony braid.

Taala's demeanor was calm, aloof, and self-assured. Though she only had two guardsmen stationed outside the entrance flaps, everything about her said *she* was in control. The plunging neckline of her silk dress, exposing a swathe of cerulean skin, leaving little to the imagination. Her willingness to surrender her weapons to her attendants. Taala expected the Resistance to do exactly what she wanted—perhaps even *beg* her for it by the end of negotiations.

Hefting a bottle of blood-red wine, General Iolus walked to his desk and tipped open the lid of a small, ornate mahogany box. "A cigar, then? Trillith make, imported straight from Badlands caravans."

"Are they always so presumptuous?" Taala asked, turning to Jis.

She blinked. "Excuse me?"

Taala pointed at the General, wine in one hand, a cigar in the other. "This one is a male, and yet he takes your place at the head of the table and raids your private stashes. The one across from me is worse." Her other upper arm flicked a finger at Rodale. "He didn't rise when you entered, drinks without permission, and reeks worse than a brood of males kept in a prison pit for weeks on end. Why do you not whip them for their insolence?"

As if on cue, Rodale leaned back, slung his boots onto the table, and belched loud enough to wake Darmatus' departed spirit.

"See?" Taala scoffed.

Rodale slammed his bottle on the table so hard Jis thought it would shatter. "Well slap Artyr's hindquarters and give scaly Reshal a sloppy kiss. It looks like miss prim and proper don't know how things work around here. That's the head honcho"—he jerked a thumb over his shoulder at a red-faced, seething Hardwick Iolus—"and I'm his number two. Pretty little Jis here works for us."

Taala's mask of composure flickered, eyes blinking rapidly as she pressed against the back of her chair. "Is this true?" she whispered.

"Yes," Jis admitted. "But I can assure you our unit is still capable of fighting the Sarconians. General Iolus trained many of our nation's best officers, and Rodale . . . " She trailed off as he winked at her and blew a kiss.

"Not a ringing endorsement. Even in your . . . *backwards* gender system"—Taala spat the phrase like a wad of poison—"I can't fathom why your leaders would elevate such pitiful stock to positions of power. One is lost in his cups and dresses like a tramp, the other can't see his toes over his bloated gut. *You* are a national hero. A powerful mage. Why don't you simply freeze them and their stones and be done with it?"

A question I ask myself every day, Jis thought, trying to keep her

444

magic from manifesting. She wanted to shoot an icicle through Rodale's half-empty bottle and splatter its contents all over his too-smug face. She wanted to trap General Iolus in a cell of ice before his temper erupted and he buried any possible alliance between their people.

Instead, Jis leaned forward, clasped her hands on the table, and said, "I trust in the decisions of our Council and the Steward we elected."

"Ha!" Taala didn't bother to restrain her laughter. "That Council is now deposed, and that Steward is imprisoned. They sent your fleet to perish at Aldona, after which most of them fled your capital in disgrace—every *man* for themselves."

"Flight seems like a pretty stellar option right now," Rodale said. "I'd join them if Ms. Ice-For-Eyes over here wouldn't turn me soprano for vamoosing. Like that. See?"

He jabbed the mouth of his bottle at Jis, around whom pinpricks of ice were beginning to sparkle. Frost spread from her hands, coating the lacquered wood in a thin white layer. She urged herself to breathe. To focus on the future. But it was impossible with these two men, both of whom continued to ruin her life and career.

Taala stood. "I think I've heard enough. Under present leadership, the Ascendancy cannot broker any deal with your . . . " She shook her head. "No, this isn't an army. It's a pack of swine rutting in the seaside muck. I shall inform the Prime Factor she was wrong to expect otherwise."

That was that. Jis bowed her head, closed her eyes, and began running potential scenarios in her mind. In some of them, the Resistance was discovered by the Empire and wiped out. In others, they ran out of supplies and starved, or disease ravaged their dwindling numbers.

The worst was the one where they gave up. Where the soldiers decided a quiet life was worth shouldering the Empire's tyranny and simply . . . drifted away, deserting their country and what she stood for. Deserting Jis and her dreams.

"Please hold a moment, Adjudicator."

Jis glanced up. General Iolus was standing beside the table, palms out, his wine and cigar abandoned on his desk. He shot a glare at Rodale, who removed his feet from the table with a roll of his eyes.

"I understand we haven't made the best impression," Iolus said.

Taala snorted. "That's putting it mildly."

"Even so," he paused, his throat bulging like he was having trouble swallowing. Pride could be sticky like that. "Even so, we haven't abandoned Darmatia. We want to save her—for the sake of our people, for the good of those the Empire is all too willing to cast aside. And *I'm willing to make changes to see that happen.*"

Iolus looked at Jis and *smiled.* He'd never favored her with anything kinder than a frown. And to be honest, it was pretty revolting. Like a vilewart-frog puffing up its cheeks before mating.

"Major Jis Reev is a trusted advisor," Iolus continued, "as well as a brilliant military mind and a heroic mage. She is completely indispensable to our operations here. But if it will set your mind at ease, Adjudicator, I will put her in charge of all interactions with you and the Ascendancy. Including"—he took a deep breath, as though the fresh air would clear away the ego rotting in his belly—"our negotiations today."

As Taala swung her gaze toward Jis, one thought echoed over and over again in her head: *What is Hardwick Iolus playing at?*

Outwardly, she nodded. The ice in the stale pavilion air and near her hands faded away. "It would be my honor to work directly with you, Adjudicator."

With a sigh, Taala swept the train of her gown aside and resumed her seat.

"Yes it is."

"Stop that!" Jis growled as she smacked Rodale's hand away. "It's not a toy."

He'd been flicking it in and out of the map covering the table, watching the ghostly blue mountains, forests, and streams reform around his fingers and arms. Its source was a tiny orb the size of the nail on Jis' pinkey—a pebble capable of projecting a full three-dimensional map of Darmatia and its surrounding territories.

"What did you call this technology?" General Iolus asked, turning to Adjudicator Lyadrin.

"I didn't call it anything," she replied, her lips turned up in a coy grin.

The orb had been encased in a bead on her gown's neckline, a storage space none of them had thought to look for weapons or secrets. Jis couldn't help wondering what else was hidden on her person. Or just how far the Hues eclipsed the rest of the continent in magtech research.

Taala snapped her fingers. In an instant, a rush of red light spilled down from the north, thrusting through the Theradas Pass, spreading through Darmatia like creeping vines. Seconds later, the entire nation was an angry crimson, and a tiny banner bearing the Sarconian crest rose out of a large dot labeled *Nemare*.

"Are the theatrics necessary?" Jis asked. Her blood boiled at the sight of her country's swift capitulation.

"I'm making a point," Taala said. "If you do nothing, this is your future."

"We'd have to wear red?" Rodale covered his mouth in mock surprise. "I'm much better with cool colors. They highlight my beard and hair. But if I have to switch, I will. It'd be much harder to see the wine stains."

Jis sent a wave of frost-dappled mist his way, which made the drunk clutch his robes to his chest and purse his trembling lips. "We understand our circumstances all too well." She waved at the pavilion around them—a small slice of heaven in the middle of a subterranean pit. "What we *need* is advice on how to fix them."

"It won't be easy." Another input, a twirl of two long blue fingers, sent a red wave crashing into the neighboring Imperium. "They have Nemare, your synth-oil reserves at Dusan, the illyrium shale mines at Kharit, and are even now pushing into Rabban. If they can strike hard and fast at the Imperium's capital, the war will be over."

"So we"—Taala tapped the Etrus Canal, the waterway that doubled as the border between the Kingdom and Ascendancy—"need to start a second front. Draw their forces away from the east, give the Rabbanite armies at Varas Fortress time to breathe."

General Iolus cupped his chin, massaging the loose skin there. He didn't seem to realize anyone was watching. "How long until the Prime Factor is ready to strike? Can you give me troop numbers? Fleet strength? Do you have a diagram of your projected invasion plans?"

"Sir . . . " Jis started, then shut her mouth.

Those *were* excellent questions—the kind she expected from a veteran field commander, not a desk jockey like Iolus. Was this the same man who'd once stood in front of her tactics class and told them the side that struck harder and faster would win?

Taala chuckled. "Her Eminence would hardly trust a band of drunks—"

"Guilty," Rodale said, raising his hand.

"—and dregs with that information."

That condescending laugh of hers was *seriously* wearing on Jis' nerves. If she heard it one more time . . . "How do you expect us to coordinate our efforts, then?"

"You'll take refuge in the Ascendancy after"—Taala placed two fingers on the Etrus region and pushed them outward, magnifying the topography beneath—"you pass a test."

"You must be joking."

"Hardly." Taala cocked her head, exposing her long, slender neck. "Let me ask you a few questions, Major."

Jis dropped back onto the wobbly stool that was her seat. If the General had something better hidden away, he hadn't brought it out on her account. "I'm all ears, *Adjudicator*."

Taala smiled and steepled her fingers. "Who runs the Ascendancy?"

"The Prime Factor and the Assembly."

"And who do they work for?"

"Wouldn't you know better than I would?"

"A question can't answer a question," Taala said, clicking her tongue. "I'll have to mark that down as incorrect, Ms. Former Professor."

"The Ascendant Bank," General Iolus said.

His interjection came barely a moment before Jis tossed the fate of the Kingdom in the proverbial waste heap and made a haughty ice sculpture out of the good ambassador. It would have felt *oh-so-wonderful* ... and been *oh-so-foolish*. Were the cadets rubbing off on her?

Taala nodded like a schoolteacher. "Precisely. And the Bank is only interested in making profitable investments. Tell me," she glanced over her shoulder at the tent flap, beneath which the muddy cavern floor was visible, "do homeless soldiers living in caves sound like a good investment?"

"With Sondek's sizzling scrotum as my witness, I'd take those odds," Rodale said, pulling a greasy bronze geldar from a pocket. "Give me the rogues, ruffians, and scamps over those tight-arse Sarcs any day." He rolled the coin toward Taala across the map.

Enough, Jis decided.

Snatching the coin off the table mid-roll, she flung it back at Rodale. He hissed as its frosted surface struck his cheek, leaving behind a red welt. "Out!" Jis roared, pointing at the tent flap.

Rodale's lower lip trembled, liquor-clouded eyes darting between her and the geldar bobbling on the table. It had landed tails side up, Sariel's lance pointed toward his heart.

"What? But I ... I didn't mean to ... "

"Out," Jis repeated, words dripping frost. "You are a disgrace to this army, Colone—*no* ... " She shook her head. " ... *Holcomb*. You don't deserve your rank. You aren't worthy of the men you lead. I've tolerated your betrayals, deceits, and vices because somehow, some way, I thought you might redeem yourself. That here, at the end—when the nation and I both needed you—you would change.

Jis' voice dropped to a whisper. "I was wrong. So . . . get out. You're not ruining Darmatia's last hope like you ruined us."

Life fled Rodale. His shoulders slumped, the grease in his beard seeming to ooze toward the floor along with the rest of him. Slowly, he cast his sunken gaze toward General Iolus, begging, pleading for aid.

Iolus coughed. "Surely Colonel Holcomb could still contribute to—"

"*My* negotiation, remember," Jis said, raising a hand toward Taala. "*My* rules."

The Adjudicator nodded, her smirk that of a spider ensnaring its prey. One less male at the table, one less headache for them both to deal with.

General Iolus sighed, chins sagging atop his stubby neck. "You're dismissed, Colonel Holcomb," he said, gesturing toward the exit.

Rodale didn't look back, didn't protest. He slumped from the room like a man headed to the gallows, back bent, steps heavy. Would he think about his mistakes? Reflect on what he'd done, what he'd almost cost them?

No. He drowned his past in drink, blaming anyone but himself for his faults. *That* was the Rodale who'd abandoned Jis, leaving her to clean up his mess.

He had no reason to change now.

"That was the first smart thing you've done," Taala said, dragging Jis' attention from the closed tent flap. How long had she been staring at it?

"I did what needed to be done," she replied, banishing the crystal vestiges floating around her head. "Please continue."

"We do not *gamble* as that . . . foolish male suggested." Taala smiled, revealing jagged, sharpened teeth. "We pick *victors*. The countries, leaders, and movements we think will one day rule Lozaria. Then we give them a push. A nudge in the right direction, so that when they succeed, we succeed. And we have picked a great many victors over the years, Major."

Her obsidian eyes narrowed into slits. "You do *not* want us as an enemy."

Like it or not, the Adjudicator was right. Supplies were dwindling. Morale was low and would continue to plummet as food and spirits became scarcer. If they were going to strike a blow against the Empire, it had to fall *now*—while Jis could still take advantage of the Triaron and what he represented.

Gun at their back, noose dangling ahead. Jis hadn't seen a worse deal in her whole life.

She wiped her eyes, straightened her uniform, and waved at the shimmering hills and forests of the Etrus region. "We'll take your hangman's bargain, Adjudicator. Tell us what we need to do, and we'll give you your victory."

One slender finger tipped with a tar-black nail reached out and traced a lazy circle around the canal's mouth, within which sat a tiny white dot.

Etrus: the coastal gem, beloved of fishers and traders alike, home to one of the finest meat markets in the Kingdom.

"Take this city," Taala said.

And soon to become a warzone.

Chapter 44

Failure No More

Adamantele 8, 697 ABH
Resistance Base, Sarconian Province of Darmatia

Renar walked the path to the executioner's block with fists clenched and head held high. This time, things would be different.

The colors of his life were back. Bright oranges and yellows lit the braziers outside the pavilion, casting twisting shadows on the marble white canvas. Subdued blues trimmed with red hung tiredly from two guards hunched over their rifles. Even the muted gray of the cavern stones seemed livelier, as though the rocks were lanterns whose flames had been hidden for far too long.

Stepping to the side, Corporal Sayles waved at the tent flap. Neither guard straightened nor made any move to block them. They might as well have been cast from stone themselves.

"Go in whenever you're ready, sir," she said, raising her fingers to her shock of blond hair in salute.

Renar didn't bother reminding her that cadets weren't officers. He returned her salute and matched her smile with his own. "Thank you."

Yes, things would be different. The Soldier had fallen silent, trapped with his despair behind a frail wall built from Unter's compassion and encouragement. Yet the rest of his darkness lay on the other side of that strip of canvas. Renar needed to face it.

Only then could he slay the Soldier.

Only then could he be *free*.

When Sayles departed, Renar grabbed the tent flap and flung it aside without hesitation. A wall of incense struck him as he stepped inside. Cloying and strong, the scent forced its way down his throat, making him gag. He swung his hands as he stumbled deeper into the tent, trying in vain to clear the air.

"General?" Renar called, squinting into the mist.

"Here!"

The man who owned him lurched into view from behind his wine cabinet, a mostly empty bottle in one hand, a pile of smoking leaves in

451

another. He cast the latter at his smoldering brazier, but most scattered across his Trillith-silk rug.

What's the occasion? Renar thought.

Then again, the General had never needed a reason to indulge himself. The belly poking from beneath his stained undershirt attested to that fact, as did the glaze over his usually angry eyes. He had lost his uniform coat somewhere, but thankfully still retained his pants and some small measure of dignity.

"I have news for you, my boy!" the General slurred, teetering one way, then the other on his way to his desk. "We're going to be saved!"

"What?" Renar shook his head, trying to clear away the incense fog. "No, never mind that. I have something I need to ask you."

"Ask me what?" His father glanced up as he fumbled with a new glass. Half the wine made it into the fluted crystal, half onto his papers. Red crept across his reports, ledgers, and books like blood from a wound.

No eruption? No spittle-spraying rant about knowing his place, about only speaking when spoken to? Renar had come prepared for a fight but almost lost his nerve staring at the incoherent wretch before him. Was this even the same man? Had he been afraid of *this*?

Approaching the desk, Renar steeled himself and spoke. "Three years ago, at Unter's first match on my team. I need to know if . . . if you knew that his suit's limiter was incorrectly calibrated. That his armor wouldn't lock no matter how much magic hit him."

"Foolish question from a—*hic*—foolish boy." The General staggered against the desk, leaning on it for support as he moved to stand before Renar. "Of course I ordered the settings altered. Getting a Blauer on the rolls was a perfect opportunity to get unique magtech data for that gearhead Archimas. How the suit worked on the big brute, what level of shock it took to bring him down, on and on."

"I knew it was you," Renar fumed, squeezing his fists.

"At first I was furious you stopped that match," the General continued, oblivious to his son's mounting rage. "But then I realized you had the right idea. Why kill the Blauer by overloading his suit in his first match when I could make money off him for years? I sold every bit of data on him to Archimas, the Council, anyone I could. Thank you for making one good decision in your life."

Renar turned to go. He had his answer. He knew the General was beyond redemption, that he'd sacrifice anything—and *anyone*—for his warped sense of ambition. Closure for Unter was the last thing he'd needed from this sack of ek-dung.

A rough hand grabbed Renar by the shoulder, spinning him around. The punch to his gut that followed doubled him over, made him blink tears and want to vomit.

Before he could fall to his knees, the General grabbed his hair and yanked his head back. "You failed," he whispered, musky, spirit-laced breath pouring right onto Renar's nose and eyes. "You didn't refer to me by the rank I've earned. You didn't stand at attention, and you didn't wait for me to address you before speaking. None of my lessons have taken root in that thick skull of yours, so perhaps it's time for another beating."

Renar's mouth moved, but no words issued forth. Through his bleary eyes, he saw the wine glass sitting upright on the desk. Saw the bottle next to it. If he could just grab one, maybe he could—

This is your fault, the Soldier taunted. *You know the General. You know his tests and tricks. Most of all, you know he can hold his liquor.*

The General saw Renar's shaking fingers reaching for the glass and immediately hit him again. "Don't you dare, boy. I will beat you into a quivering lump. And once I'm done, I'll be sure to do the same to your mother."

"Mother . . . ?" Renar croaked, closing his eyes, arms falling limp at his sides.

"Yes, your mother. I know where she is and who has her. If you do what I say, we can get her back."

His eyes popped open, staring into the General's sneering face, searching for some sign of compassion. Some hint that what he said was true.

Renar found none. Just hard eyes, a twisted grin, and a spittle-drenched chin.

"Nod if you understand me," the General said.

What choice did Renar have? On the off chance the General wasn't lying, he couldn't abandon the woman who'd birthed him. He couldn't blame her when this creature controlled them both.

Renar nodded, and the General dropped him to the floor. "Good. If all goes to plan, you won't have to lift a finger. But if it doesn't, here's what you need to do . . ."

That's right, the Soldier said, stalking around the room, floating from shadow to shadow. *Lie there and listen like a good little boy. You were never free. You never had a* chance *to be free.*

He barely heard the General's words. His mind processed them with cold, rational detachment, but the meaning behind them didn't

453

register. And though Renar was loath to admit it, some part of him *relished* the General's orders.

He *needed* Renar for a task only *he* could accomplish. In an instant, he was back in their mansion's study. The fire crackled in the hearth. He waited at attention, arms folded behind his back, and the General stood before the flames, face half-cloaked in shadow.

His words came from far, far away. Muffled by time, distorted by the light Renar had clung to for so long. His magic-wielding friends he'd never measure up to. Geniuses like Vallen, Sylette, and Matteo who he could never match.

If he just took a step to the side, away from the fire's glow—away from their radiance—he would understand. He would see what the General saw. The world he envisioned for people like them.

And then he'd let Renar call him father.

Then they could be a family—all three of them, together.

Then . . . he'd be loved.

The Soldier smiled. Darkness gushed in from the cracks, crevices, and pits of Renar's mind, sweeping away the light, drowning him in pitch.

"Do this for me, son," his father said, holding out a bundle filled with engimage tools, "and you'll no longer be a failure."

Chapter 45

Graduation Day

Adamantele 9, 697 ABH
Resistance Base, Sarconian Province of Darmatia

Three-hundred and sixty-seven.

The number haunted Jis' dreams; reminded her of the fallibility and naiveté of their leaders. She could still see their faces, bright, happy, hopeful. Their trivial greetings and goodbyes still rang in her ears.

Morning, Professor! Please say we don't have a quiz today.

Another exam? Really?

Thanks for the explanation, Professor. I think I understand Malkath's Gambit now.

See you tomorrow, Professor.

But Jis wouldn't see them tomorrow. None of the three-hundred and sixty-seven cadets who perished at Aldona would see *anyone* again. They wouldn't graduate, wouldn't have their own commands, and wouldn't have the chance to love, start a family, or do something entirely unrelated to the military. Nothing remained of them but ash.

Ash . . . and echoes that would never leave her.

Jis had once heard it was easy to have empathy for the dead. People's faults fell away, and all anyone could remember was the best of them.

It was true. In life, she'd seen most of her students as obstacles—a test she had to overcome to advance her career. Those with high marks were her favorites. Those with ink-drenched papers were headaches. Why did they insist on inconveniencing *her*? Why couldn't they just *try harder*?

Yet in death, Jis saw them. She remembered, and she would never make the same mistake again.

Stooping, Jis pulled aside the frayed flap and entered the darkened tent beyond. A single dim illyrium lamp hung from a pole running the length of the space, illuminating the only students she had left. Three-hundred and sixty-seven cadets had sailed for Aldona. Thirteen remained in camp, including the seven here.

Sylette spotted Jis and bolted to her feet. The silver-haired girl was perceptive and cunning, two excellent qualities in a commander. Jis just hoped Sylette's secrets wouldn't catch up to her before she reached her potential.

"Major's here!" she yelled, smacking the arm dangling from the netting above her. "On your feet."

A month ago, Vallen would've laughed and stayed in his hammock. But the man Jis had trained swung out of his bunk, hit the muddy floor planks with a *thud*, and straightened into a salute.

Jis couldn't help smiling at his progress—at how far *all* of them had come. Striding to the center of the room, she waved the rest of them down. "At ease, cadets. I'm just here to talk."

"You never just *talk*," Lilith said, settling back onto a scuffed-up trunk. "It's always 'training and talk.' Or 'sprints and talk.'"

Her saber was in her hands almost immediately, blade unsheathed, cleaning rag rubbing oil along its length. Jis approved of proper weapon maintenance, but there was something odd about how Lilith never let it out of her sight.

"Don't forget 'magic drills and talk,'" Velle added. "Or 'use you for target practice and talk.'"

Ever the group's mother, she was taking old laundry off a clothesline at the rear of the tent and pinning up a variety of bloody, dirt-stained pants and tunics. The largest belonged to Unter, who'd taken a beating at the hands of one of Taala's guards. He'd told Jis about their relationship after the Hue delegation's departure, but she was still having trouble processing that his own sister had ordered his execution.

Jis held up her hands. "No training, no exams, and no drills today. I promise."

"Then why are you here?" Vallen asked.

She took a quick step toward him, and he instinctively fell into a defensive stance, one foot forward, both arms raised. Excellent. "Good reflexes," Jis said, chuckling. "Keep your guard up like that, and maybe you'll survive what's coming."

"The rumors floating around camp are true, then?" Matteo sat on one of the lower hammocks, swinging back and forth, wringing his hands together. Jis could see the furtive glances he cast at Velle as she worked, which meant everyone else could too. "We're going to be deployed?"

"Not deployed," Renar corrected. "*Leaving.* In a few days, this base will be completely abandoned."

He was sprawled on the ground beside Unter, staring up at a constellation of holes in the tent's roof. Wherever he was, Jis could tell it wasn't here. His left leg was in a puddle, water was dripping onto his chest through one of those holes, and he didn't seem to realize that Lilith was dabbing excess oil on the edge of his shirt.

"Washing in lake no more?" Unter said. "Though quite refreshing, ice water was."

Vallen's eyes brightened. "No more sleeping in a hammock and waking up with rope burns?"

"You did more than *sleep* in yours," Sylette said, acting like she was covering her ears. "And I wouldn't be surprised if those burns were in . . . strange places.

Lilith snickered as Vallen spun toward the silver-haired girl. "I thought we agreed not to—"

Major Reev cleared her throat. "Regardless of nocturnal activities I would rather not be privy to, Cadet Iolus is right. We'll be abandoning the base in a few days and moving south. Official orders will come soon, along with unit assignments for the upcoming battle."

"Battle?" Velle asked. "With the army in this condition?"

"Things aren't likely to improve."

Jis waved at their surroundings. Six sagging hammocks made from fishing nets. Sun-bleached sailcloth repurposed as tent canvas. Listing support poles, a plank-covered walkway, and a cot with snapped legs that served as Unter's bed.

"Disease, morale, supplies . . . " Jis shook her head. "They're only going to get worse. A few more weeks of this and the war will end without us firing a shot."

Sylette nodded. "So, we take the fight to the Empire. I like this plan already."

And there was the problem. *We.* Taking a deep breath, Jis said what she should have a month ago. Before she knew them as more than faces and grades. Before she truly cared whether they lived or died.

"It's not *we* this time, cadets."

Silence consumed the tent. A pair of trousers fell from Velle's fingers, the wooden pin she'd held clattering across the stone floor. Lilith's rag froze midway down the blade. Unter's face was impassive. Renar didn't so much as glance up.

But the others—Vallen, Matteo, and Sylette—looked shocked. Betrayed.

"You can't be serious," Sylette mumbled, running a hand through her hair.

Vallen stepped forward. "What do you mean, Major?"

Jis stood her ground, her eyes cold, her face set like stone. This was *right*. She was doing the right thing. "Exactly what you think. I'm not taking cadets with me on another suicide mission."

"We're part of the army," Lilith said softly. "That's what being a cadet means. What we signed up—"

The temperature in the tent plummeted as Jis slashed her arm through the air. "You did *not* sign up to be butchered. High command was wrong to send you to Aldona. And *I*"—her voice cracked like thawing ice—"was wrong to agree with them. We thought the Empire was bluffing. That both sides would rattle sabers, beat their shields, and then let diplomats hash things out."

"You were wrong," Sylette cut in. "But that doesn't change our situation. You don't have enough mages, Major. And if you sideline us, remove"—she took a deep breath and gritted her teeth—"the Triaron from the equation, I don't think you'll have the manpower or morale to win a battle."

"We'll manage without you," Jis insisted.

The hushed voice of Matteo came from his hammock. It sounded like he was whispering a prayer or reciting a mantra, steeling himself for whatever came next. His knees trembled. His knuckles whitened as he squeezed his fists. Then, pushing his glasses tight against his nose, he stood and stared Jis down.

"No," he said.

Jis laughed. "This isn't up for debate, Alhan. And since when do you have the stones to stand up to me?" Pride welled in her chest at his resolve. But she had to make them see reason, even if that meant striking at his weak points.

Matteo didn't budge. "Since you trained me. Since I was forced to take a miserable trip with all these crazy fools," he said, gesturing at his comrades. "With all due respect, we aren't the same kids from your class. We survived Aldona."

"We lost Leon," Vallen added, gaze distant.

Sylette moved up beside him, standing shoulder to shoulder with the object of her loathing. "We fought our way through an entire Sarc company to escape Etrus."

"And don't forget that scrap with the Draken," Lilith said, sheathing her sword, rising to join them.

"*I* saved you," Jis pointed out. "If I hadn't been there—"

"You did save us." Laying her hand on Matteo's shoulder, Velle joined the others. He nearly stumbled away, but she grabbed his arm and held him tight, much to his evident surprise. "And then you started teaching us. You found us the right trainers, put us through void and oblivion, and never let us have a moment's rest. The journey broke us, Major ...

"But you," Velle smiled, "put us back together."

Words failed Jis. She tried to speak, but no sound passed her lips. Mother Tabitha had been right. In training these cadets, she'd found *herself* again.

Kel by Kel, the temperature in the tent returned to its usual clammy chill. Jis couldn't feel the change, but the warmth of her admiration for these young soldiers, bubbling up from inside, was something she could get used to.

"Pardon, Major."

When Unter rose, the top of his head brushed the roof, making the canvas walls shiver and shake. He quickly hunched over, large head hovering above Vallen and Sylette.

"Solution to problem simple seem," he continued. "You no cadets take with you. So, if cadets no longer"—Unter shrugged, grin splitting his face—"then no issue. Logic sound, by Vida swear."

If they aren't cadets, Jis thought, *then everything I said is meaningless.*

A laughably simple solution, yes. She had come here hoping they were the same aimless wanderers she'd rescued from Nehalena's clutches: selfish, uncooperative, and barely able to work together. Whether they stayed in the base or struck off on their own, *that* team would have accepted her decision to cut them loose, grateful for the opportunity to save their own skins.

And they still weren't perfect. Sylette elbowed Vallen in the gut when he bumped into her. Matteo whispered something in Velle's ear, but she pointedly looked elsewhere even as she held his arm. For some reason, Renar hadn't budged from the plank he was laying on.

Yet Jis didn't need perfect. She needed warriors—people with the determination to stand up and fight for each other when the darkness closed in. These cadets fit that bill.

No, Jis corrected herself. *Not cadets.*

Not today. Never again.

Unbuttoning her uniform jacket, Jis reached inside and

removed a rusty tin where she kept her valuables. The locator talisman she'd received from Mother Tabitha. A bracelet of gemstones whose purpose—the linking of two souls—would never be fulfilled.

And the pile of medals she'd taken off her breast earlier that day. Trophies meant nothing where they were going, but now she'd found another use for them.

They fell quiet as she cracked the lid and held up the first medal—a blue and white ribbon attached to a pair of crossed lances and a silver cup. The *King Darmatus Royal Chalice,* the highest honor any Darmatian could receive. Steward Metellus had personally bestowed it on Jis for rescuing hundreds of drowning sailors during the Kharit Incident.

She was happy to pass the pointless bauble on.

"There aren't any crowds here," Jis said, trying to keep her voice from cracking. "No officers in dress blues or politicians in suit-robes and silk. I can't promise you a parade afterward, and you won't be getting a traditional laurel-leaf pin and a diploma sealed with the Steward's mark. But here it is at last, cadets."

Tears filled Jis' eyes. It was all she could do to not break down, sobbing with pride and regret. They had missed out on the celebration they deserved when Aldona fell. Now, she would give it back to them.

"Step forward to begin your commissioning ceremony, cadets of Darmatia. Your long overdue Graduation Day is finally here."

"Renar Iolus," Major Reev called.

Renar approached mechanically, limbs moving on unseen strings like the puppet he was. He didn't want to accept the medal she offered him. The praise of the others, the way they cheered and clapped for him, grated against his ears like ghastly shrieks.

If only he could refuse. Turn tail, run away, and hide from both them and the General.

But Renar needed their trust to do what he'd been ordered. He needed to get aboard one of their cruisers, needed to reach the coming battlefield at Etrus.

Only once Renar was there could he betray their misplaced faith.

Major Reev clipped his skin as she pinned the medal on him, but he barely felt the prick or the blood welling beneath his tunic. Snatching his wrist, she held it in the air and announced:

"Congratulations on joining the family business, Lieutenant Iolus!"

"Unter of Clan Darmatia," Major Reev called.

The addition attached to his name stunned Unter. For an instant, he couldn't move, even with the hands of his friends tugging his arms and trying to pull him toward the front of the tent.

Clan Darmatia.

Unter had a *home* again. Friends and comrades, people to protect—a clan. He was no longer part of House Lyadrin, but that didn't matter. He was Bekshak no more, at least by how he defined these things. Once again, he *belonged.*

Blinking gratitude, Unter rushed to the front where he grabbed Major Reev with all four arms and pulled her into a tight embrace.

"You thank," he babbled. "You thank, you thank, you thank ... "

Major Reev wiggled an arm free of his grasp and patted him on the shoulder. "It's my privilege to welcome you into your new clan, Lieutenant Unter."

"Sylette Farkos," Major Reev called.

Artorios, Sylette corrected silently.

The name was wrong, but it was preferable to the truth. Straightening her back, raising her head, Sylette marched to stand before the Ice Queen.

Being an officer didn't matter to her. Winning the Ice Queen's trust, though? Well, that was another story. Sylette shook her frosty hand, then waited as Major Reev leaned in to pin a small illyrium crystal set in silver to her chest.

Warm breath tickled her ear. Why was the Major so close? She didn't need to brush her hair against Sylette's cheek to—

"*I know,*" Major Reev whispered, then withdrew. Taking Sylette's limp hand in hers, she raised it high.

"A woman I know will go far, Lieutenant Farkos!"

"Vallen Metellus," Major Reev called.

Vallen had never wanted to be a Kingdom soldier. It was something Steward Metellus had come up with, one of his fanciful plans to make the country accept him as their reincarnated hero.

But he wasn't Darmatus, not even close. He had failed Elaine. Then, in his arrogance, he'd cost Leon his life as well.

You seem to get hung up on death a lot, the darkness said, chuckling. *If it bothers you that much, just take my power. You'll never lose anyone again.*

Except himself. *That* was why Vallen had swallowed his pride, training with Jis even though she took out years of frustration on him. He needed to be strong enough to save others without surrendering to the voice's temptations.

When he reached the front, Major Reev punched him in the arm. "You did well, Metellus. Maybe we can have another go sometime where I *don't* hold back."

Vallen grinned. "Same goes for me."

As soon as she pinned his medal on his collar, Vallen thrust his fist in the air.

"Hopefully we'll still have an army when you're done with it, Lieutenant Metellus," Major Reev said.

"Matteo Alhan," Major Reev called.

Matteo was the last to 'graduate.' Lilith and Velle had gone one after the other, and the Sylph was back at his side. She gave him a slight push when she heard his name. At first, he didn't move, so Velle pushed him again, mouthed the word *'later,'* and started clapping.

Knees shaking, vision blurry, Matteo lurched forward, stumbling over the wooden planks between him and his dream. It couldn't be real, could it? He wanted to pinch himself to be sure, but the hands thumping against his back was proof enough.

Matteo wished his parents could be here, or that he could at least find out if they were safe. But that was something he'd need to determine himself. If the rumors circulating through camp were true, their objective was in the south near the Ascendancy. Only one Darmatian city fit that description:

His home, Etrus.

Steadying his breath, Matteo clicked his heels together, turned to Major Reev, and saluted. Vallen laughed at his display, but he no longer cared. This was how they handled military ceremonies in books—how it would be done if they were still at the Academy.

Major Reev smiled as she pinned a silver-and-gold cannon medallion to his breast. "I thought sending you to Holcomb might be a mistake. But instead, you improved more than anyone. Hold your head high, Lieutenant Alhan."

And he did. Even with tears streaming down his face, even as his legs and arms trembled, Matteo kept his chin up and his salute firm.

Just like a hero in the legends of old.

Chapter 46

What Was Lost

Jis had a hundred things to do.

Ammo requisitions from every squad required approval. The chief engimage aboard the cruiser *Dharmasya* insisted he needed another team of welders to finish repairs before their operation—code name, 'Fated Thrust'—commenced. Half a dozen officers wanted an audience with General Iolus, but he was holed up in his sweet-smelling ivory tower, refusing to talk to anyone. And since Rodale was equally useless, planning for the entire campaign had fallen on Jis' aching shoulders.

When Jis left her cadets—no, newly minted *lieutenants*—behind, she should have tackled her bottomless list of tasks. Instead, she ducked between a pair of sagging tents, skirted a raucous group of soldiers singing around a fire pit, and stole down the slope toward the lake. Her students were busy making merry with the bottle of Seylan gin she'd gifted them, so Jis deserved a short break as well.

A stand of boulders halfway to the north wall provided the privacy she craved. Slumping against a smooth stalagmite, Jis slid to the cave floor, legs out, eyes half closed. Corporal Sayles shouldn't be able to find her here. The clamor of the camp was a distant, muted roar, far enough away that she could ignore it for a few minutes.

Jis breathed slowly in and out, savoring the view. Crystal clear water whose placid surface sparkled like sapphires. White spikes hanging from the cavern roof, glittering in the glow from illyrium lamp panels.

If Jis blinked, she could almost see little lights floating across the mirror's surface. Tiny lanterns, pulsing souls, ready to begin their final journey. They'd disappeared over the mist-obscured waterfall at the lake's far edge, but not from her heart.

The coming battle was her offering to them.

And to you, lost cadets, Jis thought, closing her eyes, focusing on her heartbeat. *Know that your fellows have risen to the challenge. You will be avenged.* Jis didn't believe in prayer, but she hoped that somehow, some way, they heard her.

"If the Ice Queen could catch a chill, I *might* be worried about you sleeping here."

Jis' eyelids fluttered open at the familiar voice. It had pulled her from her slumber numerous times, whispering sweetly as strong arms slithered beneath their sheets to grab her waist. She'd always mumbled, "Five more minutes," at which point he'd slide his fingers to Jis' sides, tickling her until she threw off the covers, tackled him, and—

"Why are you here, Holcomb?" Jis asked. "You know, never mind. The wake-up call is appreciated. Now *leave.*"

She shouldn't have dozed off. Not now, not with the army relying on her. Every minute she dallied increased the risk that her men wouldn't distribute the correct amount of synth-oil to the ships or the wrong caliber rounds would end up in their rifle kits.

Cracking her neck, Jis leaned forward, preparing to jump to her feet. Rodale's arm caught her shoulder and pushed her back down. "Take five more minutes, Jis. I promise the war will still be there when you're done."

Did he just *touch* her? Jis let frost creep from her back, coating the boulders and floor in a white sheen. "Unless you want to chill your own ale, you'd better move your hand."

Rodale's breath misted around his beard, but his trembling fingers didn't move. "I'm not going anywhere. Not till you hear me out."

"Hear you out?" Jis laughed. "Are you really going with that line?"

"Jis, please—"

"No!" she shouted. Ice bloomed around her legs and arms, shooting out of the ground like crystal spears. One clipped Rodale's calf, slicing through his trousers, drawing a deep scarlet line across his flesh.

He winced. Gritted his teeth and swore under his breath. But still, he didn't move.

"No," Jis repeated, frosty spikes still sprouting around them. "I *was* ready to hear you out, Rodale. Five years ago, after the Kharit Incident. I waited at our apartment for you to come explain yourself. For you to tell me the accusations of the MPs and inspectors were wrong. That you hadn't tricked me with false weather data. That you hadn't convinced me to send those crews to their deaths for a voided *payday.*

"Did you ever come?" she said softly.

Rodale ducked his head, refusing to meet her gaze. "No."

"Then I think we're done here."

On impulse, Jis tore open her uniform collar. Silver buttons scattered among the icy blossoms. One of her rank insignias clattered across the slick stones and into the water. Jis didn't care. She needed to get rid of it—to dispose of the poison she'd kept near her heart all these years.

Out came her tin case. She popped the lid, pushed aside Tabitha's talisman, and snatched up the gem-studded bracelet. At its center were set two gleaming stones: an emerald for Jis to match her eyes, and a ruby for her beloved. The color of Rodale's hair, a sign of the passion he swore would never waver.

It was a betrothal bracelet. A chain that joined two souls together in the sight of the Veneer, a bond that not even death was supposed to shatter.

Jis threw it at him. "Take it! Take it and pawn it. Sell it for booze, trade it for sex, use it to flee Darmatia. I don't care what you do, just get away from me."

The bracelet thudded against Rodale's chest, then dropped atop the ice field between them. He didn't reach for it, and his arm remained pressed to Jis' shoulder like a blazing brand, a hot poker piercing her flesh. Every second he was close to her was agony.

"I don't want it, Jis," Rodale said through trembling, purpling lips. "It's yours."

"I'm not keeping the trinket you bought with blood money."

"It wasn't like that. The man I worked for didn't give me the geldars to—"

Jis threw up her hands and blasted Rodale with a gust of frigid air. Ice formed along his collar, rime clung to his beard and eyebrows, but still, he didn't budge. "Where you got the money isn't the only problem! You *left*. You had an opportunity to come clean—to me, to our friends, to the army. Instead, you disappeared. And when you reappeared, all the charges were dropped like they never existed.

"But did you come find me then?" Jis asked, shards of ice running down her face like tears. "Did you so much as *apologize*? No, you turned to the bottle and became the most irredeemable, disgusting *drunk* I've ever met."

Rodale pushed forward, forcing Jis to drop her arms lest she freeze his face off. "L-look at me . . . me, Jis."

"Five seconds," she hissed. "Then the hand goes."

"I'm . . . he-here now. I-I'm talking n-now."

"Four."

He grabbed her other shoulder and tugged her closer. Jis kept counting as she waited for the stench of old spirits and piss-stained clothes to hit her.

"Three."

"Look a-at me, J-Jis. I've bloody-well c-changed. I'm . . . t-trying to be b-better."

Ha! Jis thought, glaring hatred at the man she'd once cherished above all else. *The Void and Creator would sooner take a roll in the hay together than—*

The smell hit her. Not the scent of alcohol-laced breath, but of freshly chewed mantri leaves. Jis stared at Rodale, truly seeing him for the first time in a month. The matted wads had been trimmed from his beard, leaving it patchy but clean. Dark circles ringed his eyes, a sign he wasn't sleeping well, and sweat dribbled from his scalp despite the chill.

The naval coat Rodale wore wasn't new. A few buttons were missing, the hem was frayed, and the blue dye was all but faded. Yet there were no stains. No careless streaks of food, no splotches from spilled liquor. He even wore a proper belt to keep his trousers up.

"You're clean," Jis breathed, collapsing back against the stalagmite. "I don't believe it."

"Neither do I, to be honest." Releasing her at last, Rodale patted himself all over and shook his coat. Nothing sloshed around. No hidden flasks or glasses clinked.

"You're clean," Jis repeated.

Chuckling, Rodale started scratching his beard. His fingers bit deep enough to rub the skin red and raw. "It's a work in progress. After that meeting with Taala where I was as much use as a pair of teats on Sariel's nethers, I decided I needed to make a change."

The scratching continued, and blood dribbled down his chin. He pulled his fingers away, saw the red on them, and sighed. "Yep, a work in progress indeed. I'm shaking like a virgin on red-lantern street, not"—he waved at the now receding ice—"just because of you. Night sweats, muscle aches, vomiting. You name it, I've got it."

Jis reached out, touched his arm. Then she snatched her hand back. Why was she concerned? This wretch had left her alone at her lowest. She didn't owe him any sympathy.

"Why now?" Jis asked. *Why not while what we had could still be salvaged?* a voice deep within her mind whispered.

Content that she was no longer on the verge of flight, Rodale collapsed to the ground with a huff. He crossed his legs, picked up the betrothal bracelet, and began dusting it off with the edge of his coat.

"To save you," Rodale said at length.

Before she could tell him where to shove his concern, he raised a hand. "Running this army alone is killing you, Jis, even if you don't want to admit it. I know logistics. It was my job, both above and below board. Plus my last command was Etrus. If anybody knows the town— where the Sarcs will have their ships, how to avoid civvie casualties, how to mask our approach—it's me."

That was hard logic to argue with. Jis bit her lip, mulling Rodale's offer over while trying *not* to look at his face. A little bit of trimming, a splash of color in his cheeks, and he'd be the same handsome rogue she'd relished waking up beside each morning.

Those days were gone. Just as the waterfall couldn't give back the lanterns it had taken, what was lost would not return. Not her love, nor her trust.

But . . . Jis could swallow her pride for the sake of what could still be saved.

"Fine," she said, rising to her feet. "With General Iolus locked in his room like a petulant child, I'll take all the help I can get."

Rodale stopped polishing and sighed. "That's the other thing. You know the man I said I reported to? The man who ruined my life?"

"I'd say you did that yourself, but go on."

"It's him," Rodale said, nodding at the pavilion rising above the camp like a marble palace. "General Hardwick Iolus. And you shouldn't trust a word from that voidspawn's swollen lips."

Chapter 47
It's Treason, Then

Adamantele 10, 697 ABH
Etrus, Sarconian Province of Darmatia

Death stalked Lieutenant-Colonel Olivier Stetson. He felt its cold touch in his watery lungs, filling with fluid no spell could reach. Its skeletal hand gripped him by the throat, making every wheeze a struggle, every word a trial. His head erupted in torment at the slightest twitch or disturbance, and his muscles ached like he'd been mugged in a Sarconia back alley.

Unless Olivier returned to the capital, he would die in Etrus—a provincial backwater filled with quaint stucco buildings, jovial peasants, and the rancid stench of fish. And he would die a disgrace. Cast out by his Emperor, disowned by his noble family, still clinging to his head only by the goodwill of that barbaric rube, Rittermarschal Valescar.

Every breath Olivier took was fire. But knowing he would meet his end without redemption—without leaving a legacy men would remember—was suffering he could scarcely bear.

Olivier had one opportunity left to change his gravestone's epithet. Or, glorious emperors willing, evade his burial entirely.

Fortunately, today was a good day. The voidspawn responsible for pounding iron spikes into his skull was on sabbatical, and Olivier could string several sentences together without descending into a blood-flecked coughing fit. He could stare out the wraparound viewport of his cruiser's bridge without the coastal sun setting his eyeballs ablaze and listen to the incessant murmurs of his crew and hiss of the vessel's pipes without covering his sensitive ears.

His good bill of health, confirmed by the white-robed salvator hiding behind his command chair, gave him confidence. He'd need that confidence to outwit his commander: the Imperial *sow*, Rittermarschal Titania. Leaning forward in his cushioned seat, Olivier's thin lips pulled back as he smiled at the collection of yellow globules forming into the shape of Darmatia's governor.

Even through the LDCT transmission, he could tell Titania was beautiful. Curls the color of fire cascaded down her back and rested atop her silver shoulder pauldrons and burgundy cloak. Her skin was pale and smooth like cream, with nary an imperfection or blemish. And though she was wise enough to wear a breastplate without slots for her . . . *feminine charms*, the bulge at her chest was noticeable.

In another life, Olivier would have called in every favor, deal, and debt he could to possess her. Now, he just wanted to see the witch burn. He'd fallen from grace at the hands of that whore Lanara, the former third consort, and he believed any wench who slept her way to prominence deserved nothing but the headsman's axe.

"To what do I owe the pleasure, Rittermarschal?" Olivier asked, cadaverous fingers tapping his armrest.

"Cut the crap, Stetson." Titania's crimson locks pulsed her fury. "I can see your cruisers' transponder beacons on my campaign map. You haven't advanced north to meet the rebels. *Why?*" She ground the word between scarlet-painted lips.

Olivier shrugged, the motion barely lifting his gold-trimmed shoulder epaulets. They shouldn't be heavy, but to him, they were like cannon shells. "Technical difficulties, I'm afraid. The damp sea air is wreaking havoc on the illyrium converter circuitry. We'll have to replace the engine blades, re-lay the wiring to the main distribution station, then—"

"Spare me the details. How soon will your ships be airborne?"

"Three, maybe four days, Your Grace."

In the pit below the command deck, out of the Rittermarschal's sight, Olivier's chief engimage began to fidget. A single glare made him bury his face in his workstation's readouts. Or was it the massive, fully armored guard looming over the mousy man that made him quiver? Olivier didn't much care so long as the bridge crew of his flagship, *Ardor,* obeyed him and *only* him.

It was all a lie. Olivier's reasons for disobeying orders, his engineering woes, the repairs they needed to make. A well-crafted lie, but a lie nonetheless.

And the first person to breathe a word of it to high command would never breathe again.

"Unacceptable," Titania growled, the yellow motes of her projection writhing in tune with her irritation. "You were to be the anvil for Operation Clipped Wings—the blocking force that would catch the rebels in the open and smash them against my fleet. Now I'll have to rush everything to Etrus and *hope* we arrive in time to save your bony carcass."

Olivier *relished* her rage, smiling behind his gaunt cheeks. This sow was fifteen years his junior. When he was the commander of the Emperor's Royal Guard, she'd been writing Academy term papers about battles *he'd* fought in. How many times had this harlot lain on her back to obtain the burgundy cloak she wore? How many men had Titania serviced? *He* should be wearing the livery of the rittermarschals, not her.

"I can hold them," Olivier said, revealing his smile. "My 232nd mechanized battalion has a company of panzcraft which far outclasses anything they can field on the ground. My fighter wings will cut them from the skies. Not to mention we have Archimas' device and a trap my mages have been—"

"No."

"—working...on ... " Olivier paused. What had she said? "Please repeat that, Rittermarschal."

"*No*," Titania said again, louder and more forcefully.

Haze began to shake the projection—some sort of heat interfering with the connection. Olivier glanced at his communications officer, who shook her head. The problem wasn't on their end of the line.

"No, you will not hold them," Titania continued, baring her teeth, clenching her gauntlets. "You are removed from command, Lt. Colonel Stetson, effective immediately. You will be replaced by your second, Captain Neering, who will oversee operations until I can send a suitable replacement."

An iron spike slid into Olivier's temple, spearing him with white-hot pain. The breath caught in his throat even as his heart threatened to spring from his sunken chest. "That isn't . . . necessary, Your Grace," he babbled, trying not to cough, not to double over. "Tell His . . . Majesty that I promise him a swift . . . and decisive victory."

Titania laughed. "You? *Victory?* The Emperor nearly perished to a traitor's blade on your watch. You let his banished daughter—one measly girl and a bunch of green cadets—escape you. And then you have the gall to tell me you have mechanical troubles? You've been in Etrus for a month, you witless fool. How have I not heard about your circuitry issues before *now?*"

Oh, Olivier thought. *Undone by such a simple mistake.*

And just like that, his lies came crashing down around him like so much shattered glass. The bridge crew began to whisper amongst themselves. Lieutenant Rhest, the gangly officer who manned *Ardor's* gunnery station, rose and began walking in the direction of the ship-wide voicepipes.

"But . . . Rittermarschal Valescar assured me—" Olivier tried to gasp.

Flames licked the tips of Titania's tresses. Her scarlet eyes were now smoldering coals. Olivier could almost feel the heat of her wrath *through* the transmission. If not for the leagues separating them, he suspected she would break him in half, then burn whatever was left.

"Valescar can't save you now, Stetson," she whispered. "You will be dragged back here, bound to a rack, and flayed until not a strip of flesh remains on your craven corpse. Your head will be skewered on *Ardor's* ramming spike. Your body will be nailed to the palace balcony, and a sign hung round the stump of your neck that will read: *Stetson—The Imbecile Who Thought To Cross Titania.* All who see it will tremble and—"

The pounding in Olivier's head stopped. Calm settled over him, freeing his lungs, soothing the fires scorching his muscles. In that instant, he saw what he needed to do.

Adrenaline carried Olivier to his feet, placed his Lerchis sidearm in his hand. He was not a crack shot. But at this range, fueled by an otherworldly sense of purpose, he didn't need to be.

He *would* be remembered.

Four shots rang out. The first three pinged off the brass speaking tubes connecting the bridge to the rest of the cruiser. The last caught Lieutenant Rhest in the neck, spraying blood across the wall, drawing screams from the rest of the deck officers.

Titania's eyes went wide. "What in the Void are you doin—"

Olivier spun toward the LDCT magchine, burying the rest of his lead in the projector at its base. Sparks flew, static tore through Titania's image, and with a high-pitched squeal, the sow disappeared entirely.

Smoke filled the bridge as the magchine bled synth-oil and dun illyrium crystals. For once, the acrid stench wafting from the bubbling black fluid didn't bring Olivier to tears or reduce him to a wheezing lump. He grinned, pulled another magazine from his belt, and studied his cowering subordinates as he slotted it into his pistol.

"Why aren't the guards doing anything?" Olivier's *former* chief engimage cried, squatting beneath his desk.

Yes, *former*. Olivier fired three rounds into his chest.

"They're mercenaries," he said, answering the dead man. "I thought something like this might happen, so I brought them"— he waved the barrel of his gun at the five armored sentinels stalking around the room, patting down his officers while searching for hidden weapons—"in as an insurance policy. I think it's wonderful when people are more loyal to coin than country.

472

"Any other questions?" Olivier asked.

No one spoke. The only sounds on the bridge were the hissing of the dying LDCT, the clomp of iron boots on metal walkways, and the exultant thumping of Olivier's heart. Part one of his plan was done, even if the execution was off. As for part two ...

Olivier gazed out *Ardor's* viewport at the airfield, harbor, and city beyond. He had no eyes for the glimmering blue water, nor appreciation for the way Etrus' rising tiers and rooftop gardens glowed in the late afternoon sun. Only three things mattered to him:

The convoy of trucks crossing the bridge on their way back from the settlement, their beds packed tight with squirming bodies; the red-robed mages chanting in unison at the water's edge; and the towering bronze pole at the airfield's opposite end.

Olivier smiled, exposing rotting gums. Death might stalk him, might already have him wrapped in its embrace, but he wouldn't be going out alone. And if he caught a certain silver-haired exile in his net, perhaps he wouldn't have to go at all.

Chapter 48
A Hint of Cinnamon

Adamantele 10, 697 ABH
Nemare, Capital of the Sarconian Province of Darmatia

A wave of heat and smoke assaulted Ritterbruder Mikus Garax the instant he opened the door to the governor's office. Against his better judgment, he jumped in front of the woman beside him, shielding her with his half-cloak and body as he brought a thick sleeve up to cover his nose and mouth.

"Stay low, Rittermark," Mikus cautioned Silesia Marta. "The attackers could still be nearby." His eyes scanned the ash-choked chamber, searching for the source of the blaze.

Flames surged through the room, claiming more priceless artifacts and relics with each passing second. Once grand tapestries withered to cinders as fire climbed the walls. Trillith-silk carpets, velvet-padded couches, and a darkwood table inlaid with an engraving of King Darmatus' coronation had been lashed to pieces, scoured by blackened lines similar to whip marks. In the far corners were two blobs of molten silver—suits of antique armor from centuries past, now melted to slag.

Had a bomb gone off? Were the cultists so well-organized they could strike at the heart of the Sarconian occupation? Blinking sweat from his eyes, Mikus swore and prepared to dive into the inferno to find the Rittermarschal.

Or whatever's left of her, he thought. If the old emperors were just, he'd find a blackened, shrapnel-riddled body near her desk.

Silesia grabbed Mikus' arm and pushed him aside. "Don't be a fool, Garax." She raised her voice, shouting into the maelstrom of orange and red. "You can stop the fire sh'crackera display, Rittermarschal!"

The flames froze, stilling like pieces of radiant glass shaped by a master smith. Mikus reached for one crawling up a nearby coatrack, but Silesia batted his hand away. "They still hurt. I suggest staying where you are until she cleans up."

He raised an eyebrow. "Cleans . . . up?"

The curling length of yellow-orange fire trembled like a leaf shaking in the wind. Then it *flew* toward the opposite end of the room, accompanied by all its fellows. They tore away from half-burnt paintings, bookshelves, and chairs, leaving behind charred scars, black and ugly, but not a single smoldering ember. Mikus found himself gaping at the masterful men'ar control on display.

A condensed orb of flame sucked in every last spark. It roiled and convulsed above the mailed palm that held it, streaks of crimson shooting out at random, yearning to be free. Before Mikus could start worrying about what would happen if the orb exploded, clawed fingers snapped shut on it, leaving behind only stray fumes.

"And the smoke?" Mikus muttered, staring at the dark smog clinging to the ceiling.

Rittermarschal Titania raised her gauntlet, then swept it toward a shattered window that overlooked the palace balcony. Pinpricks of fire roared to life within the smoke and herded the gray mist through the gap into the blue sky beyond.

"Better?" the governor asked, a smile on her full lips.

Mikus nodded. Why was he surrounded by crazy mages?

Doffing her cap, Silesia picked her way through the scorched debris toward Titania. She didn't salute upon reaching the Rittermarschal's desk, nor did she bow or show subservience in any way. Chestnut hair bouncing, Silesia hopped onto the ash-smeared surface and leaned back, legs dangling over the side like she was relaxing on a bed.

The Rittermark had finally lost it. All the stress of high rank had caught up with her, and one final show of disrespect was going to get her—and more importantly, *him*—executed. Mikus went stock still, banging his fist to his breast in salute, practicing his excuses in his head.

I just work for her, Your Grace. I had no idea she was going to—

Titania climbed up beside Silesia and pulled the Rittermark's head down onto a pillow formed from the tail end of her cloak. She slowly ran her fingers through Silesia's hair, producing a contented murmur from the younger woman.

All conscious thought fled Mikus. He had no idea what he was watching, only that it drew more blood south than was healthy right now.

"Why'd you bring him with you?" Titania asked, bending so that her crimson curls brushed against Silesia's snow-kissed skin. "I might have to burn his eyes out."

Silesia giggled. "No need, my fire. A little bit of song"—she started humming a sad, somber melody—"and he'll happily forget he was ever here."

Fire sparked in the air between them, a glow that Mikus barely caught before it dissipated to smoke. Titania reared back, laughing, then gently flicked Silesia's nose. "Your charms don't work on me, little flower," the Rittermarschal said. "It's why this arrangement between us works."

"Really?" Silesia purred, pushing up on her elbows, eyes locked on the woman above her. "I suppose I'll have to find something else that does ..."

For a moment, they were lost in their own world, leaving Mikus to digest the truth of their relationship. It was more . . . *intimate* than he'd expected. The lads in his squad, especially Dar, would probably end up drooling at the news. Mikus could almost hear their first crude attempts at composing an appropriately tawdry ditty.

But I won't tell them, Mikus thought, feeling the coarse threads of an imaginary rope sliding between the fingers of his fist, still clenched in salute. This was *exactly* the information he needed to hang Silesia. To get rid of the domineering Rittermark who treated his mind and loyalty like her personal plaything.

For though it wasn't an official Imperial edict, everyone in the Ritter Order knew Auvrea Titania belonged to the power that reigned above all others: Emperor Artorios.

"Unfortunately, business calls." Titania pushed Silesia away with a clawed finger on her lips. Scooting her hips to the side, she slid out from under her subordinate's head and marched back behind her desk.

"Is that what you call this?" Silesia sat up and waved at the torched office. "Business?"

Shadows clouded Titania's face. "Stetson has turned traitor. He shot his gunnery officer, destroyed his unit's only LDCT, and is going to bugger all the work we put into Operation Clipped Wings. If only that sniveling wretch were here before me ..."

A whip of flames sprouted from her hand and lashed out at a marble bust of some Darmatian politician. It took the man's head off at the neck, separating his hawkish countenance and plaited wig from his shoulders.

Mikus gulped. He needed to leave *now,* while his limbs were still accounted for and Titania's infidelity was secure in his mind. "Rittermarschal, Rittermark, if you don't have further need of my services, I shall retire to the hall and let you talk strate—

"*Kneel,*" Silesia Ordered.

What? As if Mikus would obey such a demeaning command, even from his superior officer. He wouldn't behave like a hound just because of that loathsome nickname.

Mikus blinked, then glanced around. Piles of ash surrounded his

legs and hands as he knelt on the office floor, back bent, head bowed. He couldn't move. Or rather, he didn't want to.

The longer Mikus remained in this pose, the more peace and pleasure he felt. *This* was what he'd been called to do, and he awaited his next order—the next divine mandate from his mistress' lips—like a drowning man waits for rescue.

Only a faint whiff of cinnamon kept Mikus from diving headlong into the rapture she promised. Flailing against the waves of bliss forcing him down, he fought to keep his head above water. To keep his eyes and ears open even as his body became Silesia's slave.

"What an incredible gift," Titania said, dispelling her whip. "It's one thing to cajole and encourage His Majesty as I've done, but if we got you alone in a room with him …" The Rittermarschal chuckled softly.

"Ever since Lanara, he's always kept a cadre of sensors nearby, ready for another betrayal," Silesia said. "It would have to be during one of your nightly sessions." She tilted her head, batted her long eyelashes. "Tell him you want to invite a friend. I'm sure the lecher would *salivate* at the prospect."

Titania shook her head. "He's more cautious than you think. He'd have intelligence agents study you for years before inviting you to bed. And when they do, they'll discover—"

"Don't speak of it." Silesia planted her boots against the side of the desk, bracing like a drake preparing to pounce. Her eyes were hard, and Mikus saw something shift beneath her uniform sleeves. "It's bad enough that *you* found me. If anyone else were to find out, I'd have to take a very different approach with them."

"You *did* try to kill me, if I recall correctly," Titania said with a snicker. "Or tried to make me kill myself. I'm not sure whether magic-compelled suicide counts."

"And look where it's brought us, my fire."

Slowly, as if he were wading uphill against a mudslide, Mikus realized what he was hearing. Infidelity was the least of their crimes. They were speaking *treason,* of snaring the Emperor in Silesia's spell and manipulating him like a puppet at a mummer's show.

Mikus tried to smile, yet his muscles didn't obey. He couldn't escape. Not yet, at least. But when he did, finding proof of their treachery was his first objective. Otherwise, it would be the word of a lowly Ritterbruder against the most powerful women in the Empire.

"Fetch."

The silken command wove through Mikus' ears, ensnaring his

heart, making his pulse quicken. He leapt to his feet, dashed across the room, and took the cepyrus folder from Rittermarschal Titania without sparing her a second glance. His eyes belonged to Silesia.

"You'll find two dossiers in there," Titania said. "The first is everything the Emperor currently has on you." She raised a gauntlet to silence Silesia, who was opening her mouth to protest. "Yes, I kept back as much as I could. Your birthplace, true family name, and living relatives, for example. But after you spoke up in front of high command, he took an interest in you and I had to give him something."

"Speaking of which ..." Titania leaned over her desk and prodded Silesia in the chest. "'Marta' is a terrible choice of last name for someone trying to hide their identity. It's only missing the last three letters, so someone is bound to fill in the blanks."

"I was fourteen at the time, so go tap yourself," Silesia growled, batting the Rittermarschal's arm away.

Sparks flared across Titania's scarlet locks. Heaving a breathy sigh, she leered at her partner and whispered, "You'd like to watch that, wouldn't you, little Martavis?"

"Don't make me dunk you in the palace pond."

Titania shrugged, cloak billowing as she started pacing in front of her ruined window. "Taking a dip could be fun. *After* you rein in our Stetson problem, of course."

Martavis. Where had Mikus heard that name before? His thoughts slipped through his fingers like oil, slippery and evasive, impossible to catch.

Distantly, he saw a blurry, distorted image of a wooden scaffold. A woman with autumn brown hair knelt on the rough planks, her neck lowered over a waiting basket. Bruises coated her cheeks, calves, and every inch of pale flesh exposed by the bloody shift she wore.

The gathered crowd roared as a one-eyed man marched up the scaffold steps behind her. Hefting an axe, he aimed it at the woman's neck, glanced skyward, then swung with all his might.

Mikus turned away. He'd been on the cusp of adulthood then, and it was the first time he'd seen a beheading *or* a corpse. Now it was a sight as familiar as breakfast rations.

Silesia must have noticed Mikus' foggy, unfocused gaze, for she snapped her fingers and Sang, *"Listen."*

Thought failed him, for Mikus had no need of it. Listening to her angelic melodies was all that mattered, all that sustained him and gave him purpose. Soft and shallow came his breath—just enough to let him live to hear her words.

"Is he alright?" Titania asked, waving her gauntlet in front of Mikus' face. He didn't so much as blink.

Silesia flicked her wrist dismissively. "If he isn't, it's not a big deal. You were saying?"

Spicy and sweet, the fragrance of cinnamon wafted up Mikus' nostrils, restoring a fraction of his awareness. He made a mental tally of Silesia's intrusion: *Compulsion 174.* And those were the ones Mikus knew of, that had occurred after he began to suspect what was happening and had a special memory talisman *seared* onto his flesh where none would find it.

Purchasing enough high-quality illyrium powder, an excruciating three-day procedure, and buying the Engraver's silence. All told, it had cost Mikus more than a year's wages to secure his memories within a seal tied to his senses. But they were *his* memories again, and that was well worth the price and pain.

Oh, the exquisite torment he would visit on this whore for messing with his head. Mikus could scarcely wait for that day to arrive.

"With their only LDCT down, I have no way of communicating with Stetson's command. Which means someone has to go there and arrest him." Titania nodded at Silesia. "You're the perfect candidate. Gather a team, take my personal airship, and bring him to heel. Make him your thrall or clap him in irons—I don't care. Just make sure Stetson reaches me alive.

"I have . . . *plans* for him," the Rittermarschal murmured, tracing a silver claw down the curve of her smirk.

Silesia jumped off the desk and snatched the folder from Mikus' numb fingers. He could still feel them but couldn't make his pinky so much as twitch. Mikus was a phantom in his own flesh.

After a moment of flipping through the documents, Silesia snapped the folder shut and tucked it into her belt. "Got it. We'll leave after I take care of one more thing."

"Which is?"

Grinning, Silesia stole toward Titania on cat-quick feet. She grabbed the taller woman by the clasp of her cloak and pulled her close. "Settling a debt, my fire. You said my charms don't work on you. I aim to change that."

Mikus felt his blood quicken, entranced though he was. But before their lips could meet, Silesia drew back, glanced over her shoulder, and whispered a soft lullaby.

Sleep now, little one.
Sleep and forget.
The darkness can't claim you,
If it doesn't exist.

Heavy and leaden, Mikus' eyelids drooped, then slammed shut entirely, plunging him into shadows that were very much real.

Mikus trailed Rittermark Silesia Marta through the palace halls, scratching his neck while trying in vain to figure out how he'd fallen asleep during their meeting with Governor Titania. He remembered knocking on the door, but everything after that?

One massive blank, murky and dark.

"I apologize, Rittermark," Mikus said, inclining his head like the penitent statues lining the carpeted passageway. "I've been getting enough sleep and eating properly, so I don't understand—"

"Don't let it happen again," Silesia snarled.

Her tone suggested that was the end of the discussion, so Mikus simply stared at the crossed white sabers on the back of her black jacket as they walked. It was a view he was familiar with. Silesia always charged off somewhere and he, the loyal hound, rushed to catch up.

Except ...

Mikus caught a whiff of cinnamon floating down the hall. Strange. They were nowhere near the palace kitchens, and there wasn't a serving trolley in sight. Was it a floral fragrance, drifting in from windows above the gardens? A new perfume favored by what few noble ladies remained in the Darmatian court?

No! Mikus' mind shouted at him. *She did it* again!

Clarity hit him like a pugilist's sucker punch, breaking his stride, freezing him in place. Mikus *had* been awake during the Rittermarschal's meeting. He'd seen the extent of their indiscretion, heard them plotting treason.

But more importantly, Mikus now knew who Silesia *Martavis* was.

"What are you smiling for?" His tormentor turned and glared at him, hands on her hips. "Void out on your own time. Or when you're between me and a bullet. At least then you can still be useful."

"My apologies, Rittermark," Mikus said, erasing his grin.

481

Silesia spun on her heel and kept walking. "You're apologizing a lot lately, Garax. *Fix it.*"

The smile crept back onto his face, defiance that would, at last, be rewarded. He would soon be able to fix his biggest problem, as Silesia desired. When that happened, *she* would be the one on her knees apologizing, begging the Emperor through tear-stained eyes to forgive what she'd done and who she was.

For there was only *one* Martavis bloodline Mikus knew of: that of Lanara Martavis, former third consort, *traitor* to the Empire.

Chapter 49

Life and Death

Adamantele 11, 697 ABH
Resistance Base, Sarconian Province of Darmatia

Matteo stumbled through the chaos of the hangar bay, one arm clutching the sack holding all he owned, the other warding away passing soldiers like a trembling sword. He wasn't claustrophobic, otherwise he couldn't squeeze into a cramped airship cockpit or traipse through dark sewer tunnels as they had in Etrus. But he *did* get nervous around people, and a whole army's worth were swarming around him.

Eyes down, watch their feet, Matteo told himself. His gut churned, making him *almost* wish he could be back on the surface training with Holcomb, painful as it had been.

Up ahead, a long-bearded sergeant perched atop a stack of crates, directing the flow of traffic like an orchestra conductor. He glanced at his clipboard, then waved a rag-covered wrench to his left.

"Landin' teams that'away," he bellowed, loud as an airship's docking horn. "Transports at the bay's far end. Can't miss 'em."

The crowd shifted, and a slope-shouldered Terran knocked Matteo aside as he marched in that direction. Matteo regained his balance just in time to dodge a Hue lumbering the other way, two crates of rifles tucked under his arms, and stepped backward onto the toes of a Sylph.

"I'm so sorry!" Matteo yelled, straining to be heard above the clamor of humming engines, stomping feet, and shouted orders.

The woman glared at him, then flipped her braided hair over her shoulder and stalked off. Matteo caught a glimpse of a tattoo as she vanished from sight—a strand of blue ivy snaking up her bare arm and shoulder. His blood ran cold. If not for a push from a foul-mouthed sailor, Matteo might have frozen where he stood.

"Eyes up, void-for-brains!"

Instead, he let the shove propel him into motion, dropping his sack as he went. Matteo recognized the woman: Siena, one of the Sylph who'd turned hostile when he'd questioned them about Velle's hidden tattoo.

And the ink on Siena's arms wasn't the only thing he'd noticed. Something in the palm of her hand had glinted silver in the cavern's bright lamplight. A short dagger? A vial filled with poison?

What it was didn't matter. Matteo cut through the press of bodies, heading in the opposite direction of Siena. Following her wouldn't stop what he knew was coming. He needed to get above the crowd, find Velle, and reach her first.

"Hey, where do you think you're going?"

"There's a line here, buddy. Or are you that eager to get back in the war?"

Matteo ignored the shouts, the jostling and bumping. Thrusting off the shoulder of a small man in fitted combat armor, he landed on a pallet of grain sacks, then clambered up an illyrium crystal crate to stand beside the slack-jawed sergeant.

"Son, you need to climb back down a'fore I—"

There wasn't time for argument. Matteo pointed at the silver-gold cannon medal pinned to his collar in place of a rank insignia. "Lieutenant," he said. "And you're a sergeant." He gestured at the chevrons sewn onto the man's sweaty, grease-stained fatigues. "I outrank you, so move aside."

"Las' I checked, a medal ain't a rank badge. Don't much care who you are or what you need. This is gettin' reported to . . ."

Report it to Major Reev, Matteo thought, scanning the chamber for red-skin and flowing raven hair. *It couldn't matter less right now.*

Hundreds of bodies filled the base's drydock, forming lines to board the cruisers and transports, hauling supplies up the vessels' wide loading ramps. *Dharmasya* and *Conviction* looked far healthier than when Matteo had first laid eyes on them. The scaffolding supporting them had been removed, and off-color patches—bronze or brass instead of their natural metallic blue—covered their wounds like hastily applied bandages. Better still, their engines were aglow with a yellow sheen, and the air beneath their gravpads bucked and twisted as they floated under their own power.

Like the Resistance, there was life in them yet.

But Velle wouldn't be on the ramps, or in line to go aboard. She'd been assigned as a salvator for the ground teams. Matteo's eyes drifted toward the transports and fighter craft being lowered to the ground on thick cables.

He saw Vallen, regaling a group of wide-eyed soldiers with a tale about some exaggerated exploit. Unter stood nearby, a blue island in a swirling ocean of tan and gray. And in his shadow was . . .

Velle! Matteo's spirits soared. She was safe, and Siena was still weaving her way across the hangar toward her. There were only a few Sylph in the Darmatian army, so it was easy to find her and her comrades.

Comrades who are much, much closer to Velle than she is, Matteo realized, panic piercing his heart.

The older Sylph was two squads behind Velle in line, while the male from their gang was walking from transport to transport, a clipboard in one hand and a wrench in the other. He wore an engimage's coveralls and utility belt, but Matteo knew he wasn't part of the maintenance crew. Both were steadily easing their way toward Velle.

Why attack now? Matteo wondered.

He'd done his best to protect Velle from a distance, asking the others to never leave her alone, even at the latrine. But they were heading into battle. Surely targeting her during the coming chaos would be more logical. Did they fear dying and leaving the deed undone? Was their hatred—their desire for revenge—that intense?

Shaking his head, Matteo banished his meaningless thoughts. He needed to move. To act.

To protect Velle, even if she didn't want him near her.

Matteo closed his eyes and activated his magic. Then he leapt off the stack of crates.

The hangar came alive as he fell. Grays, browns, and blues were replaced by a vibrant array of golden yellow. Radiant stars for illyrium crystals, bright beacons for the mages, and subdued glimmers for everyone else. Matteo *heard* his pulse quicken. Felt his breath trickle down his throat like an intoxicating wine. *This* was living.

A dozen strands shot backward from his central spool—the most balancing threads Matteo could manage right now. Their matching ends, the twelve soldiers closest to him, lit up as the rest of the chamber was swallowed by shadow.

Those lights dodged away as Matteo landed. He bent into the impact, rolled, and came up running.

Next. The first dozen lights were useless now, so Matteo cast his web to the next group, and the next after that. They were prayer candles and he was their temple attendant, snuffing out ones that had burned too long, bringing flame to those in darkness.

Most cleared out of Matteo's path. Some didn't move or even tried to block him, reaching to grab his arms or uniform jacket. The light showed him how they would attack, sketching glowing outlines of the near future for him to avoid. Matteo ducked a swipe from the right, jumped a trip, and deftly squeezed between two burly lights hoping to pincer him.

His head throbbed as it processed so much sensory data, as it planned each cut, shift, and slide he needed to perform. But it didn't matter. Only Velle and this wondrous feeling of *connection*—to men'ar and everything it touched—meant anything right now.

And then Matteo was there. He skidded to a halt beside the beaming sun that was Unter, spreading his net about them in all directions.

"Unter, keep any Sylph you see away from Velle!"

"What's gotten into you, Professor?" asked a white-hot star, so brilliant Matteo had to raise a hand to shield his eyes.

Was that Vallen? He was brighter than any mage he'd ever seen— so bright it was like two infernos crammed into a single vessel. "Just protect Velle!" Matteo yelled. "Trust me."

The world went sideways. With a *pop* and a screech of pain, Matteo's magic failed him. He dropped to one knee, gasping for breath, hangar spinning around him. Just one thing remained clear: Velle rushing to his side, healing glyphs already forming in her hands.

"Matteo?" she whispered in his ear as her soft fingers found his neck. Relief washed through him, keeping the fog in his head at bay. "Everyone's staring at you! The Major's guards are heading this way, and I have no idea what stunt you were trying to pull by—"

"Behind you!" Matteo gasped.

"Die, tyrant's spawn!" Black hair flaring, the male Sylph dove from the top of the nearest transport, silver flashing in his extended right hand.

He didn't get close. One of Unter's upper arms lashed out, catching him by the throat and slamming him to the concrete floor. Blood flew from his lips and the weapon tumbled from his grasp, skittering toward them.

Matteo had been right. It was a palm-sized dagger with a vial wedged in its hilt—one filled with murky green fluid. If it wasn't poison, Matteo was a muck-fish.

As the Major's guards arrived and rushed toward the now convulsing, frothing at the mouth Sylph, another shout came from the other direction.

"We won't go back!" the Sylph matron screamed, lunging at Velle. "Not now, not ever!"

The girl's eyes went wide. Her hands were down, she was casting a healing spell, and the assassin was but three steps away. There was nothing she could do.

Matteo tried to rise. Tried to throw himself between her and the falling blade. But as strong as he'd become, his limbs still betrayed him, refusing to do more than twitch. No matter how far he'd come, weakness still held him back in the end.

No. No, no, no-no-NO! Matteo raged inside.

"Spi'ferat!"

A ball of fire swept the Sylph assassin off her feet and sent her tumbling through the crowd. Vallen chased after her, krenesh blade in hand, but Lilith materialized from the onlookers and reached the body first.

"We only need one prisoner," she said, drawing her blade and silencing the woman's agonized shrieks. A snap of her fingers snuffed out the flames crawling across the Sylph's body.

For once, Matteo agreed with their extreme measures. These were *fanatics.* Men and women bent on exacting revenge against Velle for reasons he knew nothing about. If they were willing to attack her in the middle of the army's deployment, they weren't people who could be reasoned with.

And one is still out there, Matteo thought, surveying the crowd. Not a speck of crimson flesh nor a wisp of raven-black hair could be seen among the herd of gawkers. Siena had wisely chosen to disappear, content to try again later.

For now . . . Matteo needed to learn the truth.

He glanced up at the stunned girl cradling him, her body trembling so much *he* was shaking. Just like the last time, Velle's surprise had revealed her secret. A three-pronged black star and a crescent moon glared at him from beneath her right eye.

"It's later, Velle," Matteo whispered. "I need to know what that tattoo means."

"No."

Velle pulled her hands from Matteo's neck. Raising two fingers to her cheek, she brushed them slowly across the tattoo. It evaporated at her touch, little flakes of crimson dust folding over the dark ink until her flesh was smooth and spotless.

She didn't run like before. Matteo studied her face, more beautiful than anything he'd ever seen. Like a pastel sunset or the dazzling world unveiled whenever he wielded his magic.

But Velle's obsidian eyes were cold as the stone they lay on. Beneath the molded cuirass of her combat harness, blue and black plates fitted to her body like a second skin, Matteo could see her shoulders tense, her muscles primed to flee. Her brightness and cheer were a front hiding . . .

What, exactly? Velle had once told him she wanted to save Vallen to save herself. What did that mean?

"Why?" Matteo asked, straining to grab her forearm. Velle twitched away.

"To keep you safe." Velle sighed, gesturing at the unconscious Sylph being hauled upright by two guards wearing red MP bands on their arms. "Look at what some of my people did because of that mark. Look at what *you* did."

She pointed toward the path he'd carved. Grumbling soldiers were extricating themselves from piles of supplies, each other, anywhere they'd fallen while dodging out of his way. The sergeant directing traffic had his rump stuck in a broken crate, loosing a string of curses as a Hue tried to tug him free. He must have lost his balance when Matteo leapt from the top of the stack.

A third guard approached, his rifle barrel pointed at the ground. He cleared his throat. "Miss, that man"—he nodded at Matteo—"was part of the altercation, and Sergeant Maefin wants him drawn up on insubordination charges for disrupting army operations. We'll need to take him to Major Reev."

Matteo bristled. They were going to arrest *him*? He'd saved Velle—protected her from a trio of vile assassins. He was the hero here, *not* a villain.

Stepping forward, Vallen placed an arm in the guard's way. "Lieutenant Metellus," he said, indicating the silver rank bars painted on the breastplate of his combat cuirass. Like Velle, he was part of the ground assault force. "I'll make sure he sees Major Reev once the fleet is underway, corporal."

"But, sir—"

Vallen jerked his thumb at the limp Sylph being hauled toward *Dharmasya's* ramp. "Just get a confession out of that void-stain."

A shiver raced through Velle, drawing Matteo's attention. "What's he going to confess, Velle?" he pressed. "What will he tell them? Better we know now than later, right?"

The girl looked at him with quivering, fear-filled eyes. Years melted away. The mature, compassionate woman Matteo knew vanished into a terrified child cowering before shadows he couldn't see. He wanted to hold her, to tell her all would be fine if she just trusted them.

Trusted *him*.

Velle lunged at him just like before, silencing Matteo's protests with her lips, smothering him with her kiss. There was less passion in

488

the act than the first time, and even though his heart raced and his blood exulted, Matteo knew this wasn't real.

This was how Velle buried her problems. How she blocked out a past she wasn't ready to deal with.

Some of the soldiers cheered, whistling and applauding Matteo on his good fortune. Vallen snorted. "Is . . . *that* actually happening? Please tell me someone spiked our morning gruel with something."

"I'd say it's happening," Lilith said. "Those lips don't lie."

But they did. And perhaps everything about Velle was a lie, from her reasons for enrolling at the Academy, to her kindness, to this love she pretended to feel for him. A lie Matteo would uncover no matter what.

Velle broke the kiss, pulling back while staring into Matteo's eyes. "If we survive, I'll tell you the whole story. Otherwise . . . " She bit her lip, gaze distant and full of pain. "It's not something I want as my last thought in this world."

Chapter 50

Departure

The view from *Dharmasya's* bridge gave Jis hope. She stood outside the wraparound glass windows, leaning against a narrow railing that was the only thing between her and a fifty-meter plummet to the hangar floor. From there she could see the entire Resistance: two light cruisers, twenty transports, three wings of khamer hoverjets, and the hundreds of soldiers and support personnel willing to give their lives for a Darmatia free of Sarconian tyranny.

Jis wouldn't disappoint them. *Couldn't* disappoint them. Not everyone would survive, but by the Veneer, she would ensure as many as possible reached the Ascendancy and the safety they promised.

So *of course*, the loading procedure immediately went awry. Jis watched timid Lieutenant Alhan mount a stack of crates, bowl over Sergeant Maefin, then take off sprinting across the chamber. Bodies tumbled in his wake. A Hue dodged the boy only to stumble into a pyramid of grain sacks. Bags toppled, canvas ripped, and what precious little preserved rations they had scattered beneath an army of clomping boots.

Before Jis could scream for a guard squad to grab the fool, shouts rose near the transports on the hangar's far side. She turned and ran through the bridge, knocking a stack of papers from the arms of Corporal Sayles, drawing a raised eyebrow from Rodale at the communications station.

No time for an explanation. Bursting out the opposite hatch, Jis raced to the railing and tried to process what was happening far below. A Sylph dressed in engimage coveralls was twitching on the ground, Unter's massive fist clenched about his neck. Another roared and charged Velle and Alhan, who were huddled together on the ground.

Orange flames tossed the would-be assassin through the air. She hit hard, rolled, then flopped onto her back, magic-fed fire hungrily devouring her garments and skin. Shrieks and the smell of charred flesh wafted up from below, turning Jis' stomach. Fortunately, Lilith strode to the woman and ended her misery with a flick of her blade.

"Send a squad to clean up!" Jis shouted over her shoulder. "And get someone up here to explain what in Sariel's name I just saw."

It was a mistake, she thought, fingers tightening on the rail. *Promoting the fledglings, agreeing to the Ascendancy's demands, this*

490

assault, everything.

Boots thudded on the metal walkway behind Jis. "Trouble in the heavenly halls?" Rodale asked, stepping up beside her.

He wore a black and blue combat jumpsuit fitted with thin gestalt-steel plates on the chest, legs, shoulders, and arms. Most of his ruddy hair was tucked up under an officer's beret, and the scraggly patches in his beard were starting to fill back in. The dark circles around his eyes had faded, and his breath smelled of fresh mantri leaves, evidence the Colonel hadn't run back to the bottle.

This is what could have been, a small part of Jis said. *A partner who's handsome, intelligent, supportive.* Only . . . she preferred the version in her fantasies that *didn't* have the ale paunch poking out above his belt. That would take some effort to eliminate.

"This mission is going to be a disaster," Jis sighed, slumping until her elbows rested on the railing. "The ships aren't even in the air and we already have chaos in the boarding line, weeks of grain on the hangar floor, and some sort of assassins targeting our students. I'm tempted to call the whole thing off."

Rodale grinned. "But what about our dinner reservations, dear? Do you know how hard it was to get a candlelit table at Luceno's on such short notice?"

"That little bistro in Etrus with wall-to-wall mosaics and ivy cascading down to the waterfront?"

"The very same. They have a spicy seafood carbonara that would put hair on Ellara's stones."

Jis frowned. "Ellara's *female.* She doesn't have stones."

"My point stands."

The crisis below slowly sorted itself out. Guards with red armbands forced their way through the cordon of onlookers, bound the hands of the surviving assailant, then waved for Sergeant Maefin and the other non-coms to resume boarding operations. The subdued murmur of soldiers preparing for battle rejoined the clanking of engimage hammers and the cruisers' humming engines.

Across from Jis, a maintenance crew hung halfway down *Conviction's* flank, welders sparking as they rushed to seal one final breach in her hull. They were suspended by thin cables tied to the ship's bridge railing, a match for the one she and Rodale stood at. A loose knot, a frayed line, and those engimages would plummet to their demise, the rend they'd worked so hard to close left gaping and exposed.

Mother Tabitha would see a metaphor here. Something about

491

a single mistake dooming not just the Resistance, but the whole country as well.

What was Jis doing? She might be a powerful mage, but she was a *teacher*—someone who talked about battles instead of fighting them. The Ruling Council had never given her a proper command or put her in a situation where her decisions meant life or death for those following her orders.

Even the Kharit Incident had been Jis against the elements. Succeed and save hundreds, fail and sink below the waves. The only life she'd risked had been her own.

Now Jis was supposed to lead a rebellion, a revolution? Her knuckles whitened on the railing as all her carefully laid plans, speeches, and assurances melted to slush in her mind.

"Rodale, you're a colonel," Jis said, wearing a smile that went skin deep. "If General Iolus isn't going on the expedition, I think you should have overall comm—"

"Thank you for these past few days," Rodale said, cutting her off.

The rest of Jis' resignation froze on her lips. "You're thanking *me*? I just gave you the stuff I didn't want to do. Taking stock of unit strength, ammunition, airship range, our illyrium reserves, and everything else involved *way* too much math."

"You didn't do well in our artillery physics or supply accounting classes, did you?" Rodale winked at her. "However did you graduate?"

"Not thanks to you." Jis punched his arm. "We were supposed to be studying, but *you* always distracted me."

"A prepared commander always targets his opponent's weaknesses."

She punched him again, harder this time. "Don't quote High Admiral Nysier to justify *tickling me to tears* every time I visited your dorm."

"All's fair in love and—" Rodale stopped mid-quotation and jumped aside, hands raised to ward off another blow. "Fine, fine. You win, as always."

Then the moment passed. Jis' gaze roved across the soldiers—*her* soldiers—climbing into poorly armored transports, marching up *Conviction's* lowered ramps. The weight of responsibility stole the mirth from her voice.

"Why thank me?" Jis asked. "Why thank me for *this*?" She gestured at the throng below, thinning as the fateful moment of departure ticked closer.

Rodale turned to face her, eyes the color of open sky boring into hers. "You gave me back my purpose, Jis. Asking me to train Matteo. Getting me invested in those kids. Void, even just being willing to *listen* to me after all the crud I put you through. You didn't have to let me serve with you again, but"—he tapped his polished chest plate, then reached up to give his beret a tug—"here we are."

The combat gear *did* look dashing on him, but Jis would never admit that to his face. "Are you sure you're sober? You sound a little too reasonable to be the Rodale I know."

"Clean as the Creator's nethers after a dip in the temple nectar."

"That's more like it."

They both chuckled. Then something warm touched Jis' hand. Glancing down, she saw Rodale's weathered hand settling over hers. Was he trying to make a move on her? Jis wouldn't freeze his fingers off, but she would—

Gratitude. When she looked back at Rodale, there was nothing but gratitude in his awkward, toothy smile and sunken eyes. "Don't try to give me command again, Jis. I refuse now, and I'll refuse every time because of what I just told you. I admire you more than any person alive. And it's the same for your students, your men, and this whole void-forsaken army. They look at me and see a corrupt drunk. That's what I was, and that's what I'll always be. But you?"

Rodale squeezed Jis' hand, feeding heat and reassurance into her frozen body. Her breath caught. How long had it been since she'd felt something—*anything*—when touching another person?

"They look at you and see a *leader.* A *hero.* They might follow orders from me or General Iolus, but they'll do the impossible for you."

"How do you know that?" Jis asked.

Balling his fingers into a fist, Rodale raised his arm and lightly bopped her on the chin. "Because I'm part of this loony army and I know *I* would."

Jis laughed. Laughed until she staggered into the bridge bulkhead, laughed until she had to put both hands on the railing to avoid tumbling over. A few of the officers on the command deck glanced their way but wisely kept their thoughts to themselves.

"So sappy," Jis said, clutching her gut as she straightened. "I think you could keep a cake-maker in business for *years* with your sugary one-liners. But have it your way. I'll keep the big chair"—she nodded at *Dharmasya's* captain chair, situated on a raised platform at the rear of the bridge—"until we reach the Ascendancy."

Rodale swept an arm to the side, slid his left leg back, and bowed as low as his paunch would allow. "Excellent, Madame Commander. However," his tone darkened, "there's another matter we should discuss while we can."

He strode past Jis down the walkway, motioning for her to follow. They rounded the rear of the bridge, descended a flight of maintenance steps, and stopped in the shadow of *Dharmasya's* central turret.

"So secretive," Jis said.

The outer hull was deserted in both directions, their only company the twin guns and rigging above their heads. No one but engimages frequented the airship's top deck, and most of them were probably below, prepping the engines for takeoff.

Rodale pulled her close, whispering in her ear. "Yes, because what I'm about to say is treason. Well, it would be if we still had a functioning government."

"Is it about General Iolus' decision to stay behind with a small part of his staff? The ludicrous claim that he's fallen ill and can't travel?"

"It's about . . . " Rodale paused, then raised an eyebrow. "That's exactly it. How did you know?"

"Simple. I don't trust him."

Jis didn't need to list all the reasons, but her suspicions had been mounting for weeks. How had desk-bound, magic-less Iolus escaped the Sarconian occupation of Nemare? Why had the coward agreed to Taala's terms so easily? Everything Rodale had told her—the general's shady deals with politicians and industrialists, his bribes, document forging, and a hundred other crimes that had never come to light—just cemented her opinion of the scoundrel.

"If you understand, this will be simple," Rodale said. "In the event he's working against us, we need to—"

"Corporal Sayles!" Jis yelled.

The blonde girl detached from the shadows of a nearby exhaust pipe that was taller than she was. Jis hadn't heard Sayles follow them from the bridge, but she knew her aide—and occasional protector or problem solver—was never far away.

"Here, Major," the girl chorused, waving at a slack-jawed Rodale as she approached.

"Pick six soldiers you trust and join the General's guards," Jis ordered. "If it becomes apparent he has anything other than the Resistance's best interests at heart . . . "

" . . . remove said heart," Sayles finished, still grinning cheerfully.

Jis squeezed Rodale's arm, then used a finger to push his mouth shut. "Is that about what you were thinking?"

"About," he mumbled.

"Good. Now if you'll excuse me, I have a rebellion to spark."

Turning, Jis started back up the walkway toward the bridge. The last soldiers were boarding their transports, most of the crates of ammo, crystals, and rations had been loaded onto *Conviction*, and the red warning lights above the hangar doors were flashing red as the gears adorning them began to turn. Once Jis gave the final order, their paltry fleet would set sail.

A hand grabbed her shoulder, spun her around. Before she could react, Rodale thrust a bandage-wrapped package into her hand, then closed her fingers on top of it.

"What's this?" Jis asked.

Rodale smiled. "Something I should have given you a long time ago." Stepping away, Rodale clicked his heels together and gave her a stiff salute. "Knock 'em dead, *Admiral* Reev."

Chapter 51

One for the Road

Adamantele 11, 697 ABH
Above the Phar Coast, Sarconian Province of Darmatia

Quiet was a dangerous thing.

It wormed inside Vallen's mind, dredging up thoughts he preferred buried, threatening his heavy eyelids with sleep. He needed distraction, conversation, noise. Anything was preferable to this ominous pre-battle stillness and the perilous freedom it afforded the thing inside his head.

Don't think of me that way, the darkness soothed, stroking the inside of Vallen's skull with shadowy tendrils. *We're old friends now, you and me. Two pals heading out to whet our blades on mortal blood.*

Every bump, jerk, and twist of the transport ship brought Vallen closer to a fight. He craved the sweet release of combat, of surrendering to the tempo of violence. Rushing blood. Clanging swords and frantic breath. At last, he would have a chance to avenge Leon and bury Elaine forever.

And yet . . . Vallen also feared the seconds ticking past, counted by the chronometer on his neighbor's wrist. The soldier—a monolith of a man with short blond braids and matching beard—hunched against his restraints, unconcerned with the racket of his timepiece. Each tick was a gunshot, a scream, a screech. A reminder of every loss Vallen had suffered, and of the darkness' lust for slaughter.

Another jolt shook the thinly armored craft, tossing the passengers around, rattling the weapons and gear tied down on the racks above their heads. Across the aisle, a girl squealed and clutched the boy beside her. Both were young, perhaps two or three years Vallen's juniors. Pale, freckled, and trembling, they seemed fresh off some backwater farm— kids who had enlisted to get away and see the world.

They wore the same combat armor he did: black jumpsuit, blue impact webbing on the joints, and thin steel plates where getting stabbed would hurt. But the garb was loose on them, like they didn't have the presence to fill it out.

You pity them? the darkness asked, tone mocking.

Vallen wasn't sure. But he was voiding tired of the morbid silence.

He stomped his boots on the floor. "Is everyone already dead? It's like a funeral in here. Though to be fair, I'd prefer the funeral. They usually have decent food."

That earned him a chorus of laughs and a slap on the shoulder from blond-braids, who had just unwrapped a very gray, very blocky ration bar. "Some last meal, huh?"

"Those can definitely kill you, Herj," another soldier quipped. "And if the bland brick gets you, the Sarcs won't. Look on the bright side."

"*Last meal?*" the timid girl glanced up, brown eyes shaking. "We're not going to ... I mean, the Major said ... "

In the corner by the ramp, Velle stopped rubbing her right cheek and glared at him. Vallen knew that look: *You messed up, fix it.*

He waved to draw the girl's attention. "We're going to be fine, sweetheart. Triaron's solemn promise." Vallen patted the plate over his heart with more confidence than he felt.

The boy holding her snorted. Her brother, perhaps? They certainly looked alike. "That's well and fine for you to say," the brother said. "You can mow them down in droves with your magic. But we're not mages. Void, we barely know how to *shoot*. How well do you think we'll do against Sarc elites?"

"About as well as the Triaron, to be honest," Lilith said, chipping in from her seat beside the closed cockpit door. Though her scabbard rested on her thighs, for once the blade wasn't drawn. Sharp swords getting loose in a cramped, shaking compartment was a recipe for disaster.

"I find that hard to believe."

Lilith licked her lips and winked at Vallen. "Creator as my witness, it's the truth. I've put him on his rear so many times I'm surprised he still remembers how to stand."

More guffaws filled the transport, louder than before, and even the frightened girl cracked a ghost of a grin. A month ago, Vallen would have fought tooth and nail to save face. Now he just flipped Sariel's lance at Lilith and smiled at the jeering faces around him.

"Laugh it up," he said playfully. "Get your kicks in now. But I'll remember every single one of you."

"So, you think normal people can't fight, miss ... ?"

Colonel Holcomb left the question hanging as he extended his palm toward the young girl. Vallen didn't know why Major Reev's former lover had chosen to ride in their transport, but he suspected she'd had a hand in it. He couldn't think of any other reason for the ground force commander to become their personal wet nurse.

"Miss Erika, sir," the girl finished, shaking his hand.

"A beautiful name, one that'd make Ellara blush with envy." Holcomb leaned forward, dropping his voice to a conspiratorial whisper. "But tell me, Miss Erika, why count out non-mages? Grab a rifle from that rack"—he pointed at a shelf of weapons bolted to the bulkhead beside the landing ramp—"and I'd be hard pressed to keep you from putting a bullet in my mostly rotten brain."

"He's different." Erika's brother nodded at Vallen.

"The Triaron?" Holcomb chuckled. "Let's leave that one out of the conversation for now. He's too easy a target."

Vallen's fingers twitched, but he resisted the urge to make a crude gesture at his superior. "Colonel . . ."

"Calm down, calm down. No, the story I'm imagining is of the other far more famous, far more handsome—"

"Debatable," Vallen interjected.

"—Triaron. I'm speaking, of course, of just and virtuous King Darmatus Aurelian."

Erika's brown eyes grew to the size of glazed sticky buns. *Which suggests I might be a little hungry right now,* Vallen thought, stomach rumbling.

"He wasn't always a mage?" she asked.

"Not at all," Holcomb said. "None of his brothers were. Do you want to hear the tale of how they first tasted magic?"

Vallen groaned. "Please no. The one you did at camp was torment enough."

He was quickly outvoted. Clapping and cheers filled the ship, Unter's loudest of all. The blue giant wasn't so much strapped as *squeezed* into his seat. Three lashed-together cables formed his restraint belt, and the bench beneath him protested a little more each time turbulence rocked the transport.

Let the talking mountain have his fun, the darkness murmured. *I bet he'll be the one to die for you today. You lost Elaine to the flames, Leon to the Empire, and now the gravekeeper comes calling again. If only you had the power to—*

One slam. Two. Vallen banged his head back against the cold metal bulkhead until the voice withered to static. He was in control. It would be *his* power, not the shadows in his mind, that won today.

When Vallen looked up, Velle was staring at him, worry creasing her lips and brow as she absently rubbed her face. He shook his head.

She didn't need to know. Not now, preferably not ever. Turning toward Holcomb, Vallen lost himself in a story that would stave off the quiet, if only for a time.

Fast as a striking viper, the colonel popped open a satchel on his belt and withdrew four small sacks bound with colored threads. Three were familiar to Vallen: the green, blue, and red dust pouches he'd seen at their campfire. The fourth, tied with a yellow string, was new.

"The world of the Elder Three was a dark place—"

Vallen rolled his eyes and held out his arms to encompass the rattling cabin. "It's not exactly Elysium and light around here right now."

"Do you wanna tell the story, boy?" A little of Holcomb's former fire crept into his voice. "Or do you wanna see if one-winged Artyr cares enough about sassy braggarts to catch you when you get tossed from the loading ramp? I'm good with either."

"The second sounds like fun," Herj said, digging his elbow into Vallen's side.

Lilith raised her hand. "Seconded."

"I loathe you all," Vallen said, crossing his arms and slumping against his crash restraints.

"Ah, where was I," Holcomb said, settling back into the tale. "Yes, darkness, and lots of it. The Creator was missing. His Veneer hadn't been seen for centuries. And to make matters worse, a vile plague was spreading across the land."

He tugged the red drawstring and dumped the bag. The dust should have fallen to the floor, but some unseen wind caught and whipped it into the center of the aisle. Each shudder of the transport was a breath of life to the dust, shaping it, molding it, and at last setting it in motion.

The red sands showed a dilapidated village. Bodies lay untouched in the streets, doors and windows were boarded up, and what few people still lived peeked out between the slats, unwilling to venture outside.

Vallen could see nothing wrong with the air. Rot-flies swarmed the carcasses. Mangy mutts chewed on the meals left for them, bony stomachs heaving with each bite.

But the corpses? They were another story.

Scarlet crystals jutted from them like spring blooms, deadly flowers that had killed their hosts in an effort to reach the sun. A bloated man in a fine doublet had sprouted a beard of shards around his face. Nearby, a boy of six or seven had grown to twice his original height as the crystals jutted from his legs and skull.

Vallen knew what he was seeing. There was not a being alive who hadn't heard of the Red Plague, and not one of them wanted to see it return.

Holcomb nodded at the grim reactions of his audience. "The Red Plague was doing what the Grand Alliance of Races had failed to. Terrans in the midlands were dying in their hundreds and thousands, their bodies piling up in cities and villages. To touch the crystal—to chance it getting under your skin, into your blood—was death. Children abandoned infected parents. Parents, their children. It was a dark era, and the gods seemed not to care.

"Enter our heroes." With a dramatic flourish, Holcomb took a pinch of dust from each of the other bags in his lap and cast them into the air.

In seconds, three Terrans around Vallen's age rose from the village street and wandered into the neighboring forest. Their clothes were rags, their hair long and matted by sticks and slime, and the shortest and scrawniest had a single gleaming crystal protruding from his neck. The green one, infected with the Plague, stumbled along in the wake of his blue and yellow brothers.

"At some point during their travels, Rabban was stricken with the crimson scourge. He implored his brothers, Sarcon"—Holcomb pointed at the tall, long-haired yellow figure—"and Darmatus"—he indicated the muscular blue figure with black stubble on his cheeks—"to leave him. They refused, insisting they would find a cure or share his fate. As one they had lived, as one they would die.

"Weeks passed, and with every day—with every breath—Rabban's condition worsened." The little green man slowed, then began to limp as a walking staff appeared in his hands. Though his glow had started a brilliant verdant, tendrils of crimson spread from the crystal on his neck, creeping along his veins, crawling toward his heart. Soon he was covered in red—only a speck of green left beneath his left breast.

"They tried everything," Holcomb said. "Witches' brews, shaman spells, druid ointments, every manner of cure both natural and occult. They climbed mountains, plumbed caverns, scoured forests, and explored old ruins. Every attempt failed."

Holcomb snapped his fingers, making Rabban vanish and reappear strapped to Darmatus' broad back. The poor lad's shoulders heaved with every ragged, gasping breath he took. "Their supplies dwindled, their money ran out, and Rabban was on the verge of succumbing to the plague, his body shrouded in crystals. The next attempt to save him would be their last.

"Down into the bowels of Lozaria they went, past the point miners dared not venture, past where sharp-eyed predators refused to nest. If they couldn't find a cure, the tunnels would be their tomb. For when Rabban died, the miasma his crystals emitted would also doom his brothers."

"But then a miracle occurred!" Holcomb shouted, leaning forward to cast more blue and green dust into the scene. A vast chasm appeared, one with square sides and thousands upon thousands of identical archways carved into its walls. The brothers crept toward the bottom along a winding set of steps, breath catching in their throats, eyes wide with wonder.

"The tunnels opened onto a mausoleum lit by eerie blue lights. Cold to the touch"—Darmatus stuck a finger, then his whole hand into a wall-mounted brazier—"but bright all the same. Guided by these lights, they descended the steps. Minutes passed into hours. Hours into an entire day. And at last, just as Rabban's pulse started to fade, they saw it!"

"What?" Erika asked, eyes alight. "What was it?" The rest of the cabin was dead quiet, every listener waiting on bated breath for the story's conclusion.

"Illyriite!" Holcomb exclaimed, tossing the rest of the green bag into the air. The dust gathered at the bottom of the hovering shaft, forming into a bed of emerald crystals that pulsed with white light.

Vallen's scalp tingled. He could sense the darkness inside him sitting up, suddenly invested in Holcomb's tale. Illyriite was clearly the trigger, but why? And if the thing inside him possessed such curiosity—if it wasn't his guilt made manifest and truly lived—what did it want?

"It was like a garden," Holcomb explained. "They carefully picked their way into a chamber filled with draping vines, blooming flowers, and knee-high grasses waving in an unseen wind. All glowed green. All were pure crystal—pure *Illyriite,* though the brothers didn't know it yet.

"As they walked among wonders none would believe, Rabban's limp hand brushed the tip of a leafy fern. Darmatus jerked him away, frightened at what the unknown crystal would do, but Sarcon, following behind, saw the truth of Illyriite's divine power."

Where the fern touched Rabban's fingers, the Red Plague drew back, jagged shards retracting, healthy flesh surfacing in its place. It *was* a miracle.

If only Vallen believed in them.

"Sarcon snatched Rabban from Darmatus' back and cast him into the dense Illyriite thicket. Darmatus cursed him, but Sarcon urged him to wait. Their brother was dead. Any chance at life, even from the unknown, was worth trying."

A red body, more crystal than man, disappeared into the emerald underbrush. But when the vines and grasses pulled back, a green figure devoid of blemish—without a single sliver of crimson left on him—was all that was left behind.

Holcomb flicked his wrist and a burst of light erupted from Rabban and raced up the crypt walls. "Illyriite *was* the cure they'd been searching for. It absorbed the Plague. Consumed it the same way the scourge so greedily drank of mortal blood."

Erika clapped her hands. Velle shook her head and whispered, "Lost Magic always comes with a cost."

Spreading his fingers, Holcomb pulled at the mausoleum's archways, summoning forth whatever lay inside. Ancient bones rattled. Dead teeth clattered, swords scraped free of rusty scabbards, and time-ravaged armor clanked against skeletal bodies it no longer fit. In seconds, an army of soulless, sightless undead was clambering down the shaft toward the brothers.

"Well, they're voided," Herj said with a chuckle.

Holcomb nodded at Velle. "Right you are, missy. Our heroes were as thieves, stealing power they didn't comprehend, robbing a gardener they had never met. And so, the dead turned on them, rising from their funeral biers and rushing them in their hundreds.

"They fought with all the strength they had left."

Darmatus drew a fire-blackened cudgel from his belt and laid about, staving in skinless skulls, shattering gaping ribcages. At his side, Sarcon thrust and stabbed with a chipped dagger, each desperate strike cracking it more and more.

"But no matter how many they felled, how many lifeless bones they piled at their feet, it wasn't enough. The clicking of skeletal fingers echoed up and down the chasm. The chattering of their teeth, so much like laughter, came from every direction. Rabban, healed but unconscious, lay at their backs. With each exchange, they grew bloodier, and he grew closer as they retreated. Soon all three would perish, and knowledge of the cure would die with them.

"Sarcon's dagger broke in two. A splintered buckler slammed atop Darmatus' wrist, knocking his weapon from his grasp. The horde closed in, and they prepared to breathe their last.

"'*STOP!*'" Holcomb roared. Vallen jerked away, pulse hammering. He hadn't realized he was listening so intently.

"The undead obeyed the mysterious voice," Holcomb continued, resuming his previous tone. "They stopped mid-swing, mid-thrust, mid-stab, frozen mere hand spans from skewering the brothers where they lay. Then, *it* arrived."

A sweep of Holcomb's hands split the corpse army down the middle. They shambled aside—heads bowed, backs bent—making way for something far worse.

The creature formed from dust as it walked, a shifting tapestry of *all* the colors Holcomb had used thus far. Tattered red robes hung from its shoulders. A gilt crown, ashen and faded, listed atop its cracked skull. The rest was a sickly combination, blue, greens, and blacks mixed into a palette of rot and decay.

Slimy skin clung desperately to age-worn bones, beneath which pulsed veins of dark ooze. Vallen could see no rhythm to it, no beat. It didn't seem to have a heart. The monster simply *was.*

As it lurched toward the brothers, the retreating shadows revealed it had no chest. Ribs floated where its robes lay open, but beyond was an abyss deep as the mausoleum it ruled. Something wriggled in its eye sockets. Erika scooted forward for a closer look, then squealed and grabbed her brother's arm.

Maggots nested there, squirming around, eating the dead flesh of the creature's face even as more putrefied tissue grew alongside it. Vallen's stomach turned, and he fought the urge to gag. The thing died as it lived. Was reborn even as it decomposed.

Its mouth opened, and Holcomb spoke in a deep, gravelly voice. "'*Life for life, young thieves. You have taken, now you must give.*'"

"Darmatus and Sarcon quailed before the master of the dead. There was no fighting it, no chance to outwit or outrun it. They fell to their knees, begging for Rabban's life, imploring the shade to show him mercy.

"'*You grovel not for yourselves, but for another,*' the aberration said. '*There is nobility in that.*'" Holcomb twitched his fingers. The creature walked to Rabban's side, stooping to gather a discarded fragment of gleaming crimson crystal. Skeletal digits encrusted with gems and jewels rolled the deadly shard back and forth.

"'*All these,*' the aberration said, raising his arms to encompass the silent horde, '*came here for honor, power, and prestige. They lusted after what my garden could do for them. Who they could defeat, who they could usurp with my Illyriite.'"*

"And why not?" Herj said softly. "If the stuff's as powerful as the legends say, we could solve our Sarc problem with a single chunk."

"Story moral is this," Unter rumbled, speaking for the first time in hours. "Power for own gain, use not. For others, only. Not same mistake as deathless make."

The blue giant had been quiet since that Hue delegation visited camp. Well, *quieter,* at least. Vallen hadn't quite realized he missed the big guy's slivers of wisdom until now.

"Is this a true story?" Erika asked. "Is this how the Elder Three got their Illyriite?"

Holcomb winked. "A storyteller never spoils the ending."

With a heave of his arm, the colonel cast the rest of his dust toward the transport's ceiling. It latched onto the creature, extending his shadow, making him seem as large as the mausoleum itself.

"*'For their folly, I condemned them to eternal undeath,'* the aberration bellowed. *'And for the greed of mortals, I took back the gifts I had once given, dragging my garden deep below Lozaria, far beneath their ravenous gazes. Yet still, you found me. It would seem I have no choice but to bury my crypt for good.'"*

The mausoleum walls began to shake. Cracks raced up the columns supporting the shaft, caving in arched ossuaries, splintering ornate carvings that had likely existed for millennia. Dust and rocks rained down on the crystal garden, shattering trees and buds like glass.

Little blue Darmatus, no more than a fourth the height of the ancient aberration, stood and pointed to Rabban. "*'We're different,'* Darmatus said. *'We came to cure, not take. To save, not destroy. Search our hearts. If I'm lying, kill us then. But don't assume two nights are alike simply because the same moons shine on them both.'*

"The aberration stilled, maggots dripping from his eyes like fetid tears. *'I have heard such oaths before, even from my children. They uttered them sweetly, lovingly, only for their promises to decay to lies like my flesh. If they betrayed their oaths, why would mortals do any better? Do you still think you can show me a future I haven't seen before?'"*

Holcomb raised his right arm, and with it, Darmatus grew and grew and grew. Soon he was the same size as the creature, staring it down despite his bleeding scalp, bruised ribs, and broken nose.

"*'I cannot promise you a different future ... ,'* Darmatus said. The aberration grinned, drawing back its limbs to strike. *'But I can give you hope. Hope that night will fade and day will dawn. Hope that life'*—he glanced at Rabban, whose chest quietly rose and fell—*'will triumph over death. I cannot guarantee the light will never fade, but I can promise you the chance for a radiant dawn is worth the risk of an endless night.'"*

"Laughter echoed endlessly through the chasm. *'Hope?'* the aberration snorted. *'That is your defense against an army of undead? Against me, the—'"*

The door to the cockpit banged open, revealing a man in a blue flight suit with what looked like a giant pair of earmuffs on his head. What did *those* do?

"Final approach in five," he said to Holcomb. "We'll jump the cliffs, skim the settlement, and land before they can organize. Make sure you're belted in. Things are going to get rough."

"I thought they already were," Herj joked, cinching his restraints tighter.

The pilot blinked at him, then rolled the door shut.

"Let's get ready, people," Holcomb said. "Remember which rifle is yours, run through our deployment drills in your head, and for the love of Sariel's syphilitic screw, I hope you went to the little commando's room before we left."

Someone held up their hand. "I could go again, sir."

"Not when I'm down-ship of you, you won't."

Nervous laughter and the sound of hurried preparations filled the cabin. Clinking buckles, rattling hooks, and snapping straps. Vallen rolled his bronze rod between his gloved palms, savoring the press of the metal, imagining the thrill of wielding it. His long wait was at an end.

Our wait, the darkness corrected. It seemed fixated on Holcomb, though Vallen couldn't fathom why.

"Sir!" Erika stretched across her brother to tap the colonel's leg. "That can't be how the story ends."

It was just as well the tale had been cut off. Even if it wasn't a complete fabrication, Darmatus was a liar. Sometimes doing nothing— giving up, refusing to try—was the right choice. If Vallen had never met Elaine, the girl wouldn't have died. The same was true of Leon. Any 'dawn' he might have spent with them hadn't been worth their lives.

Holcomb glanced one way, then the other. Cupping his mouth, he leaned in and whispered, "I'll let you in on a secret, Erika. The story hasn't ended. You and I—everyone in the army—*we're* the culmination of Darmatus' hope. Rumor says that mausoleum is buried deep, deep below Nemare. Our nation was *built* on the dreams of the past. So, keep your chin up, missy. As long as we survive, Darmatia's hope lives on."

A chill slithered down Vallen's spine, making him shiver, setting his legs to trembling. The darkness inside him was *elated*. He could sense its impossibly wide grin. Hear its laughter bouncing around his skull.

Oh, you clever, clever candle, it exulted, shadows whipping into a frenzy. *You hid it well, hid it in the last place I'd think to look. But now, my old, sputtering flame, I've found your Vestige. And so begins the end.*

Idyllic Days IV

Darkness fell over Nemare like a slowly drawn curtain, the sun clinging to the distant dunes as it breathed its last. The scene was beautiful. Glittering sand as far as Leon could see, gusts of wind whipping dust into dancing funnels, and a land dappled in streaks of deep orange and scarlet.

Yet Leon could not enjoy the dying of the day.

Needles pricked his scalp, probing, searching for the truths seared into his skull. A slimy feeling of wrongness slithered down his spine, making his breath run cold, setting his teeth to chattering.

The rosy battlement stones Leon leaned against had bathed in the sun's rays for a long desert day, but their still-warm touch meant *nothing* to him. He shivered and quaked, dreading the next stab of pain, the next time he'd be ripped to pieces.

He'd experienced a thousand ends. Heard hundreds of falsehoods, dozens of sweetly whispered promises, all delivered by the creature standing at Leon's side.

The creature that now wore Vallen's flesh.

A shock of messy brown hair crowned his head, falling to a pair of twinkling chestnut eyes and a grin that thought the whole world was a joke. Silks covered his shoulders and chest, a v-shaped gap at the tunic's front exposing the taut bronzed skin Vallen flaunted at every opportunity. No weapons dangled from his bead-encrusted belt—his easy smile and chiseled muscles were dangerous enough.

A bottle of honeyed Gelt whiskey materialized in his hand, cork tossed from the wall as not-Vallen brought it to his lips. He took one swig, two, then held out the liquor for his friend.

Leon didn't move. He kept his eyes fixed on the purpling horizon, willing the scene to end. Of all the days this monster showed him, those he spent with Vallen's shade were the worst.

Not-Vallen shrugged. "Your loss."

Emptying the bottle, he took two steps back toward the inner parapet, then lunged forward as he hurled it across the sands. A sliver of sunlight caught it, making it sparkle like crystal as it tumbled end over end.

A pair of guards patrolling nearby turned away, pretending

they'd seen nothing. They didn't need to see the blue-red Academy patch on Vallen's shoulder to know who he was: the Steward's adopted son, the Triaron.

Someone far above them.

But . . . they weren't real anyway. *None of this*—Leon glanced back at Nemare, at its towering minarets, marble aqueducts, and winding canals—*is real.* It was all an illusion, one fabricated with a single purpose:

To make him submit.

"What should we do after we graduate?" Not-Vallen asked, leaning over the edge. A gentle breeze caught the edge of his silk tunic, billowing it like the train of a dress. Leon should have been smiling, his heart racing as he laughed and drank and planned with the man who was his world.

Instead, he stayed silent, shivering as his nerves and body frayed like the final thread of a hangman's noose.

"I'd like to see the continent," not-Vallen continued as if nothing was wrong. "Visit the shores of Lake Lovare, travel to the Imperium and Empire, experience everything Lozaria has to offer." He nudged Leon with his elbow. "The women most of all. Sylphs and Hues and Terrans, aristocrats and actresses and courtesans—you know, the whole gambit."

Leon said nothing.

"Now, don't get me wrong." With a leap, not-Vallen hopped atop the battlements and began walking toward the nearest wall turret, arms held out for balance. "I like Velle, and I like this city. Both have been good to me."

A lie, Leon thought. *You hate Nemare, and you loathe what's beneath it even more.*

"But it's too confining. Like this shirt." Laughing, not-Vallen pulled off his shirt and cast it into the air. Leon didn't bother to watch.

Let the sun fall. Let this scene pass. *Let. It. End.*

Not-Vallen spun, summoning a sandy gust to twirl around him. "I need action, adventure, *excitement.* A journey we'll tell tales of when we're too fat to move and too old to remember anything else. Hopefully we can still string a sentence or two together at that point, but if not, Matteo can write all our escapades down for us."

Leon's silence stretched like the sun across the walls, its last rays painting the city streets orange as it reached for the domed palace in the distance.

"You understand, Leon," not-Vallen said, nodding. "I know you do, which is why I want you with me. We'll eat every kind of food there is. Drink beer with weird names, fight beasts people have never heard of, sleep in a different tavern or inn or noble's house each night, provided"—not-Vallen winked—"said noble doesn't notice we've already fleeced his vault.

"And the best part is," not-Vallen jumped off the parapet, landing in front of Leon, "you won't have to see your father ever again. No more looking over your shoulder, no more wondering when he'll drag you back home. Perfect freedom, Leon."

Not-Vallen extended his hand, fading sunlight glimmering on his sweat-streaked skin. "Let's go together. What do you say?"

"Let it end," Leon said.

Not-Vallen tilted his head. "What?"

"Let it end," Leon repeated, waving at the lengthening shadows, the mesmerizing sunset before them. "This day, this illusion, this however-many-thousandth repetition of the *worst* Vallen impression I've ever seen."

A frown creased not-Vallen's cheeks, the darkness beneath his eyes and around his feet growing, swelling. "This *is* the conceited brat you know."

"No," Leon shook his head, holding in his tears as he remembered oh-so-many little moments of their life together. "It's not."

Images flashed through his tortured, needle-ravaged mind:

A crate of old rations Vallen just *happened* to abandon in an alley near the slums.

The time Velle had fallen ill and Vallen walked across the city to fetch Sylph-made medicine because, *'I need a bite to eat, anyway.'* His stomach had growled when he returned with the pills.

Excuses. So many excuses for his small, seemingly trivial kindnesses. Because underneath all the bluster, bravado, and ego, Vallen hated only one person: *himself.*

Not-Vallen kept his arm extended. "So, this is a farce, is it? Are you ready to bring it to a close? Accept me and your torment shall end."

Turning, Leon gazed out over Nemare. It expanded in every direction like a quilt, great temples and towering libraries its patches, its gleaming waterways the threads that bound them together. Lights flickered on as daylight waned, starting beneath the wall and racing to the capital's far corners. Great spotlights framed the tiered palace gardens. Strings of festive bulbs ran along the main thoroughfares and illuminated markets and bazaars that never truly slept.

It *was* an illusion.

But, like Vallen, it was an echo of reality. Of something Leon would give anything to protect.

"I won't give you control," Leon answered. "I know what you are—what you'll do if I give you free rein."

A pitch-coated smile sprouted on not-Vallen's lips. "You have *no* idea what I am, mortal. But there may be another way to reach an accord."

He held out his palm, above which appeared a glowing portal that displayed shifting images like a recorb. As Leon watched, a man dressed in Sarconian red and gold raced across a battlefield, his comrades falling around him one by one.

"Vahn gave me his body, and in return I swore to grant his greatest desire: the salvation of his homeland."

Leon snorted. "By invading Darmatia."

"Forest fires sow new life in the soil. Storms lash the land with water necessary for growth. A soldier dies in war so that his family might escape his fate."

Not-Vallen held out his other hand, summoning a set of golden scales that hung in the air. "All things are in balance, and for a harmonious future"—a bleeding soldier in a blue uniform appeared on one side of the scale opposite a mother hugging two sniveling children—"some things and people must be sacrificed."

"So . . . " Not-Vallen smiled, a grin deep as eternity and black as midnight. "Shall I save your friends? Your country? What is it *you* desire, Leon? For what cause would you hand over your soul?"

There was wisdom in the creature's words. An understanding born of centuries of detached study and evaluation. Leon, his comrades—even nations and empires . . . they were all insects before this force. Disobedient children who couldn't be trusted to make decisions for themselves.

Pretending to cough, Leon gathered every speck of phlegm in his throat and spat it right in not-Vallen's face. "Go tap yourself. And when you're done, go tap my father. You two were made for each other."

The shade didn't lash out. Didn't hurl Leon from the wall or smash his face into the stones on which they stood. Dispelling the illusions he held, not-Vallen wiped the spittle from his nose and lips, shook it off, and raised his hand above his head.

"So be it," he said, voice placid as a lake at dawn. "There are worse things in this world than I, Leonel Descar. True monsters. Ones to whom reason means *nothing*. By rejecting me, you choose them.

"Let's see how that plays out."

Snap!

At not-Vallen's snap, the world went dark. Black as the corner of Leon's windowless cell, the door locked from the outside, the gap below the door plugged with wool so no one could hear his cries, his wails as he begged to talk to someone, *anyone*. Not a shred of light by which to see his tears, the blood dripping from fists gone numb beating at the walls.

Please, father. Please come back. I'll do better this time. I'll get the problems right, I promise.

The wall beneath his feet gave way, stones vanishing like everything else. Leon fell. Down and down and down, plummeting for what might have been short as seconds or long as years. He tried to activate his magic. To produce a spark in his hand without his staff.

But Leon's men'ar wouldn't respond. It had betrayed him, just like his father and brothers. Just like everyone in his—

Leon plunged into a pool of liquid, momentum carrying him deep below the surface. He closed his eyes, holding his breath as he kicked upward. The fluid resisted him, its touch warm and sticky. Was he in some noble's bathhouse?

He gasped as he reached open air, spitting gobs of the fluid, blinking it from his eyes. It tasted coppery—like the tang left over from biting a geldar. Paddling with his arms and legs, Leon surveyed . . .

Well, nothing. Darkness stretched in every direction, unbroken, unceasing. Leon fought the urge to panic. Swimming aimlessly would accomplish nothing, and there was something *wrong* about this place. It stank like the slums, a stomach-twisting aroma of voided bowels, rot, and death.

Vomit surged in Leon's throat, his throat tightening, his eyes watering. He knew that taste, that smell. Recognized the ooze clinging to his hair, dribbling over his ears, slipping in long, wet strands back into the pool.

It couldn't be.

Plip. Plip. Plip.

No, surely it wasn't.

Plip. Plip. Plip.

Leon struck out with his arm. He needed to move, to swim, to get away from—

His fingers brushed a soft log, the moss covering its surface fine as the hairs on his arm. He clung to it, feeling along its length to see how long it was. One side ended in five tight buds, while the other was splintered, the rotten wood around it ripped and . . . and . . .

With a scream, Leon threw the severed arm away, splashing wildly,

511

churning up the blood around him. Where was he? What was going on? *I'm covered in blood. I'm covered in blood. I'M COVERED IN BLOOD!*

"I see you've discovered your first clue," the sky said, clapping its unseen hands.

Snap!

The light returned. Leon shaded his eyes, expecting to be blinded by the sudden glare. But its touch was soft. Cold. Where normal sunlight was a warm yellow, this radiance was a pale gray, subdued and washed out.

Leon stared up at the sun.

No, not a sun at all. A *pit*. A black hole in a dead sky that dripped ink or pitch or blood.

Leon glanced around, heart hammering against his chest like cannon fire. He knew what he'd see. What he'd find. But still he looked, morbid curiosity—the need to know—overriding any sense or reason he may have once possessed.

He was on the broad thoroughfare beneath Nemare's outer wall: Nabirai Lane, a park district with cafes and boutiques that catered to Academy staff and young couples. Only . . . years had passed. Centuries, perhaps.

The trees and shrubs lining the street were withered, blossoms replaced by twisted sprouts that leaked black sludge. Whole segments of the wall had collapsed inward, huge stone blocks scattered across the cobbles and embedded in ruined storefronts on the opposite side. Broken windows gaped like sightless eyes. Shell holes pitted houses like open sores, blackened scorch marks lining the edge of their missing second stories. Every surface, even the high battlements, was weathered and worn as if sanded down by centuries of harsh storms.

And below it all was a river of scarlet—a river of blood.

Leon vomited, but nothing came out. Bodies lay around him in their hundreds, men, women, children. People of all races wearing fine vestments, uniforms, and rags. Some were skeletons, bleached bones picked clean. Most were rotting, skin sloughing off in strips, the muscles beneath slowly liquefying.

They lay where they'd perished. Draped over rusted fences, hanging from balconies, nestled together beneath an oak whose leaves would never again sprout. More floated in the river, bobbing along on an unseen current. Piles of corpses on the shore, down the road, in the park beside a crumpled temple, everywhere Leon looked, everywhere he turned.

Death. *Death. DEATH.*

"Ah," Leon chuckled, tears streaking his cheeks, unable to retch, to gag, to spit. "This must be Oblivion."

The sky rumbled, its voice like peals of thunder. "This is your future."

A distant one, no doubt. Nabirai Lane was *massive.* To fill it with blood—to fill *all* the neighboring streets and canals—would require the deaths of . . .

Everyone.

The *whole* voiding country.

Coughing, Leon swam for shore, his eyes shut tight against the horror. "You think to break me," he shouted at the heavens, "but this is centuries from now—an age far beyond the present."

"It will come to pass in mere *decades.* Look at their uniforms, at the fallen streetlamps and buried magtech vehicles of which you mortals are so proud. This is coming, Leon. This is *now."*

No.

Leon brushed aside a corpse that *deflated* as he pressed its stomach, filling the air with noxious fumes.

NO.

He struck the half-exposed ribs of a dead woman, fingers snarling in her slimy innards. Leon reeled back, took a different path, repeating the same mantra over and over and over again in his head.

This isn't real. This isn't real. This isn't real.

"I don't recommend you leave the river," the bleeding sun said.

Leon opened his eyes. The rubble ahead of him sloped upward toward a collapsed tenement, its top floors wedged against the outer wall. Shadows lurked beneath it. Deep and dark and endless, their threads seeming to twist and contort even as Leon watched.

No, not twisting.

Moving.

One detached from the ground, heaving itself up on two spindly arms made of pitch. It slid toward the river—half crawling, half floating—its spiked legs leaving sizzling imprints in its wake. One monstrous claw lashed out, stabbing into a pile of bodies, ripping free a rot-stained heart.

The creature brought it to its lips. Bit down with fangs the size of Leon's thumbs, a too-wide mouth that stretched from non-existent ear to ear. And when it chewed, shadows and blood spurted forth—the same wispy tendrils that wafted from every part of its pitch-colored flesh.

Finishing its meal, it stooped to tear open another corpse's chest. Then it stopped. Raised its pointed head, sniffing at the air.

Leon didn't move. He held his breath, kept his fingers still despite the chill seeping into his veins.

Yet those blazing embers found him anyway—two scarlet eyes that reflected nothing but empty, eternal hunger. Its face ripped open in a cruel smile, exposing its needle-sharp fangs.

And then it charged. Bounding off slanted pieces of rubble, jumping over half-eaten bodies. Thirty meters. Twenty. All four limbs pounding at the ground, gouging furrows in solid stone, determined to reach Leon and rip him—

It slammed to a halt, hissing and snarling at the thin line before it, black as pitch on one side, pale gray on the other. No matter how much it strained or raged, the monster couldn't take another step.

"They fear the sunlight," Leon said, crawling onto a sandstone slab near the river.

"For now," the sky agreed. "But the days grow shorter"—the dark sun shifted, extending the tenement's shadow, allowing the creature to move another half-meter forward—"and eventually, the sun will fade entirely."

"What are they?" Leon asked.

"This world's doom. Though," the voice paused, humming to itself, "you might know them by a different name: *voidspawn.*"

Leon wanted to protest, but the words died on his lips. It could be nothing but the truth. He shivered, his blood-soaked tunic clinging to his clammy skin.

"Did you send them?" Leon flinched as the shadows—and the voidspawn—came a step closer. "Or, rather, *will* you send them? We both know this isn't real."

"What is reality but what we perceive it to be? *This* is your existence now."

"That wasn't a 'no.'"

Thunder boomed. Was it *amused?* "Nor was it a 'yes.' Would you believe me if I told you I intend to *save* Lozaria from them? From what created them?"

Leon spat his answer. "No."

"And we remain at an impasse. Yet I hope that, given time in this realm, you will come to understand my position. One can only suffer Oblivion for so long, particularly when it affects those they care for most."

"What do you mean?"

A ray of pale light fell on the temple across the street. Its domed roof had caved in, the main worship hall below a mess of shattered pews, yellowed parchment, and broken statues. A seven-pointed star should have hung above the entryway, but the marble had been scorched clean by char and flame.

Leon didn't care for the state of the church. The Veneer had never done him any favors, no matter how much he'd begged them to. Yet seven bodies lay on the bullet-pocked steps leading to its vacant doors: one Sylph, one Hue, and five Terrans.

His friends.

Vallen.

Blood dripped from their arms and legs, poured from wounds on their chests. Their clothes were scarlet-soaked rags. Their hair was knotted with sweat and grease and grime.

What had they been through? Why were they here? Unter's massive chest rose and fell, but Leon couldn't tell if the others were still alive.

Leon took one halting step. Another. Then he stopped, stared up at the sky, and laughed. "Another trick. Void, how do I keep falling for the same trick over and over."

"It *will* come to pass," the very air replied, booming from all around him. "If not now, then later."

"How did *this* happen?" Leon asked, waving at his friends.

"They bring it upon themselves."

"By resisting you?"

The voice hesitated. When it spoke, its words held no hint of doubt. "Unless things change, this will be the fate of *all,* regardless of when or how they fall. Now ... "

Snap!

"Let's see that famous resolve of yours."

The dark sun winked out, plunging Leon back into the abyss. Roars and growls split the city's silence, echoing off the ruins, redoubling with every passing second. Leon heard claws scraping on stone. Felt the ground shake as hundreds of feet pounded toward the river, the temple, in search of fresh prey.

This is an illusion, Leon told himself, steadying his breathing, trying to calm his racing heart. He couldn't die—not permanently—and neither could his friends. The day would reset, and he'd be plunged into another attempt to claim his soul.

That was how this worked.

So . . . why was he running?

Leon dove into the river, ignoring the stench and the rot and the filth. Yes, this was an illusion. Yes, his friends weren't real.

But if Leon didn't try to save them when they were right in front of his eyes, that would be the same as betraying the love he held for them. *He* was real. *His* decisions were real.

And that was *all* that mattered.

Leathery wings snapped through the air above him. Snarls rose from the rooftops, the wall, the distant city streets. Voidspawn were closing from every direction—an entire city populated by nothing but vicious monsters.

Leon reached the far shore, slicing his knee open as he half-stumbled, half-sprinted from the bloody waters. "Vallen!" he shouted, letting the pain drive him on. "Matteo! Velle! If you can hear me, come toward the river!"

No response.

Something barreled past him, knocking Leon aside as it charged. He didn't think. Snarling, he dove after the beast, tackling it to the ground. It raked his side with its claws, setting it aflame. An elbow to the head left him reeling.

Yet Leon wasn't going to give in.

He *would* save them.

Raising his boot, he kicked and kicked until he felt the voidspawn go slack. Had he killed it? Was it a weaker type than the one he'd seen before?

Not important. Leon staggered upright, running in the direction of the temple, following the howls of Nemare's hunters. He tripped on a rock. No, a *step!* His palms struck jagged, chipped marble, shredding them instantly. Blood welled from the wounds, but Leon grabbed the steps and hurled himself forward on all fours.

One step, two, three.

Leon caught hold of a thick, muscular ankle as wide around as his knee. *Unter!* "Wake up!" he urged, jerking on it as hard as it could. "Get up *now!*"

A shadowy limb slammed into his chest, lifting him off the steps and *smashing* him into one of the entryway's columns. Cracking echoed through the air—Leon's bones, the column, he could no longer tell. Warmth trickled down his neck, driving back the numbness setting into his flesh. Had he broken a rib? His spine?

Plop-plop-plop-plop-plop!

Swaying, Leon teetered forward. He stepped into a thick puddle, nearly losing his balance. Where were his friends? He dropped to his knees, casting about with blood-slick hands. He found only marble and thick, gooey fluid.

Plop-plop-plop-plop-plop!

More liquid poured from above, plopping on the steps around Leon, soaking his hair and dribbling down his shoulders. Steam rose from the goop—a rancid smoke that smelt like days old meat left to fester in the sun.

Just like corpses, Leon realized.

Drool. Buckets of drool were dripping from the voidspawns' mouths. Leon glanced up. Saw the shadows above him twisting, roiling, writhing.

A whole host of voidspawn were clinging to the entryway ceiling. One lashed out with a spiked tendril, slashing open his forearm. Before Leon could scream, another pierced his boot, pinning his foot to the floor.

What were they waiting for? They could kill him at any time and slaughter his friends in the next breath. Why . . . ?

His friends.

Leon had crawled across the entryway floor on hands and knees, searching, praying, hoping. But he hadn't found his friends' bodies. They were gone.

Taken.

The baying and jeering crescendoed, claws clicking, fangs snapping. The voidspawn were *laughing* at Leon. Taunting him.

And why shouldn't they?

They had won.

Leon collapsed onto his side, curling into a ball as tears streamed down his face. Sobs racked his body, his cries nearly loud enough to rival the roaring monsters.

But one sound was louder still: the gnashing of teeth and claws as the voidspawn tore into flesh and sinew. Leon barely felt the rain pouring down on him, more blood and drool soaking his clothes, pooling about his limp form.

At long last, he was numb.

Leon could no longer feel the blood pounding atop his head. He couldn't hear the wails of his companions, nor the jubilant cries of Nemare's new elite, the vicious, unrelenting shades who were gorging themselves even now. It had taken a while, ten thousand . . .

No, that didn't matter. Time meant nothing, nor did the beliefs and convictions he'd once held.

He was numb.

This is the 15,532 loop you've repeated, Leon, the voice of his captor spoke directly into his mind. He'd long since cast aside his other senses.

He was numb.

Why do you stubbornly cling to this agony when I can set you free?

Leon *was* free. Death and life, struggle and hardship—these were no longer important to him. To think was to feel. To feel was to suffer. To suffer was to fall, to fail.

And Leon was tired of failing. He'd tried everything he could to save his friends, to outwit the being that held him trapped within his mind. Nothing had worked.

So . . . he'd purged it all.

He was numb.

Another matter has come up. I must step away, but rest assured that your . . . confinement . . . will continue unabated. If you wish to concede, tell me now.

The horrendous revelry swirled around Leon without end. His friends died and were reborn. The city rose and fell to ruin. Death, slaughter, and bloodshed were now Leon's closest companions, so familiar they failed to faze him.

He was numb.

Sighing, the telepathic voice withdrew. Leon was always able to tell when it was focusing on him and when it wasn't. Its attentions were like a dark shroud, a thick cloak thrown atop his already numbed consciousness. Pressing him into the dirt, grinding him into nothingness.

Tears fell from Leon's eyes, tracing the deep furrows in his face, dripping onto knees tucked up against his chin. Leon *was* numb. He couldn't feel the tears anymore, couldn't fathom why they came.

But . . . he couldn't stop them either.

And so Leon kept weeping, softly, silently, until his idyllic world reset once more.

Part 4
Water and Fire

Chapter 52

Flank Speed

Adamantele 11, 697 ABH
Above Lyndwur Forest, Sarconian Province of Darmatia

"*I know.*"

Those two words tormented Sylette. Since Major Reev had whispered them in her ear, she hadn't had a restful night. Staring at the tent canopy, she'd strained to hear the faintest tap of steel boots approaching their tent. She'd spent her days glancing over her shoulder, watching, waiting for the squad she knew was coming to arrest her.

But they never came, and Sylette was forced to wonder just what it was Major Reev knew about her. *Does she suspect my story about Aldona?* Sylette mused, finger straying toward her lips. *Did she realize I've been trying to manipulate her?*

Neither made sense. Sylette had only one secret that would break her, one hidden truth that would matter to the Ice Queen.

Major Reev knew who she was: exiled princess, third in line to the Sarconian throne. And for some reason, she wasn't acting on the information.

Sylette turned from the viewport fronting *Dharmaysa's* bridge, scanning the room for anything unusual, anything that had changed since her last check a minute prior. Matteo and Renar still stood nearby, gazing at the snow-laced fields rushing past below the cruiser.

Glasses low on his nose, mouth pinched into a frown, Matteo was as focused as she'd ever seen him. This mission was everything he'd wanted—a chance to liberate his hometown and rescue his parents.

Renar, on the other hand, was a mess. He acted like Sylette felt, eyes twitching back and forth, knuckles white as he gripped the safety railing between them and the reinforced glass windows. Words slipped from his lips, mutterings and mumbling she couldn't decipher. Was the fool that nervous about the coming battle?

Dignity and poise. Sylette's heart raced. She yearned to tear into her fingernail like a babe, shredding it until her frayed nerves calmed. But she wouldn't crack. That was a sure sign of guilt, and Sylette had nothing to feel guilty for. She was *exactly* who she was born to be.

The rest of the bridge possessed that breathless tension that always preceded battle. Orderlies rushed along the metal walkways lining the chamber's curved sides, delivering commands to officers at their stations. Communications, sensors, gunnery, steering, tactical. Sylette studied each bank of read-out panels and the crew around them, searching for signs of shock, confusion, or disbelief. Indications they might be coming for her.

A cry came from the tactical salon. Sylette spun, expecting an accusing finger aimed her way. Instead, the lanky lieutenant hovering above the map table gestured excitedly at his charts while waving Major Reev over. Another minute of freedom gained.

Sylette ran escape scenarios in her head, just to be ready. Fifteen people on the bridge, four of them armed guards, one of them the Ice Queen of Darmatia. Overhead was a thermal pipe filled with enough steam to heat the room at high altitudes. She'd need one dagger to slice the clasp binding it to the ceiling, a second to pierce a weak weld that was already leaking mist.

As smoke flooded the room, Sylette would sprint to the exit, take the stairs in the hall down two levels, then board the *Kinloss* while cutting the anchors holding it to *Dharmasya's* outer hull. Sylette didn't know the first thing about flying, but she would learn.

And if she didn't, a brief, fiery end was preferable to rotting in a cell.

Rough, muscular fingers gripped Sylette's shoulder. She ducked into the grab, wrapped her arm around her assailant's, and thrust her other palm at their face.

"Matteo?" Sylette gasped, stopping her strike a hairsbreadth from his chin.

He flinched. "Who were you expecting?"

Sylette released him and stepped away. After everything he'd done for her, Matteo didn't deserve to bear the brunt of her paranoia. "I was, I mean ..."

"*Now* which one of us is stammering?" Smiling, he adjusted his crooked glasses and flicked a few stray hairs from his eyes. "Are you alright, Sylette?"

"Fine."

She couldn't tell him the truth. He'd insist on explaining things to Major Reev, which would probably land the whole gang in an ice freezer for failing to tell her sooner. If things went worse—if the Ice Queen turned hostile—he'd throw everything away to get her out on the *Kinloss*.

How had Sylette ever thought him a coward?

"Anyway, I thought you might want to see Lyndwur Forest," Matteo said, directing her attention out the viewport. "It was dark last time we came through, and I was busy crashing, and—"

Sylette gave his arm a light jab. "*Now* which one of us is babbling?"

"... I concede the point."

It *was* a breathtaking sight, far grander than any of the forests she'd seen when the royal family had toured the Imperial countryside. Twisted and tangled, the gnarled claws of the great Weisse Elegoras trees reached up to scratch at *Dharmasya's* belly. She was flying low to avoid Sarconian sensors, but not so low that an ordinary oak or ash could reach her.

These were *massive*. Hundreds of meters tall with boughs that stretched like aqueduct arches and root systems that extended for leagues in all directions. Once they were over the forest, Sylette could see nothing but snow-dappled branches, tower-thick trunks, and roots covering the ground like cobwebs.

"It's hard to imagine we crossed that." Sylette's gaze roved the canopy, searching for where their ship went down. Not a hole could be seen, not even one small enough for a Terran to slip through.

Matteo shook his head. "Wouldn't want to do it again. Especially not now."

"And why is that, Lieutenant Alhan?"

It took deific levels of reserve *not* to fall into a defensive stance as Major Reev approached. Sylette followed Matteo's example, bringing her fingers to her brow in salute. She didn't blink or look away. *I am* not *guilty,* she thought. *I am* not *guilty.*

Major Reev waved away their salutes, then gestured at the forest flashing by outside. Matteo cleared his throat. "It's a death trap, ma'am. Winter forces predators to migrate south from the Great Divide and they wind up here."

"Still seems pretty tame," the Ice Queen said with a smirk.

"Except the predators don't win. Direwraiths, venom-stalkers, crag-howlers, every kind of nasty you can imagine, they *all* get ripped apart by the Lyndwur. They go for the succulent elegoras fruit—the seeds the forest exposes to absorb men'ar—and end up becoming a meal themselves."

"The forest sounds like a hunter."

Matteo nodded as he took a cautious step away from the railing.

"It is. Some old storytellers even say it's one gigantic tree—that all the roots are interconnected and it possesses the intellect of a Primal. Though I had friends whose mums told them the Lyndwur would pluck them from their beds if they misbehaved, so take all that with a grain of illyrium."

Sylette wondered if there was a way to weaponize the forest against the Empire. Major Reev was clearly thinking the same thing, for she motioned for them to follow her back to the tactical salon. Lost in his thoughts, eyes glued to the viewport as his hands were to the railing, Renar didn't budge.

The lanky lieutenant stepped aside at their approach, and Major Reev pointed to a smudge of shading on the map. *Lyndwur Forest* was scrawled beside it, and a dot beyond it read, *Etrus.*

"This is our approach." She traced a line through the center of the smudge, exiting the blob right on top of the coastal city. "This"—the Ice Queen drug another finger down the jagged line representing the Phar Coast—"is the route our transports and hoverjets are taking. The goal is to catch the Sarcs with their trousers down and pincer them from two sides. Sound logic?"

Major Reev glanced at Sylette, hard emerald eyes betraying nothing. Did she want an answer to that *obvious* rhetorical question? Or perhaps for her to melt into a sobbing pool and confess her heritage?

"Yes," Sylette said, voice calm, measured. "Their cruisers should be at the canal airfield. Catch them unawares from both water and city"—she tapped the two directions the Major had indicated—"and they won't be able to launch their ships. A quick victory."

"If only all our problems could be resolved so easily," Major Reev said, boring icicle spikes *through* Sylette's head with her gaze. According to her, Sylette was aboard *Dharmasya* to hone her skills as a commander.

But they both knew the *real* reason the Ice Queen wanted her here.

Why does she delay? Sylette thought, biting the inside of her cheek, letting the pain grant her focus. *Why doesn't she just accuse me and get it over with?*

"What about Nehalena?" Sylette asked. "With the might of a Primal, tactics like these would be meaningless."

Major Reev snorted. "Do *you* want to separate her from her brood? Ask her to leave her young undefended?" Sylette stayed silent. "That's what I thought."

The Ice Queen's eyes narrowed, then swung to Matteo. "We lose if the enemy knows we're coming. Is there any chance the Sarcs put scouts in the Lyndwur?"

"None," he replied. "In the past, Etrus' best woodsmen and hunters challenged the winter forest. Not one returned."

"So, luring them into the wood is also out?"

Sighing, Matteo shut his eyes. "You'd be sacrificing whatever bait you use, ma'am. And if their commander isn't a fool"—he gritted his teeth while clenching his fists—"he's already . . . interrogated the citizens and learned everything I'm telling you."

Sylette *almost* blurted that she knew their foe—that Olivier Stetson was a conniving scum-sucker that deserved a death nearly as brutal as those she'd planned for her father and brother. But Matteo already knew that. The talking corpse had executed Abbott Kinloss for aiding their escape and likely had his parents locked in a cell aboard his cruiser.

Yet even if a single word from her would improve their odds of defeating Stetson, Sylette wouldn't speak. To do so would betray her origins as surely as an Imperial crest carved into her flesh. When the crystals went dun, and the shell casings clattered to the ground, empty and smoking, only one thing mattered:

That I remain alive and free long enough to put a dagger through the Emperor's throat.

Major Reev clapped Matteo on the shoulder, then spun toward the barrel-broad woman manning *Dharmasya's* helm. "That's it, then!" she yelled, loud enough for the whole bridge to hear her. "Our plans have been laid, the wind is at our backs, and Darmatus and all the Veneer watch over us! *We go to war!*"

"*We go to victory!*" the bridge crew shouted back, stamping their feet hard enough to shake the deck.

Major Reev slashed her arm forward, toward the thinning forest and the ruddy mound sparkling beyond it. "Flank speed!"

Chapter 53

Coffin

Darmatians burned their dead.

Mother Tabitha would say the practice freed the souls of the fallen from their fleshy prisons, allowing them to rise heavenward to meet the Veneer. Vallen knew it was simply more efficient.

Corpses began to stink a day or so after death. He should know since he had looted his fair share in the waste-clogged alleys of Sewertown. But there was still honor amongst thieves. After Vallen had taken their few tins, bread scraps, and whatever rags were still wearable, he'd always yelled for the Collector before scampering off.

No one knew who the Collector was, but to the dregs of Sewertown they were both saint and reaper, angel and voidspawn. No matter who invoked their name, word passed along—mouth to mouth—until it reached them, at which point a pillar of smoke would rise above the wilting roofs and tired slum streets.

The curious always rushed to the scene, hoping to catch a glimpse of the legend. They never did. All that remained in the Collector's wake was a pile of ash and a dull marble.

Vallen reflected on the Collector's methods as the assault transport tried to shake him to pieces. He'd heard some rich noblemen preferred to go out this way, their powdered carcasses dressed up in fine suit-robes and locked inside a windowless box for all eternity.

What a foolish idea. The 'coffin' Vallen now rode in was one cannon blast—one collision with a tree—from destruction, and his only way of guessing where they were was the direction the ship tossed him.

Burn my bones, Vallen prayed, gritting his teeth as the airship accelerated. *Don't let me suffer like this once I'm gone.*

The cabin slanted up, producing grunts and curses from everyone aboard. Vallen was thrown into Herj, who grabbed his crash restraints and held on tight for both their sakes. They were rising. Up a hill? Up a cliff? Vallen couldn't say, but with each passing second his flattened lungs tried harder and harder to reach the seat beneath him.

Thought became a chore. Darkness pressed in at the corners of his eyes, his breath came in ragged gasps, and he soon lost track of what was up and down. Vallen's whole world contracted to a rattling, clanking pinprick of light.

Then his stomach shot *through* his throat, threatening to reacquaint him with the gooey gray mush he'd had for breakfast. Sucking in a mouthful of sweat-laced air, Vallen tumbled away from Herj. Why in oblivion had he agreed to come on this mission?

"We're over the city!" Holcomb said. "Hold on tight. We're gonna have to dance our way past some Sarc welcoming presents."

Vallen grabbed the coarse handles on either side of his seat, clenching them until he thought they'd snap. It was going to get *worse?*

Across the aisle, Erika started whispering a prayer. Green light came from Velle's direction as she soothed the nausea of one of her neighbors. Would they get hit? Swatted out of the sky by flak without seeing the shot that killed them? Vallen might be able to activate his lightning barrier an instant before a gale of shrapnel hit him, but someone like Unter—large and immobile—would be blasted to shreds.

This attack plan was *horrible.*

A moment passed. Then another. Vallen glanced around, wondering why they weren't doing barrel rolls or dodging wildly enough to void his bowels. He should be able to hear explosions: shells bursting and other transports screaming as they dropped from the sky.

Only the chattering of loose screws and the howl of gusting wind reached his ears. Something was wrong.

Colonel Holcomb clearly thought so as well. Frowning, he released his safety handles and banged on the cockpit door. "We're over Etrus, right?"

The hatch slid open. Through the gap between the two pilots, Vallen saw tiers of sand-colored buildings and bright greenery flowing past the curved viewport. A growing blue band twisted back and forth beside the city proper.

There were no puffs of smoke to mar the view. No jets of flame or hail of flying bullets.

"We are," the pilot on the right side said, scratching his neck. "Which is the funny thing."

Holcomb scowled. "I'm not in the mood for jokes, son."

"No joke, sir. There's just ... " He turned and waved at the cobbled streets of Etrus. Strings of pennants fluttered between buildings, colorful awnings hung from windows, and the rooftop gardens were just as vibrant as the last time Vallen had seen them. Only there was ...

" ... no one here," the pilot finished. "No Sarcs, no civvies. Not a single person. It's a ghost town, Colonel."

Chapter 54

Snatch and Grab

Etrus rushed at Matteo, the leagues eroding like sand before waves as *Dharmasya* sprinted to greet her foes.

Familiar sights were there and gone in an eye-blink. Tavel's Watch, the hut of the old hermit who lived at the Lyndwur's edge. Baudin's Boulder, the massive stone lying in the valley between forest and town. It was covered in paint, some professional murals, mostly childish handprints and scribbles. Matteo grinned, remembering when his mother had taken him to paint his own palm on the rock.

I'm coming, mom, he thought. *Dad, Sal, Vera . . . Kinloss . . . I'm back now.*

The city rose from the plain like a gem, three tiers of stucco architecture climbing to crown the tallest cliff in the region. It had no wall, just a tall archway over the main street. The place had always been peaceable, and if there was a problem, the merchants and sailors took care of it themselves.

Strands of greenery swept up the slopes, marking the gardens, courtyards, and secluded bathhouses that were the center of Etrusian tourism. Matteo followed them up to the town's peak, then glanced away from the black scar he saw there.

At that moment, he could almost smell the sweet scent of trampled neverfades and bloodlillies. Could nearly hear the babbling of the chapel's shattered fountain. Light diffracted by phantom stained-glass windows dappled the back of his eyes.

All of it was gone. Stolen by the Empire. And though the charred wound would never fade, they would take it back now. *His* town. *His* memories. *His* life.

"Aim off the starboard bow as we pass the town," Major Reev ordered the gunners. "Pummel the first cruiser you see, then move to the next in line."

"Aye, ma'am," the gunnery officer acknowledged.

Matteo's chest blazed with righteous fire as he watched *Dharmasya's* forward turrets adjust their bearing. Four guns in two turrets, gleaming against a slate gray sky. He could hardly wait to feel the rush of their first salvo. To feel the deep *thump* in his gut as they tossed lead at the men who occupied his home.

The Etrus canal came into view, its waters lapping against the carved stone banks, threatening to wash over the harbor docks. It was running higher than Matteo expected. The coming spring thaw usually filled the waterway to the brim, but if it rose a handspan or two farther, the dozens of tied-up sailing ships would be in danger of capsizing.

They closed with the town, using it to screen their approach. At the last second, the helmswoman threw the wheel to port and guided *Dharmasya* over the canal and harbor. Matteo leaned forward, gripping the rail. The airfield and Sarc base would be in sight right . . . about . . .

. . . now?

"It's empty," Sylette gasped at his side.

A solid league of bare concrete stared at them from across the Etrus canal. No cruisers in sight, not even scorch marks on the tarmac to suggest they'd recently taken off. The hangars gaped like laughing mouths, their doors thrown wide, their depths dark as the grave. Matteo couldn't spot a single soldier or a hint of red and gold.

The only construct of note was a strange bronze pole erected at the airfield's far end, concentric rings surrounding its central shaft, a bulb of gleaming metal affixed at its peak. Matteo remembered it from their escape a month prior, its presence a glaring reminder of the Sarconian occupation.

Dharmasya continued her banking turn, her sister, *Conviction*, shadowing her tail. They'd been prepared to broadside the grounded Sarc cruisers, then fight a running battle as the injured beasts lumbered into the air. Now it seemed the Empire had abandoned Etrus entirely.

The bridge erupted into a cacophony of hurried, confused whispers.

"Did they withdraw?"

"That makes no sense. Etrus controls the Ascendancy border."

"Then explain—"

Major Reev climbed the steps to the helm and pressed a button beside the wheel mount. A shrill warning klaxon warbled through the ship, making Matteo wince and cover his ears. It stopped when she removed her finger.

"Nothing's changed!" she shouted, both to the bridge crew and the rows of voicepipes next to her. They snaked down into the floor, then spread throughout the rest of the ship, carrying her words to the whole vessel. "We came to secure Etrus, so that's what we'll do. Doesn't matter if the Sarcs are here or not."

531

"I smell a trap," said a man with captain's bars on his uniform collar. Some of the soldiers beside him nodded in agreement.

Sylette turned and stepped away from the viewport. "With all due respect, Captain Hurshik, the Empire has every advantage in this war. Why do they need to set a trap?"

Captain Hurshik snorted. "Young miss, I suggest you—"

"You're both right," Major Reev snapped, forestalling an argument. "Which is why we'll proceed carefully. Sensors?"

A woman with auburn curls tucked beneath a neat cap rose from her station. "Yes, ma'am?"

"Get me a reading on those hangars, the airfield, the town, everything. If they're hiding, I want to know about it."

The sensor saluted. "Right away!"

Raven hair bouncing, Major Reev raced to the other side of the helm platform. Matteo knew she could have led from the commander's chair at the rear of the bridge, but it was just like her to want to be in the thick of things.

"Comms? Send a message to Colonel Holcomb. Get his status, then contact our fighter squadron."

Rhythmic taps rang out from the communication desk, a brass knocker piecing together short and long clicks into code. Similar devices on the transports and lead hoverjet would repeat the sequence while a code breaker translated it into something meaningful.

Update status, Matteo deciphered, closing his eyes, recalling his Kingdom Encryptions classes. *Send immediate plans.*

He saw the flight of transports leap over the summit of Etrus, then bank toward the harbor, skimming the rooftops as they went. Khamer hoverjets, long and sleek with swept wings and hooked noses, formed a protective triangle around them. Festival banners hung throughout the town whipped violently as they passed, and clouds of disturbed dust swept through the streets.

Banners? Matteo stared at the mayor's manse, its windows boarded-up, its walls smeared with crimson lettering he couldn't read at this distance. A wide flag hung from the second-story balcony, a blue background with a segmented white crustacean emblazoned on it.

Why were Sedring Festival decorations up months before the spring celebration? The giant lobsters would still be hiding in their winter grottos, waiting for the thaw to emerge and mate—which also happened to be the perfect time to trap them in well-placed cages. Matteo scanned Etrus' tiers, searching for more oddities. The market was festooned with colorful bunting. A towering bloom-pole was erected at its center, long streamers waving in the transports' wake.

A slimy feeling of wrongness pimpled the back of his neck. "Major Reev, I think you need to look at—"

"Reply from Colonel Holcomb," the silver-haired elder at the communication station said. *Jesrac*, Matteo remembered. The recent enlistee, a farmer who'd sought out the Resistance, was the oldest member of *Dharmasya's* crew.

Major Reev was behind his chair in an instant. "Let's hear it."

"Town empty. Land and check for survivors. Will snatch and grab anything useful."

"'Snatch and grab?' He really sent that?" The Ice Queen laughed. "Tell him to keep his eyes open and make it quick. We can't stay in the air forever."

She glanced at a series of dials and readouts on the bridge's rear bulkhead. Some were small, little notched vials filled with fluid that measured things like pressure or temperature. The largest was a great bronze circle, impossible to miss no matter where you were in the chamber. One end was white, the other an angry crimson, and a long silver needle hung between them, twitching ever so slightly as the deck vibrated.

The display showed *Dharmasya's* illyrium reserve, a chronometer measuring how much time was left before they plummeted from the sky. As Matteo watched, the needle crossed the vertical centerline, drifting ever closer to red.

They had burned half their fuel getting here. To reach the nearest Ascendancy settlement would require another quarter tank. There were no more back-ups, no crates of crystals in storage they could feed the cruiser's engines. The illyrium the Resistance ships were using now was the last they would get.

Missing townspeople. A vanished Imperial fleet. Mysterious banners, out-of-season festival decorations, and a clock ticking the seconds until they crashed.

Matteo's stomach twisted. Sweat beaded on his forehead, and the veins in his temple began to throb.

Ba-dump went his surging pulse.

Tick-tock mocked the chronometer on a passing orderly's wrist.

This was Aldona Fortress all over again. Matteo could see that now, as clearly as if he were swathed in the radiant threads of his magic. The pain was building. Needles were prodding his flesh, preparing to stab. Waiting to light an inferno inside his skull.

It was a warning, a prophecy. This time, he would make someone listen.

Lashing out, Matteo grabbed Sylette's wrist. "I need you," he said before she could jerk away.

"What's gotten into—"

"I need you to take my ramblings and explain them to Major Reev."

Sylette's arm went limp, and she didn't resist as Matteo tugged her toward the Ice Queen. Thank the Veneer for small blessings.

The comm officer, Jesrec, was clicking away at his knocker when they approached. Major Reev straightened up, then raised a blade-thin eyebrow when she saw Sylette's hand in Matteo's.

"I don't have time for whatever *this*"—she waved at them—"is."

Sylette thrust out her other arm, blocking the Ice Queen as she tried to slide past them. "Make time."

Cold mist formed in the space between their dueling glares, but Sylette's limb wasn't immediately reduced to a frozen stick. A good sign.

Sucking in a breath, Matteo blurted the only thing that mattered:

"We're in danger, Major Reev. And unless you listen to me, you're going to have another disaster like Aldona on your hands."

Chapter 55
Deadly Glimmer

This was not the battle Vallen had been promised.

He'd expected the transport to hurtle to a stop, bullets pinging off its flanks, soldiers inside and out screaming frantic orders. The landing ramp would drop onto a scene of chaos—a narrow blue perimeter clinging to the airships' sides while exchanging fire with rank upon rank of men in red and gold. Rod in hand, smile on his lips, he'd rush forward and break their lines, bestowing the same gift they'd given Leon with every swing and swipe of his blade.

It would have been glorious, the darkness agreed. *But it is not an impossibility. Not yet.*

Vallen didn't acknowledge the voice. Krenesh blade gripped in both hands, he crept down the ramp. Soldiers on either side swung their rifles back and forth, searching for a target. There were none. The broad harbor avenue they'd landed on was silent and empty, devoid of any noise but that they brought with them.

Where had the Sarcs gone? Why would they leave? Sure, he'd killed dozens of them and smashed up a few of their magtech toys the last time he was here, but that shouldn't have been enough to make them flee.

The clatter of their boots echoed off the deserted storefronts on Vallen's right and rose toward the still gray sky. He saw signs of life as they marched down the street. Fishing trawlers and merchant brigantines left tied to the long wooden piers, livelihoods people wouldn't just abandon. Windows and doors were locked and boarded-up, sealed so securely it was impossible to glimpse what lay inside.

Who would do such a thing? Why? The same questions bounced around his head as Vallen lowered his sword and approached a store with a cleaver dangling above its door.

Sal's Meats and— read the vandalized sign on its crimson-stained wall. Someone had taken a sword to it, then dashed bright, glittering paint over everything else. Vallen could make out a crude word here and there. *Darmi scum! Loyalist pig! Speak out again, and we'll gut you like your goods.*

Colonel Holcomb moved up beside him. "Don't get close to the buildings, son. We don't know—" He saw the graffiti, and his warning slid back down his throat.

"You're going to see worse before you see better," Holcomb said, turning around. Vallen didn't much care who Sal was or what had happened to him. It was just one more reason to hate the Sarcs.

Raising his arms, Holcomb waved together the fifty or so Darmatian troopers who'd emerged from the transports. "We're going to make this quicker than a holy man's first brothel pilgrimage," he announced, drawing a few wry chuckles. "Some of our ships landed elsewhere, some of them"—he gestured as a flight of three hoverjets screamed past, headed for the two cruisers holding position above the canal—"are staying high and dry until we get a read on things."

Holcomb pointed at Herj and the Sylph woman beside him. Her dark hair was bound in a braid that hung over her open suit back, a gap that exposed twisting blue vines tattooed on either side of her spine. Vallen found the contrast with her crimson skin alluring.

"Squads one and two, you're exploring the harbor with me. Squads three and four," Holcomb jabbed a finger at Vallen and a tall, square-jawed man with a puckered burn down his neck, "you're heading up toward the market. Search for survivors, grab any illyrium or non-perishable grub you find. Understand?"

"Yes, sir!" Vallen and the soldiers shouted.

Velle, Lilith, and Unter moved to join him. The blue giant had a bright grin on his face as he tightened the straps of the four gleaming bucklers lashed to his arms.

"New?" Vallen asked.

Unter nodded, flexing muscles his suit barely constrained, swinging his rounded shields to gauge their weight. "Scrap from cruiser repair. Major Reev tell me gift bolted to transport side. Find these when land, whole again feel."

"Glad you have them. We've been without our vanguard for too long."

"That," Velle said, chuckling, "almost sounded like something a leader would say."

"Don't get used to it," Lilith said. "I bet five tins it was a fluke and he's back to his grumbly, depressing self before the mission's over." Drawing her saber, she started stalking up the street on their right.

Vallen sighed and motioned for the others to follow her. Arguing wouldn't help, and Velle wasn't entirely wrong. He didn't see himself as a leader. Void, he didn't even *want* the title of Triaron anymore. Both labels belonged to someone better—someone whose comrades didn't wind up as bloody heaps at their feet.

But he *did* want them to survive the day, and having Unter at full strength was the best way for that to happen.

The darkness laughed, cold and cruel. *Let's see how that goes.*

After half an hour, Vallen was ready to quit the war.

His inner thighs blazed like a furnace, and the skin around his neck was raw from chafing. Yes, his combat gear wasn't fitted properly. The Resistance didn't have the resources—fabric and a good blacksmith—to tailor the skin-tight webbing to him. But at this point, charging around in his skivvies would be preferable to the hive of scum-crawlers gnawing away between his legs.

Eyes pinched, teeth gritted, Vallen *almost* asked Velle if she was having similar issues. She raised an eyebrow, then leaned to the side, scanning the street ahead of them.

"Did you see something?"

He shook his head. Velle—or Lilith, or any girl for that matter—was the wrong person to discuss his unique troubles with.

Across the sloped road, Captain Nyal raised three fingers, tapped them to his opposite palm, and waved both hands forward. The signal to move up. Vallen nodded, hugging the buildings on his left at a running crouch.

They hadn't encountered any resistance yet. Or anyone at all, for that matter. Every street, intersection, and square they reached was more of the same: locked doors, boarded-up windows, and splotches of shiny crimson paint wherever they looked.

Vallen could taste the hatred in the air, thick and noxious like Sewertown sludge. There were no eyes on him. Even so, he felt the glares, the sneers and pointed fingers. Being here made the years fall away, reducing him to the urchin no one from the surface wanted.

No one but the girl whose life he'd stolen.

"This is awful," Velle whispered, stepping around a spray of smashed glass. The home above it didn't have an intact window left, and the crimson tag scrawled on the door read, *Scarlet Witches don't belong here!*

Turning, Vallen saw Velle's hand was back on her face, obsidian nails scrubbing at her cheek. He reverted his blade to a rod and grabbed her hand before she could break the skin. "It's Sarc propaganda. Don't pay any attention to it."

"Worse," Unter rumbled behind her. Though the Hue was crouched like them, his head still reached the smashed planters beneath the first-story windows. "Sarcs no reason to smear paint on conquered homes. Darmatians to selves do this. In hearts whole time felt, war freedom to say give them."

The foul taste in Vallen's mouth grew worse still. "Let's move on."

They soon reached the market. Composed of a small square lined with flat-faced buildings, it was a far cry from the vibrant, bustling bazaars of Nemare. At street level, the stores were hollowed out. Carved pillars supported the upper floors, leaving the bottom open to shoppers who wanted to escape the day's heat.

Today there was snow on the ground, pushed into piles beside the square's four entrances. No shoppers roamed the boarded-up stores or perused the smashed and splintered stalls near the central fountain. Of the statue that had crowned it, only a mauled leg still stood. What water remained in its basin was brackish and black.

Lilith returned on silent feet, slithering from the shadows beneath a produce vendor's awning. "No civilians in any of the buildings nearby. I heard some rats clawing at the planks on the north side, but that's the only sign of life since the docks. It's just like . . . " she trailed off, lips moving without producing words.

Vallen didn't say anything. He had a habit of making things worse for people he cared about, and he was the *last* person Lilith needed reassurances from. Facing Captain Nyal and his squad, Vallen drew a circle in the air and shook his head. Their search had been in vain.

"Do you think the Sarcs killed them all?" Velle asked, gaze distant. She slowly looked from stand to stand as if seeing the past—the cheerful market and town as they had been before the Empire arrived.

"Hostages more valuable," Unter said.

Vallen stood and glanced around. "But why take hostages if you aren't going to use them? They didn't even try to fight for this place."

Metal scraping against metal broke the eerie market silence. Vallen jumped, then settled when he saw Nyal's men slotting bayonets beneath their rifle barrels. The burned captain pointed at a boarded-up store and made a two-handed stabbing motion. They were going to break in to search for usable supplies.

Not a bad idea. "Pick a store, Lilith," Vallen said, morphing his rod into an axe. "We'll open it up and see what's inside."

With Lilith leading, they stepped around the corner. Most of the buildings looked the same. Stucco walls covered with ivy draping from above. Wrought-iron railings lining the roofs and windows. Festive bunting hung from the upper levels, while lines draped with pennants crisscrossed the space between them.

The flags and banners bore the same symbol Vallen had seen from the air: a simple, blocky lobster painted in white. He stopped in front of one. What were the townsfolk thinking, trying to celebrate a *festival* under the new regime?

"A sedring," Velle explained, pointing at the lobster. "They're half as big as a Terran man and twice as fierce. A lot of coastal towns on the Etrus peninsula hunt them for their valuable shells and delicious meat."

Lilith stared at it, then used her hand to draw a line from Vallen's midriff over to her. It hit her shoulders. "How? They're almost as big as me."

"The same way most people hunt scary things: traps." Scanning around, Velle pointed at a large metal cage in one of the market's corners. "They bait the cages with little bits of illyrium, then drop the open latch when the sedring is inside. Once it's stuck, they stab it with harpoons until it dies."

"Not very fair," Lilith said.

Unter grunted. "Most battles aren't."

It soon became clear what house—or rather, *mansion*—Lilith had chosen. Outside the market proper, the estate possessed a tiny fenced-in lawn, three stories, and a wide balcony suited to entertaining guests or delivering speeches to those gathered below. Two marble columns—now defaced by vulgar slogans—supported the balcony, beneath which was another heavily boarded door.

The gate creaked as Vallen eased it open and slipped inside. Aside from the two headless statues on the front porch, their nethers smothered with red paint, the mansion wasn't so different than Elaine's estate. The bushes were neatly pruned, the walls scrubbed clean of grime, and the porch swept free of dust.

"You had to pick the biggest house, didn't you?" Vallen said.

"It only makes sense," Lilith replied. "Bigger house, more stuff."

Wait. Vallen paused as he climbed the steps. Stooping, he swept a finger across the cold stones. No dust, no snow. Someone was still caring for the house.

He held up his hand, the signal for *'Get ready.'* The sound of shuffling armor plates and adjusting weapons came from behind him. Three steps brought Vallen to the door. He put an ear to the boards hiding it.

No noise, only the shallow beat of his own heart and lungs. Stepping back, Vallen studied the walls, doors, and the curtain obscured windows to either side of the entrance. Like dripping blood, red paint coated everything. In some places it was readable, slurs such as, *"In the Council's pocket!"* or *"Better red and gold than dead and cold."*

But most of it was excessive, smears, streaks, and splashes that looked like someone had *tossed* paint at the mansion rather than taken the time to draw proper graffiti. Narrowing his eyes, Vallen leaned closer to the splatter on the door. Was it *sparkling*?

Before he could stop himself, Vallen lowered his axe and touched the glimmering paint with his opposite hand. Power surged into him. Energy, electricity, excitement. His cells came alive, his fatigue faded, and even the chafing between his legs dulled to a faint prickle.

"This is illyrium dust," Vallen mumbled, the exultant men'ar inside his body urging him to act, to move. "Enough to serve as a catalyst for magic. Why in the Void would someone grind up expensive crystals, mix them with paint, and spray it all over town?"

A gasp made him spin around, axe ready to swing. Velle held a dagger in one hand. The other covered her gaping mouth. *"All over town,"* she repeated. "We have to leave! Now!"

"What's wrong?" Vallen asked, leaping off the porch, rushing toward her.

Her whispered reply was cryptic. "Sensors only see in *black and white ...*"

Inside his head, the darkness surged, growing as if fed by the illyrium all around them. *It appears you'll get your battle after all, Triaron.*

Chapter 56
From the Deep

A gasp from the sensor station interrupted Matteo before he could speak. The girl at the desk shook her braided black hair, tore her gloves from her hands, and cast them on the deck beside her. Cursing, she plastered her bare palms to the illyrium crystal embedded in the dashboard in front of her, feeding it men'ar until it almost glowed white.

Seconds later, she slumped back in her seat. "Plague and pox. I can't get a reading. Nothing but white static everywhere."

White. The pain in Matteo's skull spiked. Without waiting for Major Reev's approval, he clomped down the steps into the recessed pit housing the sensor station, dragging Sylette with him.

"What now?" she asked. "What does a magtech failure have to do with this?"

"Repeat that," Matteo said, coming up behind the sensor tech's chair.

She jumped, spinning the chair around and clutching a hand to her chest. Her eyes—thin as river stones and just as bright—sought out the rank badge on his uniform collar and found a cannon medallion instead.

"Officer . . . ?" she mumbled, fishing for Matteo's rank.

"*Lieutenant* Alhan," Major Reev said from behind him. "Give me a full report of your scan of the city, Ensign Fayet."

"What's to report?" Fayet sighed, waving at the crystal. Matteo recognized it as a catalyst crystal—an amplifier for the girl's abilities wired to a similar crystal on *Dharmasya's* outer hull. "The voided thing is broken. Either that, or the recent snowfall was laced with illyrium. My magic shows the whole town is covered in a white sheet. Men'ar as far as the eye can see with barely a black blip in between."

Matteo's breath caught as tendrils of fire dripped down his cheek, dribbled onto his neck. "That's impossible," he grunted.

"I know, which is why I said the bloody thing is—"

Phantom flames scorched his shoulder. Searing smoke drifted into Matteo's throat, making every breath, every wheeze a struggle. Sylette saw his distress and squeezed his hand. But there was nothing she could do. By the Veneer, why couldn't his magic come with an easier warning system, like the taste of strawberries?

541

Mouthing an apology, Matteo shook off Sylette and *leapt* onto Fayet's desk. She screamed. Major Reev shouted at him. Ignoring them both, he grabbed the railing over the pit and heaved himself back onto the main deck.

Five steps—five excruciating steps—brought Matteo to the forward viewport. Every motion made him want to vomit. Every stumble was a hammer strike to his skull. Distantly, he saw Renar beside him, reaching for his shoulder, trying to push him away.

Why?

Why would Renar want Matteo to fail?

"Let it happen," he whispered through trembling lips, gaze filled with desperation.

No. Never again.

Matteo closed his eyes, opened himself to magic, and *saw*.

Threads launched in every direction, bursting from his stationary body, wrapping the world in color. Renar became a dull spark, barely touched by the golden light of men'ar. He was too dim to be a mage. Too dull to be anything more than an ordinary Terran.

How had Matteo not seen it before? But he shook off the revelation, casting his vivid sight down toward his hometown.

Where Renar was a dying candle, Etrus was a blazing inferno. It was like staring into the sun or peering at the unshrouded face of the Creator. Matteo almost brought up a hand to shield the glare, but that wouldn't hide the glow. It would simply pierce his flesh like it wasn't there.

Buildings that should be black pits, dead and devoid of men'ar, were pillars of radiance. The canal and harbor were a brilliant yellow, not a single creature visible beneath the blanket of spiritual energy they effused. What few green specks Matteo saw throughout the city—gardens, trees, and grassy parks—were all but drowned in a sea of light, mere drops in a wall of gold.

Matteo could think of no explanation for this sight. Two things glowed yellow in his sight: sentient beings, those capable of using the men'ar in their body, and illyrium crystals. Etrus clearly wasn't splattered in blood. Such a tragedy would be impossible to hide.

Which meant the town had been dusted with . . .

Everything clicked into place. The Sedring banners hung as a warning by the missing townsfolk. The unseasonal flooding of the harbor.

His pain disappeared, its purpose fulfilled.

Praying he wasn't too late, Matteo roared at the top of his lungs.

"The Empire never left! They're hiding in the buildings and under the harbor!"

Renar sighed and let his arm slide from Matteo's shoulder to fall at his side. The bridge exploded into a maelstrom of activity, Major Reev shouting orders, officers punching buttons and fiddling with their controls. *Dharmasya* lurched, throwing him against the railing as she accelerated. Hard metal bit at his gut, driving the air from his chest.

But the pain, noise, and chaos were welcome. They gave Renar something to focus on. To distract him from his self-loathing and . . . what he now had to do.

What would Unter think? Would he . . . hate him? Stare at him with the same disgust as the General, as Vallen, as every single person who thought he was useless?

Does it matter? The Soldier laid an arm across Renar's shoulders, pulling him close, whispering in his ear. *Does it matter what* any *of them think? No.*

But—

The Soldier grabbed his chin. *Do it. You want the General's approval, his love, and your 'friends'—this 'Resistance'—stand in your way. Do what must be done.*

They hadn't landed as the General had wanted. The Empire's trap was coming undone, knot by knot. Matteo—bright, determined, irrepressible Matteo—was finally the hero he'd always wanted to be.

Bravo for him, the Soldier said. *Now he can die with the rest.*

Renar nodded, grasping the railing, heaving himself upright. Thought was difficult. Moving was as hard as any exam he'd ever taken. Color had drained from his world, and all was black and gray.

But it would return. If Renar did what the General asked, he would see the color of love. Would it be red like blood? Yellow or silver like precious metals?

Renar strode through the bridge, past Sylette and Major Reev, out the door behind the captain's chair. No one noticed him. He had no magic, and no one trusted him to do anything in this situation.

Magicless. Useless. Unseen.

But not unloved. One press of a button, and Renar would finally see the color of love.

"Their cruisers are moving," Captain Neering said, tearing his eyes from the periscope. Most of the device—Olivier's personal invention—extended above *Ardor's* bulk. Up through the water illusion cast by his mages, up into the frosty air where his foes scurried about like mewling children, unable to comprehend the genius of his snare.

If Olivier could leap for joy at their ignorance, he would. But today he was confined to his command chair. The white-robed salvator waiting at his side had warned a step, a shout—any sudden movement— would leave him a blood-spitting lump on the floor.

Fortunately, Olivier's pawns would do the moving for him. "Repositioning? Landing? Give me the details, nephew."

The rat-faced whelp, long of nose with drooping whiskers to match, glanced at Olivier's plate-armored mercenaries. Eight of them hunched at the edges of *Ardor's* bridge, waiting on his orders like temple statues waiting for the Creator's return. They wouldn't harm his squeamish nephew . . . unless he told them to.

"Fleeing, it appears," Neering squeaked. "Full burn from their engines. Their ground forces are also agitated, rushing back toward their transports."

"Then the truth is known. No matter." Grinning, Olivier gripped his cane with trembling fingers and thrust its wyrm-bone tip at the shadows beyond *Ardor's* viewports. "They've already wandered too far into my web. Order all companies and squadrons to attack. Blow our ballast tanks. Full tilt, maximum angle, flank speed ascent. We'll scorch them from the land, cut them from the skies. For the Emperor!"

"For the Emperor!" his officers echoed, bending over their stations.

For my survival! Olivier added silently. At the end of the day, nothing else—not even his beloved sovereign—mattered more than his own rotting flesh.

Chapter 57

Collapse

Vallen's squad was halfway across the market square when a bright red flare shot from the harbor depths. He didn't stop running to follow its path. He barely spared a thought for why the arcing projectile was fired from the water instead of land. Getting back to the transports—warning the others—was all that mattered now.

"Back to ships!" Unter bellowed at Captain Nyal's men. "Trap it is! Run now!"

They paused and glanced up at the sprinting lieutenants, their bayonets buried in the splinters of the barricade sealing a carpet dealer's shop. Vallen saw understanding brighten Nyal's burn-pocked face an instant before a sword thrust from the shadowy wreckage into his side.

Then a screech split the air. High-pitched and warbling, like the triumphant call of a drake swooping upon its prey. Only *this* cry was amplified by magic. Vallen saw the harbor buckle and twist, lashed by vibrations unleashed by the falling flare. Buildings at the water's edge shook, roof tiles clattered, and a wall of dust came flying up the street toward them.

"Brace yourselves!" Vallen yelled, plugging his ears, shutting his eyes. The wave hit him like a mallet. He bucked backward, barely keeping his feet, and ringing filled his head as pain knifed through his skull.

So much ringing, so much throbbing. It hurt to think, to stand, to breathe. Blinking, Vallen stumbled forward, swiping at the clouds of dirt and debris hanging in the air. He saw a flash of crimson amid the dust. Velle?

Her lips moved. She pointed at something past him. Or was it above him? The market square spun, buildings blurring together, the gray of the cobblestones indistinguishable from the gray of the sky.

Fangs bared, Velle stormed toward him, fingers glowing with green light. She brushed something warm and sticky from Vallen's ears, mouthing two words his eyes couldn't process.

Sound rushed in on him from all sides. Nyal's screaming, the cries of his soldiers, the clash of steel on steel. Rifle retorts, humming engines, clanking gears. Vallen couldn't see the harbor through the swirling smog, but he could hear the distinct *whumping* of airship cannons and the roar of exploding shells.

The battle for Etrus had begun.

"That flare was a signal," Jis shouted. "They'll be coming at us from—"

"Below!" Matteo interrupted, pointing out the viewport at the canal and harbor. They glowed crimson in the spectral light of the falling Sarconian flare.

Jis didn't argue with the boy. At Aldona, the fleet had ignored the warning of a green cadet most Academy staff had considered a coward. Today, she would listen to the word of a promising *officer* she trusted with her life.

"Hard port," Jis ordered, grabbing a nearby railing. "All guns aim starboard."

"Aye, ma'am."

The helmswoman threw the wheel left, taking *Dharmasya* into a tight turn away from the bay's center. As the deck tilted, the bridge crew clung to their desks or pulled hooks from their belts and snapped them onto bulkheads, railings, anything that would support their weight. Those at their stations strapped themselves into their seat harnesses. This wouldn't be the cruiser's last extreme maneuver, and a little discomfort was preferable to being tossed into a wall at high speed.

"It's breaking," Matteo said, eyes closed, still focused on the tranquil water beneath the airship.

Sylette glanced at Jis, then at him. "What is?"

Streaks of light lit the harbor, a blinding glare that forced Jis to squint and shade her eyes. The streaks became cracks, radiating, rushing to every corner of the cliff-enclosed bay. Then it *shattered*. Collapsed into millions of yellow globules—residual men'ar from a massive spell. And as they disappeared, the fishing craft floating on the false surface plummeted toward the true water far below.

The flooded harbor had been an illusion. A trick by their foes to hide their forces. *They must have dammed the canal,* Jis thought. *Plugged the mouth of the bay. All to clear out a hollow for—*

A trio of T-shaped Sarc heavy cruisers hurtled upward from the chasm, engines blazing, forward turrets aglow with angry crimson light.

546

"Lume!" Jis shrieked

An officer at the tactical station threw a lever. The glistening soap bubble of *Dharmaysa's* shield winked into existence, only to be *buffeted* by a deluge of explosions a second later. Jis' teeth chattered. Her whole body shook as the airship bucked and twisted.

They flew free of the blast's smoke, trembling subsiding as the ripples marring the lume flattened out. *Dharmasya* had taken a hook to the ribs and kept soaring. But she couldn't take another.

"Lume down to thirty-four percent efficiency!" an orderly called. "We have holes running across our starboard flank."

Red lights pulsed throughout the bridge. On the ceiling, in the pits, across every instrument panel. Shouted damage reports came from every quarter.

"Bulkhead collapse in tail section D35. Three injured, dispatching salvators."

"Wiring to the rear turret melted. It can only be fired manually."

"Chief Engimage Darres says the engines are running hot. They can't take another pummeling like that."

"I know, I know," Jis said, waving away their concerns. She breathed deeply, trying to focus, hoping not to be overwhelmed. This was *exactly* what she'd been afraid of. Everything was going wrong. All her plans were falling apart.

Beads jangled, their clattering a distant but familiar melody. *Which means it's time for a new plan,* Mother Tabitha whispered in Jis' ear. *It is not falling that defines us, Jisarivel. It is whether we choose to rise again once we do. How we rise is far more meaningful than how we fall.*

Jis began roaring orders. "Lieutenant Farkos, you and Captain Hurshik organize our repair crews. Lieutenant Alhan, scan their ships. Warn me when they're ready to fire."

The boy's eyes snapped open. "I'm not sure I—"

"You can see their men'ar signatures, so I'm certain you can see it building up in their guns. Helm?"

"Ma'am?" The muscular helmswoman, Ensign Keleva, acknowledged. Her uniform was soaked with sweat, her knuckles white on the lacquered wood of *Dharmasya's* wheel.

Jis grinned. "Bring us around for a broadside pass."

Splinters of stone and wood blasted across the market square, enveloping Vallen's squad in a storm of flying shrapnel. Velle threw up her arms, surrounding them with white glyphs. Unter raised his bucklers to ward off debris falling from above. And Vallen? He stood still, his lightning barrier incinerating or redirecting anything that came too close.

He saw glints of silver through the smoke, murky shapes in red and gold surging from gaping market stalls with bayonets fixed to their rifle barrels. They'd blown open the barricades with some sort of pre-set charges.

Vallen heard their battle cries. Watched them tear into Captain Nyal's doomed squad, then turn their blood-slick blades toward him. Groaning panzcraft joined them, brushing aside pillars as they lumbered from their hidden berths, treads crushing fallen Darmatian bodies with sickening snaps.

"We have to run," Lilith said, launching a fireball that glanced harmlessly off a panzcraft gun turret. Its cannon started shifting toward her.

Fight, the darkness urged Vallen. *Show them your power. Take your vengeance.*

Bullets pinged against Velle's barriers, but the Sarc soldiers stopped firing after a single volley. An officer wearing a slick black cap waved at another panzcraft, then pointed at their squad. The Sarcs had learned a lot from their last engagement, including how to tear through the Sylph's shields.

Velle swung her hands, adjusting her barriers so they were layered between them and the two armored behemoths. "My glyphs can take a bit more punishment now, but not enough to stop them. We need to leave, Vallen."

The darkness scowled at her. *Don't listen. This is your moment, Triaron. Everything you wanted. Everything you've waited for.*

Chainmail armored soldiers flanked to the sides, edging to cut off the street in front of them—their only avenue of escape. But what good would escape do them? By the sound of it, Etrus was becoming a bloodbath. Screams and rifle retorts split the smoky sky. Cries of delight and cries of agony surged from hundreds of throats as fighter-craft roared through the air and airships exchanged furious broadsides.

Bucklers still directed outward, Unter stepped close to Vallen. "Save life first, deal death later. *We* choose battlefield, not them. Don't what Empire wants do."

Let me out, Triaron. The darkness loomed, stretching out a pitch-dark hand from which shadow dripped like water. *I can brush them aside like sand before the waves. Like night before a flame. Let me give you* victory.

No. What the voice offered wasn't victory, but surrender—an abdication of both pain and responsibility. Vallen wouldn't accept. Not now, not ever. He would win this battle on *his* terms, not someone else's. The Triaron of Darmatia was just that greedy.

Vallen morphed his rod into a staff. "We run," he yelled, dashing toward the market exit. "Straight on to the harbor. We'll link up with Holcomb, rally the troops, and win this bloody fight."

Matteo watched Etrus burn.

He couldn't keep his attention fixed on the Sarconian cruisers. Not when buildings were crumbling in the distance, masonry grinding beneath the treads of rampaging panzcraft. Not when the stores and homes of people he cherished were being riddled with shells and bullets.

Sal's butcher shop imploded in a gout of flame. The market was shrouded in smoke, the fountain in its midst toppled and gushing water. Matteo could see little skirmishes here and there. Spells scorching rubble barricades behind which indistinct shapes huddled. Armored soldiers chasing their foes through the streets, rifles flashing orange, bayonets glinting silver.

Who was who? Was there hope for the Resistance, or had they already lost?

And where, Matteo glanced back and forth through the haze, his flesh pimpling in a sudden chill, *are my parents? Where is anyone?*

His breath came fast and ragged. His blood thundered in his ears. This *was* Aldona all over again. Nothing had changed. Matteo had failed, and now his hometown was paying the—

"Cruisers, Alhan!"

He blinked, shaking off his stupor, focusing on Major Reev's voice. The battle wasn't over, and there was a job only *he* could do.

Raising his arms like an orchestra conductor, Matteo closed his eyes and drifted on the threads of his magic. It was a roaring ocean now. A thousand threads dappled Etrus in a shifting tapestry of light, some shining like stars, others extinguishing to darkness. Life blazing with passion and purpose. Life fading away, bleeding out until not a spark remained.

Matteo thought he saw a group of familiar lights rushing down Main Street toward the harbor—his friends, thank the Veneer. But he didn't have time to monitor their progress. The three Sarconian cruisers rushed to meet *Dharmasya*, their turrets and cannons swinging to track her swift movements. If she and *Conviction* fell, the Resistance fell with them.

He furrowed his brow, trying to go deeper into his magic than he ever had. If Holcomb and Major Reev were right, Matteo wasn't an ordinary sensory mage, which meant he should be able to do more than just *see* men'ar. Perhaps he could read it as well. Understand what it was doing now . . . and what it would do in the future.

You're not far off, boy, came a strange whisper in his ear. Matteo jerked at the intrusion, glancing over his shoulder, searching for the speaker. No one had moved from their stations. He was still alone at the viewport.

The whisper came again, now in his other ear. *Watch where the threads twitch. Where they seem to quiver in an unseen wind. Find where the energy is now, and then predict where it will be next.*

Praying he wasn't losing his mind, Matteo listened.

"Cruiser 'one' is moving to our port side," he shouted, following the trajectory of the thread tied to its engines.

The shimmering twine *was* twitching, a vibration that grew stronger as it arced to the left. The light pouring off its cannons was also growing, men'ar leeching from illyrium crystals to power its guns and aiming systems.

"'One' will fire in the next five seconds," Matteo added. "Evade in three, two, one, *GO!*"

"Dive!" Major Reev ordered.

Matteo's gut lurched as *Dharmasya* pointed its bow toward the water and flared her engines. As his breakfast mush tried to make a surprise reappearance, his boots lost contact with the deck and his body began to float. Then the airship settled out and he nearly *splattered* on the metal flooring. His arm muscles screamed as he gripped the railing for dear life.

Four or five loud whistles screeched past overhead, shaking *Dharmasya*. The volley had missed them entirely. Matteo's prediction had been right. The *whisper* had been right. "Don't let it go to your head, Alhan," Major Reev said, seeming to read his thoughts. "Get me a bead on the other cruisers."

He heard the click of her boots on the bridge's grated floor, followed by the raspy grunt of the gunnery officer. "All turrets locked and loaded, ma'am."

"Lower lume," she commanded. "Fire at will."

One of the closest and brightest threads—*Dharmasya's* shield—winked out. The two top deck turrets in front of Matteo blazed like bonfires, and the ship *leapt* under him, rocking away from the outgoing broadside.

Her target still had its lume lowered, and its course was set. Unlike *Dharmasya*, the big, lumbering vessel couldn't dodge at the last second, even if it knew the barrage was coming. Six bright blooms blossomed against the Sarc cruiser's flank, knocking out one of its turret threads and weakening the glow from its engine.

Matteo cracked one eye—just enough to see the true extent of the damage.

Cheers erupted from the entire bridge crew. The cruiser was smoking from the hits, bleeding vaporized wisps of synth-oil and a long trail of illyrium dust. An entire turret was missing, blown clean off her top deck, and the armor plating down her side was torn, blackened, and mangled.

But best of all, she was losing altitude. The cruiser's bow turned away from them, her captain likely hoping he could put her down before she took another salvo.

A grin split Matteo's face. *Dharmasya* had drawn first blood, and the Resistance was *far* from defeated.

The wall in front of Vallen blew outward, sending massive shards of tan stone careening into the neat garden across the street. Neverfade stalks were flattened, thin menja fruit trees broke in half, and the head of a topiary shaped like a dragwyrm went bouncing into the neighboring lawn.

Vallen spun his staff and yelled, "Gust'orren!" Wind blades swept down the street, knocking aside any splinters headed their way.

They did *nothing* to dissuade the armored monstrosity heaving itself out of the wreckage. Stucco and marble fragments snapped like bones beneath the panzcraft's treads as it lurched onto the street and aimed its twin barrels at Vallen's squad.

An explosion roared behind him, and a rush of heat swept against his back. Velle had her own problems—defending against shells from the panzcraft *chasing* them—and Unter was keeping them safe from rooftop snipers. He and Lilith would have to handle this foe on their own.

Rule two, Vallen recalled, glancing at the tall buildings around them. *Use the terrain to your advantage.*

"Bring that house down on it," he told Lilith, gesturing with the staff melting in his hands. He needed a larger weapon for the next step.

The girl nodded, then jabbed her saber tip at a jagged crack running from the street to the roof. "Flar'en!"

A bolt of flame shot from the blade and struck the crack where it passed a gaping window. Stone chips rained down, followed by most of the upper floor. The slab broke away from the rest of the building and collapsed atop the panzcraft, burying its cannons, denting the commander's hatch and turrets.

"Good enough?" Lilith asked.

Vallen shrugged as he raised his warhammer. "I could've done better."

"You wish, backside-boy."

He brought the thick mallet down, ramming it into the cobbles, injecting his men'ar into the earth beneath.

Rule four, Vallen thought, directing his spell through unseen soil and silt. *There is more to your opponents than their attacks.* The panzcraft wasn't just a danger because of its guns. It was a bunker. A rallying point. A *barrier.*

One that needed to be removed.

Rock spikes thrust from the street, embedding in the magchine's right tracks. The first spike slashed the rubber treads, taking away its traction. The next half-dozen impaled its undercarriage and *lifted* it off the road.

The panzcraft hung there for a moment, teetering on its one remaining track. Vallen sneered and pressed on his warhammer, jabbing it a little deeper into the ground. A final earthen spear erupted from those he'd already made and pushed the beast onto its side.

"Way's clear!" he called over his shoulder as he raced around the flailing vehicle. Its guns couldn't depress enough to hit them, and its untreaded wheels spun pointlessly in the air.

A hatch in the panzcraft's belly popped open, revealing a soot-stained man in greasy coveralls. He held a pistol but seemed too dazed to use it, his other hand clutching a bleeding slash on his forehead.

Vallen *could* bash the Sarc's head in with a single swing of his hammer. The darkness agreed. *He would've killed you if you hadn't upended his little toy. A life for a life. Claim your vengeance, then burn out his companions. They all share the guilt.*

The hammer grew heavy in Vallen's grip, its handle slick with his sweat. Blue eyes swam from side to side, settled on his weapon, then slid up to his face. The Sarc knew what was happening. Knew his life was forfeit if he didn't kill Vallen first.

But the Sarc didn't raise his pistol. His lips moved, forming words Vallen didn't understand. An apology? A plea?

Lilith rounded the back of the panzcraft, her eyes narrowing as they locked on the Sarc. She didn't hesitate. A single kick to the back of his head knocked him out, and she yanked the pistol from his limp grip.

"He's not a threat anymore," she confirmed, passing the pistol to Velle as she approached. The Sylph's other hand held a defensive glyph in the air behind them. "Let's go."

Vallen nodded. Not every Sarc needed to die, and right now staying alive was more important than slaying a defenseless enemy. Vallen couldn't bring back Leon or Elaine.

But he could ensure no one else he cared about went to join them. Not today, not ever.

Sylette was adrift in a sea of shouts and curses.

Orderlies raced up to Captain Hurshik as he hunched over the map table, a scrivle in one hand, the other gesturing to whichever station needed support at that particular instant. They were all short-staffed. Every console—every surface on the bridge, it seemed—was covered in blinking warning lights, and damage reports continued to pour in like air through a breached hull. No matter how many patches they slapped on the breach, it would never be enough.

"*Conviction* just took a broadside from cruiser 'three,'" an officer at the comm station yelled. "Her main engine's toast and harrier skimmers are pouring fire into her belly. Commander Jezricar doesn't know how long she'll last."

Captain Hurshik jotted a note on the map, blotting out the nearby island of Pharsalus. A pristine map mattered little if they didn't survive the next few minutes. "Sariel's arse! Can't Lieutenant Faerns spare a wing of hoverjets to screen for her?"

"Lieutenant Faerns is dead," an orderly said, glancing up from her notes. "Ensign Drannik commands the fighter squadron now."

"Then get him on the line right—"

The orderly shook her head, dark curls seeming to wilt along with her falling gaze. "We haven't heard from him in three minutes."

Sylette felt lost. Helpless. She hadn't been this impotent—this out of her depth—since she'd knelt on that filthy platform in Sarconia's outer ring, bleeding wrists clapped in stocks, peasants tossing refuse and rocks at her. That day she'd screamed herself hoarse as Valescar murdered her mother.

So . . . what would Sylette lose today?

Her daggers were useless compared to the fighters twisting and spinning beyond the viewport. She didn't know how to 'fight' a cruiser, to command its crew and guns in battle. And even if she did, Major Reev was vastly more experienced. Captain Hurshik knew *Dharmasya* inside and out, down to its bolts, welds, and pipes. Sylette had only memorized her escape route to the *Kinloss* in case the Ice Queen decided to arrest her.

There was nothing for her to do. No way Sylette could influence the battle, no way she could turn things in her favor with keen tactics or magic. Was this how Renar felt? Was this why he'd been clinging to the railing, staring at the chaos like it wasn't even there?

Sylette slipped away from the tactical salon, stepping around messengers headed the opposite way. No one paid her any attention. Captain Hurshik kept roaring order after order, not even aware she'd left.

The deck shook, sending Sylette staggering into the starboard bulkhead. Outside the viewport, the lume flickered as a burning hulk bearing the Darmatian crest bounced off its surface and plummeted to the harbor far below. Two sleek, hook-beaked lancerjets slashed past behind it, their swept wings painted red and gold.

"Anti-air batteries, take them down!" Major Reev shouted.

With a *pop*, the lume dissipated. Dozens of shells from the small caliber barbettes lining *Dharmasya's* flank peppered the sky, filling the air around the lancerjets with shrapnel and puffs of black smoke. One lost a wing and spiraled out of control. The other soared skyward beyond the guns' range.

"It's a trick," Matteo wheezed, voice cracking. "Cruiser 'two' is . . . ready to fire . . . "

Dharmasya bucked as an explosion ripped into her side. Sylette caught a glimpse of flames and wildly careening metal before she and most of the bridge crew were tossed to the floor. The ringing in her head met the blaring of the damage klaxons, blending into a grand symphony of irritation.

"Get that lume back up," Major Reev ordered. "Helm, get us some distance. Flank speed."

The officer at the comm station heaved himself up using his desk, then pressed his ear to a quivering voicepipe. "Chief Engimage Darres says we're down an engine. Fifty percent power is the best we can do."

"Plague and pox . . . "

Groaning, Sylette stood. Warm blood seeped from a cut on her right hand, but she was otherwise unharmed. Matteo, on the other hand . . .

Sylette picked her way across the bridge, skirting fallen orderlies, avoiding overturned tables, scattered maps, and a few sparking wires dangling from the ceiling. Reaching Matteo's side, she stooped, slid an arm under his shoulder, and lifted him up.

"You're supposed to rest *after* the battle, not during," Sylette joked.

"Uh-huh . . . " was the best he could manage.

It had barely been ten minutes since the fighting began, but constantly using his magic was taking a heavy toll on him. Color had drained from his face, leaving it haggard and pale like freshly fallen snow. Veins bulged around his eyes, blood-red and angry. There was a clear correlation between his condition and whatever his powers were showing him.

Sylette bit her lip. This went against everything she wanted—everything she craved—but . . . "You need to stop, Matteo."

"It's . . . fine," he coughed, his trembling arm reaching for the railing. Sylette took his wrist and guided it to the coarse metal.

"It's not. You're making yourself sick. Or"—she glanced at his sunken eyes—"worse."

Matteo turned to Sylette, patted her hand, and started to open his mouth.

"I need a status update on those cruisers, Alhan!" Major Reev's cry cut off whatever he'd been preparing to say.

He nodded. Winking at her, Matteo faced the viewport and closed his eyes. A second later, the veins surrounding his eyes *pulsed* with energy, their snaking tendrils expanding across his nose, toward his hairline.

What in Sarcon's venerated name was happening to him?

Sylette shook her head, marveling at his strength. If only *she* could do as much as he was. Extricating her arm from his, she scanned the bridge, searching for Renar. The least they could do was hold Matteo up as he struggled to keep *Dharmasya* afloat.

Renar wasn't at the railing. No mush of jet-black hair could be seen in the pits, on the helm platform, or strapped into a seat along the rear bulkhead. The man-child was tall—the biggest, burliest slab of raw muscle in their group except for Unter. How could he just disappear?

Holding out her hand, Sylette stopped Ensign Fayet as she passed. With Matteo handling sensor scans for the whole airship, the young officer had been reassigned to orderly duty.

"Have you seen Lieutenant Iolus?" Sylette asked. "Tall, dark hair, might be in a corner drawing?"

The girl pressed a finger to her chin. A second later, her thin eyes shot open. "I *did* see him. He left the bridge right after your buddy Alhan jumped on my desk and warned us about the Sarc trap. No idea where he is now."

Sylette mumbled a word of thanks and waved Fayet on. Why would Renar leave the bridge without orders? Was he hiding? Trying to help elsewhere on the ship?

Something *twisted* in Sylette's gut, like a dagger rooting through her organs, mangling everything as it went. She'd seen the look he'd had on his face before. Mouth open in despair. Shoulders bent in resignation. Limbs trembling with anguish.

It was the same empty gaze Sylette had worn when she collapsed in the Sarconian senate, staring at her shackled mother as her father condemned her to death.

It was the face of someone with nothing left to lose.

Bullets chased Vallen's squad onto the broad harbor thoroughfare. There were at least ten Sarcs behind them—four on the rooftops, another six hugging stairwells and doorways as they emptied rifle rounds against Velle's glyphs and Unter's shields.

They weren't close to breaking through. No cracks marred the Sylph's glowing shields, no nicks scoured Unter's men'ar-enhanced bucklers. Vallen knew their strength. Trusted their magic would hold for an hour, maybe longer.

If their foes only came at them from one side.

A sizzling round breached Vallen's lightning barrier, glancing off his breastplate, drawing a wince. More shells followed, forcing him to convert his hammer to a tower shield, tall and broad as he was. He fed men'ar into its surface, setting it ablaze and incinerating any lead slugs that came too close.

"They're here too!" Vallen screamed, struggling to be heard over the rushing flames, crackling lightning, and ricocheting bullets.

Lilith launched a fireball at the rooftops that sent a cloaked sniper tumbling away in a spray of stucco slivers and smoking fabric. "Really? I hadn't noticed."

Vallen loved her sass, but right now it was a tad irritating. He glanced around the curved edge of his shield, trying to gauge the situation. The transports were in sight, six matte gray rectangles blocking the road to the east. But they didn't promise safety. Not anymore.

Rubble from destroyed buildings had buried one and kept spilling across the cobblestones toward the harbor, forming a makeshift wall which several dozen Resistance soldiers crouched behind, their armor coated in dust, rifles pointed outward. A helm etched with a gold star marked Colonel Holcomb, but Vallen couldn't make out any other faces.

They were trading fire with a platoon of Sarcs advancing from the opposite direction, three panzcraft leading the way, huddled infantry clinging to their flanks and bringing up the rear.

The long black barrel of the lead magchine twitched down, a hair left, and belched smoke and flame. One of the surviving transports exploded from the inside out, scything down Darmatians in a spray of shrapnel, casting a plume of inky smog into the frenzied sky. Blood splattered the debris and trickled over the stone levee into the bay.

Another panzcraft noticed Vallen's squad, its turret shifting their way as its tracks squealed and exhaust jetted from its rear deck. Void it all.

"Velle!" he shouted.

"Working on it," she grunted.

Two glyphs swung around in front of him, circling the Sylph like celestial bodies. Her fingers splayed open, widening the shields, expanding the complex runes until Vallen could hardly see the panzcraft beyond the translucent barriers.

The turret bucked back. At this distance, the roar of the blast, the acrid stench of gunpowder, and the explosion itself struck him all at once. Vallen's lungs dropped into his stomach. His ears crumpled and his eyes screamed under the pressure.

Then clarity returned. Gasping for breath, Vallen willed his tower shield into a krenesh blade and stepped *through* the fading mist of Velle's shattered glyphs. Little floating shards, so much like glittering stars, touched his skin and melded with it—energy returning to energy, her residual men'ar now made his.

Vallen felt the warmth in it, the compassion that was her. The Sarcs would not take Velle from him this day, nor Lilith, Unter, or any of the rest.

Not here, not ever.

"Hold them back," Vallen said, waving his blade at the red- and gold-clad stream trickling in behind them. "I'm going to take care of their main group."

Yes. The darkness smiled, coiling about itself in anticipation. *That's more like it, Triaron.*

"Alone?" Velle gasped, arms trembling as she maintained her remaining glyphs.

Unter simply nodded. "Strength with you go, brother."

Vallen charged.

A downward slash of wind launched him into the air as he ran, raising him onto a roof overlooking the Sarc platoon. Dashing through an archway draped with blue-budded ivy, Vallen surprised a Sarc sniper, slipping his sword between his ribs before he could utter a cry of alarm. The soldier's partner swung her rifle toward him, green eyes wide, fingers fumbling at the sliding bolt.

"You lousy—"

Vallen parted her fingers from the weapon, then carved her chest and neck open on the reverse swing. Bright eyes went dark. Two bodies collapsed on the rooftop, joining the broken clay pots, dust, and crushed flowers already there. Vallen moved on.

He didn't have time to think.

The darkness agreed. *To think is to stop. To stop is to die. Keep bleeding them.*

If Vallen stopped—if he hesitated—people would die. One for every mistake he made. One for every Sarc he didn't kill or turn away.

559

Feed the furnace that blazes in your soul, the darkness whispered. *Drink in the death, offer it at the pyre of your loss. Give it to ME.*

The krenesh blade liquefied, cool fluid flowing over his hands, encasing them in sheathes of men'ar and metal. Vallen fed the power of earth into them, then slammed his fists against the roof.

Stone and mortar, rock and tile. Furniture, carpets, dishware—the trappings of ordinary life. They *all* exploded outward, cascading over the Sarconian host as a wave crests the shore. Vallen didn't see the soldiers die. Didn't see their helmets crushed in like tin cans beneath a boot, didn't witness jagged porcelain and cutlery slice their flesh to ribbons.

But he *did* hear them. Screams and wails and agony. Cries for mothers, squadmates yelling for their brethren, simple mewls and whimpers as life fled and blood ran cold among the dirt and grit.

The darkness approved, smiling, *beaming. THIS is what you were meant for, Triaron. This is the work you were entrusted with.*

Mere stone wasn't enough to stop the panzcraft. A turret tracked toward Vallen, desperate to end him before he could do more harm. Too slow. *Much* too slow.

Vallen collected wind at the base of his boots, fashioning it into engines to rival any airship's. Major Reev would be furious. He was casting without incantations, burning through his men'ar like a flame through a wick. But to speak cost time, and time was a luxury Vallen didn't have.

Roars from Darmatian throats drifted to him on the wind. Voices of squads pinned down, battling desperately to flee the city, to reach the transports. Lilith cursed as she cast fire spell after fire spell. Velle groaned under the impact of shells on her shields, and Unter bellowed as he swept fragile men and women aside with his bucklers.

It wouldn't be enough.

The darkness agreed.

Unleashing the condensed wind, Vallen *rocketed* off the roof— away from the collapsed house, away from the turning panzcraft. His gauntlets became a spear, one he aimed like a rifle as he flew. Fire lanced from its point, flashing down onto the exposed deck of the middle panzcraft. It burned straight through the thin metal grate. Melted into the rumbling heart of the armored beast.

Steam blasted skyward, missing Vallen by a hand span. A shrill whistle filled the air, growing louder and louder. Then ... the magchine's rear blossomed like a deadly flower, metal bending like petals, flame gushing like pollen. The crew inside never stood a chance. A blackened arm sticking from the commander's hatch and the nauseous tang of charred flesh were all that remained of them.

Vallen's momentum carried him out over the water, toward the sagging masts and sails of what vessels remained at the dock. Some were burning, their rigging ablaze and hulls riddled with holes from stray rounds. The one he'd chosen was still pristine. Its unfurled sails flapped softly in the heat from its dying comrades.

Curling, Vallen struck the mainsail and let himself roll with gravity until his feet were beneath him. He channeled wind, feeding it into the thick canvas, using it to right his body.

Aiming it like an arrow.

Vallen soared back the way he'd come, breeze tousling his hair and tearing at his eyes and lips. Such a small discomfort. Barely an inconvenience compared to the chasm inside his chest, the pit engraved with two names from his past.

Fill it in, the darkness urged. *With bodies and blood, until not a crevice or crack remains.*

Lightning coated Vallen's spear. Enough to fry a drake or charge a lake with energy. Vallen struck the turret of the closest panzcraft with his spear *grafted* onto his arms, cool liquid clamping to his flesh as he'd seen Bohomaz do with armor plates.

It pierced the metal. Scalded it until the surface bubbled around the spear-haft, white-hot and dripping. The Sarc commander inside screeched like a voidspawn. But not for long. Vallen converted a vast chunk of his men'ar to lightning and sent it surging through the magchine even as he leapt away. More noxious odors—cooked ozone and blistered skin—followed him to the ground.

The fluid from Vallen's weapon pursued him, droplets reforming as he stood amid the carnage, breath ragged, scalp drenched in sweat. There were still Sarc survivors. Men and women choked by dust, limbs twisted at grotesque angles, blood seeping through their chainmail links. Some could even move. They raised their rifles and bayonets toward Vallen, hatred contorting their features until they looked like voidspawn.

Which of us is the voidspawn? Vallen wondered.

He materialized his krenesh and went to work.

Vallen swung, slashed, and slew. His foes screamed, bled, and died. They tried their best, coming at him from all sides, shooting at his left flank as gleaming silver stabbed at his right. But Vallen was in complete control of the elements, catching the bullets with his lightning, dashing apart their concerted charges with bursts of flame and wind.

He stamped the ground, and an earthen spike impaled a man's

groin, thrusting through his body until it exited at his shoulder. A flaming strike broke the stock of a soldier's rifle and cut his gut at the same time. The wound cauterized instantly, leaving him shrieking as he curled into a ball around his ruined insides.

Flaring his lightning barrier left a pair of attackers scorched and blinded, their short swords discarded on the ground. Gusting winds lifted a trio from their feet and cast them into the harbor. A slow, agonizing death, given the chainmail and cuirasses they wore.

Bodies mounted as Vallen stepped and struck, danced and hacked. They formed a ring around him—a circle in which death was assured. He barely felt the blood coating him, the ooze dribbling down his combat suit and clinging to his boots. A normal blade would have caught on a rib or chipped on a skull by now, but Vallen's krenesh, charged with men'ar and fed by his fury, continued to cut and kill and maim like it was freshly sharpened.

And then they stopped coming. Rifles clattered to the cobblestones, swords dropped from shaking fingers, and ashen hands lifted in the air. Even the final panzcraft ceased moving, the man halfway out of its open hatch mouthing the same words as the other Sarcs.

"We surrender."

You *surrender?* Vallen thought with a snarl. After all the death and pain they'd dealt, the Sarcs wanted to give up? Throw down their arms and quit to save their lives?

No, the darkness agreed, riding the wave of his fury. *They didn't let Leon surrender, did they? Or any of the Kingdom soldiers at Aldona? They deserve only that which they've meted out: death.* The darkness cradled the final word, holding it on its tongue like a lover.

Vallen stepped toward the nearest soldier, a ruddy-cheeked youth who seemed greener than a fresh spring bud. Tears welled in his eyes. Snot crusted his bulbous, over-large nose and dripped onto his quivering lips.

"Please. P-please don't. I don't w-want to fight an-anymore, I want to g-go—"

Not good enough, Vallen decided, raising his blade.

A massive explosion stopped him mid-swing. Made him raise his eyes to the sky, where the battle between cruisers was being fought. Too much smoke. It was impossible to see higher than the tops of what buildings still stood.

Scowling, Vallen summoned what little men'ar remained in his veins and launched himself to another rooftop. The fading of combat's thrill—the loss of the risk and rush of it all—left him feeling drained. Empty. Vallen staggered to the roof's edge, slumped against the bullet-pocked parapet.

What he saw sucked the rest of the life from him. *Conviction* was plummeting from the air, her guts bleeding fire, her engines cold and quiet. How many hundreds would die when she crashed? How many had already perished?

Dharmasya still battled bravely, trading broadsides as she zipped between the two remaining Sarc cruisers. But she was a bird beating her wings against wolves. One swipe of their claws, one direct hit, and her defiance would be ended.

A Resistance hoverjet careened past, trailing smoke as it plowed into the harbor. Vallen glanced back the way it had come. Saw the Sarc lancerjets sighting in on the cluster of grounded transports. Too late he opened his mouth to scream, for all the good it would have accomplished.

Flashes lit their bellies, shells roared, and blasts tore through the Darmatian defensive line. The lancerjets peeled away, leaving behind another blazing landing craft and a crater filled with dead and dying.

Tired. Vallen was oh-so-very tired, his eyelids leaden, his thoughts like sludge. He'd fought, and fought, and fought. So hard, so long, with every fiber of his being. And for what? To lose anyway? Vallen could drop to the roof right now. Splay out on the hard surface and sleep until the Creator returned to right the royal mess he'd created.

Perhaps *that* would be a better use of his time.

Or you could give me control, the darkness suggested. *I can save them. I can save them all.*

No, Vallen decided, wading through the Sewertown mire that had become his mind. *I will not yield. Not now, not—*

Look there. The darkness gestured with a shadowy tendril, easing Vallen's chin back toward the battle.

Velle rose above the chaos on crimson wings, hauling a host of floating glyphs with her. She set one in the path of an attacking hoverjet, too preoccupied with its ground target to notice. Both glyph and airship exploded in an inferno of sparkling men'ar and roiling flame.

But fire from below hurtled up at her—not small arms, but shells from more panzcraft crawling through Etrus toward the Resistance. Most missed as Velle dodged, wings beating furiously from side to side, up and down. Two hit, shredding her shields, driving her closer to the ground. The Sylph's stamina and men'ar wouldn't last forever.

I can save her, the darkness whispered.

Vallen struggled to his feet. Started hobbling toward Velle, rod clutched in trembling fingers. *"I will save her."*

Oh! The darkness rushed to the other side, dragging Vallen's gaze around. *What's this? More lost lambs, come to slaughter?*

A trio of Darmatian soldiers tumbled from a side street, running from a squad of men in heavy leathers and gasmasks. Vallen watched fire leap from their fingers, a scorching torrent that seemed to *grab* the slowest Resistance trooper and consume him in a scarlet maw. When the flames withdrew, nothing was left but ash.

"I know those two," Vallen mumbled, dragging himself back to the parapet.

You do.

"Erika and her brother. From the transport. The freckle-faced twins, the ones who—"

More flames shot forth, licking at their heels, threatening to overtake them. Erika's brother glanced back at their pursuers. It was only a second of split focus, an instant of hesitation.

His foot caught on a jutting cobblestone. He tumbled, scraping his palms and knees, forcing Erika to stoop to help him. The Sarc mage squad closed the gap. Closed within range. Vallen saw the moment hope fled the girl's eyes, replaced instead by fear.

Screaming, Vallen raised his arm. Willed his rod to become a lance that would blow the Sarcs away with a storm-blessed gust of wind. The metal rippled, men'ar forming the lance-head, the hilt, and everything in between.

Vallen's spark went out, the last embers in his gut fading to smoke. The bronze alloy reverted to liquid form. Dripped between his fingers and pooled on the roof at his feet.

And on the street below, Erika shrieked as flames devoured their huddled forms.

You didn't give me control, the darkness said.

Vallen didn't respond.

I could have saved them. Could have given you access to a well of men'ar unlike any other. Boundless. Infinite. So vast you would never run dry again.

His eyes filled with tears. Vallen collapsed to his knees, his hands trying to scoop up the gleaming puddle that was his weapon and will it back to life. It was impossible to grasp. To hold.

Just like everything he loved and cherished.

The darkness turned, sightless gaze tracking Velle through the sky. *Three glyphs. No, two now. How much longer can she keep this up, I wonder? How much longer can any of them survive?*

"You've made your point," Vallen said.

Have I? Then why do you still kneel here, Triaron? Why do you still bow your head when you—when WE—could be so much more?

Vallen didn't know anymore. Every time he tried, he failed. Every time he got back up, he was beaten down again. Elaine, Leon, Erika . . . How many more would die for his vanity, his pride?

Enough.

Vallen would let the dark in. He would let it do what he could not. Right here, right now.

"I give you control," Vallen whispered, closing his eyes and letting go.

Chapter 58

Avatar

Icy wind rushed past Vallen as he fell, tugging at his sweat-matted hair, slashing at his exposed flesh. The sky grew darker as he plummeted. Gray into obsidian. Obsidian into pitch, black as a starless night.

Black as death.

Distantly, Vallen heard someone screaming. Was there someone falling alongside him? And why was he falling in the first place? He'd collapsed on a roof in Etrus, ashes and bodies all around, countrymen dead and dying. In that instant, heart bubbling over with despair, he'd . . .

"You gave me control," the darkness all around him rumbled. "Now lay there and watch what I do with it."

The scream came closer, resolving into a familiar cry: *his own.* Vallen's mouth was open, shrieking as sensation fled his limbs, leaving him numb. He tried to move. To grasp at the air, to flip over and see what he was falling toward. His fingers didn't so much as twitch.

Vallen struck water. The impact should have killed him. Instead, agony arched his spine. Stole the breath from his lungs and shot molten pain through every muscle. Thought dashed to pieces on the spears impaling him, cracking into slivers he couldn't pick back up.

Who Vallen was, what he desired—*everything* began to fade before the torment, slipping into a void from which he would never return.

And just as suddenly as it began, the pain ceased. The water's surface parted, swallowing Vallen, accepting him into its embrace. Fetid ooze raced into his mouth, plugged his nose with weeks-old rot, and slithered into his ears. His eyes burned as he kept them glued to the fading surface above.

No, *no, NO!* This was Vallen's greatest nightmare—drowning in Sewertown sludge, no one around to save him, alone and unremembered. He tried to thrash his arms and kick his feet, even though he knew fighting was useless.

Suddenly, his fingers flinched. His legs shook. Control of his body had been restored! Vallen thrust upward with all his might, blinking away sludge, forcing down the urge to vomit. Somehow, he knew that if he broke the surface, glinting above him like obsidian shale, he would be able to stop whatever the darkness was planning.

Vallen struck the surface with his left hand. Bones snapped, his fingers twisting as they struck a barrier harder than any lume. Pain exploded down his left side, needles and flames the ooze did nothing to soothe.

But Vallen didn't stop. Gritting his teeth, he beat his other fist against the glossy ceiling, smacked his head until wisps of scarlet blood dappled the grime around him. This wasn't what he'd wanted from the darkness. It was supposed to give him victory, not consign him to this . . . *prison.*

The other side of the surface flickered, changing from a murky, pitch-colored wasteland to a dust-clogged thoroughfare. Mutilated bodies and ruined panzcraft littered the rubble from collapsed buildings. Farther up the cobblestone road, two charred corpses clung to each other, bonded even in death.

Etrus, Vallen realized as he struggled. He was seeing through the darkness' eyes—*his* eyes.

"It's *precisely* what you wanted," the darkness said, standing and extending Vallen's metal rod into a gleaming two-handed blade. "To give up. To forfeit responsibility. To rely on someone else. So, I shall take your pain and burdens, *Triaron.* I have space aplenty to house your trivial suffering, a mere drop of anguish in the pit of mortal tragedy. But . . . "

Grinning, the darkness leapt from the rooftop, angling toward the throng of mages who'd claimed Erika's life. " . . . you might not like what it costs you."

Sylette raced through *Dharmasya's* trembling corridors, bouncing off walls, fighting to keep her balance as the cruiser exchanged salvos with foes the exile couldn't see. She didn't have time to look out a window, to gauge how long the airship would last.

If Sylette didn't find Renar, she suspected the outcome of the fleet battle wouldn't matter.

A four-way intersection loomed ahead—two paths curving away along the cruiser's flanks, a stairwell directly ahead. Sylette skidded to a halt, uncertain which way the imbecile had gone. The metal deck betrayed no footprints, and Renar's scent was impossible to distinguish from the heady musk of sweat and synth-oil in the refiltered air.

Movement caught her eye, a white-robed Sylph bending atop a

crumpled man a few paces down the right hall. Sylette rushed forward and grabbed the woman's shoulder.

"Did you see a Terran come this way?" she asked the salvator. "Tall, black hair, scowl chiseled on his face?"

The Sylph turned to Sylette, expression confused. Scarlet coated her already red hands, smeared the front of her vestments and leaked from the hastily wrapped bandages on the ribs of the man beneath her. His eyes were closed, his brown curls and ruddy cheeks scorched by the same blast that had nearly claimed his life. Only the slight quiver of his lips told Sylette the soldier still lived.

"I'm sorry, I—" Sylette stopped speaking as she glanced down the hall.

More limp forms crowded the passageway, some groaning or whispering frantic prayers, most still and silent. Sylette almost gagged at the stench of burnt flesh wafting off them, the tang of iron rising from the crimson-painted bulkheads and deck. A few white-robed salvators roamed among the wounded, but not enough to treat them all.

And these were the *lucky* ones.

Sylette narrowed her eyes, shutting out the carnage, distancing herself from the mewls and whimpers. She'd seen it all before. Smelt and tasted and heard it. Her pity couldn't save these soldiers, but stopping Renar might.

She shook the salvator as the Sylph stooped back to her charge. "General Iolus' brat. I need to know where he went *now*."

"Does that matter? This man is—"

Another shake, harder. "We're all dead if I don't find him."

The salvator balked, gaze flitting to a woman missing half her face, a crying soldier clutching the bloody strips of his mangled left leg. In her mind, the battle was probably already lost, her actions naught but a cork trying to stem the tide.

But Sylette didn't give up that easily.

As she released the salvator to go find someone more useful, an arm pocked by deep burns reached up to grasp her own. "That way," the brown-haired soldier gasped, his quivering finger pointing back toward the stairwell. "I saw him"—the man spluttered, coughed blood—"go down . . ."

His lips shivered. His eyelids flickered, then stilled, gaze locked not on Sylette, but on the eternity beyond her. She caught his arm as it fell. Squeezed his hand before folding it to his breast.

"Thank you," Sylette whispered. The words tasted far less bitter than when she'd said them to Vallen.

She faced the salvator, whose hands were clasped in prayer above the dead man's brow. "What's below us?"

"The engine room and—"

Sylette didn't wait for her to finish. She was already sprinting away, grabbing the safety rail at the top of the stairs, swinging herself around the corner so hard her shoulder shrieked. The steps disappeared as she vaulted them two at a time.

Engineering. Illyrium power converters, synth-oil processing, the hub for their lume projectors. It was *Dharmasya's* beating heart, a heart encased in layers of metal flesh and bulkhead bone that protected it from the outside.

But a knife from the *inside?* A blade no one saw coming?

That would end her instantly.

The Darkness summoned rubble to him as he flew, bits and pieces of mortar and brick that crumbled and reformed about his body like armor. There was no command. No order, spoken or silent, for men'ar to do his bidding.

It simply obeyed.

Needle pricks lanced Vallen's legs as the stone adhered. His bones and muscles wailed as Darkness landed *atop* a mage, staving in the man's chest, spraying blood across the cobbles. Warmth trickled down Vallen's face, rivulets of scarlet Darkness' tongue slithered out to catch. He tasted copper. Felt the searing thrill of combat bubbling inside his breast.

But Vallen couldn't move. He was a passenger in his own flesh, experiencing everything, influencing nothing.

The slaughter began.

Lightning quick, the greatsword lashed out, splitting the closest soldier head to groin. His gas mask split and fell, followed by the gushing halves of his corpse.

Once again, Vallen hadn't heard Darkness' spell. Like pulsing stars, limitless in their energy, men'ar flowed through his body, enhancing his strength, making him faster than he'd ever been. It was electrifying. The highest high he'd ever experienced, better than any pleasure of flesh or pipe he'd ever tasted. Vallen's nethers tingled, his skin flushing, pimpling. His breath came as a shivering sigh.

He *hated* it.

Give me back my body! he railed, slamming his shoulder against the barrier.

"No."

As the first of their comrades fell, the mages jumped away from Darkness, hands raised, mumbling spells beneath their masks. They thought *they* had the advantage. That *they* were encircling him.

None of that mattered.

Without moving, splinters of stone shot from Darkness' body, eviscerating two men *through* their leather armor. He leveled his blade at another, and the gust of wind it launched took the mage's shoulder off along with his outstretched arm. More blood streaked the cobbles, painted the collapsed bayside warehouses.

The remaining mages kept casting. Embers sparked at their fingertips, swelling into curtains of flame that flowed through the air between them, merging, growing. They'd summoned a hollow pillar of fire, tall as two men stacked together, with no avenue for escape but straight up into the sky.

Sweat beaded on Vallen's forehead, soaked his hair and undergarments. He could scarcely draw an ash-laced breath, which meant Darkness was suffering just as much. Some small part of Vallen hoped they'd suffocate. That they would perish together, ending whatever Darkness was.

The flames slunk closer, disintegrating fallen corpses, blowing away what remained of Erika and her brother. Darkness waited, still, silent. When the inferno was close enough to touch, he raised his hand.

Streaks of orange, red, and yellow rushed into his palm, the fabric of the maelstrom—the men'ar that bound it together—coming undone like the threads of a tattered quilt. In seconds, the spell was naught but a mesmerizing ruby hovering above Darkness' skin. An entire squad's magic, reduced to a glowing orb.

Arms clattered against leather plates as they fell. Masks twitched, their owners unable to stop their trembling. And then they broke, scrambling toward the water, up the street, screaming as they fled the voidspawn in their midst.

Vallen's hatred died. The rage in his heart beat softer, slower, until it, at last, stood still. These monsters had *murdered* Erika, but even they didn't deserve what the creature inside him was capable of.

Darkness grinned, twisting Vallen's lips as he willed. "I don't think so."

He held up his palm. Beams of light flashed from it, aimed at a dozen backs now turned to him. Vallen breathed. In the space of that breath, a dozen bodies struck the cobbles, smoking holes burned clean through to their chests.

"A fine warm-up," Darkness said, flexing his neck. "But not enough. To have an avatar after millennia of mere spectating . . . " His gaze turned inward, sending a shiver across Vallen's neck. "Well, it's exhilarating, to say the least. What say we enjoy it, hmm?"

With a laugh, Darkness launched back into the sky.

Dharmasya's deck bucked under Jis' feet, trying to cast her to the floor. She'd frozen her palms to the nearest railing, but every salvo that launched from or struck the cruiser still rattled her teeth and made her regret the pile of leave days she'd never used.

Jis had never visited Seyla's renowned white-sand beaches, and given how this battle was going, she likely never would.

"Lume status!" Jis called.

A tech in the pit glanced up at her, face pale. "Gone. We lost it in that last blast."

"Plague and pox," Jis swore.

Outside the viewport, *Dharmasya's* forward turrets shuddered, casting another volley of lead at the nearest Sarc warship. Its shimmering lume dimpled. Flickered and buckled, even cracked in a few spots along its starboard bow.

Yet it held. The Sarc cruisers simply outclassed them. More guns, more crew; bigger lume generators, stronger shields. And with *Conviction* settling into the bay below, waves coursing in every direction from her barely controlled impact, it was two versus one.

The battle was over.

Dharmasya—the Resistance—could no longer win.

Giving up rankled Jis. The thought clenched her chest like iron in a blacksmith's vice, twisted her lips into a snarl. But if this past month had taught the Ice Queen anything, it was that lives were vastly more important than pride.

Jis raised her head, emerald eyes hard as flint. "Full power to the engines, Ensign Keleva." The helmswoman nodded, gripping the ship's wheel in one hand while the other jammed the throttle lever forward.

Nothing happened. No sudden burst of speed, no disorienting lurch as the cruiser leapt forward. *Dharmasya* was still at normal combat velocity—a sitting quill-duck without a lume, hemmed in by two Sarc heavy cruisers.

Ensign Keleva yanked back on the lever, resetting it to neutral, then thrusting it toward the floor with enough force to make the metal squeal and groan.

No change.

Matteo's croaking voice, barely stronger than a whisper, came from the forward viewport. "Cruiser one . . . firing *now* . . ."

"Down-trim, evasive maneuvers!" Jis yelled as smoke blossomed along the flank of the Sarc cruiser to port.

Dharmasya tilted, slanting to starboard, changing the angle of her upper deck so the rounds would pass harmlessly overhead. Two struck anyway. The first *ripped* a turret clean off the hull, leaving behind a ragged wound which gushed flame, synth-oil, and mangled bodies.

The second punched through the bridge, a flash of silver that passed in an eye-blink. Air whistled through the head-sized gaps torn in the bulkheads. Ensign Fayet was gone, a streak of blood and bone across her station and fellow sensors all that remained of her.

Trembling hands touched gore-coated cheeks. Quivering eyes glanced up at a ceiling dripping drops of crimson—drops of their friend and comrade. One girl started hyperventilating, mouth opening to scream, but Captain Hurshik grabbed and eased her to the floor before she could shatter the final sliver of their morale.

"There-there, missy," he said, cleaning the blood from her face with his uniform sleeve. "It's fine. We're going to make it. It's all going to be fine."

Unless it isn't, Jis thought. It was a lie, one grand enough to please the Void. But for the young sensor, it was a necessary one.

The rest of the bridge looked at her, wide eyes pleading, desperate. They wanted Jis to lie to them as well. To give them a reason to not despair in what looked like their last moments.

"Get me Darres in engineering," Jis said.

Jesrac bent over his panel, gnarled fingers punching at his dials and knockers even as they trembled. A second later, he shook his head. The return knocker hadn't so much as twitched.

"Try the voicepipe."

He shouted into the bronze tube labeled 'Engineering' in flowing Darmatian script. Once, twice, thrice. The only response was the echo of his husky, fear-laced voice.

Engineering was silent. *Dead.* Jis ran through the possibilities as she scanned the bridge, watched *Dharmasya's* lone turret futilely sling shells at their closing foes.

Had the engineering block been hit? No, a blow like that would've torn the airship from the sky. A gas leak, perhaps? Some sort of chemical that knocked out Darres and his engimages? Just as improbable. Someone in an adjoining compartment would've smelt it seeping through the vents and reported the issue.

Which left Jis with a single disturbing conclusion:

Sabotage.

A muffled voice burst from the med-bay voicepipe. Jesrac hurriedly jotted the message down with a scrivle, then turned to Jis. "Odd report from the salvators. They say a silver-haired lieutenant interrupted their work demanding the location of a tall, dark-haired soldier named ..."

Jis didn't hear the rest. She didn't need to. Renar Iolus was absent from the bridge, along with Sylette Far—

No. It was time to stop thinking of the little exile in such terms. Jis' ship had been sabotaged, and the son of a corrupt general and the Emperor's wayward daughter were both missing. Even a blind man could see what was happening.

Shards of ice sparkled around Jis' head as she turned and stormed from the bridge, shouting her final orders through gritted teeth. "You have the Con, Captain Hurshik. I'm going to sort out our engineering problem."

Chapter 59
You're Not Alone

Renar stared at the long wrench in his hand, the sack of engimage tools now scattered across the grated deck of the engineering compartment. There was blood crusting on the wrench head. More blood and sweat stained the bottom of the bag where it had struck backs and necks, shattered ribs, and broken arms.

They hadn't seen him coming. A half-dozen illyrium-fed boilers hugged the room's walls, their mouths jetting flame, their bellies clinking and clanking loud enough to rouse Darmatus from the grave. No one had heard Renar's boots as he approached. No one had glanced up from shoveling crystal shards or watching their readout panels. Even if they had, the smoke the magchines produced was as dense as a hashim den.

Collar cinched about his nose and mouth, Renar had stalked through the smog. He hadn't wanted to hurt these people. They were innocent, uninvolved.

But you want your father's love, the Soldier whispered. *And for that, we'll do anything.*

Smack!

Down went a bare-scalped man with tattoos ringing his neck and shoulders.

Smack!

The wrench got caught in the next woman's braids, and Renar had to rip three strands free, rending her scalp raw and bloody. He nearly gagged at the sight, at the scarlet staining his weapon, his hands, his . . . everything.

Push on, the Soldier urged. *For what we never had. For what we'll never lack again.*

Smack! Smack! Smack!

A pile of engimages lay around him, their bodies broken and bleeding. Renar saw lips quivering, chests slowly rising and falling. They still lived.

But not for long. Not if Renar did as the General—soon to be his *father*—commanded.

He knelt beside a tall, lanky redhead, rummaging through

the pockets of his lab coat. The strange monocle he'd worn had fallen when he had, bouncing across the floor to rest against a small red fuel canister.

Renar found its gleaming lenses intriguing. Red, green, blue—a puzzle waiting to be solved. He wondered if different combinations allowed the wearer to see different things, sort of like—

Focus! the Soldier hissed. *We have no time for games, for the weakness that cost us the General's love in the first place.*

His fingers closed around a triangular pin, the object he'd been told to find. Standing, Renar walked to the station in front of the largest boiler. The flat surface was covered in twitching needles, gauges, and blinking lights, some red, some orange, some green. Renar didn't understand any of it, but he didn't need to.

Hefting his wrench, he tightened it around a bright red bolt at the panel's center and heaved it round. Once, twice. On the third spin, a cheery *pop* sounded within the device. Gears clanked, pistons whirred, and a metal slide retracted, revealing a hidden triangular slot.

It was a perfect match for the chief engimage's pin.

Renar started to insert the key, but hesitated as he read the large warning script above the slot:

EMERGENCY ENGINE OVERRIDE

"If the Sarconian trap fails," the General had said, putrid breath pouring against Renar's face as he loomed above him in the gloom of the command tent, *"Take the chief engimage's pin and activate the override. That'll put an end to that whore Reev's Resistance and earn us a spot at the Emperor's table."*

But it wouldn't be 'us.' Renar might be a fool, yet even he understood what turning off an airship's engines would do. *Dharmasya* would plummet from the sky and crash in the harbor below. Soldiers would be crushed by the impact, drowned by the water gushing in through the cruiser's wounds.

Most would die. *Renar* would probably die.

But what's the point? the Soldier asked. *Without purpose—without love—is there any reason for us to go on?*

There wasn't. Renar was an empty shell. Alone, unwanted, magicless, useless. He was already drowning in the darkness, the pitch that blotted out the feeble light of Unter and his comrades. What did it matter if his body drowned when his mind was already lost?

Put the key in.

Renar did.

Now push.

Renar—

"STOP!"

"STOP!" Sylette shouted.

A dozen daggers hung in the air around her, blades pulsing in the furnace light as her chest heaved. She took in the bodies at a glance. They were bruised, battered, but breathing.

Which meant Renar was her only concern.

He slowly turned toward her, revealing a triangular pin clutched in his fingers. Half the pin was inserted into a slot surrounded by angry red warning labels.

"What are you doing, Renar?" Sylette asked.

His lips curled in a sad, wistful smile. "I should've known you'd figure me out. You always did see more than the others."

"I've had lots of practice. Everyone at court had a dagger, real or otherwise"—Sylette glanced at her floating blades, forced a mirthless laugh—"so I got good at spotting them."

"You're too late."

"Why?" She took a step forward, palms raised. "Tell me what you're doing. Tell me how I can help you."

Renar shook his head, clenching his fingers until they were white as the pin he held. "Not another step. If you do, I'll twist this key and send *Dharmasya* to her grave."

"Engineering!" bellowed a tinny voice from a speaking tube above the engine panel. "What's your status? We need an update. Engineering? *Engineering!* Is . . . Is anyone there?"

"You aren't going to respond?" Sylette said, nodding at the still vibrating tube. Renar didn't move. Didn't give her the opening she needed to take him down.

The room shook, the pipes clogging the ceiling clanging against each other like melodic chimes. Steam spouted from new breaches, filling the chamber with a shrill whistle. It was only a matter of time until *Dharmasya* died, with or without Renar's help.

But ancestors be damned, Sylette was going to go out on *her* terms, not his.

She let a few of her daggers spin, tips and hilts rotating about their cross guards. It was a distraction. One that drew Renar's gaze, made his eyes and limbs tremble.

It also gave Sylette time to think, licking her lips, heart pounding in her chest. A blow to the head would kill him, as would a stab to the heart. Yet both ran the risk of a final twitch—a flinch of his fingers— dooming *Dharmasya* anyway.

Could Sylette slice off those fingers? Pierce his elbow and sever the nerves?

Questions, questions, questions. Ever swirling, making her blood race, her skin tingle.

In the end, only a single question mattered:

Am I willing to kill him?

Is she going to kill me? Renar wondered.

The scene was something out of a Moonlight Theatre play. Sylette was framed by the flickering lamps of the hall at her back, her tangled silver hair dappled with shifting oranges and reds from the belching furnaces. Her daggers glinted like fiery crystal. Her platinum eyes were set, her pale lips pursed in a grim line.

And above her shoulder—so faint it might be a trick of the smoke, the heat—was Angelie's ghost, come to claim its due.

What artistry! Renar thought. *What drama!*

Sylette was the beautiful heroine, blades poised to save the day, justified in the death she was prepared to deal. Renar was the dark lord, perhaps Sarcon, the Void, or another ne'er-do-well from the old stories.

There was only one way this could end. One outcome the audience would accept.

Some part of him wanted her to succeed. Renar could make a show of priming the pin, then draw back just as her daggers struck him. Smiling, he'd lament his choices and pass to the Afterplane. No more emptiness. No more yearning. No more filling himself up with dreams that could never be.

And yet you won't, the Soldier said, covering Renar's fingers in shadowy tendrils, pressing down on the pin. *You need to know. Death cannot come for us, not before we know if this final act will earn our father's love.*

Renar tore his gaze from the floating blades, focusing on Sylette's platinum eyes. Daring her to blink. To falter and give him an opening.

"I'm not backing down," Renar said.

"Think about this for a moment, Renar. Do you really—"

A snarl tore from his mouth. "I *have* thought about it. For weeks and weeks, years and years, through sleepless nights and joyless days. You don't understand, Sylette. You may have lost everything, but at least you had it once. I . . . "—Renar's voice broke—"I never had it to begin with."

Sylette's grimace softened. Raising her shoulders, she eased out of her fighting stance.

"What do you mean?" she asked.

Don't! the Soldier warned, putting more force on Renar's hand. *She can't know. Take the secret to our—*

Void it all. If Renar was going to die, he'd do so with one less anchor dragging him into the depths.

"I'm fle'bilis," he blurted. "Magicless. I've been lying to you all since the day we met, pretending I'm something I'm not. You hate lies, right, Sylette? The lies your father told you? The lies you've told us? Well, it's all out in the open. I've nothing left to hide. Now, kill me and get it over with."

Renar leaned over the pin, preparing his body so that when the end came, his lifeless bulk would take *Dharmasya* down with him.

Across the room, Sylette straightened, shadows falling from her cream-pale face as she marched fully into the furnace light. Her lips twisted. Her fists clenched. Then, with a long, shuddering sigh, all the tension left her body.

And above Sylette's head, her daggers dispelled into wisps of shimmering astral dust.

Sylette stood tall, hands to her sides, glimmering dust brushing her cheeks and neck as it faded into nothingness. She was disarmed. No more weapons, no more tricks. Completely at the mercy of whatever Renar decided to do next.

"I'm not going to kill you," Sylette said.

The boy gasped, stumbled, and nearly depressed the pin that would end them all anyway, smashing his free hand onto the engimage panel to support his weight. Sylette could have rushed him while he was off-balance. Knocked him aside, yanked the pin from his grasp.

Part of her wondered why she didn't. What was Renar compared to *her* life, compared to the vengeance she craved like a throat-dry sel-spice addict?

Nothing. A tool at best, a hindrance at worst. And yet ...

Renar heaved himself up, lips pulled back in a snarl. "You *what?*"

"I'm not going to kill you," Sylette repeated, tasting the strange words on her tongue. Foul, bitter, but somehow *right*, nonetheless.

"*Do it!*" Spittle flew from his lips.

"No."

"*DO IT!*" Renar slammed his clenched fist down, denting the metal panel, shaking the pin in its berth.

Sylette flung his rage back at him. "If you want to end it, do it on your own. Don't bring *me* into it." She pounded her chest. "Don't bring *them*"—she waved at the fallen engimages, the shaking bulkhead walls, the whole of the ship beyond—"into it."

Renar wilted, eyes darting around the bodies, then back to her. Whispers slipped from his mouth, mumbles spoken to no one at all. What was he fighting? What darkness had taken root in his soul?

"I have to do it," Renar murmured.

"Why?"

"Because if I don't ... " he paused, eyes misting, breath coming in great, heaving sobs. "Then my father ... I-I won't ever find out if . . . if he, he loves me ... "

The puzzle that was Renar clicked into place. His empty gaze, his bent back, his tear-stained cheeks. He was *her*. The Sylette that broke. The dagger that, instead of hardening into steel at her mother's execution, shattered into a thousand fragments, never to be re-forged.

Renar was her—a scared, frightened boy who desperately wanted to go back to the way things were. Only ... there was no way to put back the hourglass' drifting sands.

What if I hadn't been loved? Sylette thought, taking a small step forward.

What if my mother hadn't been at my bedside each night, ready to read me a story? What if she hadn't taught me to tell one fragrant bud from another, brushed my hair, or laughed with me about my insufferable tutors?

Sylette stepped over the ruddy-haired engimage, who groaned as he began to wake.

What if—she gritted her teeth, repressed fury roiling in her gut—*What if ... I hadn't had Valescar to train me? To play chess with? To give*

579

me refuge when ...

Renar loomed before Sylette, a statue bathed in flickering furnace light. He was so lost in his despair—his *grief*—that he didn't seem to see her. Babbled words tumbled forth, muttered pleas, vile curses. His fingers were ready to break atop the pin, clenched so tightly she could count the veins beneath.

He was her.

She was him.

Except that ...

To give me refuge when ... my father refused to love me, Sylette completed the thought.

Except that, like he'd said, she had once known love.

Stooping, her movements like a hush, a whisper, Sylette placed one hand on Renar's boiler-warmed cheek, the other on the hand that held their lives. Clarity returned to his gaze. His fingers twitched, his neck jerked up, and he peered into her eyes.

Silver and obsidian.

Love and neglect.

Past and present.

"You," Sylette soothed, brushing a tear from his cheek, "are the bravest man I know. You fought Valescar *without magic*. You faced a Draken without shining shields, flaming swords, or any of the other powers we possess. You found the Resistance when no one else could. And you, Renar Iolus, regardless of what your father says, no matter what anyone else tries to tell you, despite your own doubts and misgivings ..."

Taking a breath, Sylette lowered her hand, pressed it against Renar's thumping heart.

"You."

Ba-dump.

"Are."

Ba-dump.

"Loved."

Ba-dump-ba-dump-ba-dump!

The beat took off then, thundering, hammering against her palm. Renar's tears flowed. Sobs tore from his throat, and great gobs of snot dripped from his quivering nostrils. It was disgusting. It was *beautiful*.

As Sylette started to pry his fingers from the pin, one by one, Renar reached up and grabbed her shoulder. "Who loves me?" he begged, voice cracking like he didn't believe it was possible. "Who is it?"

Sylette smiled and told the truth—the truth that had been blossoming inside her like one of her mother's precious roses, now in full bloom.

"*Us,* Renar. You're not alone, and you never will be again."

Chapter 60
Darkness Falls

Vallen watched the world through a pane of glass, every explosion at once muffled and booming in his ears, each swing of his arms both foreign and intimate. Ash caressed his cheek from leagues away. The blood clinging to his lips was fresh and years—perhaps ages—old.

Where did he end and Darkness begin, when every act of one the other felt?

All Vallen could say for certain was that he wasn't in control. Trapped behind a bulwark of glass, buried in a prison of ice, his senses were slaved to Darkness. He tried to suppress the thrill. The burning in his loins, the rising lust for death and carnage.

But *he* was the captive now, and as Darkness rose above Etrus on coils of whipping wind, Vallen couldn't help grinning along with him.

"Where to first?" Darkness mused, voice a peal of thunder rumbling from the depths of eternity.

Velle still fought in the skies, one shield, cracked and battered, trailing her like a loyal sentinel. Her bright red wings were pitted with black wounds, rips and tears that drug her ever closer to the ground. Armor scarred, suit leaking drops of blood onto the rooftops she wove among like a fish through reefs, Velle lashed out with claw and dagger, snipers screaming as she knocked them from their perches.

It won't be enough, Vallen thought.

On a street close to the Resistance transports, Unter and Lilith fought back to back. A pile of rubble formed their flank, forcing Sarc infantry to scramble over or around the dusty, jagged slate to reach them. Flames launched from Lilith's saber, scorching the flesh of two riflemen preparing to leap onto Unter's undefended back. In the front, Unter blocked a bayonet jab with one buckler, hurled aside two swordsmen with another, and *flattened* a Sarc who'd buried his blade in the Hue's thigh.

Unter roared. Purple blood oozed from the wound, joined the swathe of crimson painting the cobbles. *It won't be enough,* Vallen thought, once more pounding against the glass confining him.

Panzcraft burned before the Resistance barricades, the coppery tang of blood, the acrid stench of char overriding the salty musk of the bay. But it hadn't been enough. The platoon Vallen had wiped out was just one of many.

More Sarc soldiers—a tide of red and gold to rival that of any sea—swept up the harbor boulevard from the opposite direction. Two panzcraft at the fore belched smoke and flame, one shell peeling apart a Darmatian transport like overripe fruit, the other torching a three-masted schooner moored to the pier.

Colonel Holcomb bellowed something Vallen couldn't hear, waved his rifle in the air and jabbed it at the approaching Sarc column. Weary and tired, their faces smeared with soot and stained with their comrades' blood, the Darmatian survivors heaved themselves up and rushed to defend their other flank. A hail of lead met them, scything down three soldiers in blue and silver, leaving their corpses twitching on the wharf's edge.

Two transports left, the others molten wrecks.

A handful of Darmatian soldiers, resignation in their eyes as they fired their final shells.

And in the sky above, *Dharmasya* bucked and twisted as two Sarc cruisers circled her, smelling her blood on the wind as fire rippled down the warship's smoking sides.

It

won't

be

enough.

Railing on the glass, hands slick with scarlet, eyes burning with tears, Vallen roared at Darkness. *You said you'd save them! That's what you promised me—why I gave up everything!*

"I *never* break my oaths," Darkness growled. "I am more than enough for this task, little Triaron. I am more than enough for *anything.*"

Darkness bolted through the air, an arrow from a marksman's quiver, a bullet streaking across the sky. Krenesh blade extended, he struck a soaring lancerjet at its hooked beak, tearing its nose from its body, rendering its pilot a warm red mist.

Laughing, Darkness called the gray skies above, whipping them into a frenzy. Before the airship could fall, he snatched it in an invisible hand—a claw of swirling gales that somehow held something a thousand, a million times their weight. Vallen couldn't fathom what he was watching. He'd never imagined his powers could be this strong.

Up Darkness soared. Up into heavens devoid of light, clouds the shade of pitch that seemed to tremble with excitement as he passed. The lancerjet came with him. A hulk of twisted metal.

A hammer poised above its anvil.

Darkness arced through the growing—*growling*—abyss around him, pausing for only an instant amid the slicing wind and booming thunder and crashing lightning.

And then he fell.

Down and down and down.

Faster and faster and faster.

Strands of fire gripped the lancerjet as it rushed before Darkness. A pocket of roiling heat, a white-hot net of flames Vallen could almost *feel* scalding his flesh through their strange link.

The meteor struck the harbor road with the force of a thousand artillery. Panzcraft went flying, armor melting, treads and turrets shattering as they tumbled. One landed *fifty meters* away in the bay, sinking to its demise. Another crashed through three blocks of stucco houses before the crumpled slag that remained came to rest.

And the bodies. Oh, the bodies.

Skin vaporized. Muscles peeled like the petals on some rotting, bubbling, *boiling* flower. Eyes vanished, armor glued to blackened bone, and—

Vallen collapsed to his knees in his prison, trying to retch. Nothing came out. *He* was the captive now. He had no stomach, no food in his belly with which to paint his utter revulsion.

"Stand, Triaron," Darkness commanded, one curled hand gesturing at a wall of stone jutting from the harbor district's ruin. "Our deal was protection, and protection they received."

Vallen cracked an eye, glimpsed the water-filling crater where the Sarc column had once marched. True to Darkness' word, a thick wall of obsidian-black stone bordered the crater, beyond which not a crack, not a *cinder*, of his devastation had passed.

The bedraggled men and women of the Resistance looked up at Darkness, mouths agape, their rifles held in slack fingers. Would they scream and shriek at what they'd witnessed? Fire on them while shouting, *"Monster?"*

No.

They *cheered* Vallen—*Darkness*—instead.

"TRIARON! TRIARON! TRIARON!"

Vallen couldn't exult with them. Loathing pressed at the back of his eyes, threatening to become tears. His breaths shuddered up and down the length of his bent spine as his lips stretched in a wordless scream.

This is wrong. This is wrong. This is—

But if it was wrong, why did it feel so . . . right?

Darkness moved on, shooting through the air on unseen wings. The surviving Sarcs were running now. Fleeing up the street away from Unter and Lilith, casting terrified glances over their shoulders at the flattened buildings, plumes of fire and smoke, and the great black monolith that had appeared from nowhere.

The pair sank against a nearby wall, too exhausted to give pursuit.

Darkness chased the Sarcs anyway.

They've given up, Vallen pled. *They aren't a threat anymore. Not to my friends, not to—*

Darkness reached *through* the glass, grabbed Vallen's head, and slammed him to the floor of his cell. "A vow is a vow. An oath is an oath. I *will* carry it out."

Rubble blasted away from Darkness as he landed, a ring of broken shrapnel that never struck the ground. It hovered in the air, bound to his will, obedient hounds awaiting the whistle of their master.

Silently, Darkness blew the whistle. Silently, his dogs were loosed from their chains, freed to the hunt. They rushed down the streets, onto rooftops, through tiny courtyards and up narrow alley stairwells. Tracking, ever tracking, not dissuaded by distance or obstacles. One by one, the ragged, heaving gasps of the Sarc runners were silenced. Their tabards and chainmail rent, their hearts lanced by shards of jagged stone.

Vallen looked up at Velle, beating her wings to stay aloft. Her gaze darted around, watching the soldiers run. Watching them meet their ends. And when Darkness smiled—when he sensed the last sliver of earth spear the last beating heart—Velle turned her glare on *him*.

She thought *he* was responsible for this. That *he* was so filled with hate he would massacre fleeing men, their spirits broken by what they'd seen.

I was, Vallen admitted before Velle's furrowed brow, her dark, accusing eyes.

But not anymore. Not after . . . this.

"We aren't finished," Darkness said.

He turned, whipped his krenesh around, and sent a razor-sharp gust soaring back down the street toward the Resistance. Vallen saw a

585

Sylph woman crouched atop a pile of rubble in its path, blue ivy tattoos curling along her arms, up her neck, and among her knotted black braids. A rifle was in her hands, its barrel pointed upward. A grim smile played atop her lips.

Vallen screamed, hoping she'd somehow hear.

She didn't.

The blade of wind sliced her fingers, the rifle stock, then separated her pretty head from her pretty shoulders. She died instantly, a spray of blood, a shock of drifting black strands her body's last gasp.

Why? Vallen screeched at Darkness.

"My oath."

The monster possessing him pointed at the corpse's bisected rifle, at Velle descending from the sky above. His meaning was clear: *she* had been the target. Why? Another assassin, the same group who'd attacked her at the Resistance base?

Vallen's thoughts were dragged away from him. They were in the air again, flying past Velle, ignoring her cries to stop and explain what in the Void was going on. The Sarc cruisers loomed ahead, their lumbering bulks and bristling weapons growing nearer by the second. In between them, *Dharmasya* listed, a lone gun turret still firing, one engine barely keeping her aloft.

Below the warships were a slate-gray harbor, an abandoned airfield lined with gaping hangars, and a solitary bronze pole standing alone amid a handful of poorly manned bunkers and sandbag entrenched guns.

Darkness ignored them all.

The cruisers were the final threat to the Resistance.

The final obstacle Darkness needed to eliminate to complete his vow.

"And then," Darkness whispered, his deep rumble shaking Vallen's prison, "I'll be free. After two long, long millennia, I'll *finally* be free."

Renar let go.

Like roots clutching at a stone deep within the earth, his fingers peeled back from the engine override pin, knuckles popping, blood recoloring his chalk-white digits. Sylette slowly eased the pin away from him, tucking it inside her breast pocket where it could do no more harm.

"It's over, Renar," she whispered, patting his chest. "You're safe now. You don't have to follow his orders anymore."

Nothing is over! The Soldier reared up, expanding from the shadows behind the boilers, trying to blot out the light of the flames—the light pouring off Sylette. *We failed the General. We ignored his commands, and now he's going to—*

Renar focused on Sylette, the incoherent rage of the Soldier fading into the background. Her skin, so pale it shone like glass. Silken silver hair, falling in sweat-mussed clumps and tangles about her shoulders. Bright eyes, soot-smeared cheeks, neck and collar drenched by the heat they bathed in.

And that smile.

A curve of the lips like the crescent of the moons, tugged up at the corners, kindness directed at him and *only* him. The sketchbook in his jacket's inner pocket burned like a red-hot coal held to his flesh, searing as it called him.

Called him to draw once more. To *live* once more.

But was it a ruse? A trick? Renar's gut churned, and the glow in his chest faded. Sylette had the pin now. The danger had passed, he was no longer a threat. Would she turn on him? Abandon him for the failure he was?

Renar stared at Sylette as she pulled away from him. "You thought me a fool, once."

"I did."

"What changed?"

A pause, a slight darkening of her eyes. Then Sylette snorted, her grin widening. "Nothing. I still think you're the same fool who needed me to win your graduation match. But perhaps you're not so bad as a certain imbecile."

See! the Soldier railed, pushing forward, trying to reclaim the pitch-stained ground the exile's words had washed clean. *She still looks down on you. Insults and tramples on the weakness YOU exposed to her.*

"Yet that doesn't mean I don't *see* you, Renar," Sylette continued, reaching up to flick his forehead. He winced, even though the blow barely stung. "You're brave but dense. Creative but obnoxious. And you're loyal to a fault, even if"—she tapped the pin beneath the blue fabric of her uniform—"the people you obey aren't worthy of your trust."

Shame flooded through Renar. Clouding his sight, drying his tongue, draining the warmth from his limbs. Leaving him *empty*.

"Dear Veneer, I tried to *kill* you all," Renar babbled, tears gathering at the dam of his eyes. "I was going to crash *Dharmasya*. I was going to end the Resistance."

"But you didn't," Sylette countered as she stood. "Thank the ancestors for colossal void-ups like that one."

Renar's breath caught. The tears stilled, black indignation swelling with the bile in his stomach. "You just said—"

"I said we loved you, not," Sylette waved at the now stirring bodies, the open override hatch, "that we'd—that *I'd*—condone everything you do. You really messed up this time."

"I had no choice," Renar said between clenched teeth. He was suddenly aware of all the barbs this girl had thrown at him in the past month, including a thinly veiled threat to use him as a dagger target.

Sylette paused, glancing at him, then at the pipe-clogged ceiling and whatever lay beyond it. "There's no such thing as 'no choice,' Renar. My father killed my mother, and I vowed vengeance on him. That was a choice. I could've walked away. Clung to my life, forgotten what he did, lived quietly in some corner of the world.

"But I didn't. I made a choice to fight back. To stand up. Was it a bad choice?" Sylette shrugged as the room shook about them. Another blow to *Dharmasya's* hull, another blast closer to the warship's demise. "Given how bleak things look right now, it probably was. But it was still a *choice,* Renar. A choice to stand. A choice to struggle, and bite, and rip and tear and claw until *that man*"—she spat the words—"pays for everything he's taken from me."

Such strength. How Renar wished he could emulate Sylette. How he wished he could buckle on the armor of her rage, wield the sword of her conviction, brush aside the tangled web of his father's influence with the fire spraying from her lips.

But even if Renar accepted her love as true, it didn't change his circumstances.

"They have my mother."

Sylette was easing the ruddy-haired engimage into a sitting position, placing his back against one of the room's four support pillars as she unclipped a canteen from her belt. The officer coughed as she brought it to his lips, poured a dribble down his throat.

"Who?" Sylette asked.

"The Empire."

"Is that why your father turned traitor?"

The word stung, but it fit. Renar and his father were both traitors now. "I . . . don't think it was the only reason. She was rarely at our

Nemare estate these past few years, and he never paid attention to her except at balls and official functions. I'm not sure if ... "

Renar bit down on the thought, realizing it was true of him as well. The General had *never* loved either of them. They were puppets—tools—to be used or discarded as the master marionette willed.

"He didn't," Sylette finished for him. She moved to the engimage with long dark braids, flipping her over, examining her blood-matted scalp.

"What will they do to her?" Renar's throat was parched as the Badlands. "I failed, which means he failed, which means—"

"We'll get her back."

"And my father?"

Sylette glanced at him, eyes hard and simmering like coals. "He's *not* your father anymore—no more than the Emperor is mine."

"But they're my ... " Renar choked on the unfamiliar word: *family.*

After everything Sylette had done, how could he tell her the General was still his relative, his blood, his kin? How could he tell her some dark, depraved part of him still cared for the man? Still wanted to love and please and win the approval of a monster that had been willing to sacrifice him?

It was a paradox. A conundrum. A puzzle.

But then again, so was life itself.

"I know," Sylette whispered, tearing off a piece of the woman's oil-stained undershirt to bind her wound. "They *were* your family. Your blood will always be their blood."

"But ... now you have a new family, Renar. *Us.*"

The tears, wellsprings of sorrow and joy in equal measure, *would* have overwhelmed Renar if not for the shadow he saw darkening the chamber door. Emerald spears stabbed from her eyes. A scowl blacker than any shadow marred her ice-cold lips. About her raven hair hung a halo of gleaming ice, razor-sharp tips pointed at him and Sylette.

"What a touching sentiment, Lieutenant *Artorios,*" Major Reev snarled.

All Matteo knew was pain.

An ache behind his eyes, weightier than the press of the Phar Sea. Fire searing his brow, the nape of his neck, the scalp beneath his sodden hair. Blood dribbled from his nose, washed around his mouth. He tasted copper. Smelt fire and ash and sweaty fear. The roar of exploding shells and the screams of desperate soldiers bombarded his ears like endless waves upon a shore.

Matteo staggered upright. One knee to the metal deck, one hand grasping the rail. Pull. *Heave.* Harder and harder still. He gasped, started to call for help.

But no one would come. They were too busy. Punching buttons at their stations, roaring orders, begging the Veneer to save them.

Above the flush of Matteo's skin—born from abusing his powers, just like the rest of his suffering—he felt the whisper-warmth of crackling flames. A soft caress, still distant. Still ignorable. Pipes and wires dangled from the ceiling, a blaze had taken root in the right crew pit, but the battle wasn't over yet.

Dharmasya still flew.

Matteo still stood.

He spat blood, then aimed his faltering, murky gaze out the viewport. Cracks laced its surface, spider-web lines growing ever wider, ever closer to the inevitable collapse. It mattered not. Matteo saw not with his eyes, but with his magic.

Shifting colors filled his vision. They were faded now, washed-out and muted as his strength began to fade. He saw one of the Sarc cruisers blaze a dull yellow, its guns preparing to fire.

"Do . . . dge," Matteo murmured, scarlet dribbling down his lips as his warning became a cough.

No one heard him. They were, as before, too busy dealing with a thousand other problems.

Blasts rocked the ship, tried to cast Matteo back to the ground. The last of *Dharmasya's* turrets turned pitch-black in his sight as it ripped from the hull and tumbled toward the bay.

But Matteo held firm. Kinloss hadn't fallen at the end. Neither had Leon, Darmatus, or any of the heroes he'd known or read about. And so, neither would he.

He looked down at the harbor, the settlement of Etrus that straddled it. Bright light still flared from its buildings and streets, the glow of illyrium dust that had hidden the Sarc ambush. It looked no different than it had at the start of the battle. No matter the blood that was spilled, the destruction that was wrought, Matteo's magic painted the scene the same.

A beautiful lie.

His knees trembled. His facade of strength began to crumble, tears wetting his eyes, raspy wheezes accelerating. Were his friends safe? What of his parents? Had they fled before the battle, been allowed to leave before Etrus became a warzone? Or had something far worse befallen them?

As the Sarc cruisers turned, coming around for another pass, one final, frightened whisper found Matteo's lips:

"Dear Veneer, I don't want to die ... "

Blinding light struck him. A scalding blaze, a furious sun. The almost physical force of the glare pushed Matteo to a knee, his aching arms struggling to hold onto the railing. He'd never seen anything so bright, so glorious. It was as if *all* the illyrium—*all* the magical energy—in the world had been gathered in one place and given form, a form that ...

No, Matteo thought, narrowing his burning eyes, refusing to look away. *It can't be.*

A form that was all-too-familiar. Wind-whipped brown hair, a cocky smile, a curved krenesh blade in his hands. Vallen was *flying* to meet the Sarc cruisers.

The questions 'how' and 'why' died on Matteo's blood-slick tongue. He cared only for 'what,' since the radiance he saw couldn't possibly belong to the Triaron. It was beyond the twin infernos he'd witnessed in the Resistance cavern, beyond the power of a Primal like the Draken Nehalena.

It was vast as the stars.

Deep as the oceans.

Endless as time.

Eternal, infinite, impossible.

And even as it raced past *Dharmasya's* viewport, even as it rushed to save him, Matteo knew one thing with startling clarity:

That thing *is not Vallen Metellus.*

The traitorous wretch glanced up from the engimage she crouched beside, hands slick with guilty crimson. Jis watched Sylette's shoulders slump. Heard a sigh deep enough to shake mountains slip from her lips as they twisted into a mirthless smile.

"Artorios, huh?" Sylette said. "So, you *did* know."

It took all of Jis' restraint—a block of ice *rapidly* melting beneath the heat of her fury—*not* to widen the girl's smile further by spearing it with an ice-lance. *"Of course,* I bloody knew! I was your teacher for *four* void-forsaken years. What kind of halfwit wouldn't know who they were teaching?"

Sylette blanched. "No one should've known. The Farkos' forged my transfer papers, my Imperium citizenship, every—"

"Servants, my dear," Jis scoffed, loathing dripping from every word. "As royalty, you grew up oblivious to them, but they see things. Hear things. All it took was Sayles dropping silvers to the right butlers and scullery maids for me to discover Undersecretary Farkos was receiving a hefty stipend from the Rabban government to care for a silver-haired orphan. It made no sense."

Jis scowled, stepping into the room, angling her ice-shards toward the Sarconian princess. "That is, until I started tracking your journey back across the Imperium," she continued. "Back into the Empire. Across the years and leagues. Through snatches of tavern rumor, tales of knife-point robberies by a thin slip of a girl, accounts by orphanage matrons whose kindness was repaid in deceit and guile."

Drip.

Something plopped to the ground near Jis' feet, hissed and smoked in the heat from *Dharmasya's* beating heart—the furnaces surrounding them like fiery statues, the clattering, clanking pipes and gauges. She was dizzy, sweat rising from her flesh, vision blurry in the muggy haze.

But Jis only needed to focus on Sylette. On the silver girl, the heir to the Empire, before her. If she could apprehend her, Renar wouldn't matter.

Drip-Drip.

Sylette stayed rooted to the floor, eyes narrowed, hands held where Jis could see them. "If you heard all that, why trust me? Why teach me? Why not slit my throat the second I entered your base?"

"Hope?" Jis laughed even as an invisible knife wrenched inside her gut. This betrayal hurt. Not as much as Rodale's—*that* had been like swallowing acid—but a close second. "After everything I learned, I thought you *hated* the Empire. Despised them with all the rage and resentment of the blackest void. And because of that, I saw you becoming my greatest ally."

Jis splayed her fingers, urged frosty men'ar to their tips. Sweat crystallized as it raced down her arms. "But I was wrong, *Your Highness.* Think about your choices while you're frozen."

"Wait!" Renar shouted, rushing to get between them. "It was me. *I'm* the traitor. *I'm* the one who tried to sabotage the ship, not—"

Drip-Drip-Drip-Drip-Drip ...

The first icicle spears launched, aimed at Sylette's feet, her hands. Intended to trap and immobilize, not kill. The girl grinned. Astral dust coalesced before her, glittering specks molding into wicked blades.

Too slow, Jis thought, preparing her next assault. *They won't form in time to—*

Her spears *splattered* against the growing daggers. Turned to slush and splashed harmlessly against Sylette, the wounded engimage, and the metal grate beneath them. The same sizzle Jis had heard before filled the chamber as smoke rose from the floor.

"You talk too much," Sylette said, rising to her feet, fully formed daggers hovering in the air around her. Smirking, she waved at the hulking, steaming monstrosities spitting flame around them. "And boy, did you pick a bad battlefield for *ice* magic."

A storm spun around Darkness.

Vallen watched it grow from within his prison walls, a thousand tendrils of oozing ink, towering thunderheads with cavernous abysses yawning between them. This wasn't a natural squall. Some freak storm blowing in from the Phar Sea to hammer the coast.

It was *reacting* to Darkness. Spinning into a frenzy, laughing with peals of thunder, reaching out to cloak Vallen's possessed flesh in shadow as they hovered alongside the battling warships. Red streaks lanced the descending night. Pinpricks of flame and muted cannon roars that were *nothing* beside the flashing lightning, howling winds, and the stinging rain that had begun to fall.

Darkness paused his ascent. Threw back his head, hair plastered to his scalp, manic grin on his face—*Vallen's* face.

And he began to laugh, a deep cackle that the sky echoed with rumble after rumble.

Though the rain couldn't touch him, Vallen shivered.

Though the wind couldn't lash him, Vallen quaked and trembled.

What have I unleashed?

A shadow-mailed hand jerked forward, krenesh blade extended. Gleeful wind raced to its tip, then shot like a rifle—once, twice, thrice.

Vallen could barely track the spells, but he saw the aftermath. The first lancerjet lost its engines in a spray of shredded shrapnel that flipped it end over end as it fell. Another burst in twain, its pilot a splash of scarlet arcing through the storm.

The last . . . disintegrated. Came apart at the seams, the welds, modern magtech no match for some ancient evil Vallen suspected had been young when men were still slaying each other with stone and club.

Enough, he begged Darkness.

"More," the entity demanded, heavens reverberating his malice.

Up Darkness raced. Higher and higher and then higher still. Streaks of white capered around him, lances of lightning that raised the hair on Vallen's arms and sent tingles of pure euphoria racing through his veins.

He could see now. Bonded with Darkness, the truth of the world became clear. These sparks, this *energy*—it was men'ar in its purest form. Dancing, leaping, painting the somber skies white for the briefest of instants.

It was beautiful.

It was *disgusting.*

Darkness stretched out his fingers, curled them in, and two bolts of crackling white flew toward his blade, wrapping around the hilt, stretching up his arm and shearing the armor from his flesh as it went. Some part of Vallen hoped the power would be too much. That it would incinerate Darkness and him along with it.

But the lightning paused at his shoulder and, like a chastised servant, slunk back into his sword. The blade gleamed. The lightning crackled and filled the air with the acrid tang of scorched ozone.

And slow as centuries, Darkness pointed the krenesh down.

Down toward the embattled cruisers, outlined against the clouds by their blasting guns and shimmering lumes.

"More," Darkness whispered.

He unleashed a torrent of lightning, a spear of white-hot fire bright enough to blind the gods themselves. Vallen shaded his eyes, wincing at the glare despite the not-glass and not-water of his prison walls. He had no doubt how this would end. What fate the cruisers below were about to suffer.

The bolt hit the right-most cruiser's lume like a hammer, bashing it in, pressing it until it shook and cracked and buckled. For an instant, it held.

Then the lightning-spear sliced through, slashing apart dozens of decks and tons of gestalt steel as a blade shears through cloth. It punched out the other side and struck the bay below, vaporizing a swathe of water, casting plumes of smoke high into the air. Flame bubbled in its wake, an explosion consuming the cruiser from the inside out.

Vallen's breath caught.

And when he released it, a bright light erupted from the warship, ripping it from bow to stern, casting twisted metal across the storm-churned sky.

Hundreds of lives. Gone in an eye-blink. A breath.

Yet Darkness wasn't satisfied.

"More," he insisted, gliding toward the boiling harbor. Like the clouds above, like the winds and shadows caressing his legs and arms, the waters climbed to meet him. Welcoming him like a long-lost brother finally returned to the plane of the living.

Fear reigned on Olivier's bridge.

Panicked cries. Shouted warnings. Requests for orders that grew increasingly desperate every time they were repeated. The *Ardor* still flew. Her lume was intact, her cannons firing, and the paint of her hull barely scorched from her exchanges with the Darmatian light cruiser limping away from them across the darkening sky.

The same could not be said for *Fervor*, her sister ship.

"*Fervor*, she's . . . she's gone," a sensor tech breathed, staring out the darkened viewport.

Olivier had eyes. He knew his second cruiser was gone, reduced to illyrium dust, flame, and wreckage by a pillar of lightning fired from above. Inside his withered chest, his heart thudded a fierce symphony. His head throbbed as spikes of agony pierced his temples from every side.

How? Why? Had Olivier not prepared enough? Should he have listened to that sow Titania? This storm had sprung up from nowhere, but even the gods' fury shouldn't be enough to—

An officer at the communications desk spun his chair toward Olivier. "We've lost contact with our lancerjet squadron! All icons show red."

Olivier's vision swam. He coughed, doubling over, covering his mouth with a white glove. When he pulled it back, red flecks dotted the once pristine surface.

No. Not yet. This battle would *not* be his grave.

"Retreat toward . . . the ground," Olivier wheezed, trying to make out the fuzzy images floating above the bridge's tactical display. One green blip. Dozens of gleaming crimson dots, some large, some small. All gone. All destroyed. "We'll lure their cruiser into a volley of panzcraft fire and—"

"Nothing but static from the ground teams," another bridge officer shouted, her fingers shaking as they darted from one angry red display to the next. "I . . . I can't raise anyone, sir."

Olivier stopped listening. Tuned out their cries and pleas as the invisible grip on his lungs tightened, strangling the life from him, setting his every breath on fire.

He was going to lose.

He was going to *die.*

"No," Olivier gasped. "Not yet."

And he *stood.* Grabbing the armrests of his command chair, tossing aside his cane, Olivier pulled himself to his full height, roaring with every scrap of strength left in his ravaged carcass.

"Dive!" he ordered *Ardor's* helmsman. "Flank speed. Back to the airfield, back to the ground. I don't care if you have to crash to get us there faster."

Captain Neering stepped toward Olivier, arms raised to support him, but he waved the cowardly pipe-rat off. This was *his* moment.

"Ready Archimas' device," he ordered his nephew, grinning as blood dribbled from his lips. "If we go down, so will they."

Sylette kept to the shadows, hiding behind rumbling boilers, striking from the darkness. There was only so much room to maneuver in the cramped compartment. The main walkway, crowded with fallen bodies. A few secondary gantries around the perimeter and a ladder leading to a narrow service ledge on the second floor.

If Sylette paused, the Ice Queen would catch her.

And in this game, being caught meant death.

Two daggers appeared in the air beside her and launched at Major Reev. Sylette didn't pause to see if they hit, moving away, slinking past the engine access panel on soft feet. Clinks sounded in the muggy air. Blades striking ice, followed by a loud *crack* as the spell shattered.

In this heat, the Ice Queen was vulnerable. Her magic was slow, her constructs flimsy and brittle. Sylette smiled. She hadn't wanted to fight Major Reev, but in this environment—in this battlefield she'd chosen—she could *win.*

"Come out and we can talk, princess!" Major Reev shouted into the swirling furnace smoke.

Sylette immediately fired three daggers in the direction of her voice, aimed high to low. Men'ar flashed. A thin ice shield appeared in front of Major Reev, gleaming in the furnace light, drops of water beading on its surface. Two daggers bounced off it. The third pierced through, ripping the hem of the Ice Queen's jacket as it passed.

I can win! Sylette thought, circling toward the nearest ladder. *I can beat her!*

"You only say that because you're at a disadvantage."

"I say that because you were my student, Sylette. Surrender, and I promise you a fair trial before a military tribunal."

Sylette scowled, thinking of her mother. Of beatings, chains, and a scarlet-stained chopping block. "I've had enough of trials for one lifetime, thank you."

She launched two more daggers while planting a third against the hissing bulk of a shuddering boiler. One missed wide, burying itself in a gap in the grated floor. The other chipped slivers from a hastily summoned arm-sheathe, which splintered down the middle.

Mouthing words under her breath, Major Reev flung her hand toward where Sylette *had* been. Jagged ice spears tore through the ash-choked air, splattered harmlessly against the bulkhead wall. The Major was doubly handicapped here. She couldn't hit the boilers, lest she damage *Dharmasya*, and her powers were weakened by the all-oppressive heat.

Yes, Sylette could win. She was *going* to win.

"I was the traitor," Renar pleaded as he huddled beneath the main engineering panel. Beside him, the red-haired engimage was blinking and shaking his head, obviously bewildered by the scene he'd woken up to. "General Iolus ordered me to sabotage *Dharmasya* if the Empire's trap—"

"And I'm supposed to believe Sylette's innocent? With all these bodies? With the engine override pin in her possession?" Major Reev laughed. "Tell your royal companion to stand down, Iolus, then we'll figure out the truth."

Another two daggers launched. Another deflection, another miss, this time into the curled tubing of a fire-suppressant hose hung near the entry hatch. The blade bit deep into the fabric, where it sat glinting in the glow from the furnaces. Watching their fight. Waiting.

Wedging another dagger into the soft metal between two wall plates, Sylette dashed between two boilers, dodged a melting shard of ice, and leapt onto the ladder. Scalding metal seared her gloveless fingers, but she bit back a cry.

A few more rungs. A little more height. A second or two more.

And then, Sylette would win.

She reached the top, splinters of watery ice splashing against the grate beneath her feet. One long, thin shard slipped through and slashed a bloody furrow from Sylette's chin to her ear. But she ignored the pain, the oozing crimson. It burned in the fires around her. Vanished before the flames of her resolve.

Sylette's eyes darted around the chamber, seeking the silver glints where she had hidden them. Where she had *placed* them.

"During training, you never asked how I would beat *you*," Sylette said, glaring at Major Reev as she raised her arms, palms up and out.

"Because you can't."

"We'll see."

As one, the daggers she'd planted rose, flipped their blades toward the Ice Queen, and rushed her from every direction.

Major Reev didn't move. Didn't raise her arms, stamp her feet, or so much as twitch her fingers. She simply *exhaled*. A long breath, dripping frost, coated with rime.

The smoke in the chamber *froze*. Turned into beads of radiant crystal that latched onto Sylette's daggers and dragged them to the floor. She had no time to gasp. No time to jump aside or flee.

For the smoke was everywhere, including atop her sweat-slicked skin.

In an instant, Sylette lost feeling in her legs and arms. They weren't cold, just . . . numb. Immobile. She glanced down, cursing as she realized her body—from the neck down—was encased in a thin sheathe of ice.

And unlike before, it wasn't melting—wasn't weakened in the slightest. Sylette had set a trap for Major Reev, only to end up trapped herself.

The Ice Queen gazed up at her, something approaching pity softening her emerald eyes. "I told you, Sylette. You never had a chance of winning."

Cold as winter's kiss, gray as a funeral sky, the waters of the bay embraced Darkness, wrapping his arms in chilling tendrils, coursing about him like stars about a sun.

Vallen heard it then. A joyful chittering, a triumphant melody. The water, the clouds, the lightning—the very *air* itself—was singing a song of reunion. The water swished, the wind whispered, and the lightning crackled, a tune that none but he and Darkness understood.

Yes, Vallen at last understood. The men'ar in all things, even his own blood, cried out to Darkness. Hailing him as friend. Savior.

Father.

Trembling, Vallen's hands dropped to his sides. Sighing, he dropped to the floor of his prison. There was no fighting this infinite, eternal *thing* inside him. He could only wait and watch, fists clenched, throat tight, eyes shaking as every fiber of his being fought his mind, yearning to give up—to join with that which gave them life.

Darkness stretched out a hand, nuzzled a tendril of water as it passed. "I'm here," he murmured. "Not in full, no, but the pieces will soon be gathered. And then the pact that binds me—that binds *us,* my sweet—shall at last be shattered, and the Eighth will resume their place at my side."

Was Darkness *speaking* to men'ar? It wasn't sentient—it did only that which it was commanded. So how was—

With a click of his tongue, Darkness stilled Vallen's thoughts, freezing them with a chill not even Major Reev could match. "Do not pretend to know *anything* about this universe, mortal."

Mute, numb, and unable to tear his eyes from the scene before him, Vallen watched Darkness raise his arms.

The *harbor* rose with them. Fish slipped from its depths to flounder on the glistening seabed. Fishing trawlers and two-masted brigantines snapped taut against their lines as they plummeted into the gap, tearing apart the Etrus pier, dragging it down with them. Wide-eyed soldiers in Darmatian blue gaped from shore, Velle, Unter, and Lilith somewhere among them. They no more comprehended what they were witnessing than Vallen did.

Darkness stretched his arms toward the final Sarc cruiser, its engines flaring like the sun as it fled toward the airfield—the warehouses, tarmac, and lonely bronze tower across the bay. The waters leaped forward, forming a frothing white whip, eager to obey his command.

They sang as they flew. Cascading, bouncing, flowing freely as they'd always desired.

The ebony clouds sang, notes reverberating in the chasms between them.

The lightning sang, a furious melody of hunger and rage.

The earth sang.

Vallen's blood sang.

And with a triumphant roar, the surging waters grabbed the Sarc cruiser about its engines and began to *squeeze.* Its lume flickered as the torrents closed. Its engines sparked and spat as water dribbled through the barrier's widening cracks, and its hull dimpled and twisted under the growing pressure.

A few seconds more, and the battle would be over.

Darkness smiled. "I've won."

Crimson bathed *Ardor's* bridge as every single warning light on every single station screamed the cruiser's impending doom. Techs shouted as one, impossible to distinguish, impossible to answer.

"Engines failing!"

"No thrust! I can't turn 'er, Cap'n!"

"Lume at forty-seven percent, thirty-four, twenty-six . . . "

"We're over the airfield, but I cannae land 'er like this. Orders, Cap'n?"

"*Orders?*"

"*ORDERS!?*"

The airship lurched, trying to throw Olivier over the railing he clung to and into the chaotic crew pit below. Metal groaned. Sparks showered from a ceiling that shuddered like a living thing. Eyes blurry, Olivier stared as a tendril of slate-gray water pierced *Ardor's* failing lume and *ripped* one of her forward turrets from her top deck like it were some petulant child's toy.

He traced the snaking limb back to its master, a young man in Darmatian combat armor hovering between the storm below and the storm above. *This* trivial voidstain had undone him. Destroyed *years* of careful planning and made a mockery of his resolve to challenge Titania.

But . . . Olivier spat blood, smiling despite the unseen sword mangling his insides and stealing his breath. *This is still*

my
MOMENT.

"Give the order, Neering!" Olivier yelled. "Activate the tower. Plunge us and that void-forsaken interloper back into the last age!"

Neering roared. The communications officer slammed a button on their instrument panel.

Outside the bridge, a solitary streak of brilliant white shot through a breach in *Ardor's* failing lume and into the sky. Across the airfield, bay, and city.

It was beautiful.

It was *victory.*

At the far end of the airfield, the bronze tower shook, concentric rings vibrating the air until it seemed to blur and shimmer. A second later, every system, every light, every magtech device aboard *Ardor* switched off. Her heart was dead. The illyrium at her core silenced by whatever lunacy Archimas had invented.

And as *Ardor* fell, as his crew shrieked and screamed and wailed, Olivier smiled.

He had won.

Matteo went blind.

He screamed at the sensation. Foreign yet familiar, a gaping abyss in his chest where his magic had always been. Why was it gone? What had happened?

Matteo grabbed his uniform in both hands. Ripped it open, scratched at the spot where his color—his *world*—should have been. *Dharmasya* tilted beneath him, angling downward. Captain Hurshik roared for a status update as men and women babbled and cried.

It didn't matter to Matteo. His only concern was the darkness spilling from his soul, the cold emptiness creeping from his core to consume him. Nails dug through his undershirt. Bit into the skin beneath and kept clawing through sweat-damp skin and sticky blood.

"Wh-where is my m-magic," Matteo muttered, toppling to the deck, curling about his bleeding flesh. "Where d-did it go, where . . . where did it g-go . . . "

Someone grabbed him. Hauled him upright, carried him to the bulkhead, and strapped him into a mesh harness with a loud *click.* "Hold on," Captain Hurshik said, patting his shoulder as he left.

Distantly, Matteo heard the captain speak again. "Aim for the Lyndwur! We'll use the trees to break our fall!"

They were crashing. Into the wild Lyndwur, of all places. But Matteo didn't care. He kept scratching, rocking, muttering, lost in this world where he couldn't see.

Where, once again, his magic meant nothing.

Where he might as well be dead.

A spear slammed into Jis' chest—a shaft that ripped through her, taking her men'ar along with it. Agony poured from the invisible wound, white-hot and searing. A great hand reached out, gripped her ribs and lungs, and clenched as if intent on breaking her in half.

Yet it was the sensations that startled her. *Heat.* Warmth, fire, and flames. The coals blazing in the furnaces around her. The press of scalding metal so close it singed the threads of her uniform.

Jis stumbled, nearly falling, nearly tumbling to her knees at the *shock* of the sweat on her cheeks, the sweltering smog ripping the breath from her lips. Normal people dealt with this *every* day? Engimages chose to work in places like this?

Movement caught her eye. The ice encasing Sylette had dissolved, splashing harmlessly to the floor. And the girl ...

She took one faltering step forward, plastered a hand to her bloodless face, and collapsed head-first *over* the service gantry's edge. Jis forgot the pain tearing at her insides. Forgot the loss of her magic, the treason she suspected. All of that could be sorted out later.

Right now, she was nothing but a teacher whose student was in danger.

Out of the corner of her eye, Jis saw Renar rush forward alongside her. Together, they raised their arms. Together, they leapt, hoping, praying they'd make it in time.

The pulse hit, dashing apart the tendrils of living water, sending the bay crashing back into the bed from which it had risen.

Vallen screamed at the blow. Raged within his prison, clutching his hands to his head as a million temple bells rang inside his skull. He couldn't see, couldn't think. And the only thing he heard was Darkness screaming along with him. Bellowing hatred at the sky, howling as he fell.

And fell.

And fell.

Until, suddenly, it was *Vallen* falling. Darkness was gone. Silent or dead, it mattered not. Vallen was *free.*

And now . . . he was going to die. His flesh was aflame, a thousand needles lancing his limbs, a hundred hungry fires ravaging his lungs as he fought to wheeze, to draw a solitary breath of ash-choked air. Darkness and magic—they'd kept him aloft, kept him from succumbing to the price of men'ar overuse.

And so Vallen fell.

And fell.

And

f

e

l

l

Chapter 61

Fle'bilis

Cold.

It seeped beneath the fabric of Unter's combat suit, chilling his flesh, making him tremble as the rush of combat drained away. He knew instantly that his flar'en spell was gone, as were the enhancements he'd applied to his arms and legs.

Unter stumbled, bucklers growing heavy, knees threatening to give out as every ache and pain was magnified a hundred-, a thousand-fold. The bayonet wound in his thigh oozed a lazy trail of purple blood. Scratches along his face and neck reopened, their warm rivulets an almost welcome relief.

Men'ar. Unter's men'ar wasn't working. His magic—his spells—had fizzled away to nothing. A dark emptiness crept through his veins instead, a hollow that left him teetering on weak legs, struggling to raise his arms, to take another breath.

How? Unter thought. *I wasn't close to running out. I should still be able to fight, to—*

He glanced down the pier toward the rest of the Darmatian survivors. They'd been clustered at the water's edge, cheering on Vallen, screaming themselves hoarse as the Triaron singlehandedly tore Imperial cruisers from the sky.

Now almost half of them were on the ground, scratching at their throats, curling around unseen wounds. A woman Unter had seen casting wind magic dropped to her knees, clawing at her forearms. She shrieked at them. Begged the bloody rends in her flesh to give it back, give her magic back.

"I can't feel anything. It's dark inside. Empty, empty, empty. A void, nothing left. Give it back. *GIVE IT BACK!*"

Others were better. Colonel Holcomb clutched his head with one hand, the other grabbing a silver flask from his belt with shaking fingers. Uncorking it, he started to raise it to his lips, then cast it into the bay with a curse.

"As if . . . I were . . . that weak."

"It's gone . . . it's gone . . . "

"Dear Creator, it hurts, it *burns!* Make it stop. Make-it-stop, make-it-stop, *make-it-stop!*"

More wails rose, the cries of those stricken, the worried shouts of medics and friends who had no idea how to aid the fallen. Velle was on her side, vomiting over the levee's edge, while Lilith huddled over her, still possessed of enough strength to stand.

Blood trickled from her thigh, a wound too fresh to have been inflicted by the Sarcs. Unter saw a dagger nearby—*Velle's* dagger, coated with fresh blood. What resolve! The little Terran had stabbed herself to relieve the shock all the mages were—

The mages!

Every single victim of the invisible attack was a mage. Which meant . . .

Unter's cloudy gaze drifted to the last two transports. Engines that had roared as the Resistance prepared to flee were deathly silent. Not a single light on the loading ramps glowed, and the illyrium on the under-wing gravpads was as lifeless as the cobblestones on which Unter stood.

No magic. No magtech. No *flight.*

With a roar, Unter bashed one of his shields into his stomach, cutting his suit, scoring a long purple line across his gut. The pain was like a bucket of glacial water pitched right at his face. It restored his clarity, reminded him of what he should be doing.

Two cruisers tumbled from the sky, one toward Lyndwur Forest, the other toward the airfield across the harbor. Beneath them was a speck, a tuft of messy brown hair on its head, a blue Darmatian combat suit flapping as it fell and fell and fell.

Down toward the roiling, frothing waters of the now freed bay.

Down toward certain death.

Unstrapping his bucklers, tossing them aside, Unter ran past Lilith and Velle and dived off the levee. He *would* save Vallen.

Renar skidded across the unforgiving metal floor, arms outstretched. Buttons tore from his jacket. The skin of his arms and side ripped and blistered. But he gritted his teeth and bore the pain.

He *would* save Sylette.

She thudded into his chest, all bones, elbows, and hard angles. Something popped in Renar's back. He gasped as the air left his lungs, as his bent arms screeched in torment. Then a wad of silver hair struck him in the face.

Renar didn't toss Sylette aside. Didn't scream that she was crushing one of his precious kidneys. Raising up slowly, carefully, he eased the exile toward Major Reev, who'd arrived a second too late.

The Ice Queen took Sylette's shoulders, cradled her limp form into her chest. Side by side, their faces appeared unnaturally pale. Sweat streaked their cheeks, and the Major's throat heaved, each breath a hiss that twisted her lips into a grimace.

"Are you alright?" Renar asked, stretching a hand toward her.

Major Reev batted it away. "You don't get to . . . ask that . . . *traitor.*"

She wasn't wrong. Renar could accept who he was—what he'd done and the consequences he'd need to face. He owed Sylette that much and more.

But the situation had clearly changed. "Something's wrong with both of you," Renar said, wincing as he rolled onto his knees. "And since we *both* wanted to catch Sylette, I say we call a truce and—"

Dharmasya bucked, the deck beneath them suddenly slanting downward. Not enough for them to fall, but steep enough that Renar had to put a hand out to steady himself. "Another blast?"

A raspy chuckle came from the direction of the engine panel. The ruddy-haired engimage was sitting up, his eyes open, chalk-white features split in a wry grin. "A bit worse than that, my friend. We're *crashing.*"

Major Reev narrowed her eyes. "How do you know, Lieutenant Darres?"

"How does a tree know when it's time to sprout buds?" He shrugged. "By the way, I told you to call me Jay—"

"Do I need to freeze the answer out of you?"

Darres—no, *Jay*—didn't look at her. He was too busy combing the floor around him, searching for something Renar couldn't see. A few seconds later, his smile brightened, and the engimage plopped a slightly cracked, slightly bent set of colored monocles over his right eye. Between his days-old blond stubble and wildly unkempt hair, he cut a ridiculous figure.

One Renar *desperately* wanted to draw.

"You can't use magic," Jay said, flicking to the red monocle.

Renar patted his jacket pocket, which hung open with three of his gold buttons missing. No sketchbook.

Major Reev huffed. "How do you know?"

"I'd say you look just as drained as that Alhan kid I tested my canceller on, but it's simpler to take a peek around the room."

Another lurch shook the ship. Unconscious bodies began to

shift. Scattered tools clattered as they slid across the deck, banging into boilers and pipes along the way.

Renar barely noticed. Pulse quickening, he jabbed his fingers into his inner pocket. Nothing. He shook his belt satchel, flipped out his trouser pockets. Nothing.

"We don't have time for games, Darres," Major Reev growled. "Spit it out."

"No power!" the engimage proclaimed grandly. "All the lights are off, the boilers are dead, the illyrium's out of juice. Haven't you noticed it getting colder? We're running on naught but embers and cinders."

"How?"

"The Sarcs have dear old Archimas' device, my dear, and they decided to use it, mad lads that they are."

"A . . . *canceller?*" she said, testing the word.

No sketchbook underneath him. Renar reached out, tapped Sylette's pockets. It wasn't on her either.

"*Magic* canceller, technically. Using energy stored up in a battery, it vibrates a series of variably sized rings to produce a wave frequency to counter the natural one given off by men'ar cells in illyrium and other—"

The deck tilted again, bulkheads moaning, shrieking as *Dharmasya* picked up speed. Major Reev snagged a vertical pipe with one arm, groaning as she strained to hold onto Sylette. Renar watched more loose items slide toward the far wall. Wrenches, welders, a rusty toolbox, an old mug with a half-naked Sylph stenciled on the side.

Jay grabbed a passing red canister by its handle, clutching it to his chest like a lover, his other arm wrapped around the engine panel. Renar ignored him. Ignored every other object, scanning, searching for his . . .

There!

His sketchbook was skidding toward him, its pages open to a charcoal-smeared drawing. Renar must have lost it when he dove to save Sylette. When his uniform ripped and his pockets turned out.

No matter. Renar scrambled across the listing deck, dodging flying tools, digging his fingers into the metal grate for traction. He didn't care how much his nails bled or his knuckles screamed in protest.

He *would* save his sketches.

One more meter. One more tug, one more grab. Bloody fingers closed atop the open pages, staining them with crimson.

Light flashed.

Energy left Renar like a heavy sigh, a long farewell.

And as it did, black ooze flowed off the sketch, across Renar's hands, up and up and up until it stood before him on the uneven engineering compartment deck. Hands took shape. Plate armor grew from its chest, a long cape unfurled from its shoulders, and two spools of thick wire spiraled from its belt. A dark eyepatch completed the ensemble, leaving one ebony eye to glare at Renar.

The specter scowled. "Ya *dare* summon me, void-stain?"

Somehow, some way, Rittermarschal Ober Valescar had risen from the pages of Renar's sketchbook, and he did *not* seem pleased.

Unter surfaced to the sight of Vallen striking the churning bay.

His doll-limp form didn't shatter. No sound of snapping bones reached Unter across the roaring bay, above the crackling of flames throughout the town.

Was Vallen dead? Sinking? An obsidian wave washed over him, pushing the Triaron farther and farther away.

He's alive, Unter decided, diving back beneath the swells, scything the frigid water with all four of his arms. *He's alive, he's alive, he's alive.*

Stroke, pull. Stroke, pull, breathe.

Unter repeated the mantra as he swam, cold seeping ever deeper into his limbs. He wasn't the best swimmer. His people looked down on the practice, believing magtech to be the *proper* way to cross the seas. Why should they sully their skin? Why should they stoop so low?

How naive. How shortsighted. It didn't matter *how* one overcame an obstacle, only that one *did.*

Stroke, pull. Stroke, pull, breathe.

Perhaps it was good the Haead had him exiled. Unter had learned so much since then: to swim, to use magic, a hundred other lessons.

Stroke, pull. Stroke, pull, breathe.

But above all, he'd found new comrades. People to protect. To laugh and fight alongside. Renar, Lilith, and the rest—even Vallen. *Friends . . .* Yes, that was the Terran word for it. Friends he cherished more than honor and ritual, laws and tradition. More than his own flesh and blood. More than *anything.*

Stroke, pull . . . Stroke, pull . . . breathe.

Unter was slowing. A gnawing emptiness filled his body, a chill that numbed both sides of his flesh. He closed his eyes, tore through a wave. Prayed to Vida and all the Veneer that he'd make it before his friend drowned. That he'd still have strength to get them back to shore.

And there Vallen was. Over the next crest, floating in a valley between swirling waves. Unter paused mid-stroke, kicking with his legs as he bobbed in place. What . . . was underneath Vallen?

It was similar to a discarded Trillith cocoon—a dingy white-gray blanket that sat between the boy and the water. Threads of the substance seemed to *ooze* from Vallen's skin, dribbling down his flesh and suit, coagulating beneath him.

What *was* it? Some kind of sickness? An aftereffect of whatever caused their magic to vanish? Unter shook his head and swam closer. Each stroke was a battle. Every labored breath a war. He didn't have time to—

"Don't touch it!"

Unter spun toward the voice. Well, flailed was more accurate. Water splashed. A bob of drenched brown hair ducked beneath the surface, then reemerged an arm-span closer to him, freckles gleaming like constellations on ice-pale skin.

"Lilith," Unter gasped. "Why here?"

The girl ignored him, paddling around Vallen with short, deft strokes. She seemed made for the water, slicing it like a ship's prow. "Can you smell that?" Lilith asked.

"Need only one to tug to shore Triaron."

Lilith glanced at him. "I'm the better swimmer. Anyway, what do you smell? It's pretty flowery . . . Lilac's blossom?"

Unter heaved a sigh, touched his aching chest. She *was* the better swimmer. Conceding the point, he drifted closer to the white cocoon, nose sampling the air.

The briny scent of salt swept up his nostrils, accompanied by the acrid tang of char and the metallic aroma of blood. It was better here than on land. Washed out and faded instead of overpowering. But beneath it all was something else. A fresh scent, like a spring breeze or a freshly ground . . .

"Crystal," Unter breathed. "White ooze like illyrium crystals smell."

Lilith tilted her head. "I thought illyrium didn't have a scent."

"*Ground* illyrium pleasant smell off give. Flowers. Perfume." Unter splashed an arm toward Vallen. "If this similar, then maybe he's leaking . . . " He paused, blinking consternation. "*Men . . . Men'ar,* yes?"

"This"—Lilith flicked a finger at the threads dripping, *slipping*

609

from Vallen's pores—"is men'ar?"

"Dead men'ar? When magic killed, it killed? Maybe?"

"Ew."

Lilith's hand lashed out, grabbed Vallen's wrist, and tugged him free of the webbing. Some still clung to him, stubborn strands matted to his hair or crusted beneath his eyes and mouth, but most detached with a wet *plop.*

Unter gaped. "You not touch said!"

"Well, if you see a better way to get him back to shore, let's hear it." He shrugged. Once again, Unter had to concede the point.

"Good. You take the other arm, I'll steer us toward our troops."

"Speak, cur," Valescar growled, stomping toward Renar. "Why did ya summon me?"

Another explosion rocked *Dharmasya.* More loose articles whizzed past, including a fist-sized gear that went right *through* the Rittermarschal's chest. Ink sprayed across the deck, but the wound quickly resealed, disappearing as though it had never been.

Valescar glanced at the shaking boilers, the trembling ceiling and clanking pipes. "And ta such a *disaster* o' all places. Ye'd think none o' ya knew how ta fly a ship."

Renar looked down at the bloody sketchbook in his hands. His raw and oozing fingers, the glow emanating from his scrapes and cuts. The open pages were blank. Empty except for the scarlet smears from his desperate grab.

And that flash he'd seen? It was the same radiance that flared when Sylette summoned daggers, or when Major Reev drew water from the air for her ice magic. There could be only one conclusion. Renar had used—

"Magic!" Jay exclaimed, grinning from ear to ear. "You used *magic.* In a zone where the effects of men'ar are canceled. Where even the Ice Queen of Darmatia"—he waved at Major Reev, who snarled at Valescar as she tried to stand—"is powerless. Can I get a blood sample, perchance? Run some tests?"

With a grunt, Major Reev collapsed backward, Sylette still unconscious in her arms. "We have more pressing worries, Darres."

One of which was the fourth most powerful mage in the Empire. Renar turned, scrambling up the slanted deck. He expected a spool of wire to pierce his back. To lift him into the air and paint the bulkhead walls with little pieces of Renar.

The blow didn't fall. Seconds passed, the deck continued to tilt, and the only noise that came from Valescar was the furious tapping of his boot on the grated floor. Renar paused. Stopped and glanced back at the thing he'd drawn—the thing that had, impossibly, leapt off the page and into real life.

It was *exactly* as he'd imagined the commander. A sharp jaw, a steely glare. Hair black as pitch shot through with streaks of white, corded muscles bulging against the mail between his plates. He towered over Renar, teeth bared, gauntlets clenched at his sides.

And yet . . . this *wasn't* Valescar. The dying furnace light at his back exposed cracks in his armor, spots Renar had left open on his sketch. Spaces where the off-white of the page conveyed the gleam of his silver armor or weren't as shaded as the chasm beneath his eyepatch.

When Valescar moved, the lines that made him shifted. Up and down. Left and right. He wasn't the real Rittermarschal, just a copy made from ticks of Renar's scrivle, smeared charcoal, and his imagination.

Yes, *his*. Renar was fle'bilis. The weak, the infirm, the *magicless*. And yet . . . here Valescar stood.

His creation. A nightmare from the depths of his darkest nights, a terror—like the General—he'd never fully overcome.

Yet it was *his,* nonetheless.

Which means it should obey my commands, Renar thought, a smile creeping onto his lips.

With a yelp, Major Reev started to slide, her knuckles trembling, her fingers bloody where they gripped the pipe. She was going to fall. *All* the engimages he'd knocked out were going to career across the chamber and smash into the still simmering boilers.

"Grab them, Valescar!" He ordered, scanning the chamber. There! Crash seats on either side of the entry hatch, buckles undone, mesh hooked to the ceiling. "Grab all of us and lash us into those seats!"

The specter scoffed. "Who are ye ta—"

"I made you," Renar said, popping his scrivle out of its slot in the sketchbook's binding. "Which means"—he held its end to the now blank page—"I can *unmake* you, too."

A weighty pause. A season of fear and uncertainty packed into one tense moment. And then, Valescar nodded. "Very well."

His ink-dark spools of wire unwound, snaking across the room, headed for Jay and Major Reev. The engimage didn't protest as the cable coiled around his waist. He was too busy prodding the line with his finger and examining the smudge it produced. Renar thought he saw Jay *lick* it as he was lowered into his seat.

Major Reev started to resist, hand fumbling at a pistol holster on her ankle. She likely believed this was a Sarconian trick. That Renar couldn't *possibly* have powers. He didn't quite believe it himself, but they could talk *after* they survived *Dharmasya's* death.

"It's safe," Renar soothed. "I drew him. He's under my control."

"Fer now," Valescar groused.

Major Reev snorted. "That doesn't fill me with confidence, Iolus."

But she relaxed and let the Rittersmarschal carry her and Sylette to the crash harnesses. Allowed him to buckle their restraints and aided the groggy engimages as he hauled them over.

Then it was Renar's turn. The cable slithered around him, lifted him into the air. It was a freeing feeling. Exhilarating. *Electrifying.* For once, Renar wasn't the weak one—the powerless one who needed others to save him.

For once, *he* was the one saving *them.*

And for a short, sweet, blessed moment, the Soldier was silent. He had no condemnation to spew. No barb to fling about how unworthy or inadequate Renar was.

Which was almost—*almost*—as thrilling as having magic.

Chapter 62

Crash

"**B**race for impact!" Captain Hurshik roared.

Matteo inhaled. Caught a breath, stored it in his hollow chest, waited for the inevitable.

But . . . what did it matter? His magic was gone. His veins lifeless, empty. The airship around him shook like a sinner before the Creator's fury, wires snapping, pipes bursting, bulkheads rattling.

Those officers who could see screamed or cried. The sensors who couldn't—the other mages stripped of *everything* they were—ranted, raged, and cursed, all but oblivious to the tower-tall trees Matteo knew were rising to greet them.

The Lyndwur was welcoming him home, spreading its vast branches like the doors of a crypt. Etrus was the land of his birth. And now . . . it would be the land of his death as well.

Matteo *should* be smiling. A *hero* would smile at such a poetic end.

He sobbed instead. "Even without magic, even empty, I don't want to die. I don't want to die, I-don't-want-to-die, *Idon'twanttodie.*"

Oh! Matteo realized.

He blinked.

Once, twice, his vision blurry. Watery and unfocused beneath his tear-stained glasses. Great ashen blobs flashed past *Dharmasya's* cracked viewport. Some gnarled and twisted. Others long and tall. They grew closer together, weaving like the threads of a carpet, blending like paint on a canvas.

Closer and closer and yet closer still, until scarcely a ray of light could be seen between the flood of gray.

How? Matteo thought. *How did I forget I could* always *see, even without magic?*

A giant bough pierced the viewport. Shattered the glass, sent it spiraling through the room like shrapnel. Another branch tore a gunnery officer in two. More iron-hard tendrils ripped through *Dharmasya's* flanks, tearing free gestalt steel slabs, sending whole instrument panels and those strapped to them hurtling into the gale beyond.

Something struck Matteo. He jolted, gasped. Felt a flush of warmth at his waist, a chill sliding up his side.

613

He saw blood.

And then, like before, he saw nothing at all.

Renar felt the crash before it happened—a great shudder that raced the length of *Dharmasya* like a beast drawing its final breath. Beneath the buckles and restraint mesh, his arms and legs trembled. His teeth chattered.

Would it be enough?

The whole cabin pitched backward as if *Dharmasya* had been struck by a deity's uppercut. Renar's head hit the metal wall, drawing a wince, clouding his vision. Beside him, Major Reev stared straight ahead, refusing to budge.

Renar thought the Ice Queen was simply focused, resolved. Then a wrench hurtled across the bucking chamber. Major Reev twisted her head right—just enough that the deadly projectile banged off the bulkhead behind her instead of turning her skull to paste.

More objects were flying around the room. Loose screws, spare nuts and bolts, the tools he'd used, even a badly dented mug painted with a Sylph in a compromising pose. They were effectively bullets in the cramped space, and the coals from the boilers would …

"You're the one with magic," Major Reev hissed, elbowing him through her crash harness. "Do something!"

"Valescar!" Renar called. The apparition faced him, arms crossed, single eye blazing like a hot poker.

"Am I some snot-nosed whelp that ye shud call on me without a *scrap* o' respect? Without the title I slew thousands ta—"

"Defend us!"

The living sketch huffed, then spat a wad of ink on the floor as he marched to the compartment's center. A wrench struck his arm, shattering the shifting patterns he was made from, casting black gobs against a nearby boiler where they smoked and sizzled. Yet as soon as the tool passed, the sketch lines *snapped* back together. Like healing muscles, only a million times faster.

Valescar was invincible.

Which meant *Renar* was invincible.

Up came Valescar's hands, the claws of his gauntlets splayed. Out flew his rapiers, his spools of cable, his armor plates. The sketch had no need for defense. Nothing that pierced his not-flesh seemed to faze him.

And so Valescar struck like the calamity Renar had drawn. A wire grabbed the wrench and *speared* it into the wall. His breastplate blocked a trio of screws trying to impale Jay, while one of his rapiers pinned the erotic mug to the ceiling.

He seemed to be everywhere at once. A beast with six limbs . . . eight . . . No. Renar shook his head, unable to count how many pieces of ink-metal Valescar was manipulating at once.

It was a storm within a storm—the chaos outside the crashing airship matched by the grace and fury of the Empire's fourth strongest mage. *Dharmasya* shook and twisted, debris flew, and *his* creation cut, slashed, and stabbed, a living wall between them and the warship's end.

How beautiful.

Renar lost track of time. Bulkheads continued to groan, metal continued to shriek, and jolt after jolt after jolt *rammed* through his neck and spine. But the buckles and restraints held. *Valescar* held.

Dharmasya slammed into something massive—a monstrous tree, a *mountain,* Renar couldn't say. She immediately stopped, but everything inside her kept moving. Renar's head, which screamed as it tried to tear off his shoulders. His chest, arms, and stomach, which burned as steel-tight restraints etched stinging welts into his flesh.

His sight grew hazy. Dark and disoriented. Distantly, he heard a colossal snap, metal tearing free from metal. Valescar roared. Flung out his cables, stabbed with his rapiers.

But the loose boiler crashed into him anyway. Smashing him against the far bulkhead, splattering the walls, floor, and several of the engimages with strands of gooey ink. None of the pieces twitched. They didn't crawl back into a ball and try to reform.

Renar gaped at the dark splotches, so much like bloodstains. Valescar was . . . gone. His creations weren't invincible, any more than he was. Renar winced as he raised his sketchbook, the fingers clutching it raw and bruised.

The pages were blank but for the crimson streaks he'd left behind. No portrait of Valescar, not even a charcoal smudge. In fact . . .

Closing his eyes, Renar tried to recall what Valescar looked like. His magic. How he'd acted. It was like trying to hold a fistful of sand. Details slipped away one by one, vanishing until the picture in his mind was as dead as the ink coating the wall.

"Fascinating . . . " Jay said, coughing as he spoke. "Your creation could manipulate its *own* metal, but not metal from our world. I've

615

never seen anything like it."

Major Reev popped her restraints. Collapsed forward onto her knees, back bent, shoulders slumped. "Study him later. We need to move before the ship does."

Renar barely heard them. Their conversation, the pops and hisses of the furnaces, the creaking of the walls and floor—*all* of it was background noise.

Yes, he had magic now. But if Renar used it—if it was *destroyed*—his mental image went with it. All the creativity, the imagination, just .. . gone in an instant. What if his sketchbook, activated by his blood, was burned to ash? Would he lose all those drawings as well?

Renar clutched his sketchbook tighter. Being a mage was *everything* he'd craved. Yet now that Renar had it, was he willing to sacrifice the art that made him who he was?

With a mighty bellow, Unter heaved Vallen onto the levee and hauled his dripping bulk up after him. He took two steps, sank to his knees, and tumbled onto his side, lungs heaving.

Vaguely, Unter saw Velle race over, pain and worry twisting her soot-smeared face. She flopped atop Vallen. Placed her hands on his pale, bloodless cheeks. Whispered a mantra that should have solved everything.

No light glowed. No glyph appeared. Baring her fangs, the Sylph slammed her fist onto the cobblestones.

Lilith approached Velle quietly, hair and suit plastered to her body, freckles glinting on her winter-white skin. She whispered something in Velle's ear, which twitched as though pricked.

Then, slowly, the healer scooted aside and let Lilith take her place. She pressed her palms to Vallen's chest, putting all of her tiny weight behind her thrusts. Press, press, press . . . On and on, trying to make him breathe. Make him live. When that didn't work, Lilith took his head in her hand, raising it as she lowered her lips to his.

With no magic, Unter knew this was the right procedure. But that surely didn't make it any easier for Velle to bear. As a friend, as their squad salvator, as his former lover.

"Useless," Velle muttered, grinding her fist in the dust. "Useless, useless, useless . . ."

"Don't say that, little missy."

Colonel Holcomb limped over, one hand clutching his side. Crimson peeked through the blue of his combat garb, the press of his ashen fingers. A graze, most likely—enough to sting, not enough to kill.

Groaning, Unter tried to rise and salute. The Colonel waved him back down. "That's enough, Lieutenant. Take a break. You fought hard—*all* of you did. So"—he winked, tried and failed to smile—"let me handle the rest."

Holcomb peered past Unter, over his shoulder, across the bay. He shifted to follow the Terran's gaze, though his magic-drained veins and muscles protested the movement.

The last Sarc cruiser was a crumpled mess on the airfield tarmac. Bent fragments of hull plates and cannons were scattered in all directions. Its engines were cold and dead, its upper deck awash with angry orange flames, and one of the wings that formed its T-shape was twisted beyond recognition. Only the high bridge tower seemed in decent shape, though its shattered viewports gaped like sightless eyes and the Imperial flag was missing.

Unter chuckled. There was some small justice in that.

Then he blinked. Scanned the sky, searching for . . .

"Where *Dharmasya?*" Unter asked.

A far-off explosion answered him. The roar of rending metal, the bellow of dying engines. Everyone spun toward the sound. It came from the other side of Etrus, past the ruined buildings, across the plain, out in the depths of Lyndwur Forest.

Memories of another crash surfaced in Unter's mind.

"*You don't want to be here during the winter,*" Matteo had said, gazing at the night-dark forest clearing around their wrecked Sarconian transport. The young Terran had been *terrified* by the Lyndwur, flinching at hooting nochlows, giving every shadow-clad tree a wide berth. If half of his warning was true . . .

Biting down a gasp, fighting the gaping chasm in his chest, Unter staggered to his feet. "Rescue them we have to."

"How?" Holcomb asked.

How? Unter unleashed a furious series of blinks. "Matter not," he said, taking a stumbling step across the broken cobblestones. "Forest dangerous is. We have to . . . them out get before . . . "

The Colonel moved forward, blocking Unter's path with an outstretched arm. Did he think that would stop him? Limbs trembling, magic drained, Unter could still knock the Terran aside with a swing of an arm.

617

"How?" Holcomb repeated. "Look around, Lieutenant." He raised his bloody hand, waved it at the cluster of Darmatian survivors. But a handful were still standing, their ash-caked, blood-drenched features grim as they hobbled between the wounded and unhinged sprawled across the street.

They had no beds. No linens or wrappings. Tattered uniforms formed their cots, ripped undergarments their bandages. Blood oozed from bullet holes, soaking their suits, mixing with the dust. Many moaned. Others cried and ranted, delirious after losing their magic. Several . . . didn't speak at all, staring up at a rain-heavy sky they could no longer see.

"We can barely save ourselves," Holcomb continued, "and we have no way of knowing if they survived the crash. Should I risk everything on a *chance* we could reach *Dharmasya* in time?"

"But no reason that's to—"

Unter paused. Gazed into Holcomb's quivering eyes. Saw his shoulders stiffen, his lips purse. *He* wanted to go. To rush to Major Reev's side, to pull her from the airship's wreckage—plate by mangled plate, if necessary.

Yet her fate wasn't his responsibility.

Nor is Renar's—or Sylette or Matteo's—mine, Unter realized, glancing back at Lilith as she ministered to Vallen.

"There you go, son," Holcomb said as the Hue took a step back. "Think with that"—he pointed at Unter's head—"instead of this"—he rapped a knuckle on Unter's dented breastplate—"from time to time."

"Still, what now do?" Unter asked. "Can't stay. More Empire troops soon come."

Nodding, Holcomb turned back toward the bay. There was only one thing he could be looking at. One towering edifice that still stood despite the destruction all around them.

Tall as a cruiser raised stem to stern, the bronze column jutted above the airfield hangars like a spear pointed at the heavens. Its tip was set with a rounded cap. Rings—large at the bottom, smaller as they rose toward the top—sprouted from it at regular intervals.

When Unter had first seen the pole, it had been still. Silent. Now it shook with violent fury, whipping the air around it into a haze, vibrating until the gleaming metal seemed to blur.

The more he stared, the more the dark pit left by his magic ached. Icy pain radiated from the unseen wound. Black tendrils clawed through his blood, seeking his heart, his *life*.

Unter had no doubts. *This* was the thing blocking his men'ar.

"Sariel's arse," Holcomb breathed, grimacing as he held his side. "The Sarcs figured out how to turn magic off. Just one more way they've learned to suck the joy out o' my life."

Turn magic off.

Magic.

Mag*tech!*

Like gears meshing for the first time, the pieces clicked together in Unter's mind. Who had the most to lose if the Sarcs perfected a magic canceller? The Darmatians, yes, but they were all but defeated. The Ascendancy, however, had *everything* to lose if their magtech—their very way of life—was brought to a screeching halt.

Unter's gums pulled back, exposing a snarl as he peered *past* the airfield. Across the Etrus canal, over the border, into the shrub-dotted foothills of the country he'd once called home.

She did this. His sister. Taala. She'd manipulated the Resistance. Convinced them to attack Etrus knowing full well the danger they'd face. The Prime Factor, the Assembly, the Bank—they cared not for the Kingdom's fate. Studying the Empire's new weapon had been their objective all along.

Tears welled in Unter's eyes. His lids moved rapidly, blinking shame, anger, and sorrow. "Sorry, am I," he whispered to Holcomb.

The Colonel craned his neck to look up at him. "For?"

"This disaster. Ascendancy fault it is."

"I don't give a foglip's rot-tainted scrotum who caused this mess," Holcomb grunted, brushing ash and dried blood from his patchy red beard. "I'm gonna get out of it first, then ram my boot so far up their backside the Creator who made them'll feel it in his stones."

Was that . . . even possible? Unter chuckled. "How?"

"Easy." Making a gun from his fingers, Holcomb aimed it at the bronze tower. "Destroy the bloody thing."

Dirt had a loamy taste to it. Not altogether unpleasant, especially when the sodden clumps of soil came apart on his parched tongue. Liquid relief cascaded down his smoke-choked throat. Sated his nauseated gut.

And then Mikus spat the wad of dirt back from whence it came. Back into the trench he was crawling out of. Back alongside the blazing ruin of Rittermarschal Titania's personal airship and the corpses roasting inside.

Mikus hated the taste of dirt.

But not more than he hated his job and the woman who ruled over him.

Two more tugs. Two more finger-nail-tearing pulls. Reaching the top of the trench, Mikus rolled over the lip and collapsed in a heap, a yawning emptiness in his chest, stinging welts welling beneath his leather armor.

Dar, his sergeant, was already there. Between his thick beard and his hulking frame, it looked like someone had dumped a bear quilt in the middle of the Etrusian plain. Laying beside him, gaunt Jotun played the perfect corpse, chest barely rising and falling. Hursch, the last of their merry band, combed through a pair of bodies *hurled* through the airship's viewport when they crashed, pocketing anything that crinkled or glittered.

The ship's engines had just . . . stopped during the flight, as had Mikus' magic. They'd nosedived, plowed into the broad plain outside Etrus, and then . . .

And then he'd woken up in a ditch. Dirt in his mouth, hatred in his belly. Of all the blasted missions Rittermark Silesia could bring him on—

"What about our second squad?" the object of his loathing asked.

Mikus glared up at Silesia. *How* was she standing? Her uniform was rent down the side, exposing a bloody undershirt, and her collar was singed with char. Synth-oil and mud caked her short brown hair. The black officer's cap that normally completed her perfect ensemble was missing, freeing her matted locks to sway in the wind.

Silesia was as battered as any of them. And yet, she stood. Defiant. Determined. For an instant—a fleeting blip so insignificant Mikus couldn't be sure it happened—he *admired* her.

Then she opened her mouth. "Get the void up already," Silesia snarled, kicking Jotun in the ribs. The man grunted, hastening to obey.

She moved toward Mikus, but he stumbled upright, eager to avoid *more* pain.

"Second squad?" the Rittermark demanded.

"Dead."

"Equipment?"

Mikus shrugged. "Lost, except for a couple pistols and a rifle."

"Lida," Dar insisted, stroking the wooden stock of his rifle. Of

course, the rifle he'd named survived the crash. Of *bloody* course.

"You and Jotun take the pistols," Silesia said, turning away. She faced the smoke- and ash-shrouded city in the distance, studying the fires and craters scattered across its ruddy tiers. More smoke rose from the nearby forest, a swathe of inky black that rose to join the looming clouds above the settlement.

Etrus. The object of their mission. The place Lt. Colonel Stetson had chosen to make a stand against both the Darmatian rebels *and* Titania.

What an imbecile.

"And what about you?" Mikus asked, unsure why he bothered.

Silesia patted her bulging forearm. Whatever lay beneath was concealed by her sleeve. "I'm fine. Now . . . let's go *massacre* a traitor."

Holstering the salvaged Lerchis pistols, Mikus and his squad trudged after her. There was no point reminding Silesia their mission was to *capture* Stetson. That was a good way to die alongside the fool, and Mikus couldn't die yet.

Not until he'd had his revenge.

Not until the Emperor knew who Silesia *Martavis* really was.

Chapter 63

The Forest Writhes

Jis stooped under a girder blocking *Dharmasya's* central stairwell, then knelt beside a crewman all but buried beneath a fallen panel. Two fingers found his blood-crusted neck. No pulse. Shaking her head, Jis rose and waved her small party up the steps.

That empty gaze. That outstretched arm, grasping, begging for aid that would never come. It haunted her. Another ghost to go with the three-hundred and sixty-seven cadets that frequented her nightmares, to take its place alongside *every* Darmatian life lost since she'd led them into this disastrous battle.

Stay strong, Mother Tabitha whispered in Jis' ear. *The rain falls, the rivers rise, but it is only when we close our eyes—when we give in to despair—that we drown. Save what can be saved, Jisarivel.*

Jis glanced back at Renar, scrambling over a bent pipe with Sylette on his back. There was a purpose to his steps now, a fire in his eyes. Had his sudden manifestation of magic banished his doubts? Or was it something Sylette had said to him?

Something Jis had misunderstood.

She saw the scene again. Renar, fingers clenched atop the engine override pin, ready to damn them to Oblivion. Sylette kneeling in front of him, hand atop his chest.

Jis had watched *Conviction* fall from the sky. Had seen panzcraft lurching through the ruins of Etrus, bearing down on her soldiers. Everything had been unraveling—the bodies mounting, her desperation growing.

And so . . . she'd given into her rage. Branded her students traitors, lashed out at them without asking for an explanation. Another mistake, on top of another mistake, on top of another mistake. Jis wanted to beat her head against the nearest bulkhead. To knock herself senseless before her tears finally fell.

But she couldn't. Not yet.

Save what can be saved, Jisarivel.

Jis paused when she reached the top of the stairs, waiting for the others to catch up. Jayden Darres and two of his engimages—a man with black whorls tattooed down his right cheek and the woman with black braids—followed behind Renar. The last of *Dharmasya's* engimages, a kindly gent with a booming laugh called Vald, had suffered a bolt to the head during the crash.

Yet another corpse for Jis' pile.

She scowled at Darres. He was the slowest of the bunch, stumbling on the uneven steps, tripping over jutting beams. Yet the man refused to part with the red canister in his arms, which was nuzzled to his breast like an infant.

It irked Jis to no end that Darres—and his darling barrel of a child—were their best hope of surviving this mess.

"Are you sure it'll work?" Major Reev asked him for the second time.

The engimage looked up. Smiled illyrium bright. "Of course, Major! My kerium is foolproof. Passed every test, checked every box. Why, your own Lieutenant Alhan was *blown away* by my last demonstration."

"And if I'm lying," Darres bowed his head and pressed the kerium canister over his heart. "May the Creator smite me where I stand."

"Ain't ya an atheist?" Tattoo-face said.

Darres shot him a glare. "Quiet, Jhorn."

So, this is probably going to kill us all, Jis thought with a sigh.

Reaching the landing, Renar shifted Sylette farther up his back. The girl stirred, groaned, but didn't wake. "This . . . *kerium,*" he said, trying the unfamiliar word. "It's going to power the whole cruiser?"

"I wish," Darres said, holding up the small fuel tank. "But alas, this is all that survived the expl . . . I mean, all I have left. It's enough to power a small airship for a few leagues—no more."

Darres grinned at Jis, a greasy, synth-oil-laced smile. But that didn't erase that he'd nearly uttered the word 'explosion.' This was going to end *terribly.*

Shaking her head, Jis waved down the darkened hall. No magtech meant what few lights weren't shattered by the crash were as dead as the rest of the ship. "Which is why we're going to use Matteo's ship, the *Kinloss.* We'll go up three more levels, check the bridge for survivors, then let Darres do whatever he needs to get the transport airborne."

They walked in silence for a time, the going slow and treacherous. Plates shifted, pipes hissed, the whole of *Dharmasya* moaning its death wails. In places, entire decks had collapsed, falling onto the compartments below and crushing everything inside.

The medical bay was one such charnel house. Jis peered into the gap in the floor, sleeve to her nose. Blood smeared the walls, the twisted metal gurneys, the shredded white sheets. An overpowering stench of copper mixed with urine, vomit, and smashed ointments and salves wafted from the hole, turning her stomach, making her eyes water.

Save what can be saved, Jisarivel.

Not one mutilated body moved. Not a twitch, not a whimper. None of them had been strapped down during the crash, and the tables, blades, and tools of the surgery suite had become deadly shrapnel once the ship began to buck and twist.

They were gone. More crimson on Jis' hands.

Save what can be saved, Jisarivel.

She waved the group away. Back to the last intersection, then down an adjoining hall that ran the length of *Dharmasya's* starboard flank. Steel-hard branches of ashen-gray pierced the warship's flesh at regular intervals, rends that cut the gloom with slivers of dim light. A few tiny snowflakes drifted through on a faint breeze, hovering in the air, sparkling like candles beside a funeral bier.

Unbidden, Jis' arms began to tremble. Her breath misted and her teeth chattered. Was she . . . cold? Jis pressed her hands together as she walked, rubbing them as she'd seen others do. A small spark of warmth blossomed between her palms, weak and faint but comforting all the same.

Cold, heat—they were such strange sensations. But not so strange as the dark void in her chest, the hole where Jis' magic should be.

"How is kerium going to help?" Renar asked, voice breaking the stillness. "I mean, illyrium doesn't work, so why would something else?"

"Wave physics," Darres replied, crawling beneath a gnarled bough. The knots dotting it were like misshapen ovals. Like wrinkled . . . *eyes,* their vertical lids pinched tight.

Jis shook her head, squeezed around a warped bulkhead. Imagining things *wasn't* going to make the situation any better.

"I don't follow," Renar said.

Sighing, Darres glanced at Jis and raised an eyebrow. "What *are* you teaching Darmatia's youth these days?"

"Important things," she said as he promptly tripped and smacked his shoulder on the next branch. "Like how to keep their balance, watch where they're going, and focus on the *bloody mission.*"

Darres flipped her Sariel's lance. Beside him, on the rough bark beneath his shoulder, something *flickered.* A flash of yellow, a soft *crack* Jis barely heard.

And then it was gone. When Darres pushed himself up and brushed off his lab coat, the wood was as it had been—drab and lifeless, unseeing eyes still closed.

"Anyway," Darres said, "a *proper* teacher should have explained that men'ar operates like ocean waves. Pulses of energy that have specific wavelengths, frequency, and amplitude, allowing them to—"

Jis glared at him, then jabbed her finger up the hall. Darres gulped. "Right'o. Simple version, keep moving, got it."

"If he finishes in less than five minutes, I'll swear off shags for good," Jhorn called from the back.

"Everyone's a critic," Darres grumbled, resuming his march. "Fine, short and sweet it is. Illyrium *isn't* fuel, my young Iolus. It *produces* fuel—gives off waves of men'ar until whatever resides at its core stops ticking."

Renar pushed aside a dangling wire that would have hit Sylette. "You don't know what's inside illyrium crystals?"

The engimage shrugged. "Ain't got a clue, and most people don't get fussed about it. As long as their gadgets work, they aren't picky about the hows or whys."

"So . . . kerium doesn't have waves?"

"Precisely!" Darres boomed, loud enough to wake the . . .

No. Jis couldn't think about the dead. Not right now. Climbing over the next obstacle, getting Darres to the *Kinloss*—*that* was her only focus.

"Kerium is magically inert," he continued. "Where illyrium gives off energy we collect and use, we *burn* kerium to obtain the same result. Nasty business, really. Lots of smoke, a small danger of an uncontrolled detonation, and a few other side effects, but it gets the job done."

"Did you say *detona*—"

Darres cut Renar off. "I *did* say magically inert. No waves, nothing for the magic canceller to block. Which is why . . . "

He stopped, spun, and stood on his tiptoes in front of the Iolus boy, eye narrowed beneath his monocle. ". . . *you* are so voiding fascinating. The good Major can't use magic. The girl you're carrying like a sack of ferras grain"—Darres gestured at the wad of silver hair draped over Renar's shoulder—"was knocked out by the canceller's anti-pulse. So why can *you* still use magic, hm?"

It was a fair question, one Jis would've spent more time on if she had the luxury. She *knew* the boy was fle'bilis—a condition he'd inherited from his father. Yes, Hardwick had gone to extreme lengths to hide it. Fake blood tests and altered doctor reports. A hollowed-out great-sword enchanted with runes to give Renar the false strength of an enhancive mage.

So . . . how *were* his drawings climbing off the page?

"Leave it, Darres," Jis cautioned. "The bridge is close. Once you get *Kinloss* airborne, you can ponder the miracle all you want."

The engimage gaped at her. "Are you daft? He's our greatest asset right now—someone who could, in theory, simply *sketch* me a new engine for the ship. You're telling me you don't want to know ho . . . "

Darres' voice trailed off, his fingers drumming on the side of his fuel canister. Then his eyes went wide. Flames lit his gaze, and a hungry sigh dripped from his lips. "What do you mean . . . *miracle?*"

"Renar's fle'bilis," Jis said. "Magicless—or at least he was. I thought you knew that?"

Laughter bubbled from Darres' mouth, echoing down the corridor, grating against Jis' ears. What was so funny? Had the last shred of his good sense come undone? She raced toward Darres, grabbing his shoulders and rooting him to the floor before he started bouncing around and hurt himself.

"Hold it together, Darres!" Jis snapped.

"I was right!" he yelled, oblivious of where he was. Of how far his cries were carrying. Of whom or what could hear him. *"I was RIGHT! Me.* Not stuck-up-his-own-arse Litaame, not stones-for-brains Farinen, not even that void-forsaken swindler Archimas. *ME!"*

"Right about what?" Renar asked.

"Magic theory. The root of *everything*. They said fle'bilis can't be cured. But *you*," Darres grinned at Renar, *"you're* the proof. A men'ar wave hit by its exact opposite cancels out, like with the Ice Queen and our engines. High meets low. Positive meets negative. But you were struck by an anti-wave and *gained* magic. Which means you were never magicless, my friend."

Renar gasped and stumbled into a branch, nearly dropping Sylette in the process. "I . . . I wasn't?"

"No! Your magic was *blocked*—you and all the other fle'bilis. By some sort of anti-wave, just like the jammer is producing now."

Creaking filled the hall, the sound of shifting girders and crumpling steel plates. Jis glanced up, over Darres' shoulder. The tears in *Dharmasya's* hull were *growing,* jagged edges gaping like fangs as they spread wider and wider and wider.

Was the ship falling again? Were they under attack?

A stray beam of light fell on the bough behind Renar. It was *writhing*, twitching and trembling as if awakened from a long slumber. One twisted knot pulled apart, exposing a filmy yellow eye. It swiveled around, blinked at Jis, then focused on Renar.

Matteo's legends were true—Lyndwur Forest *was* alive.

And it didn't seem to want them here.

" . . . two anti-waves collided, producing a massive surge that exceeded the magic production threshold," Jay said, still babbling. *"That's* why you can use spells."

"Quiet," Jis urged, shaking him.

"All the fle'bilis can be cured!"

She smacked him. No response. Wherever Darres was right now, it wasn't here.

"I was right!" he screamed. *"I WAS RIGHT!"*

And the forest screamed back. A long, low, mournful screech that seemed to come from all around. More eyes fluttered open, their lids narrowed, their yellow gaze fixed on Darres. More branches flexed and stretched, rising into the air like headless serpents. A cacophony of banging came from outside the airship—more terrors waking from their sleep.

Jis turned and pushed Darres in the direction of the central stairwell, then stooped to free the pistol from her ankle holster. They couldn't defeat a forest. Couldn't hope to slay an entity that rivaled—that likely *exceeded*—a Primal like Nehalena. Only one option remained.

Save what can be saved, Jisarivel.

Even if it seems impossible.

"Run!" Jis yelled.

Chapter 64

Ache

Rodale ached.

Void and Oblivion, did he ache.

In his legs, muscles screaming, raging with every staggering stride the Colonel took. In his tattered side, blood dribbling from a close graze. In his head, which throbbed at every word he spoke, at each hunched shoulder he gripped as he made his rounds of the makeshift Darmatian perimeter.

Worst of all, Rodale's soul ached. The blighted thing was already a mess. Blackened and twisted, rotted by deceit and betrayal, drenched in liquor and drowned in every perversion under the Creator's thrice-damned sun.

It was a hideous thing. One Rodale had *no* desire to examine.

But still the pathetic lump of void-taint lived, clinging to life just as he did. And with each slain soldier, with each blood-flecked gasp from men and women who once more looked to *him* for orders, his soul decayed a little more. Became a little fouler, a little darker. Crept a little closer to the grave.

Two gaping wounds pierced through it. The smaller was a deep pit, a bottomless crevice that swallowed Rodale's men'ar and left him cold. Empty. He bore that ache well—much better than the poor sods curled on the cobblestones or propped against ruined storefronts. Peloqun, Renerv, Pesca, and so many others, crying at the skies, clawing at their limbs as their friends tried to hold them down.

Rodale pitied them. By Sariel's plague-pocked phallus, he did. They were him, just . . . beholden to a different master, a different addiction. The bottom of a bubbling glass had been his comfort; their magic, theirs. Now *all* of them were broken.

The larger wound? That one ached like a spear rammed up his arse, broken in half, then plunged down his lower shaft for good measure. But though it made Rodale hiss through grime-caked lips—though it bled anew each time he glanced at the smoke clouds rising from the Lyndwur—*this* was a wound he could still do something about.

He could still save her.

Would save her.

"And you," Rodale said, clapping one final man on the shoulder.

"You look like you could go another round." Silt-soaked blond hair slid from the man's brow as he looked up, a few strands catching in a hook-shaped cut on his cheek that oozed clear pus.

Herj. That was the bloke's name. A womanizer and a lush, so much like himself. Herj swallowed hard. Met Rodale's gaze, then lolled his head toward a pile of rubble and bodies strewn across the mouth of the harbor road. Most of the corpses were half-buried, limbs jutting at grotesque angles, blood pooling at the base of the mound.

But a Sylph lay on top, her combat suit peeled at the back to expose wreathes of twisting blue ivy atop her scarlet skin. She was like marble. Smooth curves, supple flesh, a rear holy Ellara would've envied.

Her beauty may have matched even rot-poxed Artyr's . . . if not for her missing fingers and head. They were gone. Whisked away by wind, blast, or blade, only a smear of crimson and a wad of raven locks left behind.

Rodale hadn't a clue what slew the girl, but he recognized the look in Herj's vacant eyes. Loss. Despair. The same emptiness that had clutched his heart as he stared at an empty bottle, one of many scattered across a bar filthier than a vagrant's piss-drenched trousers. Hating himself. Wishing for another sip, another drop.

Anything to take her place.

Anything to wipe away her memory.

But those days were past. By the Veneer, he *would* save her.

"Aye," Herj muttered, grabbing his rifle, heaving himself up. "Aye, I'll do it. Ain't nothin' left fer me here besides."

"You make this sound like a suicide mission," another soldier said, grinning as Herj took his place beside her.

"Ya mean it isn't?"

Rodale studied the group he'd assembled. Ten soldiers, ten souls. Mostly uninjured, but plenty of slashes, scrapes, and purpling bruises between them. Several limped, favoring one leg or the other. A man with a beard thicker than Rodale's southern bush couldn't move his left arm, blood dripping down his sleeve, between his fingers. They carried rifles, bayonets, scavenged short swords, crooked lengths of metal—anything they could find.

It wasn't what Rodale wanted, but Plague take him, it was the best he was going to get. The rest . . . He didn't bother to look. Their screams and moans, the reek of urine and vomit, told him all he needed to know.

Drawing himself up, puffing out his chest, Rodale strode down the line. "Gentlemen and gentleladies, what we're about to do is . . . " He trailed off. Waved his hand in the air as if struggling—*hoping*—to pull the proper words out of the ash-laced air.

Rodale failed. Cursing, he kicked a half-melted pistol off the pier. Watched it splash into the murky water below. There were no words for this. No right way to ask these brave wretches to give another pound of flesh.

Their *final* pound of flesh.

He jabbed a finger at the tower across the harbor. Over the Etrus bridge, past a pair of concrete bunkers and a wall of sandbags. "We're taking that voiding thing out."

The squad grumbled, shifting in place, staring at their feet.

"We take it down, we get our magic back. *They*"—Rodale pointed at their fallen mages, at the still unconscious Triaron and the freckled girl desperately trying to revive him—"get their *lives* back."

A few sympathetic nods. Fingers clenched around rifle stocks, lips pursed atop gritted teeth.

"And then the transports will fly. Then we can leave this void-forsaken city, maybe go someplace sunny for a change." Rodale shook his fist at the abyssal clouds. "Weather 'round here is bloody atrocious. Clouds, clouds, and more blasted clouds."

"What good'll that do us?" a grizzled veteran asked. His face was blistered and charred from his chin to his neck, a vicious wound that should have laid him in the ground. "We cross that bridge, we ain't gonna see any o' it."

Rodale stumped over to him. Leaned in, close enough to smell the coming rot. "Right now, we're dead. All of us, including the Triaron who took out *two* Sarc cruisers and half a dozen panzcraft beside. No one gets in the air. No one gets out. The end of the Resistance, a tidy little footnote scribbled in Sarc history books that snot-nosed brats won't even bother to read."

He faced Herj. "Is that what you want, son?"

"No, sir," the lad mumbled, gaze still locked on the mangled Sylph.

"I said, '*Is that what you want, son?*'" Rodale stalked toward Herj, grabbing his chin, thrusting it toward the rows of wounded. Toward the blood, tears, and wailing. "She's dead, they aren't. But that's liable to change when the next group of Sarc sightseers rolls in to lop our stones off and cook 'em with a side of butter.

"So, I'll ask again—I'll ask *all* of you," he said, raising his voice until it echoed off the collapsed storefronts, the debris-choked bay. "*Is this what you want?"*

"No!" the ten souls roared.

Shaking his head, Rodale tossed Herj away. "I don't believe you! Make me feel it. Make *them* feel it." He gestured at the Sarconian fortifications around the tower. "Void, make that spineless, teat-sucking, arse-coddling prick in the heavens feel it. Make him regret creating those inbred codpiece ticklers over there in the first place!"

Rodale drew in a deep breath. Ignoring every ache in his body—every painful memory, every failure—he tilted his head back and bellowed at the dark, roiling sky:

"IS

THIS

WHAT

YOU

WANT?"

Every soul—every mouth that could still speak, whimper, or whisper—answered his cry. They stamped their feet. Beat their rifle butts on the cobbles and screamed themselves hoarse. *"NOOOOOOOO!"*

"Good," Rodale said softly.

Bending down, he grabbed a rifle. Dusted the cinders from its stock, held it up to test the simple iron sights. It would do. The sound of metal scraping filled the sullen silence as Rodale drew the bayonet on his belt, as he slotted it home beneath the gleaming silver barrel. There was butcher's work ahead, and he was ready for it.

Rodale leveled the rifle at the bridge. At the tower that lay beyond it. A short march along the harbor, a straight charge, and then ...

"Let's go," he said, locking in his fate.

Condemning them all.

Those that could stood and saluted as they passed. Whispered prayers fluttered in the air, hurried pleas, frantic murmurs. A man lying on a blood-soaked coat began humming, his notes weak and off-key. Rodale recognized it at once: *Mavketh's Ballad.* The tale of a fallen knight, of a fallen house, of a fallen kingdom. One who had every reason to give up, but who stayed true to his heart regardless.

How appropriate. Rodale took up the slow, somber tune, whistling as he walked. *And when in white they laid him down, a wreath of ivy on his brow—*

"Wait."

The booming word brought Rodale to a halt. He turned, not at all surprised to find a limping Hue and a slip of a girl wielding a broken saber behind him. Lieutenant Unter and . . . Lilith. Yes, those were the names Jis had told him.

"The answer's, 'No,'" Rodale said.

Both bristled. He could practically see the girl's hackles rise as she bared her teeth. "But—"

Rodale pointed past them. At the Triaron, at the Sylph girl draped across his too-still chest. "*He* is your responsibility. No one else, not even the rest of these brave men and women. The Major needs him."

"She also you need," Unter said, taking a step closer, raising a palm toward him.

That was a good jest. Rodale chuckled, brought a finger up to wipe away an imaginary tear. They couldn't see his clenched jaw, his trembling gaze. Couldn't know how much he wished those words were true.

But even if they were, to acknowledge them was to fail. Rodale *had* to do this.

He *would* save her.

"She doesn't," he lied. "She needs the students she chose. And the Kingdom—the *world*—needs its Triaron. I am but a bit actor." Holding his rifle to the side, Rodale placed a hand on his breastplate and bowed. "He is the leading man, and you are the only ones who can see him to that end."

His shredded side ached. His men'ar drained limbs shook even as his soul continued to bleed, to crumble. But Rodale didn't break. He held his bow, maintained his smile.

For he had finally found his role in this tale.

He *would* save her.

"Why do this?" Lilith asked. "Why go so far?"

Rodale straightened and favored her with a grin charming enough to fleece a goddess' undergarments right off her sanctified nethers. "For the same reason all stories are told, my dear:

"Hope."

Chapter 65

Voice in the Dark

Renar ran.

Barreling into the walls, tripping over his own feet, he dashed down the corridor toward the faint glimmer of light at the far end. The stairs to the bridge. Safety.

Or the closest thing to it in this voidscape, Renar thought, slamming into the wall to dodge a swinging branch. He struck with his chest, his shoulder, bearing the blow with clenched teeth.

On his back, Sylette grunted but didn't wake. Whatever Renar did, he couldn't let her get hit. Not right now. Not when she couldn't defend herself. Adjusting her weight, he roared and charged once more.

The Lyndwur roared back. Whole segments of bark peeled away from their branches like removable armor plates, rustling, chattering as they opened and closed. Branches, vines, and roots bashed against *Dharmasya's* hull, seeking a way inside. More eyes blinked awake. Dozens of them, perhaps hundreds, bathing the hall in a sickly yellow glare.

Renar had no desire to paint them. The color was wrong, their movements grotesque, and that chittering . . . He couldn't close his ears, couldn't tune them out. The ringing! Dear Veneer, that awful ringing was stabbing through his skull again and again and—

"Left, Renar!"

He stumbled to the side, caught himself on a jagged pipe that slashed his hand bloody. No staccato retort rang out. Just a muzzle flash in the gloom, a whisper of wind as something tugged at his uniform sleeve.

Ahead, three eyes exploded in jets of smoky fluid, the branches attached to them writhing and flinching away, retreating into the shadows. Renar blinked. The ringing was fading, and suddenly he could see the sharp, ooze-tipped points on the vines—*roots?*—that had been poised to rip into him.

He glanced back, nodded his thanks to Major Reev. But the Ice Queen was already swinging her pistol to cover Darres as he scampered forward, kerium canister clutched in chalk-white fingers. Two more eyes detonated, two more branches retracted through the holes in *Dharmasya's* flank.

Yet it was effective as flinging stones at a dragon. A great bough *smashed* through the nearest viewport, scattering shards of glass, warping and twisting steel like it was mere clay. Renar watched Jhorn, the tattooed engimage, bash a wrench large as his arm against the creature.

It chipped a single piece of bark free. Chittering, the limb reared up and fell, squishing Jhorn to a bloody pulp.

"Jhorn? *Jhorn? JHORN!*"

The woman in braids shrieked, flattening herself against the inner bulkhead, hands slapping at the floor as she tried to push herself away. Into the metal. Away from this horror, this *thing* from the darkest bowels of forgotten legend.

Major Reev slotted another cartridge into her gun and continued to shoot, but the bough didn't seem to notice or care. For every eye she slew, more took its place. Renar couldn't count how many dotted the limb. Yellow was all he could see, a gas seeping from the eyes, leaking like sap from each razor-edged branch. Drops struck the floor and began to hiss, filling the passage with an acrid stench.

Renar wanted to gag. To roll over, retch, and cry all at once. He hadn't smelt something so awful since fighting Neha . . . lena . . .

That was it! Renar tore open his jacket, sending what few silver buttons he had left clattering. Out came his sketchbook, binding ripped and tattered, pages stained by blood and soot. He knelt. Pressed Sylette to the wall with one hand while the other frantically flipped through his drawings.

Not the Etrus chapel.

Not Mrs. Alhan's dinner, Grozza's Moravi gang, or the Nemare palace.

No, only a monster could fight a monster.

Renar caught sight of bladed tentacles. A grisly maw filled with too many teeth, four crimson eyes boring straight through his soul. He smacked his bloody palm to the page.

Light flashed. Power raced out of him, a sudden drain that left Renar clutching his chest, gasping for breath.

And out from the sketchbook lurched a monstrous tentacle, muscles rippling, suckers dripping ebony ink. It surged across the corridor. Slammed into the coiled bough, pinning it to the far wall in a spray of glass and tortured metal.

Only a monster could fight a monster.

And this time, Renar thought with a grin, *the Primal is on* our *side.*

Dark.

It stretched on and on and on forever, an infinite chasm, an endless pit. Matteo saw nothing within its depths. Heard nothing from its shifting shadows and silent shades. He simply floated. Drifted atop its unseen eddies and currents.

On and on and on forever.

Am I ... dead?

Not an unreasonable conclusion. Matteo had been aboard *Dharmasya* when the Sarcs somehow ... *erased* magic. Her engines died. Her heart ceased beating and her blood stilled. And then the airship plummeted into Lyndwur Forest. Branches snapping, metal rending, crew screaming as everything bucked and shook and twisted.

Then ... dark.

On and on and on forever.

This wasn't the Afterplane he'd been expecting. The Tome of Testament spoke of crystalline halls where everything was fashioned from gemstones. Floors, streets, buildings. Temples, aqueducts, and— Matteo's personal favorite—*libraries.*

Light was everywhere, refracted and channeled into brilliant rainbow hues by the crystals. There was no darkness. No sadness or suffering. The Creator's eternal radiance banished even the faintest shadow, and with them any scrap of mortal grief and anguish.

Yet Matteo feared. His regrets multiplied in the gloom, wrapping his wrists like rusted chains, clinging to his body like fetid ooze. What of his comrades? Were they safe? Did they win the battle? Had Velle survived?

Matteo pictured the Sylph, her form a glowing crimson. She swam through the air on sleek wings, raven hair rippling, eyes forever fixed on him and him alone. Grace was defined by *her,* not the other way around.

Velle waved at him. Glided nearer and extended her hand to grasp his. Warmth kindled in her eyes, flowing down her cheeks, neck, and into her palm. It was light. A ray of hope and salvation in this abyssal expanse.

Scrambling forward on invisible limbs, Matteo reached for her. Their fingertips brushed. An ember sparked, growing, surging.

Darkness speared her chest, an obsidian blade that appeared

from nowhere. Velle gasped. Glanced at him with pleading, tear-filled eyes as her lips spat blood. Then she . . . evaporated. Faded to mist, blended into the boundless nothingness.

Matteo's light was gone.

He screamed, but no sound emerged. He beat his fists on the ground, but it gave way, washing over his hands like smoke. There was no way to vent his rage, his despair. Matteo could only drown in it.

More regrets flooded in, waters black as pitch.

I didn't surpass Vallen.

Rising over his bent knees.

I failed them: Unter, Lilith, Renar, even Leon.

Tugging at his arms, his chest.

Sylette was right to doubt me.

Reaching his mouth. Rushing into his nostrils, dribbling down his ears.

And I let the Empire take my parents. They're dead. Tortured, then slain, and I did nothing to—

Matteo tilted his head back. Took one last breath, one last look at the void-touched sky.

A pinprick of light appeared above him. Soft at first, but growing brighter, stronger with each passing second. Matteo squinted as the glare increased. It was like a star, cutting through the heavens, bathing Lozaria with heat wherever it touched.

And Matteo *felt* that heat.

It was a weathered hand on his cheek. A whisper in his ear that everything would be alright.

It was a kiss on his forehead. Fingers ruffling his hair, a hug that barely left him room to breathe.

It was his favorite meal, a kind word at just the right time, encouragement at his bleakest moment.

It was safety on a dark night. A bed to sneak to when the shadows held monsters and a stern word when he ripped his clothes or left the dishes unwashed.

It was a new book on his Nameday. A shelter from every storm, a steaming mug and thick blanket set between him and everything cold and chilling and frightening in the world.

In short, it was *love*.

A light in the darkness. A voice in the dark.

Wake up, Matteo, the light said.

He did. Blinking the dust from his eyes, hissing at the pain lancing through his mesh-wrapped arms and chest. Blood trickled from a slash above his left eye, blurring his vision. A hundred bruises cried out in agony.

But Matteo was alive.

He could see.

And at least one of his regrets had no meaning, for a woman with sun-worn skin and chestnut-brown hair swept back in a tidy bun knelt before him, tears coursing down her cheeks, gripping his shoulders as if she'd never let go again.

"Matteo … " she sobbed.

He smiled, dry lips parting with a crack. "Mother."

An overwhelming urge to vomit tore Sylette from the darkness. She lurched forward, fingers clawing at the grated metal floor. Gasping, dry heaving, unable to expel a single drop but desperate to purge her insides all the same.

What was this pain, this emptiness? Sylette slammed back into the wall, barely resisting the urge—the *need*—to rip and rend and gouge out the hollow in her the chest. The bottomless wound where her men'ar should be.

No! she ordered her hands, stilling them as they touched the fabric above her heart. *She* was Sylette Artorios. Exile. Survivor. *She* would tell her body what to do. *She* would not be controlled. Not by her father, the Empire, or her disobedient magic.

A branch thick as a steel beam smashed into the bulkhead above her head, crumpling it like paper, showering her with sticky pieces of bark. Something hurtled after it. A rope, a tentacle, Sylette couldn't tell. Still panting, she rolled to the side as the great ebony cord coiled around the branch, drug it loose, and flung it out the gaping hole in the opposite wall.

"What the void … " Sylette breathed.

She started to rise, one shaky hand gripping what was left of the wall. Hammers wailed at her skull. Her body was lead. But Sylette retained enough sense to run, to flee.

That's what one did when there was no hope of winning.

Fingers closed around her waist as an arm slid under hers. "This way, princess," said a familiar voice.

Sylette half-expected to see Vallen. No one else referred to her so flippantly, so carelessly, so ...

But no, it was Renar. Cheeks smudged by soot and ink, black hair and stubble singed by furnace flames. She should have pulled away. Insisted she was fine walking on her own two feet.

Then the emptiness surged, and Sylette clutched at Renar's back and dry heaved into his chest. "Your magic ... " he whispered, trailing off as she glared at him.

"Not ... important," she hissed.

And it wasn't. Not when they were being attacked by what appeared to be a sentient *tree* and the roiling tentacles of a—

A *Draken?*

No, Sylette thought. *It couldn't be.*

She glanced back. Watched a sucker-coated appendage wrap around a trio of vines and *squeeze* until they exploded in a splatter of yellow goop. Anything the fluid hit melted. *Dharmasya's* hull, the deck, the gory remains of a body dressed in engimage coveralls. Sylette saw Major Reev stagger as some splashed on her uniform jacket, but she tore the garment free and cast it aside before the acid could reach her flesh.

The Ice Queen should've blocked the attack with a shield of ice. Should have frozen *all* the flailing roots, vines, and tentacles in place, as she'd done with Nehalena. What was stopping her? What was—

"The Ice Queen can't use magic," Sylette realized as they limped up the hall.

"Worse than that, missy." A red-haired man wearing a bizarre monocle materialized from the shadows of an open compartment. Where he should have held a weapon, the fool instead hugged a red canister the size of a desert melon.

"Not a single mage for a radius of," he paused, tapping a finger to his lip, "—Oh, I'd say three leagues, given the time ol' Archie's had to tinker with *my* design—can use magic. Wish I had time to run some calculations, but ... "

He waved at the battle raging around them. Tentacles strangling branches. Jagged roots slashing through tentacles. Metal buckling, glass cracking. Yellow slime dribbling down the vines, pooling on the trembling, tilting deck.

Ahead, two roots slithered through a hole in the ceiling, brushing aside pipes and wires as they came. Renar stepped forward, edging in front of Sylette. He held up his other hand, the sketchbook in it open to a bloody page.

Noble? Yes, but Sylette's heart wasn't moved by the pointless gesture. What did he hope to do? Give the tree a *paper cut?*

Muscles shrieking in torment, Sylette raised her left arm. Pointing it at the vines. *Willing* daggers to shred them to splinters.

The emptiness yawned, an infinite, unending void. Her arm fell. The roots charged, tips glinting with deadly sap.

"Take them, Nehalena!" Renar yelled.

Light flared as something *lunged* from the sketchbook. It was massive. Larger than Unter, covered in overlapping scales, dripping water as it rose. Four slotted eyes locked on the vines, narrowing as a crest of spines flared along its neck.

Her neck.

Nehalena the *Primal's* neck.

A crunch of her glittering fangs was all it took. She snagged the roots. Ripped them from the ceiling, tossed back her head, and devoured them in a single gulp.

Black ooze sprayed from the Draken's jowls as she swallowed, a drop of which struck Sylette's cheek. She flinched away, expecting her skin to burn, but no pain came. Hesitant, she touched it. Rolled it between her fingers. Was this ...

"Ink?" Sylette said.

She looked at the open sketchbook. At the thin wisps of pitch dangling from its cepyrus pages, down to the deck, along the hall, growing, expanding until they resolved into the massive tentacles that were keeping the forest at bay.

Realization struck like a dagger to the gut. "You have magic!" Sylette gasped.

"Thank you for stating the obvious, Lieutenant *Artorios*," Major Reev said, slotting a new magazine into her pistol as she and a cowering female engimage joined them. The Ice Queen still spat Sylette's true name like a curse against the Creator, but she pointed the reloaded gun toward the branches instead of her.

Progress, right?

"*You* have *magic*," Sylette repeated. "This is, I mean ... "

Renar glanced at her, then the floor. "I know. I'm sorry I do and you don't. We'll get things sorted out, and then—"

"Are you *kidding?*" she interrupted, waving at Nehalena's floating head. At the dozens of muscle-corded limbs beating back the fury of a *legendary forest.* "You're amazing, Renar! You could wipe out entire

639

Imperial platoons with this kind of magic. Tear down bunkers, destroy airships. Why"—Sylette glanced at Major Reev, a coy smile on her lips—"you might even be able to beat—"

"No," the Ice Queen growled as she shot the glowing eye of a root that came too close. "Not happening."

"So ..." Renar said. "I'm not ... useless?"

Sylette shook her head. "You never were."

He gulped, clenching the spine of his sketchbook as if dreading what he was about to say. "That's not what you told me at the Academy. Or the last time we were in Etrus."

"True."

Sylette swallowed her pride. Stuffed it into the chasm where her men'ar should be, spoke three words that curled her tongue like rancid milk.

"I ... was wrong."

A sharp cough slew the moment. With a sigh, Sylette turned to the red-haired engimage. "Yes?"

"A touching moment," he said. "Top marks for sentimentality, lovely little admission of fault there at the end. I think I may have shed not one, but *two* tears. However"—the engimage pointed at the stairs to the bridge—"it appears our exit is slightly more closed than your very warm, very open hearts."

Countless roots clogged the hall's far end, winding in from the lower decks, creeping down from the ceiling. They intertwined like snakes in a Vladisvar execution pit. Embracing as they coiled and twisted. Binding into cables stronger than steel, forming a living wall that could withstand a dreadnaught strike.

Metal groaned. The cruiser shook beneath them, shuddering as more branches, roots, and vines pierced her flesh. Was the forest trying to rip *Dharmasya* in half? Or was it cunning enough to *intentionally* block off its next meal's escape?

Sylette didn't much care which. "We need to get through that?"

"The *Kinloss* is on the other side," Major Reev said, "and it's our way out."

Raising his sketchbook, Renar grinned. "Time for some magic, Nehalena."

The Draken's mouth opened, rows of dagger-sharp teeth pulling back as a trio of hovering runes—each larger than the last—spawned within her gaping maw. Beads of moisture materialized from the air and drifted toward the orb of frothing white gathering in front of the Primal.

Sylette smiled as well. It was good to see Renar confident in his abilities, at last assured that his worth had *nothing* to do with what his fool of a father thought. And his new magic? A bonus.

One that will make him an excellent tool—no . . . comrade, Sylette corrected as a beam of roaring water shot down the corridor, *in the battles to come.*

She was *here.*

His mother. Anathea.

Matteo had longed for this moment. Imagined it a thousand different ways, including nightmares where it didn't happen at all. In those dark dreams, Matteo watched her die—watched Imperial torturers peel the flesh from her bones or behead her before a jeering crowd.

But here she was. After all his worries, tears, and struggles, she was—

His mother released him, grabbed a faded waterskin from her belt, and poured its contents on his head. Sticky fluid oozed down his forehead, trickling past his glasses, dripping onto his lips. It smelt *awful,* like weeks-old vegetable compost mixed with rancid fish and buckets of raw sewage.

Matteo gagged, thrashing at his restraints as his eyes watered. He needed to pinch his nose shut. To flee, to . . .

A drop hit his tongue.

He nearly vomited. Sylette's cooking, synth-oil, that strange mushroom dish he'd failed to make as a child—none of them were *half* as revolting as this . . . slime. Matteo opened his eyes, fury building in his burning throat.

"Why are you—"

"Stay still," his mother ordered.

More fluid struck his chest, staining his uniform a sickly shade of yellow, bleeding down his trousers. In seconds, Matteo was all but *drenched* in the foul concoction. He glared at Anathea, then past her at the rest of the bridge, searching for the reason behind her baffling actions.

She hadn't come alone. Other townspeople were with her, perhaps a half dozen in total. Sal stood at the bridge entrance, a ragged homespun robe draped from his shoulders, his customary grin and jolly belly missing. Instead of a knife, the butcher gripped an old, rusty blunderbuss in his meaty fingers. Orethia the apothecary knelt beside a fallen sensory mage, wizened fingers to the girl's neck, head slowly shaking.

Like Matteo, they were filthy. Garbed in thick rags, wielding an assortment of outdated firearms, blades, and knife-hewn spears, covered in a yellowish film. He lifted his head, sniffed the air. The same pungent aroma clinging to his clothes wafted from his mother, from *all* of them.

But why?

A soft scraping filled the bridge. A rustling like fabric or bark being dragged across metal. Matteo glanced at his mother, who placed a finger to her lips and nodded at the viewport. The glass was broken. Shattered into a thousand pieces, scattered across the floor, embedded in a trio of unlucky corpses.

One of which was moving. Captain Hurshik slid across the deck, his countless wounds leaving behind a crimson smear. Matteo forced down a shout. Hurshik had saved him. Sacrificed himself to get *him* to safety. And now he was ...

His eyes wandered to Hurshik's leg, and there they froze along with his breath and thoughts. A green-gray vine was wrapped about the man's ankle, sap seeping from its tip, dozens of glowing eyes blinking along its length.

It tugged the carcass through the glass.

Move! Matteo begged his trembling body. *MOVE!*

Over the mangled railing went Hurshik's corpse, his uniform ripping loudly in the somber silence.

Matteo leaned forward, pushing against the mesh that bound him. Hurshik was dead, but he still deserved a better end than—

A sun-worn hand blocked his way. "No," Anathea whispered. "He's gone."

And so he was. The vine dragged him through the viewport and over the lip, both disappearing into the white, snow-dotted forest beyond.

"Why did it ignore us?" Matteo asked.

Anathea rose, pulling out a chipped dagger and setting to work on his restraints. "More will be coming. We need to go." She looked over her shoulder at Sal and another tall, thick-bearded man. "Any other survivors?"

"Two." Sal pointed at the crash-seats right of the entrance, where a pair of delirious and bloody bridge techs were being helped to their feet.

Two? Was that it? After all their planning, Major Reev's determination, their training and sweat and grit, *two* was what remained of *Dharmasya's* bridge crew? It couldn't be. *It couldn't be, itcouldn'tbe, it—*

"Why?" Matteo asked again.

A strap snapped beneath his mother's blade, freeing his right arm. "I . . . think you know."

"The fluid. This *stench*." He nodded. "How long?"

She pursed her lips. Looked down at him, eyes narrowed, wrinkles creasing. "How long *what?*"

"How long have you been able to make the bloody miracle tincture that keeps the Lyndwur at bay?"

Matteo understood now. The yellow of the fluid, the yellow of the sap and the eyes. It was the same, a mixture distilled from the liquid running through the Lyndwur's veins that seemed to make it recognize them as parts of itself. They'd managed to reduce its acidic nature. A normal drop would melt through tissue, muscle, and bone, eating down and down and down as the victim shrieked and wailed.

Instead, Matteo's skin was simply reddening, a stinging rash that pricked like swarmites gnawing at his flesh. The pain was a far cry from the agony of his mother's stories. Her tales of hunters gone missing in the bowels of the winter forest. Of children lost in its frigid depths, never to be seen again.

"How long?" Matteo repeated when Anathea failed to answer.

His mother sighed. "As long as I've been alive, at least. Probably longer. But it doesn't matt—"

"Of course it matters!" Matteo snatched the dagger from her quivering fingers as she took a step back. Was she shocked at how upset he was? If so, *good*.

He hacked at the netting.

"Think of all the lives you could have saved."

The strands came loose, one at a time, ends pulling apart thread by thread.

"Merchants. Hunters. *Children*. Void," Matteo cursed as he cut, not caring that his mother heard. She couldn't wash his mouth out with soap anymore. "Even all the soldiers on this ship. We could have planned our assault differently if we'd had your serum. Used the forest as a staging area or lured the Empire into it."

"She didn't know," said a creaky, age-worn voice. Matteo turned toward Orethia, who was fixing the hem of her robe as she rose from the floor. "Until a month ago, only I did. And my predecessor. And her predecessor, and so on, just as it's always been from the time of the Veneer until now."

"So, you've kept up the lie," Matteo accused.

Orethia shook her head. "I've held on to the *truth*."

"What truth?"

"The Lyndwur is sacred, young Alhan."

Orethia waved out the viewport, where more vines, branches, and roots were crawling up *Dharmasya's* hull. They slithered into the charred blasts inflicted by the Sarcs, crept down the gaping chasms where her turrets should have been.

It was like worms reveling atop a fallen beast, its carcass barely cold. Matteo's stomach churned at the thought. At the memory of the comrades this . . . *thing* was taking from him.

"How many other sentient forests dot Lozaria?" Orethia continued. "How many organisms that span leagues—that have an intelligent mind and can communicate over vast distances? We of Etrus are called to protect this marvel given us by the gods—"

Matteo snorted. *"You* were called to protect this *death trap*."

"—which is why I only shared my secret to save the town." Orethia gestured at Anathea. At Sal, at thick-beard, at the others Matteo vaguely recognized but whose names were lost to him. "When the Empire began their persecution—when they began to take *hostages*—I told the others we could hide in the forest. That we'd be safe there."

"We laughed at her at first," his mother said.

"Until," Sal chuckled, a bit of warmth returning to his flabby cheeks, "she spent the night inside and returned unscathed. That was all the convincing we needed."

"Some reacted as you did," thick-beard added as he collected discarded weapons. "Lost, betrayed. But we did what we needed to survive."

"The Lyndwur *saved* us, Matteo." Anathea reached toward him, tears forming beneath her eyes. "Mother Junica helped us escape through Kinloss' tunnels, a few at a time, slowly and carefully, until one day everybody who wanted out was free. If not for our presence here, we wouldn't have seen your ship crash, wouldn't have been able to come to your aid. We protected the forest for generations, and now it's protecting us."

Matteo slashed through the last strap around his waist, casting it aside and standing up. His muscles ached. His skin burned, his eyes throbbed, and the hole in his chest yawned like he'd been pierced by three spears tied together. Every fiber of his being *screamed* for Matteo to lie down, curl up, and surrender.

But his friends needed him.

Velle needed him.

Tucking the dagger into his belt, Matteo took one shaky step, then another, only stopping when he was shoulder to shoulder with his mother. The woman he loved more than any other. The woman who, along with Orethia and all of Etrus, had failed him and the Resistance.

Had failed the entire Kingdom.

He asked one final question: "Father?"

"Alive," Anathea said, brown eyes boring into his. "He's with the others."

Matteo nodded, then bent to kiss her forehead.

Yes, he still loved her. More than the stars loved the heavens or day loved the dawn. She was his voice in the dark. His safe haven from every storm, every fear, and *all* his suffering.

And despite his misgivings, despite his distrust, Matteo would not let her down.

Chapter 66

On the Precipice

Vines clashed with tentacles, bark chips flying, ink splashing on the stairwell's walls and ceiling like bloody brush strokes. Renar dashed straight through the carnage, sketchbook held before him. The worn, leather-bound pages had always been his refuge, the world he retreated to when reality became too much to bear.

And now . . .

Now they were saving him again.

Even as Renar's heart hammered against his ribs, even as stray branches slashed shallow furrows in his arms, he couldn't help smiling at that thought. His father had been wrong. The soldier had been wrong.

His art—his passions—*were* useful.

"Renar!" Sylette yelled, pointing over his shoulder at a tangle of roots twisting together to block their path again.

Drawing in a breath, Renar slammed his bloody palm atop the crimson-stained page. "Nehalena!"

The Draken's head reappeared, scales rendered in oozing black, fangs a chalky white. Coils of ink gathered at the apparition's snout, launched with the fury of storm-driven waves. The vines withered before the frothing onslaught. Yellow fluid erupted from hundreds of cuts, and the tattered, dismembered remains collapsed to the floor, lifeless.

"Push on!" Major Reev shouted from the rear, pistol retorts echoing up the steps along with her voice.

Renar needed no encouragement. He plowed through the listless vines, emerging into a circular chamber larger than any of the halls they'd passed through. Pipes and wires dangled from the ceiling, and a spray of glass shards from curved viewports on either side crunched beneath his boots.

There were no bodies, no corpses, though the acrid tang of iron and forest ooze was everywhere. Strange scarlet smears led across the floor, up the walls, and out the windows. Out into the chittering, groaning forest.

No, Renar thought, stomach churning as his throat tightened. *It couldn't be . . .* eating *them, could it?*

"Don't think about it," Sylette said, following his gaze. She brushed past him, dodging holes in the deck, sidestepping steel beams that jutted through the room like broken ribs.

"Where are we?" Renar asked.

"Central hub. Bridge is on the next level, but what we need is . . . "

Sylette reached the right wall, then poked her head out the ruined viewport. Was she insane? Sticking her head in a *dragwyrm's maw* was probably less dangerous than going out in this twisted forest.

Renar raced toward her, hand on his sketchbook, pages glowing with a soft light. Power left him, surging through the air, morphing into living ink and paint. He didn't know how his magic worked, but Jay could theorize over that later.

For now, it only mattered *that* it worked.

Tentacles shot from the hull beneath Sylette, reaching up and covering her in a shield of scales and twitching muscles. The vines struck an instant later, sharpened barbs thudding into Renar's barrier, ripping free gobs of wispy Draken flesh that smeared the window frame black.

Yet Nehalena didn't cry out. She was a copy, a phantom with the original's abilities but no life of their own. Or at least that's how it seemed to Renar. As Sylette darted away from the viewport, the Draken's tentacles uncurled and wrapped about their assailants, hugging them tighter and tighter and tighter until they popped in an explosion of yellow mist.

"Such a handy ability," Sylette said, raising her arm and flexing her fingers. When nothing happened, she sighed and shook her head. "Still nothing."

Renar took a step toward her. "What were you thinking, getting that close to—"

"The ship's still there." *Aaannnd* Sylette was moving again, making for a circular hatch in the right wall. Injuries, losing her magic, a deadly forest . . . *nothing* slowed the girl down.

"The *Kinloss?*" he asked.

Sylette stopped at a control panel beside the hatch, the light above it as dark as the forest gloom outside. She punched a few buttons.

No response.

Grabbed the edge of the hatch and tugged until her cheeks turned red.

The metal refused to budge.

"Yes," Sylette huffed, placing her hands on her hips. "But the code doesn't work and there's no power to operate the blasted thing manually."

Hurried footfalls sounded behind them. Jay, still clutching his

647

canister of kerium, hurtled from the stairwell. He stumbled around a yawning tear in the deck that pierced the next three levels, then collapsed against a beam that trembled and groaned as it took his weight.

Sylette cocked an eyebrow. "Is now a good time to relax?"

"Rest is the mind's fuel, my dear," Jay replied, using his lab coat's sleeve to wipe sweat from his cheeks. "Just give me a moment and I'll be in tip-top shape."

More gunfire echoed through the room, along with flashes of bright light. "You're going to be resting permanently if you don't get that voided airship flying in the next five minutes."

Major Reev staggered backward into the room, pushing the last surviving engimage ahead of her with one hand while the other fired her pistol at something just out of sight.

Click! Click!

Renar knew that dreadful sound—an empty magazine. Cursing, the Ice Queen fumbled at her belt for another clip, but her bandolier was bare. She'd used the last of her ammo.

Vines slithered up the steps, along the darkened walls and ceiling. Major Reev tossed her sidearm at them, then turned to run. But . . . where were they supposed to flee to? They could retreat to the bridge above, but without the *Kinloss,* they'd have no way off the ship.

Either they made their stand here, or they'd perish with *Dharmasya.*

Renar pressed his fingers to his sketchbook, blurring the ink strokes he'd labored to create, blotting the ragged pages with his blood. He *could* match the forest. He *would* give them the time they needed.

More tentacles shot from the deck, the roof, the bulkheads, joining, twisting, melding. Their spearhead tips clasped together, forming a wall across the stairwell. A chittering louder than a swarm of flit-gnats rose on the other side as untold vines railed against the barrier. Smacking and tearing. Striking and stabbing.

But they couldn't get through. Not through Nehalena the Primal. Not through *his* magic.

Then the pain hit Renar.

He gasped, clutching at his chest, feeling a trickle of warmth slide from his nose and over his lips. Blood. He tasted blood and something *searing* was stabbing into his skull, rooting around in his guts. His fingers ached as if they'd been smashed by a hammer and . . . Yes, there was a hollow growing in his breast, an emptiness, a *chill.* Like someone had ripped out his heart and left him to freeze on a snowy mountaintop.

Cold, cold, *cold* ...

"Renar, you're bleeding!"

Something swiped at his nose, brushing away the blood. Sylette? He felt her heave him up, the blessed warmth of her body seeping into his icy veins.

"It's MIS," she said, voice coming from a thousand leagues away. "He's not used to using magic. I doubt he can last much longer. Get that door open!"

Renar blinked. He *would* stay standing. He *would* last. Gritting his teeth, growling against the pain, he straightened his back and raised his sketchbook in trembling arms.

The Lyndwur was crafty. It stopped attacking Nehalena, going instead for the non-magical pipes, wires, and metal flanking her tentacles. Every time a vine broke through, Renar pushed another finger to the page and summoned a new piece of the Draken to block the gap. It was agonizing, like jabbing his finger into blazing coals.

But he *would* endure.

He *would* last.

"The hatch's stuck tighter than my gran in her chair after a Festivus feast!" Jay grunted.

"We need a crowbar," Major Reev suggested. "A beam, a pipe, something for leverage."

Not fast enough. But he ...

Renar chuckled, more blood pooling in his mouth. *I* am *fast enough.* He slid his fingers across the book, leaving behind a streak of blackest scarlet. They were one color now—one soul, connected to his own.

Two tentacles spawned inside the hatch, gripping its halves, forcing them apart with a tortured squeal. Renar coughed, the cold inside him spreading. Claiming his neck, creeping down his spine. Was that enough? Had he done enough to be useful?

Jay cheered, rushing into the shadowy umbilical tube connecting the *Kinloss* to *Dharmasya*. Distantly, Renar heard metal shifting. A grate being lifted? Had Jay found the ship's engine?

"How long will it take to modify?" Major Reev asked.

A pause, long as years. "With just me and Hanni? Twenty minutes at best."

Sylette squeezed Renar's arm, peering up at him with eyes he could barely see. She was little more than a silver blob with ears and lips. "You've got . . . five," Sylette said, glancing between him and the thrashing forest. "Maybe." Vines were beginning to crawl in through the ruined viewports, and Renar would soon have to split his focus.

"Not possible," Jay called back. "Hanni doesn't know how kerium interacts with the fuel injectors, so it's basically down to me to update this last-gen hunk of junk. Seriously, is that *goompa gum* holding the illyrium collection rods together? If there were two of me, then I'd have this done in a flash, but ... " The engimage's grumbling trailed off as Major Reev started shouting threats at him.

Two of him.

Two of him.

Renar sought the edge of his sketchbook, shivering fingers trying and failing to turn the page. Void and Oblivion! He needed a blank page, a new canvas.

Sylette's fingers found his, their warmth flowing into him like rays of pure sunlight. "What is it?" she asked. "What do you need?"

"F-flip the page," Renar said through chattering lips. "And ... and hand me the scrivle hidden inside the binding."

"What are you going to do?"

He gave her a weak grin. "I'm going to ... *draw* Jay the help he needs."

Etrus, the coastal gem, was no more.

Rodale watched her death throes from behind a pile of rubble near the city's grand bridge. His men were still getting in position to assault the Sarc jammer, and it wasn't as though there was anything else to look at. Destruction was everywhere he bloody well turned.

Fires raging across the rooftop gardens, climbing toward Etrus' peak, leaving ash and cinders in their wake.

No more greenery, no more beauty.

Blocks of leveled buildings, their sand-colored remnants stained a deep scarlet by Darmatian blood.

No more boisterous market stalls, no more bright festival squares.

Twisted metal hulks jutting from a debris-clogged harbor, straining like skeletal fingers for a sky they'd never again reach.

No more lively dockyards, no more joyous tavern nights.

Rodale heard phantom screams on the wind, the cries of comrades whose magic had been torn from them. He tasted copper on his lips— his own blood and that of those who'd fallen beside him. The stench of burned flesh mixed with the swirling smoke, clinging to his throat, turning his hollow stomach. Rodale buried his nose in his suit's collar, wishing he could smell Jis' scent, *any* scent but the death around him.

Why had they come here? What were they fighting for? And if *this* was what they left in their wake . . . what was the point of it all?

Rodale clenched his fist on his rifle stock. Steadied his breathing to match the rhythm of the voidspawn pounding on his skull, the ache in his rotten heart. By Ellara's engorged twat and all her debauched siblings, he *would* save her.

That was the only point that still mattered.

A soft scuffle preceded Herj as he crawled up beside Rodale, careful not to expose his sun-scorched blond hair above the rubble. The Sarcs on the far side of the bridge were flustered—they *had* lost two cruisers to a floating brat, which was a hoot—but not so disoriented they wouldn't plug anyone trying to cross the canal.

"Everyone's in position," Herj whispered, waving at the groups of Resistance soldiers huddling behind other piles of debris.

Rodale nodded. They weren't going to get closer than this without being seen. Quick as a pimple-faced deckhand on his first brothel visit, he rose and glanced over the collapsed pillar. One last peek to see if maybe— *maybe*—there was an approach that *wouldn't* get their stones shot off.

Sure enough, the bridge was a kill zone. A shell had struck the center, leaving behind a blackened crater that narrowed the bridge from ten to six meters at its midpoint. Any statues, benches, or columns that might have given them cover had been shredded by the blast, dotting the span with marble shards—a hand here, a head there, centuries of history obliterated in an instant.

And the bridge itself shook with every distant peal of thunder, trembling like a virgin bride on her, well . . . Rodale chuckled. Jis had never fully appreciated his . . . *deviant* sense of humor. Perhaps it was time to lay off the warped analogies.

Here at the end.

For her.

Herj chanced his own peek, sighing as he pulled back. "That gun's gonna rip us ta shreds."

An eighty-eight-millimeter flak cannon, the kind of artillery Rodale expected to see on a dreadnaught, not mounted on a bunker between him and Jis' freedom. It was a *nasty* piece with rounds that could pierce a panzcraft and peel it open like Vida's succulent . . .

Void and Oblivion, am I going to have to work on that, Rodale thought, scratching crusted blood from his stubble.

"Don't worry about that gun," he said, holding up his hands so his other squad members could see. Sticking out a finger, he mimed pointing it away from himself, across the bridge toward the not-so-distant Ascendancy border. "It's aimed the wrong way, and they don't have the illyrium juice to swing it around quickly. By the time they crank it to face us, we'll have taken the bunker."

"And the rows o' rifles lined up 'hind those sandbags?" Herj asked. His fingers fidgeted, drumming against his weapon, plucking at the trigger guard.

"That's ... " Rodale shrugged. "Well, at least half of them left to check on their downed cruisers. That leaves, what? Ten? Fifteen? Those are fair odds." *If this were an open field,* he added silently.

Herj nodded, but his twitching fingers and darting eyes betrayed him. The lad wasn't reassured, not in the least. Rodale couldn't blame him. His girl, that headless Sylph draped across the rubble down the harbor thoroughfare, was gone. And now he was liable to join her.

What a twisted world this was.

"Why?"

Rodale blinked, realizing he'd drifted off somewhere. Off into dark thoughts, ones that bubbled up from the blighted abyss of his soul despite his best efforts to resist them: *will she weep for me when* I'm *gone?*

"Why what?" Rodale replied, popping the clip from his rifle, counting the rounds inside. Six bullets, then six more on his belt. A bayonet, a knife, and an illyrium grenade as dun and dead as his magic. That was all he had to fight with.

All he had to save her.

Herj grabbed Rodale's arm, squeezing it with ash-white fingers, pleading eyes boring into his. "Why are ya here, sir? Ya could've ordered us ta do this ourselves, put Farrod"—he pointed at the man with the freshly burned face—"or someone else in charge. With all due respect, this ain't a job fo' brass, so I can't figger out why yer here instead o' hangin' back like General Iolus an' his ilk."

Rodale took the soldier's hand and gently removed it. "If General Iolus ordered you to take out that jammer, would you do it?"

"I ... I'm not sure I understand—"

"After everything that's happened—your dead comrades, the blood and the screams and the tears—would you take another step on

652

that man's orders?"

Iron filled Herj's gaze. "No."

"Then you have your answer." Rodale rose to a crouch and chambered a round with a soft click. "Words are lovely things, Herj. They can tell inspiring stories, paint breathtaking pictures, sway hearts and minds. But words alone accomplish nothing unless someone is willing to *act* on them. Which is why I ... "

Rodale placed one palm on the fallen pillar and swung himself over the top. " ... would never ask a soldier to do something I wouldn't do myself."

He roared no battle cries. Shouted no curses nor bellowed to steel his courage.

He didn't need to.

He *would* save her.

The sight of Etrus burning didn't bother Mikus as it might other men. He'd seen the same scene play out again and again throughout his military service. Villages reduced to rubble. Smoke-clogged skies and corpse-littered streets. Hollow eyes set in ash-smeared faces, survivors who stared at the wreckage of their lives and saw in it their own reflections.

Mikus pitied them—the kind of pity one has for the corner drunk or a filthy back alley vagrant covered in his own piss. Better them than him, right?

Wrong.

Rittermark Silesia was leading Mikus' squad *toward* the devastation, not away from it as he'd so very much prefer. Step by torturous step, his battered body screaming with each footfall, a throbbing hole in his chest where his magic should be.

How does she do it? Mikus wondered for the umpteenth time, gazing at Silesia's silt-stained back as they marched. At her matted hair, torn jacket, and the crimson patch peeking through her undershirt. He ached like he'd gone three rounds with Sergeant Jard the Dreadnaught *after* visiting four pubs and five brothels the night before.

Silesia had to be feeling at least a fraction of his pain, right? And if so, why was she pushing herself—and more importantly, *him*—so hard? For the sake of her plot with Rittermarschal Titania? Or did it go deeper than that?

"Are we winning?" Jotun asked from the rear of their small column.

Mikus glanced over the top of the drainage ditch they were following. The warehouses and hangars to their right were mostly undamaged, just a few gaps in their walls and roofs where airship debris had plummeted from above. Those skies were now clear. Empty except for ash, smoke, and the occasional flash of distant lightning. A slow rain fell, chilling Mikus through his leathers, adding another stone to the pile of grievances he had against Silesia.

The quiet was eerie. Without his magic, Mikus heard nothing but the soft plopping of the rain and the squelching of their boots as they waded up the channel. The tang of char overwhelmed his weakened nostrils. Yes, fires raged in the city across the bay, but where were the soldiers who had set them? The explosions and carnage of a battle being waged?

Silesia answered Jotun without breaking stride. "We're losing."

"How can you tell?"

Cursing under his breath, Mikus glared over his shoulder at Hursch, who was prodding the cracked canopy of a crashed lancerjet with his bayonet, trying to wedge it open. Didn't the brat know better than to press the Rittermark for details?

"Our crash," Silesia said. "It was the work of Archimas' device— the prototype Stetson was forbidden to use. Even *he* isn't foolish enough to activate it unless he had no choice."

Dar chuckled, shaking beads of water from his thick beard. "I reckon he didn't get command's memo. Just like this"—he snagged Hursch's collar as he passed, hauling the scrawny youth back into line— "little thief."

"I was gonna check on the pilot," Hursch grumbled, jerking free of the bear-man's grip.

Jotun narrowed his skeletal eyes. "Sure you were."

"Mission first, loot later," Mikus hissed, hoping Silesia wouldn't hear.

For once, the Rittermark was lost in her thoughts, staring through the misty rain at a hill on their left. A few twisted trees clung to its crown while a scree of chalky stones poured down toward a fence at its base. Mikus' eyes weren't what they'd been, but it was impossible to miss the rusted red sign clinging to the fence's sagging iron links:

DARMATIA-ASCENDANCY BORDER
NOT AN OFFICIAL CROSSING

"Do you see them?" Silesia asked, tilting her head up. Water snaked off her hair in rivulets, running over her lips, dripping along her ice-pale neck.

She almost—*almost*—looked like an ordinary woman instead of the voidspawn she was.

"See who?"

Mikus squinted at the hilltop, seeing only the hazy outlines of two trees and a mass of shifting shadows beneath them. How did ordinary people function without enhancive magic?

Dar raised his rifle, sighting down its scope. "I've got 'em, Rittermark. Couple o' Blauers who forgot they're too fat ta hide under a camo cloak. An' is that . . . "

The sergeant's eyes went wide as his tongue ran along his upper lip, slowly, sensually. Dear ancestors, the combat-nut was getting riled up.

"Dar . . . " Mikus cautioned, still trying to locate the Hues his squadmate had seen. Behind those scraggly bushes? That pile of rocks that was just a *bit* too orderly?

Dar's fingers tightened atop his rifle. "They didn't come out for a stroll. No ma'am, they have *artillery* up there. Permission ta plug the buggers and see what happens?"

"Denied," Silesia said, turning back toward the airfield. "It isn't our mission, so it's not our problem."

"But—"

Crack! Crack-crack!

Gunfire broke the sodden stillness, sporadic at first but growing in strength as more rifles joined the staccato symphony. Mikus snapped his head around as he slammed shoulder-first into the muddy slope of the ditch. He was already soaked, and a little dirt was better than a bullet to the brain.

"Where's it coming from?" he shouted.

Jotun pointed past the hangars. "They're not shooting at us. It's coming from the bridge."

A glance confirmed his words. The airfield complex opened onto a broad field at its southern end, a swathe of greenery that nestled against the canal waterfront and the broad bridge fording it. Yet most of the bushes, shrubs, and trees had been cleared away, replaced by cement bunkers, trenches topped with sandbags, and a long-barreled artillery piece. Above the new construction loomed a bronze tower, the rings jutting from it shaking fast enough to blur.

And past it, crossing the rain-slick bridge, was a charging squad of what Mikus could only assume were Darmatian rebels. They came on in a thin wave, snapping off shots with their rifles as they ran, trying to spread out to present harder targets.

It worked . . . for a few seconds. Then a man with a beard to rival Dar's took a round through his breastplate, going down in a tumble of splayed limbs and blood. A woman at the edge lost her jaw in a spray of gore, staggering over the bullet-chipped parapet, falling into the dark waters below.

A wild shot caught a defender in the shoulder, knocking him back into the trench. Two white-robed salvators rushed down the line to help him, ducking low to avoid the same fate.

"Shouldn't we go reinforce them?" Dar asked. His fingers were stroking the barrel of his gun—his *Lida*—and his breathing was short and ragged.

Hursch snorted. "Why bother? The Darms are getting massacred."

Another Darmatian stumbled, calf pierced and gushing blood. His screams railed against Mikus' ears until another shell silenced them for good. The odds weren't in the rebels' favor: perhaps half a dozen attackers with no cover against twice as many defenders in pillboxes and trenches. Even *he* wouldn't mind sticking his neck out for such an easy victory, provided there was bonus combat pay.

"And that . . . cock-shaped thing?" Dar waved at the tower. "We're not worried about protectin' it?"

"*Jammer,*" Jotun corrected, rolling his eyes. "It has a ball on *top*, Dar, not the bottom. One ball. *One.* Ancestors, does *everything* have to be about teats and stones with you?"

"It's long, it's tan, an' it's juttin' straight toward the sky, hard as can be. What do ya want me ta call it?"

"Anything but a . . . "

Ignoring them, Mikus turned to Silesia, only to find her rounding the next bend in the drainage ditch. "That's Archimas' device, right? Do you think the Rittermarschal would want us to—"

"No."

The Rittermark didn't pause. She kept marching, eyes forward, attention fixed on the far end of the airfield. A wrecked heavy cruiser lay there, dead engines spewing ebony smoke, ravenous flames devouring her upper decks. Only the bridge remained untouched, like a heretic hung above the executioner's blaze.

"We have a mission," Silesia said, "and until it's accomplished, nothing else matters."

Mikus gulped. He knew *precisely* who the executioner was here. And the heretic? Well, for his sake, Mikus hoped he'd already perished.

The alternative was far, far worse.

Dear Veneer, there were *two* of him.

Two Jaydens.

Two insufferable engimages who wouldn't shut up about how difficult this job was, how they'd love to shove this invention in Dr. Archimas Descar's face, and how bloody clever they were for creating kerium in the first place. Jis had never been the praying type, but beset by their incessant jabbering and unable to freeze them in a block of ice, she was warming to the idea.

That, or she could just throw herself out the nearest window. Death by stab-happy vines was looking more and more attractive right now.

"If we connect this pipe to this one, we can bypass the old illyrium manifold and increase output by about twelve percent," Jay-One said, digging his oil-stained hands deeper into the *Kinloss'* open engine compartment.

Jay-Two nodded. "Brilliant idea! Fantastic, superb. And while you're in there, why not reroute power from the pistons past the crystal collection chamber and straight into the drive shaft? It's a waste of fuel as it is."

The likeness was uncanny. Everything from Jay's unkempt hair, to his baggy lab coat, to that ridiculous multi-colored monocle he wore had been reproduced in flowing lines of ink. Yes, the eyes of Renar's creation were pitch-black, the textures on his clothes less detailed, and his flesh rendered with smudged shadow instead of ruddy tones. But the rest—including his personality—was so spot on it made Jis' skin crawl.

"Excellent suggestion, me," Jay-One replied. "It's been *ages* since I worked with someone competent."

"Are you paying yourself a compliment?"

Jay-One grinned, smudging his cheek with grease as he wiped sweat from his face. "Of course! If I'm a genius, there's no reason *not* to say so."

"Quite right. Now ... "

Jis tried to tune them out, tightening her grip on the twisted pipe in her hands, focusing on the entry hatch linking the *Kinloss* to *Dharmasya*. The chamber beyond was a mess of thrashing tentacles and whipping vines. Streaks of ink coated the floor, the walls, the ceiling. Yellow goop dribbled from the shattered viewports and pooled in the room's corners.

The tattered, shriveled husks of lifeless roots lay *everywhere.*

She couldn't see Renar, or Sylette who was doing her best to support him. *How?* Jis thought, her stomach twisting with a pain different than the empty ache in her chest. *How did I ever think they'd betray us?*

If not for them, the ship would already be lost. And if that happened, they couldn't reach their soldiers stranded in Etrus. She wouldn't be able to reach—

Jis blinked, gritting her teeth. She couldn't think about Rodale now, not until they'd solved their own problems. He would be alright. He *would* be alright.

A tap on her shoulder made her spin, pipe lashing out toward the throat of her attacker. Jis saw the glint of blue glass, a shock of messy red hair. She stopped her strike a hairsbreadth from Jay's . . . Jay-*One's* throat.

"What?" Jis growled.

Jay-One jerked his thumb over his shoulder. "We're just about done. Hanni's ready to spark the ignition chamber, and my other half is closing up the last few piston chambers."

"And?"

"And it would be mighty nice if you sent someone up front to fly this thing."

Jis' breath caught. "You . . . you don't know how to operate an airship?"

"No," Jay-One said, shrugging. "I just want to build the things. I'm more than happy to leave dangerous stuff like piloting my metal monstrosities to people a few shards short of a full crystal."

"You can't be serious . . . "

Jis turned, placing one hand on the wall of the cargo compartment as she limped back onto the trembling gantry connecting the two airships. There was no time for this nonsense. Every second they delayed cost her more lives, comrades who had trusted *her* to lead them. Who saw her as a hero when she was truly anything but.

She saw the crimson stains on *Dharmasya's* decks. The discarded, mangled weapons, the ragged strips of uniforms snagged on jagged sheets of metal. How many had already been lost? How many more would die because she, because she . . .

A pilot. Jis needed a pilot. She stumbled forward, pipe held up to ward off the vines she knew would come, bleary, aching eyes staring at nothing at all.

"Renar," she called, stopping at the edge of the hatch. "We need to clear a path to the bridge. We need . . . to find . . . Matteo."

The chasm in Jis' chest yawned. Dozens of scratches, scrapes, and bruises tugged on her like lead weights, bidding her to fall. To lay down and submit. Blood soaked her undershirt, dripping down her pants, sucking the warmth from her flesh. Heat. Cold. Such strange, strange sensations.

But, Jis smiled as she toppled, *at least I finally got to feel them.*

Arms caught her, clutching her shoulders as they righted her. Straining her neck, Jis peered into a pair of cracked glasses barely clinging to an ashen, blood-flecked face.

"You look like crap," she whispered, letting her head fall against Matteo's shoulder.

The boy winced but didn't try to remove her. "Good to see you too, Major."

It *was* good to see him. If Matteo was safe, then their pilot issue was—

Jis recoiled, nostrils wide and eyes burning. His clothes, his hair, his cheeks . . . all of it was awash with a yellow fluid that was as rancid as—no, *worse* than—the Academy locker rooms after a flag-brawl match. She spun away, coughing, spitting, doing everything she could to eliminate the foul stench.

A tan woman with tawny hair drawn up in a bun knelt before Jis, wrinkles creased in an apologetic smile. "You'll get used to the smell," she said, tossing the contents of a faded waterskin at Jis.

"You could have warned her," Matteo said, easing one of Major Reev's arms over his shoulder.

"Too slow."

His mother cinched the waterskin back onto her belt, then counted the remaining pouches of their special tincture. Only two of the sacks were still full, bouncing against her belt as she moved.

"Is that it?" Matteo asked, chest tightening. "Is that all you have left?"

"It takes a long time to brew. If you want the recipe, then—"

He shook his head, eyes scanning the circular chamber. Sylette stood in the middle, Renar draped across her shoulders. Dark circles ringed his eyes, and the skin of his cheeks and arms was sallow like aged paper. His every breath was a struggle, hoarse and shallow, and his outstretched arm trembled as if ready to shatter and break.

Why was he . . .

Matteo's gaze fell on the notebook in Renar's hand. Ebony tentacles rose from its pages, surging forth to strike at the vines and branches piercing through the walls, ceiling, and floor. For now, the battle was evenly matched. Vines were squeezed until they burst or ripped from their stalks. Branches sliced through tentacles, splattering the deck with gobs of what looked like black paint or ink.

Could . . . could Renar use *magic* now? He shouldn't be able to, yet Matteo couldn't deny the evidence. Light blossomed within the sketchbook, drawing a cry from Renar as blood dribbled from his nose. A monstrous head appeared before him, a terrifyingly familiar visage crowned with spikes and filled with fangs long as Matteo's arms.

His heart skipped a beat as it lunged forward—not at him, thank the Veneer, but at a tangle of vines forcing their way through the window. Fangs flashed, the Draken roared, and acrid goop exploded from the mauled pieces of the Lyndwur.

Renar stumbled, turning as he and Sylette sank to their knees. His head lolled, gaze distant, unfocused. Then his eyes found Matteo. A grin split his scarlet-streaked lips, and he nodded. Just a tilt of the head, the best he could manage.

And Matteo smiled back. For the briefest of instants, he'd been jealous of Renar. *Why should* he *have magic when there's a gaping void in my stomach? When* I *can't so much as touch my men'ar?*

But Renar was fighting. Defending their comrades, protecting their ship. How he'd obtained his magic didn't matter, so long as he was wielding it for the right reasons.

Matteo bent, cupping his mother's cheek with his free hand. "My friends need me. No one else can fly the ship, you see. If there was someone who could do it, I'd stay with you, but . . . Father . . . he'll understand, right? I mean, I have to—"

Taking his hand in hers, she leaned forward and kissed his forehead, his cheeks, his chin, and finally his nose. It was their sign of love. A magic spell that made scrapes and aches disappear, that could right every wrong in the world, no matter how tragic or awful.

It nearly broke Matteo. He wanted nothing more than to wrap her in his arms, to return with her, meet his father, and flee somewhere this wretched war hadn't touched.

But . . .

"Go," Anathea whispered, eyes twinkling as her tears swelled.

"I've saved my family. Now you need to save yours."

Robes rustling, she stood and crossed the room, joining Sal, Orethia, and the other Etrusians at the stairs to the lower decks. She didn't look back. Not a peek, not a glance. To do so, to let Matteo see her cry, would shatter his resolve into a thousand fragments.

And for that, mother, I thank you from the bottom of my heart.

"She's a good woman," Major Reev said, her breath weak against his ear.

Matteo didn't jump or flail with embarrassment as he might once have. Careful not to drop the Major, he slowly turned, entering the dark hatch. Stepping onto his ship.

Returning to the only home he still possessed.

And, for now, that was enough.

"I know," he said, letting his tears fall.

Chapter 67

Last Gasp

A little more.

Just a little more and Renar could lie down. Rest his eyes, curl into a ball. Still his shrieking fingers, let go of his sketchbook and finally, finally know an end to the agony burning him from the inside out.

It was as if his blood was boiling beneath flesh stabbed through by a hundred thousand needles. The flames surged, trying to get free. Pushing up and up and up, pressing against his eyes, pounding at his skull.

Renar could barely think. Each activation of his magic was now an instinctive thing. A flash of light, a surge of power. Beyond the oblivion that was his pain, a piece of Nehalena would appear, tear into a pack of vines, then deteriorate into a puddle of ink. Renar couldn't maintain her form any longer than that.

Not with his own coming undone, second by second, heartbeat by heartbeat.

"Hang in there, Renar," Sylette soothed. She was touching him—rubbing his back, holding him up. But he didn't feel her fingers. The pain, the torment of forcing too much men'ar out of too small a vessel, was his whole world.

He groaned. An assurance that all was well, only it didn't come out as such. His gaze, ever darker at the edges, drifted around the room.

Another barbed root with a hooked tip broke through from the lower deck, whipping toward Sylette.

Renar mumbled, light flashed, and a tentacle sheared the attacker in half.

The floor began to shake, the forest railing against it, its strikes loud as rolling thunder.

Renar mumbled, light flashed, and Nehalena's clawed legs slammed atop the metal plates, stilling them. Blood trickled from his nose, bubbled inside his throat. Renar's right ear went numb even as the chill on his back spread to his hip, to his knee, down and down and down, claiming him as it went.

Yet his spell wouldn't hold. It never did. What was one weak Terran—a fledgling mage, newly birthed to his powers—to do against a forest ancient as the ages?

Nothing, General Iolus spat, spilling a goblet of wine atop Renar's bowed head. *You will fail. Just as you always have, just as you always will.*

No!

Renar planted his foot, rose to one knee. That one movement left him gasping for breath, but he made it anyway. It was defiance. It was *victory.*

A cry came from behind him, the shrill squeak of that engimage, Jay. "Matteo's ready to fire up the engine! Let's go, let's go, *let's go!*"

"You heard him," Sylette said, tugging at Renar's armpits. "You've held on long enough, so now—"

Squealing and shrieking, the bulkhead on the far wall gave way, imploding in a spray of jagged metal slivers, twisted bolts, and stinking globs of forest fluid. Renar summoned Nehalena's scaly torso, deflecting most of the shrapnel aimed at them.

"Dear ancestors," Sylette breathed, staring at the monstrosity heaving itself through the newly torn hole.

If he could speak, Renar would've agreed. The creature was like a living seedpod with countless roots for legs, branches for arms, and acid-coated vines jutting from its too-large mouth. Beautiful petals rounded that gaping maw, some pink, some blue, a wondrous array of colors that Renar would love to paint.

But inside . . . Renar's stomach twisted, his throat heaving though he hadn't the strength to retch. Past gnarled shoots of bark shaped like teeth, past the waving vines and down the sickly yellow tunnel that formed the beast's gullet, was an arm half-clothed in the blue and silver of a Darmatian naval coat. Renar could see the familiar buttons, the rank insignia of an ensign emblazoned on the cufflink.

Yet beneath it was sizzling flesh, skin peeling away to expose raw muscles and white bone. This . . . *thing* was dissolving them, *eating* them as Renar had suspected. He knew he shouldn't look, yet look he did. There, a skull, gleaming as eyes melted and lips fell away. Beside it, a mangled torso, glittering medals rusting to nothing as the one who'd earned them became nothing more than food.

Sightless sockets, jutting bones, the withering flesh of legs and hands and oh, so many corpses. Renar wanted to run. To flee this revolting horror. To escape his pain, his father—*everything.*

The roots began to move, clacking as they punctured the deck with each footfall.

Clunk. Clunk. Clunk.

Vines arced through the air, tearing wires from the ceiling, smashing bulkheads and shearing through pipes.

Crack. Slam. Snap.

The Lyndwur felt no pain. It knew no quarter, no surrender. Survival was its only concern, and to do so, it needed to eat. The forest was a stomach, and they were its prey.

Yet, at the edge of his limits, when *all* he knew was pain, Renar was also unwilling to give in. He pushed off Sylette's waiting arms, gaining his feet, extending his sketchbook.

This would be the end.

The maw opened, stretching like a grisly ear-to-ear smile. And from it launched dozens of bark-teeth shards, wicked tips gleaming in the dim light.

"Neha . . . lena," Renar murmured.

The sketchbook—or was it the Draken herself?—read his intent as if they'd always been linked. Her snout appeared, the leftmost of her four slotted eyes covered with a spinning runic circle. Orbs of ink materialized between them and the pod-monster, sliding through the room on unseen strands, intercepting and absorbing every projectile.

No roar of rage left the creature's mouth. It was part of the Lyndwur, and Renar suspected concepts like fury and anger were beneath it. More bark spears fired. More ink globules spawned to catch them, so many Renar could scarcely see through the fluid screen.

He felt the vine slice through him before he saw it. A sting like a thorn-prick, a burning that *paled* in comparison to the inferno roaring inside him. Was there a hole in his side? Was he missing ribs, bleeding out onto the deck?

Renar heard Sylette's shouts as muffled drops of water striking a lake—tiny splashes, little waves, there and gone in an instant. She was worried. Desperate, for *him* of all people.

And that touched him like nothing else ever had.

More runic circles wove into existence, threading themselves atop Nehalena's rightmost eyes. Ice spears shot through the ink wall even as Renar let it fade, impaling the pod's roots, making it stumble. It crashed *hard*—hard enough to shake *Dharmasya*, to leave her trembling even after the initial impact. Would she hold? Or would she fall deeper into the forest, taking them with her?

For now, that wasn't Renar's concern.

More radiance beamed from the sketchbook, light born from his blood and given will by his men'ar. It flowed out, through Nehalena, and became disks of spiraling water, so fast, so sharp they seemed more white than blue.

Renar fired them. From the left, the right. Up and down. Bringing them in on more vectors, more angles than the beast could respond to. It shot bark teeth as quickly as it could, knocking disks from the air in showers of splinters and acidic ooze.

But some got through, carving away its hovering vines, slicing into its open maw. Yellow fluid splashed on the deck, the walls. Half of its mouth slipped forward, disgorging pools of digestive juice and the bodies of Renar's comrades onto the floor.

Forest or foe, mindless or aware, it would pay for that. This was *his* family. The people who loved and cherished him for ...

Yes, Renar thought, reaching within himself for one last gasp of power, *I'll admit it.*

... the first time in his life.

"Open," he gasped, pulling the sketchbook back, plastering it to his bleeding side.

Blinding light flared, banishing every shadow in the chamber as Nehalena's fourth and final eye opened. The runic circles hovering before them overlapped, joining, merging into a greater rune that covered the Draken's head from jaw to crown. Power sparked within it, white-hot and deadly.

Not water nor ice, as the Draken was known for.

It was a more primal magic, the fruit of the heavens, the beacon of the gods.

Arcing, dancing, it grew between Nehalena's fangs until Renar could no longer hold it back. He raised his sketchbook, pointing its open pages at the creature that had dared attack his ship.

His friends.

His *family.*

The lightning struck faster than he could see, carving through the creature, incinerating its central pod. Shriveled vines splattered against the walls. Roots and branches burned in a blue fire, leaving behind naught but ash. In place of its core—its stomach—a scorch mark marred the half-melted panels upon which it had stood.

And, out in the dark, the Lyndwur *did* finally cry. A long, mournful shriek. The sound of a thousand wounded beasts screeching in agony.

Renar heard it as if from the bottom of an ocean. His ears were numb, his eyes so blurry the world was reduced to spots of light and color. He was beyond his pain. So cold, so scorched he felt nothing at all.

Hands grabbed Renar as he fell, one set delicate but firm, the other coarse and weathered. They dragged him across a slick floor. But slick with what? The forest ooze? His blood?

Nehalena was gone, reduced to drops of ink scattered throughout the failing warship. His sketchbook was ruined, so tattered, so worn that its pages would rip the instant he pressed down with his scrivle.

No more drawing.

No more creating.

Well, at least for now. There would always be tomorrow. And the day after that, and the one after that. Now ... that Renar had ... cast aside the Soldier, his father ... everything else that weighed him down.

Now ... that he ... had a family.

Now ... that ...

He

was

l

o

v

e

d

Chapter 68
Save Her

Muzzle flashes blossomed along the Sarconian line, little stabs of light and puffs of smoke that the unending drizzle quickly whisked away. Rodale saw them fire, casting himself down on the damp bridge stones even as he opened his mouth to shout.

The bullets struck, zipping over his head, burying themselves in wood and marble and flesh. Blood spurted from a thigh wound as one of his soldiers shrieked and dropped her rifle. The man beside her tumbled backward, breastplate cleanly pierced, sightless eyes rolled back in his head.

Then—*only* then—did the sound hit. The roar of gunpowder igniting. The whizz of shells scything through the air, chipping the stones, thudding through skin and bone.

"Get down!" Rodale shouted, far too late to change anything.

Screams echoed in the rain-muffled wind. Pleas for mercy, cries for mothers, fathers, lovers. "Reload!" a Sarc officer bellowed, peaked cap visible above the trench some hundred meters distant.

A hundred meters ...

A fraction of a flag-brawl field or a military parade ground.

The distance from which Rodale had bid Jis a silent farewell as he disappeared years ago, never entering their apartment, never seeing her face. He'd been too much of a coward then. The opposite balcony was the closest he could get.

A hundred meters ...

It seemed an impossible gulf. An eternity of slick cobbles, shell craters, and bullets flying like hail.

But not today. He *would* save her.

Growling, Rodale surged to his feet. He brought his rifle up and sighted down the scope, lining up the iron spike with the oversized codpiece that whoreson Sarc officer thought was a hat. Rodale didn't expect to hit, but void if he was going to die without shooting his weapon.

Crack!

The butt of the gun slammed into his shoulder, giving him a firm kiss to let him know it was working properly. Rodale swung the weapon down and popped free his spent shell casing. There was no time to stop, no time to follow his round. Waving to the rest of his squad, he charged forward again.

Cries rose from the Sarc ranks. Confusion, dismay. Shouts of rage and shock and disbelief. By Artyr's arrogant anus, he must've plugged the arsehole!

Eighty meters.

Blood thundered in Rodale's ears, his breath a ragged hammer in his throat and chest. As he ran, the mist ahead pulled back, revealing a host of polished steel helmets and glinting barrels behind a low wall of sandbags. Two squat bunkers, gray as the weeping sky, huddled a few meters past the trench. The first supported an artillery piece long as most lordlings imagined their own armament to be, while the other sprouted the bronze tower that was the source of all Rodale's woes.

Sixty meters.

Someone sensible took charge of the Sarc platoon. The barrels stiffened, the spike-topped helms behind them focused squarely on Rodale and his men. Shouts of, "Crank it 'round, crank it 'round!" drifted from inside the bunkers as the torturous squeal of grinding gears reached his ears. Two Sarcs were heaving on a giant wheel set in the side of the great flak gun, turning it toward them degree by ponderous degree.

Too slow. They would—

Crack-crack-crack!

More lead lanced from the trench. Rodale closed his eyes and kept running, begging the gods he scorned they'd miss, picturing Jis in his head. Her enthralling emerald eyes. Full, smooth lips, equally quick with both curse and compliment. She was ice to everyone else, but to him she'd been …

A bullet tugged at his coat, tearing open his hip pocket, scattering coins in his wake. Rodale barely felt the furrow it left in his side. It was just another graze, another tear, slowly leaking blood.

Not enough to kill him. Not yet.

Out of the corner of his eye, another Darmatian staggered into the bridge's bullet-pocked parapet, then flipped over the side without a scream. Gore splattered his right arm and cheek as a freckle-faced youth keeping pace with him took a round through his neck.

Rodale wanted to stop, to scream, to rage. Was the lad sixteen? Seventeen?

But he couldn't stop.

He *would* save her.

Fifty meters.

Herj sprinted beside him, shoulder matted with scarlet from a wound Rodale couldn't see. "We're not gonna make it!" he roared. "We've lost Farrod, Jassale . . . Void, *half* the squad, sir. We gotta jump off an' take our chances in the water!"

Rifles lowered along the Sarc line, barrels nestled atop sandbags for support. Plague and pox, Herj was right. Same number of guns over there, half the targets running toward them and getting closer and closer by the second. The next salvo would finish them.

Yet . . . If Rodale stopped, the whole Resistance would perish. *Jis* would perish.

Boots pounding the cobbles, parched tongue *shrieking* for a drop of liquor, he scanned the bridge. The crater was just ahead, and beyond it, the Sarc lines. No columns, no alcoves, no cover of any kind. The only debris in sight was a mangled lancerjet wing that must have ripped free as the airship crashed. But since it was flat, they couldn't hide . . . behind it . . .

Rodale jabbed at the wing with his bayonet. "Make for that wing!" he shouted, hoping his squad heard him.

Herj gaped. "What will that—"

"Just do it!"

Skidding to a halt, Rodale tossed aside his rifle and dropped to his knees beside the wing. The tip was bent skyward and the surface was riddled with shrapnel holes and black scorch marks. Still, it looked solid. Four meters across, a meter wide—a gestalt steel shield *just* large enough to keep lead from finding their hearts.

Rodale grabbed a pair of handles at the edge—likely part of a ladder the pilot climbed to reach the cockpit—and heaved.

The wing groaned but didn't shift.

Void and Oblivion! If only he had—

Herj leapt into place beside Rodale, sliding his bulging arms beneath the jagged surface. Blood spilled from his palms as the metal bit deep. A gasp escaped his mouth as he bit his lip and pinched his eyes shut.

The wing moved, rising off the ground, beginning to tilt. Seconds. They only had seconds until the Sarcs fired.

Another soldier staggered into place next to Herj, the others grabbing handles, pipes, anything they could as they took positions alongside Rodale. Curses slipped from their mouths. The scuffling of boots and their frenzied grunting overwhelmed the dripping of the rain, the shouts of the Sarcs. Lifting the wing became their whole world.

Higher.

And higher.

And higher still as frantic breaths misted in the air, as rain plastered Rodale's uniform to his back, as blood dribbled from his side to join that of his comrades pooling on the ground.

"HEAVE!" Rodale yelled.

"FIRE!" a Sarconian sergeant bellowed.

Crack-crack-crack!

Plink-plunk-plink!

Rodale smiled as vibrations rattled his screaming muscles. The wing was *up,* supported by the arms of his final squadmates, shielding them from the Sarc barrage. It wasn't a perfect barrier. There was a blackened gap at head-level he could squint through, and their feet were partially exposed.

But it was leagues better than charging forward, waving their stones in the air and all but begging the Sarcs to blast them off.

Looking left, then right, Rodale nodded and took a deep breath. "Right leg first, on my mark . . . *STEP!"*

Thirty meters to the Sarc line.

He *would* save her.

"Are you *sure* this will work?"

Matteo swiveled his pilot's seat around, jerking the rag-wrapped armrests to overcome resistance from the rust *caking* its suspension. It was a dream come true to be back aboard the *Kinloss.* His father's ship, now his. A cherished refuge that had been with him his entire life.

But . . . Matteo could do without the mechanical failures, the disrepair, and the fog of ancient grease and crusted synth-oil that permeated every compartment. He wasn't sure which smelled fouler— the ship or its new occupants.

Jay glanced up at Matteo from an open hatch in the cockpit floor, ruddy hair in perpetual disarray, grinning ear-to-muck-smeared-ear. "Of course," he soothed, massaging the rounded top of the *Kinloss'* exposed engine a bit *too* familiarly. "It worked the first time you saw it, remember?"

"It exploded."

"Exploded, worked, they're basically the same thing."

Pushing back against her headrest, Major Reev sighed. "Just get on with it already. If I'm going to die, I'd like it to be quick so I don't have to put up with the rest of my aches. *Or* a world with two of Lieutenant Darres."

"I'll have you know our effectiveness increased by fifty-seven percent working in tandem," a second Jay said from the cockpit door. Matteo had heard he was a creation of Renar's, though the sight of a fully formed Terran made of shifting, oozing strands of ink left him a touch unsettled.

"Don't care. Let's go, Alhan."

Matteo nodded. He did a quick scan of his instrument panel, making sure the correct buttons were flipped, the dials were set properly, and the half-moon viewport was clear of gunk and debris. The *Kinloss* didn't have power now, but she needed to be ready to move the instant she regained it.

"We're ready," Matteo said. Raising his voice, he peered past ink-Jay into the cargo compartment. "Everyone aboard?"

A weak chorus of, "Ayes!" came in response. Sylette was strapping Renar's limp body onto one of the bay's long benches, while the surviving members of *Dharmasya's* crew were pressing their shoulders against the sealed hatch connecting them to the cruiser. Rhythmic thumps came from the other side, the metal shaking and warping with each blow.

One of them glanced at Matteo, revealing three curved slashes across his shredded right eye. "Yes, yes. Anyone who's gettin' on is here. Now get this tub flyin' afore the blasted forest joins us fer the trip."

Matteo didn't bother reminding the soldier they'd be taking off into the *heart* of the Lyndwur. One problem at a time, right? Twisting his chair around, he took hold of the control stick jutting between his legs with one hand—Holcomb would have a quip ready for that one—and laid the other against the primary ignition key.

"Fire it up, Jay," Matteo said, every muscle in his body clenching. *No explosions,* he begged any Veneer who might be listening. *No explosions.*

Jay nodded to Hanni, who was kneeling between the seats, her long raven braids all but draped across Matteo's lap. Flint in one hand, dagger in the other, she bent over a dark hole at the top of the engine, whispered a prayer, and cracked them together.

Sparks flew, a spray of embers that fell down, down, down.

An explosion shook the engine. The pistons atop it shot up and

671

down, cranking the shaft to which they were attached with violent energy, making the whole deck tremble. Jay grinned even as the quaking monstrosity tried to knock him from his feet.

"We're . . . not dead," Major Reev muttered. "I can't believe it."

Jay turned and smacked palms with his double. *"HAHA! IT WORKS!* Power to the thrusters, Matteo. Let's see what she can do!"

"He," Matteo corrected softly.

He jammed his key down and twisted, transferring the engine's power to the rear thrusters. *Kinloss* was alive. The monk who'd been his tutor, friend, and savior was rescuing him again. Somehow, someday, Matteo would repay that debt.

The ship surged with energy, straining against the binds that held her fast to *Dharmasya's* side. One snapped immediately, ricocheting off *Kinloss'* hull before falling away into the murky gloom below. Just how high up *were* they?

Matteo's fingers flew across the dashboard, flicking the switches that disengaged the remaining three docking tethers. *Kinloss* came loose, skidding along *Dharmasya's* rounded flank as she fell. A horrid screeching filled the cabin, sparks erupting beyond the viewport, the whole ship rattling as if coming apart. Matteo activated the gravpads, engaged the forward floodlamps, and whipped the yoke to the left, sending them into a spin.

Screams came from the cargo bay, but he ignored them. Matteo knew what he was doing now. He wasn't a green pilot anymore, and though his fingers and legs were trembling, he knew what he needed to do to save them.

Major Reev spun toward him, tugging against her crash restraints. "If you kill us, Alhan, I swear I'll put you on latrine duty in the Afterplane."

"I won't."

Kinloss bounced off *Dharmasya's* hull, propelled by a concentrated burst of force from her belly gravpads. For an instant, they were weightless, their bodies hovering as the airship beneath them started to fall.

Matteo's blood raced, the thrill of total control—of perfect freedom—washing over him. Nothing could take this ecstasy from him. Not the war, the abyss gnawing at his chest, his worries for Velle and his city. In flight, he found his *life*.

The moment faded. Before *Kinloss* could nosedive, Matteo

rammed the thrusters to maximum. With *Dharmasya* at its back, the transport jumped forward, shooting away between the Lyndwur's massive trunks.

Light from *Kinloss*' pointed nose drove back the forest's murk, revealing a vast tapestry of interwoven branches connected to pillars that stretched down and down until they were lost to sight. The branches were diverse as a Nemare bazaar: big and small, thick and narrow, twisted and straight, all ash-gray and stripped of foliage. Something within their bark glistened, reflecting the floodlamps' glare, illuminating a network of channels tracing across each and every tree.

As ever, the Lyndwur made Matteo feel small. Trapped. Like he was a flit-gnat staring up at the walls of a colossal labyrinth.

"It's beautiful," Hanni said, standing and leaning against the cockpit wall.

Major Reev snorted. "If only it hadn't tried to murder us."

Matteo angled the ship up, gently gliding around branches, doing his best to keep the airship level. "Given how tightly the branches are packed together, it looks like *Dharmasya* got caught in the upper canopy. A few minutes of easy flying should clear the top, and then we can—"

A glowing fissure on the branch ahead of them *exploded*, thrusting a jagged lance of obsidian bark directly in *Kinloss*' path. Matteo threw the control stick to the right, tilting the transport, swerving around it. He wasn't about to test if his tattered ship could survive a collision with a piece of the Lyndwur.

"Careful!" Sylette shouted from the back. "Not everyone's buckled in yet."

Hanni gulped, raising a shaking arm toward the viewport. "Then they better get strapped in quick."

The forest was aglow around them, the gaps between branches spreading, tearing as more spikes, vines, and petal-laced seedpods sprouted from them. It was like watching the birth of a hundred constellations, only far, far more grotesque. Each growth emerged in a spray of sickly yellow fluid, as if the trees were covered in popping cysts.

Gazing up toward the unseen sky, Matteo licked his lips and tightened his grip on the yoke. "Did you install any weapons while *Kinloss* was docked, Jay?"

"Two fifty-cal cannons under her wings, but ... "

"But what?"

The engimage gave a nervous chuckle. "We only have enough kerium to fuel the engines."

"And my lume?" Matteo asked, dreading the answer.

"As you might expect . . . that would also . . . "

" . . . take too much power," Matteo finished. He tipped the *Kinloss* down, dodging the spike-tipped club attached to the end of a whipping vine. A thump sounded from the rear compartment after he made the maneuver, followed by a groan.

How did that old saying go? Escape the dragon's claws, food for its maw? If that didn't describe this moment perfectly, Matteo would eat the pants Holcomb was so fond of not wearing.

He jerked the stick left, turning the ship vertical to pass between two branches closing like the halves of a mighty gate. A deeper darkness fell around them, smothering the light, wrapping them in its embrace. *A little more,* Matteo thought, counting down in his head. *Three seconds. Two. One.*

A massive boom shook the *Kinloss* as it shot out the other side, not a single scratch on what little remained of its paint. "Well," Matteo said, heart racing, cold-sweat beading on his skin, "this is going to get a *whole* lot worse before it gets better."

"Almost there," Rodale grunted. "The worst is behind us. Just a little more, and . . . *STEP!*"

With a mountain-shaking groan, the lancerjet wing and those clutching it staggered forward another step. Rodale's muscles screamed at him, begging for release. Pleading for him to drop the load biting into his hands, to give in and let the others bear it alone.

Blood welled from his numb palms as the coarse handles melded with his flesh. They were a part of him now, imprinted on his skin, embedded in his very definition of pain.

But Rodale would *not* give in.

Nothing could dissuade him from his goal. Not the unseen flames scorching his lungs, making his every gasp a living void. Not the ripping of his joints, grating, popping as they sent white-hot jolts of agony shooting down his spine.

He

would

save

her.

Ragged breaths slipped from bloody lips as knees locked and the squad paused beneath their load. Rodale blinked away the rain clinging to his eyes. Glanced at Herj, who looked about as happy as a virgin who'd been told the alley strumpet *wouldn't* open her legs for the two bronze coins he'd scrounged from his pocket.

Oh, Rodale thought, emitting a chuckle that became a haggard cough. *I'm supposed to be working on that, aren't I? For her.*

Spitting a wad of phlegm, blood, and silt, he raised his eye to the diagonal slash some bullet or piece of shrapnel had carved through the wing. The Sarcs in the trench still had their rifles trained on them but had stopped firing after a few ineffective volleys. Was their morale shot after seeing their cruisers fall? Would they flee, or fix bayonets and rush them?

Rodale didn't much care. One way or another, he was going to bring down that jammer.

"Enough rest, you slackers!" he shouted. "Three, two, one . . . *STEP!*"

Another round of curses, grinding teeth, and splashes echoed along the bridge as boots slid across the rain-slick cobbles. Ten meters now.

Just *ten* void-forsaken meters left.

Movement disturbed the Sarc line. A sergeant in a drab olive cloak bustled behind his riflemen, whispering in their ears, pointing at Rodale's moving barricade. They were close now. Close enough he could see the pitiful worm of a mustache the Sarc was trying to cultivate. Close enough he could see fingers twitching atop trigger guards, hands reaching up to wipe rain from gunpowder-smudged cheeks.

Fingers stiffened. Eyes narrowed. Were they going to shoot again? Lancerjet wings weren't thick, but they were still gestalt steel—more than enough to repel small arms fire.

"Brace," Rodale cautioned. "Let them fire, then—"

Crack-crack-crack!

Shots rang out. Screams followed. The wing tilted, sagging as the two soldiers on Rodale's right stumbled.

"Hold! Hold, void you!" Rodale glanced down even though he knew what he'd find. Crimson was spurting from a hole in his neighbor's boot, while the woman past him had been pierced clean through her shin. She tried to hold, as he'd ordered. Tried to stand as tears streamed from her eyes to join the rain and sweat and blood trickling down her face.

But it was like asking a man to hold up the sun. Getting burned was the only possible conclusion.

Her leg *snapped,* twisting to the side at a grotesque angle as she screeched like a voidspawn. Rodale saw milk-white bone jutting through, glistening, glaring at him. Then the wing slammed down on her gut, silencing her cries.

"Hold!" Rodale continued to roar, heaving with strength he didn't possess. The wing kept shifting, scraping the skin from his palms as it fell, carving his hands into a tortured, mangled mess.

But he didn't feel the pain.

They had to raise the wing. They had to reach the trench. If they didn't . . .

"Hold! Hold, Creator void you! HOLD!"

The leftmost squad members crawled forward, one step, two. Herj was red in the face, tugging at the wing like a schoolboy who'd just discovered a very firm stick resting between his—

You promised, came Jis' voice in Rodale's ear.

He looked up through the tear in the wing at the bunkers, the jamming tower, and the sagging clouds beyond, so full of rain and sorrow. A grinding sound filled the air. Not the grinding of his bones, nor the shriek of the right wingtip as it dragged across the cobblestones.

It was the squeal of a rusted metal wheel. Turning and turning and turning, round and round and round.

Until it stopped with a weighty *click*.

Rodale's gaze dropped, settling on the dark maw at the rifled end of five meters of deadly Sarconian steel. The flak gun had finished its turn.

Slowly, dispassionately, the Sarc seated on the attached gunner's platform yanked back on the firing lever. Light flared from the muzzle. The whole cannon assembly jerked backward, recoiling in on itself.

Rodale didn't see the shell launch. Wind ripped at his hair and uniform as it punched through the wing, casting shards of metal and guts and bone in every direction. He barely registered Herj's death. One second, he was there, and the next . . . he was splattered across Rodale's coat, the wing, the stones—*everywhere*.

Before he could collapse or retch or cry, the round struck the bridge behind him. Heat surged in a wave, sweeping Rodale up its embrace, casting him forward. The wing became a toy in his hands. Small, weightless. Both of them flipped through the air.

End.

Over end.

Over end.

On and on and on, rolling, sliding, skidding. Then Rodale

struck something soft. A corpse? A sandbag? He raised his head, vision blurry, ears ringing, left eye clouded with blood from one of the cuts lacing his scalp.

Everything ached, everything hurt. Each wheeze had to fight its way from his ash-choked throat, each twinge of his limbs was accompanied by a pulse of scalding torment.

But the trench lay before him, filled with Sarcs huddled against the blast. The bunkers rose beyond them, and atop the second towered the jammer, its frame shrouded by swirling smoke and rain.

Five meters to his goal.

A dagger and a dead illyrium grenade his only remaining weapons. Even so ...

... Rodale *would* save her.

The hardest flight simulation at the Academy—affectionately nicknamed Ego's End—pitted cadets in a last-gen Khamer mark-II against ten Imperial lancerjets and their light cruiser tender. Matteo had never completed the trial. Blessed Veneer, he hadn't even scored a *hit* before getting blasted to pieces.

Now he faced a dozen times the enemies with no weapons, no shields, and an airship that had been obsolete when the Khamer mark-II was still a prototype in the Descar laboratory.

Vines rushed the *Kinloss* from all angles, too many to count, too many to dodge. So, Matteo didn't try. Yanking back the yoke, slamming forward the throttle, he aimed the transport at the dark forest ceiling.

Wet squelches pounded the hull, vines ripping, tearing as *Kinloss'* tapered half-moon wings scythed through them. Each impact shook the ship from stem to stern, bucking it up and down, left and right like a leaf in a storm. Jay hunkered down in the engine compartment, tucking his legs to his chest and gripping the edges for dear life. Sylette's curses grew louder with every strike the craft suffered.

Licking his ivory lips, ink-Jay clung to the cockpit doorframe. "I'm not sure *ramming* your way through the forest is the best idea. There seem to be more trees than we have wings, so we're likely to run out of—"

Something smacked the roof above their heads, denting the steel and cracking the ceiling panels. Sparks rained atop ink-Jay, distorting his lines, melting his face. Matteo didn't so much as glance back. Surviving was *infinitely* more important than helping a puddle of living paint.

"Here's your ear, buddy," Jay said, bending to scoop something off the floor.

The response was garbled, like someone trying to speak with a mouth full of water. "... 'ank ... ou ... "

"And your mouth. I'll just push up this bit, straighten out this part, and—"

Matteo jerked the stick right, avoiding a cluster of spikes ejecting from the branch below. He heard a shriek, a splash, then the clatter of someone rolling around the cargo compartment. For the love of everything sacred, why couldn't Jay be normal?

He glanced down at his instrument panel. The tallest elegoras trees in the Lyndwur peaked at around a thousand meters, so they only had ...

What? Matteo blinked, then grunted as a barb-tipped spear flashed by, missing the canopy by mere handspans. Distraction was death. He didn't have time to split his attention, even if the bloody altimeter was *frozen* in place. The needle was locked on *'0 meters,'* not moving, not twitching in the slightest.

His other displays were equally useless. Air pressure ... blank. Airspeed ... a null reading. Even his damage indicators were dead, their usually bright diodes still and silent. The *Kinloss* should be screaming its pain at him, but all Matteo heard were Jay's groans and Sylette's frustration.

"Jay," he called over the roar of crashing, splattering vines, "why don't my instruments work?"

"Um, yeah ... Suppose I should have mentioned the tiny, almost insignificant possibility that we wouldn't have—"

"—enough power to run *anything* on this scrap heap," Major Reev fumed, striking the bulkhead with her fist. "I'm wondering why we even agreed to try this void-touched plan of yours."

Focus, Matteo told himself, tuning out the noise around him. Voices raised in fear and anger. Vines lashing his ship, tearing through her plates, digging into the wiring beneath. Shards of bark striking the glass canopy, cracking it bit, by bit, by bit.

He had no magic. His chest was a gaping abyss, cold and bottomless, threatening to drag him down and never let go. Aches plagued his battered side, his bruised and swelling arm. Matteo could rely on nothing but his ordinary eyes, his reflexes, and ...

... and my companions—just as I always have.

Smiling, Matteo reached up and pushed the bent frame of his glasses tight against his nose. They didn't fit well, one scuffed lens too high, the other too low. But he *could* see, and that was enough. "Major, can you get ready to activate the flaps and landing gear on my signal?"

The Ice Queen's emerald gaze bored through him. "Landing gear? Won't that slow us down?"

"Trust me."

She chuckled, then nodded. "Why not? Let's see what you can do, *Lieutenant* Alhan."

Warmth flooded Matteo's chest, surging up his spine, rushing down his arms. Was this praise? Was this what it was to be *needed*?

No. Matteo fought down the swell of pride, the elation from her words. There was still a job to do.

Friends to save.

"Hanni," he continued, dodging erupting spikes, bashing through vines as he spoke. "Grab what's left of Jay's kerium. When I tell you to, dump it *directly* into the first piston."

Jay's moan floated from the cargo compartment. *"All* of it?"

"All of it. One wild burst of power."

"Will we live through it?" Major Reev asked.

Fear knotted Matteo's guts, urging him to reconsider. His skin was covered in a sheen of sweat, his tattered uniform plastered to his pimpling flesh. But beyond the worry, past the doubt, blazed the fire of conviction.

He knew what he was doing.

Matteo shrugged. "Guess we'll find out."

Without warning, he pointed *Kinloss'* nose down and dove toward the nearest seedpod. It was a wretched, monstrous thing. Goo-coated petals glistened in the light of the floodlamps. Countless fangs of sharpened bark lined its open maw, shaking, rustling in anticipation of its coming meal. A horde of vines uncurled from its sides and slithered out from its throat like serpents, tasting the air with their barbed tips.

"Matteo . . . " Major Reev whispered, grip tightening on her switches.

"Not yet."

Closer and closer Matteo flew, barely adjusting course to avoid the forest's other attacks. A bark spear pierced the canopy, its point impaling the bulkhead behind his head. Wind whistled through the opening, adding a loamy scent to the greasy stench of synth-oil, mixing with the all-encompassing symphony of clanks, crashes, and curses.

Matteo didn't blink, didn't move. He ignored the sweat dribbling down the yoke. Spared not a glance for the gnarled piece of ooze-coated timber that had nearly claimed his life. They had one shot at this. *One.* And by the Veneer, Matteo was going to make it a good one.

More vines shadowed them. From above, below, all angling to block their escape. To drive them right into the now opening gullet of the seedpod. Its petals peeled back like the rind of an overripe fruit, exposing folds upon folds of sickly, rotting tissue. It was as if Matteo was looking at a dragwyrm from the inside-out, its stomach—its guts and viscera—on full display.

Tears welled at the corners of his eyes. He wanted to vomit, to void his bowels to gain a *sliver* of relief. But he wouldn't submit. He wouldn't fall or fail. Not now, not with so many depending on him. One hand on the yoke, one pressing at his quivering throat, Matteo homed in on his target.

Decaying yellow flesh filled the viewport, growing larger by the second. Vines railed at *Kinloss'* fuselage, canopy, wings—*everywhere*—threatening to tear the airship to shreds. To rip it apart and claim the juicy meat bags inside.

"Matteo?" Major Reev hissed again, glaring at him.

Jay appeared behind him in the doorway. "What in the Void are you doing? Turn! For the love of Pylanorit's Unsolved Conundrum, *TURN!*"

Matteo didn't. He kept his course.

Closer.

And closer.

And closer.

"Major! *NOW!*"

Matteo hauled the control stick back, ramming it against the front of his seat with enough force to dent the metal. *Kinloss'* wing flaps and landing gear deployed at the same time, arresting the craft's momentum, altering its trajectory.

Everything on the ship quaked. The bulkhead welds, the bolts straining to hold it together, Matteo's teeth and the lungs of every passenger. Then, arm trembling against the forces pressing down on him, he stretched forward and slammed his fist atop the gravpad ignition.

Right before the seedpod could close its putrid 'lips' around *Kinloss'* beak, the airship jerked skyward. The combined air resistance of the flaps, the landing gear, and the gravpads swung the transport upward like a pendulum, its engines directed at the branch below.

At the seedpod and the hundreds of vines that had been all but glued to their stern.

"Dump the kerium!" Matteo roared. *"NOW!"*

He heard fluid slosh into the piston. A tortured mechanical cough split the cabin, followed by a puff of acrid smoke that made him scrunch his nose as he squinted through watery eyes. For an instant—a dreadful, eternal instant—there was silence.

Had he misjudged kerium's power? How quickly the engine processed it?

Kinloss jumped forward, pressing Matteo into the worn leather of his seat, sending everything not latched down streaking toward the rear of the ship. Mouth open in a wordless scream, Jay clutched the edge of the cockpit hatch for dear life. Major Reev strained to keep her neck straight, her lips pursed, eyes narrowed, raven hair streaming around her headrest.

Branches whizzed past, ashen blurs that *Kinloss'* floodlamps touched for but a second. No vines could keep up with their speed, and those blocking the transport's path disappeared in puffs of mist. *Poof-poof-poof!*

Yet the receding glare from *Kinloss'* topside mirror was Matteo's favorite view. Fires raged behind them, little rivulets of flame coursing outwards from a blackened crater that had nearly sheared the great branch in half. There was no sign of the seedpod, nor of the hundreds of vines that had been chasing them.

All of them had been vaporized by the sudden flare from *Kinloss'* engines. Blasted and cooked until naught but charcoal and ash remained.

Serves this bloody forest right, he thought, smiling as a low, mournful warble drifted through the crack in the canopy.

Kinloss continued to rise. Higher and higher, dodging around branches with small taps of the stick. Soon the press of boughs began to thin, the gloom receding until narrow pillars of light could be seen filtering from above.

The exit was in sight.

Laughter and tears welled up from deep inside Matteo, his mask of confidence finally slipping. "We . . . we did it, didn't we?" he cried, wiping his eyes with a finger. Back and forth, again and again, unable to stem the flow in the slightest. Void, his smile was so wide it hurt. "We really did it . . .

"We survived."

Flayed fingers drifted to Rodale's belt, closing about the hilt of his dagger.

The leather wrap stung his open wounds, old salt and fresh rain mingling as they joined the blood weeping from his countless cuts. Rodale could barely hold on. His fingers refused to close, the bones beneath ravaged to the point of breaking. Trembling seized his limbs, trying to tear the dagger from his grasp, whispering for him to remain on the mud-caked cobbles.

Wait. Lay still and let the heavens wash away your worries, cares, and sorrows.

No.

Rodale clenched his fist tight. Bent his neck back and roared defiance at the heavy clouds as bones and joints snapped and piercing pain coursed through his arm. He didn't bother standing. Forward was the only direction he needed to go. Pushing off with his right arm, kicking with his tattered boots, Rodale dove into the Sarconian trench.

He *would* save her.

Sarc soldiers glanced up in shock and confusion, mouths wide, hands cupped around their ears to deafen the artillery blast. Rodale took the first in the neck. A blond youth with fuzz just budding on his lip whose gasp was cut short by the blade penetrating his throat.

Crimson gushed, splashing Rodale's cheeks, deepening the stain on his uniform. He didn't feel the warmth. Right now, he hardly felt anything at all.

He slid the dagger into his neighbor's armpit. In and out, right below the cuirass, then shunted him back into two Sarcs drawing their short swords. Cursing, they fell into a rapidly reddening puddle.

"Calm down!" the sergeant bellowed. "He's one man. Keep your distance and use your bayonets." His cloak was drawn up to his mouth, muffling his orders, making them hard to hear above the rain.

Rodale took advantage of that, charging down the trench as the sergeant struggled to raise his rifle. He bounded off a crate of ammo and led with his raised knee.

Crack!

Knee met chin, toppling the sergeant against a pile of untied sandbags. Disoriented, flailing, the man grabbed handfuls of silt and cast them at Rodale. Fool. He didn't need to see, close together as they were. Shutting his eyes, Rodale clenched his dagger in both hands and rammed it straight down.

Over and over and over again.

Punching through the sergeant's thin breastplate, splitting the flesh beneath. The man squealed like a voidspawn, spitting blood, begging for mercy. But Rodale was past caring.

Stab!

For Erika and her brother.

Stab!

For Herj.

Stab!

For his entire squad. For every single comrade these void-forsaken whoresons had taken from him. May they rot in Oblivion with their stones shoved down their throats and a spike rammed so far up their arse they could taste their own—

Rodale jerked forward, a small gasp slipping from his lips. His eyes fell of their own accord. Down and left to the long, slender bayonet jutting from his ribs below his chest plate. It didn't burn, didn't blaze as he expected it to. With all the aches, all the pains, and the absence of his magic, it was just another stick cast into the fire—a fire that would soon be naught but ash and embers.

He spun and threw his dagger. The point was bent, the blade useless, but the Sarc dodged all the same, yanking free his bayonet-tipped rifle as he stumbled aside. Rodale hauled himself upright, clutched his mangled side, and climbed over the sergeant's corpse.

Up toward the top of the trench.

Up toward the bunkers, the vibrating jammer. Rodale could feel its pulse here. A physical force that made the rain hover as if standing still and filled his ears with an eerie humming. Hand over hand he crawled, tossing back sand, mud, rocks—anything to buy him another second. He kicked someone who grabbed his leg, feeling a satisfying crunch as his boot connected. A blade bit into his right calf, carving down into the bone, but Rodale growled and kept moving.

He *would* save her.

"What's with this guy?" one Sarc yelled.

Another breathless voice answered him. "Enough with the blades. Just plug him with a bullet and finish it."

Rodale reached the top of the trench and waded through the muck and grass on his knees. A few more meters, just a few more. The tower swam in his vision, bronze shaft shaking and splitting, rings waving and convulsing as it reached for the callous gray sky.

Archimas, you pompous fool, Rodale thought, planting his scarlet palms on the bunker's concrete wall, his whole body heaving with each ragged wheeze. *You tried to . . . play god and we're . . . paying the price.* Rodale didn't expect he'd ever see the scum-sucker again. But if he did, no one would stop him from feeding the good doctor his own genitals with a side of burning coals.

He started to stand. To reach for the rain-slick rungs that would take him to the bunker roof.

Two rounds struck him. One in the shoulder, the other in the right arse cheek. Rodale would've laughed if not for the chance he'd spit out his lungs instead. Fingers slackening, he slipped to the side, tracing a crimson crescent along the wall as he fell.

Of all the bloody things to do him in, only the gods could've predicted it'd be a shot to his bum. It must be their revenge. For all the times he'd blasphemed them, for all the lewd comments he'd made about their nethers, and teats, and every other body part besides.

And if he could do it all over again?

Void, he'd curse them even *harder* the second time round.

Ice crept from the chasm in his chest, the wounds in his side, shoulder, and legs. It was a slow sensation. Like laying on a shore, the frigid autumn waves coming higher and higher as the tide came in. Rodale's feet went numb, then his legs, darkness crawling up his body with whisper-soft steps.

But death couldn't claim him yet.

He *would* save her.

"Don't move."

Rodale let his head loll to the side. The artilleryman stood there—the one who'd fired the flak gun at them. A pistol quivered in his outstretched arms, muzzle aimed at Rodale's chest.

"Can't," Rodale muttered.

Then, doing his best *not* to cough up a lung, he chuckled and raised his left arm. Dragging it up his side. Plastering the object in his oh-so-cold fingers to the last of his warmth, the blood welling from his ribs.

Drip . . . Drip . . . Drip . . .

"Well," Rodale sighed, his world darkening, "except for this."

The gunner's eyes went wide at the sight of the illyrium grenade. He dove for the trench, which was the wisest response to a dead man whipping out an explosive. Only . . . it wouldn't activate. The crystal at its heart was dun, dead and lifeless as every other hunk of magtech for leagues around.

Yet men'ar dwelled in blood, as it did in illyrium and every other living thing. If Rodale could spark it with the last of his life—a direct infusion to bypass the jammer—then maybe, just maybe, his end could still mean something.

It was a slim hope.

But like I told that whip of a girl, Lilith, stories are founded on hope. The hope they give us, certainly, but also the hope we give each other. We nurture it inside, little fires that we protect from rains, gusts, and gales—all the things in this world that seek to snuff them out. And when they grow bright enough to sustain us, when the flames can beat back darkness within and without, we have to pass them on.

To warm others with the same hope that saved us.

To give them the means to conquer their own darkness.

This is your *story now, Jis. Let my hope be enough to save you.*

Failing lips parted one final time. "Let my . . . sacrifice . . . save you."

Time stopped. For a glorious instant, the rain around Rodale was suspended like shards of crystal. The gunner hung mid-dive, arm extended as he cast his pistol away, his mouth open in a soundless scream.

Rodale felt rather than saw the hands touch his side, clasping the illyrium grenade he held there. Light radiated from the contact. Not a visible glow, but one that raced along his veins, through his blood, directly into his mind.

It was blinding, as if he was falling into the sun. Over and over again without ever touching its surface, without burning to a cinder as he surely should. There was no bottom to the power. No darkness or shadow to mark where it began or ended. It was endless. Infinite.

Pure.

"Who . . . are you?" Rodale murmured, words echoing around his unmoving head. Was he already dead? Was this the Afterplane?

The light smiled. No, its luminance *fell* on him like a smile—rays bright as a summer's day, warm as Jis' laughter. A love she'd reserved for none but him.

Then Rodale was flying. Thousands of images flashed through his mind, there and gone before he could so much as blink. Seven great crystals painted a deep-purple hue. Fleets falling to ruin as a massive raven-scaled dragon surged through their midst. A wing of white feathers matched by one of darkest night. And an empty plain of shadows that seemed to stretch forever, its tendrils slinking toward a single pillar of light on the far horizon.

He didn't understand. *Couldn't* understand.

But then again, Rodale didn't have to. He'd passed on the torch. Time for someone else to do the bloody heavy lifting, eh?

The light nodded, and a distant voice whispered in his ear.

Your sacrifice is accepted.

"Voiding . . . right . . . it is."

Light gushed from the illyrium grenade, enveloping Rodale, wrapping him in its embrace.

Ending

his.

story.

Chapter 69

The Way of All Flesh

Rain leaked around the root spear jammed through *Kinloss'* canopy, dripping down its length and pooling on the floor behind Matteo.

Plip. Plop. Plip.

Wind whipped through the hole, tousling his hair, carrying with it the stench of smoke rising from below. It turned his stomach—not because of the smell, but because of what it meant.

Etrus was a ruin, the hill upon which she stood now little more than a cairn covered with ashen funerary stones. The city's famed rooftop gardens had withered to dust. Her harbor, once full of colorful sails, vibrant market stalls, and boisterous traders, was clogged with flotsam from its mouth to the canal. Stray festival pennants hung limp, their ends burnt and tattered. Bullet and shell holes pocked the streets like open sores, blood leaking from them as they filled and filled and filled.

Matteo tried not to look. To focus on flying the airship and staring at his blank instruments. But the smell . . . It was a horrid mix of burnt flesh, melting metal, and damp gunpowder. The same scent had flooded his nostrils at Aldona, bringing him to the verge of tears, to the cusp of voiding his innards. Now . . .

Now Matteo just did his best to ignore it.

This was no longer his home. His mother, father, Junica, and most of the townsfolk had escaped into the tunnels and forest. Stores, taverns, churches—these things could be rebuilt. So long as the people survived, Etrus lived on.

"Here," Sylette said, entering the cockpit and tossing a thin blanket around Matteo's shoulders. "We've got a few dozen holes in the back, so the temperature's dropping quickly."

He glanced up at the cracks spreading across the viewport, at the panels and bolts creaking and clattering as *Kinloss* descended toward the settlement. "Huh. I hadn't noticed. Thanks."

The silver-haired girl nodded, then turned to Major Reev. "I've got an extra."

"I'm sorry," the Ice Queen said softly. Then she shook her head. "No. No blanket for me. I . . . I want to feel the cold for a little while longer."

Sylette didn't explode, shout, or hurl accusations at the woman who'd attacked her. Folding up the patchwork scrap of cloth, she stepped back and leaned against the rear bulkhead, platinum eyes glaring past Matteo toward the horizon. He understood the hurt she must feel, the pain of opening herself up and being betrayed under the worst possible circumstances. They'd all lost more than their magic this day.

And what of Major Reev? Matteo watched her out of the corner of his eye, shivering as she huddled in her seat. Her jacket was gone, lost to the Lyndwur, and her pale chest heaved beneath her undershirt as she gazed at the smoldering city. One white-knuckled hand clutched the dashboard, while the other traced absent circles over a bulge in her left pants pocket.

Was she *worried*?

Matteo cleared his throat. "Major, I—"

Kinloss jerked, falling several meters before bouncing like a rubber ball. Matteo's guts leapt into his throat. Sylette gasped, and a string of inventive curses came from the rear compartment.

His eyes flicked to the *Kinloss'* readouts, which were still dead and useless. Was it turbulence? Damage from the vines?

Behind Matteo, the engine gave a haggard cough—the kind of rasp he'd expect to hear from a dying man. More smoke filled the cabin and the rear thrusters stuttered, tossing *Kinloss* forward then slowing it to a crawl.

"Jay!" Matteo screamed.

A grease-smudged monocle popped up beside him a second later. "We're out of kerium. What do you want me to do?"

The craft plummeted again—one second, two, three—before the gravpads reengaged and sent everyone in the cockpit tumbling toward the floor. Jay screeched as his chin struck the instrument panel, while Sylette clung to the back of Matteo's seat.

Groaning in distress, the old chair started to pull away from the control stick. "Uhh, Sylette, now isn't a good time to get clingy."

She kicked the chair. "Was that a *joke?*"

"No, I just . . . Can't you do something, Jay?"

Jay lifted his head, one hand massaging his swelling face. "I could try spitting in the fuel intake, see if it'll buy us a few more seconds."

"Then—"

"*That* was a joke. I've always been a fan of gallows humor."

Before Matteo could slap the grin off the engimage's face, the engine gave a shuddering wheeze, spat a ring of black smog, and stopped moving. Pistons frozen. Gears frozen. Completely and utterly dead.

Kinloss followed it an instant later. Its nose tipped toward the ground, picking up speed, angling toward a block of toppled homes that had once included the governor's estate. Matteo heaved against the yoke, trying to alter their trajectory. A field, a street, the bay—he *had* to crash them somewhere that wouldn't mean certain death.

The stick was locked in place. Without power, Matteo couldn't move the flaps, couldn't adjust their course by a single handspan. The ground rushed up at them as *Kinloss* shook itself to pieces. A wing panel peeled away and flipped end over end in their wake. Popping bolts echoed through the ship like gunfire.

So, this was it. Matteo saw the governor's mansion ahead of them, its grounds growing larger by the second. The mangled gates, the collapsed marble balcony, the statue of King Darmatus in the courtyard with his sacred lance held toward the sky. They were going to hit that lance, weren't they?

What a laughable way to go.

The roar of an explosion washed over them. For a moment, Matteo thought something on the *Kinloss* had exploded: some residual fuel in the thrusters or one of the wing cannons Jay had installed.

Then his instrument panel lit up like the floating lanterns at a Nemare festival. Most were an angry red, blinking their fury at him. Warning klaxons boomed from the ceiling, deafening him, drowning out every other noise.

Well, every noise but the sweet, merry sound of a purring airship engine.

Matteo barely noticed the trickle of heat flowing into his breast, thawing the ice around his core, freeing the threads of his spirit. His magic could wait. Right now, he had a ship to save.

Tugging back on the yoke, Matteo pulled them out of their dive and flared the gravpads. Terracotta roof tiles snapped beneath *Kinloss* as it raced along the mansion's roof, knocking aside char-streaked chimneys, flattening what few plants had survived the fires.

"Someone destroyed the jammer!" Jay said, laughing as he stumbled upright.

"Which means . . . " Sylette held out her hand. Glittering dust coalesced above it, forming the hilt, crossguard, and silver blade of a throwing dagger. " . . . we've got our magic back!" She twisted the dagger round and round on unseen strings, soot-smudged lips spread in a beaming smile.

Matteo grinned, recalling a similar scene from a lifetime ago. "You wouldn't fire that in here, would you?"

"Not if you stay awake this time," Sylette replied with a wink.

A sword of ice flashed through the cabin, cleaving through the bark spear and resealing the gap it had torn in *Kinloss'* canopy. The temperature dropped along with the jagged branch, making Matteo's breath mist and his arms tremble.

Major Reev didn't seem to realize that frost was seeping from her, creeping across her seat, painting patterns on the rain-slick walls and ceiling. Her gaze was fixed past the rooftops flashing beneath them. On the harbor, the wreckage littered airfield, and the smoke-shrouded pile of scrap burning at its far end.

"Get to our men, Alhan," she said, one hand still rubbing the object in her pocket. "It's time we leave this place."

Alive.

Olivier Stetson was still alive, if only just.

He knew not how far he'd flown when *Ardor* crashed. That moment had been chaos. Screaming deck officers, crumpling metal. Collapsing beams and sparking wires and blood splashing, spurting, pooling. Bones snapping, rain dripping, feeble voices moaning as they pled for someone—*anyone*—to help them.

Olivier raised his head, blinking in the ash-choked gloom. His command chair was across the bridge, laying on its side. It had torn free of the deck as they plowed into the airfield, ripping his restraints, casting him from its relative safety.

Traitor, Olivier thought.

Just like his nephew, Neering. His mercenaries, his men, his entire battalion. Treasonous voidspawn, the lot of them. How else could they lose to the Darmatians? Only willful sabotage could've undone his meticulous plans and left him in this—

In what state, exactly?

He was no stranger to the coils of fire racing through his veins. The spikes driving through his skull were familiar, as was the mighty gauntlet pressing against his ribs, squeezing the breath from his lungs.

Olivier coughed, spitting up gobs of dust and blood. The top of his head was damp, his hair plastered to his skull by something sticky. His own blood? Yet he could still think clearly, rationally. If he'd suffered a head wound, it hadn't gone deep.

Placing both hands on the metal deck, Olivier tried to heave himself up. It would be a struggle to do alone, yes, but so was everything in his life. He scanned the bridge as he squirmed, noting which bodies lay still and which were beginning to stir.

Most of those clad in Sarconian gray were broken, arms twisted at grotesque angles, legs bent in shapes they were never meant to take. But a few of his armored sentinels were shifting, raising their helms, patting themselves over for wounds.

Olivier could still salvage this defeat. He would drag his Etrusian hostages from the hangars, parade them before the rebels with guns to their heads. He could still force their surrender.

He could still . . .

Why was moving *this* hard?

Slowly, Olivier glanced over his epaulet-adorned shoulder.

A mound of debris pinned him to the deck from the waist down. Pipes fallen from the ceiling, the wreckage of the gunnery station, warped and melted panels of glass that had been blown inward by the force of the crash. Olivier may have still been able to wriggle free, bit by bit, but the ceiling had collapsed atop the rest, burying the front half of the bridge.

No.

No-no-no-no-no!

Stretching out his arms, Olivier clawed at the deck, digging his fingernails into the narrow gaps in the grate, heaving with what little strength he still possessed. He kicked with his legs. Bucked with his hips and back.

Except . . . he couldn't. Nothing from his waist down responded. His legs, his feet . . . they were numb. Cold and unfeeling as ice.

After a few moments of struggle, Olivier fell into a coughing fit, hacking up more phlegm and blood as he tried to roll over, to see what had made his legs turn traitor like everything else in his world. Crimson stained the back of his uniform, a splotch of deep red seeping from a jagged pipe embedded near his spine. The flow was weak now, but if Olivier moved—if the pipe was removed—he would surely . . .

Die.

No.

No, he wouldn't. Not after coming this far. Not after betraying that sow Titania, groveling to that halfwit Valescar. Not after striving and conniving and crawling his way back from the abyss that whore

Lanara cast him into.

This wouldn't be the end of Olivier Stetson.

"You," he gasped, waving weakly at the nearest mercenary. "Grab bandages from *that*"—he pointed at the reddening robe of his personal salvator, draped over a nearby railing—"and then plaster them on my back *precisely* where I tell you to."

Grunting, the man rose and crossed the bridge, footfalls heavy on the metal floor. So heavy neither of them heard the *tap-tap-tap* of boots clomping up the hall to the bridge.

Massive gauntlets gripped the half-open hatch and *heaved* it aside hard enough to shake the entire room. The debris atop Olivier shook, dust showering on him as it threatened to collapse. But, for now, it held firm.

The mercenary turned toward the door, hand going for the short sword on his belt. He grabbed the hilt. Tugged the blade free with a glorious *clang*.

A rifle cracked, muzzle flare blinding in the near darkness. Olivier saw smoke and blood spurt from his mercenary's helmet. Then the guard crumpled to his knees, dead.

Five shapes stood where his command chair once had. Four were clad in soaked leathers, the skin-tight tunics beneath woven of blackest ebony—the color of the Ritter order. But Olivier couldn't be bothered with men who were clearly lackeys. The woman at the front, short brown hair slick against her scalp, eyes and lips narrowed to a blade's edge, was their leader.

She approached the railing above the crew pits with slow, measured steps. Her uniform was tattered and torn. Dark circles ringed her eyes and drops of rain dribbled down her milk-white skin. Yet there was no mistaking the crossed sabers on her sole surviving epaulet, the silver claw marks peaking from beneath the char on her collar.

Rittermark Silesia Marta. Another whore, another traitor.

"What does Titania's *pet* want with me?" Olivier spat, pitching a glob of blood as far across the bridge as he could. The girl didn't so much as blink. What was Sarconia coming to, promoting whelps like her far beyond their station?

"For failure to follow orders and gross misuse of the 232nd Mechanized Battalion of the Fifth Fleet, you, Lt. Colonel Olivier Stetson, have been charged with high treason against His Majesty and the Empire," Silesia said as if reading from a script. "You will be stripped of your rank, remanded to Rittermarschal Titania's custody, and assigned a court martial date at her earliest convenience. Do you have anything to say in your defense?"

A thousand protests perished on Olivier's bloody lips. He had *nothing* to say to this wench, this *tool* of the harlot queen herself. Piling every drop of his hatred into his sneer, Olivier glared at her and said, "That whore can go tap herself."

Silesia snorted. "I've told her that myself on a few occasions." Raising two fingers, she waved her men forward. "Take him alive. The Rittermarschal wants his hide run up her flagpole, and it'll be infinitely harder to remove after he stops breathing."

Something moved in the darkness at the rear of the bridge: his nephew, Captain Neering, carefully rising with a pistol in his hand. Two mercenaries in full plate were with him, tensing to charge the instant he fired.

Olivier held in his laugh, channeling it into one final lie. "You know, we could work together, Rittermark. Titania is only where she is because of how eagerly she hops onto her back. But if we defeat the Darmatian remnants I've all but snuffed out, His Majesty will—"

An explosion cut through the stillness—too loud to be a pistol retort, too near to have come from outside Etrus. What weapon could still work despite Archimas' jammer?

Silesia's eyes went wide. Then slowly, softly, her mouth split into a predatory grin. "Cover your ears, boys. Looks like the magic's back on."

Her four subordinates immediately complied, dropping to their knees and plastering their hands to the sides of their heads. Fools! Olivier nodded at Neering, who pointed his pistol at the first one in line and—

"*KILL YOURSELVES,*" Silesia Ordered.

Olivier's mind went blank. Distantly, he saw Neering point the pistol at one of his mercenaries, who had already rammed his blade to the hilt in his comrade's gut.

Crack!

The round took the surviving guard through the helm, splattering blood, bone, and metal out the other side. Before his corpse struck the floor, Neering turned the gun around, stuck it to his chin, and pulled the trigger a second time.

Crack!

Olivier barely heard the noise. He had something important to do, something that oh-so-sweet voice had Ordered him to do. Glancing up, he met her bright face, her warm and glowing smile. Olivier had to

693

please this perfect being.

Nothing—not his plans, his dreams, or his life—mattered anymore.

Only her.

Forever her.

He cast around for a pistol, a sword, anything sharp with which to carry out her command. *No!* There was nothing suitable within reach. His mind recoiled with each passing second, slipping into despair, sinking beneath a pain unlike any he'd ever known. It was from her—Olivier understood that much. But unlike her rapturous words, it burned him with the fury of a thousand suns, scalding his flesh, peeling back his muscles, searing him until ...

Every thought.

Every word.

Every letter he saw in his mind's eye.

Was

a

g

o

n

y

Ah, Olivier realized, smiling as the pain evaporated. He had but to remove the pipe embedded in his back. Such a simple solution. How could he have missed it?

Reaching over his shoulder, Olivier grabbed the pipe and yanked it free without a second's hesitation. Blood bubbled from the wound, faster and faster and faster, staining his uniform, pooling around him in an ever-widening ring.

He felt cold. Hot as the fluid was, he couldn't stop himself from shivering, couldn't keep his teeth from chattering. His vision began to fade. His thoughts drifted away from him as if borne by shifting sands, farther, and farther, and ...

Olivier turned around.

Faced his perfect idol. The one to whom *all* his worship was due.

Why had Olivier ever wanted more than this?

Eyelids drooping, breath slowing, he stared at Silesia.

And stared.

And stared until he could stare no more.

Trembling, Mikus rose to his feet.

Stetson was dead. The three men who'd intended to ambush them were dead.

And at the center of it was Silesia Martavis, feet shoulder-width apart, arms clasped behind her back. She looked like she'd just finished reviewing her troops, not murdering the man she'd been sent to capture.

Worst of all, the grin Mikus saw on her twisted lips was *euphoric.* She had *enjoyed* watching these men—formerly their comrades—kill each other. Derived some sort of perverse pleasure from it.

What warped a woman into . . . *this?* Mikus glanced at Stetson, smile imprinted on his still lips, once spiteful eyes forever closed. He held no compassion for the traitor, but their orders had been to bring him in alive. Orders Silesia had willfully disobeyed.

Why? Weren't she and Titania working together?

Questions bounced around his head as he looked at each of his men in turn. Jotun and Hursch were bone-white, their knees shaking as they desperately tried to remain at attention. Dar wasn't shaking, but for the first time since Mikus had known him, the big man's permanent grin was missing from his face, a scowl in its place.

They'd never seen Silesia do this before, which meant a mind-wipe was coming. Did he have time to use his magic to preserve their memories? His eyesight was improving, brightening the dark room until it was as day to him. Scents flooded in: the sharp cologne Stetson had used, the overwhelming tang of iron, the aromas of salt and sea and death. If Silesia stayed put for just a minute—

Boot heels echoed across the bridge as Silesia spun to face them.

"I have two Orders for you. Search the ship and find all the survivors from Stetson's battalion. I'll be taking charge of his unit, and I need to know what I'm working with.

"After that," her eyes narrowed as her words became a soft, haunting lullaby, *"I'll need you to FORGET . . . "*

Chapter 70

No Safe Haven

Unter lumbered among the Darmatian wounded, left leg dragging behind him, purple blood oozing from beneath a frayed bandage on his thigh. He didn't know who had applied it. Velle, most likely. The Sylph girl had thrown herself into treating their casualties, leaving Vallen's care to Lilith.

Neither of them had gotten him to open his eyes, to so much as move his lips. The Triaron lived. Blood thundered through his veins, elevating his pulse, flushing his skin as if afflicted by fever. And yet the Terran didn't breathe. Not a gasp, not a moan like the rest of their tormented mages.

It was an unnatural sickness. And since Unter couldn't help Vallen, he did what he could to assist Velle. Hauling buckets of water up from a shattered well. Scrounging nearby gardens for usable herbs not taken by the flames. Sagewort, vivenna bells, rowt berries—any ingredients Unter recognized from his distant life in the Ascendant Guard.

A life that still haunted him.

A life that is determined to destroy the one I have now, he thought, glancing across the canal toward the land that had abandoned him.

Raven hair pinned behind her pointed ears, Velle hunched over a large piece of rubble she was using as a makeshift mortar. Her shoulders were pinched tight beneath her combat suit, her sunken eyes fixed on the paste she was grinding. She hadn't rested for a moment since Colonel Holcomb had left with his squad, not even to wipe away the tear streaks marring her cheeks.

"Last of martyr's bramble," Unter grunted, holding out the collection of seeds and leaves in his lower right hand. "All buildings on harbor left side search, nothing more to find."

"Thank you." Velle took the herbs from him without looking, then pointed at a pile of cloth strips smeared with an algae-like paste. "These are done."

Blinking his appreciation, Unter picked up the scraps and hobbled back the way he'd come. Fire, mud, and rain had done their best to ruin the cloths he held, but their faded blue and silver embroidery still peeked through. Here, a piece of Darmatia's sacred silver chalice. There, the proud lance sigil of the royal family.

Groaning, Unter knelt beside a Terran whose chest was a mess of pus-filled sores and blackened flesh. He plastered the poultice to the wound, massaging it so the paste seeped into the ravaged tissue, drawing a pained sigh from his patient. It didn't matter that the strips he held were part of his nation's—his clan's—flag. The symbol could never be more important than the people it represented.

Drifting through the Darmatian cordon, Unter repeated the same process again and again. Stoop, apply Velle's salve, whisper a word of hope, move on. Screams accompanied him as he walked. The whimpers of the dying, the cries of those empty shells whose magic had been ripped from them.

Unter pitied them because he *was* them. Tendrils of ice crawled from the void in his chest, tugging at his eyes, begging him to stop, to sleep.

Ah, to let go. To lay down on the cobbles and escape it all.

But Unter couldn't. Not when the actions of his kin—his own *sister*—had cost them so dearly. He must bear the responsibility they would not.

Rifle fire from across the bay drew Unter's gaze as he worked, rising and falling as the skirmish on Etrus' bridge played out. He had seen flames in Holcomb's gaze when the colonel left—the conviction of a man prepared to die, who *knew* he was going to die. Yet despite the odds, Holcomb had refused his aid, insisting he protect Vallen instead.

Yes, the Triaron was vital to their cause, but . . . *could* Unter still protect anyone?

He looked down at his calloused, blood-drenched hands. Hands that had failed to hold onto his dearest Jesrah, to shield her from the Haead Assembly's accusations. Hands that had brought dishonor upon his family, his clan. Hands that had let go of Leon, leaving him to his fate, relying on him to do and be what Unter could not.

Four hands that couldn't match the strength of Holcomb's two.

Unter blinked. The gunfire at the canal mouth had ceased, leaving behind a pall of gray smoke the rain slowly washed away. Above the bullet-pocked bridge columns, the trenches, and the bunkers, the jammer still stood. Tall, imposing, and still very much active.

"He . . . failed."

Lilith stood beside him, hand to her mouth, tears welling in her eyes. She was the strongest among them, the fiercest and most determined. But at that instant, she looked so very small and afraid.

Reaching out, Unter took her other hand in his. It *was* small, able

697

to fit inside his palm without even touching his massive fingers. He forced himself to smile at her, blinking reassurance he didn't feel. "Faith have. Colonel come through will."

An explosion erupted at the base of the tower, casting slivers of concrete and timber high into the sky, blowing clouds of ash and dust and rain in all directions. The long barrel of a flak gun flipped end over end toward the canal as the shockwave rushed toward them, whipping the harbor waters into a frenzy.

Unter stepped into the blast, shielding Lilith and the nearest wounded with his bulk. Tattered pennants and sheets snapped taut in the gale. Empty shell casings rolled across the ground and the two surviving transports rocked back and forth on their struts.

The roar died, replaced by the groan of metal strained to the breaking point. Unter turned back toward the jammer. Watched it shake, then tilt, then fall and fall and fall until it crashed onto the bridge, cracking it down the middle.

Like ice before the sun, the cold gripping Unter's chest shattered, freeing his lungs, restoring the fire in his veins. His flar'en spell returned, banishing the rain's damp chill. He swung his upper arms, each movement swift and easy as he remembered.

Colonel Holcomb had done it.

He had saved them all.

For an instant, no one moved.

Confused mages rose on unsteady legs, glancing at the deep scratches on their mangled arms, examining their shredded armor and uniforms. They couldn't comprehend their injuries, let alone the horror the jammer had unleashed on them.

No one knew what was happening. No one wanted to take charge.

Lilith squeezed Unter's palm. "You've got the loudest voice, big guy."

He nodded, then let go and strode to stand beside the transports. Freed from the jammer's effects, their illyrium cores were already humming as wisps of exhaust streamed from their bellies.

"Ampli," Unter whispered, touching his neck. He didn't much care if the Sarconians heard him. "Attention!" he bellowed, magic-enhanced voice echoing up and down the harbor thoroughfare.

Every Resistance soldier turned toward Unter, breaking off their conversations and bickering. He counted perhaps three dozen of them, their gear worn and ragged, their faces smeared by soot and grime and blood. Most were injured in some way. Deep burns, vicious slashes, festering bullet holes. Missing fingers and limbs, bandaged-wrapped eyes that saw no more. Some propped themselves up on their elbows, straining to rise from the pitiful sheets they'd been laid on.

Some didn't move at all.

"Where pilots are?" Unter asked.

A woman with a crimson-stained wrap tied around her left arm raised her other hand. Off to the right, atop a curved piece of metal slag, the burned man Unter had treated weakly pointed at himself.

"Aboard ships, get them," he said, waving to a group whose wounds weren't visible. "Fly help. Rest between ships split. Shoving no, pushing no. We in together come, out together go."

"We're . . . we're leaving?" mumbled a mage with gouges along her forehead, nose, and cheeks. In her delirium, she'd ripped out clumps of her hair, then attacked her face until her comrades could pin her down.

"Is it over?"

"We can go home?"

Unter wanted to tell them 'yes.' To assure them that everything would be alright, that they would see their families and loved ones soon.

He couldn't tell that lie. They may have devastated Etrus' Imperial garrison, but more would be coming. Whether because of Taala's treachery or some other betrayal, the Empire had known their plans. Another wave of enemies was sure to arrive soon—more airships, panzcraft, and troops than they could possibly deal with.

The Resistance—these weary, battered souls before him—was no more.

This rebellion was dead.

"We're leaving," Unter said simply, patting the hull of the nearest transport. "Over, it is."

He waded through their midst as they rushed him, bumping into each other, fighting to be first onto the ships. It was the exact opposite of what he'd asked of them. Yet, after the oblivion they'd been through, he couldn't fault their desperation.

Unter made straight for Vallen's limp form. Unlike the other mages, the Triaron hadn't awoken. Did his stupor have something to do with the bizarre white threads that had poured from his flesh? Or had his deific display of power broken something deep inside him?

Kneeling, Unter pressed two fingers to his lips, then raised them to the weeping clouds. "Over him watch, Vida. His will restore, Sariel."

He took Vallen in his arms. Rose with a grunt and began trudging back toward the transports. Lilith was standing atop a mound of rubble doing her best to direct traffic, while Velle—

The Sylph materialized from the crowd, hollow eyes fixed on Vallen. "He didn't wake?"

Unter shook his head. There wasn't anything else to say.

A sudden gust of wind buffeted them as an airship swerved low over the waterfront shops, twisted in midair, and slammed onto the street with a clatter of squealing gears and hissing steam. One of the landing struts snapped, dropping the craft onto its cracked and mangled beak, but the other two held firm, leaving just enough space for its rear ramp to depress.

Its crescent-moon wings were mangled, steel shot through with slime-coated spears of bark, whole panels ripped clean away, ailerons bent and twisted. Not a square meter of the craft had escaped without a scrape, dent, or synth-oil dripping hole. Its landing flaps were missing, shorn off in some maneuver, and only one of its two cannons was still attached . . . if that half-melted slag counted as a gun.

"How is it able to fly?" Velle muttered.

Smiling, Unter shrugged and headed for the ramp. "Hope."

"That's *not* an answer."

Three faces Unter didn't recognize were the first to disembark. They limped past him toward the other Darmatians, worry-creased gazes sweeping the crowd. Light brightened the eyes of a woman with a bandage wrapped head, her black braids swaying as she broke into a sprint. She leapt at two soot-caked soldiers, wrapping her arms around them, pulling their faces to hers. Soon, all of them were crying.

Some bonds survived, and hope lived on.

Sylette and Major Reev met Unter at the bottom of *Kinloss'* ramp, both worn and ragged as the rest of the survivors. The Ice Queen was missing her jacket, revealing arms covered in shallow cuts, bruises, and glistening yellow goop. Unter didn't bother asking what they'd been through. That story could wait for later.

"What's wrong with him? What happened?" Sylette leaned forward, staring at Vallen. For an instant, it looked like the princess was going to reach out and touch his char-blackened arm—the place where some spell had ripped apart his armor and scorched the shoulder and chest beneath. Then she jerked back, clutching her disobedient fingers with her other hand.

"He's been comatose since the jammer went off," Velle replied. "For some reason, he didn't wake up with the other mages."

"Intriguing," came a voice from the cargo compartment. "If you let me run some tests, I can isolate whatever variable is causing our dear Triaron to behave differently than—"

Major Reev huffed, spraying glittering frost through the air. "Stow it, Darres." Turning, she pointed at Vallen. "Get him aboard. We're leaving as soon as everyone's accounted for."

"How many . . . how many made it?" Sylette grabbed one of the pistons supporting the ramp, swinging out to watch the chaotic loading of the other transports.

"Too few," Unter said. It was the only answer that mattered.

He limped up into the *Kinloss*, grunting as each step sent fresh agony through his torn thigh. The rush of combat was fading. The worry, the anxiety over what the next second, moment, or minute would bring. Stumbling, Unter tossed Vallen into the first available seat, then collapsed beside him. He didn't bother strapping himself in. None of the crash restraints would fit him anyway.

Quick, light footfalls trailed them up the ramp. A bob of tawny hair burst into view, followed by snow-fair cheeks dotted with constellations of freckles. Lilith had made it and—Unter couldn't help chuckling as he glimpsed the thin, tapered blade slotted through her belt—had brought *another* Sarconian saber with her.

"The transports are loaded," Lilith said, sketching a lazy, two-finger salute at Major Reev. "I've told them to follow our lead, but"— she sighed—"it's anyone's guess what they'll do given how voided up everything is."

Major Reev nodded, though her eyes kept drifting to the now closing ramp as if expecting someone else to walk up it. "Good enough. Get us in the air, Alhan."

She doesn't know, Unter realized, shivering despite his flar'en spell. "Major—"

The *Kinloss* shuddered as its gravpads engaged, shaking the bulkheads, rattling every bolt, panel, and latch on the airship. The dim lights on the ceiling flickered in time with the engine's groans, and a puff of smoke jetted from the cockpit entrance.

"Fix that leak, Jay!" Matteo's plucky voice shouted from the forward cabin.

"Should I spit on it? 'Cause if not, there's not a lot I can do for this slag of a ship. Besides, I think it'll hold. I'm like"—the odd man who'd wanted to experiment on Vallen paused—"sixty-two percent sure it will."

Matteo groaned. "Ink-Jay would've been able to do something."

"And now that Renar's lost his magic, my slightly-less-handsome twin will be sorely missed. Creator preserve his soul."

Renar? *Magic?* Unter stared across the narrow aisle at the huddled form of his best friend. He was sleeping now, black hair matted to his head by sweat and sap, his uniform slashed to ribbons and dangling from his shoulders. Crusted blood clung to his lips, dribbled along his chin.

He'd clearly been put through the wringer, just as they all had.

The rumbling of the vessel increased, vibrating through Unter like a second pulse, a new heartbeat. Then *Kinloss* was off, turning about its axis, speeding off toward ...

Unter frowned. Based on how far they'd turned, they were heading south. The only things in that direction were the airfield and the Ascendancy border.

The Ascendancy border!

Grabbing the storage rack above his head, Unter hauled himself upright and squeezed his way past Velle and Lilith toward the forward hatch. He needed to warn them. To get them to alter course before the next phase of Taala's treachery could be revealed.

She'd always hated loose ends, even during the silly games they'd played as children. And right now, the Resistance remnants were the *only* evidence that the Ascendancy wasn't walking in lockstep with the empire they bankrolled.

Killing her Bekshak brother—expunging the Liadrin clan's secret shame—would just be a bonus.

Unter poked his head in the cockpit door, unable to force his shoulders through the frame. Beyond the cracked, quivering canopy in front of him, the two surviving Darmatian transports rushed toward the scraggly foothills of the Tesset mountains, which rose above the coastal plain like giant claws.

Yellow-illyrium dust blasted from their engines, each second extending their lead over the ravaged *Kinloss*. Unter looked down, catching sight of the tall, storms-rusted fence that marked the border. Dear Vida ... The other ships were already in Ascendancy airspace.

"Taala betrayed us has!" he bellowed. "Course change, *NOW!*"

Everyone in the cramped compartment spun toward him except Matteo, their brief calm giving way to alarm. Major Reev leaned forward in the co-pilot seat, eyes darting between her transports, the

702

barren, shale-littered slopes, and Unter. One second passed. Five. The Ice Queen bit her lower lip, ice shimmering on her cheeks, glittering in her grit-streaked hair.

What was she waiting for?

Unter reached for the instrument panel. "Them signal. Tell back over border get, regroup elsewhere."

"We . . . can't." Matteo gestured at their com-crystal, which was half-melted and coated in a sizzling glob of sap.

Sylette groaned. "Is there anything on this ship that *isn't* destroyed?"

"The crapper?" Jay suggested with a lopsided grin.

"She wouldn't." Frost crept down Major Reev's cheeks, her neck, her arms, turning her sweat into crystal shards that tumbled to the floor. "We signed a treaty, and the terms were clear: attack Etrus, defeat the garrison, and the Ascendancy would shelter us. Would take *our* side in the war. She signed it. The voiding *Prime Factor's* seal was on it. There's no way an ambassador would risk their nation's reputation like that."

Sylette's gaze was cold as the Ice Queen's rampant magic as she leaned against Matteo's headrest and stared at the ships they couldn't save. "It's politics. If no one's left from our side, who's to say the treaty ever existed?"

And there it was: Taala's winning play, a knife in the back of the pawns she'd so effortlessly manipulated.

But Unter wouldn't let her win. He jabbed a finger at the blocky transports, now rising up the tree-dotted slope, heading farther inland. "Overtake them can? Gun fire? Anything to attention draw?"

Sighing, Matteo threw the thrust-lever to maximum. The entire ship immediately began to rattle and shake. "We are *so* going to regret—"

Smoke and fire blossomed from the foothills before them, uprooting shriveled ferns and bushes, casting pillars of dirt and grass and stone into the sky. Light flared behind the crumbling soil, great, gleaming barrels being rolled from hidden alcoves into the pale light of day for the first time.

The Ascendancy had never believed the Darmatians would invade them. *But as my mother loved to say: complacency is the death of preparedness,* Unter thought, watching the cannons aim skyward.

The guns recoiled, spitting shells and flame and ash. At a hundred meters, the shells split open, filling the air with a horde of whizzing shrapnel. They tore through the first transport. Rent its wings from its hull, savaged the engines in bright scarlet explosions. Trailing pitch-

703

black fumes, the mangled remnants struck a nearby hillside and pitched stem over stern down its side.

There would be no survivors.

Screaming, Matteo flung the yoke left and activated the lume. Unter braced himself in the doorframe and reached out to wrap Sylette and Jay in his lower arms. There was little else he *could* do, now that his sister's trap had been revealed.

Everything trembled. Unter's vision, his arms, the heart racing inside his chest. Puffs of gray exploded against the shimmering lume, dimpling its surface, casting ever widening—ever *closer*—ripples as it shrank inward. Matteo jerked the *Kinloss* in erratic patterns, drawing cries from the cargo compartment as anyone not strapped in was thrown around.

Yet the chaos had no effect on Major Reev.

She simply stared at the viewport, wide eyes fixed on the spot she'd watched the first transport fall from the sky. Tears welled in their corners. Shaking, her hand drifted to her leggings, clutching at a round outline in her pocket.

"Lilith!" Major Reev yelled. She tugged at her restraints, trying to rise despite the maelstrom assailing their ship. "That ship. Was Rodale"—her voice quavered, breath caught in her throat—"Was Rodale on that ship? Was he?"

Something bucked the *Kinloss*. Had they taken a hit to the stern? Lilith shouted, but Unter couldn't make out her words over the roar of the shells, the groaning of the ship, and the Ice Queen's babbling.

"I need to know which transport he was on. He's alright, I'm sure he's alright, but ... "

Crash! Snap!

More clattering came from the cargo compartment. Unter wanted to turn and see what was happening, but he *literally* had his hands full.

Major Reev grabbed Matteo's arm. "We need to go find the other transport. Then we can check the wreckage—"

He shook her off, jammed the yoke down to avoid a cluster of explosions. "They broke right, Major. We can't go back without flying back through that voidstorm. Now let me save my ship."

She pulled away as if stung, then twisted her seat around toward Unter. The Major had removed her safety harness, but his bulk still blocked the doorframe. Packed tightly as they were, she had nowhere to go. They were trapped in this crumbling, stinking cesspit of sweat, grease, and blood together.

"Let me through," Major Reev said, ice tracing her veins atop her skin, rimming her gleaming emerald eyes. There was steel in her tone, frost wafting from her mouth and nostrils. Unter wouldn't be surprised if her blood was frozen solid.

"Let me through," she repeated. Icicles spawned from her raven locks, draping over her shoulders as they grew, framing her in a cloak of shimmering crystal. "I have my magic back, *Lieutenant*. I will *waste* those gun emplacements. Slaughter those who betrayed us, eradicate the Imperial holdouts and whatever feeble reinforcements they send. I'll bury *all* of them under a glacier that will never melt."

Major Reev's voice dropped to a rime-coated whisper. "Do not stop me, Unter. *Let. Me. Through.*"

Unter had no chance of stopping her. This was the Ice Queen of Darmatia. The hero of Kharit and Lake Lovare, the woman who had risked *everything* to save hundreds of drowning sailors.

She had defeated a Primal. Led the faltering Resistance back from the brink of defeat. Those winter-deep eyes held the truth of her words. She meant everything she said—an inviolable promise, an oath of rage and fury and carnage.

But then what?

What happened when her men'ar ran dry? When the ice shattered and she drowned in the very rivers of blood she created?

Unter saw that distant day, clear as a sparkling pane of glass. Jesrah before the Assembly, gaze downcast, eyes hidden beneath her ebony bangs. He'd been pierced twice that day—condemned *and* betrayed. Too inept to conceal their bond, too weak to protect it from the Ascendancy's petty laws. Yet still he could've fought. Rallied those loyal to him, taken a stand against the injustice of the clans and the Bank they propped up.

That day . . . he'd faced a similar choice.

And he'd chosen exile over hate. Life over death.

The future over the past.

Today, Unter thought, closing his eyes, *she will have to make the same choice.*

He spoke the truth Major Reev had no desire to hear. Slowly, carefully, determined not to stumble over the foreign words as he so often did.

"Colonel Holcomb . . . is dead. He . . . blew up jammer. Saved us all. He is hero, yes? Greatest hero I have . . . ever known."

705

"He's . . . He's *dead* . . . ?"

Cracks appeared in Major Reev's icy armor. Her eyes drifted closed as her lips trembled, her fists clenching tighter and tighter until a trickle of blood dribbled down her left thumb.

Then the moment passed. Matteo hauled the stick back as *Kinloss* spasmed and tumbled toward the ground. "What in the Seven Abyssal Names is going on back there?" he screamed.

Unter grunted as a wave of fire washed over his back. He heard the crackle of electricity. Smelt the acrid tang of flash-cooked air and singed flesh. A massive clank sounded as one of the storage racks collapsed, scraping along the inner hull as it fell.

"Calm down!" Lilith shouted, words hoarse and strained. "I don't know who you're talking about, but I'll listen. I'll help you. Just breathe, *breathe.*" Was she fighting someone? If so, whom could it possibly—

Blinking apology, Unter dropped Sylette and Jay and turned toward the cargo compartment. Vallen's cries greeted him, as did a surge of magic so strong it made the hairs on his arms stand on end.

"I killed her! Void and Oblivion,

I

killed

her!"

Chapter 71

I Killed Her

Vallen fell.

Down and down, end over end, screaming the whole way.

At some point, the slate-gray sky disappeared. The roar of battle faded away, as did the stench of burned bodies, the stomach-curdling tang of blood. Nothingness replaced them. A blanket of darkest pitch cast over his whole world, so complete not a sliver of light remained.

It stretched in every direction, on and on and on forever. There was no horizon. Nothing to delineate up from down, left from right. Just an endless, fathomless abyss.

Eternal.

Infinite.

For a spine-chilling instant, Vallen thought Darkness had returned. That the creature had cast him into an even deeper prison—the one within his own mind. Yet there was no noise to mar the stillness of this space between. No taunting cries or whispered promises of power he could not control.

For once his dreams—his *nightmares*—belonged to him alone.

A light appeared before Vallen, unraveling from top to bottom like a ream of purest silk. Its radiance was blinding, forcing him to twist his head, to cover his eyes. Was this some new trick?

Or, Vallen chuckled, *do I have yet* another *passenger hitching a ride inside my head?*

The radiance faded, growing darker, blacker by the second. He removed his hands to find a familiar sight: a mirror as tall as he was, its surface not a reflection, but a portal onto a world of shifting, blurry images.

Flames danced within its confines. Smoke curled about its edges, seeped from the mirror's frame. It had once been trimmed with silver, graceful floral patterns that swept and flowed like running water. Now it crumbled, the char at its edges cracking away piece by piece, tumbling away into the infinity above.

No.

No, no, no. Not now, not ever.

Though Vallen was still falling, he tried to paddle backward, legs flailing, arms groping and swiping through the shadows. He was *not* going through that doorway. That was a memory he had sealed away. Drowned with spirits and sex and sel-spice.

He didn't want to see the truth.

Didn't want to know who'd claimed Elaine's life, who was responsible for turning her perfect smile crimson. He didn't want to see that day play out again.

Another portal. There had to be another portal he could escape into. Vallen kicked out at the mirror, breaking off an ember-laced sliver that stuck to his boot. He gained a bit of distance, flipping around, scything through the air with his arms.

But even after Elaine's instruction, he'd never been a good swimmer.

The mirror soared after him, somehow unconstrained by the supernatural physics that bound him. Vallen shrieked, paddling harder, his combat suit drenched with the sweat of his desperation.

He kicked and kicked and kicked.

More char came away, sticking to him, slowing him down like lead weights. The more Vallen struggled, the closer the mirror came. His legs stopped moving. His fingers and arms froze mid-stroke as the shadows turned to viscous Sewertown sludge.

And closer came the mirror. Floating above him, tilting on its axis, pressing itself to his face. So close he could make out the blazing bookshelves and torn, bloody pages covering the floor of the room beyond. So close he could *smell* burning flowers and leather and flesh.

"*NO!*" Vallen screamed.

The mirror didn't listen. Its glass liquified, glittering tendrils reaching out and snagging his arms and legs. It took but a moment to pull him in, to swallow him whole.

And so, Vallen fell again, this time into the nightmare he'd spent the past decade fleeing.

Vallen awoke screaming, and with his scream came magic.

White-hot, pure, and powerful. Streaks of fire, coils of lightning, furious winds and gales. He cared not who or what he struck. It just needed to be released, to be poured out onto the world until not a shred, not a drop remained in his filthy veins.

I want it gone, Vallen thought, drawing his legs to his chest, cradling his head in his arms. *Take this curse from me, someone,* anyone.

You can have my body, Darkness.

Take

it

all!

Yet Darkness didn't respond. The vile creature had abandoned Vallen.

Vile? Vallen laughed, ejecting streams of wind from his throat to slice gouges in the metal ceiling that swam past his endless tears. What right had *he* to name anyone vile?

He had killed her.

Murdered her and her family. Burned down her estate, her books, her life before falling asleep in the ashes. The circumstances didn't matter. The who, the how, the what.

None of that would change the result.

"I killed her!" Vallen shouted, leaping to his feet in a spray of scorching flames. "I killed her, I killed her, *I killed her, I-killed-her-Ikilledher!*"

His words slurred together, tripping over each other as he wept, laughed, and danced like a drunkard. Vallen punched the wall, blowing a jagged hole in the thick steel. He stamped the floor, searing it black—black as the char on the mirror in his dreams, black as his void-forsaken heart.

Distantly, as if from beneath a mound of fallen rubble, Vallen heard a voice. Begging him to stop. Pleading for him to talk, to explain.

Cocking his head, Vallen turned toward the voice. How could the corpses be speaking? He'd buried them beneath their fine wardrobes and armoires, their paintings and their bookshelves. Ash didn't speak. Cinder couldn't talk.

More lies and more deception.

"I killed her," Vallen whispered, snot dribbling down his chin and mixing with his tears. That was the only truth that mattered now.

He raised his hand to incinerate the voice, only to be lifted off his feet and *slammed* into the wall. Four bulging arms gripped him tight, pinning him, holding him in place.

Yes! This was what Vallen deserved. Pain, punishment, *death.* He'd fled from it for so long. Forgotten the trauma he'd inflicted. Buried it under his ego, pleasure-seeking, and Metellus' soothing lies of the hero he could be.

709

But this was

who

he

was.

A monster. Giggling, Vallen spat the truth in his attacker's face. *"I KILLED HER!"*

And sent with it a surge of energy, crackling lightning that expanded from his body like a shell. It struck his assailant. Hurled him across the room, his weighty impact with the far wall shaking and spinning the world around them.

"Stop!" someone pled.

Vallen was beyond stopping. Raising his arms, he reached into the metal hulk surrounding him, seeking *its* truth. The impurities, the shards of earth and soil and clay that once defined it. And though Vallen's touch was far from perfect, it was enough.

He *yanked,* tugging pieces of the floor into the air. Letting them float around him like the moons above. They'd watch him kill her, smiling on the scene as grotesque shadows twisted across their distant bodies. Now they'd watch Vallen rid himself of his curse.

This magic that had ruined her life, then his own.

"Are you that far gone, you imbecile?"

Daggers rained against his shields, clanging off them with hardly a dent. It wasn't enough. They needed to try harder to end him.

Glowing white barriers pressed against Vallen's metal plates, stilling their orbit, holding them in place. "I saw, Vallen," yelled a voice on the verge of tears. A voice that had once murmured in his ear as he drifted to sleep, his arm draped across crimson shoulders. "You killed the Sylph girl, but you did it for me. She was going to shoot me. So . . . don't blame yourself."

Vallen laughed. "Not her. Do you think I'd be this torn up about killing a traitorous wench? No, my crime runs far deeper. I killed *my sun.* I. Killed. *Her.*"

Bolts of lightning shot from his palms, punctuating each of his words. The barriers shifted, catching the blasts, containing them. Why? Why wouldn't they just let him vent his magic?

The barriers dropped, releasing Vallen's shields to smash against the walls. Leaving him open to attack. A flood of ice raced toward him, encasing his feet, creeping up his legs. The frigid chill lancing through his flesh was *blissful.* It numbed him, inside and out. Taking away the agony, freeing him to fall into infinite emptiness.

"Yes!" Vallen roared. "I killed her! Give me what I deserve!"

"My pleasure, voidstain."

An angel wreathed in white launched toward him, frost wings flaring behind her, a spear of green ice melded with her oh-so-pale arm. Vallen gasped as it pierced his stomach below his half-melted breastplate. Smiled as the pain spiked, then began to fade. His eyelids drooped, slipping, falling.

He let his head drop atop Major Reev's, burying his nose in her grit-caked hair.

"I . . . killed her," Vallen mumbled.

"Sleep well, Triaron. We'll deal with your delusions when next you wake."

A surge of panic swept through him, chill as her touch. If Vallen slept, he'd dream. He'd be forced to relive that nightmare again.

Gradually, the dread faded beneath the knock-out venom flooding his system. Numbing him, as he'd so desperately desired. Soon, only one thought—one truth—remained.

"I

killed

Elaine . . ."

Chapter 72

Cut Off the Head

Four daggers.

That was all that had kept Sylette from death.

Blades scraping, hilts twitching, they bent and cracked as they strained to cast off the slab of warped metal pinning Sylette to the wall. She'd let her guard down. Believed the fighting was past, that she could trust her comrades.

As always, that imbecile Vallen strived to make her regret every scrap of armor she stripped from her heart.

Pain radiated from Sylette's leg in crashing waves. A sharp bolt, a jagged sliver of metal—something had impaled her left calf, shredding her uniform, spilling her blood onto the ruined airship floor. Oh, that imbecile would *pay* for this.

Grunting, Sylette turned her rage into energy, funneling it through her chest, sending it forth on streams of men'ar. More daggers formed, pressing at the panel Vallen had ripped from *Kinloss'* deck. Pushing it back, bit by bit, until they finally toppled it over with a resounding *clang*.

The touch of her magic was like lightning coursing through Sylette's veins, thrilling and rapturous. Yet her joy had been the Triaron's loss. Upon regaining his powers, he'd flown at them like a rabid beast, all but foaming at the mouth. Tears had spilled from his eyes as he cast spell after spell, heedless of who or what he struck. The same phrase had slipped time and again from his trembling, spittle-flecked lips:

I killed her.

I killed Elaine.

But . . . who the void was Elaine?

Sylette's daggers dissolved back into the ether of their own accord. She took a halting step, placed her hand on the bulkhead, and sank to the deck beside the cockpit door. Sweat and char stained her tattered uniform. Her silver hair had faded to a dingy gray, matted by clumps of blood and sap, streaked through with ash.

Every breath was a wheeze. Each flicker of her eyes like raising a portcullis with nothing but her scrawny arms. Sylette wanted to sleep until the sun set, rose, then set again. And before that, she wanted to bathe three times—once each for the blood, sap, and sweat clinging to her flesh.

Yet before that ...

Sighing, Sylette glanced up. The inside of the *Kinloss'* cargo bay had been bombed. There simply wasn't a better way to describe it.

Scorch marks marred the walls, floor, and ceiling. Whole panels had been torn from the deck, revealing gears and pipes that smoked, sparked, and clattered as they strained to keep the airship afloat. A fist-sized hole in the wall shrieked as howling gusts tried to widen it further.

And the Darmatian remnants? The *army* Sylette had pinned her hopes on?

Looking at the survivors, she wanted to laugh—to curse her own naiveté that *they* could somehow defeat the Empire.

'Heroic' Major Reev knelt beside Vallen's limp form, one hand on the wound she'd inflicted, the other forever tracing a curved bundle in her pocket. Velle hovered over Unter, who had nearly crushed Renar when Vallen sent him flying. Light radiated from glyphs on her palms, slowly removing the vicious burns lacing the blue giant's arms and torso.

Lilith squatted on Vallen's other side, pressing his pale fingers between her own. Sickening. Sylette stared at the saber still belted to Lilith's side. How could she not have drawn her sword the entire battle? She should have fought *with* them. Instead, she'd tried to talk Vallen down, spouting compassionate gibberish as the deranged Triaron tried to tear them from the sky.

Who could ever think of that—Sylette glanced at the imbecile's crumpled from—*fondly?*

Releasing a world-weary sigh, Sylette placed her elbows on her knees and leaned forward. "I'll say it if no one else will. What the *void* was that?"

"MIS?" Jay suggested. He peeked around the cockpit entrance, beady eyes and small nose making him look like a rat—a cowardly one, at that. "Or maybe some sort of magic-repression feedback—"

Sylette shot him a glare. "That's not what this was. The rest of us lost our magic and we're fine."

"Possession?" Velle stood, wiping her hand across her brow as she dispelled her runes. Taking a deep breath, she moved to Vallen's head, knelt, and resumed her ministrations.

Fool, Sylette thought. He'd admitted to killing another companion, one obviously precious to him. Was it such a stretch to think he'd do the same to them?

Unter nodded. "Point fair. Triaron great warrior, but fight with wings like Vida—like Veneer—against Empire. Nothing like it seen have I."

"You must be joking," Sylette said. "*Our* Vallen? Always on his *rear*, Vallen?"

The Hue blinked twice, then shook his head. "Triaron sweep panzcraft aside like toys. Burn whole platoons, swat lancerjets from sky." His voice trembled, but not from pain. Was the giant . . . *afraid?* "Float in heavens. Same as deity, like your Terran winged god—Sariel. Down struck cruiser with light-from-clouds. Water command to down other hurl."

Sylette gaped at Vallen, eyeing his charred and twisted shoulder, the half-melted armor plates clinging to his ragged combat suit. She noted the way his eyes and mouth twitched even as he slept. Was he trying to say something?

Trying to repeat those awful, condemning words?

I killed her.

"*He* destroyed those Imperial cruisers? All that wreckage in the bay, throughout the town—that was *him?*"

"Just so."

"He's a monster," Sylette whispered, smile tugging at her lips, chills surging down her arms. Like threads dancing at a weaver's touch, a faint plan was spinning together in her mind.

"He's our *squadmate*," Lilith insisted, raising her gaze to meet Sylette's. "And yet all of you attacked him without asking what was wrong—without trying to understand his pain and suffering."

Lilith pointed at the blackened flesh peeling from his exposed shoulder, the sores and crusted scabs riddling his bare cheeks, neck, and arms. "We'd be dead if not for . . . " Lilith sniffled, tears threatening to flood her eyes. "If not for . . . *whatever* it was he became."

Velle curled her fingers and pulled at Vallen's chest wound, drawing globs of dark crimson into her glyph as the flesh beneath knit shut. "I agree with Lilith," she said. "The look I saw in Vallen's eyes as he fought, the pleasure, the *glee* he took in the slaughter . . . " The Sylph shuddered. "That was *not* Vallen."

Sylette shrugged. "Doesn't sound much different from the imbecile I know."

Baring her fangs, Velle leaned forward. "No one asked you, *princess*."

714

Kinloss gave a sudden lurch, throwing Sylette against the wall, tossing everyone toward the cockpit. The ship was leveling out, reducing its speed and settling onto a straight course. Matteo must have evaded the last of the Ascendancy's gunners.

Or the yoke locked up and they were going to die in three, two, one . . .

"What in the Creator's blessed name have you been doing to my ship?" Matteo asked, standing in the cockpit doorway with his arms crossed.

His eyes had sunken deep into the sallow flesh of his face, the veins around them radiating like creeping spider webs. White streaked his auburn hair—roots turning the color of snow for some reason Sylette could only guess at. Blood crusted on his lips, around his nose and ears. Somehow, this battle had taken more out of Matteo than most of them.

Yet still, he stood.

All of them stood.

And perhaps, Sylette thought with a grin, *that's enough to work with.*

Now she saw. Now she *understood.* They'd been going about this war the wrong way.

Defeating the Empire in the field was meaningless. Take down a single army, or even one of the Seven Fleets, and the Emperor and his slavish senators would simply replace it. Her former nation accepted the war. It was a part of them, as surely as their breath, their skin, their blood. Even if they hated it, they bowed their heads and sent their children to die.

It was the way things had always been.

Unless they cut off the head of the snake.

Vallen and Major Reev were Primal-grade monsters. Matteo could see *and* predict the flow of men'ar, to say nothing of his telepathic abilities. No one could match Unter's brawn, Lilith was a peerless swordswoman, and Velle could stop panzcraft rounds with her glyphs.

And Renar? Well, perhaps Sylette had a *small* soft spot for the man whose father was as rotten as her own. Even if she couldn't find a way to coax out his hidden magic, he'd still be an asset.

This was *possible.*

At long last, after more than a decade on the run, Sylette had a path to *His Majesty's* throat. A team that could avenge her mother—that could avenge every filthy sewer, every starving night, and every rib-cracking beating she'd suffered at the whim of that wretched void-stain who lounged atop the Sarconian throne.

Yes, it was high time to cut off his head.

"I have a proposition for you all," Sylette said, interrupting Matteo's heated argument with Lilith. Something about there being more smoke *inside* the ship than *outside*. Completely unimportant.

"What now?" Velle asked, sighing.

Ignoring her, Sylette rose and limped toward Matteo. She took his hand. Stood on her tiptoes, leaned in, and—soft as a snowflake—kissed his cheek.

"Thank you. I'll repair *Kinloss* after our next mission. Wait, I can do better than that." She turned away from the wide-eyed boy, facing the whole team. "I'll get him a *new* ship *and* buy all of you whatever you want."

"She's lost it," Lilith said with a snort. "All those sour thoughts finally rotted her brain."

Sylette laughed. "No, Lilith. I'm finally thinking *clearly*. For the first time in months—*years,* even. Defeating the Empire is simple. So laughably easy, I'm a fool for not seeing it earlier."

Major Reev spun around, gaze hollow, blood-smeared fingers *clenched* atop the object in her pocket. "You said 'mission,' *princess.*" The Ice Queen spat the word—which was a step up from firing ice shards at Sylette's face. "What's your plan?"

"Nothing complicated." Sylette turned to the side, raising her arm and pointing toward the distant horizon. Toward Nemare, the First Fleet, and that sneering whoreson garbed in purple robes. "We're just going to murder my father, the Emperor."

"Yep," Lilith said, nodding. "Totally void-touched."

Chapter 73

Wait

Rays of late-evening sun pierced the clouds on the horizon, dappling the damp hills and vales passing beneath the *Kinloss* in warm, ruddy tones. Orange here, mauve there, drifting ever closer to purple the higher Matteo looked. Even the twisting Etrus canal sparkled, calm surface reflecting none of the brutality that had taken place mere leagues upstream.

It was like he was flying through another world.

A beautiful land completely detached from the blood, death, and misery of the previous day.

Matteo's limbs were lead. His eyes ached, the skin around them pinched tight as if in the grip of some unseen vice. And despite the weight of his flesh, the groans of his bones, sleep eluded him.

Yes, not collapsing while piloting the ship was a good thing. Sylette would kill him if he crashed again, regardless of how valuable she thought he was. Matteo pawed at his cheek, skin still tingling from the phantom touch of her lips.

But it was odd that he felt not the least bit tired. In fact, he was on edge. Like something was scratching at the back of his eyeballs, urging him to look past the flowing Darmatian fields, the stalks of grain, and the little hamlets clustered along the canal's edge. Matteo could almost hear a voice, a whisper speaking of the truths he could know if he only dove deeper into his magic.

He shook his head. The blood Velle had wiped from his nose, lips, and ears was warning enough of what awaited him if he tried to use his magic now. *I will keep practicing,* Matteo promised, glancing up at the darkening sky—at the Afterplane that supposedly lay beyond it. *For your sake, Holcomb. And for all the others who perished that I might get this far.*

No tears came as he pictured his mentor, scraggly beard stained by mead and legs bare as the day he was born. Nor had they earlier, when Matteo first heard the news. Did he have any tears left to shed? Or was he becoming so accustomed to loss that another death was, well, just that?

Another.

Then another.

And another after that.

"When will it end?" Matteo whispered, sorrow weighting his words.

"When will what end?" asked a soft voice in his ear.

Turning, his cheek met Velle's lips. She kissed him, lightly, tenderly, then passed half of a tattered blanket about his shoulders. "That was to erase Sylette's," she said, curling up in the empty co-pilot's chair and wrapping herself in the blanket's other half.

Matteo tried to smile. He failed. "Are you jealous?"

"No."

"Then ... "

"Is it wrong to want to kiss you?"

A scene drifted in front of Matteo's throbbing eyes: the two of them behind Etrus' chapel, sprawled in the grass of Kinloss' garden, hands clasped together as they watched the sun set over Lyndwur Forest. Even then, he'd been innocent. His heart pounding, palms sweaty, unable to appreciate the gorgeous view because the one he loved was at his side.

It should be the same now. With *this* sunset. With *this* Velle.

And yet ...

Matteo stared at her. Streaks of ash couldn't hide the glow of her scarlet skin. Her raven hair was a mess, full of knots and tangles, matted by sweat and grease. Yet the way it fell across her ears and shoulders made his pulse quicken. Made him want to take it in his fingers and brush it clean, strand by strand by strand. Her eyes were full, her quivering lips parted as she waited for his reply.

Dear Veneer, *Velle* was nervous around *him*.

And yet ...

"Velle," Matteo said, taking her hand. Slipping his fingers between hers. "Please tell me about your past."

She met his gaze. Cocked her head to the side, leaned across the space between them, and nuzzled her shoulder into his. "I want to, Matteo. I do. But I'm afraid."

"It won't change how I—"

An obsidian-clawed finger pressed against his lips. "It will. And not in the way you think."

For an instant, Matteo bristled. How could *she* know how *he* would react? "I will always lo—"

A second finger joined the first, tapping him like he was a disobedient child. "Don't use that word. Not yet, anyway."

"So, what *do* you want me to do?" Matteo huffed.

"Wait." Velle's hand drifted down his uniform, pointed out the viewport. "And watch the sunset with me. Just the two of us, sitting together, enjoying . . . the moment. As we . . . are now. Not . . . who we were . . . before."

Her words started to slur, slowing as her eyelids drooped. Pausing as they closed completely and her head rested on Matteo's shoulder. A quiet moment passed, her breath tickling his neck, her arm draped across his lap.

One of Velle's eyes popped open, locking with his. Its crimson depths entranced him. *She* entranced him.

"Wait and sit . . . Matteo. That's all I want. All I . . . need, right now. And . . . just be glad. Glad that . . . we're still . . . alive . . .

Still together . . .

Despite it . . .

All . . . "

Chapter 74

Forever, Always, and Only Yours

Night had fallen, shrouding the *Kinloss* in an inky blackness broken only by the lonely gaze of the moons and the dim running lights scattered throughout the cargo bay. Two souls were still awake. The rest slept where they had collapsed, draped across the narrow benches, huddled against bulkheads, or curled up on the floor. What few thin blankets they'd found in the storage bins were scant comfort against the seeping chill of high altitude, but bone-weary exhaustion had shut their eyes all the same.

Only two souls still clung to the waking world.

The pilot, and a woman who had lost her love not once, but twice.

After telling Matteo to fly toward Seyla, Jis stumbled toward the far corner of the cargo bay. The Empire's influence shouldn't have reached …

Shouldn't have reached *where,* exactly? Her thoughts were crystal, shattering the instant she tried to grasp them, crumbling into the hole at the center of her soul. Jis should be planning right now. Figuring out what was wrong with Vallen, determining which of her contacts could still be trusted, assessing …

Assessing *what,* again?

Jis glanced down as her knee struck the bench above Unter's head. She … she wasn't quite sure how her legs worked. Was it left, then right? Right, then left?

Nothing made sense right now. Not with a chasm ripping apart Jis' chest, a void that left her on the verge of falling—of curling in on herself—with every step she took. She had her magic back. The slivers of frost orbiting her were evidence of that.

But she had lost something else.

Something that, somehow, pierced her more deeply than it had the first time.

He's dead.

Rodale is dead.

It couldn't be true. No, Rodale was gone again. That must be it. The crafty voidstain was setting her up, pulling the strings in the shadows, plotting to make her a hero like he had before.

Then he'd reappear. Let Jis lash him with ice, insults, and threats. Let her rail against him, unflinching, unmoving, until her heart began to melt. Until she started to think that maybe, just maybe, they had a chance . . . again . . .

Jis struck the side of the closed ramp, slid down it until she reached the floor. She hadn't the energy to pull herself onto the bench. Hadn't the will to unlace her boots, wipe her ash-smeared face, or find a jacket to replace the one she'd lost.

The cold no longer affected her. As before, the Ice Queen felt neither the glow of heat nor the chill of frost.

She was empty.

A void into which love, like everything else, disappeared.

He's dead.

Rodale is dead.

Jis wanted to cry, but the tears wouldn't come.

She wanted to rage, but her powers would rip the vessel apart—just as that fool Triaron had tried to do.

There was nothing for Jis to do but sit, stare at the forward bulkhead, and wait for—

Her fingers brushed the package in her pants pocket, the wrapped parcel she'd carried through the entire battle of Etrus. A gift from Rodale.

The epitaph he'd never intended.

Should Jis open it? Wouldn't that just remind her of him?

She chuckled. *Not as if there's anything else on my mind.*

Unlacing her pocket, Jis took out the package and unwrapped it layer by layer. The bandages Rodale had used were filthy now, stained dark by her blood, slimy with strands of forest ooze. Yet the gauze at its core was still white. Pure and untainted, like they had been during their Academy da—

Jis tore through the cloth. She didn't need another painful memory, another reminder of the joy and laughs and love they'd shared.

Clink-clink!

Silver flashed in the dim light as two metal bracelets tumbled free and clattered on the deck between her legs. Two gleaming stones were set in each: an emerald for Jis to match her eyes, and a ruby for her beloved. The color of Rodale's hair, a sign of the passion he swore would never waver.

Betrothal bracelets. Two of them. The one he'd given her, and the one she'd given him.

Jis snatched them up. Made to fling them across the room, to cast them as far from her as she could. *Why did you have to go? Why, when we were finally together again? When I'd begun to trust you, to rely on you, to . . . to . . .*

To need you in my life again.

Trembling, Jis lowered the bracelets. Clutched them to her chest and rocked slowly back and forth. *Why, why, why . . .*

Something slipped between Jis' fingers. It fell on her leg, then tumbled to the floor where it stood on v-shaped legs. A piece of paper! Folded again and again until it had fit inside the hollow gap beneath her betrothal bracelet.

Jis didn't think. She grabbed the paper, unfolding it and pressing it close to the faint light at the base of the ramp.

To the Coldest Woman Alive,

It's a pun, you see. About your ice magic and your frosty demeanor. Most people would laugh. You, on the other hand, are probably thinking about how to bring me back just so you can freeze my stones off and shove them down my throat. I should warn you that I'm rather attached to said stones and don't think they'd make a choice meal for any throat you attempted to insert them into.

Yes, my phrasing was deliberate. 'Back' is the correct term, I'm afraid. If you're reading this, I'm no longer among the living. Because if I was, you can bet Sariel's sacred scrotum I'd never let this see the light of the crystals. It's too bloody embarrassing, even for a man of my age. What age, you ask? Younger than you! Twenty-four, for the record, and not a season older.

You know, scratch all of that. Just stop reading. Full halt, not another word, another letter. Just. Say. No! Rip this letter up, burn it, then scatter the ashes on a Seylan beach and get a drink with an umbrella in it while you're there. Always wanted to see if the little doo-dads made the booze taste better.

That's all, remember me as I was.

You're . . . you're still reading, aren't you?

"I am," Jis whispered.

Good, because now it's time for me to get serious.

"Were you ever, though?" Jis said, chuckling.

Yes, I can be serious. Yes, you can stop laughing now.

She didn't. Her grin grew wider. So wide it hurt.

You are my crystal, Jis. That might sound cliché or corny, but I truly mean it. You showed the world one face—that of a hero who couldn't be beaten down. Who would keep working for justice no matter how many times you failed, no matter how many times the system got in your way. That you was mesmerizing. So bright even I had to shade my eyes from time to time.

"Was that what prompted the shade-goggle phase?"

Yes, that's what prompted the shade-goggle phase. Now you get the joke.
But there were more sides to you, Jis. More layers than I could count. The slither-slug that hated getting up in the mornings despite being in the army. The girl who'd skip meals just so she could eat more for dessert. The most beautiful woman I've known, who knew how to make me go crazy with that thing you did using—

Jis rolled her eyes, feeling the mist gathering at their edges. "You don't need to say it."

You're right. I don't need to write it here. We both know what you did.
But you were smart and funny, moody and exuberant. You may have been an ice-mage, Jis, but to me, you were my sun. The light that greeted me when I opened my eyes. The radiance that filled my days with joy. The sunset that kissed my lips as I drifted to sleep. You were my everything, Jis.
And somehow, I still managed to void it all up.

"It was your . . . special gift," Jis murmured.

Don't you dare apologize for me. Even if I told you in person, I need to write these words. I need to own my mistakes so my only regret . . .

"Is

    that

        we

           won't

                have

                    more

                        time

                            together."

Jis nodded. "I understand."

Do you? I left you, Jis. I took our perfect life and threw it away for a voidstain like Iolus. I will never hurt as much as you do, but it burns me like a raging fire. Searing my insides, scorching me to ash bit by bit by bit.

So, if I ever get the chance to save you.

If I ever have the opportunity to trade my life for yours.

I'd do it in a heartbeat and thank the Veneer I loathe that they gave me the chance.

"I would've done the same for you."

You better not be thinking, "I would've done the same for you." I want you to live, Jis. Don't die with me. Don't throw your life away to follow me into some happily-never-after that's probably as real as the miracle wart treatment I've been seeking for . . . reasons. Those brats need you. Most of them have never had a real mother, the rest have crappy fathers, and ALL of them are some sort of void-touched.

Jis laughed, wiping at her eyes. "You're telling me."

As if you needed the reminder. But in case you do, let me say it again.
LIVE.
And again . . .
LIVE.
I can keep writing this till it sinks in.
LIVE.

"Alright, I've got it."

No. No, I don't think you've got it yet.

LIVE, Jis. LIVE for me, LIVE for those kids, LIVE until you're so fed up with your perfectly happy life and your delicious desserts and the wonderful, peaceful world you created that you can't think of a single thing you'd regret if you died that moment.

Then KEEP living until you're old and gray, until that face I love so much is wrecked with wrinkles, your hair falls out, and Darmatia's given you an airship-sized medal for being the oldest voiding hag on the continent.

Then, only then, can you join me, Jis.
I'll wait for you.

"I'll be there," Jis promised.

With a love that warmed us both.

She felt it. Dear Veneer, Jis *felt* it. Pulsing in her empty heart, driving back the chill with little wisps of fire, tiny rays of light. It was just a flicker. But even so, she was warmer than she'd been in her entire life.

That thawed your heart, if just a bit, and melted my crusty old soul to goo.

"It did." Jis' tears overwhelmed her, running along her nose, dripping down her cheeks. "It did, didn't it?"

> "*That's*
> how
> *much*
> I
> *loved* …
> *No,*
> that's
> *not*
> right.
> That's

725

> how
>> much
>>> *I*
>>>> LOVE
>>>>> *you, Jis …*
>>>>>> Rodale … "

Forever, Always, and Only Yours,
Rodale

The tears kept falling, blending with Jis' snot, striking the page in great plops that made the ink blur and run. She folded it quickly, drawing it to her chest, holding it as if it were the man himself as she heaved and shook and sobbed.

She'd lost so much.

Years she'd given to Darmatia. Cadets and soldiers who'd died at her command.

But the spear shoved through Jis' gut had been driven home by a man she'd loved and hated more than any other.

And even though he'd asked her to live, even though he'd begged her to move on, she couldn't. Not this night. Not yet, at least.

And so, her tears fell.

Drenching her sleeves.

Puddling on the floor.

Down and down, over and over again.

A flood for the man who'd warmed her frozen heart.

Jis' tears fell.

And fell.

And

f

e

l

l

726

Epilogue

Vestiges of Decay

Adamantele 12, 697 ABH
Sarconia, Imperial Seat of the Sarconian Empire

Vasuron Artorios was a light sleeper.

The slightest noise could wake him. The scuff of a scullery maid's slippers in the hall, the twitter of a songbird risen before its fellows, or even the phantom sliding of bookcases in the vault far beneath the palace plateau.

Sometimes, Vasuron stirred without hearing anything at all, the thrumming of his blood, the *thrill* of a scheme or plan or idea tearing him from his slumber.

Tonight, was one such night.

Casting aside his Trillith-silk sheets, Vasuron slid to the end of his canopy bed, parted the thick curtains, and planted his bare feet on the lacquered darkwood floor. Groans followed him, his concubines clutching the sheets tighter about their pale breasts and snuggling deeper into the mattress.

Vasuron considered waking them. Reaching out, he stroked a finger along the blonde girl's exposed leg, tracing her freckles, smiling as she shivered in her sleep. He did the same with the scarlet-haired beauty on the right, then tugged at her covers. Once, twice, chuckling when she turned over and yanked the sheets from his grasp.

His smile faded, crushed beneath the weight of indifference. What a trivial game. How boring. *All of this*—Vasuron gazed around his spacious chambers—*is boring.*

The racks of exotic weapons he'd long since mastered gathered dust near the windows. Beyond his tightly drawn drapes, the rows of foreign flowers and spices he'd briefly cultivated withered, rotting boughs drooping toward the balcony floor. Tomes and missals by Lozaria's greatest minds lay half-read on the tables, the shelves, the ground, pages covered in symbols he'd scrawled during fits of inspiration.

None of it brought Vasuron joy anymore. Not the sel-spice still floating in the air, tickling his nostrils with its touch. Not the pitcher of 541 Ithran wine on the nightstand, nor the untouched shank of veal beside it, its dried juices glimmering in a stray strand of moonlight.

The crown prince of the Sarconian Empire, the one who'd inherit the world, was sick of his banal existence.

Or, at least, he *had* been.

Purpose drove Vasuron across the room, brought him to stand before his dresser. A broad mirror stood atop it, but he indulged his image for but a moment. Flowing raven locks, high Artorios cheekbones, sculpted flesh and muscles toned by years of training . . .

None of it mattered. It brought Vasuron no more than a spark of pleasure, a spike of joy and life and fulfillment. There and gone, just like the release his maids allowed him.

Only his obsidian eyes gave him pause. Whenever he gazed into their depths, Vasuron sensed something gazing back. *That* made him smile. *That* was interesting.

As was the folder laying open on the dresser's surface. Vasuron started flipping through the crinkled, yellowing documents with one hand, the other reaching out to ruffle the crystalline fur of a crysahund curled nearby. It didn't whimper, flinch, or pant with delight. No, the stuffed hound just maintained its eternal slumber atop the mahogany plaque he'd set it on.

Vasuron hadn't killed Sylette's pet out of malice. No, he'd simply been bored and wanted to experiment with taxidermy. The urge had quickly passed, but his handiwork was impeccable. Illyrium shards made the creature's eyes glow and gave the crystal fur a haunting blue sheen. Its claws had been sharpened to a point, its fangs glossed in amber, and its tail strengthened with wire to let it move. Perhaps Sylette would even appreciate the gesture—her beloved Tyxt, perfectly preserved forevermore.

It was one more reason to anticipate their coming reunion.

Yes, Vasuron smiled, shivers racing along his naked flesh, breath coming quicker with every ornate family tree and genealogical record he perused. *With this, our reunion is all but ordained, dearest sister.*

He'd been right to demand the original from that spy, who'd been given a copy in its place. The grain of the text, the cracking seals emblazoned with chalice and lance, angel and scepter . . . These would provide Vasuron with no end of entertainment.

And should the war be prolonged . . .

Should the truth come to light . . .

Should *he* reveal it himself . . .

Then, little sister, little brother . . . the three of us shall experience amusement unlike any we have before.

And I, Vasuron shuddered with ecstasy, eyes of blackest pitch rolling back in his head. *I shall never know boredom again.*

Hans Ulrich had lost track of time.

Down and down he wandered, tracing drafty spiral staircases lit by flickering candles, marching along vast hallways with not a living soul in sight. How deep did the Nemare palace extend? Why build all these corridors and rooms yet fill them with . . . nothing?

And what lay at the bottom?

Cinching his uniform collar tight against the chill, clutching Vier's folder beneath his arm, Hans exited another empty passageway and entered the next curving stairwell. Stone was all he saw—great slabs of granite stacked one atop the other in endless rows and columns. No carpets lined the floor, no tapestries or banners hung from the walls. Not a single chair lay along his path to offer weary visitors rest.

Candles were the only evidence someone had been here before Hans, their glow driving back the subterranean gloom, guiding him ever onward.

Clomp-clomp, went Hans' boots.

Drip-snap went the candles, wax dribbling down their sides, flames crackling like distant laughter.

Unease prickled the back of Hans' neck, shivers that had nothing to do with the moisture-slick stones. Every noise he didn't make made him want to run for the surface. Every breath he took was quicker than the last.

Keep going, Hans told himself. *For Elycia, for Meira, for Sirus.*

Keep going, because if you stop, Lord Sarcon will never forgive you.

And so he walked, twisting and turning, down and down.

Eventually, the sound of groaning reached his ears—the muddled grunts of dozens of sick, tired, or beaten people shoved into too small a space. Hans knew their cries well. Had heard them countless times in the Sarconia slums when plagues ripped through their streets or rations became scarcer than normal. Rattling and clicking soon joined the symphony of suffering, along with the rough shuffle of flesh on stone.

What in the Void was happening down here?

Hans reached the bottom and stepped out into a long chamber with a high, arched ceiling. The only light was an illyrium lamp fixed to a cluttered workbench at the far end, behind which stood a man dressed in loose Darmatian silks.

Sarcon.

He appeared little different than the last time Hans had seen him. No decay marred his host's fair features, and his curly golden hair beamed like the sunlight Darmatia was so proud of. Sea-blue eyes glanced up. Settled on Hans as rosy lips parted in a grin.

"Good, good, you've returned. I was beginning to worry you'd lost your way."

Warmth drained from Hans' cheeks. He'd never lose his way, not when the consequences would be so dire. "O-of course, My Lord. I have the documents you requested right here." His fingers tapped a frantic rhythm on the folder clutched in his right hand.

"Bring them to me."

Hans started across the chamber, gaze drifting despite his best efforts to focus. The whole left wall was comprised of long metal bars with narrow gaps between them, much like he'd have expected to see in a prison. The ceiling receded into shadow above the cells, no light—and therefore no escape—to be found above.

Was this an old Darmatian dungeon? The dusty, murk-shrouded cells suggested it might be. But where were the lifts for hauling prisoners and supplies? The guard barracks, the food cellar, and all the other necessities for restraining criminals?

Something glinted within the darkness, little flashes of scarlet that brought Hans to a halt. He blinked. Reached up and wiped the grit from the corners of his eyes. Hans craved the embrace of a real bed after six days on another transport hauler, but he shouldn't be so exhausted he started seeing things.

The bars are rusty, Hans told himself, nodding and moving on. *It's just a trick of the light.* And if there *were* prisoners inside?

For those he cherished, he would look the other way.

Sarcon's voice echoed like thunder in the prison chamber. "How goes the war? I haven't left my work for weeks now, let alone heard what goes on beyond these walls."

Weeks? And yet the warlock's flesh was ruddy and hale, not a spot, not a blemish to be seen. Was the cadet boy such a superior host that he no longer needed to eat, drink, or rest?

"Rittermarschal Valescar has pacified Beiras and prepares to encircle the bulk of Rabban's forces at Varas Fortress," Hans replied. "If all goes well, the war could be over by the Renewal festivities next month." *And I might be able to spend my first holiday season with my family,* he added silently.

"And Sychon?" Sarcon cast the Emperor's name like a curse. "I expect he's still fouling things up with his *adoring* citizens?"

Hans didn't rise to defend his sovereign. By contracting Vier—by sending a spy into the heart of the Imperial palace—he'd made his choice. The lies he'd written to the Grand Marschal corroborating Sarcon's reliance on Cimbri's text for his grand spell were merely the final drops in the poisoned goblet of his treason.

Either Sarcon would emerge victorious, or Hans and those dear to him would die.

That was his future.

"Nemare is on the brink of rebellion," Hans said, nearing the workbench. "Ritter troops clash with Sariel cultists nightly, armed protestors gather at the bridges to the government district, and Rittermarschal Titania is positioning warships over the slums."

"Kindling waiting for embers," Sarcon murmured, holding a strange crimson crystal up in front of his lamp. "And with embers shall come fire, with fire a rush of wind, and with wind a storm of ashes. The Emperor moves his pieces poorly, but we shall make use of their shattering all the same."

"My Lord?" Hans slid the folder across the table, then stepped back, awaiting orders.

Sarcon waved his hand. "Just musings, my friend. Every death is a rebirth, you see. Every ending, a beginning. Every loss"—he clenched his hand into a fist, crushing the crystal—"a gain. I told that brat Leon as much, but he didn't seem inclined to listen."

Leon? Was Sarcon speaking of the boy he'd possessed?

Turning, the immortal opened his hand. Light jetted from it in a wide arc. White, pure, dazzling. It drove back the shadows at the chamber's far end, revealing a great crimson door carved directly into the stone around it. It had no handles or knobs, no hinges to swing on nor means to slide it open. Only a faint slit slicing it from top to bottom suggested the portal was intended to be opened at all.

The whole surface sparkled, reflecting Sarcon's light, filling the chamber with radiance. Glowing runes dotted its twin faces. Ancient symbols and lines of text that made as much sense to Hans as ancient

Eliassi. He couldn't look directly at it. Shielding his eyes with his arms, he staggered backward one step, two.

He struck the cell bars on his third step. Manacles rattled. Chains clanked as they scraped across the floor, snapped taut as those they bound rushed toward the bars. An arm clothed in grimy rags thrust over Hans' shoulder, grabbing, clawing for his throat. Hoarse growls roared in his ears. Drool dribbled from the thing's mouth, soaking the back of his collar.

Hans ducked the limb, then dove forward as more arms, legs—even gaping mouths—lunged for him. He struck shoulder first, rolled, and came up in a defensive stance facing the cells. "What in oblivion is going on?" Hans screamed.

Sarcon rounded his table, blazing palm held before him. "Back! Back, you wretches!"

The light afforded Hans his first good look at the monstrosities. They were . . . *people*. Dear ancestors, they were *Terrans* just like him, only . . . twisted. Malformed by strange scarlet crystals that coated their bodies like grotesque flowers, budding from eyes, sprouting from throats, ripping and tearing the flesh above as they blossomed.

They shied away from Sarcon, raising bloated limbs to block the light. Skin sloughed from their faces, their limbs, revealing glittering seedbeds of crystal still waiting to sprout. Sores pocked what tissue remained, seeping puss, weeping tears their eyes no longer could.

And their groans, their cries! They were in *pain*—wailing, moaning, shrieking though their minds were already broken. Though the tattered strips they wore were all that remained of who they'd once been.

"You."

Sarcon lowered his light, gesturing to the creature whose mangled arm was still caught between the bars. It had tried to attack Hans, but now it hadn't the intelligence to squeeze its crystal-riddled limb back through.

What a pitiful soul, Hans thought, touching his throat.

He could almost feel its rotting fingers reaching for him. Could almost smell the putrid stench of decay wafting from its blackened gums, clogging his nostrils, drowning him completely. Hans wanted to retch, to cry, to run. Instead, he collapsed to his knees, frozen.

"What are they? Who *were* they?"

"Red Plague victims," Sarcon said. He took one step toward the still howling creature, which thrust more of its arm through the bars, tearing open its shoulder, ripping out gobs of sallow flesh that plopped to the floor.

Yet it didn't bleed. Didn't seem to care that it was in agony.

It only wanted Sarcon—or whatever it sensed inside him.

The sorcerer dodged its clumsy swipes, then lashed out and tore a fist-sized clump of crimson crystals from its elbow. Holding up the gemstone, Sarcon turned to Hans.

"Every loss, a gain," he repeated, grin twisting his shadow-shrouded features. "These crystals are pure spiritual energy, Hans. Men'ar in pristine condition. Movable, transportable, usable by anyone, anywhere. This is our way into Har'muth. This is how we reclaim my body.

"This is how we *win*."

Hans had to choke out his words. "A-against *whom?*"

Sarcon's face clouded, eyes flooding with pitch, tendrils of darkness creeping along his cheeks and down his neck. Chasms yawned in the shadows of his robes, sprouted from the stones at his feet. Hans watched the light die. Watched it fall into those depths, down and down and down until it was gone forever.

What had he chosen for a master?

"Against what comes next," Sarcon rumbled, voice loud as thunder and deep as eternity.

END OF REMNANT

Thank You! Please Read!

I cannot thank you enough for reading *Divinity's Twilight: Remnant,* the second book in my combined multiverse of worlds, characters, and magic called the Constella. Each entry will reveal more intrigue about this universe, so be sure to catch them all.

If you enjoyed *Remnant,* PLEASE consider rating and reviewing it on Amazon or any of your favorite book sites and social media platforms. There are countless amazing tales for readers to connect with these days, and leaving a review is the single best way a reader can help an author they love succeed. Bookshelves and hearts only have so much space, but your reviews enable stories like *Remnant* to stand out among the millions of other choices available.

Lastly, it is your support that makes it possible for me to take the worlds, stories, and characters in my mind and bring them to life on the page before you. I truly value your thoughts, opinions, and comments, and would love to hear your feedback. Feel free to email me at chrisrusselldivinitystwilight@gmail.com and I will respond as soon as I am able.

Once again, thank you, and I hope you'll check out the rest of the works in my Constella universe at
https://www.christopherrussellauthor.com/

Forever Yours,
Christopher Russell

Glossary of the Unfamiliar and Arcane

ABH: Acronym for "After the Battle of Har'muth." Most Terran calendars use this event to delineate the start of the modern era.

League: A unit of length equivalent to the distance a Terran man could walk in about one hour.

Veneer: Seven immeasurably powerful deities formed from portions of the Creator's essence and fashioned after each of Lozaria's seven races. Their appearances, abilities, and personalities reflect the temperament and qualities of said race. They were originally Lozaria's stewards, its caretakers, but have long since vanished along with their maker.

Illyriite (Glows Green): Immensely potent spirit stone and an unlimited source of energy (men'ar) for performing magic. After the disappearance of the three Aurelian brothers (Sarcon, Darmatus, and Rabban), knowledge of existing shards was lost, and now Illyriite is considered little more than a fable.

Men'ar: Unconfirmed component dwelling within all forms of matter. In mortals, it is believed to be carried on blood vessels. It is by harnessing its latent connection to ambient men'ar in the environment that mages are capable of performing the miracles known as magic. Known to function via wave mechanics similar to those emitted by projectostands.

Illyrium (Glows Yellow): A weaker version of Illyriite that serves as the foundation of modern society. Everything from airships to catalysts to lamps use it as an energy source. Unlike Illyriite, this mineable yellow mineral breaks down over time, becoming dun and useless. Comprised of compressed men'ar somehow trapped within its crystalline structure.

Creator: Ultimate deity responsible for the creation of Lozaria and its people. His true name is unknown. Worshipped by the Church of Light, who depict him as a radiant pillar of light that burns away darkness. Church teaching cites that he and his Veneer are presently withdrawn from the world and its affairs.

Void or Oblivion: The twin names of the infinite nothingness from

735

which life is said to have originated. Whether or not the Void is sentient is the subject of much debate, and there are religious sects that pay it homage instead of the Creator.

Sensor: Mage capable of sensing the flow of men'ar in living things. Sensor skills do not inhibit the development of any of the ten schools of magic. Only see in black and white, the absence and presence of men'ar, respectively.

Telepath: Mage who can project their essence into the minds of others, seeking to either directly communicate, persuade, or manipulate. Telepath skills do not inhibit the development of any of the ten schools of magic.

Red Plague (Glows Red): A vicious pestilence that swept across Lozaria during the second century EOA (Era of Abandonment). Infection first became apparent when the victim's veins changed from blue to red. Intense coughing fits and expulsion of blood from every orifice followed, along with the gradual, painful growth of crimson crystals within the bloodstream. Death occurred after the sprouting of these beautiful buds, which ejected a dense mist that was contagious for ten days after death. There are no records of recovery prior to its total eradication by the Aurelian brothers.

Dragwyrm: A rare interbreeding of the mighty land-bound wyrm and the graceful, semi-sentient dragons of the sky. While there is not a more powerful beast on the face of Lozaria, magic and magtech advancements have enabled mortals to hunt down or capture many of them. Most known dragwyrms are now bred in captivity, raised as servient haulers of artillery and other heavy cargo.

Empyrean Relics: Mythological weapons and mystical items rumored to have been wielded by the Veneer prior to their disappearance. References to them are confined to the realm of storybooks.

Firing-Arm: Prototype firearms engineered to fire piercing bolts using a series of springs and cables, much like a crossbow. Application of the user's men'ar increased their range, accuracy, and effectiveness.

Elysium (Glows Dark Purple): Seven obsidian shards of varying sizes and shapes said to have power over the very fabric of the universe. Legends tell of a ritual by which one may sacrifice a portion of one's soul—one's life force—to an Elysium fragment to have their deepest desires granted.

Scrying Orb: Illyrium infused hand-held recording device capable of capturing visual and audio data for later playback. Central crystal encodes information as men'ar waves—pure magical energy.

Lume: Luminescent barrier projected by a generator infused with men'ar, typically via direct transference from connected illyrium crystals. Capable of absorbing and dissipating an equivalent amount of physical or magical energy.

Esta and Exal: Lozaria's twin moons, considered female and male respectively. They are perpetually out of sync with each other, one waxing while the other wans and vice versa. The presence of these two bodies causes Lozaria's tidal patterns to be stronger than normal, and the effects of gravity have been lessened compared to a planet with fewer orbiting bodies. Their combined luminescence is enough to make nocturnal travel easy unless cloud cover is present.

Scrivening Magchine: An autonomous copying device powered by illyrium that can perform a range of scribing functions from copying to critique based on the enchantments applied to it.

Casting Catalyst: Weapon or accessory imprinted with illyrium dust in the form of runes and symbols. These etchings are tailored to the type of magic utilized by a mage, enabling them to bolster their internal men'ar with ambient energy absorbed from their surroundings. While the body's own men'ar reserves are more potent, since they are familiar to the user, casting spells with men'ar channeled through a catalyst will prevent destruction of the mage's physical vessel through MIS (Men'ar Imbalance Syndrome).

MIS (Men'ar Imbalance Syndrome): Degradation of the mind and flesh as a result of a body holding more or less men'ar than it is capable of. In other words, the size of the "soul" must match the sturdiness of its "container."

Projectomic: Input system that uses magic to convert auditory input into vibrations and waves that can be transmitted across varying distances. Handheld versions can modulate the speaker's volume, and brass knockers can be attached to send short-range, codified transmissions.

Projectostand: Output system that deciphers projectomic signals and converts them back to sound. Small, in-home units are becoming more popular for news and entertainment, but most still occupy stadiums and cities to quickly broadcast information to large crowds.

Telescriber: Screen based display system that projects visual data acquired by either scrying orb or recorb.

Recorbs: Short-range, direct transmission device consisting of a hovering sphere, a lens, and a low quality illyrium crystal that can only hold a few minutes of optical information at a time. Since they're cheaper than scrying orbs and can indirectly offload their data to nearby telescribers, they are often used to relay sporting events, speeches, or special events.

Flag-Brawl: A popular Lozarian sport played by two teams of four mages each. While the basic premise is the same as capture the flag, a children's game, its brutal execution involves far more rules and violence. Many professional players are former soldiers and mercenaries, a fact that is indicative of Lozaria's belligerent nature.

Seven Fleets: Nickname for the Sarconian navy—its world-renowned air fleet. Each fleet is commanded by a rittermarschal, one of the nation's preeminent mages and tacticians.

Great/Lost Magic: Capable of altering the landscape and leaving behind whole armies of mutilated corpses, these incredible spells were banned by a council of nations, never to again be used in war. Originally wielded by the Veneer before their disappearance, mortals were capable of duplicating them through the efforts of entire battalions of mages, most of whom perished or were deformed in the process.

Long Chants: Several dozen incantations translated from ancient Eliassi to Common over numerous generations. The difficulty of learning and casting them is made up for by their potency and effects—

which often seem to possess minds of their own. Every boon they grant is balanced by a cost.

Afterplane: Grey, drab, endless space occupying the region between the physical realm— Lozaria—and Oblivion. The souls of the dead wait here, suspended in vacant emptiness, until they are claimed by either the Creator or the Void.

MP: A member of the military police responsible for enforcing order within a nation's armed forces.

Talisman: Single-use spells crafted by skilled artisans. Four things are required to produce a talisman: high-quality paper such as cepyrus to act as a casting catalyst, an appropriate amount of illyrium dust, the men'ar of someone who knows the desired spell, and sufficient time for the artisan to Engrave the necessary sigils and runes onto the paper. Etching the runes is performed with an ink made using illyrium dust infused with men'ar. It should be noted that talismans can be Engraved on things other than paper, such as flesh, walls, and other suitable surfaces.

Mother Superior: The leader of the Way of the Will, a prominent branch of the Church of Light that worships the Creator and Veneer.

Engraving/Engraver: The use of men'ar, illyrium, and runes to craft talismans or inscribe other artifacts—such as weapons, furniture, or buildings—with magic spells and capabilities. Those skilled at Engraving are called Engravers.

Non-Com: A non-commissioned officer, such as a sergeant.

Sleds: A game similar to dominos that involves tiles placed atop a surface like upward facing sleds. Each sled has a value and a direction—the way the sled's tip is facing—that can be combined with other sleds to form hands of varying worth. Play progresses around a table in a circular fashion, with each player trading in sleds until one player assembles a hand with all tips facing the same direction, at which point hands are revealed and scores are tallied. Betting on sleds is a common pastime among soldiers, despite the Church's distaste for gambling.

Voidspawn: Demonic creatures believed to have been birthed from the darkness between the stars at the height of the Void's power. Consigned to myth and bedtime fables.

Primal: A class of legendary creatures resulting from the experiments of ancient sorcerers, the foremost of which was Sarcon Aurelian. Most, like the Draken, are chimeras—a blend of the features of their constituent species.

Draken: An aqua Primal with masterful command of water, ink, and lightning—the forces of the sea. Has the head and torso of a dragon but the limbs and healing capabilities of a kraken.

Favorre Medal: A token exchanged between Sewertown crime syndicates that allows a single inviolable request from the recipient to the giver. Sealed in blood.

Kata: A martial arts form, typically conducted for training or exercise.

Sensor's Labyrinth: Training exercises in which sensors set aside their five primary senses and navigate a maze or series of obstacles using only their ability to distinguish men'ar.

Orabairos: Shadowy organization of assassins dwelling in the underbelly of the Imperial capital, Sarconia.

Bekshak: A Hue/Haead cast out of the Ascendancy who may be killed on sight. Committed an offense so egregious that a period of absolute shame—not immediate death—is the only suitable punishment.

Alteration: Magtech enhancements applied or inserted directly into organic tissue. Considered evolution by some and an abomination by those who see the body as a sacred gift from the Veneer.

Ascendant Bank: The largest bank in Lozaria, headquartered in the Hue Ascendancy. It is rumored that those who run the Bank and the Ascendancy are one and the same.

Adjudicator: An agent of the Ascendancy granted the powers of both diplomat and judge. Many covet the title.

LDCT: Long distance communication transceiver. Expensive, cutting-edge technology developed by the Sarconian Empire to enable visual communication across long distances. Each of their fleets will likely possess no more than *one* of the devices.

Fle'bilis: Weak, infirm, and feeble in the old tongue. A person whose men'ar—that all creatures possess—is inert and unresponsive. While many people choose not to develop their magic due to modern magtech conveniences, the majority *could* conceivably become mages. The minority that can't, ten to twenty percent of the population, were once disparaged by the ancient Eliassi word, fle'bilis, which has since gone out of style.

Illyrium Grenade: An explosive charge centered around an illyrium shard whose detonation is primed by a concentrated infusion of men'ar.

Mimeo: Derogatory slang for a morphic mage, someone who uses illusion magic.

Blauer: Derogatory slang for a Hue/Haead. Translation, "Blue Beast."

Feuergrer: Derogatory slang for a Sylph. Translation, "Scarlet Witch."

Gravpads: Magtech devices that emit constant pulses of concussive force against the air and ground to maintain or increase an airship's altitude.

Panzcraft: A large, heavily armored vehicle mounted on treads and powered by an illyrium engine. Built around one to two cannons in rotatable turrets. Slow and unwieldy but powerful and hard to stop. Usually crewed by two to five soldiers, depending on size.

Seven Races of Lozaria

Terrans: A race of bipedal beings who, in comparison to their fellows, are average in almost every way. Lacking the brawn, longevity, or hardiness of other races, they have invested heavily in the development of magic and magtech. Though they lose out to the Sylph in the former and the Hues in the latter, their population far exceeds either, which has enabled them to expand all across Lozaria. Responsibility for many of the continent's conflicts can be laid at their feet, and the three principal Terran states—Darmatia, Sarconia, and Rabban—remain embroiled in what outsiders view as a "Terran Civil War."

Vladisvar: The most prepared warrior is the one whose arm *is* his sword.

The foremost of Lozaria's martial races, the Vladisvar possess an appropriately imposing physiology. Standing at almost three meters tall, they possess coarse, leathery grey skin, long claws, and horns growing from the sides of their temples. As tradition mandates, most Vladisvar, both male and female, are tattooed with a variety of permanent dyes as they age. These symbols, along with the armor plates their mercenaries graft to their flesh, tell the story of their life through recountings of important events. While their religion worships cosmic balance— equalizing good and evil in the world—most Vladisvar that stray from their nomadic origins take work as mercenaries. Though outsiders speculate on their apparent hypocrisy, no one can say for sure why they almost desperately seek battle.

Hue/Haead: Give a Hue—or Haead, as they call themselves—a new invention, and she'll return it to you a few days later with two improvements you'd thought of and three you hadn't.

This matriarchal society of four-armed, blue-skinned beings occupy half of the Etrus Peninsula, a territory they grudgingly share with the Sylph. The largest, tallest beings on Lozaria, they are quick-witted and deft with their many limbs, making them the continent's foremost authority on magtech. It is believed that their obsession with technology stemmed from a population with a low men'ar factor. While every living creature possesses men'ar, not all can wield it, and a Hue child capable of wielding magic is a rarity. Even should a Hue develop magic, sorceries are frowned upon in their society, perhaps because of their country's proximity to the men'ar adored Sylph. The practice of 'Alteration,' enhancing one's body with magtech implants and grafts, is a newly popular trend to overcome magical deficiencies, though there is considerable pushback against it by traditionalists.

In addition, it should be noted that Hue gender roles are flipped not just in government, but across the spectrum. Males are viewed as breeding stock first and individuals second, and their advancement in society is only at the whims of their female superiors or mates.

Sylph: Grace and elegance are paramount to a Sylph. If you are born with magic and beauty, you'll go far in life. If you must choose just one, pick magic, for with it you can grasp the other. But if you have neither … slavery or a swift death are the best you can hope for.

Like their neighbors, the Hues, the Sylph are particularly isolationist, believing themselves superior to the other races. Their base features are similar to Terrans, with the exception of their red pigmentation, the curvature of their ears, and their innate ability to manipulate their body structure using the men'ar in their blood. By doing so, they can sprout wings, expand their muscles, and even rearrange their organs to avoid or mitigate lethal wounds. This ability stems from their command of magic, which is—as a collective race—only second to the Eliade.

Since political power stems from magical aptitude, magtech is almost completely banned within their borders. Foreigners are confined to a special district in their cities. Visiting dignitaries are suffered rather than honored. Though a tenuous peace currently exists between them and the Hues, their disputed ownership of the Tesset Lode, a massive illyrium deposit sitting astride the border between them, means that a renewal of hostilities is all but guaranteed.

Eliade: What is the difference between Illyriite and Eliade? While a person is unlikely to encounter either in their lifetime, Eliade are *supposed* to still exist. However, none have been seen since the Illyriite War, so accounts of them are confined to myths and fables.

Their bodies are wispy, almost ethereal. Solid substance makes up their core, but everything beyond that—their roving sensory appendages, clothing, and skin—is hazy, like flowing mist. It is theorized that this nebulous state brings them closer to ambient men'ar than any other creature, thereby enabling them to wield incredibly potent magic.

When they did engage in mortal affairs, their immortal council, the Eliassa, governed over the other races like a stern parent. Their longevity, which brought them to the cusp of divinity, gave them the right to rule. Now, like the Veneer they worked alongside, they have all but vanished from Lozaria.

Moravi: There is no deal a Moravi won't make, nor cesspit to which he will not travel to make it.

An extremely prolific reptilian race hailing from the southern atoll that bears their name, the Moravi, once conquerors, are now proficient traders. They can walk on two or four legs, using their tail for balance in the former orientation. Similar to the Sylph, Moravi can rapidly produce bone marrow within their bodies, enabling them to modify or eject portions of their skeleton. This ability is handy during a variety of situations, including combat. The color, size, and positioning of their scales and spinal spikes is the primary distinguisher of sex. To outsiders, the slight bulge of a Moravi female's chest is practically imperceptible. In addition to being highly sensitive, their long, forked tongue plays a role in intraspecies communication.

Though they previously dominated much of present Rabban, Darmatia, and the Etrus Peninsula, the Moravi have since been driven back to their isles, where the aristocracy enjoy lives of indolence and the most ambitious travel far afield as merchants and crime bosses. Since each clan-pack numbers in the hundreds, and clan-packs often pursue the same interests, the organizations Moravi establish are incredibly powerful.

Trillith: The individual is nothing; the Hive is all.

Trillith culture is almost as mysterious as that of the Eliade. They certainly *do* exist; their silk products, spun from gossamer threads certain members of their species produce, can be found adorning manses and palaces all across Lozaria. Yet the expansive diffusion of these wondrous fabrics and tapestries is misleading. A foreign merchant wishing to establish a trade relationship with them will not succeed in his lifetime. In fact, it's possible that his grandchildren may still be struggling to earn the Trillith's trust generations later. The only outsiders the insectoid beings truly accept are those who are outsiders no longer. Even a Hue or Vladisvar who willingly relinquishes their sense of self and melds with the collective Hive may join them, at which point they are merely one more appendage of a million limbed whole.

There are as many kinds of Trillith as there are communal roles to be fulfilled. Some have six legs and walk low to the ground. Others are bipedal, and still others fly. The only commonality is that they all go through larva, pupa, and adult stages, with the latter possessing a chitin exoskeleton. Most communicate mind to mind telepathically, through the Hive, but some few possess . . . unsettling features similar to other races, such as vocal cords and distorted faces to go along with them. Scholars speculate that these evolutions were developed to interact with other races, but remain uncertain—or unwilling to guess—how the adaptations were acquired.

The principal Trillith nesting grounds are the Great Southern Forest and the Badlands. Other Hives have yet to be confirmed.

Principal Styles of Magic Use

Engravate (Tier 1 caster): A mage who uses a paired catalyst—on which is carved illyrium infused runes often laced with their own blood—to cast spells by drawing upon the ambient men'ar in their environment. They must establish a special bond with the catalyst in order for the transference of men'ar from surroundings, to device, to caster to function properly. Most still use a verbal incantation to direct their spells and reduce men'ar consumption.

Invoker (Tier 2 caster): A mage, typically an Engravate, who can cast spells without using a spoken incantation. Instead, they compute the directives of their magic (type, spread, range, potency, target, etc.) internally using a second "injection" of men'ar. This process is best examined using two analogies. While the men'ar for the incantation is molded separately from the men'ar for the physical formula, like two hearts beating in parallel, Invoking is akin to holding one's breath during the swiftest of sprints. Approximately twice the men'ar will be consumed for the spell—all directly from the user's bloodstream. The benefits from Invoking a spell (speed and secrecy) must always be weighed against its cost, as Invokers are far more likely to suffer MIS (Men'ar Imbalance Syndrome) than any other type of mage. It should be noted that an Invoker is *not* required to Invoke with every cast. Provided they recall the Eliassi diction, they can revert to utilizing verbal methods of invocation.

Armsmage (Tier 2 caster): Armsmages are the inverse of Invokers in that they can cast spells utilizing any tool or weapon—including their own body, in many cases. Though practitioners of some schools of magic are known for tattooing their bodies with runes after the style of Engraving, neither an Armsmage's flesh nor weapon needs be covered in arcane symbols. They can pick up a stick and wield it just as effectively as an enchanted blade. In fact, their magic is expelled from the "Arms" themselves, whether by swing or block, stab or shot. However, as with Invokers, this convenience comes with an increased drain on men'ar, one accomplished by crafting a men'ar link between their essence and the implement. The perception of both merges, and, for an instant, they become extensions of each other.

Triaron (Tier 3 caster): The Triaron is a classification of mage referring to an elementalist sorcerer who possesses the properties of both an Invoker and Armsmage. When all of these are used in conjunction, the Triaron can cast any elemental spell from any weapon without an Engraved or verbal catalyst. While this does make the wielder extremely versatile, capable of launching wave after wave of magic with no warning or delay between them, they are still bound by the laws of men'ar usage. Where an Invoker exhausts men'ar at twice the rate of an ordinary mage, the Triaron will expend it at three times that speed. There are rumors that Darmatus Aurelian, the first Triaron, found a way to circumvent this severe handicap, but contemporary magic scientists have yet to uncover the secrets of his power. Aside from Darmatus, only one other Triaron has ever been identified.

NOTE: Tier 0 casting requires a series of formulaic drawings and the chanting of a lengthy quotation. This archaic method of casting has been accelerated in the modern era, where magtech and a mage's individual skill combine to evolve their casting into a flowing, graceful art.

Gerjunia Halsruf's Classification of Magical Attributes
(Ten Schools of Magic)

Elemental: The School of Physical Manifestation

Time and Space: The School of Axial Manipulation

Curative: The School of Rejuvenation

Blood: The School of Seals and Pacts

Enhancive: The School of Reinforcement

Morphic: The School of Alteration and Perception

Degenerative: The School of Separation

Necromantic: The School of Preservation

Dark: The School of Shadows and Eternity

Light: The School of Radiance and Infinity

The vast majority of mages fall into one of these categories. Those that don't, approximately a percent of known magic users or less, are grouped in an eleventh set called "Unique." Unlike the vast array of abilities comprising the ten main schools, there is no common ground among the powers of Unique mages. One may be able to control quantities of metal with magnetism, while another might use soothing song and dance to manipulate people's actions and feelings. Why or how these marked deviations manifest has yet to be determined.

Seven Blessings (Seven Holy Tenets)

Order (Justice) — Trillith

Understanding (Charity) — Moravi

Strength (Honor) — Vladisvar

Curiosity (Knowledge) — Hue/Haead

Knowledge (Dedication) — Sylph

Wisdom (Unity) — Eliade

Will (Conviction) — Terran

Each Blessing, bestowed as a boon upon a specific race by the Creator, is paired with a related Tenet: an aspiration or ideal that they should strive to achieve. Part of a faithful believer's responsibility is to meditate on how to live a life that will connect the two. Any adherent to the Church of Light should endeavor to practice all seven Tenets, but, whether because of racial schisms or the difficulty of that task, most choose to focus on the one directly associated with their race and Veneer.

Knowledge is both a Blessing and a Tenet, a curious occurrence that many priests point to as a sign of its importance. Divisiveness between various races and factions of the Church has led to the marginalization of this teaching outside of Nemare and other prominent centers of learning.

Lozarian Calendar

Jenuvant

Illyssuil

Charkur

Aegiq

Kusselaf

Venare

Fulminos

Orpexaz

Festivus

Hetrachia

Adamantele

Mesmeri

NOTE: Four seven-day weeks = Twenty-eight days = One month

Order of Military Ranks for Embattled Nations

Sarconian Empire

Gefreiter
Unteroffizier
Sergeant
Ritterbruder Second Class (Equivalent to regular army captain)
Ritterbruder First Class (Equivalent to regular army major)
Rittermark (Equivalent to regular army colonel)
Vice Admiral
General or Admiral
Rittermarschal
Grand Marschal

Kingdom of Darmatia

Private
Corporal
(Not active duty) Cadet
(Not active duty) Senior Cadet
Ensign
Lieutenant
Captain
Major
Lieutenant Colonel
Colonel
General or Admiral

Airship Classifications Ordered by Size and Crew Complement

Civilian

Skimmer
Yacht
Freighter / Transport

Military

Hoverskiff (fighter)
Hoverjet / Lancerjet (fighter)
Transport / Lander
Light Cruiser / Corvette
Heavy Cruiser / Frigate
Carrier
Dreadnought (Capital Ship)

Dramatis Personae

Darmatia

Vallen Metellus (Terran—Senior Cadet): Second Triaron and adopted son of Steward Rowan Metellus. Formerly known as Kit. Wielder of elemental magic.

Sylette Artorios (Terran—Senior Cadet): Exiled third princess of the Sarconian Empire, daughter of Third Consort Lanara, deceased. Taken in by Undersecretary Farkos of the Rabban Imperium and uses the family name as a cover. Wielder of spatial manipulation magic.

Matteo Alhan (Terran—Senior Cadet): Son of Anathea and Martan Alhan, heir to the Antares Shipping Company. Nominal squad pilot. Wielder of sensory and telepathic magic.

Velle'assa Me'andara (Sylph—Senior Cadet): "Velle." Wandering Sylph who earned a scholarship to the Darmatian Military Academy. Formerly Vallen's lover. Empath and wielder of blood, curative, and enhancive magic.

Leonel Descar (Terran—Senior Cadet): "Leon." Third son of Archimas Redora Descar, best friend to Vallen Metellus. Wielder of light magic. Presumed deceased.

Unter (Hue/Haead—Senior Cadet): Wandering Hue who earned a scholarship to the Darmatian Military Academy, best friend to Renar Iolus. Speaks poor Common. Wielder of enhancive magic.

Renar Iolus (Terran—Senior Cadet): Only son of General Hardwick Iolus, heir to House Iolus. Best friend to Unter. Wielder of enhancive magic.

Lilith (Terran—Senior Cadet): Daughter of merchants who paid for her to attend the Darmatian Military Academy. Wielder of explosive-type elemental magic.

Rowan Metellus (Terran—Steward): Fourth elected Steward of the Kingdom of Darmatia, adoptive father of Vallen Metellus. Imprisoned by Sychon Artorios.

Hardwick Iolus (Terran—General): Commandant of the Darmatian Military Academy and commander of the Royal City Defense Forces. Father of Renar Iolus. Post-Aldona status unknown.

Jis Reev (Terran—Major): Instructor at the Darmatian Military Academy, heralded as the heroic "Ice Queen of Darmatia." Wielder of ice-type elemental magic. Post-Aldona status unknown.

Ur Contus (Terran—Admiral): Commander of the Darmatian

armed forces. Was aboard the *King Darmatus* at the battle of Aldona Fortress. Presumed deceased.

Anathea Alhan (Terran—Mother): Wife of Martan and mother of Matteo. Sickly woman who fusses over her son's wellbeing.

Martan Alhan (Terran—Businessman): Husband of Anathea and father of Matteo. Owner of the Antares Shipping Company in Sarconian occupied Etrus.

Elaine Gennesaret (Terran—Aristocrat): "Aristo girl." Young girl "Kit," now known as Vallen, attempted to steal from. After saving him from drowning, she took him home, gave him a *real* name, and became the center of his world. Deceased.

Reesa (Terran—Maidservant): Servant in the employ of Elaine and the Gennesaret family. Presumed deceased.

Bernard Foltran (Terran—Councilman): Member of the Ruling Council / Council of Overseers and Foreign Minister of Darmatia. Post-Aldona status unknown.

Ich'oth (Moravi—Senior Cadet): Former member of Renar's squad recalled to the Moravi Atoll for their mating rituals. Replaced by Sylette.

Cappie (Terran—Captain): Captain of the *Feywind*, a supply freighter supporting the Darmatian fleet at the Battle of Aldona Fortress. Presumed deceased.

Sal Stenberg (Terran—Butcher): Owner of Sal's Eats and Meats Emporium in Etrus. Gave Matteo and Velle feuersteer steaks to celebrate their "marriage."

Sarconia

Sarcon Aurelian (Terran—Immortal): Older brother of Darmatus and Rabban. Founder of the Sarconian Empire who gathered all seven shards of Elysium only to be thwarted by his brothers. After breaking free of his prison, he possesses first Vahn, then Leon.

Sychon Artorios (Terran—Emperor): Sovereign of the Sarconian Empire, former husband of Third Consort Lanara Artorios, father of Sylette, Vasuron, and an unnamed third child. Wielder of gravity magic, a potent subset of spatial manipulation magic.

Vasuron Artorios (Terran—Crown Prince): Eldest son of Sychon and heir apparent to the Sarconian Empire. Tricked Sylette, resulting in her banishment. Wielder of unknown spatial manipulation magic.

Lanara Artorios (Terran—Third Consort): Former wife of Sychon Artorios and mother to Sylette. Executed for attempted regicide, the reasons for which are unknown.

Konig Zaratus (Unknown—Grand Marschal): Commander of the Rittermarschals and the Sarconian Empire's armed forces. Magic is unknown.

Ober Valescar (Terran—Rittermarschal): "The Wall of the Empire." Commander of the Empire's Seventh Airfleet and mentor of Sylette. Executed Lanara in front of her daughter. Wielder of unique magnetism magic.

Auvrea Titania (Terran—Rittermarschal): "The Imperial Rose." Commander of the Empire's Fifth Airfleet and newly appointed governor of the Sarconian Province of Darmatia. Only female Rittermarschal. Wielder of fire/explosive elemental magic.

Galran (Terran—Rittermarschal): Commander of the defeated Eighth Imperial Airfleet. Deceased.

Vahn Badenschiff (Terran—Ritterbruder First Class): Leader of a special forces mission to steal Rabbanite magtech secrets. After the mission failed, he traded his body to Sarcon in exchange for saving Hans and Sarconia. Wielder of fire elemental magic. Deceased.

Hans Ulrich (Terran—Second Lieutenant): Former squadmate of Vahn Badenschiff. Current aide of Sarcon. Husband of Elycia, father of Meira and Sirus. Wielder of sensory and curative magic.

Dr. Archimas Redora Descar (Terran—Engimage): Foremost authority on airship design in Lozaria. Father of Leon, Ernst, and Julian. Husband of Anjalise, now deceased. Defected from the Kingdom to the Empire after the former's unconditional surrender.

Olivier Stetson (Terran—Lieutenant Colonel): Former captain of the royal guard, demoted one grade for failing to stop Lanara's assassination attempt.

Wilhelm Badenschiff (Terran—Minister of Agriculture): Father of Vahn. Minister of Agriculture for the Sarconian Empire.

Tannen Holler (Terran—Broadcaster): Former celebrity projectostand and flagbrawl caster, current Sarconian propaganda announcer.

Faltro Gustavus (Terran—Foreign Minister): Foreign minister of the Sarconian Empire.

Seb and Tremon (Terran—Gefreiters): Enlisted Sarconian soldiers ambushed by Sariel cultists while off-duty in the Darmatian capital, Nemare. Deceased.

Sewertown

Bohomaz (Vladisvar—Crime Boss): Leader of the gang of street urchins and thieves Kit/Vallen was part of as a youth. Former warrior of some renown.

Jomori (Moravi—Fence): Owner of the *Safe Haven* pawnshop, a front business for Bohomaz's gang. Referred to as "Uncle" by other members.

Pockey (Terran—Pickpocket): Young Kit/Vallen's best friend and go-to pickpocket for Bohomaz's gang.

Singe (Terran—Gang Lieutenant): Senior member of Bohomaz's gang who lords his authority over younger members. Wielder of fire elemental magic.

Unaffiliated

Grozza (Moravi—Trader/Thief): Leader of a small group of Moravi who attempted to sell the cadets to Sarconian forces. Status unknown.

Mother Junica (Terran—Nun): Elderly sister in the religious organization, The Way of the Will. Helped deliver Matteo and served as the Alhan family physician during his youth.

Abbott Kinloss (Terran—Priest): Church of Light pastor servicing the city of Etrus. Slain by Lt. Colonel Stetson for assisting cadets.

Historical

Darmatus Aurelian (Terran—Triaron): First Triaron and founder of Darmatia. Younger brother of Sarcon, older brother of Rabban. Defeated his brother, Sarcon, but was forced to sacrifice his life to stop the Oblivion Well he unleashed. Wielder of all elemental magic. Deceased.

Rabban Aurelian (Terran—Lord): Younger brother of Sarcon and Darmatus. Defeated his brother, Sarcon, alongside Darmatus, but was forced to sacrifice his life to stop the Oblivion Well he unleashed. Enterprising designer of weapons and wielder of sensory and telepathic magic. Deceased.

Saris Aurelian (Terran—Lady): Wife of Darmatus. Survived him and bore an heir to the Darmatian royal line. Deceased.

Jarrik Savane (Terran—Aide): Adjutant to Darmatus during the Battle of Har'muth. Deceased.

Kanar'kren (Hue/Haead—Prime Factor): Prime Factor of the Hue Ascendancy during the Battle of Har'muth. Deceased.

Faratul (Sylph—Grand Magister): Grand Magister of the Sylph Magerium during the Battle of Har'muth. Deceased.

Ilitharia (Eliade—Her Grace): Immortal leader of the Eliade and chairwoman of the Eliassa, their divine council.

Syvas Artorios (Terran—General): Commander of Sarcon's forces during the Battle of Har'muth. Progenitor of the Artorios bloodline that assumed rule of the Empire after Sarcon's imprisonment. Deceased.

Ephalia Aurelian (Terran—Queen): Last Queen of Darmatia assassinated during the Theradas Dispute with the Sarconian Empire. Died without an heir, ending the Aurelian bloodline.

Gerjunia Halsruf (Terran—Magic Scholar): Second century ABH magic scholar who introduced the modern system of magic classification.

Archelaus Heisden (Terran—Poet): Fourth century poet and author who composed the "Sea God's Crest," a poem used by an unknown Darmatian army operative as a coded cipher.

The Seven Veneer

Sariel: Veneer of the Terrans
Artyr: Veneer of the Sylph
Vida: Veneer of the Hues/Haead
Ellara: Veneer of the Eliade
Sondek: Veneer of the Vladisvar
Chi'Chotath: Veneer of the Trillith
Reshal: Veneer of the Moravi

The Story Thus Far

Seven centuries ago, the forces of order won the Illyriite War on the plains of Har'muth. Darmatus and Rabban Aurelian slew their elder brother, Sarcon, the despotic architect of the conflict, then sacrificed themselves to banish the cataclysmic vortex opened with his dying breath. The first advent of the Oblivion Well was thwarted. Even without their vanished gods, the seven races of Lozaria proved themselves capable of safeguarding their world.

In the present, three nations carry on the brothers' dreams. Sarconia, land of law and order. Darmatia, kingdom of light and wisdom. Rabban, realm of progress and advancement. Since the time of their progenitors, they have fought a near ceaseless battle for supremacy, no faction gaining more than a slight edge on the others.

Until now.

A new magtech weapon allows Rabban to conquer Varas Fortress, a crucial fortification defending the Sarconian Empire's eastern provinces. With the loss of the fortress and one of their eight airfleets, the Empire launches a desperate covert operation to steal or disable Rabban's revolutionary device.

It fails. Subordinates dead and dying, the mission's commander, Vahn Badenschiff, takes refuge in the ancient battleground of Har'muth. Instead of sanctuary, he discovers a prison—a weakening magical seal that has bound the dark sorcerer Sarcon since the time of his downfall.

Mind enthralled by Sarcon's power, Vahn strikes a bargain. He will give up his body as a vessel for the sorcerer's escape in exchange for two inviolable promises: Sarcon will save the Empire, and he will keep Hans Ulrich—Vahn's last surviving soldier—alive.

Three months later, the Kingdom of Darmatia celebrates a host of festivals culminating in their Royal Military Academy's Graduation Day events. Much to the chagrin of Matteo Alhan, Vallen Metellus—his squad leader—chooses to flunk the written portion of their final exam. The arrogant mage, second Triaron and heir to the abilities of the Hero King Darmatus, believes he can ace the practical exam and pass anyway.

Vallen is sorely mistaken. Their flag-brawl match turns into a disaster as Sylette Farkos, an honor student from the Rabban Imperium, outmaneuvers or KOs his teammates Velle'assa Me'andara and Leonel Descar. During a one-on-one engagement, Sylette lures Vallen into attacking her right as Matteo snipes at her from afar. The shot hits Vallen square in the back, incapacitating him.

Before Sylette can claim victory, the match is halted. The Sarconian Empire has broken the terms of the Theradas Accord by besieging Aldona Fortress. All Academy cadets are called up to serve alongside the regular army in defense of the Kingdom.

Unfortunately for Vallen's squad, his refusal to throw the graduation match lands him in hot water with General Hardwick Iolus, commandant of the Academy. Vallen and the general's son, Renar, end up assigned to the same rundown freighter at the rear of the Darmatian defense fleet—far from any chance at glory. Their squads trade barbs while waiting for the Empire to rattle their sabers, fire a warning shot, and go home.

But Sarcon has not spent his freedom idly. With Hans in tow, Sarcon returned to the Sarconian capital and forcefully secured Emperor Sychon Artorios' cooperation in retrieving his yet imprisoned body. In exchange, the ancient mage promises Sychon a shard of Elysium—the very same wish-granting stone his flesh is trapped within.

Wielding taboo Great Magic—battalion-level spells banned by international law—Sarcon obliterates half the Kingdom fleet and crushes Aldona Fortress. His current vessel, Vahn, succumbs in the process, disintegrating until only a blackened husk remains.

The freighter *Feywind* is clipped by Sarcon's spell and begins a slow plummet to the ground. Vallen, Matteo, and company rush to escape, but find their way blocked by one of the Empire's top military commanders, Rittermarschal Ober Valescar. The one-eyed magnetism mage has been ordered to bring home the exiled third princess: Sylette *Artorios.*

She refuses to go, railing against a father who murdered her mother and the general—Valescar—who carried out the sentence. Vallen uses the opening to rush Valescar, who outclasses him in every way. Within a few passes, Vallen is on the ground, unconscious and drained of men'ar, the spiritual energy that enables magic.

To save him, Leon and Sylette hatch a desperate plan. Using Valescar's orders to retrieve her against him, Sylette distracts the Rittermarschal while Leon casts a mighty long chant—a slow activating spell with incredible power. Leon succeeds, enabling the remaining cadets to steal the landing craft Valescar used to board the *Feywind*. However, his long chant doesn't allow him to move while it's active. They are forced to leave Leon behind as the freighter crashes.

Thanks to Leon's spell and a scrap-metal shield crafted by Valescar, both survive the impact. Valescar takes the comatose Leon back to Emperor Sychon as an offering, who turns him over to Sarcon. Unable to survive in Vahn's broken vessel, Sarcon transfers his soul into the young cadet—an *unwilling* possession.

Fleeing Sarconian pursuit, the traumatized cadets take refuge in Matteo's hometown of Etrus. His parents, Anathea and Martan Alhan, shelter them with no questions asked. As Vallen struggles to recover from a dangerous medical condition—MIS, Men'ar Imbalance Syndrome—his unconscious mind takes him on a journey to his past.

Vallen was once Kit, a street urchin and member of a Sewertown thieving crew. Sewertown is a cesspit forgotten by Nemare, the shining Darmatian capital above. Poor and desperate, with basic necessities like water worth as much as gold, the people of Sewertown prey on each other and any surfacers foolish enough to cross their paths.

On the day of a religious festival, Kit steals from a young noblewoman, Elaine, who seems an easy mark. She chases after him, leading to a game of cat and mouse that results in Kit being trapped in her family estate. After arguing him into submission, a friendship between them blossoms and she gives him a name to replace the label bestowed by his crime boss: Vallen.

A week later, Vallen's fever breaks. He awakens to a city and country occupied by the Sarconian Empire. In order to avoid pointless casualties, his adoptive father—Steward Rowan Metellus—signed an unconditional surrender. The Kingdom is no more.

In Nemare, the Darmatian capital, Sarcon tells Sychon that he will need more magic power to overcome the defenses surrounding his Har'muth prison. He recommends draining the life-force of the whole country, a suggestion the Emperor balks at.

His newest retainer and Kingdom traitor, Dr. Archimas Redora Descar, concurs with Sarcon's assessment. Though the immortal sorcerer wears his son Leon like a set of clothes, he shows nothing but excitement at the prospect of magtech experimentation using the Empire's vast resources. In order to make an example, Sychon orchestrates an attack on his own victory parade so he can destroy a band of 'insurgents' lurking in the Cathedral of Sariel, one of the seven divine Veneer.

Back in Etrus, Sylette insists the cadets travel to Rabban or seek out a resistance group to continue the fight. She has spent twelve years planning her vengeance against her father, and she sees her new comrades as tools to that end.

During the course of their discussion, Matteo lets slip the news of Leon's death. Already overwhelmed by memories of Elaine, whose death Vallen feels responsible for, he descends into a deep depression and leaves the meeting. Afterward, the remaining cadets challenge Sylette's leadership. Why should they trust an enemy princess? Why should they keep fighting?

Sylette rolls back the clock to the day of her mother's execution. At the time, Valescar had been like an uncle to her—her closest friend and teacher. A disturbance in the Sarconian Royal Palace interrupts their daily chess match. Sylette is sent off with another tutor, while Valescar is summoned by the Emperor's personal guards.

Later, Sylette's eldest brother and heir to the throne, Vasuron, informs her that her mother, Third Consort Lanara, is going to be put on trial. She demands he sneak her into the proceedings, which he agrees to out of boredom. What they witness is a farce. The gathered dignitaries accuse Lanara of attempted regicide without allowing her a chance to defend herself.

When Sylette turns to go for help, Vasuron shoves her from their hiding place, pushing her onto the Sarconian Senate floor. A wounded Sychon orders Sylette banished for crimes of insolence—interrupting the trial—and relation to a traitor. Sylette is slapped in stocks and forced to watch Lanara's execution at the hands of a sobbing Valescar before being cast from the city gates.

As Sylette finishes her tale, a late-night projectostand broadcast relays a coded Darmatian army message. Renar, secretly an artist and fan of cryptology, manages to decipher news of a hidden army base where survivors are gathering. Since the group is unwilling to abandon Sylette to her father, they agree to stick with her until they can get her there.

But news of their stay in Etrus has reached Sarconian ears. A group of Moravi traders who witnessed their arrival sell the cadets out to their enemies, resulting in a town-wide lockdown. When the Sarcs start searching house-to-house, Matteo's parents give him the key to their airship and send them out the back door.

Their flight is soon discovered, resulting in a desperate last stand in the town square. Velle expends all her men'ar, Unter the Hue giant is grievously injured, and Imperial war magchines close in around them, closing off any chance of escape.

In a last ditch attempt to produce a miracle, Sylette throws away her pride and begs Vallen to wake up from his comatose despair. Her offer of vengeance lights a fire in him—a fire that results in him shattering the square with a pulse of earth magic.

Wounded and weary, the cadets stumble into a nearby chapel. Abbott Kinloss, the pastor and Matteo's friend, leads them to a hidden entrance to the Etrus sewers, which they use to bypass most of the Imperial forces and reach the airfield. During the hours-long trip, Matteo carries Velle on his back, deepening their relationship.

Lilith, the last member of their band, uses her magic to set fire to the fuel barrels in the airship hangar. The ensuing blaze forces the Sarcs to open the hangar doors, and the cadets blend in with the firefighting crews. Once inside, they board Matteo's airship, evade two patrolling heavy cruisers, and take off along the Phar Coast toward the source of the resistance message.

Their last sight of Etrus is an explosion. For aiding in their escape, Kinloss and his chapel are bombarded from above.

In Nemare, the peaceful Sarconian occupation turns bloody. Religious zealots claiming to serve Sariel, the Veneer of Terrans, rise up across the city and slaughter any Imperial soldiers they can get their hands on. The city is on the verge of becoming a battlefield.

Content Warning

Divinity's Twilight: Remnant contains several sections and themes that could be triggering or difficult to read. I have no wish to unintentionally cause a reader discomfort, so please be aware of the following:

Remnant contains instances of fantasy violence, mild gore, slavery, racism, sexism, child abuse, bullying, gaslighting, alcohol abuse, magic-induced suicide, and fade-to-black sex. Additionally, events involving genocide, starvation, prostitution, eugenics, and animal cruelty are alluded to.

None of these depictions reflect my personal views, especially those related to the horrid practices of slavery and racism. Rather, these occurrences aim to discuss hardship and injustice in a fantasy setting detached from our real-world experiences. As such, I took care to explore difficult and disturbing topics while clearly depicting them for the evil that they are. These acts are never glorified, and the characters who suffer through them are given opportunities to rise above their trauma.

However, I acknowledge that many people read to distance themselves from the world's darkness or do not wish to explore these difficult and potentially triggering subjects. Please proceed with caution, and always strive to stay safe and healthy.

Acknowledgements

Writing a book isn't easy.

This seems like common sense, but it takes having written, published, and marketed a first book to realize how hard it is to repeat the process. Almost two years ago to the day I released *Divinity's Twilight: Rebirth,* and during that span I've experienced the whole gambit of human emotion.

Elation at wonderful awards like the 2020 OZMA award for Best Fantasy or the 2021 American Fiction Award for Best Epic Fantasy. Anxiety and worry over negative reviews and disparaging remarks, the kind that make you wonder if your writing has meaning.

And then there's the best emotion of all: pure, unfiltered joy. The kind that creeps across your face as a smile and cascades along your arms in little twitches and tingles. *That* joy comes from the love and excitement of readers like you, expressed in countless different ways. Glowing reviews and breathtaking fan art. Social media shares, book recommendations, and people who gush about my work to everyone they meet.

So, writing a book isn't easy.

But the joy you give me—the *love* you give back to me—that's what makes it all worthwhile in the end.

Thus I present to you *Divinity's Twilight: Remnant,* book two in the *Divinity's Twilight* series. A book that is, in many ways, about love.

The love of parents for their children. First loves and last loves. Twisted love, manipulative love, lustful love, and everything in between. Love of country, love of duty, and, more meaningful than all the rest, love of self. I found myself crying SO many times while writing *Remnant,* so I would be thrilled if even the tiniest fraction of that emotion reaches you.

Without a doubt, this is the best book I've ever written. I've learned so much about writing in the past two years, so much so that I pitched out the first draft of *Remnant* and started again from scratch. More than ninety-five percent of the novel was replaced, but what was inserted in its stead is, in the words of my fabulous editor Sarah Chorn, "Going to go off like a nuclear bomb."

Many people aided in my growth. *All* my talents and abilities come from Jesus Christ, my savior, and every step forward I take is with His hand in mine. No matter how far I go, it is due to His boundless love.

My parents, Marvin and Darlene Russell, are my bedrock—my firm foundation. Through all the ups and downs of writing, they never wavered in their support or commitment to what I believe is my life's calling. Every word I wrote, every chapter I revised, every nagging 11th hour editorial change I made, they read and scanned and heard and bore it all without complaint. Never has an author had two stauncher allies.

My extended family chipped in as well; all the Russells and Conroes who bought books, shared my newsletters, or dropped my name to their fantasy-loving friends. Thank you for being my voice where I couldn't speak and my ears where I couldn't listen—particularly *you*, Uncle Barry!

Next comes my dear co-author (of books we've yet to release, but will!), Allegra Pescatore. I can honestly say that the countless hours we spent brainstorming whacky ideas, talking about plot structure, and writing the tales of Luca Fieldtreader and the Williston Gang are what took my storytelling to the next level. Thank you for being the best of friends—you, and everyone on the Plot Mom Discord server. Justin, Jessica, Lisa, Danielle, Dash, Erica, Arlene, Rachel, and yes, even Pippin, will forever hold a special place in my heart.

Now on to the list of amazing people who helped take this book from a jumble of words to the entrancing finished product before you:

Sarah Chorn was not my original editor, but she is *absolutely* the woman I want helming this ship going forward. As an editor for New York Times Bestsellers and big name Indie authors—along with being an award-winning author in her own right—I knew she would do exactly what was needed to elevate my work to compete on the international stage. Thank you so much for joining the *Divinity's Twilight* team, Sarah.

Somehow, some way, Chris McGrath managed to outdo *Rebirth's* cover. Velle looks fantastic—fierce, beautiful, and completely in command of her surroundings. Her wings seem real enough to touch, and her armor is so well-crafted and intricate that I discover new details every time I look at it. And those airships in the background? *Breathtaking.* His art makes *me* want to craft an even better story, which means I have a stellar cover artist.

Maps, maps, and *more* maps! Every fantasy lover's dream! Thanks to a connection with Ryan Cahill *(The Bound and the Broken),* I was able to bring the supremely talented Keir Scott onto the project. His Lozaria map takes what you knew about the world and expands it by five or more times. More valleys, mountains, and caverns to explore. More seas, rivers, and forests to cross. *That* alone was an impressive achievement, but then he added a pipe-and-crystal steampunk border, *two* magnificent illustrations, and a whole bunch of detailed location bubbles.

Oh, and that's only the *first* of his maps. The other is a campaign map annotated by an in-world character that just *screams* authentic. A round of applause for Keir, please.

As you start flipping through the pages, you may notice something … *different* about *Remnant*. Something it has that *Rebirth* doesn't. Have you figured it out yet? Yes, it has interior sketches and drawings! Ten of them, all rendered by the astounding Raphael Lucchini. Drakens, voidspawn, and airships. Spoilers, spoilers, and spoilers. Suffice to say many of them are characters—some new, some old—and *all* of them are brilliant. I can't wait to see what Raphael will draw next for the series.

Returning to the cover, I once again have to give my profuse appreciation to Allegra Pescatore. Not only is she a masterful word-weaver, but she's also the skilled graphic designer who set the cover fonts, designed the book wrap, and produced the pretty packaging you have in your hand. But her accolades don't stop there. Allegra was my only professional beta reader and helped add, remove, and rearrange scenes to craft the novel you're reading. So, if you know Allegra, be sure to thank her thrice over—I know I have!

And last but certainly not least is my interior formatter, Ailish Brundage. She received *Remnant* with a narrow turnaround window and still made the text on your pages sing. Every illustration, map, word, and letter you see was placed by her, so remember to thank formatters for putting together the books you love.

No acknowledgement's section would be complete without recognizing the dog that started it all: Vallen, the blue merle Sheltie. He and his five family members—Maddie, Matteo, Meira, Merle, and Meila—bring me no end of love and joy. If I ever have a bad writing day, I simply need to snuggle up with one of them and all will be well again. Plus they sell books *way* better than I do since they roll over for belly scratches—something I'm *still* trying to cut back on.

Lastly, I wish to extend one final round of appreciation to you, the readers. Without your love, praise, and support, the *Divinity's Twilight* series wouldn't be growing like it is. Along with Vallen, Matteo, Sylette, and the rest of the cast, I thank you from the bottom of my heart.

And always remember, no matter what you've said, no matter what you've done, *how we rise is FAR more meaningful than how we fall* …

About the Author

Christopher Russell (native of Williamsburg, VA) is a 30-year-old mechanical and aerospace engineer (graduate of the University of Virginia) who has loved reading since the day he picked up a book and writing since he could scrawl his first letters. After voraciously consuming titles from every genre—ranging from Star Wars to Lord of the Rings—he decided to combine the expertise from his professional education, passions, and Christian faith into a fantasy epic bridging the gap between magic and science. He currently  resides in Charlottesville, Virginia, with his loyal dog, Vallen, named after the protagonist of his first work. For behind-the-scenes information on all of Christopher Russell's works, visit christopherrussellauthor.com.

Printed in Great Britain
by Amazon

86187754R10440